LOVE'S PERILOUS ROAD

A Bluestocking Belles Collection with Friends

RUE ALLYN   ELIZABETH ELLEN CARTER

CERISE DELAND   SHERRY EWING

ALINA K. FIELD   JUDE KNIGHT

CAROLINE WARFIELD   MARY LANCASTER

BARBARA MONAJEM   MEARA PLATT

CONTENTS

CONTENTS

THE CASEBOOK OF PRINCIPAL OFFICER ROBERT PIERCE

The Office of the Magistrates' Court, Bow Street, London

It seems that I am off to the seaside. Larcenous Lucy, as some of the wits here at the Office have taken to calling her, is working the London to Brighton road. I've been told to look into a highwayman problem while I am there. There's someone plaguing both the main highway and some of the lesser roads. The local dignitaries have posted a reward, so that would be a nice bonus.

My colleagues have also been joking that smugglers and ghosts abound in the region, and that I might collect some of those while I am there. I told them, I shall leave the smugglers to the excise officers and ghosts to the duly authorized ministers of the church.

ONE GOOD WAGER
LEADS TO ANOTHER

BARBARA MONAJEM

One Good Wager Leads to Another
By Barbara Monajem

Thisbe Rose moves into the haunted cottage she inherited. She's not afraid of ghosts, smugglers, and highwaymen—but she's not so sure about the oddest housekeeper she's ever met.

Gervaise Transom wagers a friend he can spend months in disguise without being caught. When Thisbe moves into the haunted cottage, he should leave, to protect her reputation—but he also must stay, to keep her safe.

Not only that, he's sure he met her once years ago...

CHAPTER 1

The estate of Lord Wrapton, near Guildford, Surrey

Thisbe Wrapton knew the ability to see ghosts would be her downfall one day.

One morning, she was a little worried, and since there was a convenient ghost to whom to pour out her troubles, she forgot to take her customary care. Usually, she made a point of speaking to ghosts in privacy. Although such a quirk was considered amusing in a child, it was a definite hindrance to a young lady only a few months from her first London season.

The ghost of Wrapton House was a cheerful Elizabethan lady with an enormous ruff who looked benignly upon Thisbe, so perhaps she wouldn't be enraged at her question. The lady had had several children, so she would certainly know the answer, and although she was unable to speak aloud, she could write in the air or perhaps mime her response.

Thisbe glanced about, making certain she was alone. Bertha, the maid she shared with her aunt, had left the room to fetch some hair-pins, but she wouldn't take long.

"Dear lady," Thisbe said softly, "I beg your pardon for being so forward, but I have an urgent question, and there is no one else I dare ask."

The ghost poised the needle above her exquisite blackwork embroidery and raised an amused eyebrow.

"It's about a man," Thisbe said, "a handsome young man with whom I behaved shockingly, I'm ashamed to say."

The ghost shook her head reprovingly, although amusement still lurked in her eyes.

"But he's gone to the Continent, and I don't think he'll ever return, and what if—" Oh, dear. Even from this sympathetic ghost, Thisbe hesitated to ask for such information.

That hesitation led to her downfall. Ten seconds too late, she took a deep breath, plucked up her courage, and asked, "I fear that I may be with child, but how will I *know*?"

"Miss *Thisbe*!" Bertha cried from the doorway.

Thisbe whirled, cringing.

"You had carnal knowledge of a *man*?" Bertha cried.

Thisbe said nothing to this silly question, for why else would she ask about knowing whether she was with child?

"You let a man put—put that—that disgusting part of himself *inside you*?" Bertha gasped.

Actually, it had been quite pleasant, but Thisbe had a feeling that saying so wouldn't help matters. Miserably, she nodded.

Bertha ran from the room, shrieking, "Miss Wrapton! Oh, please come! It's Miss Thisbe! Whatever shall we do?"

Aunt Andrea hurtled down the corridor from her own bedchamber, bleating, "What happened? What's wrong?"

Bertha clapped a hand to her heaving breast. "Ruined, my lady. Miss Thisbe is *ruined*!"

"Ruined?" repeated Aunt Andrea, trembling so much that both her earbobs fell off. "But *how*? Thisbe is most carefully chaperoned and never left alone in the company of a man...except..." Her hands flew to her cheeks. "Oh, my poor child—it was that frightfully rude young man at the assembly when we were visiting Chichester, wasn't it? With a funny name, something to do with boats, I think. Oh, woe!"

His name is Mr. Transom, Thisbe corrected, but not aloud. What a disaster. Meanwhile, the ghost rolled her eyes and shrugged, returning to her embroidery.

Aunt Andrea moaned. "How is it possible? Granted, you went out on the terrace with him, but we found you quickly..."

Not quickly enough, though. He'd been so strong, so masculine, so thrilling, so... Aromatic wasn't quite the right word, but he'd smelled exquisitely pleasurable to Thisbe. And so *safe*.

What a fool she'd been.

"He was a nobody, although he may have been born a gentleman—for how else would he get into the assembly rooms? In any event, he was a dastard unworthy of the daughter of a baron, even a newly minted one." Aunt Andrea was extremely proud of Papa's elevation to a barony in recognition of signal services to the Crown.

By now the ghost had vanished, leaving Thisbe feeling very alone. Not that a ghost could do much but commiserate, but at least she wouldn't rant and rave. Ghosts, being no longer of this nether world, were somewhat detached from its worries and cares.

"How could you?" Aunt Andrea wailed, wringing her hands. "Why didn't you stop him before it was too late?"

"I couldn't stop him," Thisbe said. "He, ah, did what he did. I felt utterly helpless, and—" And blissful, were the truth to be told, but she wasn't about to say that aloud either, or at least not to any living person. The dead were not so eager to judge. "It all happened so fast." Far too fast, actually. She would have preferred it to take much longer.

"Carnal knowledge doesn't take long," Bertha said, snapping her fingers. "From kisses to babies, just like *that*." As a widow, she knew that sort of thing (and had warned Thisbe more than once).

Aunt Andrea, who was an innocent spinster, blushed. "Whatever shall we do with you now?" she moaned. "No decent man will wed you!"

"What the devil is all this bother?" Lord Wrapton—who refused to be addressed in any way but *my lord* since his elevation to the peerage—stalked into the bedchamber.

Aunt Andrea burst into tears. "That frightful young man at the assembly has ruined our Thisbe!"

Papa—*beg pardon*, Thisbe thought to herself, *my lord*—turned alarmingly red in the face. A horrid snarling sound issued from his throat. "He *what?*"

Thisbe bit her lip and said nothing. Papa wouldn't want to hear her excuses.

"Stupid girl!" he bellowed. "No sooner has the House of Wrapton been created by the Crown, than you have destroyed it."

"Surely it's not that bad," Aunt Andrea said. "All we must do is require him to marry her immediately."

"That impudent scoundrel wed the daughter of the House of Wrapton?" Papa shouted. "Never!"

"He can't marry me anyway, Auntie," Thisbe said. "He left the very next day for the Continent."

"You got yourself ruined by a *common soldier?*" thundered Papa.

Mr. Transom had seemed attractive and fun-loving to Thisbe in a very *un*common way. In fact, he'd kissed her for a wager, which she'd found hilariously funny, for it made no sense. He was supposed to kiss the most beautiful lady at the assembly, which she definitely wasn't. 'You are to me,' he'd said, which was charming and kind.

And then he was gone, off to the Continent to become, as he put it, 'a ghost'. On the verge of tears, she'd watched him go. How horrid to be so sure one would never return alive.

"No one else will wed her, either," Aunt Andrea said forlornly.

"Don't be a fool, Andrea," Papa scoffed. "We shan't advertise her shame to the whole world."

"But what if she is with child, Harold dear? My lord, that is." Aunt Andrea asked.

"Plenty of men will marry a ruined woman, even one with child, given the proper incentive." Papa narrowed his eyes at Thisbe. "Foolishly enamored of soldiers, are you?"

Not at all, thought Thisbe, but again didn't say.

"Well! If that's the case," Papa said, "I know just whom to ask."

After two days in her bedchamber with only bread, water, the one book they didn't find because it was under her pillow, and a great deal of time to fret about whom she might be forced to wed, Papa pronounced her punishment. She was to marry her second cousin, Eddie Rose.

It could have been much worse. Eddie was not unpleasant-looking, not unkind by nature, and by no means a fool. He was army-mad but too poor to purchase a commission. By dangling the carrot of a cornetcy before him, Papa had convinced him to marry Thisbe and accept her child as his.

At least she didn't have to run away to join the gypsies. Or traveling players, perhaps; she would have resorted to one of these dubious alternatives if Papa had chosen someone intolerable. She would never see Mr. Transom again, so it was no use pining for him and his intoxicating aroma.

The wedding took place almost immediately by special license, and Eddie was to leave for the army the following day. Papa had settled a sum on him to provide for the expenses of an officer—which were many—and to give Thisbe a little pin money. She would remain at home, of course, as at only seventeen, even though married, she was too young to live unsupervised.

Or so Papa decreed. She would have loved to have a little cottage of her own with only one or two servants, but that would make Papa look miserly. Un-baronial. Not only that, he now feared she would share her favors with any man who happened along. It was his duty, he proclaimed, to ensure her fidelity to Eddie.

That evening, when she and her husband were left together in a chamber with a bed they were to share, Eddie said kindly, "I suppose we should get on with consummating our marriage. Then at least there will be a chance the child is mine."

"Very well," she said. Perhaps he kissed nicely. She would soon find out.

"Shall I undress you, Thisbe, or do you prefer to disrobe yourself?" he asked.

"Undress me?" she asked, astonished. "Whatever for?"

"It's usual, when it comes to carnal knowledge, but if you're shy..."

"I'm not. It's just that I don't see *why* one must disrobe," she said.

"Ah," he said. "I understand, but a quick coupling on a dark terrace is nothing like what goes on between a man and his wife."

And he proceeded to show her what *carnal knowledge* really meant.

CHAPTER 2

Four years later, on a lonely stretch of road not far from Brighton

The gig carrying Thisbe Rose and her baggage pulled up at the entrance to a cart track, and the groom who drove it waved a hand toward an old stone house nestled back from the road in a sea of weeds. "That there is Lucky Cottage. Don't know how lucky you are to own it, though, ma'am. You want we should go up the track, or maybe just turn around and leave?"

Leave? Not the slightest chance of that, when the only alternative was to return home. She now had a house of her own and a little money. Somehow, with thrift and industry, she would get by.

Despite the evident neglect of the grounds, the house looked to be in tolerable condition. It had three floors—ground, first, and attic dormers, as well as a cellar, and plenty of windows to let in the light.

"The track seems relatively clear," she replied, "so please drive up and help me unload my belongings." As the gig rattled toward the house, she added, "Mr. Dent said there were servants here—a housekeeper and a man of all work." Mr. Dent was the landlord of the Old Oak Inn on the outskirts of Brighton, where she had spent the night.

"Aye, ma'am, but they're not the sort you're used to, that's for sure. The housekeeper's a surly old woman, but no one else would stay, because of the ghost."

"As I told Mr. Dent, I'm not afraid of ghosts." Nor would she allow the innkeeper, the groom, or any other man to frighten her back to her father's house.

The groom, a gloomy middle-aged man, tutted. "As for the man of all work..." He indicated the vast expanse of tall grass, unpruned bushes, dense, dark yews, and looming over all a massive, half-dead oak with its remaining leaves already on the turn in this chilly October.

"He doesn't seem to have done much lately," Thisbe admitted, wondering if leaving the place untidy made it useful for smugglers. Not that Mr. Dent had mentioned such a possibility; he almost certainly bought smuggled brandy but was, she suspected, far too shrewd to be so obvious about discouraging her. However, they weren't far from the coast, so she wouldn't be surprised if smugglers used her outbuildings. Perhaps it was they who kept the track clear.

If she were a smuggler, though, she would cultivate a façade of respectability, not neglect.

"I expect it's too much for one man to handle," she said. "I understand there's an orchard behind the house, as well as a stable and a few sheep as well."

"Aye." The groom nodded glumly and halted before the front door. "I hope Mr. Dent warned you that a highwayman rides this road."

"What would he want with me? I have nothing of value to tempt such a person."

The groom sighed and helped her down, then strode forward to knock on the heavy oak front door. While they waited, Thisbe had a good, long look at the house. The mullioned windows had lovely diamond panes, but the curtains were closed. Why, on such a beautiful autumn morning?

A minute passed, and the groom banged his fist hard on the door. A curtain at one of the front windows twitched open, and a long, dour face peered through. "Hold your horses," came a grumpy voice, followed by the sound of bolts being drawn back. The door opened enough for the same face, under a tattered mobcap and framed by untidy yellow curls, to glance suspiciously at the groom, and then, as if fascinated, at Thisbe.

"This is Mrs. Rose, the new owner of Lucky Cottage," the groom said. "Inherited it from her husband, Captain Rose, what died in the war."

The housekeeper couldn't seem to decide whether to glare or...to laugh? A rusty chuckle escaped her mostly black teeth. She dug a pair of spectacles from an apron pocket and put them on, the better to stare at Thisbe, it seemed.

Thisbe trod firmly forward. "Open the door properly, if you please. We must move my belongings inside so this good man may return to the Old Oak Inn."

The housekeeper grudgingly obliged. She was tall for a woman and sturdy, dressed in a round gown with a muddy hem, around which was tied a voluminous apron. She wiped her hands on it, sending puffs of flour into the air.

Thisbe marched past her into a surprisingly clean entrance hall with a bench for visitors and a table with some candles and a lamp. To one side was the door to what looked to be a drawing room. On the other side was a dining room and ahead was a flight of stairs. From somewhere in the rear wafted the enticing smell of mutton and onions. Seemingly, the woman was able to cook.

The groom followed with Thisbe's worldly goods. She hadn't taken much from home—mostly clothing and books, as well as a few sheets and blankets in case she found nothing useful in the cottage, which supposedly had been all but empty for years.

"Where shall I put these?" the groom asked. "Upstairs?" He glowered at the housekeeper, who was still staring. "Look lively, woman. This lady is your mistress now."

"I'll be fine," Thisbe told the groom, pressing a coin into his hand. She turned to the housekeeper. "Mrs. ah—?"

"Wix," the woman said in a creaky voice, dipping into a gawky curtsey.

"Pleased to meet you," Thisbe said and dismissed the hovering groom. "Mrs. Wix and I shall take it from here."

"Right you are, ma'am." The groom shook his head and took himself off.

❦

Gervaise Hervé Olivier Storm Transom wasn't often taken aback—one couldn't afford it while spying for the English in various disguises in France—but the war had been over for two years now. Evidently, he was out of practice.

Surely—*surely* he had met this lady before, but where? She didn't look particularly memorable—petite like many other women, hair scraped back unappealingly like a governess, and wearing a frown which rendered her regular features far less pleasing than they would otherwise be. And yet...

He shook away the memory, which didn't matter for now. So... this was Eddie Rose's widow.

He shouldn't be surprised at her sudden arrival. Eddie had confided in him one drunken night in Vienna not long after Napoleon's escape from Elba. He'd just received his captaincy and looked forward to fighting once again. "We'll get Boney for good this time, although I have a feeling my luck has run out," Eddie said in cheerful and correct prediction, "but I fear for my hapless little wife."

By what Gervaise understood, she was a cousin who'd been taken advantage of by a dastard and forced into marriage with Eddie for the sake of her reputation. Eddie had left the girl everything he possessed, including Lucky Cottage, in the care of a solicitor until her twenty-first birthday, after which she was free to do what she chose with it.

If she dared. Her father, apparently, was a brutal old tyrant who would consider it his right to control his daughter and her property now and forever, no matter what.

Judging by the way she had marched in, she did indeed dare. Good for her, he thought, but inconvenient for him that she'd taken her life into her own hands just at the time when Gervaise needed to remain holed up here in disguise.

Only for a few more days, though, thank God. He was itching to get back into comfortable men's clothing again. His own fault, of course. He should have known better than to make another wager with his friend since boyhood, Sir Simon Best.

In Simon's study one night, they'd smoked cheroots and spoken about Gervaise's years as a spy, and avoided the forbidden topic: how unfit he felt for life at home in England, and where he might run to next.

Simon had got the calculating look that should have warned Gervaise, and said, "You can't mean to say you disguised yourself successfully as a woman!"

"Several times," Gervaise said. "The French were always looking for a young man, not an old woman."

"You managed for a few days at most, I assume," Simon said. "Fifty quid says you can't do it for longer. Six months, with no one realizing you're a man."

"Done!" Gervaise retorted idiotically. He knew full well that Simon wanted to keep him from vanishing for months again, but he wouldn't refuse a wager with his oldest friend. They set the terms: Gervaise to occupy Lucky Cottage as its housekeeper. Simon was keeping an eye on the place for the owner's man of business, and the previous housekeeper had left because of a supposed ghost.

"My man will have to know," Gervaise said, having hired one the day before. "No one else."

Now, with only a few days to go, he smiled to himself. Inconvenience just made the wager more of a challenge.

"Tell you what, missus," he said, slipping into the uncultured speech he used in this role. "The rooms on the first floor are under Holland covers and such." He champed his teeth, making vulgar sucking noises before adding, "Let's leave your bags here, shall we? How 'bout a cuppa tea while I get the pie in the oven, and then I'll clean them rooms."

"I shall only need one room for now," Mrs. Rose said. "I shall inspect the rooms first and have tea later. Go ahead and prepare your pie, while I choose which bedchamber I prefer."

Gervaise muttered under his breath and returned to the kitchen, pondering what to say when she came down and confronted him in righteous indignation.

⚜

Thisbe headed up the stairs as the sound of the housekeeper's heavy gait receded. The woman disappeared into the rear of the house, and Thisbe heaved a sigh of relief at being alone.

In her very own house. With no one to tell her what to do. Or think. Or say.

Except for Eddie's ghost, who waited at the top of the stairs. He grinned at her, indicating his pride in the cottage with a sweep of his spectral arm.

"Yes, it's lovely, Eddie," she said, "just what I have longed for ever since our wedding. Now if only I can prove Papa wrong." After a pause, she added, "I must say I'm not impressed by the housekeeper. Whatever was the solicitor thinking of to hire such a person? I believe she just cursed under her breath at me."

Eddie shook with silent ghostly laughter. He was a happy ghost, as cheerful in the afterlife as he'd been in this earthly existence. He'd appeared at her father's house on her twenty-first birthday and urged her, with gestures and ghostly writing, to move to Lucky Cottage.

"Let's have a look round, shall we?" She found herself in a paneled gallery that ran the length of the house, with tall windows facing the front and at both ends, and four doors on the opposite side. Paintings on the walls were covered with dust sheets.

She turned left and went to the end of the gallery to look out the window. She ran her gloved finger along the grimy pane and immediately regretted it. Eddie's ghost seemed mightily amused at her dirty fingertip. The window revealed only a ragged path toward what she assumed was the stable—and also the housekeeper rounding the corner to meet a tall, gaunt man just below.

They spoke for a while, the man casting uneasy glances at the house. Mrs. Wix gestured towards the stable, then back at the house. She looked up, noticed Thisbe in the window, and said something to the man, who raised his head just enough to see her—and for her to see a scar down one side of his face. He bowed jerkily and hastened away.

Was this the man of all work? Poor man, was he perhaps a former soldier who had been wounded in the war? The sort Papa would never hire, for he deemed them all feckless and lazy. She felt sure this judgment was, in general, unkind and unfair, but given the condition of the grounds it might not be so in this case. However, she wished to be helpful to those less fortunate, so she must wait and see. Even so, the property required at least two able-bodied men.

Unfortunately, she couldn't afford more than one, if that.

Thisbe made her way along the gallery from room to room. The first bedchamber had two windows, a tester bed with hangings desperately in need of cleaning, and a sofa and chair under Holland covers. The shrubbery below had been maintained just enough that one could discern the paths from above—and to see that one would get a great many scratches if one tried navigating them below.

The next two chambers were much like the first, although the second was also used as a lumber room. As well as a bed, dressing table, washstand, and chair, it contained a sofa missing two legs, a backgammon table with bits of inlay missing, a cracked stool, and a vase containing cobwebby dried flowers. At this end of the house, the windows gave onto a kitchen garden which seemed reasonably well maintained. Mrs. Wix was below, plucking this and that from beds of evergreen herbs.

The last bedchamber had been inhabited more recently. In the first place, it smelled faintly of occupation. A male sort of smell? What a strange thought, as she had very little experience of rooms occupied mostly by men, and she had come to dislike her father's personal odor as well as the scent he used, an unpleasant mixture which permeated the rooms where he spent most of his time.

After that first impression, she saw that the room was free of dust and the bed neatly made. A book lay on the bedside table—and a man's coat hung over the chair! It seemed her nose had informed her correctly. She opened the clothes press and found shirts, cravats, and various undergarments that a lady should not inspect.

Nor did she wish to. Nor could she stay here if a man occupied this room!

She controlled her indignation—evidently, the solicitor had not overseen the servants properly—and found her way to the kitchen. It was unexpectedly clean and tidy, with pots hanging from the walls and shelves of crockery, and a new-looking cast-iron stove.

The housekeeper had rolled out the crust, and now glanced up from placing a pie bird in the middle of a pan. That glance was the extent of her acknowledgement of Thisbe's arrival in the kitchen.

Obviously, the woman had very little notion of the appropriate behavior of a servant towards her mistress.

"Mrs. Wix!" Thisbe said. "The room I wish to use—the only clean room up there—contains the clothing and other personal effects of a man."

"Aye," she said in her creaky voice. "They belongs to Mr. Storm, the paying guest." She spooned meat filling into the pan. "Don't this smell good, missus?"

Yes, it was the same mouthwatering aroma of mutton with onions, and also mushrooms, herbs, and something else. Despite the woman's lack of proper respect, Thisbe couldn't bring herself to object. Mrs. Wix was clearly proud of her pie. "Yes, it smells wonderful."

The housekeeper smirked. "Wait till you see how wonderful it tastes."

"I look forward to that, but the thing is, Mrs. Wix, that my husband's solicitor did not mention anything to me about a paying guest."

Mrs. Wix continued to spoon the filling gently around the pie bird. "Did he not, then?"

"Either he lied, which I doubt, or he didn't know—in which case you were lining your own pockets." Thisbe sighed. "For which I cannot blame you."

The housekeeper gaped briefly at Thisbe—not surprising, since most employers, such as her father, would deem renting that room without the owner's knowledge a form of theft. However, it meant the room was cleaned regularly. Perhaps it also explained the tolerable dining and drawing rooms.

"I know what it is to have very little money, and renting it did no harm," Thisbe said. "In fact, with several empty bedchambers, paying guests are quite a good idea, but they will have to be female. Mr. Storm must leave immediately."

The housekeeper cut an X in the center of the pie crust and lowered it gently over the filling. The bird's perky head peeked through the hole.

Finally, she deigned to speak. "He can't do that, missus." She patted the crust gently around the bird. "He ain't here. Can't say when he'll be back."

"Then why are his belongings in that room?"

"For when he comes." She gave a long-suffering sigh. "I'll pack 'em up, shall I? And send them to the inn?"

"Kindly do so," Thisbe said.

"Aye, missus, but what about his gelding? There ain't no room for him at the inn, and Sergeant Dolman—that's the man of all work you saw me a-talking to—he takes good care of him, he does. Wouldn't want to upset Mr. Storm."

"Very well, he may stay for now," Thisbe said, wondering if she could rent out the stable, too.

Ladies traveling alone were unlikely, but one with a servant or two might like to stay with her rather than at a noisy hostelry. Not only that, a woman alone often had difficulty securing a room at an inn, due to stupid prejudices about what was proper and what was not. Such nonsense.

Thisbe approved of independently-minded women. The world needed more of them.

"I'm sure Sergeant Dolman does his best, but there is work here for three men at least." She had to ask. "He seemed...uneasy this morning. Is it because of the scar? Does he fear I will dismiss him?"

"He don't take well to people," Mrs. Wix said. "Came back from the war with a scar on his face and a chip on his shoulder. Too many people are afraid of him 'cause of that scar."

"Which he got defending England!" Thisbe said indignantly. "You may tell him I'm not afraid of scars. As long as he does his job, we shall do fine." *And as long as you do yours*, she thought, but didn't say.

Drat! She'd decided to speak her mind from now on, instead of stifling herself as she had in Papa's house, and here she was hesitating... But she couldn't make up her mind what to think about Mrs. Wix.

"I don't know much about stoves, but that looks to be in excellent condition," Thisbe said. The stove was better than the old hearth in Wrapton House, for certain—but how had Eddie Rose been able to afford such a thing?

"She's a beauty, and I keeps her clean and polished," Mrs. Wix said. "Safer than cooking over a hearth."

This was true, and it might be needed if she had lodgers, but who had authorized such an expense?

It was too late to do anything about that. Thisbe seated herself at the deal table. "I'll have tea now."

Mrs. Wix frowned. "Here? In the kitchen?"

"Why not? It's warm and cozy, and I enjoy watching you cook."

"Whatever you say, missus." The housekeeper spooned tea leaves into a pot and poured water from the kettle that steamed gently on the stove.

Thisbe's father had forbidden her to enter the kitchen; it was unladylike to show an interest in cookery, or so he said. If so, she refused to be ladylike. This was her house, and she could spend as much time in the kitchen as she liked.

Except that she had a feeling Mrs. Wix didn't want her there. "I'll have my meals in the dining room, though," she added placatingly. "Or better, how about a tray in the drawing room for tonight? There's no sense having a fire in both rooms. I can't afford to waste fuel."

"You're really planning to live here, missus? All on your own?"

"With what few servants I can afford." It was vulgar to discuss money, but this was her house and her money or lack of it. "My resources are limited. The solicitor will do his best to sell my husband's commission, but with the army so much smaller now, it may take a while. In the meantime, and perhaps even afterwards, I shall have to pinch my pennies."

The housekeeper said nothing, perhaps wondering about her own chances of remaining at Lucky Cottage. She placed the teapot, a cup, and a plate with two rock cakes in front of Thisbe.

The cakes more than lived up to their name, but Thisbe politely refrained from saying so, merely dipping them in the tea to soften them a little. Perhaps she should learn how to bake them herself. She might even learn to cook simple meals. With a maid and a competent man of all work, she would do fine.

Was there a kind, polite way to get rid of Mrs. Wix? Something about the woman made her uneasy, but she couldn't quite pin it down. The housekeeper was disrespectful in a rough sort of way, but not disobliging.

Mrs. Wix opened the oven, waved a hand inside it, muttered, "Hot enough," and put the pie in to bake.

"Which herbs did you use in the pie filling?" Thisbe asked. "I smell savory and sweet marjoram, and you surely used parsley, but there's something else…"

"You've a powerful good sense of smell, missus." Mrs. Wix sounded surprised.

Thisbe smiled and inhaled. "Hmm. It's not one of the savory herbs. Perhaps a spice?"

"Aye," Mrs. Wix said. "Take a guess, love."

Thisbe closed her eyes and inhaled the delightful aroma. "Not pepper, not exactly nutmeg…I have it! Mace!"

"Got it in one!" the housekeeper said.

CHAPTER 3

W hat a dazzling smile! It transformed her entire face.

Gervaise was beginning to like Mrs. Rose. A prickly little thing, but he could hardly blame her. By what Eddie had told him, her father was the domineering sort. No doubt she wanted to be out from under his thumb.

Nevertheless, she was far too young and pretty to live here on her own. Did she expect to be accepted by local society?

Not if she meant to make Lucky Cottage into a boarding house. She might no longer be seen as a lady, and that would put her even more at risk. Brighton was full of downright snobs and worse, predatory men.

Which Gervaise was not, although he shouldn't have called her *love*, but her smile, the sheer pleasure on her face had stolen his commonsense. When and where had he met her before?

Not recently, of that he was sure. It must have been years ago, before he left to play the spy in France. Before she'd been forced to wed Eddie Rose.

A few days from now, after he'd won the wager of six months without being revealed as a man, he would leave, so as not to risk her reputation.

Which she was already risking by living alone, but he couldn't do much about that.

Or could he?

He left her with the tea and rock cakes and nipped up to the top floor to remove the signs of recent use there. Then he returned to the first floor, removed the sheets from his bed, put a fresh set on for Mrs. Rose, packed up his belongings, and brought them down to the butler's pantry for now.

He would have to sleep in the housekeeper's room to keep up appearances. He didn't much like that bed, but needs must. Luckily, he already kept all his women's clothing there.

No, it wasn't luck, just standard practice when playing a role. As a spy, he'd *become* the person he was pretending to be. It was a matter of life and death.

Now, it was only a wager, but after years when any slipup could spell disaster, a silly bet with an old friend was a welcome relief.

Except that even traveling all over England and the Continent for over a year and then six months of solitude here, away from family and society and their expectations of him, he wasn't ready to return. He wasn't the same man as four years ago. He never would be. Didn't want to be. Nor was he comfortable simply being himself. Whoever that was.

Once she'd finished her tea and cakes, Mrs. Rose went over the whole house from attics to cellar, murmuring softly to herself, detailing everything in a notebook. Perhaps she meant to sell what she could to help make ends meet.

She shouldn't have to, damn it all. And if she did, she needed help. This was a lonely stretch of road, a little too far from Brighton for both convenience and safety. The small band of smugglers who passed their goods nearby wouldn't do her any harm; most were good fellows, family men in need of a little extra money. Nevertheless...

When he went to the drawing room to fetch her supper tray— she'd polished off her share of the pie, as well as an apple, a wedge of cheese, and another rock cake—he asked, "Did Mr. Dent at the Old Oak warn you about the ghost, missus?"

She rolled her eyes. "I wondered when you would get around to mentioning it. I'm not afraid of ghosts. They are quite harmless, and in any event, there are no ghosts here except that of my deceased husband."

He stifled a laugh. "Captain Rose's ghost is here?"

"You needn't look at me like that. I see ghosts—always have—and the only one I see here is his. He's over by the mantlepiece, pointing at you and laughing."

Gervaise barely stopped himself from turning; instead, he looked himself up and down. "Why would he laugh at me?" If Eddie's ghost really was there, Gervaise knew the answer. "Well now, that explains it."

"Explains what?"

"The rattling windows in the attic, even when there's no wind. Would that be your Captain Rose's ghost?"

She chuckled. "Yes, he's grinning at me, very proud of himself. It's not easy for ghosts to move physical objects. I assume he was just having fun."

That sounded like Eddie Rose. "There's talk of the ghost of a soldier over by Devil's Dyke, missus. Seems he frightened the smugglers and excisemen alike."

"Eddie is taking credit for that, too," she said. "Which reminds me, I thought perhaps the ghost stories about this cottage were spread by smugglers, but I saw no sign that such men use this house for hiding contraband."

"Far as I know, they don't, missus," he said. "The outbuildings neither."

"Mr. Dent also mentioned a highwayman, but I fail to see what he would want with me."

What any man would want of a pretty woman, but fortunately, Captain Moonlight was a gentleman, a good sort with, Gervaise suspected, a lovely young woman already in possession of his heart. "He's not a burglar. Stay home after dark, and you'll be fine."

"I have nowhere else to go," she said.

He would have to do something about that, too, while ensuring her safety as well.

Fortunately, she was tired enough to retire early. He hurried her up to bed with a glass of hot milk, changed into his own clothes, cleaned his teeth, tied his overlong hair back in a queue, saddled Strider, his bay gelding, and sent Sergeant Dolman from the stable over to the house.

"I don't like her to be all alone in there," he said. "With any luck she'll go right to sleep, but if she comes down to the kitchen, have an excuse ready." He paused at the aghast expression in the man's eyes. "She's a pleasant lady, Sergeant. Sympathetic and kind. I'll be back as quickly as I can, but if I'm late, you'll have to man the signal light."

Dolman gave him a dirty look. "The light, fine, but I ain't playing no ghost. You may think it's a lark, sir, but I only tried to rob you out of desperation. I'd rather be an honest man."

"I know, Sergeant, and I'm probably too old for larks." Dolman, destitute and starving, had unsuccessfully tried to hold Gervaise up on the road to Brighton. Gervaise had fed him, hired him as a groom, then made the damned wager and put him to work at Lucky Cottage.

Gervaise set off at a canter, and before long rode up the long dark drive between ancient yews to the home of Sir Simon Best, JP. He realized, before he even made it halfway up the drive, that something was going on there tonight. Light gleamed from too many windows for latish on an evening in the country.

He couldn't have chosen a worse moment to drop in for a quick chat and a cigarillo—and to ask a favor. The last thing he wanted to do the pretty to Lady Best's friends, but in order to ask that favor, he had no choice.

His timing proved even worse when, on riding around to the stable, he recognized one of the coaches in the yard. It belonged to his father. "Who's here?" he asked Martin, a groom he'd known since boyhood visits. "Surely not my parents?" If so, he would turn around and leave, and send Best a note instead.

"Nay, Master Ghost, ah, Mr. Transom, I *should* say," the groom corrected himself. "Only your sister, Miss Transom, to stay for a while."

Not good, but better than having to explain to his parents once again that he wasn't ready to return to society, or at least not the sort of society they enjoyed.

"A curate and his daughter came to dine," Martin added. "Captain Somerville, too."

Gervaise squared his shoulders and made his way, like the coward he had become, through the back garden to the French door of Simon's study. Sure enough, the gentlemen had come here to smoke their cigarillos before joining the ladies in the drawing room.

"Ghost!" Simon cried. "You're a sight for sore eyes. What brings you here at this odd hour?" He raised his brows in a silent question: *Have I won the bet?*

Gervaise gave an infinitesimal shake of the head in response. "Only the opportunity to blow a cloud." He shook his friend's hand, then those of Robin Somerville and the curate. "And to ask a small favor for a friend of mine. But that can wait. I'd hoped not to disturb the ladies—as you can see, I'm not in evening attire—but I hear my sister is here."

"She is indeed," Mr. Pendleton, the curate, said. "She is wishful to attend an assembly in Brighton. These young ladies, you know—always on the lookout for a fine young man to catch unsuspecting on their hook!" He gave a cheerful laugh. "On the subject of fine young fellows, we were just speaking of you, Mr. Transom. Your dear sister was saying how much they miss you. She will be utterly delighted that you are back in England, hopefully for good. She said you were visiting relatives in France?"

That's what he'd led everyone to believe. If people thought he was elsewhere, they were less likely to penetrate his disguise. Nor would family members try to find him.

He didn't need to answer, for the curate rambled on about how delightful it must be to visit the Continent again. Gervaise shared a glance with Robin Somerville; they'd both been to war in their separate ways. He liked the man, whose eyes always held a touch of mockery.

"Have you come to stay with us?" Simon asked. "Lily would like that. She misses you."

"Not just yet," Gervaise said, "although I've been turfed out of my pied-à-terre at Lucky Cottage. Eddie Rose's widow arrived to take possession, and the housekeeper promptly packed me up and sent me away. I've a room at an inn for tonight. Then I'll be away again for I don't know how long."

"Why, you fool? You know you're always welcome here," Simon retorted, while Robin Somerville's amused expression deepened. Not for the first time, Gervaise wondered if Robin had penetrated his disguise.

They'd taken no more than a few puffs of their cigarillos before Lady Best came in, scolding. "Dearest, you really shouldn't encourage the poor curate to partake of such a ghastly vice—*Ghostie*! What a delightful surprise!"

Her shriek brought Lily, his sister, running from the drawing room, a flutter of pale muslin and lace, eyes brimming with happy tears. Gervaise did his best to seem pleased to see her—he loved his sister dearly—but she would tell his parents, and they would expect him to go home and *stay* there, being made much of and introduced to innumerable young ladies. He had no objection to ladies, but he'd never met one for whom he would make a good husband. No sane woman wants to marry a ghost.

"Shall you come to the assembly in Brighton?" Lily asked. "Oh, please do, Ghostie darling! But you mustn't fall in love with any of the ladies there," she added gaily, "because I have quite made up my mind that you shall marry one of my friends, for if you do, we shall see each other much more often."

And so it went, drinking tea and talking nonsense—he couldn't possibly tell them what France was like after years of revolution and war, and how eaten up he was with self-disgust—until the guests left and the ladies retired, and he finally had a few minutes with Simon Best in the study.

"Damn it, Ghost," his friend said, "how many days left? Three? Why risk coming here out of disguise?"

Gervaise threw himself into a chair in the study. "The arrival of Eddie Rose's widow changes everything."

"Inconvenient," Simon said. "As I said earlier, you're welcome to come here, but that would end the wager, I think."

"To hell with the wager," Gervaise said.

Simon snorted. "I've never heard you say that before."

"I'm not giving in just yet," Gervaise said, "nor have I gone to an inn. Staying where I am is more important than winning."

"Wonders will never cease. But—"

"In any event, no one will find me out." Unless Robin Somerville already had, but he had secrets of his own and would likely never let on, even to Gervaise himself. "As you say, it's only a few days."

"You can't stay there, Ghost! She's a young woman, admittedly a widow, but if it's learned that you were there, it will tarnish her reputation."

"I can't leave her alone there, either."

"But, my dear fellow, why didn't she stay with her parents, as a young widow should? She must be scarcely more than a child."

"She's twenty-one years old. By what Eddie told me, her father, Lord Wrapton, is a brute."

Simon grimaced. "I've met him once or twice. Estate near Guildford, as I recall. I can't say I like him much. Fancies himself above everyone. King of all he surveys sort of chap. I don't blame her for wanting to be out from under his thumb."

"Yes, inheriting the house is her chance of escape. She is determined to make a go of living there. She's short of funds, but I believe she can manage with what little Rose left her, added to the income from the orchard and the sheep." He paused. "Better than turning it into a boarding house."

"Good God," muttered Simon. "That would never do."

"She's innocent as a lamb and about as helpless, which is why I'm here. You're right, I can't stay there for long, but for now, I feel responsible for her."

"Why? You hardly knew Rose. Met him on the Continent, didn't you?"

"He confided in me about her," Gervaise said. "Felt sure he wouldn't make it home alive, which proved to be the case. If she means to make a go of it, she needs friends. Neighbors to give her countenance and an aura of protection."

"Ah," Simon said. "You want my wife to befriend her, introduce her to the locals, and so on?"

"If she wouldn't mind." Gervaise glanced at the ormolu clock on the mantel. "Damn, I'm late. I must be off."

"Because?"

"Of something a JP is better off not knowing about," Gervaise said, and fled.

❧

Thisbe fell asleep almost at once but woke some hours later to the sound of a thump. And then nothing, which made her wonder if the thumping sound was part of a dream—one she didn't recall. She sat up, turned up the lamp burning low by her bedside, and listened hard.

Nothing. No thumping except that of her own heart.

It wasn't really surprising. She'd fallen asleep only because she'd been too exhausted for uneasiness to keep her awake. She didn't like being alone in the house with only that strange old woman downstairs.

Suddenly, Eddie's ghost appeared, motioning to her to get up.

Thisbe shook her head at him. "It's the middle of the night. I have a great deal to do tomorrow." She couldn't afford to let a ghost, or a grumpy servant for that matter, prevent her from getting a good sleep. She turned the lamp down and settled under the coverlet, determined to fall asleep again immediately.

Creak!

She sat up, heart thumping again, but this time she knew where the sound had come from—the squeaky board in the room directly over her bedchamber. She'd noticed it when inspecting the house that afternoon. Annoyed, she turned up the lamp again, slid out of bed, and donned her robe and slippers. She lit a candle and followed the triumphant ghost to the door.

The gallery was in darkness, save for a faint light from the windows. She crept toward the staircase. No light showed either below or above. She must have been mistaken. Old houses did creak sometimes in the night, so why was Eddie pestering her?

The ghost pointed upward and made a shooing motion, as if to urge her to take the stairs.

She balked. Ghosts didn't understand human fears, since earthly danger didn't affect them anymore. Who could possibly be up there? And why? Surely for something underhanded and perhaps dangerous!

Eddie rolled his spectral eyes—an unpleasant sight—and made an even more urgent motion with his hand, mouthing, "Hurry!"

She could ignore him, but on the other hand, he might have a good reason for wishing her to investigate that sound. She couldn't afford to succumb to anxiety. *No hesitation*, she told herself. This was her house. She had every right to know what was going on.

She picked up another candlestick—the closest she could find to a weapon—and trod firmly up the stairs. Let the intruder hear her approach and tremble.

Good advice if the intention was to help her remain determined and unafraid. Unfortunately, there was no response from above, trembling or otherwise. Nothing but a nod and a grin from Eddie.

It was too late to turn around, so Thisbe trod gamely upward. Just as she expected, a flicker of light showed beneath the door of the garret above her bedchamber.

She thrust the door open. "What in heaven's name is—"

A female figure by the window tossed a brief glance at Thisbe and said, "Hush!" Then she opened her mouth wide and let out a wail that would drown out a banshee.

It was Mrs. Wix, wrapped in a heavy cloak with a hood obscuring most of her face. She proceeded to open and close the shutters of a lantern several times. Eddie stood next to the housekeeper, looking mighty pleased with himself.

"How dare you order me to hush!" Thisbe said, but in a softer voice. "This is my house, my garret, and you have no business being up here pretending to be a ghost!"

"I'll explain in a minute," the woman hissed, a finger to her lips, astonishing Thisbe so much that a furious retort died.

So much for respect for one's betters. Not that Thisbe really believed that some people were better than others merely because of an accident of birth, but surely an employee should be polite to her employer—especially such an understanding one as herself.

Mrs. Wix continued opening and closing the lantern in a strange, rhythmic pattern. The air movement of the shutters, combined with the breeze from outdoors, wafted the scents of night and dead leaves, and closer by, horse and dirt. What had she been doing in the stable? The woman surely needed a bath.

Suddenly, Thisbe knew what was going on. "You're signaling to smugglers!" she said.

"I am not." Mrs. Wix glanced at her again with a wide, mischievous grin. "I'm signaling to the revenue men."

CHAPTER 4

With difficulty, Gervaise refrained from laughing at Mrs. Rose's appalled expression. It was damned hard to maintain that whispery creak of a voice, and laughter would betray him for certain. So would letting her see him properly. He'd had no time to do more than rub dust all over his face and hope the hood of his cloak would suffice.

A pity, because she was delectable with her long, dark hair down her back, wispy waves of it framing her face, and a candlestick clutched like a weapon in one hand. He would far rather stare, drinking in her loveliness, her eagerness for enjoyment and life.

"How *could* you?" she demanded. "Stop it right now!"

Fortunately, Gervaise had signaled enough, so he obliged her by shutting the lantern.

She launched into a rant. "Those poor men, who are only trying to make a few extra shillings, will be torn from their families, hanged or transported! Have you no compassion?"

"What about the law?" he asked, avoiding her eye, trying not to smirk—unsuccessfully, judging by her expression.

"It's a stupid law. If the government would simply lower the tariffs, smuggling would no longer be profitable. The men and their families might suffer from the lower income, but at least they would still be together."

"You're a kindly woman, missus," he said. "The signal is to fool the revenue men, keep them busy while the goods are transported elsewhere."

"Oh," she said. "How clever."

"Won't work for much longer, if at all," Gervaise said. "Been four days already. The revenuers will work out that it was a decoy." He paused. "Your ghost gave us the idea. The house was already known to be haunted, so it fooled them for a while."

"Fine, but I can't allow my house to be used for illegal purposes." She glowered. "I hope they paid you well."

A lady of many contradictions, he thought, turning toward the door to avoid her eye. "Nothing at all, missus. Did it out of the goodness of my heart." And boredom, if the truth were told.

Might boredom be a good sign? An indication that he was almost ready to return to society? That it might not be too painful going home again?

Or just that he was bored. Full stop.

Except that since Mrs. Rose had arrived that morning, he wasn't bored at all.

He held the door open for her. "Shall I warm up more milk for you, Mrs. Rose?"

☙❧

Thisbe slept late, woke to a bright, chilly day, and hurried down for breakfast. Mrs. Wix had already lit the fire and set the table in the dining room, which put paid to any hope she had of eating in the cozy kitchen.

She sighed, feeling rather lonely, but that was only to be expected; it was a different sort of loneliness from at home, where she disliked her father and had nothing in common with her aunt, and felt sorry for her stepmother, who wasn't much older than she was. Her baby half-brother was a darling, and she would miss him.

She'd not been close friends with any of the gentlewomen nearby, although she rather liked some of the villagers.

One shouldn't impose upon the domain of a servant, or expect more than competent service from such people, and certainly not friendship. And, she asked herself, why would she want friendship from such a grumpy—and lawless—character as Mrs. Wix?

Although that brief, engaging smile last night had startled her with its astonishing warmth, and had led her to hope.

Thisbe was on the first floor, wearing a faded round gown and an apron, dusting the paintings and sweeping the gallery, when a coach and pair pulled up before the house. After a brief panic, she realized with relief that it wasn't her father's coach. She hoped he wouldn't come to Lucky Cottage, but instead wait for her to come crawling home. Unfortunately, one never knew what he might decide to do, but she wasn't yet ready to defy him again.

A groom leapt down from his perch, opened the door to let down the steps, and hastened up to the house to knock. Two ladies descended from the coach, one very young and sprightly, with fair hair peeping from beneath her bonnet; the other several years older, dark-haired and more composed.

The groom knocked again, knocked a third time, and the ladies waited. Where was Mrs. Wix? Soon the ladies would assume no one was home, and drive away before Thisbe even knew who had called, and why.

A lady never answered her own door, but if Mrs. Wix didn't come, what was she to do?

Break with custom once again, she told herself, wrenched open the casement, and cried, "I'll be right down!"

She stripped off her apron and hurried down the stairs, to find Sergeant Dolman peering out the same window where she'd first seen Mrs. Wix.

"Open the door, for heaven's sake!" she cried.

He turned, glowering defiantly. "I didn't want to frighten the ladies, ma'am." Poor man, even at this distance she could smell his fear of people's reaction to his scar.

"I understand your hesitation, although they are fools to be frightened by a scar. However, why didn't Mrs. Wix come?" She flapped a hand. "Don't fret, Sergeant. I'll speak to her about it. You'd best get back to work." She opened the door and put on a welcoming smile.

"So sorry, ladies, to keep you waiting, but I arrived only yesterday and have no servants to speak of. Well, except that the housekeeper is quite a good cook." And would shortly hear Thisbe's opinion of her gross dereliction of duty. "Do please come in!"

The ladies trod up the steps, apologizing for the intrusion. "I'm Lady Best and this is Lily Transom."

Transom? thought Thisbe, startled, but Lady Best kept on talking. "You must be Mrs. Rose. We heard you were here and simply had to drop by to welcome you."

"Heard?" Thisbe asked, immediately anxious. "From whom?"

"My husband told me," Lady Best said. "He's the JP, you know— Sir Simon Best. I expect he heard it from a servant. They always have the news before anyone else."

"So true," Thisbe said, a little less uneasy. The solicitor had certainly mentioned Sir Simon as the man to ask for assistance with getting settled in. Which she'd hoped not to have to do, because for all she knew, he would report right back to her father.

She ushered them indoors. "How very kind of you to come."

"Not at all. It was on our way," Lady Best said. "I knew Eddie Rose as a boy. Such a sweet lad, and a valiant soldier. You must miss him dreadfully."

"Yes, he was a wonderful man," Thisbe said, while Eddie's ghost swept off his shako and bowed invisibly to her guests.

"How courageous of you to take on Lucky Cottage all on your own. No servants, you said?"

Thisbe glanced into the chilly drawing room and said, "Let's sit in the dining room. There's already a fire there." She ushered the ladies in and said, "Two servants were here when I arrived. One is a man of all work with far too much to do, and the housekeeper is an eccentric with little concept of proper respect. Do sit down, and I'll see if I can persuade her to provide us with tea."

"Oh, we mustn't stay," Lady Best said. "In fact, we came by to see if you would like to ride into Brighton with us. Just a little shopping trip, you know."

Temptation assailed her. She'd only been sweeping for half an hour, and she already had blisters on her thumbs. However did servants manage? And yet, the work must be done.

But...here was someone named Transom! She had to learn more —although maybe she was a fool to want to. Just because she had relived that astonishing kiss in daydreams, she didn't seriously expect to meet that man again. He had probably died on the Continent. But what if he were alive? "I'm not dressed for—"

"Surely that can be remedied," Lady Best said.

The lively young lady named Transom added, "Do please come, Mrs. Rose. There will be an assembly on this side of Brighton tomorrow evening. We shall have such fun choosing fresh trim for our gowns. Oh! Would you like to come to the assembly, too, Mrs. Rose?"

The girl was probably from an entirely different Transom family, and much as Thisbe enjoyed social occasions, she should probably start as she meant to continue. What was the point of attending an assembly? She wasn't looking for a husband. "I don't think—"

"Don't say *no* just yet," Lady Best said. "Think it over; it's a good way to get to know people in the area. We'll take you there and bring you home afterwards."

Even if Lily Transom were related to that charming man, Thisbe knew better now—that a kiss didn't get one with child, but kissing could easily lead to what did, and the last thing she wanted was to take that sort of risk. Best to stay away from charming men —not that she expected to meet anyone as wonderful as the Transom who had kissed her. "You're most kind," Thisbe said, "but—"

"A lady alone needs friends," Lady Best said. "Do at least come with us today."

Thisbe gave in. "I should love to," she said, and hastened away to change her clothes.

At least I am well-dressed, thought Thisbe as she hurried down-stairs in her blue wool walking dress with the matching pelisse and bonnet. She even had an evening gown that might do for an assembly, if she could summon the courage to go.

She had sufficient fashionable clothing for now, thanks to Lord Wrapton's obsession with appearances. His daughter, however much he despised her, must be well turned-out or it affected his status. Not that she gave a feather for his status, but being out from under his thumb meant she would not be able to afford anything new for ages. Would people be willing to befriend an impoverished gentlewoman?

It didn't matter. It was far better to be alone and poor than obliged to marry one of Lord Wrapton's friends. The instant her year of mourning was over, he'd begun looking for someone to palm her off onto, with the legacy from Eddie as an inducement.

And yet, it was the legacy that had saved her, for it belonged to her, not to Papa, and he couldn't do a thing about that. At least, she hoped not. She feared he would exert whatever authority he could muster to take her back home.

On the way downstairs, she heard Mrs. Wix's voice from above. "Sorry, missus, I was up top getting rid of all sign of ghosts and such. Didn't hear the door."

"Nonsense," Thisbe said, turning to glare up at her. "It was sheer laziness, and as for subjecting Sergeant Dolman to unnecessary embarrassment, you should be ashamed of yourself." She continued down, then stopped, sniffing. Did the woman never bathe? She always smelled of meat and onions, which was to be expected of a cook, but last night of dirt and horse as well. Those powerful odors still lingered. "By the way, Mrs. Wix, I believe you would benefit from a bath."

Soon they were in Lady Best's well-sprung carriage, rolling along the road to Brighton. "Thank heavens summer is over, for Brighton is ghastly when it's full of holidaymakers," Lady Best said.

"Are you familiar with Brighton?" Miss Transom asked.

"Not really," Thisbe said. "I have spent most of my life at my father's estate in Surrey, but we came here once for a brief holiday. Papa wanted to see the place that had so captured the imagination of the Regent." He'd praised it to the skies; he always followed the Prince's lead.

She was about to enquire into Miss Transom's family, when Lady Best changed the subject, pointing out landmarks along the way and discussing families in the area, and giving her no chance to ask her burning questions. Which, Thisbe reminded herself, was all for the best.

The shopping trip proved delightful. They stopped at Lady Best's modiste, a charming lady with whom Thisbe sympathized—it was frightfully hard for a gentlewoman to be obliged to earn her keep. Next, they visited a millinery, a haberdashery, and a fabric ware-house. All Thisbe could bring herself to buy was some ribbons to change the appearance of a few gowns and a bonnet, as well as pins, needles, thread, and a thimble, none of which she'd thought to bring from her father's house.

They encountered two ladies to whom Lady Best introduced her —Lady Josephine Cranfield and her cousin and chaperone, Mrs. Julia Elford. Thisbe's circle of acquaintances was growing remarkably quickly. If only she could keep up appearances! Perhaps she should start helping Sergeant Dolman. She could wield a pair of shears well enough to clip the hedges.

All the while, the urge to learn about her handsome Mr. Transom ate away at her.

Lady Best treated them to tea and cakes at the Old Oak Inn and outlined their plans for the coming weeks. "Lady Somerville's house party will end with a grand ball—I'll see if I can get you an invita-tion, Mrs. Rose—after which Lily will return to her parents' estate."

Thisbe leapt into this opening. "Where is your family home, Miss Transom?"

"North of Chichester," Miss Transom said.

Ah! "I danced some years ago with a Mr. Transom at an assembly in Chichester. A relation of yours?"

"My brother Gervaise, most likely. Was he very charming?"

"Exceptionally so," Thisbe said, unable to prevent herself from smiling. "Handsome, too, fair-haired like you, and an excellent dancer. He said he was about to leave for the Continent. Was he a soldier?"

"No, he was a diplomatic aide-de-camp," Lady Best said.

"Whatever that means," Miss Transom said. "I believe he was a spy."

"Perhaps that is so," Lady Best said, "but you must not say so aloud." She cast a glance at Thisbe. "I'm sure Mrs. Rose will not mention it to anyone."

"Of course, I shall not," Thisbe said.

"Your parents would be mortified if people learned of it, Lily dear," Lady Best said. "Spying is an ungentlemanly occupation. It does not redound to your family's credit."

"It should do!" Miss Transom said.

"I agree," Thisbe said. "It's an important occupation in wartime, an extremely dangerous one requiring courage and daring."

"Dear Gervaise," Miss Transom said sadly. "He always had plenty of that. I miss him so much!"

Thisbe's heart plummeted. "Oh no, did he die?"

"No, he's alive," Miss Transom said, "but he's not at all well. I don't mean physically. He's healthy, but he has become restless and impatient, and he won't stay at home. Shortly after he returned from the war, he left us again, travelling all over England. He even returned to France. One would think he'd had enough of the place!"

"But he is in England now?"

"Yes!" she cried. "Imagine my surprise and—and *delight* when he came to Best Manor briefly last evening. It was lovely to see him, but…" She bit her lip, and a tear winked in her eye.

"But he's not the same Ghostie we knew, and I don't know that he ever will be," Lady Best said.

"Ghostie?" Thisbe asked.

"His initials spell the world *ghost*, which I suppose gave him the idea," Miss Transom said. "He played ghost at school to frighten the masters and wagered he wouldn't get caught, and he never did!"

"He's still my husband's close friend, which gives me hope. I think they've got another of their silly wagers going on." Lady Best rolled her eyes. "God knows what it is about, but to me it's a sign that he's on the mend."

Thisbe was too embarrassed to mention that he'd wagered he would steal a kiss from her. *Dear heaven, will I meet him again someday?*

CHAPTER 5

Gervaise doubled over laughing the instant Thisbe left the house. What an archwife—and utterly delectable as she scolded him. He'd reveled in her loose hair about her shoulders last night, and now he appreciated how it framed her sweet face under the bonnet.

She was right on one count. He'd heard the door but couldn't risk being recognized by Lily or Lady Best. On the other hand, she was wrong about Dolman. He would have to get over his shyness or live a lonely life. What he needed was a woman, preferably a wife.

A good loving wife was a lifetime comfort to be wished for—and Gervaise did wish for one for himself as well—but if all he did was make the lady uncomfortable, what was the point? And uncomfortable she would surely be, unable to understand his inability to behave like a man who had never been a spy. If she could forgive his having been a spy in the first place.

Mrs. Rose was right about his needing a bath, though, with the result that he was clean as a whistle and even wearing a clean if shabby gown by the time she came home.

He'd been watching for her. Hoping she'd enjoyed herself with Lady Best, and that friendship with her would mean introductions to more ladies of the area. If she had friends, he would no longer feel responsible for her and therefore would be free to leave. The wager was almost over, and he couldn't remain and risk her reputation. He had to move on to some other disguise, some other persona to keep himself busy and mostly alone.

She all but pranced down the steps of the carriage, turned for a word of thanks and a cheerful wave goodbye, and then hurried up the stairs and opened the front door. He barely had time to back away and pretend he was just coming from the kitchen.

She danced in, beaming with happiness. With utter joy.

Gervaise stood transfixed, for all at once he knew who she was— the most beautiful girl at the ball. It was the last occasion he'd attended before being smuggled to the Continent to spy for England, the country of his ancestors, against France, the country of his other ancestors. Not that this was unusual; the upper classes of the two countries were much interrelated. However, he felt himself to be both patriot and traitor, and it tore him up inside.

Mrs. Rose halted. "Evening, Mrs. Wix! What have we for dinner? We had tea and cakes at the Old Oak Inn, but I'm sure I shall be ravenous soon." She paused, blinking, as he simply stood and stared at her flushed cheeks, her rosy lips, her sparkling eyes. "Mrs. Wix?"

He pulled himself together and cleared his throat. "Yes, missus," he croaked, hopefully enough to disguise his voice, for he wasn't as prepared as he should be. "Chicken and the last of the sorrel, and after that a blackberry pie. Shall I take your packages?"

"No, thank you," Mrs. Rose said, "it's only ribbons and needles and such. I've been invited to an assembly in Brighton, so I must get to work preparing my evening gown."

"Invited? By whom?" Damn, he was making a mull of this. Mrs. Wix never used the word *whom*. Nonetheless, he couldn't let her go jaunting off with just anyone.

"Lady Best. She and Sir Simon will fetch me in their coach and bring me home. Isn't she the kindest lady ever? And Miss Transom, too. I believe I met her brother once, many years ago, shortly before I married Mr. Rose."

Indeed you did, thought Gervaise, but evidently he hadn't made much of an impression on her, if she'd succumbed all but immediately to some rake or other and been forced to marry Eddie Rose so soon afterwards.

Not that he could have married anyone at the time. He hadn't even allowed himself to think in such terms. He was a spy—a ghost —and like Eddie, would likely die. Except that unlike Eddie, he hadn't.

"I took a bath, missus," he said.

⚜

"Excellent," Thisbe said. "Doesn't it feel better to be clean?"

"Aye, missus, much better. I'll go finish the supper, shall I?" She returned to the kitchen, and Thisbe hurried upstairs. It would soon be dusk, so she wouldn't get much done tonight, but at least she could put her purchases away and refresh herself for dinner.

Five minutes later, a loud, determined knocking sounded on the door.

Hopefully, Mrs. Wix would answer it, but perhaps not. However obliging she'd been about bathing, she might not answer the door, and nor would Sergeant Dolman. Quickly drying her face, Thisbe went down the stairs. Mrs. Wix, unsurprisingly, was nowhere to be seen.

She peered out the window and saw three men—a Customs riding officer and two others. The riding officer snapped his crop impatiently against his breeches, and one of his men pounded on the door again.

How ghastly! They must have realized that someone in league with the smugglers had decoyed them from here. Would they arrest Mrs. Wix? Thisbe couldn't let that happen. She turned away from the window, meaning to run to warn her, when the door flew open. "Halt!" the officer shouted. "Come back here, woman!"

Thisbe turned, and Eddie's ghost marched up beside her, stern and forbidding—which was kind of him but useless, since they couldn't see him. Well! If she had learned one thing from her father, it was how intimidating haughtiness could be.

"I *beg* your pardon!" she exclaimed, nose in the air. "Who do you think you are, bursting into my house without so much as a by-your-leave?"

The officer stiffened, but amended his tone somewhat. "*Your* house, miss?" Not nearly respectful enough.

"Yes, indeed! I am Mrs. Rose, the owner of this house. And who, may I ask, are you?"

"Lieutenant Miles, Customs' Land Guard," he said. "You don't look old enough to own anything, much less a house. We were told no one lives here."

"No one did until yesterday, when I arrived to take possession. How dare you speak to me in such an impolite fashion? I shall report your behavior to Sir Simon Best. His wife is a friend of mine."

He frowned at that but didn't back down. "*No one* lived here?"

"Only a few servants, and I fail to see what business it is of yours!"

"Oy, what's going on here, missus? Sorry, I was picking rosemary for garnish, like." It was Mrs. Wix. "What's this, now? Oh, revenuers." She made one of her nasty chomping noises. "Nosy sorts." For a second, Thisbe wondered if Mrs. Wix would spit, which would not help at all. If only she had stayed away!

"With reason, my good woman." He turned to Thisbe again. "We believe this house is being used by smugglers."

"To store contraband? Nonsense!" Thisbe said. "I went over the entire house yesterday from attics to cellars, and there's nothing but dust, mildew, and broken furniture."

"Aw, missus, it ain't that bad," Mrs. Wix whined. "I kept the drawing room nice, didn't I? And the dining room, too."

"Yes, yes, there are a few decent rooms," Thisbe said, imagining herself in the role of an unsympathetic mistress. "Don't start weeping on me again. I'm sure you've done your best."

"Nevertheless, ma'am," the lieutenant said, "someone was signaling from here last night."

"Signaling to whom?"

"To the smugglers, obviously, and if it wasn't you, and it wasn't your cook here, who was it?"

"You must be mistaken," she said, thinking furiously. She couldn't let them arrest Sergeant Dolman, either. "Only Mrs. Wix and I were in the house, both of us fast asleep..." A brilliant notion descended on her. She clapped her hands to her face. "Oh, my heavens—so *that's* what it was last night!"

She sank onto a chair. "It does make more sense than ghosts, doesn't it, Mrs. Wix?"

"Mayhap it does," Mrs. Wix said grumpily, "leastways this time. Mark my words, though, this house is haunted. Everybody knows that."

"I don't believe in ghosts," the revenue officer snapped. "Tell me what happened, Mrs. Rose."

"I was wakened by a horrid shriek in the middle of the night," Thisbe said.

One of the other revenuers nodded glumly.

"Did you hear it too?" Thisbe asked him, infusing sympathy into her voice.

"Not last night, but a couple of nights ago. Chilled my bones, it did." He glanced sheepishly at his superior. "To tell the truth, I was right glad we was ordered not to go in alone."

"Yes, it was dreadful, wasn't it?" Thisbe said. "At first, I thought it was only a nightmare—since my husband died in battle, I am subject to simply *ghastly* dreams—but then I heard a board creak in the attic. I peered out into the gallery, but it was pitch dark, so I thought it must be the house settling, as old houses do at night."

"And?" the lieutenant asked eagerly.

"I was about to shut my door again when I heard footsteps, and I called out, 'Who's up there?' I was frightened, Lieutenant, but this is *my* house, and no one has the right to be here without my permission. I called for Mrs. Wix and was about to go up and tell the intruder to leave, when a man came positively *hurtling* down the stairs. He almost knocked me over and kept on down, then shoved poor Mrs. Wix out of the way and disappeared into the night, leaving the door wide open." She shuddered. "Mrs. Wix made sure all the doors were bolted, but I hardly slept the rest of the night."

"Poor lamb," the housekeeper cooed, putting an arm around her. Mrs. Wix smelled beautifully clean. And...distracting.

"Did you recognize the man?" Lieutenant Miles asked.

"Of course not!" Thisbe tried to ignore the strange distraction. "It was pitch dark, Lieutenant, and I don't know anyone here. It wasn't one of my servants, though. It was a smallish man, and my man-of-all-work is too big and too old to run down stairs like that. It must have been a smuggler, just as you said. But why would he signal from my house?"

"Because of rumors the house is haunted. I assume it gave them the idea to decoy our men here instead of where the goods were," the lieutenant said with a sigh. "From now on, ma'am, make sure your house is locked up tight at night, and that all the windows are bolted, too. You're lucky you weren't harmed."

"Yes, I see that," she said faintly, realizing that Mrs. Wix smelled not only *male* in an attractive sort of way, but headily *familiar*.

"It can be dangerous for a woman to live alone," the revenuer said. "Begging your pardon, ma'am, but you look too young to be on your own. Don't you have family to take care of you?"

Mrs. Wix's arm tightened a fraction. "She has me."

"Thank you, Mrs. Wix. I'm a widow," she said firmly, "and old enough to manage for myself." She softened, for he was only trying to be kind. "I appreciate your concern, Lieutenant, but now that I've been warned, I'll hire a footman to guard the house at night."

"Aye, but...if any other revenue officers come here, don't let them in. There are some who won't hesitate to take advantage." He sighed again, shaking his head, and they left.

"It was kind of him to warn me," she said uneasily.

"Aye, he's a good man, and he knows what he's talking about," Mrs. Wix said. "There's a revenuer along the coast who's a right bastard, begging your pardon, missus, but he'll get his comeuppance soon, never you fear. For now, as I said, you have me."

Reluctantly, Gervaise removed his arm from around the delectable Mrs. Rose. He bolted the door after the revenue men and chuckled. "You handled them nicely, missus."

"I thought so," she said vaguely, as if her mind were elsewhere. Surely, she wasn't taken with that riding officer! A decent sort, no doubt, doing a thankless job, but he wasn't right for her.

"You did well, too," she added. "I shall go upstairs and finish, ah, what I was doing." She headed for the stairs, then turned. "I hope you have informed the smugglers that we shall no longer signal from here?"

"Aye, missus, I took care of that today." Why was she frowning at him?

"I feel sorry for the lieutenant. I didn't like to deceive him, but nor could I let him arrest you or Sergeant Dolman. By the way, where is he?"

"In the kitchen, missus. He'll eat there with me."

"Good. I wouldn't put it past the revenuers to question him."

"Right, missus. I'll keep him safely here."

At the foot of the stairs, she turned again, her brows knit. "I apologize for accusing you of weeping, for I'm almost certain that is something you rarely, if ever, do."

What the devil did she mean by that? "It was a nice touch, but you're right, love. All my tears dried up years ago."

⚜

She—he?—had called her *love* again.

Mrs. Wix was a woman, not a man, so how could she smell like one?

Specifically, like the one who had kissed her four years ago!

Thisbe tried to look at it rationally. Surely a man's scent wasn't completely unique. She'd caught the personal aromas of various men when dancing with them, but although there was sometimes a similarity, it wasn't the same. Eddie, for example, had smelled quite pleasant, more so than many others. And of course, too many men wore bottled scent which competed with their own personal odors, often with distressingly unpleasant results.

But not the man who had kissed her. He'd simply smelled like himself.

Perhaps her memory was at fault. Surely one didn't remember aromas, particularly those from years ago, so very exactly. And yet...

Gervaise Transom had visited Sir Simon Best the previous evening, only a few miles away. He could have ridden back to Lucky Cottage in time to signal in the middle of the night.

Mrs. Wix was tallish for a woman, but about medium height for a man. So, she recalled, was Mr. Transom, but Thisbe was petite, so she'd gazed up, entranced, at his smiling face.

Mrs. Wix had a creaky voice, and she kept clearing her throat and making those horrid champing noises... Could that all be Mr. Transom's way of disguising his voice?

Something else popped into her mind—a memory of that wide, mischievous grin last night—with completely clean teeth. And a long cloak over...what? A man's clothing?

Unbelievable!

Yes, that was precisely what it was. Unbelievable, and she was foolish to even imagine such a thing, but she couldn't help doing so. Miss Transom had called him what...Ghostie? He'd tricked the masters at school, so why not trick people now?

No. She wanted to meet that man again, which was a foolish sort of wish, and she mustn't let that folly color her perception now. She must consider Mrs. Wix more carefully before reaching such an unlikely conclusion. However, if the housekeeper really were Gervaise Transom...

Thisbe sat in the chair by her dressing table, flummoxed. No wonder he didn't want her here, for if anyone found out she was sharing the house with a gentleman, her reputation would indeed be ruined. But why would he dress as a woman and live alone, cooking and cleaning? He certainly knew a great deal about smugglers and revenue officers—far more than a mere housekeeper would know. Was he a fugitive, accused of some dreadful crime, who daren't risk being unmasked?

No, she thought suddenly, remembering something Lady Best had said about a wager with Sir Simon, just like when he'd been a boy. Like when he'd kissed her at the ball. What fun! And yet...

There was also Miss Transom's concern for her brother, who had come back from the war a different man—restless, impatient, unwilling to return to home and family.

A man who had cried all his tears.

CHAPTER 6

The next morning, Thisbe decided that considering Mrs. Wix more carefully was well-nigh impossible. Staring at the housekeeper would look extremely odd, and sniffing her even odder.

Not only that, what if Mrs. Wix truly were Mr. Transom, and he realized he had been unmasked? He might feel obliged to leave.

She wanted him to stay, at least for now. She wasn't exactly frightened of being alone, but she wasn't comfortable, either. She felt safer with him—her—there.

Which was pure selfishness. She should be ashamed of herself. Mr. Transom—if it truly were he—must have his own reasons for remaining in disguise. He wanted to be alone, away from family, perhaps from their expectations. He would doubtless leave as soon as possible, whether or not she saw through his disguise.

"I'll have to hire another housekeeper," she told Eddie's ghost. He had joined her in the drawing room, which had excellent light for sewing.

The ghost nodded agreement, grinning widely, cheerfully, and annoyingly.

"I don't know what you're so pleased about," she retorted. "I like Mrs. Wix very much. I wish she could stay."

He nodded and grinned even more widely at that, which made no sense at all.

She turned her mind to the assembly that very evening. She intended to enjoy herself, meet new people, and hopefully cultivate friendships. She might even dance, if anyone asked, and do a little comparison of scents—although she rather hoped not to garner any admirers just yet. Before considering another marriage, which was the safest way to avoid her father, she must dismiss Mr. Transom—whether or not he was also Mrs. Wix—from her mind and heart.

She finished adding trim to the flounce and sleeves and gold ribbons to the bodice of her green ball gown. She drank tea and ate more rock cakes—taking care to smile and thank Mrs. Wix while not looking at her too closely—then went upstairs to change.

Suddenly, she found herself with an awkward problem. She'd made a point of bringing clothing she could don without assistance from a maid. She even had corsets that laced at the front—but for the ball gown, she needed help.

"What am I to do?" she asked Eddie's ghost. "I have no choice but to ask Mrs. Wix to do up the buttons at the back."

Eddie well-nigh doubled up with silent laughter. She didn't understand his amusement, but she *was* rather excited. Mr. Transom would have no choice but to touch her, and she would have another chance to inhale his intoxicating aroma. Thisbe put a shawl around her shoulders and went partway down the stairs.

"Mrs. Wix!" she called. "I need some help with my gown."

"Aye, missus?"

Thisbe assumed her sweetest voice. "Will you please come up to my chamber? Wash your hands first with plenty of soap. I'd rather not smell of onions."

There was a pause, and then a grumbling assent. "In a minute, missus."

Thisbe waited on tenterhooks and did her best to do no more than glance up when the housekeeper appeared. "Kindly do up the buttons at the back of my gown."

The housekeeper sniffed her fingers. "They seems all right to me. You want to sniff them first, missus?"

Thisbe suppressed a giggle. "No, thank you. I'm sure you washed them as best you could." She turned to face the mirror, her back to Mrs. Wix.

The housekeeper approached. She did smell a little of various herbs, but the intoxicating personal aroma was overwhelmingly there. Thisbe took a deep breath and closed her eyes. When she opened them again, she realized she could freely watch Mrs. Wix in the mirror while the housekeeper's attention was on the row of tiny buttons.

She shivered a little at the touch of her—his?—hands on her corset, and then on her bare flesh. She—he?—glanced up, and their eyes met. Thisbe felt herself flush but refused to look away.

It was Mrs. Wix who dropped her gaze, in order to fasten the last few buttons. "You look perfectly lovely, missus," she said. "You surely will slay some lucky gentleman's heart tonight."

"Oh, dear, I hope not," Thisbe said.

"Why? Don't you wish to marry again? Might help you get rid of the unpleasant dreams."

"I don't really have bad dreams about my husband," she said, seeing an opening to probe into Mr. Transom's feelings. "Eddie's ghost is a happy one, so I know he's fine where he is. I just said that for...for verisimilitude. I've heard that many people who went to war have such dreams."

"Aye, so they do," Mrs. Wix said, without much interest.

Thisbe tried again. "Or—or much sadness because of what they have seen and done and can never undo. One of the Squire's sons where I grew up in Surrey is melancholy like that."

"Missing your home already, missus?" Which was a clear attempt to change the subject.

"It's not really a home." She picked up her gold locket, one of her few pieces of jewelry, to judge how it would look with the gown. "My father is...unpleasant and unkind. All he cares about is his status. He believes I must be strictly controlled, or I will embarrass him."

"Why? Did you embarrass him in the past?"

"Yes, but it was all nonsense, and now he means to marry me off to one or other of his elderly friends. I am *so* thankful to Eddie for bequeathing me this house, and I shall manage somehow. I hope Papa will forget about me. Out of sight, out of mind."

"The man sounds like a fool," Mrs. Wix said. "Let me help you with the clasp." Thisbe shivered at the touch of those capable hands. "So, it's not marriage you wish to avoid, but marriage to the wrong man."

"Yes." Thisbe shivered. Why was her heart racing? She took a deep breath to calm herself.

"Did you never meet the right man, missus?"

Thisbe shrugged, feigning indifference. "I thought I did once, but it was not meant to be, and then I married Eddie, which was pleasant for a night and a day. Then he left for the Continent, and I never saw him alive again."

"A night and a day!" Mrs. Wix said. "Let us hope your next marriage lasts much longer."

Thisbe didn't want to talk about marriage. She was almost certain Mrs. Wix was Gervaise Transom—he wasn't controlling his voice and vocabulary as well as before—but if he didn't want her, she refused to want him in return. "And let us hope the highwayman doesn't steal my locket," she said.

Mrs. Wix stood back. "He's no fool. He won't rob Sir Simon's coach."

"Do you know who the highwayman is?"

Mrs. Wix shrugged and went to the door. "I'll get back to my kitchen. Call if you need me, love."

Thisbe donned her evening cloak of blue velvet, stowed her slippers in the pocket, and went down to wait for Sir Simon's coach. She felt a little dreary; wishing and hoping Mr. Transom would confide in her had proven useless. She tried to drum up some enthusiasm for meeting new gentlemen, but none of them would smell as good, as desirable, as safe, as the man who had kissed her so many years before.

The sound of hooves and carriage wheels roused her from this doleful reverie. Eddie's ghost appeared, frowning and flapping his arms, silently shouting something, but she couldn't make out what he said. Perhaps he meant she should wait for a servant to open the door, but judging by the sounds coming from the kitchen, Mrs. Wix was chopping something, so she wasn't likely to come.

Thisbe hurried to open the door—and gasped.

"Oh, no!" She tried to compose herself, she really did, but she was already trembling. What was Papa doing here?

He clambered down from the coach, and too late she knew what to do—slam the door shut, throw the bolt, and run for the safety of Mrs. Wix.

"Don't you dare!" He shoved hard against the door, almost knocking her to the floor. "You're coming home with me."

Eddie's ghost marched up, drew a sword from nowhere, and brandished it at Papa.

That helped a little, made her feel stronger. Surer. "This is my home now," she retorted. "Eddie left it to me, and this is where I shall stay."

"This hovel?" he cried, and Eddie dealt him a useless buffet, then vanished. "The grounds are unkempt, and I haven't a doubt the interior is just as bad."

"As a matter of fact," she said as calmly as she could, "the drawing room is perfectly fine, so is the dining room, and the housekeeper and I are working on the other rooms—"

"Working? The daughter of a baron doesn't *work*. Why are you answering your own door? Can't afford any decent servants, can you? No daughter of mine will answer her own door, I can tell you that. And where do you think you're going, all dressed up so fine? Wearing your mother's locket, too, while you go gallivanting about. How dare you?"

"I've been invited to an assembly in Brighton," she said.

"Ha! Escorted by whom? Have you already found a lover, you little trollop? I knew you'd be back to your old ways the minute you were out of my sight. We're leaving *now*!"

"No!" she cried, backing away. "I'm not going with you."

Papa grabbed her arm, and she opened her mouth to shriek—but suddenly, Mrs. Wix was there, swathed in an apron, a bloody cleaver in her hand, Eddie right behind, cheering her—him—on.

"Let her go," Mrs. Wix said.

"Who the devil are you?" Papa demanded, towing Thisbe toward the door.

"The cook. I said, let her *go*." Her—his voice was that of a very dangerous male.

"Go to hell, you stupid woman." Papa tightened his grip and tugged Thisbe hard.

"Stop it!" she cried. "You're hurting me!"

"It's nothing to what I'll do to you when we get home," Papa snarled.

Mrs. Wix grabbed hold of Papa's wrist and squeezed. "I said, *let her go.*"

Papa yelped, struggling, released Thisbe, and bellowed for his footman, Jerome, who hurried into the house, spied the bloody cleaver in Mrs. Wix's hand, and paled.

"Thank you, Mrs. Wix," Thisbe said, rubbing her wrist.

"I'll show you whom to thank," Papa said. "Don't just stand there, Jerome. Move this disgusting female out of the way, and take Miss Thisbe to the coach."

"I am not coming with you!" Thisbe retreated behind her rescuer.

"That's right, she ain't," Mrs. Wix said, brandishing the cleaver. Jerome didn't move.

"Fools and cowards, all of you!" Papa glared at Mrs. Wix. "I shall report this attack on my person to the appropriate authorities."

Mrs. Wix cackled. "The JP will be here any minute to fetch Mrs. Rose, but I doubt he'll have time for you now."

"She's tupping a JP?" Papa roared, and suddenly found himself pushed against the wall and held in a relentless grip.

"Take those foul words back, or I'll shove them down your throat," Mrs. Wix said.

Jerome merely gaped, and Papa croaked, "Do something, you useless fellow!" Eddie's ghost hovered behind Mrs. Wix, silently urging her on, a sword in one hand and a pistol in the other.

"Please don't kill him," Thisbe whispered.

Eddie desisted, looking abashed, and Mrs. Wix said, "Never fret, love. I shan't, or at least not yet." He let Papa go and grinned at Jerome. "Come work for Miss Thisbe. She's much more fun."

Poor Jerome looked so very tempted. No one liked working for Papa.

Fortunately, since Papa was rubbing his throat while working himself up to another outburst of venom, a second carriage rolled up outside.

Thisbe slumped. All anticipation of a pleasurable evening fled. What Mr. Transom must think of her! Yes, he had rescued her, but he would surely tell Sir Simon about Papa's horrid accusations. The JP would tell his wife and Miss Transom, and they would turn their backs, likely without giving her a chance to explain.

She needed to tell him all about it, and do it now!

"Looks like Sir Simon and his ladies are here, Mrs. Rose," the housekeeper said, sticking her head out the door and giving a piercing whistle. "Off you go. Dance to your heart's content, and mayhap a handsome stranger will fall in love with you."

"Don't say such things!" she cried. "I need to—I must explain something to you."

"Later will do. Trust me, all will be well." Mrs. Wix gave her a little push towards the door.

"What the devil?" Papa tried to follow her, but Mrs. Wix held him back, while a very proper gentleman in evening wear descended from the coach.

"Run along, love. Go enjoy the ball," Mrs. Wix said. "I'll have a word with Sir Simon, and he'll keep you safe."

Thisbe scurried out the door past her father and scrambled into Sir Simon's coach.

CHAPTER 7

Simon came into the house—he'd responded to that whistle, bless him—and closed the door behind him. At last, Gervaise let the struggling Lord Wrapton go.

"What's going on here?" Simon demanded, at his most magisterial. "This had better be important. I'm on the way to an assembly."

"Why, you foul debaucher! How dare you?" Wrapton began, advancing on him.

Gervaise got in the way again. He still held the bloody cleaver, which helped. He wasn't quite ready to drop the disguise completely —but by God, maybe he should have. He'd been merrily chopping meat for the next day while avoiding being seen by his sister or Lady Best, when a gust of wind almost blew him out of the kitchen, and suddenly he knew Thisbe was in danger.

This disguise, and the stupid wager, had almost cost her dearly.

"Sir Simon, this is Lord Wrapton, Mrs. Rose's father," he said. "He should be put in irons. He tried to force Mrs. Rose out of her own house and threatened to beat her if she disobeyed. Now, God knows why, he seems to think you are enamored of her."

"What? I've not yet met Mrs. Rose. She's a friend of my wife's." He turned an astonished gaze on Wrapton. "Are you quite mad, sir?"

"Not *sir*, but *my lord*," Wrapton snapped. "I don't give a tinker's damn who you are. The proper form of address is *your lordship* or *my lord*, and this woman attacked me. She is the one who must be put in irons."

"But, my dear sir, you'll look such a fool." Simon chuckled. "Surely you could defend yourself against a hysterical female, even one holding a cleaver." He looked Wrapton up and down. "I see no sign that you're bleeding."

"Been chopping meat," Gervaise said, wiping the cleaver on his apron. "Steak and kidney pie tomorrow."

"*My lord*," Wrapton insisted. "Address me *properly*. She attacked me, damn you!"

"Good God. I have seldom met such a pompous ass." Simon sighed. "Get into your carriage, *my lord*, and go back where you came from. I'm busy this evening, but if you are still here tomorrow, trespassing on private property and assaulting innocent women, you will regret it."

"I'll find a real JP," Wrapton shouted, "and I'll take my daughter away, as is my right as her father, and you'll be the one to regret your impudence!"

Simon gave Gervaise a look that said clearly, *Now it's up to you.* He folded his arms and waited while Lord Wrapton, muttering curses, stomped out to his coach and climbed in. The footman closed the door, but instead of jumping to his perch, he waved to the coachman to leave while he remained behind. The coachman nodded understandingly and drove off.

Gervaise doubted Lord Wrapton even noticed Jerome's defection, so caught up was he in his own bitter, prideful thoughts. He must never be allowed near Thisbe again. Not only that, if Gervaise had his way, he would someday find himself pleading to be accepted by his own daughter.

So what if it meant returning home? His parents couldn't understand what had driven him to solitude, but it seemed Thisbe could and did...and not only that, Gervaise had had enough of being alone. With Thisbe, he could build an interesting, worthwhile life.

If she would have him. He was almost certain she had penetrated his disguise, but she had never let on. Why not?

"Good man," he said to Jerome, making no attempt to disguise his voice. "You're hired. You and Sergeant Dolman may guard the house tonight. I've other matters to take care of—first of all, getting out of this damned uncomfortable women's clothing. Do you like oxtail soup?"

The astonished footman said, "Yes, ah, sir," and followed Gervaise into Lucky Cottage.

※

Lady Best hustled Thisbe into the coach and settled her on the far side, where Papa couldn't reach her if he tried. She didn't think he would; he wasn't courageous enough, or fit enough, or possibly even stupid enough to try.

"Thank you," she whispered, taking deep shuddering breaths.

"You poor dear," Lady Best said. "Whatever happened? No, don't answer. You need to calm down first."

"I'm well," she said. "My father tried to take me home by force." She dashed away tears. "I thought—I hoped he would be glad that I was gone. He—he dislikes me. He kept trying to get rid of me by marrying me off to one of his friends. I thought that once I left, he might leave me be."

"Heavens, how horrid of him! Well, you're safe now," Lady Best said. "In fact, you'd better come home with us after the ball until everything is sorted out."

"Oh, no," Thisbe said. "Surely that's not necessary. I have a housekeeper and a man of all work. I'll be fine."

"Servants are no use against a peer," Lady Best said. "But my dear, why would he dislike you?"

"It's a long story," Thisbe said, and she didn't intend to confess it all now if she could avoid it. "What it boils down to is that he is afraid I will embarrass him."

Sir Simon Best climbed into the coach in time to hear this. "The man's an embarrassment to himself! My apologies, Mrs. Rose—

happy to meet you, by the way—but your father is most strange. He kept ordering me to address him as *my lord*."

"I'm so sorry, Sir Simon. He's been unbearable ever since he was made a peer."

"Prinny should know better," Sir Simon grumbled. "You'll stay with us until we sort your father out. Get you some proper protection."

"But—"

"No buts," he said. "I have a feeling everything will work out very, very soon. In the meantime, enjoy the assembly tonight. You'll dance with me, I hope?"

"Thank you, I should like that," she said, relieved. At least no one was shunning her yet.

Sir Simon couldn't possibly know that everything would work out, but it was nevertheless kind of him to reassure her. Perhaps Mr. Transom would say nothing. He'd been protective of her, and he, too, had said all would be well—whatever that meant. That a handsome stranger was sure to fall in love with her?

But what was the use of meeting some handsome stranger, when Mr. Transom was the only man she wanted and would ever want? Yet couldn't have.

Papa might retreat for now, but he would return. She could stay a few days with the Bests, but after that, what would she do? What kind of protection could she afford? No servant would dare resist a nobleman.

They all chatted of minor matters until they arrived at their destination. The assembly rooms were a dazzling display of light—chandeliers ablaze with candles, and mirrors reflecting them along one wall. Lady Best introduced both her and Lily Transom to a great many ladies and gentlemen. Everyone was cordial; Sir Simon asked her to dance, which soon led to dances with other gentlemen, some of whom had pleasing aromas. Nothing like Mr. Transom's, alas.

She shook herself. She mustn't be foolish. He wasn't the only man in the world. She'd married Eddie, and it hadn't been unpleasant. Although her inheritance wasn't much, it might suffice to make a respectable man willing to offer for her—and if her so-called wanton tendencies came up for discussion, perhaps he would allow her to explain the mistake she'd made so long ago: a simple misunderstanding, not a sin.

Soon the ball would be over. She had met many new people. So far, so good. She must simply persevere, and take what help and protection she could find, and—

"Ghostie!" Lily Transom's shriek startled her out of her reverie.

Thisbe looked up, heart thumping. There he was, elegant as ever, striding toward them. Lily dashed up to him and hugged him. "Gervaise! You came!"

"I did, sister dear, in the hope that you would introduce me to some of your friends, as promised." He winked over Lily's shoulder. "But I believe this lady and I have met before."

Thisbe realized her mouth was hanging open. Hurriedly, she shut it and clapped a hand to her breast. He was here!

Mr. Transom bowed over Thisbe's hand. Her heart beat so fast she could almost hear it. "Have we not?" he asked.

"Yes," she whispered, "in Chichester, years ago. How—how kind of you to remember me, sir."

He grinned. "How could I forget the most beautiful girl at the ball?"

Lord, could she blush any more than this? The musicians struck up for a waltz, and he asked, "Might I have this dance, Mrs. Rose?"

And just like that, he swept her into his arms, like so many years ago.

* * *

At last, thought Gervaise, twirling Thisbe around the floor. He'd expected to arrive much earlier—it didn't take long to bathe and shave—but he hadn't expected to be delayed by Captain Moonlight.

Not robbing *him*, of course; this highwayman was known for robbing people who deserved it. As soon as Gervaise heard shots up ahead, followed by frightened horses and Lord Wrapton's unpleasant bellow, he reined in and waited politely for the robbery to be over. Soon, Captain Moonlight cantered past, raised a hand to Gervaise in the shadows at the roadside, and vanished into the night. A mighty observant sort, that man—one needed to be, to succeed at highway robbery.

Gervaise chuckled to himself, waited several minutes, then made his way to where Lord Wrapton's coach still stood. Thisbe's father was shouting at the hapless coachman, berating him for not shooting the highwayman—which he couldn't have done while controlling the agitated team, even if he had a gun in his hand and was a crack shot, which coachmen seldom were.

Gervaise pondered inviting the coachman to work for him instead, thus leaving the old blusterer completely stranded. Much as Wrapton deserved it, Gervaise couldn't bring himself to put the coachman in such an awkward situation; a decent chap, who cared about his horses, wouldn't agree to it anyway.

Instead, Gervaise reined in, doffed his hat, and asked if he might be of any assistance.

"Such as what?" Lord Wrapton snapped. "The highwayman got my purse, my watch, and my signet ring, thanks to this fool coachman of mine." He frowned at Gervaise in the dim light of the coach's lantern. "Do I know you? You look familiar."

"Perhaps," Gervaise said languidly. "I really can't say. If you have no need of assistance, I'll be on my way."

"Hold on a minute. Did a scoundrel on a big, dark bay—rather like yours, in fact—just pass you on the road?"

"If you mean the highwayman, no, he did not," Gervaise said. "If he had, he would have robbed me, don't you think?"

The pompous old windbag scowled. "Impudent! If you want to help, find me a magistrate. I'll see that fellow hanged if it's the last thing I do."

Gervaise doubted that. "It's late to drag a magistrate out, and for what? The highwayman's long gone. You'd best wait till morning."

"Not on your life. What if he attacks me again? Where is the nearest magistrate?"

Gervaise sighed. "Ask at the Old Oak Inn. I'll show you the way."

If it was possible to be in heaven on earth, Thisbe was there now. Dancing with Mr. Transom was like floating on air.

"Did you fear I wouldn't come?" he asked as they circled the ballroom. "I would have arrived sooner, but what with shaving and bathing, and a slight delay along the way, I'm later than I'd hoped."

"But—but what about the wager?" she asked.

"The wager be damned," he said. "It was time to end it. In any case, your safety matters more." He raised a brow. "How did you know about the wager?"

"I guessed from something Lady Best said, and remembered that you kissed me in Chichester because of a wager."

"*Thanks to* a wager. It was the perfect excuse." He smiled down at her, whirling her around, a devilish gleam in his eyes. "Do I need an excuse to kiss you again?"

Oh, dear. "I wish you could, but if you knew what trouble that kiss caused me, and is likely to cause me in the future, you wouldn't dare ask."

"What trouble?"

"I was forced to marry Eddie Rose because of that kiss," she said. "Not that it was entirely your fault, but..."

Just as he'd done four years earlier, he danced her onto the terrace, but instead of kissing her, he regarded her with knit brows. "You'd better explain."

"I thought you'd got me with child," she said. "Which was of course impossible, but my aunt's maid had always warned me that kisses led straight to babies, and she asked if you had put that horrid thing of yours inside me, and I said yes, meaning your tongue, not that I thought it was horrid at all, but she thought it was that other thing, your, ah—"

He burst into gusts of laughter. "My cock," he said unsteadily. "Oh, my dear girl, how hilarious."

When he'd calmed a little, she said indignantly, "It wasn't funny at the time. Papa forced me to marry Eddie, who taught me what I would have known if my poor aunt, who is a spinster, had known what to tell me, but by then it was too late for explanations. So, Papa believes I'm a wanton, which isn't true at all, but—"

"You darling." He pulled her into his arms and kissed her. This kiss was gentle and sweet, and it sent tremors through her, and how she wished it could go on forever. Too soon, he released her lips, but held her close. He smiled down at her. "I couldn't ask you this at the time, because I was obliged to go to the Continent and feared I would never return, but now—will you marry me?"

Oh, how she wished! She turned away; she couldn't bear to look into his eyes. "You're very kind, Mr. Transom, but you need not marry me. No one need know that we lived in the same house unchaperoned."

He chuckled. "My name is Gervaise, or Ghost if you prefer. When did you know who Mrs. Wix really was?"

"When I got a chance to smell you properly," she said. "You have the most delightful personal aroma, like no one else ever."

"You recognized me by how I *smelled?*"

"Yes, although a few other things hinted that something was amiss." But this distraction was irrelevant. "Sir Simon knows you were playing a part, so I suppose his wife does too, but surely they will not tell anyone. They wouldn't wish you to be forced into marriage."

"Didn't you hear what I said?" he demanded. "I wanted to ask you four years ago but couldn't because of a commitment to go to the Continent. Now I can. Dear, sweet Thisbe, will you please marry me?"

What could she say but, "Yes!"

CHAPTER 8

No sooner had she done so—and been kissed thoroughly in response, not to mention caressed in a delightfully arousing way—when than an outraged voice boomed from the ballroom. "I was robbed, I tell you! A masked man on a huge bay jumped out of the hedgerow, brandishing a pistol. No, not one pistol, but two!"

"Oh, dear," Thisbe said. "How dreadful for Papa."

"Serves him right," Gervaise said, letting go of her bum, which had felt so good in his big, warm hands. So had the feeling of his erection pressing against her belly. She would insist on marrying him very, very soon.

"Didn't you say you were the JP?" Papa shouted. "I knew you were a liar."

"I expect Sir Simon will do his best to send him away," Gervaise murmured, "but he has no jurisdiction in Brighton."

"Where's my daughter, damn you?" Papa bellowed. "I'll wager she's already run off with some rake, thanks to your inattention."

"Ah, well," Gervaise sighed. "Nothing like an irate parent to get in the way of such lovely lust. Perhaps we should give him some good news to counteract the bad."

"It won't be good news to him," Thisbe said. "He disapproved of you then and will do so now."

"He'll change his tune soon enough." Gervaise offered his arm, and she took it. How could he be so confident? She was already trembling at the prospect of confronting Papa again.

"What the devil?" Papa thundered the instant they reentered the ballroom. "I knew I recognized you! Unhand my daughter, you scoundrel!" He rounded on Sir Simon, jabbing a finger toward Gervaise. "That is the man who robbed me."

Sir Simon raised incredulous brows. "A moment ago, you told me the highwayman was so well covered by his hat and mask that no one could recognize him by daylight, much less in the dark."

"Aye, but this man rode up offering help not five minutes after I was robbed, and I recognized his horse. He's just the sort who would steal from innocent travelers. He is a dastard, I tell you. A wastrel, a libertine, a—"

"He's the son and heir of a respected peer," Sir Simon said. Beside Thisbe, Gervaise heaved a sigh.

He was *what*?

"I don't believe you," Papa barked. "You're no JP. You're in *league* with the rogue."

Sir Simon stiffened. "Do you accuse me of lying?" he demanded in a voice of ice.

By now the whole room was watching and listening. A bluff older gentleman of military bearing stepped forward. "Here now, what's going on?"

"Colonel Janes," Sir Simon said, "am I or am I not a Justice of the Peace?"

"You are indeed a JP, Sir Simon," he answered, looking down his nose at Papa. "Does this gentleman doubt both your word *and* mine?"

"This is Lord Wrapton, who I suspect is quite mad. He seems to think Mr. Transom is a highwayman, and that I am in league with him."

"Well now, sir, you were definitely in league with Mr. Transom as a lad, up to all sorts of mischief!" He chuckled. "But Lord Upforth's son and heir is unlikely to take to highway robbery, wouldn't you say?" He laughed heartily, and several other people joined in.

"You're what?" Thisbe whispered.

"Heir to a viscountcy, alas," Gervaise said, as chagrin suffused Lord Wrapton's face.

"Poor Papa. He must be so mortified," she said, but when Gervaise said nothing, she frowned up at him. "And poor you? You'd rather not be the heir?"

"I'm not looking forward to it—to returning to society and behaving as my bedamned status requires. It all seems so meaningless now. That's why I left my father's estate not long after returning from the Continent and eventually made a wager with Sir Simon that would keep me out of sight of the *ton*." He sighed again. "I would much rather be a cook, if I had the choice."

"You do have a choice!" Thisbe said. "If a viscount—or his heir—chooses to cook his own meals, who can stop him? But not as Mrs. Wix, please."

"You wouldn't object?"

"Of course not, as long as you don't find me lacking in the skills required of a viscountess," she said. "I hope I have a while to learn. Perhaps managing the house and estate of Lucky Cottage will give us both some practice, but without the unnecessary pomp that goes along with a peerage."

"We'll learn together," he said, "while cooking and doing whatever else we please." He laughed. "Let's go tell Best he won the wager."

※

Thisbe Rose and Gervaise Transom wed by special license a week later, at the home of Sir Simon and Lady Best. Gervaise's parents, Lord and Lady Upforth, and his sister Lily attended, as well as Thisbe's Aunt Andrea, who twittered happily, and her father, who didn't remain suitably abashed for long.

After the wedding feast they drove away, and arrived at Lucky Cottage at dusk. "Home at last," Gervaise said. They'd hardly seen each other for the past week, what with Gervaise hastening to London to acquire a special license, as well as a spanking new coach and pair, while Thisbe remained with the Bests and spent a great deal of time shopping for bride clothes.

Now, at last, they could be alone together—with all the pleasures that entailed.

Jerome the footman came out to take their baggage, and Sergeant Dolman appeared on the doorstep to wish them well. They walked into the house hand in hand—and there stood the ghost of Eddie Rose, bowing to them in welcome.

"Thank you, Eddie," she said softly and turned to Gervaise. "He warned you about my father that horrible evening. Did you realize?"

"The gust of wind," Gervaise ventured, "that practically blew me out of the kitchen? I wondered, for it came in the very nick of time."

"He's proud of his role in bringing about our marriage," Thisbe said.

The ghost grinned and motioned them up the stairs.

Thisbe giggled. "He wants us to go to our bedchamber." She sucked in a breath. "Eddie, that's frightfully vulgar of you."

"Now what?" Gervaise demanded.

"He made what I believe is a very crude gesture." She giggled again. "He wants us to get on with it."

"The devil he does," Gervaise said. "If he thinks he's going to watch—"

"He's shaking his head," Thisbe said. "He looks as appalled as you. I don't think he's interested in matters of the flesh anymore—ghosts usually aren't. He's just happy we're married at last, and wants us to enjoy ourselves."

And enjoy themselves they did.

THE END

If you enjoyed this novella, try *The Right to Remain Single*:

Faced with the ghastly suitors her father chooses, Thomasina

Warren decides to lose her virginity so that no respectable man will have her. Who better to ruin her than handsome, charming James Blakely? But James is an honorable man and refuses point-blank. Humiliated, she resorts to outright refusal to wed, with the help of a ghost who scares her suitors away. But four years later, her father has arranged her marriage to a stodgy gentleman who insists that the ghost must be banished forever

James Blakely never forgot the lovely girl who asked him to ruin her, and when he offers to get rid of the ghost, he thinks he'll be doing a good deed. Instead, he is faced with the hostile Thomasina, her cowardly suitor, pigheaded father, lecherous cousin, an exorcist monk, and a ghost who warns of danger and deadly peril—and a few short days in which to convince Thomasina that with the right man, she might just want to marry after all.

http://www.barbaramonajem.com/the-right-to-remain-single.html

SOCIAL MEDIA LINKS FOR BARBARA MONAJEM

Website: http://www.BarbaraMonajem.com

Facebook: https://www.facebook.com/barbara.monajem/

Instagram: https://www.instagram.com/barbaramonajem/

BookBub: https://www.bookbub.com/authors/barbara-monajem

Goodreads: https://www.goodreads.com/author/show/3270624.
Barbara_Monajem

ABOUT THE AUTHOR

Winner of the Holt Medallion, Maggie, Daphne du Maurier, Reviewer's Choice and Epic awards, USA Today Bestselling Author Barbara Monajem wrote her first story at eight years old about apple tree gnomes. She published a middle-grade fantasy when her children were young, then moved on to paranormal mysteries and Regency romances with intrepid heroines and long-suffering heroes (or vice versa).

Barbara loves to cook, especially soups. She used to have two items on her bucket list: to make asparagus pudding (because it was too weird to resist) and succeed at knitting socks. She managed the first (it was dreadful) and doubts she'll ever accomplish the second. This is not a bid for immortality, but merely the dismal truth. She lives near Atlanta, Georgia with an ever-shifting population of relatives, friends, and feline strays.

Learn more at www.BarbaraMonajem.com

THE CASEBOOK OF
PRINCIPAL OFFICER ROBERT
PIERCE

Brighton and surrounding districts

I had another mug of beer today with Lieutenant Miles of the Customs' Land Guard. He has solved the ghost problem he told me about the other day. Apparently, the supposed ghost that was signaling from an abandoned cottage was one of his smugglers. The man made the mistake of breaking in after the new owner took up residence, and was chased off by the owner and her cook. I've seen the cook. I would have run, too.

No leads to Larcenous Lucy, and far too many to the highwayman. In fact, I'm beginning to believe there may be two of the wretches. One of them held up the father of Miles's cottage owner, but the victim was of no use to me. He tried to pin the crime on a respectable war hero who is betrothed to the man's daughter! I can do without help like that.

MY GIFT TO YOU

MARY LANCASTER

My Gift To You
By Mary Lancaster

A rocky marriage and too many secrets...

The young Marchioness of Corey comes from a family of expensive rakehells. The world knows she married the marquis for his money—a conclusion Corey reached the day after their wedding.

Only, it was never true...

Attending the Normanton House party, each hopes for happiness. Only her wretched family gets in the way again, as does the local highwayman, and it seems their secret love is perpetually doomed...

CHAPTER 1

E veryone had told him not to marry her.
There was bad blood in the Raymonds, they said. They were all going to the devil, and her father and brothers would bleed him dry. Besides which, she, being wild to a fault like the rest of her kin, would disgrace him sooner or later.

It was not that Leopold, Marquis of Corey, had ignored them. Rather, he had already known the worst and suspected the rest, but by God it was worth it for these few occasions when he came upon her unexpectedly like this.

He stood for a moment in the open doorway of his wife's sitting room, watching her waltz extravagantly around the sofa and between the tables. She hummed her own music, which tugged a chord of his memory, a smile on her shapely lips and shining in her brilliant eyes as she danced. Her arms were raised slightly as though she touched a partner's shoulder and hand, every movement of her delectable body graceful and sensual.

She took his breath away. Even after four months of marriage and a certain amount of bitter disillusion, the sight of her like this, ebullient and natural and incomparably beautiful, hit him in the gut. Not merely with desire, but with tenderness, for he still saw in her what he always had—beauty, passion, an unquenchable spirit of fun, rare sweetness, and a kind of half-spoiled innocence that totally beguiled him.

This was the woman he had married. And heaven help him, it was worth all the trouble and heartache. He wanted nothing more than to fit into her hold, and dance with her. Alone, where no one could see.

But he was not the man she longed for. He was merely her husband.

That much was obvious as she became aware of him and instantly halted, dropping her arms to her side. Her smile died, and her expression changed to one of distant, almost insolent indifference.

"My lord," she drawled. "Behold the marchioness, practicing for the Somerville ball."

He inclined his head. "Behold the marquis, overwhelmed with joy at the prospect of my lady's company."

She lifted one corner of her mouth, a teasing challenge in her eyes now. "It looks remarkably similar to your displeasure. You need not be afraid I shall cling to you in the midst of strangers. They may be largely your friends but I daresay a few of my own acquaintances will also be present. We need not be so unfashionable as to seek each other's company."

"Let us at all costs be fashionable."

Her half-teasing eyes hardened. "Are we back to costs, my lord? I believe I might make do without new gowns or jewels I would only pawn."

My lord. Once she had called him Leo. For one magical day and one glorious night.

"It depends on your definition of new," he said glacially. He took the jewel case from behind his back and instead of giving it into her hands, laid it on the table beside him. "The Corey rubies, if you wish to take them. If not, return them to Scrivens to go back in the vault. Good morning, my lady."

He turned and walked out, aware of another chance lost, another moment ruined, another nail in the coffin of their ill-advised marriage.

Stricken, Gaby gazed after her husband. Why did he always do this to her? Put her in the wrong?

Why did she always give him the opportunity? By assuming his displeasure and countering it with defiance and mockery?

Her breath caught. What would he do if she ran after him, threw her arms around his neck and thanked him? Would his arms close around her? Would he give the slow, almost lazy smile that had first won her heart? Might he kiss her with the aching tenderness of their wedding night?

Her shoulders drooped.

No. He would look down his aristocratic nose at her, wait politely for her to remove her vulgarly effusive self, and walk away.

Had he always been like this and she had refused to see? That first time she had ever met him, he had called on her father about some piece of land or other, and she, all of sixteen years old, had fallen out of the apple tree into his arms. Had she imagined the laughter in his eyes above the seriousness of his mouth? The conspiratorial closing of one eyelid as he had later pretended to her parents the incident had not occurred? Perhaps. But she had *not* imagined the way he stood up for her and routed her bullying brothers, all without starting a fight. Instead, they had, briefly, wanted to be on his side.

No doubt it was just the stark reality of Gabriella Raymond he could not stomach.

Well, what was he thinking about, marrying into the Raymond family? Everyone knew they had been going to the devil for at least three generations, and her own was probably the worst, bidding fair to cast even her profligate, wicked old father into the shade.

She had met the Marquis of Corey only twice before he had asked for her hand. There had been the apple tree incident, when he had become her hero; and then, three years later, the dance at her godmother's ball. The very next day, he had offered for her.

Would he be disgusted if he knew he had just caught her reliving that waltz with him? Or merely indifferent?

Heroically, she re-summoned the hope that the forthcoming change of scene from Sanford Park to the neutral territory at the Somervilles' country seat would help her to win him. His mistress would be there, of course—the kind gossips had made a point of telling her so—but Gaby had every intention of eclipsing the dreadful woman in every way.

With this in mind, she straightened and went to the jewel case he had left behind. He had given her the Corey rubies, a stunning set worn by each marchioness since the seventeenth century. They were so valuable nowadays that they were only brought out of the vault for special occasions. And yet he had put them into her hands as though he trusted her. While she carped at him about his previous scold for her once pawning some trinket for her brother Arthur.

The dazzling beauty of the rubies in their gold setting caught at her breath. *Oh Leo...* Reverently, she lifted the necklace and hurried to the looking glass before holding it to her throat.

"Majestic," she breathed.

"So it is," said her brother Arthur, strolling into the room. "Change of style, Gab?"

Gaby blinked at the unexpected sight. "Art? What the devil are you doing here? Have you come to stay?"

"Lord, no. On my way to meet friends at a prize fight, then I have other plans. Just dropped in to pay you back."

Gaby's jaw dropped. "Your horse won?"

Art grinned. "Astonishing, isn't it? Knew my luck would turn, eventually. In fact, while I'm on this roll, I'll do you a favor, if you like." He held out a bundle of bank notes to her. "Happy to turn this pony into a monkey for you."

"Thanks," she said dryly. "I'll take my five-and-twenty pounds while I can."

Art's black eyebrows flew up. "Never tell me Corey keeps you short? Always seemed a very generous fellow to me."

"He is."

"He give you that gewgaw? Want me to pawn it for you in town?"

"No, I do not! That *gewgaw* is part of the Corey rubies."

"Oh," Art said without much interest. "Just thought you must be short, that's all, when you practically grabbed the pony out of my hand."

"I might have been a little extravagant," she admitted, replacing the necklace in its case on the table. "And Corey's already been so generous, I don't want to ask him for more. We're going to Normanton House tomorrow—it's near Brighton, now I come to think of it— and it will be good to have a few shillings to play cards with."

"Ah." Art dropped his careless, lanky person onto her elegant sofa. "That's the other reason I popped in. Snowy's going too."

"To Brighton?"

"To Lady Sommerville's party. At Normanton."

"Really? I wouldn't have thought it was his thing."

"It isn't," Art said restlessly. "Silly gudgeon's decided he needs to take the plunge and get leg-shackled."

"Snowy wants to be *married?*" she said, diverted. She had known the amiable Snowy most of her life and regarded him in much the same light as the relentlessly hedonistic Arthur, who was the only one of her disreputable brothers whom she could stand. "Who on earth to?"

Art studied his fingernails. "Lady Winmore. Wealthy widow. Don't think you know her."

Gaby scowled. "I'm not that naïve, Art. I know she is Corey's mistress." Saying the words felt like a knife in the heart, but they *were* only words and even Art should never guess how much the truth behind them hurt.

"*Was*, Gaby," Art said gruffly. His eyes kindled. "And I'd like to know who's been blabbering to you about such matters."

Gaby laughed. "Getting strait-laced in your old age, Arty?"

"No, but you are," he said frankly. "Can't think how in our family, but there it is. Don't suppose you've got a glass of brandy for a fellow before I clear off?"

"Not here, I haven't. Come on, there will be some in the drawing room."

"You struck lucky with Corey," Art said admiringly as they walked through the bright, well-maintained galleries and halls to the elegant drawing room. "This is quite the nobleman's seat. Pity the Old Devil will bleed him dry in a decade."

Gaby had no difficulty in recognizing her father, the Earl of Blockton, in this disrespectful epithet. "Actually, I wouldn't count on it. Corey is not the soft touch you all think him."

"Don't mind telling you the settlements he made on you were eye-watering. The Old Devil was rubbing his hands in glee. Has the rest of the pack been swarming yet?"

"Nicholas asked me for a hundred guineas, and Caroline tried to borrow the pearls Corey gave me as a wedding gift."

"Spongers," said Art, with the righteousness of one who had just paid his own debt.

She led him into the drawing room and pointed him at the decanter. He helped himself and took an appreciative sip while Gaby paced restlessly around the room.

Arthur threw himself into a chair to savor his brandy and his surroundings. "Is this the room you redecorated?"

"I just lightened it a bit," she said vaguely. "Made it more comfortable. I think Corey likes it." He had said he did, but he joined her here so seldom she suspected he was being merely polite. At least their neighbors enjoyed it when they came for dinner.

"Everything well with you, Gaby?" Art asked unexpectedly.

"Of course. Why wouldn't it be?"

"You seem a bit...off."

"I'm fine."

A short pause. "Corey well?"

"He is in excellent health."

"Not surprised with brandy as good as this. You quarreled with him, Gab?"

"No, of course not." She cast a quick glance at him to make sure he believed her and caught the skeptical expression in his eyes. More than that, she read his unease at stepping where he really did not want to tread.

"Don't give me that," he said heroically. "You're a Raymond. What have you done, and can I fix it? Happy to put myself out."

"Thank you, Art," she replied, genuinely touched. "But there is nothing you can do." She could not even blame the family. The fault was hers. Art continued to hold her gaze. She tried to smile. "I think...I am not quite the wife he wanted."

Art knocked back the rest of the brandy. "Rot. He shelled out thousands to the Old Devil for you. There's no doubt he wanted you, so don't be a goose."

He didn't know me. He only thought he wanted me, and now every sight of me disappoints him.

Art stood up, eyeing the decanter, and sighed. "Best not." He set down the glass. "I'll be on my way."

Gaby went with him to the door, and they walked along the Long Gallery just as Corey came out of the library in front of them.

He checked in surprise, and came toward them, his hand held out. "Arthur. I didn't know you had joined us."

"Oh, I haven't," Art said, clasping the offered hand briefly. "Just passing and dropped in for a moment—on my way to meet a party of friends. Very tolerable brandy you keep, Corey!"

Corey's lips twitched. "Thank you," he said gravely. "I endeavor to please."

Art grinned at him. "It's a treat for me. No need to see me out." He cast a glance at Gaby. "Remember what I said," he commanded with unusual severity, and strode off with an airy wave over his shoulder.

"What on earth did he say?" Corey asked, amusement in his voice.

That you wanted me so much once you let my father bleed you. The impossibility of repeating such a thing to him flustered her. "God knows. I don't listen to him."

And again, though he still sounded amused, the smile vanished from his face. "Don't look so appalled. I shan't pry into the family secrets." And he strolled on toward the staircase.

Smothering a sigh. Gaby instructed the nearest footman to send her maid to her. They might as well pack for the Somerville party. After all, it would be an early start tomorrow.

CHAPTER 2

By the morning, Gaby's spirits had revived to the extent that she actually looked forward to spending several hours alone with the marquis in his extremely comfortable traveling coach. She was glad he had chosen not to ride, and that her maid would travel with Corey's valet and their baggage in the other coach. His horses and his favorite curricle would also travel in their cavalcade, and they would be protected on the road by his own outriders.

Gaby knew she looked well in her new carriage dress of dark green wool with its warm matching pelisse and elegant little chip hat.

"Good morning, my lady," he said, smiling as he bowed and handed her in. They had elected to break their fast on the road rather than at home, so it was their first encounter of the day.

"Good morning, my lord. It is indeed a fine day." She clasped his strong fingers and stepped up into the carriage.

A large hamper sat on the opposite seat. Corey climbed in and sat beside it, with his back to the horses. The civility gave Gaby the opening she wanted for a casual, friendly overture.

She shifted a little to the left and indicated the space beside her. "Please, be comfortable, my lord. There is plenty of space."

"Thank you." He rose and sat beside her instead.

Immediately, despite the inches between them, she felt his nearness like a magnet, at once disturbing and deeply pleasurable.

The horses set off down the gracious drive at a good pace—Corey preferred to travel as quickly as comfort allowed. Sweeping around the bend, the carriage swerved to avoid a solitary horseman on his way up. The horseman halted and removed his hat, allowing Gaby an unwelcome glimpse of Nicholas, probably her least favorite brother. There was no affection in his nickname, Young Devil. It was merely to distinguish him from their father, the Old Devil.

"What on earth is *he* doing here?" she said, scowling.

"Do you wish to stop?" Corey asked politely.

"Lord, no. We've had a lucky escape."

Corey eyed her with amused puzzlement. "There really is no love lost between any of you, is there?"

"No. They are unrelievedly awful. Except Arthur, who only has awful tendencies. Like me."

He smiled. "And what are your awful tendencies?"

"Levity," she said lightly. "And an attraction to mischief. Although beneath this worthless exterior, lurks a deeply serious nature. Like yours."

"You find me serious?"

"You are, about some things. Your parliamentary causes for one—oh, I meant to say, if you are still looking for Lord Barhead's support for your Bill, I can probably extract a promise from him at the party."

He blinked. "How on earth will you do that?"

"He's a friend of my father's, and I am more than a pretty face. You should make use of me."

His brow twitched. "You're my wife, not a spare piece of furniture."

"I see myself as more of a secret weapon." She spoke lightly, to disguise her fear that he would reject her with contempt.

Instead, he continued to regard her as though intrigued. "I didn't know you had an interest in Parliament and politics."

"Well, there are many things about me you don't know."

Their eyes met and held, and her heart began to beat harder.

"I would like to," he said softly, and she smiled with true happiness.

Oh yes, there was hope.

***

Gaby enjoyed the journey to Normanton more than she had enjoyed anything since her wedding night. They talked of his Bill, of his parliamentary allies and enemies, and how to change the minds of the latter. The discussion was not without humor and their laughter led them down lighter roads.

Their al fresco breakfast brought them physically closer. Her heart leapt foolishly at every accidental touch, and she did not move away. Neither did he. Gaby was enchanted, for that secret smile was back in his eyes. She loved his dry, subtle humor that was rarely unkind. During their brief courtship between betrothal and marriage, this had been a revelation to her who had grown among loud, jeering people focused entirely on their own pleasure.

Once, when they were discussing the entertainments likely to be on offer at the party, she said lightly, "The rubies are even more beautiful than I expected. Thank you for trusting me with the family treasure."

He looked for the jest, of course, and she didn't blame him. She had used flippancy as protective armor too often.

"I mean it," she said ruefully.

"They're more than family treasure. They are my gift to you."

Pleasure brought a flush to her face. Impulsively, she touched her cheek to his shoulder. "Thank you," she whispered. Then, afraid he would dislike such a demonstration, she straightened. "Should I save them for the grand ball?" she wondered. "Or tease the company with a few pieces beforehand?"

"Whatever amuses you."

She was actually sorry to arrive at Normanton House, a large and gracious property, but the excitement stayed with her. She could swear this new friendliness was not mere politeness on his part. He did seem to genuinely like her still.

Which begged the question, why had he drawn away from her after that first night? Had she disappointed him so badly in bed? Or in other ways?

It doesn't matter, as long as we are truly together now...

They arrived late in the afternoon, and both host and hostess greeted them warmly.

"Welcome to Normanton House," Lady Sommerville cried. "I quite feel you have handed us the coup of the year by your presence."

"I trust your journey was unremarkable?" Sir Peter added. "We've had bother with a highwayman on the Brighton roads."

"Really?" Gaby was almost disappointed to have been spared such excitement until she realized that such a miscreant would almost certainly have stolen the Corey rubies. And the pearls.

"I expect your outriders made him think twice," Sir Peter said with approval.

"Come, I'll show to your rooms," Lady Sommerville said. "Where you may rest in comfort before tea, when you will meet all our other guests. I do hope you will be comfortable..."

Gaby had been sure that, in a house so full of guests, she and her husband would share a bedchamber. But she had reckoned without their rank. The marquis and marchioness were given their own rooms, each with a sitting room.

Just like at home, they had no need ever to meet except in company.

Her trunk already sat alone in the middle of the floor. She sat on it and watched Lady Sommerville bustle off with Corey. After the unexpected fun and companionship of the journey, loneliness was closing in.

She rose only when Hawkins, her maid, walked briskly through the sitting room, looking critically about her, and into the bedchamber.

"Not bad," Hawkins pronounced. "Let me put all your things away, my lady, and then we can get you dressed for tea."

Where is Lord Corey's room? she wanted to ask the maid, but didn't dare.

She was dressed in an elegant white muslin and was crossing the sitting room calling to Hawkins for her reticule, when a door she had never even noticed opened in the wall paneling and Corey himself wandered in.

"Ah," he said. "Forgive the intrusion. I wondered where the door led."

"A secret door!" Gaby exclaimed, rushing past him to see.

"Merely connecting to my rooms, which appear to mirror yours. In a much more lordly, masculine way, of course."

She laughed, for a connecting door was better than none.

"Shall we go down to tea?" he suggested, offering his arm.

"We shall."

It felt good to walk into Lady Sommerville's drawing room on her husband's arm, with the return of friendliness at least between them. Although Gaby gave no sign of it, she spotted Lady Winmore at once.

A glacially beautiful young widow with shining gold hair, perfect features, and unsurpassable grace, she was everything Gaby was not. Naturally, she was surrounded by gentlemen, including Art's friend, Snowy—otherwise Mr. Algernon Livesay-White—who cast her a quick, almost sheepish grin as she entered.

A positive sea of introductions followed. Gaby knew very few of the guests, but she refused to play the country mouse. Having grown up without discipline or lessons in etiquette —there had not been money to pay a governess by the time she had come along, and her mother had rarely been in residence—she had little chance of impressing the company by her manners. But the marquis had liked her as she was and that would have to be good enough for the rest of the company.

So, she made the effort to loosen her tongue, to make people laugh and to say what she thought. No doubt some thought her opinionated and eccentric, but on the whole, they seemed to like her. Once, she caught laughter in the marquis's face and a definite gleam of approval, which meant even more than the fact that Lady Winmore's gaze lingered on her too often.

Snowy ambled over with his teacup to greet her. "I don't mind telling you," he said confidentially, lowering himself into the just vacated place beside her on the sofa, "I'm very glad to see you here. Not really my sort of gathering."

"Too tame for you, Snowy?" she teased.

"Oh, no, some great fellows here. It's doing the pretty all the time that wears me out."

"If you don't like her, don't do it," Gaby said seriously. "It isn't fair on either of you."

"No, but look at her, Gab," he breathed with rare reverence. "She's so perfect, so... *unattainable*, and yet she smiles at me."

"Why?" Gaby said. "I'm not saying you're not an amusing fellow, Snowy, because you are, but is she truly considering marriage with you?"

"I think—I hope—she wants to settle down. Corey..." He broke off, clearly appalled. Blushing furiously, he glanced around to be sure no one had overheard. Since the tea party was breaking up, there happened to be no one near them.

"Lord Corey is married to me," Gaby said flatly. "And you are worth more than a consolation prize."

"I told Art you would know all about his past," Snowy said with apparent relief. "Thing is, it isn't good for either of us if they are thrown together again. You and I could help each other, keeping them occupied."

Her eyebrows flew up. "Are you suggesting I seduce my husband just to give you a chance with *her*? Have you no pride?"

"Sh-sh," he hushed her frantically, urging her to her feet. Everyone else was on their way out the door. "I'm just saying, you're still newly wed. No need to make a cake of yourself, but—"

"Likewise," she interrupted.

"I need an ally, Gab," he said frankly.

So do I...

After a pleasant walk about the formal gardens, escorted by their host's brother, Captain Somerville, lately of the Royal Navy, who was a particularly charming young man, Gaby repaired to her bedchamber.

She felt exhilarated by the pleasure of company after her weeks of isolation, by her first social success, and most of all by the fact that her husband had not gone near Lady Winmore. She had an ally in Snowy, even though she suspected the widow smiled upon him largely to annoy Corey. And she was looking forward to dinner, when she hoped to further win her husband's approval and notice.

Hawkins had laid out two evening gowns for her to choose from. "The one with the scarlet trim on the bodice," Gaby said at once. "It will look delightful with the ruby earrings."

"What ruby earrings?" Hawkins asked blankly.

"They're part of the set, the Corey rubies in the leather case."

"Oh." Hawkins stared at her, her pale skin whitening further. For the first time in their acquaintance, she looked both anxious and guilty. "I didn't bring them, my lady. I thought you'd left the case out for Scrivens to put in the vault."

"They're not here?" Gaby said, wilting a little, for her husband's words had wrapped themselves warmly about her heart.

"They're more than family treasure. They are my gift to you."

She had meant to show him how much she valued that gift.

Hawkins shook her head. "I'm sorry, my lady. I didn't know you wanted them."

"It isn't your fault," Gaby realized. "I didn't tell you." She had been so full of them herself she had just expected the maid to know. *Stupid, stupid...*

"You can send for them," Hawkins said eagerly. "Then you'd have them for tomorrow evening, or at least, the day after."

Gaby straightened. "Of course I can! Excellent idea."

Only then she remembered something else that knocked the breath out of her body.

Her brother Nicholas had arrived at Sanford Park just as they had left. What if he, like Art before him, had simply walked into her sitting room and seen the jewel case sitting there on the table...

Art wouldn't have touched them. But Nicholas, not known as the Young Devil for nothing, would pocket them without a second thought. He'd pawn them, even sell them... Her blood seemed to turn to ice in her veins.

"He *trusted* me," she whispered.

CHAPTER 3

Corey, encouraged by the better understanding established with his wife during their journey from Sanford Park, had entered the drawing room for tea feeling unforgivably smug with his lovely young wife on his arm.

The unexpected presence of Barbara Winmore had pulled him up enough to wonder if he should have warned Gabriella about her —though he baulked rather at sullying her with such explanations. What could he say? *Although it ended before our betrothal, Lady Winmore and I once enjoyed a mutually convenient relationship of an intimate nature, and it's just possible she may try and take out her spite upon you.*

What on earth had he been doing with such a woman in the first place? In the second place, it was over and done with, and Barbara would only make herself ridiculous by the slightest word against his marchioness.

Then all thought of his former mistress fled his mind, totally eclipsed by the much less palatable sight of Livesey-Bloody-White. What the devil was he doing here? And then he caught the smile the blackguard exchanged with Gabriella.

Dear God, was this planned? Had their rare, delightful

rapprochement on the journey merely been an act on her part to divert suspicion from her assignation with the unspeakable Snowy?

For an instant, the fires of jealousy roared in his head, reminding him of the day after their wedding day, when he had been replete with happiness, because his bride loved him and had shown him such passion and trust that he felt his heart would burst. And then, about to set off on their wedding journey, he had seen her from the town-house doorway. She had walked toward the carriage, and from nowhere was accosted by Livesey-White.

She had given him one of her brilliant smiles, and he had discreetly passed something from his fingers into hers. She had taken it without surprise or clumsiness, and even pressed the man's hand before climbing into the carriage with his aid.

Livesey-White had possessed the impudence to throw Corey a wave as he'd emerged from the house.

Even then, Corey had been aware that his surge of jealousy was both foolish and demeaning. But when he'd asked his wife casually what Livesey-White had wanted, she had said, "Oh, nothing. He was just passing."

He had waited, but she said no more on the subject, not even when he said lightly, "Not passing on good wishes from your brother?"

She had only laughed and replied, "God, no."

His love had not ended that day, but his trust had. And that soured everything. He had slept alone that night from choice. And when he had tried to make up for his unforgivable coldness to her, he had become merely "my lord" or "Corey" to her. He had never heard his Christian name on her lips since.

It was not so much that she loved Livesey-White that hurt—he was a neighbor and old family friend whom she had known forever. It was that she had never told him. That, loving another, she had married Corey for his fortune and to please her worthless family.

All this and more he recalled behind his armor of civility during tea. And when he glimpsed the pair on the sofa with their heads together in private conversation, he wanted to murder the amiable Snowy.

Instead, he went to his own rooms and stared at the connecting door. Could she even guess at the turbulent emotions raging in his heart?

The woman who had made love with him with such sweetness and abandon would understand. Pride and hurt had made him foolish before. He had handled her badly and she had returned cold-ness with ice and a certain style he could only admire, even while driven mad with lust.

What he hadn't done was make any effort to win her for himself. Until he had given her the rubies, which he knew now she had appre-ciated. For there had been sweet companionship today in the carriage.

And there would be tonight...

She seemed flustered when he sauntered through the connecting door to her sitting room. Even so, she took his breath away. Why had he been so stupid as to waste these weeks alone with her, nursing his own pride rather than winning her heart?

"You look very beautiful," he said.

She blushed adorably, all the sophistication she had aimed at him during their encounters at Sanford Park vanishing into tongue-tied pleasure. He hoped.

He was slightly disappointed that she had not chosen to wear any of the Corey rubies, but perhaps he had a little more to prove before she would wear his gifts. Instead, she wore a simple gold locket around her neck, distinctive in its simplicity.

Inevitably, they were separated almost as soon as they entered the salon for pre-prandial sherry, and Corey was given the honor of escorting their hostess to dinner. Rather to his annoyance, he found Barbara Winmore on his other side. Of more concern to him was that Gabriella, who had minimal experience of dining among the ton, should be comfortably situated.

She appeared to be, seated between two gentlemen he did not know but who appeared to be vying for her attention and hanging on her every word. She was smiling and coping and yet to his critical eye, her shoulders looked just a trifle tense.

"My lord," Barbara said beside him. "An unexpected pleasure to see you here."

"Somerville and I are old friends," he said. "And the pleasure is all mine. You are looking well."

"I am well. And glad of this chance to pick your notoriously dispassionate brains. What do you know of Mr. Livesey-White?"

"Very little," he replied neutrally.

"Truly? I thought he was some kind of relation to you these days. Via the Raymonds."

"Not at all. Though I believe he and Arthur Raymond are very thick."

"Well, he has become such a persistent suitor that I thought I would at least inquire about him. He is not a *gazetted* fortune hunter, is he?"

"I have never heard any such gossip."

"But then, every man is hanging out for a rich wife." She smiled, giving him an instant's warning. "Except you."

He smiled back. "Well, no one has ever accused me of vulgarity." Casually, he turned to Lady Somerville.

After dinner, when the gentlemen had finished with their port and followed Sir Peter to the drawing room, Corey's gaze went straight to his wife who sat in a group of other young women, her eyes searching the newcomers. He hoped she was looking for him, but it would have been bad form to rush immediately to her side as though he feared she could not behave in public.

He spoke instead to a Mrs. Denby and her daughter, a decision he came to regret, for when he next saw his wife, she was standing by the window with Livesey-White engrossed in an intense conversation.

❧

"Where is Arthur?" she demanded of Snowy without introduction.

"No idea."

"Yes, you have, Snowy. Think. I need him."

"Can't I help?"

"Not unless you're prepared to turn Nicholas upside down and shake him."

Snowy blanched. "Not a fighting man," he said apologetically.

"So where is Art?"

"Not perfectly sure," Snowy said cautiously. "He was going to— er... meet up with friends..."

"To go to some dreadful prize fight, yes, I know about that, but would it not have been last night or today? Where did he go afterward?"

"Brighton," Snowy said, giving up.

"Well, that's not so far from here, is it? Where will I find him?"

"Nowhere you can possibly go," Snowy said frankly.

"I see." She scowled. "What if I just write and persuade him to meet me? Do you know the direction?"

Snowy eyed her with growing unease. "Even if I did, you can't go jaunting about the countryside alone. There are highwaymen around here."

More to the point, she could not go without Corey finding out, and that rather defeated the whole object.

Snowy sighed. "I owe you a few favors, don't I?"

"No," she said honestly, touching the chain at her neck. "You redeemed my locket for me."

"That was Art. I was only the messenger. Again. Give me a note for him and I'll track him down first thing. With luck I can be back before luncheon."

"Thank you, Snowy," she said and fled to her own rooms, where she knew there were writing materials.

Dear Art,

Nicholas came to Sanford Park just as I left. Am afraid he took the rubies. Please will you find him, get the rubies back, and bring them to me here at Normanton House? It's IMPORTANT. Also URGENT.

Gabriella

She read it over quickly, then underlined IMPORTANT and URGENT several times, before sanding it and tearing off the note.

She folded it as small as she could, palmed it, and hurried back to the drawing room, where some debutante was murdering one of her favorite songs.

While all eyes were fixed somewhat glassily upon the performer, Gaby sidled up to Snowy and stood beside him. From practice as children, it was easy to slip the note into his palm. He knew enough not to look at her, only nodded infinitesimally. But as she strolled away, she noticed her husband's gaze upon her.

She smiled, trying not to look guilty or uncertain, and sat down with her cup of tea.

She did not see him again until the party began to break up for the evening, the staider to retire for the night or to discuss important matters of state in the library, the younger to play cards or billiards into the small hours. Although Corey was young, she expected him to go to the library—she had already primed Lord Barhead to expect something interesting from him—but she met her husband unexpectedly in the hallway.

"Care for a stroll before bed?" he suggested.

It was so exactly what she wanted—most especially with him—that she smiled with pleasure and led the way to the nearest door.

On the other side of it, the sharp October air cooled her cheeks. He took the shawl from her numb hands and wrapped it around her shoulders. Gentle, attentive, as he had been in the short period of their betrothal and the morning of their wedding. Something had changed after that. She had stopped trying to guess what.

What benefit had he ever got out of their marriage? She had got his name, his title, his fortune. Her family had got whatever generous settlements the Old Devil had wheedled out of him. But what had Corey got, except an ill-trained wife who answered him back, and whom he did not even like?

"Why did you marry me?" she blurted. There was a distinct pause. Even in the darkness, she felt his gaze burning into her face. Appalled at her own question, she shook her head, "You need not—"

"Don't you know?" he interrupted.

"I thought I did. After all, there seems nothing else for you to gain out of the match."

"*Gain?*" he repeated with distaste. "Is that what you think of me?"

"Of course, a man in your position must marry," she allowed. "My best guess is that you were getting it over with, while shutting the door on the annoying matchmaking mamas, which allows you to live much more as you please. Or at least, you thought it would." She turned to meet his gaze at last. "I am not the wife you wanted, am I?"

"You are the only wife I wanted."

"How polite you are," she mocked.

Abruptly she was swung around against a hedge, both his arms hard around her. His eyes blazed down at her, frightening and yet somehow exciting.

"Polite?" he said savagely, and kissed her.

Her heart soared. Her stomach dived. For he had not kissed her like this since that first morning, and even then... She could only yield, melt, opening wide to his demanding mouth, which quickly gentled into something much more sensual and tender. Desire flamed to the caress of his body, to his growing arousal pressed so excitingly against her that a small, inarticulate moan escaped her.

He let her go as suddenly as he had seized her. Her hands, clinging to his neck, to his faintly stubbled cheek, fell to her sides.

"I beg your pardon," he said hoarsely. "I regret I am not the husband *you* wanted."

This floored her so completely that she could only stare after him as he strode back up the path. What on earth did he mean? Her mouth opened but no words came out, and in any case, he was getting away from her again.

She sped after him to the lit French doors he was aiming for. As she caught up with him, she grasped his arm and was whisked inside to a blaze of light and noise, a room where several people were playing cards, and the air already smelled of brandy.

"Corey!" someone called. "Will you and your lady join us?"

"My lady is tired after our journey," Corey said.

Her hackles rose that he should speak for her without consultation, but in truth she did not want to play cards. She wanted to be alone with her husband, who conducted her through the room to the grand hall and the staircase.

Her heart beat like a drum. What did he intend? She should give him no choice. He had made the first move. At the very least, he still wanted her. This was where, she should turn into his arms, wrap her own around him and kiss him back, seduce him into her bed, tell him she had always loved him...

And then, like a blast of cold water on her burning body, she remembered the rubies.

If he found out she had been so careless as to lose them—to Nicholas of all people!— he would not believe in her apparently sudden change of heart. He would think she was cozening him for her own or her family's benefit, and they had already squeezed so much out of him.

"I regret I am not the husband you wanted." What on earth had he meant by that? She had *had* no other suitors. Unsurprising. No one wanted to marry a Raymond. Her sister Caroline's revolting husband had won her in a card game with the Old Devil. Avoiding such a catastrophe was yet another reason to be grateful to Corey...

Somehow, they had reached the passage to their rooms in total silence. Panic surged. What should she do?

Her heart threatened to jump out of her breast as he opened her door, led her inside, and closed it with a portentous click.

Slowly, he turned to face her. "I am not a complacent husband, Gabriella. Never think it. You are mine."

I have always been yours. The words stuck in her throat, blocked not now by pride but by the damned rubies. But she was not blind to the invitation in his stormy, clouded eyes as they devoured her face. She longed to take that half-step that would bring her up against him, to lift her face and kiss the beloved lips that could give such pleasure...

Damn my stupidity, damn Nicholas.

She swallowed. "I am yours," she said hoarsely, and a flame seemed to ignite in those eyes that could be hard as slate or liquid with passion. "But you must give me time. We have become strangers again."

He leaned closer, his breath tickling her cheek, her ear. "I can make you forget him."

"Who?" she whispered, a thousand tiny thrills skittering along her veins.

His lips twitched. "You see?"

In spite of everything, laughter caught at her breath. Surely one brush of her lips on his was permissible...

He turned the handle of the door and was gone.

Despite the turbulent emotions of the evening, Corey was not displeased as he left his wife and returned to the card room.

He was sure she had slipped Livesey-White something, and yet she had been in no hurry to be rid of her husband. Perhaps she was giving the wretched Snowy his congé. After all, Corey had reason to know there had been no physical contact between them since she had been immured at Sanford Park. If she had received any messages from him, they must have been extremely discreet. And tonight, although he had not meant to kiss her so quickly or so roughly, she had not appeared to mind. She had definitely kissed him back. The magic of their wedding night had not left her either. Surely that had been real?

Yes, they had finally begun something today, something they should have done weeks ago—spent time together. What had he been thinking of, sulking like a schoolgirl in distant parts of the house, neglecting her, *blaming* her?

She was nineteen years old, and despite the ramshackle nature of her father's household, she had been an innocent given to a stranger. Throughout the brief fortnight of their betrothal and even their wedding night, he had tried to address that, courting her like any honorable gentleman.

In three years, the wild, delightful child who had once dropped into his arms from an apple tree on her father's estate, had grown into a madly intriguing young woman of beauty and passion and breathtaking zest for life. Why had he never considered that other men might have been bowled over before him? That she might already have given her heart to another?

The raging hurt he had felt when he had seen her secretly accept Livesey-White's gift was a testament to his own feelings. And there had been pity for her situation amongst the pride that caused him to stay away from her subsequently. But that was no excuse.

He had behaved badly, stupidly. When he should have been erasing his rival from her mind and heart and earning her love himself, he had neglected her. She had only taken her cooly sardonic attitude from his lead and, he now suspected, from her own hurt.

Corey who, despite his youth, had already made his name as the great diplomat of Parliament, with his perceptive negotiations and solutions, had forgotten in his own marriage the one thing necessary to any understanding—talk.

And so, he played a few somewhat mechanical games of cards. Livesey-White avoided him by retiring early.

Only then did he retire himself.

He wondered if Gabriella were awake, thinking of him. She had been willing to entertain him earlier, despite her somewhat missish request for time. But this time he wanted her whole heart. Even so, the temptation had been profound. And urgent. It was still urgent.

He hesitated for several moments beside the connecting door to her sitting room. He even reached for the handle, imagining her welcome, her naked passion...

Or her squeak of protest.

Or, worse, her indifferent submission.

He dropped his hand to his side. She was right. They did need time. Blind lust—or even blind love—was no use to them now. They needed understanding and trust. And that had to be earned.

CHAPTER 4

Although he was happy enough to avoid Lord Corey, Snowy's main motive for retiring early was to rise early the following morning and ride to Brighton. Which, rather to his own surprise, he achieved in very good time.

He discovered the Honorable Arthur Raymond more or less exactly where he expected him to be. The rakehell had clearly been up all night and, about to retire to the cozy armful of femininity in the bedchamber beyond, he was not at his most welcoming.

"Snowy? What the devil are you doing here?"

"Got a message from your sister," Snowy said, brushing past him. "It's something to do with the Young Devil and she says it's urgent."

"I don't care about bloody Nicholas," Art said wrathfully.

"Neither do I, but I've done my duty by bringing you this. Read it and do what you like. I'll need to let my horse rest before I go back. I've got my own fish to fry."

Art snatched the tiny, folded note from him, but retained enough civility to ask how Snowy's suit flourished with Lady Winmore.

"She's a magnificent woman," Snowy said appreciatively. "And I think she likes me. Trouble is, I suspect she likes Corey more. She might be keeping me on a string just to make him jealous."

Art, unfolding the paper with some difficulty since he was not exactly sober, paused in his efforts to scowl at Snowy. "I thought they'd parted. I told Gaby they had."

"Oh, I think they did. Only *she* might not be averse to starting it up again. And I'm pretty sure Corey don't like me."

"Oh, that's probably just because you're a friend of mine." Art finally managed to spread out the note and peered at it owlishly.

"Damn it, if that doesn't take the cake," he exploded. "Bloody Nicholas! What the devil did she leave it there for? And where in hell *is* Nicholas? I'm damned sure those snooty servants of Corey's won't let him stay there in their master's absence."

"Might have gone home to Brockton," Snowy suggested. "Not so far from Sanford, and I expect he needs to rusticate."

"Not with the Corey rubies in his hands, he doesn't."

Snowy blinked. "Well, he can't sell those *any*where in the country. They're bound to be recognized, and he'll be arrested."

"I don't think that's exactly what Gaby needs, do you? The arrest of her brother for stealing from her husband? She's bound to be caught in the crossfire. Between you and me, things are a little tricky with that pair, and if you repeat that, I'll—"

"When have I ever blabbed your family's damned secrets?" Snowy demanded in outrage.

"Of course you haven't," Art muttered. "Sorry, Snow. Not exactly sober, you know, and now I'll have to waste my damned time tracking the Young Devil down."

"How will you make him give you the rubies?" Snowy asked curiously, for though Art was quicker with his fists than he was, Nicholas had always seemed a nasty piece of work.

"Give him a choice between a broken nose and what's left of the monkey I won at the races."

"Sorry, Art," Snowy said sincerely.

"Don't be. He might take the broken nose. Either way, I'll get Gaby's damned necklace, but she won't get it back without a severe lecture on responsibility."

Snowy goggled at him in disbelief, and Art had the grace to grin. "I know, but it's for her own good."

Art's head was pounding by the time he reached London. He had just been in time to catch the mail coach, having used yet more of his winnings to vastly overpay a very large woman for the use of her ticket. It was still the cheapest and quickest way to get back to London.

The rooms where Nicholas once resided had been relet, and Art began to suspect his brother might try to leave the country and sell the rubies abroad. However, a few inquiries in low places eventually led Art to other rooms occupied by the Young Devil's mistress, an aging but tolerant actress who let him in with a hopeful smile.

Nicholas, in his shirt sleeves and looking somewhat squalid, glared at him from a table in the middle of the room's faded splendor and swore. "What in hell do you want?"

"Gaby's rubies," Art said, getting straight to the point. "Hand them over."

"Think they'll go with your eyes?" Nicholas sneered.

"Probably, but they'll match your bloody nose a damned sight better."

"Go to hell," Nicholas said, sitting down and helping himself to a cup of tea from the pot on the table. He didn't offer Art one.

It was the actress, Margy, who brought him a fresh cup and then departed tactfully into the other room while the brothers glared at each other.

Eventually, Nicholas's curiosity got the better of him. "What do you want with the rubies? You can't sell them, you know. Can't even pawn them."

Art pounced. "How do you know? Did you try?"

Nicholas laughed. "Wouldn't you like to know?"

"Look, Nick, I'm in a hurry, so I'll give you a choice. I'll give you a hundred for them. Or I'll knock you down—which we both know I can do—and take the damned baubles anyway."

Nicholas's lips curled. "Where would *you* get a spare hundred?"

"Races."

Perhaps the rumor of Art's unprecedented good luck had reached his elder brother, for Nick did not immediately dismiss the idea. Instead, a thoughtful, almost cunning look entered his expression.

"Guineas?" he asked.

"Pounds," Art said firmly.

Nicholas looked around the room with distaste. "Very well. Hand 'em over."

Art threw the roll of banknotes onto the table. He had already counted them out and separated them from the pitifully few notes remaining. Oh well, no doubt Gaby would reimburse him. Eventually.

"The rubies."

Nicholas stood to snatch up the notes. "Do you take me for an imbecile? They're at Sanford Park, where the silly chit abandoned them. Of course I didn't take them! I'm not so stupid as to get on the wrong side of Corey, who's a lot harder than he looks. Mind you, I did pocket a gold paper knife and a purse full of coins she'd left lying in a drawer. How flash has our little sister become?"

Furious to be cheated and outraged on Gaby's behalf, Art sprang to his feet, fists clenched. But Nick, wise to his little brother's temper, was already bolting for the other room. Art pursued, but when the door slammed in his face, he realized his heart was not in it. He had to get to Sanford, now. And persuade the damned butler to give him the rubies to take to Gaby. If Art bribed him, would the man blab to Corey?

He would have to risk it.

Since there were no stage or mail coaches to anywhere near Sanford scheduled until the morning, and it was already dark, he threw his last caution to the wind and hired a post-chaise, where at least he could sprawl and sleep until morning.

One of the postilions shook Art awake when it was only just light. The good thing was, his head no longer ached. The bad part was, everything else did, since the damned yellow bounder had lived up to its nickname and rattled all his bones.

He alighted stiffly, stretched, and walked to the front steps of the imposing house.

"Payment, sir?" the postilion reminded him politely.

"Hold on, will you? I might need you again."

"Costs extra," the postilion warned.

Ignoring him, Art smiled at the maidservant scrubbing the steps.

She sprang up and curtseyed. "Good morning, sir. Neither his lordship nor his ladyship are at home."

"Oh, I know that. I'm on an errand for her ladyship." He regarded it as luck that she was not the Friday-faced butler. In fact, Art had flirted with her the last time he was here, so she definitely knew him, and she was not immune to his charm. He decided to risk his good fortune one further step. It was just possible that no one had been in Gaby's rooms since she'd left. Her personal maid was with her, and she was not expected back for a fortnight. Conceivably, the jewels were still exactly where he had seen them on his last visit.

He smiled winningly and produced one of his last remaining gold coins. "Be a good girl and run up to her ladyship's private sitting room. She wants the jewel case that's sitting on the table just inside the door. Square leather case with pretty gold tooling."

The girl looked scared. "I think you'd better speak to Mr. Scrivens, sir. I don't go into her ladyship's rooms."

"Neither does Scrivens, I hope! I know my sister would far rather you went in than he did. I'll tell her ladyship—and Hawkins," he added, as the abigail's name came to him in a moment of inspiration, "that you were extremely helpful. No need to mention the guinea."

While he walked along the drive a little to deflect any officious grooms coming to deal with the horses, he felt the postilions watching him, as though they suspected him of attempting not to pay. However, the graciousness of Corey's home seemed to reassure them to some degree, for they said nothing.

Even so, he was highly relieved when the pretty maid reappeared in the doorway. She carried the ruby case in both hands, looking petrified.

"Bless you," he said, kissing her cheek.

She blushed beetroot red, but her eyes were still large and frightened. "You will tell her ladyship? Wouldn't you please speak to Mr. Scrivens?"

"Her ladyship's orders definitely trump the butler's," Art said cheerfully. "Her ladyship will be really pleased with you. Best carry on with those steps before you get in trouble. I'll look out for you next time I call."

With that, he dropped the case into the large pocket of his great coat and swaggered back to the post chaise. "On to Normanton House, just on the edge of the South Downs," he told them. "I'll show you on the map, if you like."

"You can show us the money first, if you please," the postilion said insolently.

Clearly, they knew exactly who he was and what his circumstances were.

"Now, look here," Art began, glaring at him. But since he really didn't want a squabble here where it would attract attention from the house, he bit back his temper. With as much hauteur as he could muster, he threw his purse to the postilion, who, after the briefest inspection, condescended to get back on his horse. Art climbed back into the chaise, and off they went.

Only then did he think to check that the jewels were, in fact, in their case. If Nick had lied to him... Or Gaby had stashed the baubles somewhere without the case... But. No, there they lay in their velvet nest, glittering and breathtakingly lovely. No wonder Gaby wanted them back so urgently. She would dazzle all eyes in this collection. And in the circumstances of their somewhat frail marriage, he could quite see that keeping her carelessness from Corey was essential.

The real mystery was how Nicholas had managed to keep his hands off them. Even if he'd known he couldn't sell them, it would be just like him to hang them on Margy to show off. No, there was something else at work here, and he began to think it was his "soft touch" brother-in-law.

He had never seen Corey lose his temper, let alone strike someone. And although the Old Devil had been mighty pleased with himself over the marriage settlements, no one had screwed as much as a shilling out of him since. He would never let the Raymonds ravage his estates as they had done their own. Art's attempt to borrow money from Corey had been met with a polite refusal which he had cheerfully accepted, and yet he had never tried again.

There was something about Corey, some inner strength of character, a fearlessness even in the face of the combined Raymond rabble, that intimidated the likes of Nicholas and the Old Devil himself. Art did not care to go up against him either, though he could not put his finger on why.

Perhaps he just liked the man. Gaby clearly did—so why the devil was she keeping things from him? Why was she so tense and un-Gaby-like around him?

Not one of life's great ponderers, Art soon gave up solving the puzzle and closed his eyes.

He only opened them again when the chaise door opened to reveal the insolent postilion.

"Here we are, sir."

Art peered past him. They were in an inn yard. "This is not Normanton House. Is it the village inn?" Actually, that would be more sensible, because he needn't then encounter Corey or their hosts, who might ask awkward questions about his sudden, uninvited appearance. He could easily send a messenger from the inn to Gaby, to get her to come down and take the rubies off his hands. And lend him enough blunt to see him back to Brighton and the delectable Bettina.

"It's *a* village inn," the postilion replied. "The Red Lion at Little Plunkett."

"Where the devil is Little Plunkett?"

"On the Chichester to Brighton road."

"Then it's not where you're instructed to take me. I want to be in Normanton."

"Not without more money."

"Now, look here, you damned thieves—"

"No need for insults, sir," said the postilion with dignity. "You must feel free to take grievances up with the office. For our part, we've already done you the favor of taking you further than you were booked for. And Little Plunkett's as far as your money goes."

"Damn it, you'll get paid at Normanton!"

"No, sir. We're bound for London."

And that appeared to be that.

CHAPTER 5

G aby willed herself to wake early on the morning after she had given Snowy the note for her brother Art. She didn't entirely trust Snowy to rise at a reasonable hour, and she was prepared to have the servants rouse him if necessary.

It meant she did not sleep particularly soundly, and when she did, her dreams were fragmented and disturbing, featuring as they did her husband in all his naked glory, making exquisite love to her—and yet only a confusing moment later it was not Gaby but Lady Winmore who was the recipient of his attentions. Confusion, grief and anger accompanied her into wakefulness. Snowy had been in the dreams somewhere too, as had Nicholas, worst of her brothers, bashing away at the Corey rubies with a hammer in order to break them out of their settings to sell.

Fortunately, the full horror faded quickly into the very real sounds of a solitary horse trotting through the gravel on the drive below. She sprang out of bed and rushed to the window in time to glimpse a horseman moving just out of her line of vision. Bolting into the sitting room for a better view, she caught him heading down the drive. His shape had long been familiar, as was the rakish angle of his hat.

Snowy, she thought with relief. *Good man!*

Pleased, she turned from the window just as a soft knock sounded at the connecting door to Corey's rooms. Her heart gave a huge leap, paralyzing her somewhere between calling "Come in!" and bolting back to the protection of her bed. In that moment, a hundred possibilities, hopes, and desires flitted through her mind, but she was so stupid with surprise that she did nothing but stand there, poised for flight but staring at the door.

Until her husband strolled in and paused, apparently as frozen as she.

She had not seen him in anything but formal dress since the morning after their wedding. Now, he wore only a loose, white shirt tucked casually into riding breeches. The strong column of his exposed throat led down to a glimpse of muscled, masculine chest, where once she had lain her head and kissed his glistening skin...

She swallowed, raising her gaze back to his face. His eyes seemed to have darkened, not with displeasure but with desire. Her whole body flushed in response. She could think of nothing to say.

"Good morning," he said lightly. "I was not sure you would be awake. Since you are, would you care to accompany me on a morning ride? There is some pretty country here."

Never, in all their weeks together at Sanford Park, had he invited her to ride with him. In the early days, she had hoped to come upon him by accident or design, to take him by surprise and see if that might melt his ice. She never had and came to the conclusion that he simply avoided her.

For a very small instant, wicked pride urged her to drawl, *Oh, not this morning, my lord. I am much too fatigued.* But that was the kind of nonsense that had kept them apart. Last night he had kissed her, for the first time in months. And there were many things she needed to get to the bottom of.

So she followed her heart. "Why not?" she said lightly. "Give me five minutes to dress."

"I'll give you twenty."

Deliberately, she sauntered rather than fled toward the bedchamber, and she knew with novel exultation that his gaze followed her.

She could feel his eyes burning into the fine lawn of her night rail, which revealed far more of her outline than was seemly. She let her hips sway and longed for him to charge after her and seize her in his arms...

He didn't. But neither did he leave. She had shut her bedchamber door several seconds before she heard the click of the connecting door closing. Smiling with excitement, she ran to the bell pull and rang for Hawkins before rummaging in her wardrobe for her riding habit.

⚘

"You are quite the bruising rider," Corey said admiringly when they slowed from their exhilarating gallop across the Downs. "Did your father teach you?"

She laughed. "Lord, no. He never taught us anything. Art and I learned for ourselves, with the odd bit of advice from our old groom, who did his best to be sure we didn't ride any horse that would throw us to our doom. It was he who persuaded me to ride with a lady's saddle, which seemed extremely stupid to me at the time. Actually, it still does, but even a Raymond must bow to *some* rules of society."

His eyes gleamed. "You are right, of course. It *is* stupid, not to say dangerous. I sometimes wonder if men invented such a saddle just to make sure women would never be able to out-ride them."

She eyed him. "You think I cannot out-ride you?"

"After that performance, I am not so foolish."

They rode on, talking desultorily about horses, and then lapsed into a companionable silence.

Into it, Corey said casually, "If I answer your question, will you answer one of mine?"

She blinked. "What question?"

"Last night, you asked why I had married you. If I tell you, will you answer me honestly in return?"

"Yes," she said, without having to think about it. Her heart beat quickened, for she was far from sure she would like his answer, but if they were ever to make their marriage successful on any level, then she needed to know.

She heard the catch in his breath, saw the faint tensing of his fingers on the reins. This was not easy for him. Was that a good or a bad sign?

He gazed upward at the clear, bright autumn sky, as though for inspiration. "I offered for you on an overwhelming impulse, because you were like no one else I had ever met or imagined. Because your natural spirit and laughter enchanted me, because your every word intrigued and fascinated me. Because of how you felt in my arms when we danced. And because I liked—more than liked—how you looked. In short, I desired your body and your soul more intensely than I had ever felt anything."

His words washed over her with shock and triumph. She had been right in the beginning! And it was so sweet to hear that she could not yet even wonder what had gone wrong.

He turned and caught her no-doubt adoring gaze. His own eyes were guarded, but steady and warm. "Why did *you* marry *me*?"

"Because I loved you." She did not even think of lying. It was the unvarnished truth.

And yet he did not smile. He did not reach for her, nor show any joy in his expression. Instead, he looked almost...desperate. And thoroughly disappointed.

He cannot bear me, not in reality... Nor did he want a loving wife. He wanted a comfortable marriage of convenience so that he could cavort with the likes of Lady Winmore, unencumbered by guilt. She should have noticed that in his charming speech he had never once mentioned love.

She let out a bitter laugh and urged her tired horse back into a canter, just to get away from the unbearable sight of her husband's dissatisfaction.

"Don't let it embarrass you, Leo," she threw over her shoulder. "I don't. Naturally, there was also your fortune."

In truth, Gabriella *had* disappointed him. She had not returned his honesty by explaining about Livesey-White. She had not trusted him enough to give more than the stock lie of love. One did not tumble into love in a day, which was why he had avoided using the word. The fall might have begun, full of sweet promise and pleasure. But there could be no true love without trust. And clearly, she still did not trust him.

He urged his horse after hers, but the fun as well as the companionship had gone. They were almost back at Normanton House before he realized the significance of her parting shot.

Leo. She had called him Leo for the first time since their wedding night.

And that, spoken while in the grip of some turbulent emotion he could not grasp, gave him hope.

And so, he made sure it was he who lifted her from the saddle, smiling down at her with his hands still lightly on her waist.

"Thank you for your company. Shall we do it again?"

Confusion entered her cool, withdrawn eyes.

"Excellent," he said, as though she had answered. "I think we must be in good time for breakfast."

It was only a beginning. He had, after all, given her little reason to trust him. But he had started the conversation.

Careful not to crowd her, he gave her time to think over his words, to realize he was not angry with her, merely wanted the greater closeness of truth. So, he did not seek her out particularly during the rest of the day's entertainments, or the next day's, merely acknowledged her with open pleasure whenever they were thrown together. He had the impression she was bewildered, but she also began to look tense and worried to his eyes, and that he could not bear.

So, as it approached the dinner hour on the day after their morning ride, he knocked once more on the connecting door and entered her sitting room. For a disappointing moment, he thought he was too late to catch her, and then he heard the faint sound of voices in the bedchamber.

"Gabriella?" he called.

The voices cut off like a tap. The door to the bedchamber opened and the maid, Hawkins, came out.

"My lady is just choosing jewelry, my lord."

"I can help with that, so you may go," he said. "If your mistress needs you for nothing else?" he added, strolling past Hawkins into the bedchamber.

His wife, elegantly coiffured and dressed in an exquisite evening gown of dusky rose silk, was seated at the dressing table. She twisted round to face him, her eyes wide with either alarm or astonishment at his unprecedented invasion.

"Yes, you may go, Hawkins," she said hurriedly. "Thank you."

A small, chest-shaped jewelry box stood open in front of her. One of its several drawers was open to reveal the pearl necklace that had been his wedding gift. The matching earrings already adorned her pretty ears.

"I shan't be long," she said cooly. "But do go down without me."

"I would rather be with you." He walked across the room to her, and, yes, that was definitely alarm in her face. Not fear, at least, but he could almost see her striving for the cool, half-amused indifference with which she had treated him for months. As though she was hurt that he hadn't believed her reason for marrying him.

"Because I loved you."

What had it cost her to say those words? As much as it had cost him to speak the truth of his profound attraction?

He leaned toward her and reached over her shoulder to the open drawer of her jewelry box. It looked like a child's box, lined with soft but faded purple velvet. It was hardly worthy of the Marchioness of Corey, and she had clearly not replaced it when she had bought her trousseau—at Corey's expense as per the agreement he had made with her grasping father.

Her soft, floral perfume disturbed him. He thought her breathing had quickened. So had his, at the tempting nearness of her decolletage. He grasped the pearl necklace.

"Is this what you wished to wear? Allow me."

Although she went very still, she did not demur. He placed the pearls around her creamy throat, letting them drop a little toward her tantalizing breasts, and closed the fastening at her delicate nape.

For an instant, their eyes met in the glass. He could not read her confused expression.

"Do you know how very beautiful you are?"

She rose abruptly, forcing him to step back. "I do not need flattery to survive, my lord. I don't even like it."

"I never flatter," he said in genuine surprise. "And yesterday morning you called me Leo."

"That morning, I said too many unwise things."

He raised one eyebrow. "You wish to change your answer to my question?"

A stab of anger flashed from her eyes. "To make you feel better? You must be the only man in Christendom who does not care to be loved." She spun around to face him, her cheeks flushed.

"I did not say that. In fact, I care to be the *only* man who is loved."

A frown tugged at her brows. "You make no sense."

"Apparently not." And her incomprehension seemed genuine. Had he got this wrong somehow? Hope surged, catching at his breath.

Giving himself time, he stepped further back and examined his wife's overall appearance. "Almost perfection. Perhaps a bracelet to emphasize your slender wrist? The ruby bracelet would look well with your gown."

"I disagree," she said at once. "Besides, I have decided to keep the rubies for the grand ball at the end of our stay."

He brushed past her, pulling open the other drawers in that childish chest. "What else do you have?"

The modest gold locket she had worn last night—and on several previous occasions, he recalled—lay in one drawer. The others were empty.

He frowned. "Is this all you brought?"

"It's all I have," she said shortly, then added, "Apart from the rubies, of course, which are in their own case. Shall we join the party? Or shall I forgo dinner, if my lord is dissatisfied with my appearance?"

He turned to her in some consternation. She strode to the bed, swiping up the gloves and reticule which lay there. She was *ashamed* of having so little. But it was he who should be ashamed. He had always known she had come to him with nothing. And yet he had made her only one gift, which she kept in a child's jewelry box. Because he had been too proud, too hurt to pay attention to her.

Even the rubies, his grandiose gesture of trust, had not been the thoughtful, personally chosen gift she deserved.

Already, she was sweeping out of the bedchamber, her head held high. His throat tightened. Hastily, he strode after her and offered her his arm.

He paused, his hand on the door. "I believe the evening's entertainment is a card party. Do you have enough coin to see you through?"

"Of course," she said with icy grandeur. Then her eyes flickered. "Art just paid me back five-and-twenty pounds I had lent him for the races."

His eyebrows flew up involuntarily. "Art *won?*"

"Astonishing, isn't it?" The smile was almost back in her eyes.

So that was the reason for Art's brief visit before they left Sanford. He was only paying her back, not carrying love notes from his crony, Livesey-White. Or not necessarily.

"Before you ask," she said in a rush, "I have never lent anything to the rest of them. I knew Art would pay me back eventually."

This was the honesty he had always associated with her, that had always stood out like a beacon amongst the murky, grasping deceit of the rest of the Raymonds. With the possible exception of Art, who was a mere rakehell and whom she seemed to hold in some affection. The others, even her parents, she had been happy to leave behind. No wonder she had married him to escape them.

It was all food for thought, and for his growing belief that he had maligned her in his mind. A fierce surge of longing for her love took him by surprise. He shoved it aside as he conducted her downstairs to join the party. But he could never suppress it entirely.

CHAPTER 6

I t was another enjoyable and useful evening for Corey. Against the backdrop of cards and witty conversation, he furthered his political alliances, listened to some important discussions, made a little money and a few new friends. Blanketing everything, though, was the presence of his wife.

Although it was beneath his dignity and hers to watch her jealously the whole time, he was always aware of her position in the room. She and Livesey-White never played together and only found themselves at the same table once, when only the most innocent of interactions occurred. Had it not been for the significant nod Livesay-White had given her at luncheon yesterday, and her quick smile of response, Corey could have imagined himself completely wrong in his assumptions.

He could not doubt there was something between them. And yet in his heart he knew Gabriella was the honest person he had always believed her to be. An innocent love for Livesey-White, broken apart by Corey and by her father's greed, was pitiable. But he would not stand back and allow it to continue.

And so, when the main party retired, he accompanied her from the room.

"A short walk before we retire?" he suggested, glancing around and finding Barbara Winmore gazing right at him.

"I believe I am too fatigued," Gabriella said in a bored voice.

Damnation, had she seen and misinterpreted the direction of his accidental glance? Did she *know* about his past with Barbara? Or did she really just want to be rid of him? Panic that he could lose her forever swept up from his toes. He was not used to losing when he put his mind and heart into something, but dear God, he was making a mess of this...

"Then allow me to light you to your room," he said, placing her hand on his arm.

"I remember the way," she drawled.

"Then you light me to mine," he said, and almost surprised a smile.

She did not make a scene by refusing, but neither did she chatter with delight as they climbed the stairs, bidding various people good night as they went. In fact, she was regal and distant, and he had never admired her more.

She might have been hiding behind her familiar armor because of Livesey-White. Equally, it could be because Corey had hurt her.

He had let her carry their shared candle, in keeping with his mild joke, and so he led her first to his room, where she lit the candle just inside. He closed the door and brushed past her.

"I was thinking of running into Brighton in the curricle tomorrow," he said casually. "Would you like to come? We might look at some shops, walk along the shore. I can show you Prinny's mad pavilion, from the outside at least."

He caught the flicker of surprise on her brow. For a moment, he thought she would refuse, and the same panic as before began to mount.

"Why not?" she said. "I have never been there."

"Then that is settled. Shall we go immediately after an early breakfast?"

"Of course."

Deliberately, he took the night candle from her and walked through the connecting door.

He lit the lamp in her sitting room, then set the candle down beside it. "We seem to have gone one step forward in our relationship, then another backwards. I would be a better husband."

"Would you?" she asked doubtfully.

He took her gloved hand. "I will try. I know I have been selfish and considered you too little."

"I do not want *effort*," she said with loathing aimed, apparently, at the word more than at him.

"There has to be some in order to understand each other better. We married as strangers."

"You were not a stranger to me," she said, gazing at their joined hands. "At least, I thought you were not."

"I have made mistakes. I'm sorry."

He let his fingers stray over her palm to her naked forearm and slowly peeled back her glove. Her breath hitched as he bent and pressed his lips to her wrist. Her pulse galloped beneath his mouth, so he let it linger.

Her free hand lifted, and for one sweet, glorious moment, her fingertips touched his cheek as though in wonder.

And then she snatched it back, though her other hand still lay in his. "You have said you are not a complacent husband, that you insist on being the only one—*my* only one, I can only assume. What exactly is it you suspect me of? Adultery?"

There was plain speaking with a vengeance. He could do no less. "Not yet. Merely of harboring another man in your heart."

She stared at him, her lips parting in total astonishment. "Me? Who on earth...?"

"Livesey-White," he said steadily.

Her eyes widened. And then, stunningly, she went off into a peel of laughter.

"*Snowy?*" she gasped. "Why, he is almost my brother, and a better brother too than any of them except Art."

"And yet I saw you with him," he said, hating the stiffness in his own voice. "When we were about to set off on our wedding journey. He gave you something. Something you hid from me."

A moment longer she stared. "You want to know what it was? Wait."

Pulling her hand free, she marched into the bedchamber and returned bare moments later with something small that she held out to him. He raised his palm, and she dropped her small, gold locket in it.

"Open it," she commanded.

Inside lay a small lock of grey hair. Snowy's hair was brown.

"It was my grandmother's. She left it to me, and I kept this lock of her hair in gratitude. I defended it from all my siblings all my life until our betrothal, when I pawned it to buy a square of cotton and some silk to embroider you a handkerchief, the only gift I could afford."

He took the handkerchief from his pocket, where, perhaps foolishly, he always carried it.

"That's the one," she said. "Because you understood my circumstance, I thought, you gave me a purse full of gold coins on the day before our wedding. I sent Art to redeem the necklace because I didn't want to come to you with absolutely nothing. But being Art, he forgot until the next day, and sent it via Snowy, which was no doubt his idea of discretion. And you have hated me all these weeks because of *this*? You truly trust me so little?"

His fingers shook slightly as he closed the locket and returned it to her.

"I was an idiot," he said hoarsely, "who could not believe in his good fortune in winning you."

She smiled a little ruefully. "You need not coat it in sugar. I understand. You took a huge risk in marrying into my family. For what it's worth, I took a risk too. Everyone was at pains to tell me about Lady Winmore."

"I ended that before I even spoke to your father," he said impatiently. "Gabriella, why did we never talk?"

"I didn't know how. My family shouts and quarrels and bullies and—"

"And I believed the worst and ignored you. You must hate me."

"I tried," she admitted, dropping her eyes. "Quite hard."

She would have turned away, but he caught her chin in his hand and raised her face. His heart ached for them both, and yet the moment could not be rushed.

He smiled into her eyes. "Shall we begin again? Let me court you properly, this time, beginning with our trip to Brighton."

Her lips parted, perhaps in surprise, perhaps in invitation. Either way, he kissed them, softly, and felt the press of her mouth in response.

Happier than he had been in months, his mind found it easy to part for the night, with all the promise of tomorrow. His body objected quite strongly to such abstinence, but he did his best to ignore it.

❁❁❁

Gaby woke with joy in her heart. She had slept better than she had in weeks, and she was eager for the excursion to Brighton with her husband—who had not, it seemed, withdrawn from her because she disgusted him or because she had failed him somehow on their wedding night, but from simple jealousy.

Of Snowy.

Well, looked on from another's perspective, Snowy was an attractive man. Attractive enough to interest Lady Winmore. Who was not Leo's mistress.

Leo. She allowed herself to call him by name in her mind once more. He was her husband, and he was at least open to her love.

She rang for Hawkins and was already dressed in her warm carriage gown by the time her husband sauntered through the connecting door, handsome as always in his correct morning dress of buff pantaloons and blue coat, to escort her to breakfast.

"It looks to be a fine day," he remarked. "A good omen for our trip."

The morning's post had been left as usual on the hall table. Leo rifled through it on his way past and took two letters from the pile.

"One for each of us," he said, passing the thinner of them to her and striding on to the breakfast parlor.

With shock, Gaby recognized Art's scrawl on the address of her letter. She had forgotten all about the wretched rubies in all the turbulence of yesterday evening. She knew from Snowy that Art had agreed to fetch them back and it was past time she should have heard from him.

She must not give away her excitement. With luck Art could return the rubies to her room, or at least to Hawkins, while she and Leo were in Brighton. And then she could go to her husband's arms with a clear conscience, and confess her foolishness.

She waited until they had chosen their breakfasts and sat down with the scattering of other early-rising guests, before she unsealed the missive. It was dated yesterday and was extremely brief.

Got them. At the Blue Toad Inn on the Chichester to Brighton Road. Bring money. A.

What the devil was he doing at the Blue Toad? Come to that, *where* was the Blue Toad?

"Bad news?" Leo asked with some concern.

"Oh no. It's just Art." *What do I do? What do I say to him?* More than anything, she wanted to go to Brighton with him, to relax into his company and enjoy being alone with him, loving him... But surely the rubies would always come between them? Once she had them safe, all would be well. Perhaps she could send Snowy for them... But he was not at breakfast, and she could hardly beard him in his bedchamber or even send him a note since there was no time. *Oh hell and the devil confound it!* "Do you know, I think I'll go and clear this up with my brother. We could go to Brighton later on, Corey? Or tomorrow, perhaps?"

"We're all going on an excursion there tomorrow," Lady Somerville said. "Come with us."

"What do you think?" Gaby asked her husband nervously.

He looked up from his own letter, but he had clearly heard everything for his eyes were hard as flint. She knew before he spoke that she had chosen disastrously.

"Why, do as you like, my dear. I shall do perfectly well by myself in Brighton. Give Arthur my regards."

Stricken, she stared at her breakfast, pushing it around the plate a little while he silently read on. It was excruciating.

At last, she rose and excused herself and hurried from the room.

Since it seemed foolish to take the massive Corey travelling carriage and four horses for one person on a presumably short distance, she asked Sir Peter, encountered in the hall, if she might borrow a small vehicle for a short trip.

"Of course," he said jovially. "I'll send to the stables for you."

Two hours later, she stormed into her brother's room at the Blue Toad and glared at him.

"Why are you still in bed while I...!" she began in a towering rage.

"Because there's nothing else to do here," he interrupted, sitting up and revealing his very crumpled shirt. "I can't even go out, let alone walk all the way to Normanton for fear of losing the damned baubles to vagrants or highwaymen!"

"Then why couldn't you come to Normanton in the first place? There's a perfectly good inn there if you're avoiding Corey."

"I'm not avoiding Corey," he retorted, scowling. "You are. And I couldn't go to Normanton because I ran out of funds and the damned postilions rumbled me."

"Oh." Pulled up short by her realization of the difficulties she had put him through, she sat on the edge of the bed. "Sorry. But you got the rubies?"

"No thanks to you. Nicholas didn't have them. So, I had to go to Sanford, and they were just where you'd left them, silly chit."

She opened her mouth to retaliate but ended by sighing and admitting, "I am a silly chit. I was quite sure Nicholas couldn't have passed over them. How did you talk Scrivens round to parting with them?"

"I didn't." Art told her about the little maid fetching them, and warned her not to let anyone dismiss the girl.

Gaby promised she would not, and he extracted the familiar case from under his pillow. She hugged it.

"That was clever of you," she said generously. "Thanks, Arty. Scrivens can't have let Nicholas into the house, which is an excellent thing."

"Oh, he got in, pinched your paper knife and a few coins, but seems to me he was too in awe of Corey to nab the family heirloom."

Gaby, remembering with a chill in her heart the cold flint of her husband's eyes, shivered. For the first time ever, she understood Nicholas's behavior. She would do anything too to avoid that look. Though she was likely to see little else from her husband now.

She took the purse from her reticule. Most of it was the money Art had so recently paid her back, plus the few guineas she had won at cards last night. "Will this pay your shot and get you back to Brighton?"

"Should do," Art said, weighing it in his hand.

"I can take you as far as Normanton, if you like."

"No, you go back to Corey and stop playing games, Gaby. The only sign of weakness I've ever seen in him is that he loves you."

"I love him," she whispered. "And I think I've messed it up again."

"Tell him everything," Art said severely. "And all will be well."

"Do you really think so?"

He groaned. "Go away, Gaby. I can't stand you going all pathetic on me."

Heartened by this encouragement, she laughed and rose to her feet. "Thanks, Art. I do owe you. Again!"

❧

Back in the unassuming coach, with a change of horses, Gaby hoped to make good time on the return journey. She hugged the case of rubies to her heart and prayed that Leo would not have gone to Brighton without her. She meant to go straight to him with the rubies and tell him the whole silly story.

And it *was* silly. After last night's admissions, she should have told Leo the rest and gone to Brighton with him, via the Blue Toad if necessary.

"Wrong, wrong, wrong," she muttered. "We have both been wrong the whole way..."

Quite suddenly, she thought of another thing that could have gone wrong, and all but wrenched open the jewel case. To her relief, all the ruby pieces lay there just as she had first seen them.

Thank...

The carriage, which had been bowling along at a good clip, slowed so abruptly that she was thrown forward almost to her knees. Shouting amidst the sounds of more hooves came from the road, and the carriage lurched to a halt.

Still clutching the case, she leaned forward to see out of the window—just as the door was wrenched open.

A masked man stared at her, a pistol in his gloved hand. Only his eyes were visible, and they stared at her for what felt like a pregnant moment. Then he muttered something under his breath, wrenched the jewel case from her hold, and slammed the door in her stunned face.

As if in a bad dream, she heard him ride away with the rubies.

CHAPTER 7

H is wife, it seemed, could always take him by surprise. Raging hurt that she should still choose her thoroughly unpleasant family over him warred with overwhelming disappointment that she was so careless of the relationship he was trying to build between them.

And he missed her. God, he missed her.

At first, he drove his horses at reckless speeds along the country lanes that led to the main Brighton road, forcing his tiger to hold on grimly to his perch at the back. He could imagine Gabriella sitting by his side, laughing with excitement. Fortunately for all concerned, his thinking half began to reassert itself over the emotional, and he slowed his horses before he exhausted them or overturned the curricle.

He had set off to Brighton merely to prove he did not care. But such defensiveness achieved nothing. Corey was determined by nature, and as he analyzed what had actually happened this morning, he knew he should simply have gone with Gabriella. Or followed her. Because that letter signified some kind of trouble for her, a trouble she had not yet been ready to tell him about. That was not her fault. It was his for not yet winning her trust.

And it was nothing to do with Snowy, who remained at Normanton House, making sheep's eyes at Barbara Winmore.

Since it was too late to go after her, he carried on his way to Brighton and fulfilled the business he had always intended—which was to buy her some pretty jewels and other trinkets of her own, pieces he thought she would like. He chose them with care and unusual thoughtfulness.

Then, with his horses rested, he pointed them back toward Normanton with sweet anticipation in his heart—not for her gratitude, for he could never buy her in this way—just to be with her.

He was only a mile or so from the house when he came upon a horseman who tugged at his hat and indicated he wanted to talk. Impatiently, Corey halted his team, and the man introduced himself as a constable of the parish.

"There's been another holdup, sir, and I was wondering if you'd seen any signs of a suspicious horseman hereabouts, masked or otherwise."

Corey shook his head. "No, I haven't seen anyone except a couple of farm laborers on foot."

"We think it's the same miscreant who's already caused so much trouble," the constable said grimly, "but Sir Peter is especially furious about this one because it was one of his guests what was threatened."

A weird tingle of foreboding passed through Corey. "Who? Who was held up?"

"A lady, sir. Lady Corey."

The world tilted. "Is she hurt?" he croaked at the constable, who took off his hat and scratched his head with maddening slowness.

"Couldn't rightly say, sir, but I reckon she were, because Sir Peter seemed terribly upset over her. On—"

Corey heard no more. Awash with the sort of terror he had never known before, he jerked his hands on the ribbons, urging his startled horses into motion. He had no idea of his speed, only of his need to get to Gabriella. Fear for her obliterated everything else from his mind. His one instinct was to reach her.

Her pain, her hurt, was unbearable to him, and if she died...

The blood sang in his ears, but he could not afford to lose concentration now. He had to find her, make her well...

Before the front door, he leapt down from the curricle, abandoning his horses without a word, and charged up the front steps into the house.

"Where is Lady Corey?" he barked at the startled footman as he strode in like a hurricane.

"One m-moment, my lord," the footman stammered. "I'll find out."

"Corey." It was Somerville himself, emerging from the back of the hall. "A word, if you please."

"Later. My wife—"

"Lady Corey is well," Somerville said.

Corey almost sank to his knees. As it was, he wobbled, and had to halt in his impetuous tracks. Somerville grasped his arm and urged him toward his study. "We need to talk."

All for nothing. It was all for nothing.

One day, she would laugh at her ridiculous antics, even at her rage when Sir Peter's coachman refused to pursue the highwayman who had stolen the rubies. Now, pacing constantly through the connecting door across Leo's sitting room and back again to her own, she could think only of her foolishness, of all the reasons she had given her husband not to trust her.

Her first thought had been to tell no one, at least not until she had laid the whole mess before Leo. But of course, there was the coachman, who was bound to tell Sir Peter, and so she had reported the incident to her host, omitting the rubies from her tale, muttering only that she'd had nothing to steal.

At last, hearing the scrunch of wheels and hooves in the gravel outside, she ran to her sitting room window. Those were Leo's horses, his curricle, his tiger, but Leo himself had already vanished into the house. His tiger, looking entirely unconcerned, began to lead the horses away to the stables. So at least Leo was fine. *He* had not encountered the wretched highwayman.

She strode back to his sitting room. Why was he taking so long? She felt she would burst with the need to tell all, to throw herself upon his mercy for what she had done. There was no point in pleading for his love. She had destroyed that possibility with lies and stupidity and gross negligence with his priceless heirloom.

In the end, she did not even hear him approach. She was halfway across his room when the door to the passage opened quietly and he walked in.

For an instant, their eyes met. His looked troubled, turbulent, but not angry at least. God knew what he read in hers.

"My lord, I must speak." Something beyond her control propelled her across the room to him. She even grasped his arms. "I have lost your rubies through my own idiocy, and I am so very sorry!"

And then it all spilled out, how she had been too distracted to realize the rubies were not packed, her certainty that Nicholas had stolen them, her reluctance to tell Leo in case he thought she did not value his gift or his trust, her note to Art in Brighton via Snowy, Art's difficulties in getting the rubies to her, and the final, calamitous theft this afternoon.

At some point in her incoherent tale, his arm had crept around her.

"I know you can never forgive me, but—"

"Gabriella."

"But there must be some way to get the rubies back. They will surely be impossible to sell, and the Bow Street Runners might…"

"Gabriella."

His arm at her back urged her to the sofa, where he sat her down. He lowered himself beside her and placed something in her lap.

She blinked at it. Her lips parted. She was afraid to touch it.

Leo opened the square leather case, and the rubies, bright and serene, sparkled at her in all their glory.

Slowly, she raised her eyes to his face. "How…?"

"Somerville has just handed them over to me. No, I don't know how they came into his possession, for the highwayman is not yet caught, and I'm not going to ask. No one else knows the rubies are involved."

She swallowed and somehow managed a tremulous smile. "I am so glad you got them back."

"*We* got them back. They are my gift to you, remember?"

"I remember everything. I thought if only I could get them back, then you would have more chance of believing me, of loving me."

He took both her hands in his, resting them on the jewels in her lap. "Gabriella. The rubies are nothing, only a token. It's the love that is important. It is *you* who must forgive *me*. I only understood the truth when I feared you had been taken from me forever. There is only one reason I was so hurt and behaved so appallingly. Logic and time span count for nothing. I *loved* you from the very beginning."

Before she had even thought it, she fused her mouth to his. His arms closed around her and the kiss became his, deeper and wilder and utterly overwhelming, There were no words, it seemed, for the intensity of this feeling, it had to be shown, with caresses and sighs and tenderness, and nothing could stop it.

While the other guests gathered with their hosts for tea, the marquis finally took his wife to bed again. All had come right for them in this moment. Their worlds became one, and their road to continued joy and happiness together wound on and on.

THE END

꧁꧂

If you enjoyed **My Gift to You,** you might like to try Mary's longer Regency romance novels. You can find them listed by series on her website at http://www.MaryLancaster.com.

SOCIAL MEDIA FOR MARY LANCASTER

You can learn more about Mary Lancaster at these social medial links:

Website: http://www.MaryLancaster.com
Newsletter sign-up: https://landing.mailerlite.com/webforms/landing/e2p7c6
Facebook: https://www.facebook.com/mary.lancaster.1656
Facebook Author Page: https://www.facebook.com/MaryLancasterNovelist/
X: https://X.com/MaryLancNovels
Bluesky: https://bsky.app/profile/MaryLancaster.bsky.social
BookBub: https://www.bookbub.com/authors/mary-lancaster
TikTok: https://www.tiktok.com/@mary.lancaster1

ABOUT MARY LANCASTER

Mary Lancaster is a USA Today bestselling author of romantic historical fiction. She lives in Scotland with her husband, one of three grown-up kids, and a small dog with a big personality.

Her first literary love was historical fiction, a genre which she relishes mixing up with romance and adventure in her own writing. Several of her novels feature actual historical characters as diverse as Hungarian revolutionaries, medieval English outlaws, and a family of eternally rebellious royal Scots. To say nothing of Vlad the Impaler.

Her most recent books are light fun Regency romances, with occasional forays into historical mystery.

Connect with Mary on-line – she loves to hear from readers.

Learn more about Mary at
Website: http://www.MaryLancaster.com
Newsletter sign-up: https://www.MaryLancaster.com/Newsletter

THE CASEBOOK OF PRINCIPAL OFFICER ROBERT PIERCE

Brighton and surrounding districts

I've become convinced that there are two highwaymen, and one of them fancies himself a philanthropist. The local countryfolk are full of stories about the persecutors of widows finding themselves robbed and shamed in some way, and coins turning up in hens' nests.

These stories cluster in the neighborhood south of the Chichester to Brighton road. Therefore, I'm focusing my attention on the London to Brighton road, though not because this Captain Moonlight fellow doesn't deserve to be arrested. Breaking the law is still breaking the law. However, the other villain is more dangerous to life and limb.

Also, I hope to find clues to Larcenous Lucy. She is out there somewhere.

FALLING INTO YOU

SHERRY EWING

Falling Into You
By Sherry Ewing

Sometimes a memory is hard to forget...

Milton Sutton, Earl of Langley has one regret in life... that he left behind a lady that owned his heart in order to take over his father's businesses to prevent bankruptcy. One year later, he has a second chance to win her back, but is he too late?

Lady Josephine Cranfield is determined to move on after her heart was broken by the love of her life. However, her feelings for Milton awaken upon his return, but his eagerness to pick up where they left off only makes her resolved to forget him.

Can Milton and Josephine find a way back to one another, or will someone else find his way into Josephine's heart?

PROLOGUE

Bath Assembly Rooms
Autumn 1816

Lady Josephine Cranfield entered the brightly decorated ballroom on the arm of her brother Richard. Her distant cousin and chaperone Mrs. Julia Elford followed close behind. The room was already abuzz with sparkling conversation, and Josephine heard the musicians in the gallery tuning their instruments. Her parents had instructed Richard to take Josephine to Bath for the Season in the hopes she would finally find a husband, having run through any possible suitors in London. None of them had held any interest for her, and who could blame her? The men put before her by her parents were ready to put one foot in the grave, and the others only wanted her for her dowry.

She searched the crowded room for the one man who had caught her eye this summer. He was one of London's most eligible bachelors and as handsome as sin. If someone had told her months ago that she and her brother's best friend would be romantically involved, she would have laughed. She had known Lord Milton Sutton for most of her life, along with several others in Richard's close circle of friends, even before their days together at Oxford. But secretly, she had always held a crush on the man. Her eyes met his, and Milton nodded in her direction from across the room.

It seemed like hours passed before he finally made his way to her, and she wondered why he seemed to be avoiding her. Considering the amount of time they had spent together in recent months, it was unusual. He gave her a bow and she returned the formality with a curtsy.

"May I have the next dance, Lady Josephine?" he asked with a charming smile.

"Yes. Yes, of course, Lord Langley," she murmured after taking his arm, still wondering why it had taken him so long to come to her. Was it her imagination, or did he seem somewhat aloof instead of the affectionate way he had been with her for the past months?

There was no further time to discuss pleasantries when the beginning chords to a quadrille sounded and the dancers took their places. She became breathless as she hopped and skipped to the patterns of the dance, and when the dying chords faded away, Milton asked if he could have a moment to speak with her privately.

This is it, she thought happily to herself. He was finally going to declare himself, and she nodded her head in agreement as he escorted her out into the moonlight. She knew she was safe with Milton and trusted he would not take advantage of her. She was thankful they would have a private word together.

He led her into the garden and she took a seat on a marble bench. She waited for him to join her, but instead he began to pace back and forth in front of her. Now she *was* worried. Something was terribly wrong. He should have been sitting next to her and kissing her senseless, not wearing a path in the grass beneath his shoes. He rubbed the back of his neck in apparent agitation, and she held her breath waiting for whatever news he was about to impart.

"There's no easy way to say this, Josephine," he began, dropping any formalities previously put in place between them.

"Whatever is wrong and troubling you, we can find a solution together," she said with pleading eyes, although he avoided looking at her. In fact, he was doing his best to cast his gaze anywhere but on her. "Milton... please... tell me what's wrong."

He ran his fingers through his thick black hair, causing several strands to stand up on end. She wanted to reach out to him and push them gently back into place, but the seriousness of his features made her stay where she was. A feeling of dread filled her heart when his blue eyes finally turned to her with what she could only term as regret.

"I'm afraid any plans I may have had for our future together will have to be put on hold," he finally answered, taking a seat next to her and reaching for her gloved hands.

"You're worrying me, Milton. What's wrong?"

"My father has been terribly ill, and I must take over his business dealings. Unfortunately, that entails a lengthy journey that will take me far away from England's shores," he said, while his thumb traced the fabric of her glove.

She swallowed hard, trying to keep her composure. "For how long?"

"I may be gone for close to a year, maybe more. At the moment, I have no way of knowing when I'll return. I'm sorry, Josephine."

She frowned, thinking back to previous conversations. She knew his father had not been well for some time. She began to surmise that Milton knew more than he was telling her. "How long have you known you would be leaving? That you'd have to travel in order to take care of your father's investments?"

"I knew you wouldn't take this well," he sighed, wiping his hand across his eyes before tugging at the edge of his cravat as though it was too tight. "But... I realized I was going to have to leave about a month ago."

"And you're only telling me this now?" she cried out.

"There's nothing that can be done to change the course my life will now take. My father is depending on me, and I cannot let him and my mother down."

"But what about us?"

He reached over to wipe the tear that cascaded down her cheek. "I cannot ask you to wait for me, Josephine. Go live your life and find yourself a worthy husband. I cannot make you an offer for your hand."

She rose angrily to her feet. "You led me to believe you would marry me. How could you lead me on like this? Was I just a game to you?"

"That's not fair. You know I have feelings for you." He stood reaching for her hand, but she darted out of his grasp.

"Apparently your so-called feelings are not very strong, or you'd be asking to marry me so I could come with you," she said, as a sob caught in her throat. All her hopes and dreams were being dashed away, and she didn't know how she could keep Milton from leaving.

He gave a heavy sigh and ran his hand across his nape again. "Since I don't know what my future will bring, that wouldn't be fair to you. I'm sorry to disappoint you, Josephine. It was never my intention to hurt you."

"I'll never forgive you..."

She gave one last glimpse upon his handsome face before she picked up the hem of her gown and ran back inside to look for her brother. She spotted him. He appeared as bad as she felt, and for a moment, she wondered what had happened that caused him to appear so lost. There would be plenty of time to discuss their evening once they were in their carriage.

"Can we go home?" she asked, trying to keep from making a scene by sobbing out her heartbreak. Such behaviour was sure to end up in the latest column in *The Teatime Tattler*.

"What's happened?" Richard asked, in brotherly concern.

"I just want to leave. Is there anything wrong with that?"

"We're at a ball, and you were enjoying yourself, earlier. If I recall, you were happily dancing with Milton. Where is he?"

"Who cares! I want to go home, Richard. Now." Her raised voice caused several nearby couples to turn in their direction.

He watched her suspiciously, clearly wondering what happened. "Do I need to call Milton out?"

Her eyes widened and tears pooled in their depths before she shook her head. "No. We had a falling out. Now, can you please take me home?"

"Of course." He took her arm after sending a servant in search of her chaperone, and escorted Josephine from the Assembly room.

Any thoughts of becoming Milton's wife were now completely dashed. With no other prospects for a husband, Josephine began to wonder if she would live out the rest of her life as a spinster.

CHAPTER 1

White's, London
One year later...

Milton Sutton, Earl of Langley, strode through the doors of White's after a year's absence. To be on solid ground and not standing on the swaying boards of a ship was a welcome change. He handed his cloak to a servant, took a brandy from the tray of another, and scanned the tables for his friends. Taking a sip of his drink, he finally spotted them sitting near the hearth and began to make his way in their direction.

Most were all too familiar faces from the days of his youth. Frederick Maddox, Viscount Beacham, and Digby, Viscount Osgood, were both happily married long before Milton had left on business for his father. That Richard Cranfield had wed shouldn't have surprised him either, since it was inevitable they all must do so at some point in their lives, so their titles would go on with their heirs.

The Chadwick brothers were laughing at something Milton couldn't yet hear. George looked resplendent, as was his usual custom when it came to his clothes. His older brother David, who was in line to inherit the duchy, was far more relaxed. George had managed to get his brother from his country estate, which must have taken a miracle. The other gentleman seated with them looked familiar, but he couldn't place the name. Viscount... something. Milton really had been gone a long time.

He approached the group of friends with a welcoming smile. "Seems like some things never change," he murmured in greeting.

"Are my eyes deceiving me or has our long-lost friend finally decide to return from his journeys?" Richard joked lifting his glass in a silent toast toward Milton.

"Milton!" George chimed in. "It's good to see you. Thought maybe you forgot where to find home."

Milton shrugged good naturedly. "As if I could forget."

Digby took a sip of his drink. "What's it been? A year at least?" he asked.

"More or less," Milton answered with a nod.

Frederick waved to the empty space. "Pull up a chair and join us. There have been lots of changes since you've been gone."

Milton lifted a brow. "I've read from the correspondence that reached me that Richard is now married. What else have I missed?"

George happily clapped his hands. "Richard's little sister is finally engaged to this fine gent," he proclaimed with a grin before he gave the man seated next to him a good slap to his shoulder. "We're all very happy for them."

The chair Milton was pulling over rattled on the floor and he took a firmer grip on it before it tipped over. George seemed unaware of how uncomfortable Milton had become, and the men around him were absorbed in their drinks. Milton finally sat, afraid his legs might buckle from such news. He had hoped... no... he should have never held out hope that Josephine was still unwed.

"Nothing has been made official," the gentleman stated, looking toward Richard.

Richard cleared his throat. "As Frederick mentioned, you've missed a great deal. This is Philip, Viscount Upton, who has been escorting Josephine to events this Season. Philip, meet Lord Langley."

Philip nodded. "A pleasure."

Milton acknowledged the man, but his focus was on Richard. Bloody hell! He really had been gone too long, if Josephine was to possibly marry.

David stood. "Perhaps we should give Richard and Milton time to catch up. I for one wouldn't mind a game of billiards. Does anyone care to join me?"

The men agreed, and after their friends left, including Philip, Milton turned his angry gaze to Richard. "Why didn't you write me of such news?"

"And where exactly was I to send such a message?" Richard snapped. "The last letter I received months ago stated you were getting ready to leave the Americas and would be sailing to France. How was I to know when you would arrive back in England or if you were still at sea? Besides, who Josephine sees isn't any concern of yours. You told me you couldn't ask for her hand when I confronted you before you left."

"That didn't mean I didn't still care for her," he fumed as he relived his last encounter with Josephine, as he had every night since he left England's shores. He couldn't have offered for the lady, not when his family was facing complete financial ruin. Milton glanced at his best friend, knowing he had even kept the truth hidden from Richard and the rest of his friends. His pride kept him from revealing to them and Josephine the full truth of the matter and why he would be gone for at least a year. He had been desperate to save his family fortune and vowed he wouldn't return until he had done so.

Richard gave him a grim look. "Then you should have made your intentions known and done something about it. She's now practically spoken for, Milton. Be happy for her."

Silence stretched between them. "Does she love him?" Milton asked softly, though his heart was breaking all over again at the thought of losing Josephine so completely.

Richard arched one brow before he finally answered. "They are... well suited for one another."

Milton frowned. "But does she *love* him?" he repeated.

Richard sighed heavily. "To be honest, I don't believe Josephine is capable of loving someone again. The last time she gave away her heart, she became completely broken. She never really recovered."

Such a statement told Milton much, and he hated that he was the cause of Josephine's broken heart. "You knew I had to leave from the little I told you. My father's estate depended on me to keep it afloat."

Richard lifted his glass to his lips and drank. "You made your decisions that were in the best interest of your family. Josephine is about to make hers."

"Then there's still hope I can make amends," Milton replied, thinking that perhaps if he could just talk to Richard's sister, then he could persuade her to not marry anyone else but him.

Richard leaned forward in his chair and pointed a finger at him. "I won't have you opening old wounds, Milton. She barely survived your rejection of her last year. Let the past stay where it belongs and let her move on."

Milton swiped a hand over his eyes. "I can't."

"Whyever not?" Richard asked with a scowl.

Surely his face betrayed his feelings for Josephine, but he still voiced his thoughts aloud. "Because I still love her."

"*Bloody hell*, Milton," Richard swore before sitting back in his chair, clearly frustrated by their conversation.

"I know... if I could just talk to her. Maybe then, I can begin to mend the rift between us."

Richard shook his head. "It's more than just a disagreement you had with her, my friend. You left a hole in her heart that is as wide as the ocean."

"And I'm certain that a lot of groveling on my part will be required," Milton declared before pressing onward. "Where is she?"

Richard gave another heavy sigh before he finally answered. "Still here in London, but not for long. She will be traveling soon to Brighton with our distant cousin Julia Elford as her chaperone. She's to meet Philip's family who reside there. Josephine will be staying at Julia's townhouse. They've been waiting for word that it has been readied for them to arrive before they left."

"Then Upton hasn't formally asked for her hand in marriage?" He hated to ask but still held his breath, hoping Richard had yet to give his blessing.

"No, but I expect him to do so before he leaves for Brighton by the end of the week. You may still have time to convince her. Otherwise, you'd best be prepared to open your own place in the countryside so you can be near at hand to do... as you said... grovel at her feet."

"Then you wouldn't object to Josephine becoming my wife?"

Richard smirked. "You're one of my best friends, Milton, but before I give you my blessing, you need to convince Josephine of your intentions. She's very bitter, with good reason, so you'd best be prepared to do whatever it takes to win her heart again."

"She's worth whatever I must do to earn her love."

"Hurt her again, and you'll answer to me. Understood?" Richard warned, but Milton could see he was pleased with the prospect of Milton winning over his sister.

"Understood. Shall we join our friends for a game or two?" Milton asked, while Richard stood.

The two men shook hands and went into the other room to join in a game. But Milton was already thinking of how he would handle his first meeting with Josephine, and if the lady would even allow him past the front door. There was only one way to find out.

CHAPTER 2

Josephine stared out the bedroom window of her London townhouse. The garden below was all but bare at this time of autumn. Although her eyes lingered on the few remaining flowers that still bloomed, she wasn't really seeing what was before her. Instead, her mind floated back to days long gone, to a summer filled with promises of love. Her heart shouldn't linger in the past, but she couldn't seem to keep herself from remembering when she had fallen in love with a handsome earl.

That she had been in love with him for most of her life was no coincidence, since Milton had spent a lot of his days with her brother Richard. He was one of his closest friends, and she had admired him from when he came to visit both in town and their country estates. The lanky boy with the dark brown hair and sparkling mischievous blue eyes had grown into a handsome man with whom any girl or woman could easily fall in love. She had such hope for a future with him and yet, everything changed a year ago when he left.

How long had it taken for her to get over the anger and disappointment that he wouldn't offer for her hand in marriage? She grimaced at the memories that still revealed too much of how she truly still felt about the man. It was hard to get over someone whom you held in affection for your entire life. She shouldn't be dwelling so much on Milton and instead should be thinking about what her future might hold for her very soon.

Philip, Viscount Upton, had been a welcome relief and had thawed her melancholy mood when she was introduced to him earlier this year by her distant cousin and chaperone Julia Elford. She remembered how his blonde hair stood on end when they met in the park after he took his hat off and bowed to her. And while she covered her mouth to hide her laughter at the sight, she watched his brown eyes gaze upon her with interest. He, too, was a handsome man and completely different from Milton, which maybe was a good thing. Philip had a personality that was serious but polite, whereas Milton had always found a way to make her laugh.

And when Richard became aware that Josephine had an admirer, he had even gone so far as to remind her that it was well past time she moved on with her life. She hated to admit her brother was right. And while Philip didn't necessarily make her heart soar each time they were together, she did at least have a small affection for him that could be considered promising. She wasn't in love with him, but he would still make her a good husband. That is, if he proposed to her. She expected him to ask for her hand any day now, if she read the signs he had given her correctly. Still, she worried, thinking how she had been wrong before when she thought a proposal of marriage would be offered.

She gave a heavy sigh, took the discarded book off her lap, and went to the bookshelf and put the tome away. Somehow, a romantic novel gave her false hope of living a happily-ever-after life. She didn't think love would play any part in her possible marriage to the viscount, but they would suit one another well enough.

A knock on her door sounded, and she turned as the portal opened. Julia stood there with a smile that seemed... well... amused, although Josephine had no idea what was keeping the lady so entertained.

"You have a visitor downstairs. He's very handsome," Julia said with a wink.

Josephine looked at the clock sitting on the fireplace mantle and frowned. "Philip is earlier than expected. Why is he here at this time of day?" she asked in confusion.

Julia shrugged. "You'll have to go see for yourself," her cousin responded as they walked into the hallway, but she stopped at her own bedroom door to open it.

Josephine placed her hand on her cousin's arm. "You're not coming down with me to act as my chaperone?"

Julia patted her cheek. "I believe you might require a few minutes of privacy. I think you'll be safe enough in your own house. I'll be down in a few minutes to ensure nothing untoward is going on between you and your gentleman caller."

"This is highly irregular," Josephine insisted, knowing how closely Julia had watched over her and her reputation in the past year.

"He's in the front parlor. You shouldn't keep him waiting, dearest," Julia said, and entered her bedroom.

Knowing how much Philip was a stickler for being punctual, she hurried along the rest of the hallway, descended the stairway, and made her way toward the front parlor. She began speaking before she even entered the room.

"You're very early, Philip. Is something wrong?" she declared before she came to a sudden halt. She took hold of the doorframe to steady herself when she witnessed the gentleman standing near the window, afraid that her knees might buckle.

He turned to face her with the sun streaming through the glass to make him appear almost angelic. She drank in the sight of him as though she was dying of thirst. The cut of his suit and waistcoat was immaculate. His dark brown hair streaked with lighter shades was neatly combed into place and touched the edges of his coat. His skin appeared tanned from time spent in the sun, and he appeared far more muscular than she remembered. His linen shirt stretched across his muscled chest, while his blue eyes seemingly danced in delight to see her. She just might swoon.

"Hello, Josephine," he said, giving her a bow. The old memory of his husky baritone branded her heart with sorrow, as all the old hurt came rushing back to the surface.

"Milton..." she began, attempting to find her voice. "I wasn't expecting you."

"I know this is highly irregular, but I had to see you," he said, stepping forward.

"Why?" she gasped out as her knees began to shake, and she had the overwhelming need to sit down.

The sound of the tea trolley being rolled through the hallway gave her the moment she needed to clear her head and compose herself. She went into the room and sat in a chair near the hearth, knowing that to sit on the couch would allow him to be far too close. Once the servant put the trolley near at hand, she poured tea into two cups and offered him one as he took the opposite chair. He reached for the one she held out for him, and when their fingers touched, a zing of emotion overcame her. It wasn't fair he could still have such an effect on her after all this time. It wasn't fair at all!

He continued to stare at her, searching her face for some sign of... *what*? That she was still *in love* with him? She couldn't be certain, but what did it matter if she still cared for this man? He was her past, and Philip was her future.

"You were one of the first people I wanted to see upon my return," he confessed, setting down his tea without taking a sip.

"Oh? And who was the first?" she said in a snippy tone.

A slight chuckle left those lips she remembered all too well, having kissed them a dozen times or more. "Your brother," he finally answered.

"I see. Considering your friendship all your lives, I can see how you might have missed him."

"And you."

She raised a brow at his admission. "I don't see why you'd have missed me, Milton. After all, it was you who ended our association."

A heavy sigh left him. "I was hoping with time you would understand why I had to leave."

She gave a shrug. "I did, after months of self-pity," she admitted before continuing. "But I have moved on with my life as you, yourself, suggested. I assumed you would do the same."

A frown now marred his brow. "Yes. I heard about the possibility of your engagement."

"Weren't you the one who told me to find another for a husband?" Her sharp retort brought back the agony of every memory of Milton she had buried deep down in her soul. She wasn't certain how much more of this conversation she could endure.

"I know what I said, Josephine. That doesn't mean I didn't still care for you. I still do," he replied quietly.

She nodded, trying to remain indifferent to what she was currently feeling. Her heart was racing with Milton being this close. She closed her eyes briefly, before opening them to stare at the man who once owned her heart.

"Yes. Well... I suppose, considering you are my brother's beloved friend, it would only be natural to ensure that you and I would be able to see one another without any animosity between us. I can assure you that I will treat you as I always have at any other time in our past."

"That's not why I came here today, Josephine."

It was her turn to let out a heavy sigh. "Then *why* exactly *are* you here, Milton?"

"I was hoping I wasn't too late."

"Too late for what?" she asked with her heart hammering inside her chest.

He stood and began to pace in front of her, before he stopped to kneel down before her. Shocked, he took her hands in his, while her heart betrayed her yet again.

"I was hoping you would forgive me and give us a second chance." He appeared to search her face, and for an instant she almost gave in to what every fiber of her being was telling her. She was still in love with Milton Sutton, Earl of Langley.

She shook her head and pulled her hands from his, causing him to rise again to his feet. She stood as well, but went toward the window to put some distance between them. When she turned to face him, she had resolved the matter inside her head.

"You cannot just show up here after being gone a year to disrupt my life again," Josephine began, keeping her voice calm and even. She held up her hand to halt whatever he was about to say. "The course of my life is now set. I suggest you also move on with yours."

"I came to make amends," he declared, stepping toward her. "I never meant to hurt you, Josie. I'm so sorry."

She choked back a gasp at hearing the nickname he called her in their youth. "I forgave you a long time ago, Milton, but that doesn't mean you can just step back into my life as if you never left."

"I promise to make it up to you," he said, taking her hands again when he reached her side. He brought her fingertips to his lips to kiss them.

Once again, she pulled out of his reach, and disappointment flashed across his features. "There is nothing to make up. Whatever was between us is long since over." She huffed in annoyance that her words rang false. His next words proved to her that he knew all too clearly how she still felt about him.

"I can see for myself you still care for me, Josie. Won't you allow me to court you again and prove to you how much you mean to me?"

"What part of this conversation are you not hearing? I have moved on with my life."

Unexpectedly, he pulled her into his arms and held her close. "Your pupils are dilated, and I can see the pulse at your neck is beating far too rapidly to be anything else but excited at the prospect of what could still be between us."

A growl of outrage left her lips, and she stomped on his foot. He immediately released her, and she stepped away from him, knowing she had probably hurt her own foot more than any damage she might have done to his.

"You pompous arse!" she said. "There is no *us* nor will there ever be again. Now, if you'll excuse me, I need to get ready to go out for the evening." She went around him and stood in the doorway to the room waiting for him to leave.

"I understand you are heading to Brighton soon. I'll plan to follow you there," Milton replied with a knowing look.

"Richard talks too much," she said with pressed lips.

He gave a chuckle, before taking one finger and sliding it down her cheek in a gentle caress. "I think he has high hopes that I can convince you to love me again."

"When hell freezes over, Milton," she managed to say, as she listened to him laugh.

"I look forward to the challenge of proving my worth, my dear. I'll see you in Brighton," he said, before he quickly kissed her lips and left her standing there, dumbfounded.

Once she heard the front door close, her knees buckled and she slowly slid down the frame of the door. She raised her fingers to touch her lips where it seemed as though Milton had branded her as his. It took her several minutes before her composure was restored and she rose from the floor. Milton's overconfidence might be his undoing, and yet there was a small part of her that thought she might enjoy watching Milton grovel at her feet.

CHAPTER 3

Milton sat in his study, watching Richard from across the room while his friend downed his brandy and began fidgeting with his pocket watch for the third time. Whatever he had on his mind must be dire, if he would abuse the liquor in his glass. Richard poured another draught while Milton glanced at George sitting next to him. Their friend shrugged, before bringing his own drink to his lips and taking a slow sip to savor the liquor.

Milton went to the sideboard to refill his drink, and returned to his chair. "Whatever you're worried about, Richard, you might as well spit it out," Milton said, with growing frustration in his gut.

Richard emerged from contemplating whatever thoughts were spinning inside his head. "You know I wouldn't ask this of you if I didn't think it was important," he finally managed to say. He strode across the room and took a seat.

Milton sighed. "You haven't asked anything of me as yet," he said, before turning toward George. "Is this why you're here? For reinforcement?"

George smirked. "Richard asked me to join him here without explanation. Call me curious."

Milton raised his glass to his lips, having the notion he was going to need the spirits to calm him. "Very well. What's on your mind?"

Richard leaned his head back, closing his eyes. "Josephine and our cousin will be heading to Brighton," he began, as he stared between the two men.

"And?" Milton urged Richard to continue, since Milton was already aware of Josephine's plans from the conversation that the men had had at White's.

"And I have learned from good sources that a highwayman has been plaguing the road north of Brighton, which is the road Josephine must travel."

A snort left George. "Scoundrels in that area are hardly anything new. Smugglers are well known," he replied.

Richard stood again and began to pace in front of the hearth, before looking directly at Milton. "I would like you to accompany the ladies on their trip to Brighton to ensure their safety. I thought George could join you if he wasn't too busy."

Milton swore softly. "I don't see how this will help my cause to win over your sister, especially since she's upset with me. I highly doubt she will appreciate my company."

Richard shook his head and gave a heavy sigh. "Since I can't go myself at this time, I need someone I can trust with my sister's and cousin's safety. Someone I am familiar with who I know can protect them."

"Hire guards to protect them. You can afford the expense," Milton suggested.

Richard scowled. "Since you told me of your own plans to go to Brighton, why hire men to guard them when you'd be more than capable of performing the task?"

"Because right now Josephine hates me," Milton fumed. "I want her to come to love me again. Being stuck inside a carriage with her for hours will only cause her to distance herself from me at any function we might attend together. If she refuses to spend time with me, how will this work in my favor?"

Richard returned to this seat but leaned forward, placing his forearms upon his legs. "I need you to keep her safe, Milton, and I trust you. Will you travel with them, please?" he asked quietly.

Inwardly, Milton cursed again. This was not how he envisioned winning over the lady. Or was it? Close proximity when she couldn't escape him could work in his favor if he played his cards right. He thought about her reaction, and his own, when he left her the other day after a quick kiss upon her mouth. Afterward, her chest rose and fell, and he knew then and there that she still cared for him, whether she voiced her feelings aloud or not.

"Milton?" Richard looked at him expectingly.

"You know I will, especially knowing that Josephine and Julia might encounter danger on their journey," Milton finally answered, and relief swept across Richard's features. He turned his blue eyes upon George. "You're going with me..."

George looked down at his nails, examining them as if he appeared bored. "Are you asking me or telling me?"

"Asking."

"You know how much I detest the country."

Richard chuckled. "Brighton is very popular with the *ton*. The Prince of Wales himself bought a house there years ago, as you know. He is rebuilding it, and now Brighton is becoming quite the spot to be seen."

George raised one brow. "Well, if the prince is there... why not? I suppose a change of scenery couldn't harm me overly much."

Milton nodded before he tossed a smirk toward the two men. "And who exactly is going to tell Josephine she's to have my sparkling conversation to keep her company on the road to Brighton?"

George stood. "I'll do it," he said with a mischievous grin. "Josephine actually likes *me*, and I doubt Richard would remain in her good graces if *he* tells her, especially if she's hoping for an offer from Upton soon."

"I never gave my blessing, but then again, I didn't give Philip the time to ask. He's a good chap, but if I had my way, Milton would be my choice for a husband for my sister," Richard said, looking uncomfortable.

"That's reassuring. Now if only I can convince your sister," Milton said with a grimace.

"You will... with a fair bit of time," Richard commented before turning toward George. "You're a good friend to inform Josephine of the change of plans."

"Yes, I am, and don't either of you forget it. However, don't let the word get out, or it may ruin my reputation of being indifferent to the outside world," George said, smiling before he frowned with apparent thoughts about his upcoming conversation with Josephine. "She's not going to like having her plans go awry."

Milton agreed. "But she'll adapt, and I'll be thankful for the extra company, George, in Brighton. I've already sent word to open the country house. It's been a while since I've been there. It shouldn't be too much trouble for them to ready an extra room."

Richard stood. "You both have my gratitude. Now, if you'll excuse me, I need to get home to my wife and the children."

"And I'd best be on my way to Josephine," George said.

Richard cleared his throat. "Take the long way," he suggested.

Both men stared at him, wondering what else was going on.

"Why?" George finally asked.

"My mother may already be over at Josephine's," he said, looking guilty.

George swore as Milton watched them both leave. He made his way over to his desk, as there were important matters he needed to see to regarding business before he left London. He could only hope Josephine would take George's news with an open heart.

CHAPTER 4

Josephine bit her lip in angry frustration as her mother Eudora, Countess of Harrington, ranted about the fact that her only daughter was a spinster at the ripe old age of six and twenty. Julia, who was a cousin on Josephine's father's side of the family, sat primly in a chair with her hands folded in her lap. From her pursed lips she was feeling much like Josephine. She, too, kept her thoughts to herself. But when Eudora started her lecture about Josephine losing an earl for a potential husband last season, Julia had had enough.

"Really, Eudora," Julia began with a scowl etched across her features, "you treat your daughter as though she will be forever on the shelf. When the right gentleman comes along, she will do her duty to the family and marry."

Eudora turned her mutinous hazel eyes upon Julia. "As if your situation is any better. Why, if it wasn't for Randall, you would hardly be in a position to escort our daughter as her companion. I suppose a spinster of your age would recognize one of her own kind."

"Mother! You are well aware that Julia is a widow."

"And she should be remarried, so she isn't a burden to her family," Eudora shouted.

Josephine fumed, coming to her feet. "You will not treat Julia as though she is beneath you in my home."

Eudora pointed a finger at her daughter. "A home that is paid for by your father, along with all your expenses."

Josephine defiantly lifted her chin. "You can no longer hold that over my head. Richard told me he has taken over my living arrangements."

"You're lucky that you are not living under my roof still. Otherwise, I would have married you off to the Earl of Dexmore two seasons ago!"

"I refused him for a reason, if you recall. He's a lecherous old man who couldn't keep his hands to himself, along with being old enough to be my own father," she retaliated harshly.

"He may be old, but he has enough money to see you and your children well provided for," Eudora complained bitterly. "I understand from your father that he is still willing to make you an offer, if you would but learn to curb some of your habits."

"My habits?" she shouted. "Like speaking up for myself when he dares to touch me? He's lucky he didn't draw back a nub the last time he made advances toward me."

"If you accepted his offer, he would have been well within his rights," her mother said offhandedly.

Julia came to her feet and went to Josephine, who was trying her best not to sob. "Eudora, you've had your say. Josephine won't be marrying the Earl of Dexmore, not while I draw a breath from my body. Besides, she is expecting an offer any day now from Viscount Upton, if your spies haven't already informed you."

"Bah! A mere viscount when she could have an earl is hardly any sort of an improvement," Eudora declared with a flip of her head. She narrowed her eyes to peer directly at her daughter. "I've been informed that you are traveling to Brighton. I swear by all I hold dear, if you don't find yourself engaged by the end of your trip, I shall wash my hands of you."

Josephine could stand no more from this woman who may have been her mother, but had never treated her kindly at any time in her entire life. "Don't bother to wait until then, madam. You have no further say in how I live my life, and I never wish to see you again!" She went to the doorway of her parlor and called for her butler. He appeared quickly. "Marshall... Show the Countess of Harrington out. She is no longer welcome in this home."

"Well, I never," Eudora hissed as her eyes swept up and down Josephine. "We'll see how soon you come running back to us."

Josephine gazed directly at this woman who cared more for her money and wealth than either of her children. "When hell freezes over, Countess."

Marshall led her mother from the room, while Josephine went to the settee. Her knees buckled as she all but fell onto the cushion.

"I'm so sorry you had to witness such a scene, Julia," she cried, allowing the tears to finally fall, since her mother was now gone.

Julia squeezed her hand. "There's nothing to apologize for. You did the right thing, and I applaud you for standing up for yourself. Most young ladies would never dare to be so bold as to confront a parent in such a way, but Eudora deserved it. I have no idea how I could ever be related to Randall. Those two deserve one another."

Josephine patted her cheeks. "I don't even know why she bothered to come here. She makes a habit of sweeping in when I least expect it, which is why Richard took over my expenses."

"Thank goodness you have such an understanding brother, but you know why she and your father keep contact with you. They expect you to marry well so they can somehow benefit financially from your marriage," Julia replied with a grim expression.

"Richard and I have put up with a lot from our parents over the years. I am very thankful I am no longer under their roof, for obvious reasons."

Marshall returned to the entryway. "Lord Chadwick, my lady."

Josephine quickly turned to pat dry her cheeks before turning a welcoming smile to one of Richard's dearest friends. Impeccably dressed as was his style, he bowed low while the ladies curtseyed as he entered the room.

"Georgie. What a pleasant surprise. What brings you to see me?" She held out her hands to him while his grey eyes sparkled in delight. He kissed the air between his mouth and her knuckles.

"You are a vision, darling Josie," he declared, reverting to the name he, along with the rest of Richard's friends, called her in their younger days.

She reached up and pushed a strand of his black hair back into place. "And you are looking as resplendent as always. But really... what brings you here today?"

"I... umm..." He suddenly appeared uncomfortable, and Josephine put her guard up. She wasn't sure how much more she could take in one day.

"Georgie..."

"Perhaps we should sit," he suggested, as he put a finger to his neck and yanked on his cravat, as though the linen was suddenly too tight.

Julia raised her brow before she went to sit in a chair. Josephine returned to her place on the settee and motioned for George to join her there. Instead, he began to pace much like Richard, leaving Josephine the impression she wasn't going to like whatever he was about to say.

"You might as well get whatever you need to say over with, Georgie. I'm prepared for almost anything given I just banished my mother from this house."

He stopped his pacing. "Yes. I encountered her as I was coming up the walk," he said. "You threw her out?"

"It's a story for another time, but let me just say she won't be coming back anytime soon," Josephine replied, folding her hands in her lap.

"Long overdue, if you ask me," George declared, finally taking a seat and turning his gray eyes toward her. "Richard sent me."

That tidbit was interesting. "Really? And why is my brother sending you here? I assume this visit is on his behalf."

"In a roundabout way. Yes... I suppose," he grumbled, and then cleared his throat. "I'm afraid I'm to be the bearer of bad news... or good news is probably a better way to put it."

Josephine put her hand to her forehead. More bad news seemed to be what her day would be riddled with. "Just tell me, Georgie."

"Richard can't accompany you to Brighton right now because of business matters. He's concerned about you and Mrs. Elford arriving safely to your destination. He has heard that highwaymen have been robbing people on the road north of Normanton on the South Downs."

She arched one brow. "And..."

"He has asked myself and Milton to accompany you," he blurted out.

"What!" she shouted, coming to her feet, before she calmly sat back down.

"I'm certain you can understand his concern that no harm befalls you. You are, after all, his beloved sister," George said softly.

"That's really not necessary, Georgie, and I'd hate to inconvenience you. I happen to know how much you enjoy London."

He gave a wave of his hand. "I understand Brighton is quite the spot to relax and enjoy the coast. Besides, Milton would go to any lengths to ensure you arrive safe and sound."

"You mean Richard," she said, folding her arms over her chest.

"Of course, all of us have always been concerned for your well-being, dearest Josie. You are like a little sister to us, too," George proclaimed, taking her hand and raising her fingertips toward his lips. Once again, he kissed the air as he had done a hundred times or more. George was always the proper gentleman, and Josephine wondered why he wasn't already married and having children. It was well past time he, too, was wed.

"I suppose there's no way to talk any of you out of this?" she asked, already knowing his answer.

"Richard has made up his mind, and you know how he is once he's made his decisions. Besides, Milton and I were already heading to Brighton, so this trip isn't exactly like we are going out of our way," George said as he came to his feet. "Now, I must be going. Need to pack my things and all. We'll be here bright and early in the morning to begin our travels."

She stood and watched him leave before she turned to Julia. "That was most unexpected."

Julia shrugged. "I will be thankful for the extra protection, to be honest with you, Josephine," she said, as they made their way up the stairs to finish packing.

As Josephine entered her bedroom, her mind spun with all the possibilities of spending additional time with Milton. He had been on her mind since he left her days ago. Instead, she should be thinking of her answer to Philip when he finally asked for her hand in marriage. And as she began to plan all the items she needed to pack, she realized that unfortunately, since Milton's kiss, she hadn't thought of Philip in days until just now.

CHAPTER 5

Milton stood in the foyer of Josephine's townhouse waiting for the lady to come down from upstairs. George had already escorted Julia to the waiting carriage that would take them to Brighton. The trip had been planned with a stop in Normanton to rest the horses before continuing on. Their wagons carrying their belongings, along with the men hired to guard them, had already departed. He and George would see the ladies to their destination before continuing to his country house the next day. George had already sent word for his townhouse to be opened for an overnight stay. Milton didn't wish to leave until he knew Josephine was settled.

He had quickly begun to realize that his not being in town would present a problem. How else was he to convince her not to wed Viscount Upton, if he wasn't near enough to prove to her that he still cared? He might need to rethink his plans so he could continue to pursue her; otherwise he might lose her forever. He couldn't imagine his life without Josephine beside him.

She was a vision of loveliness when she descended the staircase. Her blonde hair with darker highlights was fashionably set in a pleasing coiffure. Her hat was set at a jaunty angle while a few curls fell across her cheeks. She was donning a pair of silk gloves as she reached the last step. He watched her take a deep breath before she turned those stunning hazel eyes in his direction. His breath caught in his throat as he realized, for the hundredth time, that he should have never left without her a year ago. He had been such a fool!

"Good morning, Josie," he said softly, giving her a bow. "You look enchanting today."

"Lord Langley," she returned, dropping into a curtsey.

The correctness of using his title was not lost upon him, much to his dismay. "So formal, my lady? You've called me by my first name all our lives whenever we were alone together."

"Times change," she said, keeping her voice low.

"It would grieve me deeply if we couldn't at the very least remain friends, Josephine. We've known one another since we were children," he added quietly, while reaching for her hand. He rubbed the back in a gentle caress.

"Can you blame me that I am not happy with the situation that I have been placed in? Richard gave me no say in the matter, and just made this outrageous plan without even consulting me."

"I understand completely how upset you must be, but we only have your best interest and, of course, your safety as our main concerns. I would think you would also understand how dear you are to all of us, and we wouldn't like to see any harm befall you."

She gave a heavy sigh. "I suppose," she replied, although Milton could see it was reluctant.

He gave her the briefest of nods. "George and Julia are already waiting outside in the carriage, if you're ready to leave," he said, while watching her intently. That she remained aloof with him shouldn't have surprised him in the least, but that didn't mean the snub of her indifference didn't sting.

"Since Richard left me with no choice on who would accompany us, then I am as ready as I'll ever be," she declared sharply. One of her brows rose when she continued, "Unless you've changed your mind."

"Why would I deprive myself of your lovely company, Josephine?" he asked with a crooked grin.

"Because you are well aware that I am spoken for," she snapped.

Amused by her answer, he couldn't help but make his own sharp retort. "Really? According to Richard, such is not the case. Did Upton ask you to marry him without your brother's blessing?"

"The only reason I am going to Brighton is to meet his family," she said firmly.

"So, he has not asked for your hand as yet. Good! That still leaves me time to change your mind about how you currently feel about me," he said with another grin.

"I have already informed you that whatever we had between us ended over a year ago. What part of our most recent conversation of *I have moved on and so should you* didn't sink into your head?" she inquired, with a frown.

He lifted her fingertips to his lips, wishing he could feel her skin beneath his mouth instead of the fabric of her glove. "Call me a hopeless romantic."

A half snort, half laugh left her lips. "Romantic? You? I believe any notion I had of you in such a manner has been tarnished by a year's absence."

"I hope to make my departure up to you with what I assume will be a fair amount of groveling at your feet, no doubt."

The briefest smile lifted the corner of her lip before she hid her amusement once more. It gave him a slim amount of hope.

"Dare I ask for a truce between us, Josie?"

She peered up at him from those hazel eyes he remembered getting lost in while he courted her. "We shall see. In the meantime, we shouldn't keep George and Julia waiting any longer than we have. Shall we go?"

"Of course, my lady," he replied, holding out his arm for her to take. She gently placed her fingertips in the crook of his arm, and inwardly he was pleased that she allowed him this small concession.

They went outside to the waiting carriage, As Josephine went inside, Milton stood at the door while she looked at George and her companion sitting together in the backward facing seat. George appeared as though he had already dozed off and Milton was thankful for the possible ruse.

Josephine scooted over on the seat. "Julia," she whispered softly, "change places with me."

Julia shook her head. "Get yourself settled, Josephine," she said with a small smile, while Milton finally came to sit next to his lady. "I know how the motion of sitting backwards doesn't agree with you. Enjoy the forward-facing scenery and trip."

Once Milton saw that everyone was indeed settled, he rapped on the roof to signal the driver to be off. The carriage wheels began to roll down the street, and while Josephine pretended to ignore him by looking out the window, he knew without any doubt that there was no way they wouldn't have any sort of conversation on the long road trip to Brighton.

CHAPTER 6

Josephine snuggled into the warmth next to her that felt like a comforting cocoon keeping her safe and content. A smile crept over her lips as she inhaled the familiar smell that reminded her of Milton. How many times in the past had she remembered the scent of his cologne? Too many to count, and with this gentle reminder from their past encounters her arm tightened around the figment of her imagination. This dream was more real than any other she had recently.

The pressure around her shoulder moved, and with the motion she felt a gentle squeeze. Josephine's eyes opened wide with the realization this was *no* dream! As she came fully awake, the constant rhythm of a heartbeat steadily thumped beneath her ear.

A gasp escaped her until the man above her gave a quiet *shhh,* so she didn't wake the other occupants of the carriage. "Good heavens," she murmured quietly, as she raised her head. She meant to right herself and sit up straight, but Milton held her in place.

Leaning his head forward, Milton stared back at her with mischievous blue eyes. "Hello, my love." His sultry tone was almost her undoing, sending shivers racing through her entire body.

"Milton... I-I'm so embarrassed." She hid her face in her hands before she finally disentangled herself from him. Josephine had to admit she immediately felt the loss of his warmth. She noticed George and Julia still fast asleep... or so she assumed, since they both could be faking their slumber.

"There's no need to feel embarrassed, dearest Josie," he purred in her ear as he relaxed in his seat while watching her intently. His smile told her much, and she knew it wouldn't take a great deal of effort on her part to give her heart away to him for a second time. "I am more than willing to be your pillow any time you need to nap."

She shook her head. The heat of her embarrassment flushed her cheeks. "I promise you this will never occur again. I am sorry I inconvenienced you."

A low chuckle left him. "Never is a long time. I am just as certain *that* vow is one you will soon break," he declared with another knowing grin.

"How can you be so sure?" she asked, annoyed that he was so full of himself. He then leaned forward as if he was going to kiss her. She quickly glanced at the other occupants of the carriage, but they continued to appear as though asleep.

"Because once you become my wife, there will be plenty of opportunities to use my shoulder as your place to rest, my dearest love."

Her breath hitched at the underlying intimacy of his words. Just the thought of being married to Milton made her traitorous heart soar. She choked back a sob, trying to remember her resolve to remain indifferent to this man. She thought of Philip and tried to bring his image to mind, but to no avail. And when Milton reached over to her and tipped her chin upward with his fingertips, she became lost in thought to everything but him.

"Tell me I haven't lost you completely," he urged, as his lips inched ever closer.

"I—"

The sudden lurching of the carriage caused Josephine to reach out to steady herself, even as George and Julia lunged forward in their seats at the unexpected movement. The driver shouted out at the horses, and they heard another man's voice demanding they stop.

Josephine shared a worried frown with Milton before he then cast a look at George. They both quickly reached for the weapons they had brought with them, but before they could reach them, the door to the carriage was jerked open. A masked man poked his head inside. He was holding a pistol.

"I'll be relieving you of your valuables," the highway man ordered in a steady tone. "Hand them over and be quick about it."

Josephine moved closer to Milton and took hold of his arm. His eyes were full of concern. "Milton?" She barely recognized her shaky voice while she trembled in terror as the bandit aimed his pistol at each of the occupants in turn.

Milton scowled before fixing his attention on the robber. "Don't do anything foolish by shooting anyone. We'll cooperate," he said, through clenched teeth.

"Hurry up, then," the masked man warned. "I can't stand here waiting all day."

Josephine watched as Milton handed over a small purse of coins while George did the same. The gunman pointed to the necklace around her neck, and she clasped the gems in her gloved hand.

She cast worried eyes at Milton. "They were a gift from Richard," she said quietly, hating to part with the memory of when her brother presented them to her on her last birthday.

Milton reached over to unfasten the clasp. "And they can be replaced. You, however, cannot," he said gently, handing over the expensive jewelry.

The highwayman then turned his gaze toward Julia, but she wasn't wearing anything costly. His eyes then turned to George.

"I'll take that ruby stickpin and your ring, my lord," he declared, pointing the gun at George.

George cursed in outrage but handed over the items. "I'll be getting these back soon," he warned in a low tone.

"You can try," the bandit said, laughing. "If it makes you feel any better parting with your treasures, you might wish to know your contributions today will go to a good cause. Enjoy the rest of your journey." He gave them a jaunty salute before slamming the door. Outside the carriage, he was heard ordering the driver to proceed.

Josephine turned toward the window to witness the bandit disappearing into the woods. "Whatever did he mean, our property is going to a good cause?" she asked when she finally found her voice.

Milton took her hand bringing it up to his lips. "It doesn't matter. I'm just happy nothing happened to you other than the loss of your necklace."

George cursed in outrage. "We didn't even have time to grab our pistols to protect ourselves."

Julia gave Josephine a worried look. "At least we are unharmed and only lost a few valuables. I have heard rumors that some traveling to Brighton have been killed while resisting their demands."

Josephine turned to Milton. "Promise me you won't do anything foolish if this happens to you again. I know you'll be traveling the roads to reach your country estate once you've seen us safely to Julia's," she said, nodding toward the weapon next to him.

"Worried for my welfare, my dear?" he asked with a roguish grin.

She gave a little huff. "Well, if I was, I'd never admit it."

He tipped her chin up again. "You more or less just did, sweet Josie," he murmured huskily.

Julia cleared her throat, breaking off the contact that made Josephine feel as though they were completely alone. Perhaps it was for the best, as she mulled over the fact that others had encountered the highwayman on the road to Brighton. For once, she kept silent, thankful that Milton had been escorting her on their journey.

CHAPTER 7

As their group came into The Devil's Dyke Inn north of Brighton, Milton arranged for a room for the ladies to freshen up before they continued on their travels. Once he had seen to their comfort and ordered tea to be brought up, he motioned for George to follow him into the tavern. Frustration that they had been robbed by a highwayman while Josephine was under his watch continued to gnaw at him. Richard would have his head once he learned the news, although how Milton and George could have prevented the robbery was beyond him.

The small purse Milton had lost was nothing compared to having to hand over Josephine's gems to the bandit. And poor George... he had been complaining about the loss of his stickpin and Onyx ring as if these were the last items of any value that he owned. Milton was perfectly aware that the jewelry items were two of many that George was fond of wearing.

"I need a drink," George said in a nasty tone. "I shouldn't have agreed to come with you to the country. Nothing good ever comes of my leaving the city."

Milton chuckled. "I'm sure there will be a house party or two to attend in or near Brighton," Milton informed his friend as he took a seat and waved a hand to a servant to bring them drinks. "Besides, I thought you'd enjoy the fun."

"A house party, yes. Getting my jewelry stolen by some no-account thief, absolutely not," he grumbled as he ordered an ale.

"You still look your resplendent self, Georgie," Milton declared with a smirk.

George dusted off an imaginary speck from his jacket. "Of course, I look resplendent. I would hardly go out looking like anything else but magnificent."

Milton's eyes traveled to the stairs, waiting for a glimpse of Josephine. He worried over her and how she handled being accosted and robbed of her jewelry. She had more or less managed everything well, considering the piece was sentimental to her. He wished there was a way he could find the necklace again and return it to her possession. The odds of that were slim.

George took a sip of his drink. "Will you propose to our girl soon?" he asked with a knowing grin.

Milton gave a heavy sigh. "She hasn't forgiven me as yet, but maybe soon."

"I was certain the way she automatically dozed off on you that you would persuade her at your first opportunity. Anyone with eyes in their head can see for themselves you are meant to be together."

Milton raised his glass to his lips and drank. "Tell that to Josie. She's still of a mind to marry the viscount, I believe."

"Bah!" George muttered. "He's a nice enough chap, but he'll never have a piece of her heart. You already claimed it long ago."

"A fact of which I plan to remind her as much as I humanly can," Milton declared, wondering how long such an admission might take.

"Stop being such a braying arse, then," George suggested. "You're being way too cocky, as if you've already won the girl. Josie isn't a fool and can certainly see right through your ruse."

Milton scowled. "You heard our conversation."

"You really didn't think I was dozing, did you?" George smirked.

"I had hoped," Milton muttered, listening as George chuckled in amusement.

The door of the inn opened, allowing entrance to those seeking the warmth of the room, and George muttered a curse. "This is bad luck," he grumbled.

Milton shook his head. "I doubt we need any more. What is happening that I can't see to make you say such a thing?"

"Look who just arrived," George replied, with a nod of his head toward the entrance to the inn.

Milton swiveled in his chair, and if he hadn't been seated, he might well have fallen over. "Well... this is bad luck, isn't it?" he finally answered when he found his voice, as he witnessed Viscount Upton entering the tavern as though they had conjured the man up from thin air.

The viscount gave a wave to George, who was far more familiar with the man than Milton. "Lord Chadwick... and Lord Langley," Philip said, performing a short bow. "I didn't expect to see you here."

George nodded. "An unexpected change of plans, Philip. Richard asked us to accompany his sister to Brighton. Unfortunately, we were accosted along the way," George explained, waving for a servant to bring another drink.

"*Bloody hell*, you too?" Philip cursed. "I was held up just north of here. Are Lady Josephine and Mrs. Elford well from the ordeal?" he asked with a frown of worry.

Milton nodded. "As well as can be expected. I had a room readied for them so they might freshen up before we continue our journey."

Philip's gaze turned toward the stairs much as Milton had done just moments ago. He began to realize this younger man cared for Josephine probably as much as he himself did. Milton didn't mind competition for Josephine's hand if it meant that he would have the lady at his side in the end. His thoughts of the lovely lady upstairs were interrupted by George's invitation to the viscount.

"You might as well join us, Philip. No sense in standing there waiting for the ladies' arrival," George said, sweeping his hand to one of the vacant chairs. "They'll be down once they're done, and that could still be a while."

Milton couldn't hide his disapproval at George's suggestion as he tossed his friend a meaningful glare that George shrugged off. Philip took a seat and the conversation turned to mundane things. Milton had no other option but to contribute, as their discussion circled around current affairs. But as much as he wanted to dislike the viscount, Milton was quickly learning that George was right in one assumption. Philip was a nice enough gentleman, and Milton could begin to understand why Josephine might wish to marry him. But Milton was just as determined that he could convince the lady otherwise.

And then... there she stood, and it was as though all the air rushed from his lungs, knowing she was near. Her blonde hair had been put back into place, and she looked refreshed, much like a newly budded spring rose. When their eyes locked from across the room, a becoming blush rushed to her cheeks. That was... until her hazel eyes widened upon noticing who else was seated at their table. Milton watched her features as she adjusted to this new development while she and Julia came to their table. The men stood and bowed until Philip held out a chair for Josephine.

She took a seat while Philip held her hand. She finally found her voice. "Lord Upton... I didn't expect to see you until tomorrow at Julia's house," she said in a low tone, her eyes on the viscount, much to Milton's annoyance.

"You are a vision of loveliness this afternoon, my lady," Philip answered, beaming as he bent forward to kiss the air between his mouth and her fingertips.

She gave a hint of a smile before pulling back her hand, causing a part of Milton to stir in jealousy because he wasn't the recipient of such a sweet look. He might have more competition for Josephine's hand than he originally thought, and he began to worry that he had perhaps actually lost her to another.

"You are too kind, my lord," she murmured softly, before her gaze went around to those seated. When her face turned to his, Milton swore the day was all the brighter just because Josephine smiled at him. "If you're done with your drinks, Julia and I are more than ready to proceed to her house. It will be a welcome relief to finally get off these roads."

Milton nodded and reached for her hand, taking advantage that he now had her undivided attention. He caressed its back while staring into her eyes. "We only waited for your return. We can begin the last part of our journey whenever you are ready, my dear," he said now, bringing her hand up to his lips. Protocol be damned as he heard her startled gasp of surprise leave her lips.

"Perhaps you and Mrs. Elford would like to ride in my carriage. It's not far to Brighton, and I can ensure you arrive there safely," Philip urged, with another look of longing at the lady. Not one to be ignored, Milton observed Philip as he, too, reached for Josephine, and if they weren't careful, they'd end up having a tug-of-war for her attention.

Josephine appeared torn between the two men, causing George to laugh. The look of reprimand she sharply tossed at him ended his merriment. She tugged both of her hands from the two men's grasp.

Milton stood, and the rest in their party did the same. "I gave my word to Richard that I would see these two ladies to their destination. I'm certain you can understand that I must keep my word," he proclaimed, ending any further suggestion that the viscount would steal the women away.

Philip nodded but he didn't look pleased. "Of course," he replied giving a short bow. "I will see you tomorrow, Lady Josephine, when you will have the pleasure of meeting my parents."

Josephine nodded. "I look forward to meeting them, Viscount Upton."

With that last exchange, Milton offered Josephine his arm, and he was pleased she readily accepted as he placed her hand in the crook of his elbow. The rest of the ride to Brighton remained uneventful, and Milton was relieved they didn't run into any more highwaymen after their valuables. Still... he just might need to stay in town longer than anticipated, if he wanted any chance of winning Josephine.

CHAPTER 8

Josephine studied the scenery outside the moving carriage but was lost in thought. That she had fallen asleep on Milton had been an embarrassment, but what was worse was how her heart had betrayed her. How was she to continue to move forward with Philip, if Milton was constantly in her thoughts, wreaking havoc with her heart? Philip deserved better than a woman who was torn between two men. She had been determined to give her full attention to Philip and his parents today in the hope she could move forward with her life and leave Milton in her past. If only the situation was that easy.

"It was a shame Philip was distracted with business and not able to come to your house to take us directly to meet his parents," Josephine mused as their carriage continued to roll down the street.

"Did you plan to accept the invitation to the Somerville affair? Sir Peter and his wife Penelope are a delight," Julia asked instead of commenting on Philip's absence.

"I saw the invitation this morning but haven't given it much thought, although I do appreciate that they invited us to stay at their country estate. I have heard that Normanton House and its grounds are magnificent," Josephine remarked, turning her attention to Julia.

"But there's a ball planned, and I certainly didn't bring a gown for such an event. I thought we'd stay only here for a short time to meet Philip's parents. I didn't plan on an extended visit."

Julia waved her hand in the air. "No need to fret about a gown or anything you may need. I know of a remarkable seamstress in town. Miss Aria Roccati will be able to run up anything we might need."

"In such a short time? The invitation said the ball was in only two weeks," Josephine said in surprise. "She'd have to sew far into the night to make such a short turnaround."

"Let's stop by her shop after our visit with Viscount Upton's parents. That way, we can see if she can accommodate our needs," Julia suggested as the carriage began to slow. Josephine gazed out the window and realized they had reached their destination. Julia took hold of her hand, and turned worried eyes in her direction. "Are you certain you wish to proceed with a possible union with Viscount Upton?"

"Philip is perfectly acceptable as a possible husband," Josephine sputtered.

"And he would be completely suitable for any lady he might offer for if said lady's heart wasn't already spoken for," Julia reminded her.

Josephine tore her hand away. "My heart isn't spoken for."

"You might want to keep reminding yourself of that, my dear, because what I see happening between you and Lord Langley says differently," Julia declared, with a knowing smile.

"Milton and George are childhood friends of my brother. It is only natural to feel a closeness to both of them since we all grew up together," she said, scoffing at the idea that she and Milton were anything more than just friends.

A snort left Julia's lips, causing Josephine to raise one brow. "George... yes... you are both certainly friends. But you and Lord Langley? You'd be a fool, dearest cousin, to easily dismiss your feelings for the gentleman."

"I closed off any feelings toward Lord Langley when he left a year ago and didn't propose. How long was I to wait for him to conclude his business?" she snapped sharply and then realized her mistake. "I'm sorry, Julia. I didn't mean to sound so... shrewish."

Julia patted her hand. "I rest my case, Josephine. You can keep telling yourself that you wish to move on, but the heart knows what the heart knows. You and Lord Langley belong together."

Josephine choked back a sob of denial. "I... I... just can't give my heart to Milton again to have it broken. My future lies with Philip."

Julia shook her head. "But you don't love him, my dear."

She saw Philip leaving the townhouse and begin walking toward their carriage. "I can learn to love him."

"If you say so, cousin," Julia replied softly.

There was no time for a reply, not when Philip came and opened the carriage door himself. He assisted Julia, who then began walking toward the house and leaving Josephine alone with Philip. He really was a handsome man with his blonde hair swept to one side while his brown eyes looked at her with a fair amount of affection, if she read the signs correctly. Well-dressed and attentive, he held out his hand, and she placed hers in his palm as he helped her from the carriage.

He turned toward her once she was on the ground, and as he stepped closer, she waited in breathless anticipation for him to take advantage of their situation. She wanted him to kiss her, if only to substantiate her claim that her words to Julia would prove true. She *could* learn to love him given enough time, and then she could let go of the memories of Milton that still tormented her every day and night.

Philip cupped her cheek before leaning forward. "I'm so glad you're finally here, dearest Josephine," he murmured, dropping all formality between them while inching even closer.

"We waited a long time for this moment... Philip," she declared, waiting for her heart to begin racing as he lowered his head.

"Yes... yes we have," he answered, running his thumb over her cheek.

She closed her eyes waiting in anticipation for his kiss, but the sound of two women giggling quickly broke Philip and Josephine apart. Josephine's eyes swept the sidewalk, only to see none other than the Danvers sisters. Prudence and Abigail always appeared at the right place at the wrong time, and Josephine began to dread when this latest bit of tittle-tattle showed up in the *Teatime Tattler*.

Rumors circulated in London that the two sisters were the source of most of the latest gossip supplied to the editor, Samuel Clemons.

Philip held out his elbow to Josephine, and she placed her hand in the crook of his arm. "Good afternoon, ladies," he said to the sisters, as he gave them a brief nod.

"Viscount Upton," Abigail answered with a quick bob before she turned curious eyes to her. "Good to see you again, Lady Josephine."

"Lady Abigail. Lady Prudence," Josephine murmured, not trusting herself to say anything more.

Instead, she forgot about the sisters and focused on being introduced to Philip's parents and getting to know the couple who could one day be her relations. They made her feel welcome in their home, and she was grateful they seemed to accept her as a possible bride for their son.

Now, if only she could convince herself that this was truly where she belonged. And when the memory of Milton unexpectedly popped into her head, it was his blue eyes that she couldn't escape. May God help her, but Milton was going to be harder to forget than she thought.

CHAPTER 9

Somerville Estate
October 1817

M ilton and George casually strolled the grounds near the lake at the Somerville estate on an unusually warm and sunny day. After receiving an invitation to stay at Normanton House, Milton had urged George to accompany him in order to have reinforcement to hopefully convince Josephine that they would suit. While George had muttered his displeasure, he finally gave in to Milton's demands. Not that George was of much use, nor had Milton made any headway even in spending any quality time with the fair lady.

Milton had spent some time with Robin Somerville this morning, telling him of the robbery north of Brighton and how he wanted to somehow find the necklace that Josephine lost. Robin had mentioned the trouble that had been happening on the road and how there were apparently two highwaymen. One was named Captain Moonlight, but Robin didn't think he went as far afield as the highway north. This left Milton feeling even more at a loss over how to possibly recover what Josephine had lost.

His thoughts turned back to the lady who was a constant in his mind. It was difficult to make any sort of an impression with Josephine, when the lady and her chaperone spent all of their time either with the other ladies who were present for the festivities or with Viscount Upton, as she was now. Jealousy reared its ugly head as he saw the lady who owned his heart laugh at something the viscount said from the other side of the lake. It was hard to dismiss that, over the past two weeks of being here, they had seemed to grow closer while Milton was forced to keep his distance.

"Perhaps we should return to the house," George suggested, as Milton continued onward. If they continued in this direction, they would eventually meet up with Josephine, unless the couple changed their current path.

Milton finally halted his steps. "And do what? I'm only here because I learned Josephine would be attending. There is nothing of interest inside the manor unless Josephine returns there as well."

A snort left George. "You're becoming a melancholy fool, chasing her around as you have for the past two weeks. Get out of your current mood and do something, old man, before you lose her completely."

"Unless I make a spectacle of myself, what more do you want me to do?" he complained bitterly.

"Maybe that's exactly what you need to do. You'll never win the lady watching her from across a lake or a dining table. I thought you were made of sterner stuff, my friend," George suggested with a smirk.

"I'm a guest here. Making a scene will hardly win the lady over."

"You'd better resort to better tactics, then, unless you'd rather be offering your congratulations to the happy couple," George taunted him. "There are rumors circulating among the women that they're expecting an engagement announcement during tonight's ball."

Milton cursed. "How the devil did you hear that horrible news?"

George shrugged. "I have ears. Besides, servants talk, and the women here are hardly keeping quiet over the matter. Seems as though love is in the air at Normanton Hall. Luckily, I've stayed far away from any temptation that the single ladies think might sway me to consider one of them for a wife."

"Josephine can't marry Upton. She doesn't love him," Milton groaned, as he once again swept his gaze toward the lady.

"Then you'd better make your case to her fast, otherwise you're going to lose her."

"Come along, then. Perhaps, besides berating me about what I should be doing, you can be of some help and keep Upton and Julia busy while I talk with Josephine," Milton declared, as he picked up his stride.

When they came up to the lady and gentleman, Josephine's hand appeared to tighten on Upton's arm, or so it seemed to Milton. After the formalities were offered, George persuaded Philip to walk with him to the edge of the water, and Julia automatically followed. Not that this left Milton completely alone with the lady, but it was as much privacy as he would be allowed... at least for now.

"Can we walk?" he finally asked after the awkward silence became too much.

She turned her hazel eyes up at him, and he could see the torment laying just beneath the surface of the calm façade she portrayed. "Why?" she finally asked.

"I'm only asking to have a few words with you, Josie," he began, holding out his arm.

"I don't see what purpose this will serve, my lord," she stated firmly. "We have already had this discussion, and anything further you wish to say will not persuade me from the course my life will now lead."

He looked around and saw a nearby tree well within the sight of her chaperone and the others. He nodded, and she finally took his arm as he led her a few feet away.

"Tell me you are not planning to marry a man you don't love?" he burst out, even though this was not how he thought he should begin this conversation.

A sharp laugh left her. "And what if I am? It's certainly none of your business. You are not my brother nor my parent who can tell me who I can or cannot wed."

"You shouldn't settle into a marriage with someone you don't love! That's no way to lead your life, Josie."

"It's *my* life to live, Milton! Besides, I love Philip," she said raising her chin in defiance.

Milton stepped closer. Her breathing became elevated. Her eyes dilated, and he watched in satisfaction as the pulse in her neck began to beat rapidly. "Then why is your body reacting to mine in such a fashion, sweet Josephine," he said in a husky whisper.

"I have no idea what you're talking about," she declared in a shaky voice. He could see that she was just as affected as he was that she was almost in his arms.

"Yes, you do. If you would only allow me the opportunity to spend some time with you, you would remember what we once had between us."

"Past tense, Milton. Apparently I must remind you yet again. You are my past. Philip is my future."

"You and I are meant to be together, Josephine. Let me prove to you how sorry I am for the mistake I made last year. I should have never left like I did, and I promise I will make the loss up to you," Milton urged. He reached out to caress her cheek, and for the briefest moment he thought she might give in to his suggestion. Instead, she stepped away from him.

"Please leave me alone, Milton. Falling into you... in love with you last year, was our one chance at happiness, and you failed me. I cannot take the heartbreak loving you will cause me again," she pleaded with tears threatening to race down her face.

"I love you, Josephine, and I'll prove myself to you before this house party is over," Milton vowed.

She shook her head. "You don't have enough time."

Milton watched her walk away and return to Philip who escorted her from the lake and back to the house. Josephine was right about one thing. With the ball this evening, he didn't have a lot of time left to convince her that she would make a mistake by marrying the wrong man. He might just need to do something extremely drastic to prove to her once and for all that they were meant to be together.

CHAPTER 10

Josephine stopped a servant for a glass of wine after Philip escorted her from the dance floor. She had already danced with him twice and regretted that she had to decline for him to place his signature in another place on her dance card. A third time would be pushing the boundaries of propriety, and she didn't wish to have any further gossip circulating around her that the Danvers sisters hadn't already started.

They were here again. In fact, Josephine couldn't seem to get rid of the pair. They turned up everywhere she went. It was like they were conspiring against her, waiting to pounce at the exact moment when even a momentary lapse in judgement might be a costly mistake she couldn't recover from. She thought of the incident with Philip in front of his parent's house and other stolen moments that never came to fruition while they had been at the Somervilles'. Anytime she thought Philip was going to kiss her was interrupted by some untimely person breaking them apart.

She took another drink of her wine, as her gaze landed on Milton watching her from across the room. Her heart leapt into her throat just knowing he was observing her. Why couldn't Philip make her feel this lightheaded? No matter how much she had tried in the past several weeks to have some deeper connection to the viscount, there just wasn't anything there that would give her a good enough reason they should marry. He might be a polite enough gentleman, but he didn't make her feel the way Milton did every time he was near.

She hated that he was right, and her stubborn pride would no doubt take a blow when she finally admitted it to the man. She couldn't marry Philip, no matter how much she thought she could learn to love him. Milton had already stolen her heart years ago. It had always belonged to him and always would. She would have to swallow her pride and let both men know her decision. She hated to disappoint Philip, but she had no choice. She was in love with Milton Sutton, and nothing could change that.

"Are you finally going to tell Milton you love him, putting the poor man out of his misery? Or will you make him grovel at your feet to make amends and prolong his agony?" George inquired, coming to stand next to her.

"Milton doesn't need to grovel or beg for my affection," she murmured softly.

"He'll be glad to hear it, but maybe he should, at least a little, or you'll have a devil of a time living with him, thinking he won you so easily," George said with a chuckle.

She barely glanced up at him. "You're very annoying sometimes. You know that, right?" she said with a raised brow.

"Yes, but you love me like another brother, so you forgive me for speaking my mind," he said. "Come... let's take a turn about the dance floor, and I can show you what an accomplished dancer I am."

"And conceited," she said, laughing, but taking his arm as the musicians began a lively tune.

"Just think how dazzling you'll look on my arm as I twirl you about the floor," he teased.

"Then lead on, my lord, so we might make the other guests jealous," she said with another laugh.

If there was anything to be said about George, it was that he was true to his word. He cut a nice figure in his well-fitted clothes, and his dancing was impeccable. He was a delight as long as you didn't take him too seriously, and was a good friend, not only to herself but to her brother. One day a woman would come along and steal this man's heart, and she looked forward to the day when George finally met his match.

The dance ended, and instead of taking her back to where she had been standing, she shouldn't have been surprised that George took her to Milton's side. He bowed, and she curtsied before George quickly disappeared into the crowded ballroom.

"You look beautiful this evening, my lady, but then you are always lovely, in my opinion," Milton said, while his blue eyes glanced over her.

"You are too kind, my lord. You look quite dashing as well."

One corner of his lip lifted up at her compliment. "Your gown complements the green color hidden in your hazel eyes. You should don the shade more often."

"I'll mention it to my seamstress that you approve of her choice in color," she said as she took his arm. His surprise flashed across his features, and she was happy for the first time in a long while that she was on his arm.

He began to walk her through the ballroom until they went out onto a balcony. "Josephine, I—"

She reached up and placed her gloved fingertips on his mouth before she remembered herself. "Wait... let me have my say first," she said softly.

"Normally, I would allow you such a concession but on this I must stand firm. I have already waited too long to confess my motives for leaving you behind," he said with a worried frown.

She considered his words for only a moment before she nodded for him to continue. "Then you have my undivided attention, Milton," she answered, as she waited patiently for him to have his say.

He gave a heavy sigh, as though the weight of the world rested on his broad shoulders. Taking her hands, he pulled her forward and then bent down to rest his forehead upon her own. "I should have confessed the real reason why I had to leave so suddenly, but I was embarrassed that my family's situation was so dire."

She squeezed his hands. "A lot of families find themselves in financial trouble from time to time, Milton. I would have stood by you no matter what."

"But mine was on the verge of complete bankruptcy. My pride wouldn't allow me to put you through the strain of a year living on the edge of uncertainty. I honestly didn't know if I could feed myself, let alone a wife."

"Oh, Milton," she whispered, caressing his cheek. His confession now made so much sense. He hadn't left her because he didn't love her and had a few investments fail. He left her because he loved her *that* much that he would let her go rather than have her suffer even one day if he couldn't make ends meet.

He lifted his head to stare into her eyes. His were brimming with tears, and she never thought she'd see the day when the man she adored was so consumed with grief from what he had put her through. He got down on one knee and looked up at her. "Please forgive me, my dearest Josephine. I always wanted you for my wife."

"Is that a proposal, my lord?" she asked, in an attempt to lighten the mood.

"Not until you say you forgive me," he murmured softly, before hanging his head as if in shame.

She leaned down and pulled on his arm until he once again stood before her. "I forgave you a long time ago, my love." As he smiled at her, he took her arm and gently pulled her away from the light coming from inside and into the shadows of the night. And then she could barely think when Milton took her into his arms.

"I've been a fool," she murmured, resting her hands upon his chest.

"As have I."

"Yes, but I'm sorry I didn't listen to you when you returned from abroad. I was just so angry that you had left me for over a year," she began, as another range of emotions rushed across his face.

"None of that matters now, my love, as long as you forgive my own foolishness. I should have never let my pride get in the way of being truthful with you. If I had only told you how bad the situation was, perhaps I could have then asked you to wait for me," he said with a worried frown.

"And perhaps I could have been more understanding on your return," she confessed honestly.

"The thought of losing you to another during my absence has tormented me for so long, and I have no idea how I can make it up to you other than to say how sorry I am."

He hung his head again, and Josephine reached out to cup his cheek. He raised his tormented eyes to hers, and a part of her heart cracked wide open with love for this man. "We're together now, Milton, and that's all that matters," she replied, giving him a smile.

"I never stopped loving you, Josie. I hope you realize that now," Milton murmured in a husky baritone that was again her undoing as her heart flipped end over end.

"I love you, too, Milton," she said in a breathy whisper.

"At last... you've given me hope."

He lowered his head, and his lips ran across the seam of her mouth. All further thoughts left her when Milton claimed her in a kiss. Gentle at first and then more persuasive, her arms went around his neck, and he pulled her completely into his body. Finally, she was where she always belonged, and she never wanted to leave his side again.

Unfortunately, giggling coming closer on the balcony gave them only the slightest warning that they were not alone. Of course, it would be the Danvers sisters politely muttering a muffled *excuse us* before disappearing into the house.

Josephine covered her face in her hands in embarrassment that they had been discovered. "We'll be the latest news now in the next edition of the *Teatime Tattler*," she said with worried eyes.

He kissed her cheek. "We'll be old news, especially when everyone is aware that we'll be married," he said, bringing her close again. "You will marry me, won't you, my dearest love?"

"I thought you would never ask," she whispered, rising on the tips of her toes to seal her answer with another kiss. She was lost again, until she realized that there was another waiting in the ballroom for her. "I'll need to break the news to Philip."

"Then let's be about it now, because I doubt I'll let you out of my sight," Milton confessed.

"I never want to be parted from you again," she said softly before he raised her hand to his lips.

Josephine was never happier than to have finally listened to what her heart had been telling her all along. Milton was the other half of herself that made her whole. Life without him would be unbearable, and she could now be happy that she had a lifetime with the man she truly loved at her side.

EPILOGUE

One Year Later
Autumn 1818

M ilton fondly watched his wife from across the crowded ballroom at his country estate near Brighton. That he had envisioned her gowned in her wedding finery holding court to their guests had run rampant through his mind for over a year. She had wanted him to call in favors so they could immediately wed, but in this instance he had to refuse her. He owed her after all the anguish he had put her through, and he had spent the last year courting her properly as any young lady of Society deserved. Besides, Josephine deserved all the details of a full wedding and everything that any future bride looked forward to leading up to the event. She had been worth the wait.

"I expect you to never let her forget how much you love her," a male voice calmly stated next to him.

Milton gazed over at the man who had made his best attempt to woo Josephine as his own bride. He had become friends with Philip, which might seem a bit odd, but Milton harbored no ill feelings toward the man.

"I'll be sure that I do," Milton said with a small smile of under-standing. He wasn't exactly sure that Philip was completely over Josephine but that would come with time.

"Daily," Philip added.

Milton chuckled. "Of course."

Philip went off to stand near George, who raised his flute of champagne in a silent toast to Milton. He gave a nod while Richard, Frederick, and Digby came to his side. The four friends stood silently for a few minutes, enjoying the view of their wives talking together.

Frederick finally spoke up. "Do you suppose Georgie will find his own lovely lady soon or remain a bachelor forever?" he asked, with an amused look upon his face.

Digby laughed. "He has no idea what he's missing out on. My Constance is the love of my life, and she was everything I could have ever asked for in a wife."

Richard nodded, agreeing. "I inherited a ready-made family when I married Patience, but I never regret the choice I made when I fell in love with her."

Milton raised his glass to his lips. "Clearly, there is much to be said for marital bliss. Just look at Frederick staring all moon-eyed at his lady."

Frederick smiled. "I'm as much in love with Margaret as I was the first time I met her in a London art gallery. She fits in perfectly with the ladies of Society, as though she has always belonged there."

Milton smiled. "I'm certain her father the vicar misses her great-ly." As he observed his own wife across the room, a part of him stirred, and he wondered if it was too early to make their excuses to their guests. But when her hazel eyes met his with a seductive gleam, he realized they could have left over an hour ago. "Gentleman... if you'll excuse me."

His friends began chuckling while their words of *about time* echoed in Milton's mind. He came up to his wife, kissed her cheek, and whispered in her ear before she also excused herself from the ladies.

Once upstairs, he locked their bedroom door and went to a table that had a small banquet for them to enjoy, along with a bottle of champagne. He popped the cork and poured two glasses, handing one of them to her.

"I have a surprise for you," he said with a mischievous wink.

She giggled as the bubbles from her drink tickled her nose. "I am certain you do," she said, apparently thinking of the night ahead of them, or so he supposed.

"Not that, my lady, but I like what you're thinking." He set his glass down and went over to the vanity for her use that he had brought into his bedroom. He picked up a box and handed it to her.

"Milton... you shouldn't have. You already gave me these pearl earrings and necklace as a wedding gift that I'm wearing." Her fingers caressed the lid of the box.

"Just open it, Josie," he urged, with a knowing grin.

A gasp escaped her when she finally saw what was inside. "Milton! How did you—" The rest of her words escaped her as she lifted the necklace that the highwayman had taken from her over a year ago.

He kissed her temple. "I knew you would be pleased," he said, taking the gems from her hands and putting them back down. "Apparently the highwayman had a conscience. They were found inside the local church along with several other valuables. It took a while to sort out who the owners were, but I'm glad I am finally able to return them to you."

"I can't believe you found them. I'm so thankful."

He pulled her into his arms and kissed her. "I've been waiting hours to do that," he murmured, nuzzling her rose-scented hair.

"I thought you'd never come and whisk me away, my darling husband," she said, winding her arms around his neck. "What took you so long?"

"I wanted you to enjoy every moment of our wedding celebration," he said huskily as she began untying his cravat.

"I would have enjoyed it more if you had just taken me upstairs hours ago," she said in a breathy whisper.

"I've waited a lifetime for you, Josephine. A few hours more wasn't a sacrifice, so long as you enjoyed the day to its fullest potential. But I'm glad I have you here now," he said turning her around as he began undoing the back of her gown and corset. "I hope you don't mind that I brought you here to my bedroom instead of the connecting one next door made for the lady of the house."

She looked over her shoulder with a mischievous gaze. "I'm never sleeping in that room, Milton. We can make it into a nursery once we're blessed with children."

"Thinking of our future already, my dear?" he teased.

"Always. As you just mentioned, I've been falling into you and the love I have always felt for you all my life, Milton. I couldn't be any happier than I am right now."

"Hold that thought, and tell me if I can change your mind once I make you mine completely," he murmured as he picked her up and carried her to their bed. The covers had already been pulled down, and he proceeded to place her on his bed before tearing off his own clothes to join her. As he pulled her again into his arms, a breathy sigh escaped her.

She pushed back a lock of his dark hair and cupped his cheek. "I love you so much, Milton, and I'm so happy I am finally your wife."

He leaned into her hand before taking it and kissing the inside of her wrist. "And I love you, my sweet Josie. Forever and always will I be falling into you."

And with those final words of devotion, Milton began to make Josephine his in every way, which took them far into the night. The vow he made this day to love and cherish her was always at the forefront of his mind, and he looked forward to a lifetime of never letting Josephine forget how much he loved and cherished her. They had somehow found a way back to each other, and forever and always would their two hearts beat as one.

THE END

Book reviews help readers to find books, and authors to find readers. Please consider writing a review for ***Falling Into You*** within the

Bluestocking Belles boxset *Love's Perilous Road*. Even a few sentences telling people what you liked about the story is helpful. Reviews can be posted on eRetailer sites including BookBub and Goodreads.

I hope you enjoyed this novella with Milton and Josephine and their journey to finding love. Hopefully you remember Milton from my other novellas with the Belles where he was the secondary character. Josephine made her recent appearance in her brother's story, *A Countess to Remember*. You can learn more about all my work that includes my medieval, time travel, and Regency era stories on my website at https://www.sherryewing.com/.

SOCIAL MEDIA FOR SHERRY EWING

You can learn more about Sherry Ewing at these social media links:

Bluesky: https://bsky.app/profile/sherryewing.bsky.social
Bookbub: www.bookbub.com/authors/sherry-ewing
Dragonblade Publishing: https://www.dragonbladepublishing.com/team/sherry-ewing/
Facebook: www.Facebook.com/SherryEwingAuthor
Goodreads: www.Goodreads.com/author/show/8382315.Sherry_Ewing
Instagram: https://instagram.com/sherry.ewing
Pinterest: www.Pinterest.com/SherryLEwing
Threads: https://www.threads.com/@sherry.ewing
TikTok: https://www.tiktok.com/@sherryewingauthor
Tumblr: https://sherryewing.tumblr.com/
X: www.X.com/Sherry_Ewing
YouTube: http://www.youtube.com/SherryEwingauthor

Newsletter Sign Up: http://bit.ly/2vGrqQM
Facebook Street Team:
www.facebook.com/groups/799623313455472/
Facebook Official Fan page: https://www.facebook.com/groups/356905935241836/

ABOUT SHERRY EWING

Sherry Ewing picked up her first historical romance when she was a teenager and has been hooked ever since. An award-winning and bestselling author, she writes historical and time travel romances to awaken the soul one heart at a time. When not writing, she can be found in the San Francisco Bay Area at her day job as an Information Technology Specialist. You can learn more about Sherry and her books on her website where a new adventure awaits you on every page

Learn more about Sherry at:
Website: www.SherryEwing.com
Email: Sherry@SherryEwing.com

THE CASEBOOK OF
PRINCIPAL OFFICER ROBERT
PIERCE

Brighton and surrounding districts

The clue of the trousers on the church steeple led nowhere. No one knows who put the trousers up there, and the curate swears he was the only man with a key. The locals are protective of "their" Captain Moonlight, but there will be a break soon. I am certain of it. Everyone makes a mistake sometime.

The second highwayman robbed another coach. Had ladies not been present, I am certain the man would have been shot, for the ladies were accompanied by some very competent gentlemen. It is a risky business, being a highwayman without a gang.

I am getting closer to Larcenous Lucy! Word has it she has been active in Brighton itself, so I am heading there in the morning.

SIR WESTCOTT STEALS
A HEART

ALINA K. FIELD

Sir Westcott Steals a Heart
By Alina K. Field

Sir Westcott Twisden didn't know he wanted to marry until the tallest lady he'd ever met crossed his path. Curious when a local smuggler shows up to visit her,

Wes follows her into trouble.
Sybil Dunsford lives to protect her brothers and their home. And so, one night she disguises herself as a boy to help shift contraband. But when the night goes awry, Sir Westcott appears, and they're locked in together. Will romance follow?

CHAPTER 1

Late September 1817

The drizzle started up again just as Sir Westcott Twisden stepped out of the farrier's barn.

Pulling the curled brim of his hat lower, he looked around. The high street was bustling just as if Normanton had been a market town. It was a homely and pleasant place, much like Stakeley, the town near Twisden Manor, his estate in the far northern county of Westmoreland.

The locals here exchanged pleasant greetings and sent him nods and inquisitive smiles even though he was, in the jargon of Sussex, a *foreigner*, one who'd strayed beyond the usual bounds of nearby Brighton. He nodded back and continued on to the local inn, the Duck and Spoon, where his friend and host, Captain Reginald Dalrymple, a bandy-legged, brown-haired captain on half-pay, awaited him.

"Oof." Almost six feet of giggling youth slammed into him, knocking his hat into a muddy rut.

As he grabbed the fellow's collar, another fellow slammed into the first one, and Wes grabbed that one as well.

He yanked them around, and their mouths dropped open. His own too, probably.

They were twins, dark haired, hazel-eyed, and identical... or not quite. One was broader, his face fuller, with a scar on his chin that the slighter, more freckled one was lacking.

"I say." Wes gave them a little shake and watched both sets of eyes start to twinkle. "What horseplay is this? That beaver came from Lock's of St. James's Street. Bought it last month. Didn't at all plan on christening it in a mud puddle."

They exchanged a glance and both squashed smiles.

"Sorry, sir," the bigger lad said in the scratchy voice of burgeoning youth.

"Deepest apologies," said the other one. "I'll fetch your hat, shall I?"

Wes released him, and he limped over, retrieving the hat and handing it to the other rapscallion, who used the tails of his neck-cloth to wipe off the worst of the mud.

A wagon stopped directly in front of them, and the woman holding the reins looked over. "Cass, Paul, what are you doing with your neckcloth?"

Her gaze met his, and his pulse quickened. Curly dark hair peeked out the sides of her chip bonnet, but her eyes were as blue as bluebells.

Was she their mother? If so, she'd been a child bride.

Her redingote was a worn lavender worsted, but from what he could discern, it was quality. She might not be a lady of the ton, such as he'd met in London over the summer, but she was at least gentry. A gentleman's widow down on her luck?

And she was very pretty.

Conscious that he'd been staring too long, he took the hat from the boy. It wasn't entirely ruined.

"A minor mishap," he said. "Sir Westcott Twisden at your service, madam. I'd tip my hat to you if it wasn't, er, damp."

She shot the boys a frown before returning a dignified gaze back to Wes.

"I do beg your pardon, Sir... Sir Westcott. The boys did this? I'm so very sorry. If there is a... a cost... for the cleaning, I—"

"No, no, madam. If there's to be a reckoning it will be with... Cass was it? And Paul? May I know your last name, gentlemen?"

"It's Picard," the slighter boy said.

"Picard." He nudged them to the plain, serviceable wagon and its cargo of crates and sacks.

The boys clambered into the back with all the gawky lankiness of boys much younger than they appeared. Which they probably were, though they had more height than most grown men he knew. "The Picards of Normanton?" he asked.

"The Picards of Devil's Dyke Grange," the one called Paul said.

Ah. They were farmers. "Good day to you, Masters Picard, Mrs. Picard."

She murmured a farewell, color rising to paint her cheeks a rosy pink, while the two in the back broke into broad grins, and, as they drove away, laughter.

The back of the lady holding the reins seemed to grow impossibly straighter.

The joke was apparently on him, and he hoped it wouldn't hamper his chances, if she was in fact unmarried. His host, Reggie, was the son and brother of a local squire. He'd grown up in these parts and would know the answer to that question.

"How could you?"

Miss Sybil Dunsford glanced back at her stepbrothers. Their mother had christened them Castor and Pollux, out of some notion that classical names would give them a leg up at Eton and Oxford.

Unfortunately, soon after their birth, the boys' father had gone down with the ship and the cargo that would have given them, and their older brother Langston, the means for a first-class education. Left with a boy of nine and infant twins, the late Mrs. Picard married her husband's widowed distant cousin, Sybil's father.

Richard Dunsford had once been a Picard, but he adopted Sybil's mother's surname as the price for his first bride's sizeable inheritance —the farm and the capital to maintain it. Under his stewardship, both had dwindled.

A short year after that second marriage, the twins' mother died. Langston was sent off to school, and the twins were put in the care of twelve-year old Sybil until they were old enough to go away also.

Then just as the disastrous year without summer got underway, Sybil's father died, leaving the struggling Devil's Dyke Grange to her.

After a close look at the accounts, she'd brought the twins home for good.

Lang had left school a couple of years earlier. He helped with the farm and ran with the local smugglers on the nights with no moon. That had lasted until a few months ago, when the new riding officer hired him. She'd been holding her breath, praying he wouldn't be found working both sides of the law.

"*Fegs*, Sybie," Cass said. "'Twere accidental. That foreigner weren't mad at us."

Paul giggled. "Seems like he got a look at you, Sybs, and didn't mind at all."

A shiver went through her. She was used to the ogling; her great height drew men's attention, but so did her ownership of the farm which, as long as she could manage the mortgage, was wholly hers now.

None of the usual oglers were as tall or as handsome or as gentlemanly as Sir Westcott Twisden.

Was he taller than her? Would he be attending the local assembly in a few days?

She shook off the thought.

"Speak proper English, Cass," she said. "You know how. Say, 'Heavens! The gentleman wasn't angry.' And neither of you are yokels. You know he's no foreigner, but a proper Englishman."

"Sir Westcott Twisden," Cass pronounced in a sonorous voice, and snickered.

She sighed. "How fared your lesson at the vicarage today?"

For a small fee, the curate was tutoring the twins in Latin and Greek. Cass was indifferent, but Paul had dreams of studying law.

"We're reading Plato," Paul said.

"Boring stuff." Cass clambered over the seat back to join her. "Paul's the scholarly one. Me, I *will* go off to sea. I'll find a way."

She would happily send him off to sea, if she could find a suitable place for him. With the war ending, there were few openings for midshipmen. Robin Somerville was home from the navy and might be able to help. She'd been searching out relatives of the boys' merchant father, so far to no avail.

As for the bookish Paul, who limped from a leg break at school years earlier, her fervent hope was to apprentice him to a solicitor or some other man of business who could appreciate his intellect.

"Best you behave, Cass," she said, "or you'll be having a sea voyage to Botany Bay."

⚜

A few days later

"Stacking up to be a bore, Reggie." Wes braced one hand on the terrace balustrade and surveyed the partygoers inside through the open French doors.

He might as well be attending one of the local assemblies at home. "Not a single interesting lady."

"Hah. *Interesting* and *lady* don't fit together. That sort don't get invited by this sort."

Reggie wasn't long out of the army where ladies of any sort had, apparently, been scarce on the ground.

They'd met in the summer, when Wes had accompanied his grandmother, the dowager Lady Twisden, a bosom friend of Reggie's mother, to London.

"You promised me a highwayman and a ghost on this seaside sojourn," Wes said, "and all I've seen are dark lanes where folks have been robbed by Captain Moonlight and the ghost has been spotted. What's that ghostie's name? Eddie Rose?"

Reggie favored Wes with a smirk.

In fact, Reggie had been a fine host, opening his home—actually his brother's home near Normanton, a few miles from Brighton, for an open-ended invitation that extended to Wes's stepmother and stepfather when they arrived home from their travels on the Continent.

"Serve you right if Captain Moonlight slips your purse one night when out and about." Reggie chuckled. "That's what the Major would say."

The Major was Major Augustus Kellborn, Reggie's former commanding officer and Wes's... well, Gus was more than Wes's distant cousin now. He'd married Honoria Twisden, Wes's stepmother, in the spring. In his letter, Gus said they were offered passage on a friend's yacht and would arrive at Shoreham in the autumn.

They might decide to stay near Brighton for a few months. Gus's letter had included shocking news about the dear, diminutive lady who'd raised Wes since the age of seven, news that set Wes's perception of her on its head. Or, given the shock he'd had when she and Gus announced their betrothal, on its head *again*.

Stepmama was with child.

Wes chuckled at his own... naivety. He would miss her presence at Twisden Manor, but was glad for Gus, who'd taken Wes under his wing, at times none too gently, in ways Wes's father never had.

From his father, his father's hunting friends, and the fellows at school, he'd heard the more salacious lessons of manhood. Gus's lessons had been more about the practicalities of navigating the temptations open to a young man of good fortune. The sort of lessons Gus had knocked into the men serving under him, like Reggie.

"There's Somerville and his wife," Reggie said. "Capital fellow. He's planning a grand house party."

Sir Peter Somerville was Reggie's neighbor and one of the higher-ranking men in the area.

"Oh, ho. And Robin." Reggie waved, but the darkly tanned gentleman didn't seem to notice. "Somerville's brother. Navy man. Put out of work by the peace, just like me."

While Reggie waxed ineloquently about the hijinks he and Robin had got up to as children, movement near the door caught Wes's eyes.

A young man and woman had entered, both dark haired, both taller than almost everyone here tonight except Wes himself.

As the woman's gaze traveled the room, he let out a breath. Eyes the color of bluebells sent him a defiant look to match the pouty turned-down lips.

It was her, and gad, she was beautiful. Even more beautiful than when she'd stopped her wagon in front of him in Normanton a few days earlier. By the time he'd reached the Duck and Spoon that afternoon, Reggie had been too jug-bitten to answer questions. But now...

"Who is that?" Wes asked.

"Eh?" Interrupted in his reverie, Reggie glanced up at him.

"The party that just entered. No, don't point."

"The matron in the dun-colored gown?"

"No, no. The woman just ahead of her. Tall."

"Oh. Hah. Why, I believe that's Sybil Dunsford, all grown up, and with that wild brother of hers, Lang. Lang Picard. Stepbrother. One of 'em. He's with the revenuers now, I hear. Lucrative trade I'll wager... for *him*, if he don't get caught with his hand out."

"She has other brothers?"

"Two. A set of twins. Just babies when I left. Surprised they're not here."

That would be Cass and Paul.

"Single, or married?"

"Her? Single, I think." Reggie waggled his eyebrows. "Don't tell me you're smitten by that Long Meg."

Wes smiled. "Smitten?" He laughed and clapped his friend on the back. "Introduce me."

❦

Sybil Dunsford handed over her cloak and tucked a loose curl behind her ear.

She wished she had another ballgown to wear, something better than the lavender she'd made when she came out of full mourning for her father. Now, she didn't have the coin for a length of new fabric, nor, in truth, the skills to make something more elegant.

The assembly room was filled with people she'd known all her life. Cass and Paul would have loved it. But Paul was abed with a bout of the ague that sometimes afflicted him, and Cass had, on a silly dare from their young groom, tumbled out of the barn loft, landing awkwardly and spraining his ankle so badly, she and Lang had to support him hopping one-legged all the way into the house.

"Quite a turnout tonight," Langston said.

Langston had only just reached his majority and gained control of the small inheritance left to him by a relative of his mother. It wasn't a great deal of money, and, unlike Sybil's inheritance, there'd been no land attached to it. Which was just as well; the Picard boys had dreams well beyond what Sussex could offer, and she would ensure they had a place to call home between adventures.

Her brother's gaze traveled the room and came to a stop on a man of middling years, a miller who'd acquired the Lewis farm next to Devil's Dyke Grange.

Her heart sank, followed by rising anxiety. "Stay away from Crofton, Lang."

Crofton might pose as a legitimate businessman, but his barns, storerooms, and millhouses were often filled with contraband goods.

"You have an honest position now. A chance to impress Sir Peter Somerville." Sir Peter was the principal landholder on this edge of the downs and an honorable man with connections that might help all three of her brothers.

"Don't worry, Syb. I was never all that involved before."

Of course, she worried. If he was compromised, he could hang. Or if he gave evidence, Crofton might have him killed.

His attention focused on something past her shoulder. "Look there. Isn't that Reggie Dalrymple approaching? Who's the fellow with him?"

Reggie Dalrymple was a close neighbor she'd known since childhood. Though she'd been one of the younger children, she'd also been one of the tallest, and thus welcomed onto the cricket and pall mall fields with the boys.

At the sight of his companion, a ripple of awareness went through her. Sir Westcott Twisden loomed above everyone. Besides height, he had shaggy, too-long hair the color of ripened grain, eyes that were more gray than blue, and wide shoulders that hinted at a rangy strength. He wasn't *prettily* handsome like her stepbrothers, but the firm jaw and aquiline nose gave him a look of masculine strength, and the twinkle in his eyes signaled good humor.

And he was taller than her.

Lines were forming in the ballroom for the Roger de Coverley. Would he ask her to dance? Her heart stuttered, wondering what it would be like to not gaze down at a dance partner's pomaded head.

"Sybie," Reggie called, jostling a couple out of their way without begging their pardon.

Dear Reggie—he was still a lummox.

She acknowledged his greeting with a dip of her head and found both men standing near. Nor had Lang deserted her, too curious by half about Reggie's companion.

"And which scapegrace is this, eh?" Reggie teased. "Is this Lang, all grown up?"

"Good evening, Mr. Dalrymple," Sybil said, teasing him back. "This gentleman is my stepbrother, Mr. Langston Picard."

Reggie's smile broadened, and he puffed out his chest. "And I'm *Captain* Dalrymple, Sybie. Well-met, Mr. Langston Picard. Miss Sybil Dunsford, this here is my good, upstanding friend, Sir Westcott Twisden." He winked. "Anxious to meet you, Syb. Might be he'll want you on his cricket team."

Sir Westcott clapped his friend on the back. "Don't mind Reggie, Miss Dunsford," he said. "I wouldn't trouble you with cricket tonight, but I'd dearly like to lead you out in a dance."

Before she could answer, he reached for her. Without thinking, she set her hand in his, and the smug smile he sent her had her questioning her good sense. His blustery confidence reminded her too much of her brothers.

"Do not worry," he said. "I've been practicing my steps for years. Enough to not step on your toes. Though I certainly flattened my stepmama's a few times when the dancing master brought her in to partner me. She always complained my feet were far too big for her tiny ones to dodge them."

"Did you consider the size of my feet before deciding to ask me to dance?"

A shocked look flashed on his face and then he laughed. "Beg pardon. That's another thing Stepmama used to drill me on—how to avoid sticking my large foot in my equally large mouth."

While he seemed to be taking a deep breath, she wondered if this proper and diminutive stepmama was also attending this party.

"No, Miss Dunsford," Sir Westcott said solemnly, "when I saw you, I said to myself, *that is the most beautiful girl in the room, and I must have a dance with her.*"

She stumbled and his hand came to her elbow, supporting her.

"Most beautiful?" she asked. "Do you not mean the tallest?"

His eyes twinkled. "Both."

While she felt her cheeks warming, mercifully the music started, and she tamed her unexpected emotions. Which were... What? Embarrassment? She was used to being the Long Meg on every occasion. But this sudden rush of warmth, of awareness... Was she *attracted* to Sir Westcott Twisden?

CHAPTER 2

Sir Westcott Twisden was taller than any man here, true, and he wasn't exactly a lumbering ox. He managed the steps of the dance quite adroitly. He managed polite conversation as well.

In the moments they came together, he told her he owned an estate in the far north and had escorted his grandmother to London where he attended to business and met up with Reggie. Upon Reggie's invitation, Sir Westcott had come further south to Brighton to await the return of his stepmother and her new husband from their honeymoon on the Continent. His new stepfather was a prince of a fellow, a retired army man who'd been Reggie's commanding officer. He'd wanted to await them because his stepmama was expecting a happy event.

That had been said with a puzzled grin that had her wondering if Sir Westcott was simple. Or if he didn't understand how happy events came about.

"Has me thinking about setting up my own nursery."

In the midst of performing a Hole in the Wall cross, his gaze held hers, the look in his darkening eyes so earnest, so intense, her face heated again.

They came together, and she stomped on his toe.

His eyes sparkled, his grin held steady, and he was blissfully silent for the rest of the dance while inside, her nerves were skipping and leaping.

When the dance ended, he tucked her hand over his arm. "Where shall we walk while we wait for the next dance?"

"Perhaps we can find you another partner."

"Who won't step on my toes? Surely, that was a reprimand. Perhaps you thought I was being too forward? I've always been told not to rush my fences."

"More advice from your stepmama?"

"She's a gem. You'll like her. Loves to paint buildings. Pictures of them, that is, not the walls. Miss Dunsford, I would like to court you. Is there anyone whose permission I should ask?"

Lang was coming their way. Sir Westcott opened his mouth.

"Don't you dare raise the subject with him," she said.

He turned his gaze down on her.

Down on her. A tingle ran through her. Next to him, she felt *small*, in the best possible way.

His eyes glinted again. "I know that Reggie will want to call on you and pay his respects. I'll tag along when he does."

She dragged Sir Westcott away and introduced him to the first group of young ladies they encountered.

"Save a waltz for me," he said, and stepped out with a new partner.

She didn't speak with him again until the waltz. That glorious waltz had her wondering if perhaps she would *like* him to court her.

But it didn't keep her from noticing Lang's long conversation with Crofton.

⚜

Breakfast at Highcross Keep, the Dalrymple family estate, was a singularly masculine meal, preceded every morning by an invigorating ride with Reggie and his great uncle Quinton Dalrymple. Reggie's older brother was away in London with the only lady of the house, their mother, who preferred the shopping in London to what she could find in Brighton.

Wes had met the fashionable widow, Mrs. Dalrymple, in London. He'd been happy at first about her matchmaking endeavors. But though he'd met a few pretty girls, and a few jolly ones, no one had caught his fancy for more than a quarter hour. There were no country girls among the misses he'd met in London through the summer, leastwise none who wanted to go as far afield as West-moreland.

Miss Sybil Dunsford might not wish to go that far afield either, but she was definitely a country girl. He'd learned last night that Sybil was actively involved in the work of the farm left her by her father.

Sybil. Did anyone besides Reggie call her Sybie?

Wes filled his plate from the sideboard—eggs, rashers, kidneys, beans, and toast with marmalade. Reggie's family kept a good table.

Grellin, the Dalrymple butler, hurried in and whispered something to Reggie, who laughed out loud.

"No need to whisper, Grelly. Tell everyone."

The butler cleared his throat. "Cook has heard from the apothecary's boy who was delivering Mr. Quinton's, er—"

"Yes, yes," Reggie said. "Uncle Quinton's purge medicine. We all know about his ailment." He beamed a smile at Wes. "Captain Moonlight has finally struck again."

Wes set his plate down awkwardly, sending a piece of bacon flying. "About demmed time."

"Promised you a highwayman," Reggie crowed.

"You also promised me a ghost."

Reggie waved Wes's comment away. "Who was the mark, Grelly?"

"The miller, Mr. Crofton."

Crofton. Wes's brainbox had been so full of Sybil Dunsford, other introductions had washed over him. "Was he there last night?"

"Big fellow," Reggie said. "Built like a side of beef. Hair—what he has of it—pulled back in a queue."

"Yes. I remember. He left before you could introduce me." Wes picked up his fork and attacked the plate. After their waltz, Sybil had hurried over to this Crofton, who at the time happened to be bending her brother's ear.

The conversation had seemed intense, and Crofton called for his carriage soon after.

On his way to see what was being discussed, Wes had been pulled aside by Reggie to meet other attendees. By the time he'd freed himself, Sybil had left also.

"Anyone hurt?" Reggie asked.

"Not as was reported." Grellin picked up the coffee urn and sent the footman off to refill it.

"The apothecary's boy heard that from one of the Somerville servants, who received a report of the robbery from the farrier," Grellin said. "Sir Peter was planning to pay a call on Crofton. The guests for his house party will be arriving soon. That is all I know. If you'll excuse me, I'll just have this platter refilled."

Reggie, his mouth filled with sausage, waved the butler away.

"Demmed dutiful magistrate you have here," Wes said. "I suppose he's either really concerned about the safety of his lady and the guests coming for his house party, or he's bored."

Reggie swallowed and took a sip of his ale. "Dutiful. Been more than one highway robbery lately."

The thought crossed Wes's mind that Sybil had left around the same time as the victim. She might have been in danger.

"Curious, though," Reggie said. "Seems like t'only ones robbed are ones you might say deserved it."

"What do you mean?"

Reggie shrugged. "Crofton's been picking up land here and there, besides the barns and storehouses he owns hereabouts. Known to fill them sometimes when the moon is dark."

"He's a smuggler?" Wes asked.

Reggie nodded his answer, having just forked in some beans.

"Of course, he's a smuggler." The gravelly pronouncement came from Reggie's uncle, who entered and strode to the sideboard. "A swindler as well. He just cheated Lewis out of an old manor house near Devil's Dyke Grange. Crofton bought out loans from a thieving banker friend in Brighton before the fellow cleaned out the deposits and scarpered. Crofton's capital isn't coming from his mills. It's from good French brandy. Gin from the low countries, and..." He waggled his eyebrows. "Silk so fine it would make a lady agree to anything."

Reggie sputtered and sent Wes a wink.

"Yes, Reginald. You may laugh in your inelegance, but the ladies appreciate fine gifts. In my day..." He shook his head. "Ah well, mark my word. On any given night, you'll find a line of pack animals crossing the weald, both two and four-legged ones, carrying merchandise right along the Devil's Dyke."

Devil's Dyke was a nearby land feature, a great, long valley. Reggie, with his usual nonsense, said it had been dug by the devil himself. Wes had seen it, but only from a distance.

"I'd like to see this Devil's Dyke up close."

Reggie's eyes gleamed. "Said you wanted to call on Sybie."

"Sybil Dunsford?" Uncle Quinton's eyes gleamed. "I once spent an intoxicating interlude with a girl as tall as her. Perhaps I should ride along with you."

"Not after taking that physic the apothecary sent," Reggie said. "Sybie's place is right there, Wes. Devil's Dyke Grange."

"Crofton's her neighbor?" Wes tossed down his napkin. "I'll get my hat."

Reggie laughed. "It's a hop, skip, and a jump. No hurry. Eat up. Might not get tea and biscuits there."

৩২৩

"I told you not to come, Uncle Quinton." Reggie reined up near the older man who was doubled over his saddle and groaning.

Devil's Dyke Grange lay within sight of the three riders, in a curve of the valley sheltered by trees. Reggie had pointed out the flintstone house and the outbuildings, structures so weathered they almost blended in with the browning slopes and dark shadows.

"They'll have a privy there," Wes said. Now that he was so close, he was anxious to see Sybil Dunsford again in the flesh.

That conversation she'd had with Crofton, now that he'd had

time to recall more, had looked serious. Was she involved with the fellow's schemes?

And if she was, what did that mean for a possible courtship?

Quinton steered his horse to a chest-high clump of thick bushes. "Can't wait," he called over his shoulder. "Come and hold my mount, Reginald."

Reggie shrugged. "Go on, Wes. We'll catch you up."

While his horse picked its way down the grassy slope, Wes contemplated his meeting with Miss Sybil Dunsford and how to approach the topic of smuggling.

If she was, in fact, in league with the smugglers, it couldn't be that dangerous. Would she let him come along? He'd like to see for himself what all the excitement was about.

The muddy, rutted lane leading up to the manor house bore the imprints of hoofs and wheels. The path skirted a small brook that passed close to the farm buildings and splashed off at an angle toward Brighton and the sea. As Wes drew nearer, he heard shouts and loud voices, and he quickened his pace.

"Are you just going to stand there, Lang?" Sybil brandished a basket and broom while Emmet Hayward, their elderly all-around stockman, hobbled in a circuit around the pen. Mud covered his boots and trousers and splashed up onto the front of his smock, soiling it more than normal. His wife, Ruth, Devil's Dyke Grange's housekeeper and cook, would ring him a peal.

Their prey, a black and white pig, zig-zagged away from them both.

"New boots, Syb," Lang said.

"Go change into the old ones."

"No time," he said. "I'm off in a moment to meet Lieutenant Miles in town."

She stalked closer and crooned. "Come along now, little maiden."

"A shilling on Emmet," Cass said, gripping the stick he'd hobbled out with.

"And I'm to bet on Syb?" Lang laughed. "You're on."

"If you had a shilling, Cass," she teased, "I'd like to know where you got it."

"Why d'ye want this pig anyway?" Cass asked. "Shoo him back into his shed and leave him be."

"This is a *she*, and this little maiden gilt is going along to a new home. Cass, go and bring the cart around. You can drive her over to the Simpsons'."

The pig raced by, and Emmet slipped, falling face down into the mud and slurry, sending the boys into howls of laughter.

"You big boobies." Stifling her own laugh, she hurried over to haul the old man up. "Are you hurt, Emmet?"

He grunted and groaned his way up, smearing her skirts with mud as he staggered to standing.

"Ought to be helping your sister instead of standing around like a couple of clods," Emmet said.

"And that's a fact," said a man.

Sybil spun around. Shocked recognition was followed swiftly by her awareness of her appearance, attired in an old gown, mud spattered, and with her hair falling about her face.

And chasing a pig.

But that was nothing compared to the shock she experienced when Sir Westcott Twisden vaulted the side of the pen, flashing shiny boots only slightly speckled with dust.

He snatched up the basket Emmet had dropped and made a direct assault on their quarry.

❧

"I hope those were not your only pair of boots," Sybil said. "No, no, don't get up."

Sybil settled the tea tray on the table near the hearth and caught sight of the long stockinged feet propped on the fender. "Take care not to burn your toes."

Sir Westcott flashed her a grin. He'd settled in as comfortably as one of her brothers, lounging his long body in the chair he'd moved close to the fireplace.

"My boots are no worse off than that gown of yours. Apologies for—"

"Knocking me into the mud?"

He laughed. "Spritely little pig you have there. Expect she'll be one of those sows eating her piglets if they misbehave."

His charm was disquieting—and probably too good to be true. Better he should be one of those gentlemen looking down his nose, so she could dismiss him like those haughty local gentlemen her brothers encouraged her to consider.

"What do you know about pigs, Sir Westcott?"

"About your little black and white ones?" He shrugged. "Ours in the north, the Cumberlands, are white and hardy enough for colder weather." His brows furrowed, and then he grinned. "It's only a bit colder there than here. We keep a good fire in all the rooms. You'll never have cause to be chilled."

Given the heat pulsing in her cheeks, she didn't have cause to be chilled now, only mortally embarrassed.

And unchaperoned.

"I'll just go and see where my brother is." Cass ought to have returned.

The big feet hit the floor, and Sir Westcott stood. "The parlor door is open, and I promise to behave. Do sit down, Miss Dunsford. This is a pretty lay of land, is Devil's Dyke. While I have some fertile dales at home, I also have some rocky fells. How is the land in these parts?"

"Are you looking to buy? Devil's Dyke Grange is not for sale."

Sir Westcott's face froze for a few beats of her heart, and then a wide smile broke.

"Always hold onto land, my grandmama says. A man with land is a man with prospects." The smile deepened to reveal a dimple. "A woman, too, I suppose."

The tone wasn't flirtatious, and some of her unease fizzled. Not all, because he was a handsome young man, and he was stirring feelings in her that she hadn't truly felt from any of her other suitors.

There had been more than a few, given her farm and her brothers' attempts at matchmaking. They hoped to marry her off and then take their inheritances and go off adventuring. She didn't expect them to stay—she would hire the help she needed—but each in his own way had displayed an endearing loyalty. Not a loyalty that brought coin with it, but still...

She shook off her woolgathering and asked him about his land in the north. The topic was obviously dear to his heart, but not so dear that he waxed on ad nauseum. They compared notes on the difficulties of the last two years' crops. Twisden Manor had made economies and had not needed to borrow money. She told him the bank holding the loan her father had taken a few years earlier had failed, but she'd been able to keep up with payments to her new creditor, and he listened as she discussed her livestock and plans for the spring planting.

Cass poked his nose in once, then hobbled away. When Mrs. Hayward appeared with Sir Westcott's freshly cleaned boots, she was accompanied by Reggie, who had come to fetch Sir Westcott home to Highcross Keep.

Unfortunately, not long after they left, she spotted Crofton on the drive.

In their conversation at the assembly, Crofton had demanded help this night. He dangled the mortgage he'd bought from the banker, reminding her he'd just foreclosed on and moved into the Lewis's farm.

His end goal was taking Devil Dyke's Grange. Even before he held the mortgage, he'd let it be known through sly innuendos, through unwelcome touches, that he thought to acquire Devil's Dyke Grange through marriage. To her.

As soon, that is, as his wife, who was ill, and wisely being cared for at her brother's home in Tunbridge Wells, departed this life for the next.

Before he could knock on the door, Sybil hastily retreated to the stable, where Emmet's widowed son and grandson were tending their plough horses.

Crofton hunted her down and found her there.

⊗⁂⊗

A bleary-eyed Reggie refilled Quinton's glass. "I'm going, too. Need some adventure. Not you, though, Uncle. Blasted bore today waiting for your bowels to—"

"You hold, young sirrah." Quinton stood, the martial light in his eyes dimmed by inebriation.

"Yes, hold." Wes had heard more than enough about Quinton's ailment.

"Your glass, Wes," Reggie demanded.

He covered it with his hand and shook his head. "Put a stopper in it. If you're coming with me, you'll want to have your wits about you."

Reggie laughed and raised his glass. "To smugglers."

"And ghosties." Quinton winked. "Ah, young Sir Westcott, it's not a view of a ghost you're after, but a look into a lady's window."

"Long Meg's window, eh?" Reggie chuckled.

Wes shrugged and peered into the empty glass, frowning. He was worried about her. He'd forgotten to broach the subject of smuggling with her, but after they left, from a vantage point at the top of the fell he'd seen Crofton paying a call at Devil's Dyke Grange.

He might not be the cleverest chap, but this fellow Crofton had Wes's nose twitching. Sybil had to make payments on a loan, which explained her rutted lane, unkempt lawn, and worn-out furnishings. She had a new creditor, who must certainly be Crofton.

Reggie and Quinton might tell him more, if they'd bother to let their glasses sit full for a while, and if he was willing to pay the price of their teasing and innuendos.

He'd do his own investigating. Devil's Dyke Grange was as good a place as any to start looking for smugglers. Perhaps ghosts and high-waymen as well.

A sudden thought propelled him upright. Considering what a dastardly fellow Crofton was, might one of the Picard boys be the one robbing travelers or playing ghost? Surely not Sybil—she wouldn't be so foolhardy for the first role nor so crackbrained for the second.

CHAPTER 3

S ybil watched Lang ride off and then quickly changed into some of his clothing.

"You ought to let me go in Lang's stead." Cass helped Sybil into the bulky jacket that would help disguise her shape.

Cass had been shocked when she came down in trousers and guessed what she was doing. He didn't know she was going in *his* stead, not Lang's. Lang was with the revenue force now, and she wouldn't let Crofton's demands jeopardize her brother's chances.

Lang's Riding Officer was a friend of his from school and knew his past history with the local smugglers—that was one of the reasons he took Lang on. Unfortunately, Crofton was holding the mortgage over her head and demanded Cass go in Lang's place.

Even if either twin was hale and hardy, she wouldn't have allowed it.

"Crofton will recognize you," Cass said.

"He won't be with these fellows. He's left Butley in charge and gone off to meet with someone further north."

"With who?"

"With *whom*, little brother. And best we not know which squire or clergyman is storing his contraband."

Crofton had access to barns, buildings, caves, even churches and vicarage cellars.

"There," she said, tightening the belt holding her trousers and buttoning her coat. "I will pass, or I won't. Take care of Paul. We'll send for the apothecary if he's still ill tomorrow."

Cass handed over a sheathed knife. "Put this in your boot. In case someone sees through your disguise and tries to, er, bother you."

Suppressing a shiver, she shoved that worry aside and took the weapon.

Her brother's eyes sparkled. "Will you have to fight with a revenue agent?" he teased.

She hadn't thought that far ahead... Being taken up by the revenuers. Held for trial. Transported. Or worse...

She shook her head. Lang had influence. If the worst happened, he'd have to help her. She was doing this one time for the sake of her brothers, and then she'd find a way to pay Crofton off. Perhaps Sir Peter Somerville might know someone who would loan her money.

"Of course not. I'll be shifting casks is all." She hoped. "Fixing them to the pack horses."

With luck, she herself wouldn't be weighted down with barrels. She was strong—the work here kept her so—but she didn't quite have a man's strength.

Hopefully Crofton's men would expect a skinny youth and assign the appropriate task.

"It's a wonder Crofton doesn't worry about Lang giving evidence against him," Cass said.

Crofton had once trusted Lang, but no longer—that was one reason he'd bought out the mortgage and now demanded what amounted to a hostage.

"You're not to worry," she said.

He limped with her through the kitchen and to the door that led out to the yard.

"Here," he said handing her a paper-wrapped package and a flask. "It's a sandwich. And in case your nerves fail, some gin. Good gin. Tasted it myself."

She ruffled her brother's hair. "A wee taste is fine, but don't make it a habit."

Adding a candle stub and tinderbox to her supplies, and lighting a small lantern, she eased the door open.

Cass would have followed her out into the night, but she pushed him back. No telling whether one of Crofton's men was watching.

* * *

Wes left his horse grazing in a stand of trees near Devil's Dyke Grange and waited.

A rider on a large bay trotted down the lane. He'd seen Lang Picard on that same horse earlier in the day.

While he debated knocking on Sybil's door before all the lights inside dimmed, a figure in a bulky coat and droopy hat passed by the barn and glanced quickly around before shuttering a lantern.

A split-second instinct set him to follow.

Light gleamed in the curtain-shrouded window of a cottage behind the outbuildings where their man, Emmett, lived with his family. That left Sybil and the twins, one sick, the other too injured to walk.

He stifled the urge to call out.

Surely that was Sybil, dressed as a man and off to do who knew what?

He would follow her; smugglers, ghosts, and highwaymen be damned.

Crackbrained woman. There was something about her that put him in mind of... no, not his stepmother. Stepmama had independent notions he'd been unaware of before, but her oddness was restricted to dabbling with paints. Nor his granny, the dowager Lady Twisden. Strong-willed as she was, she limited her adventures to haring off to spas to take the waters and keeping up a flow of gossipy correspondence.

Nor was Sybil Dunsford like any of the other females, respectable and otherwise, who he'd encountered at home or in the social circles of York or London.

Sybil Dunsford was a curiosity, an attractive one, an intriguing one. One that had to be investigated.

He damped down his exhilaration and set off, like one of the natives of North America he'd read about in stories, stalking this doe silently, wishing he'd thought to dress differently, worn a dark jumper and a dark wooly hat over his light hair.

Though in fact, his wardrobe was deficient in both of those items.

The figure moved quickly, slowing only when brush became dense, squeaking and uttering a muffled oath when a holly leaf snagged the coat.

The curse had been low-pitched. The squeak, utterly feminine.

She moved beyond the tree line onto a narrow path worn into the grassy rim of the valley. With a rustle of gravel, a rider came upon her, and she jumped to the side.

"I say. You startled me," the rider said in a cultured voice. "What are you about tonight?"

Wes lingered in the tree line, straining his ears to listen. Nothing in Sybil's demeanor reflected fear. She might know this fellow. In fact, Wes himself sensed something familiar about him.

"Looking for…"

The voices lowered to almost a whisper, and he couldn't hear the rest. But the rider soon saluted and rode on.

❦

Sybil pulled her coat tighter and looked around. Robin Somerville had come upon her so suddenly she wondered at first if he was the one stalking her, because her nerves and the occasional snap of a twig or rustle of dead leaves told her she wasn't alone.

"What are you about tonight," Robin repeated, leaning closer.

She took a step back, buying time to settle her butterflies and clear her throat.

Remember, you are Cass, not Sybil.

"Looking for…" Scrunching her face and taking a breath, she

lowered her voice to a conspiratorial whisper, "you know," and then waggled her hand and ducked her head quickly.

"Ah," he whispered, "one of the Picard brats. Which one, I can't tell. Off to meet the local free traders, and you with a brother who's one of the King's gaugers. Yes, I saw him on the road heading west, presumably to meet up with his lieutenant. How odd when you're going east."

Sybil stood silent, studying the damp path. She was not going east, but north and east. Fresh boot prints imprinted in the mud told her at least part of the party had passed this way ahead of her.

But Lang... was he steering the revenuers west at Crofton's behest?

If not, perhaps the revenuers were going to circle around and put her in danger of arrest.

Her brother wouldn't allow that, would he?

The thought sent chills down her back. She might have to give evidence against Crofton to escape punishment, and then she'd have to leave Devil's Dyke Grange and the wrath of his gang.

"Does he know you're off to meet your Lady Geneva?" Robin's question shook her out of her catastrophizing.

A girl from these parts knew what Lady Geneva was, and she had no idea whether the cargo was in fact gin, or some other luxury the government was eager to tax.

"Don't know anything about that. I'm out fetching one of the pigs that got out."

"Hah. Of course, you are." He leaned even closer. "Do you have a weapon?"

She hesitated and then nodded.

"Good. Stay to the verge, and to the tree line when there is one. We're not alone out here. Besides the free traders, and ghosts, there's that highwayman to be wary of. Play stupid again. It might work."

He saluted and rode off.

When he was out of sight, she dropped to her knees and gulped in deep breaths. She wasn't a timid girl, and she'd grown up on this land and knew it well. There was always a risk—smugglers, wandering sailors who'd jumped ship, or the occasional ex-soldier roaming the country looking for work.

Her hand went to her pocket where the flask offered ease to her nerves, but she fingered the smooth metal, remembering she needed her wits about her.

Standing, she dusted her hands and continued down the path. Robin had turned to travel cross country, though why he would risk his horse in the dark, she had no idea.

She kept to the verge and trees as he'd recommended. The clouds cleared, and the moon and stars kept her on track.

There'd been humor in Robin's voice. He knew many of the smugglers might be local people, and that worthy fellow Captain Moonlight was too selective to rob the empty pockets of the residents of Devil's Dyke Grange. Robin, brother of a baronet, was a far better target for the fellow.

Sir Westcott Twisden as well, or perhaps more *especially*, since he was a newcomer to the area and rumored to be very rich and just arrogant enough—one might say muffin-headed enough—to go roaming about the countryside alone at night.

A picture of him as he'd looked that afternoon flashed in her mind: Sir Westcott shedding his coats to reveal broad, muscled shoulders; mud plastering his tight buckskins and outlining well-shaped limbs...

A shiver went through her. With his height and muscles, he ought to be able to take on a highwayman. The free traders though, there would be too many of them.

The stupid man. She must stop woolgathering about Twisden and thinking the sort of girlish thoughts that might give her away.

Nothing to worry about. She eased in a breath. The highwayman wouldn't bother such as herself. Sir Westcott of the long limbs and wide shoulders wasn't here to stir blushes. All she had to do was act like a pathetic youth and cough a little to make them think Cass had caught his brother's ailment. Perhaps then they would send her home.

Deep in thought, she passed into a dark dale and almost stumbled into a group of men.

"Who're you?"

"Picard," she said in the gruffest voice she could manage.

A big fellow she recognized as Crofton's man, Butley, held a lantern and looked her over.

"You ain't Lang Picard."

"I'm his brother."

"Picard's with the gaugers," another man said. "Best tie this one up."

"Crofton sent me."

Crofton's man shrugged, grunted, and said, "Yeah. Heard him say somethin'. Reckon ye can do. He's the last." He beckoned, and they all fell in behind him. She blew out her lantern and tied it to her belt under the heavy coat as they walked.

She had no idea where they were going, but it was best to keep her mouth shut.

◈

Wes leaned against a beech tree watching the transfer of crates to dog carts, holding his breath each time Sybil entered the old barn until she came out again. He was near enough to hear the orders given by the overseer, a brute of a man in dark clothing who chided her and the others with each heavy load.

Case by case, cart by cart, the crates were loaded and the carts departed, some pulled by donkeys, others by men. Only three people were left—Sybil, the brute in charge, and a scrawny fellow in dark ragged clothes.

Sybil had gone in and not come out. One cart remained, and there was no animal to pull it.

"This here's the last of 'em," the thin man said. "Picard'll pull it."

Anger spiked in him, and he pushed away from the tree. Like hell she would. He was no warrior, but he had his fists and a bit of training with Gentleman Jim, and if all else failed, he had a knife in his boot.

Sybil struggled out juggling a crate.

As Wes drew nearer, he saw the scrawny bugger stick out his

foot. Sybil tripped and the crate clattered with a sound of shattering glass. Liquid spurted, and the air filled with the strong fruity smell of wine.

"God's bones, man." The brute's fist flew, just missing Sybil as she ducked.

Wes charged from the tree, decked the fellow, and shoved the scrawny one away.

"Come away from here." He yanked Sybil up by the hand.

While the fool woman tried to pull away, two men on horseback emerged out of the darkness.

"It's Crofton," the scrawny one whispered.

"What's afoot here?" One of the new arrivals rolled off his saddle.

Before anyone could answer, the brute who'd attacked Sybil bellowed. Wes dodged his fist, but a blow from the shorter fellow glanced off his shoulder.

"Stow your wids."

Wes recognized Crofton.

"Your fists too. Loud enough to raise the dead, you are. Who broke those bottles? I'll take it out of your hide, Butley. And who is this?"

Crofton approached Wes, who, still gripping Sybil's hand, had pulled her behind him.

Someone yanked his wrist around and growled, "I've got him."

Sybil. It was Sybil pretending a wrist lock on him. Had to be, since the four men stood before him.

He'd best play along.

"Sir Westcott Twisden," Wes said. "At your service, Crofton. I saw yon shabby Jack nasty-face trip the lad carrying the crate. And this fat bully here beat on the wrong person for the offense."

"Ain't your business," the shabby one said. "Anyway, you're lying. Picard's been slacking since he came."

To call a gentleman a liar... Wes started to lunge for the fellow, then remembered Sybil hidden behind him.

The brute pointed their way. "'Twas Picard dropped the crate."

"That true, Cass?" Crofton asked. He motioned to the fellow

who'd arrived with him, and he and the big brute who'd smacked Sybil each grabbed one of Wes's arms.

Sybil stood back and ducked her head at the lantern raised in front of her.

"'Twas the ghost," she said. "'Twas Eddie Rose. I saw him. I can see him." Crofton grabbed her chin and raised it, studying the mulish look she'd put on for him.

Not so different than what Wes had seen on her younger brother's face when she'd asked them to help that afternoon.

Crofton grunted. "Is all cleared from the barn?"

"Aye, all 'cept the ones you wanted left," the scrawny one said.

Crofton lowered the lantern. "Tie Twisden up and put him inside. This one," he jerked his head at Sybil, "will watch him until we come back, and then we'll decide what to do with *him*."

"What of the gaugers?" the brute asked. "If Lang Picard brings 'em here—"

"If he does, they can take Twisden." He sent Sybil a steely look. "You'll keep your mouth shut and make sure Twisden does the same, or that brother of yours will hang for a traitor."

۞

Sybil held back the curse rising in her throat and watched as the thug tied Sir Westcott's hands behind his back.

Threaten her, would he? If she was meant to stay and guard Sir Westcott... Well, she wouldn't. As soon as the smugglers were on their way, she'd let him go and head home herself. What she'd do after that...

She'd find a way to battle Crofton. He wasn't swindling her out of her home, or harming any one of her brothers. She wouldn't allow it.

When Sir Westcott's bonds were tied, they shoved him into the tomb-like interior of the old flintstone building. As she watched him enter, a hand clamped onto her shoulder and gin breath wafted past her ear.

"I'll have Devil's Dyke Grange, then, I will." Crofton chuckled, shoving her inside as well. "Best leave him tied. You know how these lords and sirs are. He'll have his way with you. And if he doesn't, if someone else finds you with him, it's a sure bet he won't marry you to save your reputation. You won't be so stiff-rumped about marrying *me* then."

The curse she'd held back exploded. Crofton only laughed again and slammed the door. The sound of the bar falling into place sent fear bubbling inside her.

Blast it all. She should have expected this.

Rage exploded in her, at Crofton, at Sir Westcott, at her own stupid self. She pounded on the door and shouted, but the creaking of cartwheels faded away into quiet and then a shiver went through her, panic clogging her throat and making her hands shake.

She took in a few ragged breaths and tried to steady her nerves. It was pitch dark in the barn. What she'd seen of the inside earlier wasn't promising.

"Well, this is a fine pickle," Sir Westcott said.

He'd moved close to her, too close. She nudged him away.

It was like trying to knock over one of the thick timbers that kept the roof in place.

"Perhaps if we work together, we can find a way to lift that bar," he said amicably.

"Don't be a bird-wit. Do you not see how well-sealed that door is?"

"Is there another door? This was what? A barn? A storage building? Might there be a door to a tack room? An opening in a hay loft?"

"I don't know." She'd seen the dark corners, not all of them filled with crates. The ceiling, though, had been swallowed in darkness.

"You had light before, and you were busy being bullied by that jackanapes. You probably didn't notice the glimmer from up there."

She craned her neck and glanced around. In the far end of the structure, a patch of fog lightened the wall, high up.

"Can we reach it?" she mused.

"If Eddie Rose is around, maybe you can ask him to help us." He laughed. "Or maybe there's a ladder? Ahem. Perhaps I can help look around if you would be so kind as to untie me?"

CHAPTER 4

The villains had taken pleasure in yanking Wes's arms back and pulling the ropes to cut into his wrists.

It was a good thing, or he'd have flattened Crofton.

He'd save that until later. The tense silence coming from the woman standing next to him pained him. What a night she'd had, and though it was her own fault... Damn, but he should have jumped in sooner.

"I won't harm you, Sybil," he said. "May I call you Sybil? I heard what Crofton said—that last parting shot. I am a gentleman, and though you are an enticing bundle of woman, I would never force myself on you."

Furthermore, he was inclined to be cautious. Enticing bundle or not, he wanted to know why she was out and about dressed as a boy and engaged in illegal activities.

"Let's find a way out before Crofton returns, or before anyone else comes along and discovers us," he said.

He heard an exasperated sigh. "You recognized me."

"Yes, of course. Crofton did as well. Those other fellows must have porridge for brains not to have noticed."

A loud huff followed. "I am still Miss Dunsford to you. If anyone else comes along, I can simply continue to pretend to be my brother."

"Discovered in a locked barn, with me, a gentleman who's tied up? Unless it's one of your fellow free traders, whoever discovers us will free me and haul you off to the magistrate, and your secret will come out. Not that I would give evidence against you, but you must admit it would appear odd."

She huffed again, and he heard rustling cloth and saw a spark striking and flaring into light.

"You have a lantern. You clever girl. Lucky, they didn't take it away from you."

She held the lantern handle with her teeth and moved behind him, grumbling.

Long moments passed as her hands moved exploring the ropes binding him, and she grumbled more.

"I have a knife in my boot," he said.

Her exploration paused, and she must have set the lantern down, as the light shone about his ankles. "And I have one in mine also, but we might need this length of rope."

"Quite right. Good thinking."

"Do hold still. The knot is loosening. I can't see well, but I can feel."

So could he. Her words whispered tantalizingly past his neck, and he glanced over his shoulder. The brim of her hat nearly touched his collar, and he saw dark curls peeking out underneath.

She murmured an unladylike curse and continued to work.

It was shocking for a lady to curse, wasn't it? He chuckled, thinking of his stepmother and grandmother. Once or twice when they thought he wasn't around, he'd heard them swear.

Sybil must have removed the gloves she'd been wearing. The cold fingers touching his wrists unaccountably sent warmth up his arms and to other parts of his body.

She slid a finger under his cuff and his heart jolted. If she kept that up, he might find himself leg-shackled, and not unwillingly.

Perhaps before the night was over, he'd have a chance to warm her hands. And more. This godforsaken place was dark enough to have his thoughts embracing the notion of a tryst and a special license.

"Stop moving," she said. "These knots are the devil."

The scold shook him out of his lustful thoughts and brought to mind his stepmother's treatment by a neighbor and friend of his father, who'd followed her to York in the spring and tried to importune her one afternoon while Wes was out.

Stepmama had absolutely forbade him from challenging the fellow because he was, she said, no worse than other friends of Wes's late father.

His father. The late Sir Twisden's passions had all been for his hounds and his hunting, not his duties as the local squire, not his wife, nor even his son. It had been Wes's stepmother raising Wes to be a gentleman.

The marriage had been a mismatch for her, an impoverished young lady who hadn't known his father at all before marrying him.

What did Wes know about Sybil Dunsford? He'd do well to slow down and not rush his fences with her.

But... what did Crofton say... *You won't be so stiff-rumped about marrying me then.*

Crofton wanted to marry her?

A stubborn determination rose in him. Crofton wouldn't have Sybil.

The bindings on his wrists loosened, bringing him back to the challenge at hand. While he'd been ruminating, she'd worked away until finally the ropes fell, and Wes shook out his arms and rolled the stiffness out of his shoulders.

He saw her rubbing her fingers, and he caught her hands up, holding them as she tried to pull away. Even in this dim light, he could see they were scratched and bleeding from working the hemp rope.

"Damn and blast it, I'll take a horsewhip to those fellows, I will," he said.

"Your wrists are not much better," she said.

"I'm so sorry, my dear."

The shiver that went through her coursed up his arms.

She pulled away. "And you should be. We wouldn't be in this spot if you hadn't decided to play Sir Galahad."

"Sir Galahad, is it? I've never had the honor of rescuing a damsel in distress before. Did you think I would stand there and let you take a beating?"

She crossed her arms and huffed. "Yes, well, you had best be prepared to do more if we're to find a way out of here."

He glanced around. The light on the floor didn't do much to illuminate the building's interior. He hadn't exactly made a careful note of the structure either. The walls were made of some coarse stone, probably flint, like those that he'd seen at Devil's Dyke Grange. The stone might provide toeholds to climb up to the window. On the other hand...

"Let's look. Maybe there's a ladder." He bent and picked up the lantern and gathered the rope. The length wasn't nearly enough to throw over a beam—if there were any beams handy—and reach that high window opening.

Somehow, they would contrive. Or not. And then they would be locked in here until Crofton's men returned and they had to fight their way out, or until someone else wandered by or came searching and discovered them.

In which case, he would have to marry her.

Would it be a good round of fisticuffs tonight, or a trip to the altar with a challenging, delectable handful of a lady tomorrow?

The thought cheered him—either outcome would do. Or perhaps both.

⊗⊗⊗

Sybil ran her hands over the rough stone of the barn wall, feeling for footholds.

"There are a few crates here," Sir Westcott said from a nearby corner.

The lantern light shimmered and moved from side to side as he searched for anything that would aid their escape. She heard a squeal of wood and a startled laugh.

"Gadzooks. Champagne. Perhaps we'll take a bottle with us. Is this Crofton's private cache?"

She ignored the question. "Can we stack the crates to climb on?"

"I said *a few*. I meant three. Not likely to be high enough." The light bobbed, and he came and stood next to her. "No ladder around that I can see."

He raised the lantern and looked up. "Those shadows... Does it look like there are beams up there? Part of a loft floor?"

The fog must have shifted, because a few stars glimmered in the opening and cold air drifted in. If there'd ever been a window or wooden door, it had long since disappeared.

"If we can get to the beams... Here." He set down the bottle, handed her the lantern, and went to retrieve the crates, hauling them over one by one while she peered through the darkness at the wall.

When they were stacked, he set the lantern away and studied them.

"Let's try this." He arranged them two on the bottom and one on top so he could step up, and she handed him the lantern.

"That won't work," she muttered.

How long would it take Crofton to drop his cargo and return? They needed to escape soon.

"Nothing within reach," he said, feeling around. "But up there..."

He hopped down and rearranged the crates, stacking them three high and took the rope and tied a loop with a slipknot.

"Now, if I can just hoist myself up—"

"Let me," Sybil said. "I'm not as tall as you, but I have a good arm."

Before she had to endure the expected lecture about ladylike behavior, his hands, large, strong, and sure came under her arms, and he'd set her atop the crates.

"Light as a feather," he said, handing up the rope. "Can you manage the lantern as well?"

Breathless and heart pounding, her thoughts muddled in a war between feelings of vulnerability and... desire? Was that what she was feeling? Sir Westcott had picked her up like she was in fact as light as a feather, like she was *feminine*.

She prayed he really was a gentleman, else, with the feelings he was stirring she might find herself truly in jeopardy and *liking* it. And then what would become of her brothers? What would become of Devil's Dyke Grange? A man like Sir Westcott would not want to take on two lads, and he didn't need her farm in Sussex. He'd probably want to sell it.

Sell her birthright. That thought tamed her wild longings.

"Are you all right, my dear?"

"Give me the lantern," she said, finding his good manners suddenly irritating.

He couldn't be that amicable. The men in her family—her father, her brothers, even Emmett—each would, in these circumstances, throw a masculine tantrum. Surely Sir Westcott would too, once they got out of here. He'd ring a peal over her all the way back to the Grange.

She raised the lantern and saw the jutting piece of wood he'd spotted. It might be the remains of a broken crossbeam.

It was a wonder the whole building hadn't tumbled down. She tossed the knotted rope and missed the first two times. On the third try, the loop caught.

"The rope is on," she said, handing down the lantern.

Thank heavens. Now to climb up and shimmy through the opening and pray that she didn't break a bone going down the other side. The barn was on a slope that fell to a small stream. She had no idea how far the drop was.

"Are you sure you don't want me to make this attempt?" he called up to her.

"Are you sure this rope would hold you? Or are you afraid I'll leave you stranded here?"

"Would you?" There was no fear in his tone, no anger, not even any sense of urgency.

"The thought is tempting."

His chuckle floated up to her, easing her nerves, and she wondered what sort of boy Sir Westcott had been. If she ever met this stepmother he spoke of so fondly, she would ask her.

Taking a deep breath, she gripped the rope and tugged it. It seemed to be holding firmly. She braced one boot in a chink in the wall, and with the other, searched for a foot hold, sliding the toe of her boot into a space where the mortar was missing. Hand over hand, very slowly, she'd almost reached the jutting timber, when a loud crack sliced the air around her head. A piece of timber whizzed past her ear, and the rope dropped from her hands as she clawed at the wall, and then at open air.

With a scream and a *whoosh*, she flew, landing sprawled on her stomach, caught by strong arms. The loud *oof* she heard came from Sir Westcott, knocked backwards to the floor.

Long moments passed before she could catch her breath, and then more long moments as her heart pounded and all her senses alerted.

She'd not only landed on Sir Westcott, she'd landed *atop* him, her breasts smashed against his waistcoat, her heart pounding in time with his, his arms holding her close. The lantern had gone out. They were submerged in darkness.

But her other senses were working quite well; too well. His breathing was as ragged as hers. Dear Lord, she could feel the taut muscles of his chest moving up and down, and smell the starch in his neckcloth.

She lifted her head, and her nose touched his chin, scratchy with evening stubble. If she just lifted her head a little higher...

"I say, Sybil. Are you injured?"

How did he not sound breathless? There was real concern in his tone.

"N-n-no," she said on another ragged breath, and the shock of the fall, of flailing about in the air hit her. She choked back a sob.

His hand stroked her back. "Shhh."

The tenderness in his voice sent warmth spiraling through her. Perhaps he'd rail at her later, but for now...

"Apologies," she said, rallying. "Are you all right?"

A long pause followed, and he finally said. "In truth, never better."

There'd been nothing flirtatious in his tone. He'd been dead serious, and that intensity had her senses reeling again with awareness.

She ought to roll off him. She ought to... Dear Lord, she wondered about kissing him. She had to get hold of herself.

"Not light as a feather then, am I?" she asked, trying to break the spell.

His chuckle vibrated near her ear, sending more warmth through her and a growing, dazzling, mad temptation. He smelled so delicious—of good soap and some pleasant masculine scent. Despite chasing her across half of Devil's Dyke, he smelled *clean*.

As she lifted her head, the clouds outside moved and faint light glimmered through the high window, illuminating his lips. They were curved up in a smile.

In all her twenty-four years, she'd never let a man kiss her. She'd never initiated a kiss.

She'd never felt this way before.

His hand moved to the back of her head. His eyes gleamed up at her, and the smile on his lips faltered and transformed to a look of wonder.

"Sybil," he said.

Dragging her hand up, she cupped his jaw, dipped her head, and pressed her lips to his. Warmth, softness, the scent of brandy made her dizzy, unable to think, unable to do anything but feel ripples of pleasure as his hands moved over her.

⚜

Wes's brain functioned feebly for a few minutes more. He'd kissed and been kissed before, but he'd never been flattened. Which he had been in all ways except, well, *that* one.

He'd managed to catch Sybil and then roll back awkwardly without bashing his head on the crates. He'd managed to cushion her fall to this floor, which was not the hard-packed earth he was expecting. Between the shock of it and her luscious body pressing into him, his brains were addled.

Hers must be, too. When he kissed her—or was it her kissing him?—her lips touched his ever so gently, ever so briefly. As she lifted away, his fingers found her head, tunneling in the soft curls and sliding away the tie that restrained them. He was a gentleman, that was true, but she was a handful of woman laid out atop him.

She needed to stop him. He prayed she would stop him.

"Oh," she said, and her lips came down on his again, and now she truly was pressing and moving her lips over his.

He angled her head and parted his lips and entered her with his tongue and felt her pause, but for only a moment until she joined him in a proper kiss that had her writhing, and him grasping for sanity, for the part of him that knew he mustn't go any further.

He pushed them both up to sitting with her still atop him and buried his face in her neck, searching for the spot that drove women wild. Sybil's legs straddled him—thank heavens she wore trousers. She sighed loudly and then stiffened.

"S-sir Westcott," she said.

"Call me Wes," he murmured into her neck, and tugged her tighter. And then remembered... he *was* a gentleman. This was Sybil, the girl he was meant to be courting.

Courting, not trying to swive.

"You're right," he said. "Apologies."

She scooted off him, none too gently, and they both got to their feet. "I kissed you first. I'm... I'm not sorry. I've never been kissed."

"Never been kissed?"

"Never allowed it. Did you notice," she said, rattling on, "under the layers of dust and dirt, this floor is wooden? This must have been a granary. It's set on a slope, but it's level, held up by staddle stones, you know, to keep out the vermin. To keep out water as well. We're right above a stream that surely must swell in heavy rains. These lower walls are flint and bungaroosh—perhaps we could kick a hole in them. Or pick out a hole with our blades. Or maybe pry up a loose floorboard."

CHAPTER 5

Sybil's race through so many topics set Wes's head spinning. His attention had stalled at the notion that she'd *never been kissed*. And she thought she had kissed him first. And wasn't sorry about it.

He took a step closer.

"You've *never* been kissed? I've been wanting to do that since the first day I saw you. I thought we would be standing up, though."

It had been heaps more compelling lying down. Yes, he preferred that.

"What?" A long pause followed. "Ah," she said finally, her voice shaky, "forget about the kissing."

"I don't want to. How could I?"

She stepped into a faint beam of light and his gaze followed hers up to the window. The fog had shifted again and the night sky appeared brighter.

How long had it been since they were locked in? He'd best get his brain back to working out how they could escape. The high window seemed more and more unlikely.

"Sir Westcott, did you not hear anything I said?"

"Vermin," he said. "Rats. You're right, I haven't heard any scurrying, or smelled them for that matter. Could there be a trap door somewhere to let out the grain?"

"We can look for one while we're looking for loose planks or holes in the wall that we can widen."

"The bungaroosh walls I saw in Brighton looked awfully sturdy." Bungaroosh was the curious name for a kind of cement being used in the buildings going up like wildfire in the fashionable seaside town.

"This building is much older. And the walls have more bungaroosh than stone."

"Well then," he said, gathering up the fallen rope. "Let's find that lantern and relight it."

❦

A surprisingly short time later, Sybil held her breath and wriggled through a gap made by prying up two wide planks with the crowbar they'd found in a dark corner.

Sir Westcott wanted the honors, in case there were dangers outside, he said. She convinced him that for his shoulders to fit, they'd have to spend precious time loosening the next board.

There might not have been vermin inside the storehouse, but something had nested between the floorboards and the damp ground. The sound of scattering feet sent chills up her spine, and the smell of scat and algae made her stomach twist. Dampness slicked her back and belly and then her knees as she scooted and then crawled down the slope.

The wind soughed through the nearby trees, and somewhere below water trickled. Easing herself out from the narrow space, she set her aching legs into motion and made her way up the slope and around to the door.

The heavy bar resisted. She shook out her sore arms and with one frantic heave, lifted the bar out of the way, and stepped aside.

The door opened and Sir Westcott peered out, looking around, his head cocked.

He stepped out and handed over her hat. "I hear something."

Tilting her head, she strained her ears, but all she heard was her own heavy breathing and the sound of the door closing and the heavy bar falling back into place.

"It may be your man," he said.

He meant Crofton. "He's not my man."

He shushed her and took her hand, leading her to a nearby clump of yew and beech trees.

As his greatcoat came around her, she heard it—the clops of horses on the gravel road.

"It might be the revenuers, or maybe Robin Somerville again." She spoke softly, mindful that sound carried more in the fog.

"That was Somerville you met on the road?" He whispered the words into her ear, sending a wave of trembling down her spine.

He took her hand again. She was damp from her crawl under the granary. With the fog lying heavy and wet, he would soon be as wet and cold as she was, from the top of his hat to the soles of his boots.

"Planks are back in place." His breath tickled her ear again. "Brought this too." Reaching around he brought out the crowbar.

He helped her slip her arms through the sleeves of the greatcoat and then handed her the heavy tool.

Two riders broke through the fog and dismounted. Crofton and Butley.

Heart pounding, she watched the two men approach the brush where she and Sir Westcott were hiding. When they tied their mounts to a sapling and stepped away, her breath returned.

"No sound from inside," Butley said. "Might be sleeping." He laughed. "Or going at it. Think she untied him?"

"Without a doubt," Crofton said. "But that namby-pamby wouldn't know what to do with a woman."

"What're *we* going to do with *him*?" Butley asked. "I know your plans for her. Serve her right, but we don't want him talking, do we? Mayhap, have it look like that highwayman—"

"Shut your trap and light a lantern," Crofton said.

Shaking with anger, she gripped the crowbar. There'd be no rape tonight, but there might be a murder or two, and not Sir Westcott's. They could blame *those* on Captain Moonlight.

"Bring that rope," Crofton said. "Tie him and take him out while

I have private *words* with her. Plenty of time before those casks come up from Beachy Head."

She squeezed Sir Westcott's hand. No wonder Crofton had needed extra men. He was bringing up a new load from east of Brighton.

They needed to get out of here. When dawn broke, there'd be no good place to hide themselves.

While Butley fumbled with the lantern and Crofton cursed the man's clumsiness, Sir Westcott leaned close.

"Let's detain them."

She took in a sharp breath and then huffed out a silent laugh. *Of course.* It was a prank worthy of the Picard boys.

And a perfect payback.

She nodded and moved into a crouch.

The door opened, the two men disappeared inside, and she followed Sir Westcott on silent feet watching the lantern light bob further into the darkness.

"Too quiet in here," Butley said.

"Come out now, Sybil, there's a good girl," Crofton called.

"*Oof,*" Butley cursed. "Reckon that ghost might—"

"Shut up, you fool. There's no ghost. Keep an eye on that do—"

Sybil pushed the door closed and Sir Westcott slammed the heavy bar into place.

Shouting and curses erupted, spurring a gleeful panic in her and setting her feet into motion.

A long, mournful, masculine wail behind her, a ghostly wail, made her pause.

The shouting inside turned into worried whispers.

Grinning, Sir Westcott grabbed her hand and pulled her back to the sapling and the waiting horses. "We'll just borrow these," he whispered.

Smuggling, and now stealing horses?

"I never believed that ghost story." He freed the reins, threw her up on one of the horses, and mounted the other.

They picked their way carefully across a field until they reached a clump of trees before halting.

"Thank heavens the war with France is over," she said.

"What?" Sir Westcott asked. "Why?"

"I'll have to flee there when Crofton sends the constable to arrest me for horse theft."

He chuckled. "Gus and my stepmama went to France for their honeymoon. I'll flee with you."

She scoffed. "*Sir Westcott...*"

"Sybil, I have an idea," he said, going on as if he hadn't just offered... What had he offered? He was only flirting again. He didn't mean any of it.

"Crofton has land near you, doesn't he?" he asked. "We'll take these fellows home. Let him think they slipped their tethers and found their way there on their own."

He threw back his head and sent up the same ghostly wail, and then laughed so hard and so contagiously that she found herself joining in.

☙❧

"So, Crofton lives *here?*" Wes asked as they stopped at a gate. Crofton's farm house wasn't visible from this far field, but all seemed quiet.

"He does now."

"Who's there with him? His wife? Children? Servants?"

"His wife is in Tunbridge Wells with her brother. No children. He has a woman come in during the day. The only servant I know of is Butley."

"You've made a study of this."

"He's holding my loan papers somewhere. Mine and other people's. Come on, let's open this gate." She slid from the horse. "It's been a long night."

"Which way to Devil's Dyke Grange?" Wes said a few minutes later, closing the gate. They watched the horses trot off to look for grazing on their home ground.

She was right. It had been a very long night. It was all well and good to be a gentleman—Sybil still had his greatcoat, and he was glad of that—but the damp chill had penetrated all the way to his shirt. He'd relish a chance to sit by a warm fire.

"Not far," she said.

No mincing miss was Sybil Dunsford, nor did she need to be constantly engaged in polite conversation. He liked that about her.

He stepped up beside her on the road. "My stomach's been rumbling for the past hour. Let's stop for a moment. I have a flask in one of those pockets."

She paused and began shrugging out of his greatcoat.

"No, no." He tucked the coat back around her. "Stand there and I'll find it."

The search gave him an opportunity to move closer, to delve into pockets, and to feel her warm breath touching his cheeks. He'd like to delve under the layers of coats and feel more than wet wool and steal another kiss. She hadn't seemed to mind the first one.

He retrieved the flask, opened it, and passed it to her. After one sip, she spluttered and coughed.

"I'm not used to spirits."

Wes chuckled and accepted the flask back. When he'd tossed back a drink, she offered another flask.

"Will you have some?" she offered. "My brother insisted I take it. He said it's good gin."

He took a taste of the drink and then a longer draught. "Not rotgut," he said, wiping his mouth. "Lang has good taste."

"That was Cass's. He's too young, I know. He's... he's incorrigible."

She dug into another one of her own pockets and brought out a cloth-wrapped package. "I've a sandwich too. You may have it."

His stomach rumbled again. "You must be peckish as well. Maybe more so after carting out all those crates."

She shook her head. "No. Or, after a night like this, I don't know whether I'm hungry or not. Maybe I am." She laughed, but there was no humor in her voice. "Shall we share it?"

She was done in. And she ought to be. This night's activities had been dangerous, and with a man like Crofton, if he'd been released, there might be more danger awaiting her at home.

"I'll take but a bite or two, and thank you," he said. "Miss Dunsford, I don't want to say it but—"

"Then don't, Sir Westcott. Don't tell me how foolish this night's work was."

He took a bite and chewed, calming the temptation to scold, putting his brain to work on a better approach. He wouldn't want his wife to go haring off with a passel of smugglers.

On the other hand, he'd always said he wanted a lady with spirit, one who would stand up for her children like Sybil stood up for her brothers.

"You did this for your brothers, didn't you?"

She shrugged.

"And Crofton bought your mortgage when the bank failed."

"Yes. And I've kept up with the payments."

And probably struggled to do so after the last year's terrible harvest.

"But he, what? Threatened to call in the whole loan? Is that what he did to your neighbor?"

"Mr. Lewis lost his wife, and then his children, one after the other. He gave up. I'm not giving up." She took a swig of the gin and coughed. "Finish this."

She handed him the rest of the sandwich and tucked away the cloth it had been wrapped in.

Wes devoured the remains of the food and dusted off his hands. "What time do you suppose it is?"

The fog wasn't as dark as it had been.

"Not sunrise yet. I'd say, maybe three, or four. I'm weary enough for it to be that late. Or early. It's not far to the Grange. If you want to go on to Highcross Keep, I'll be fine. We're coming to that turning in a moment."

"I'm going to escort you all the way home," Wes said as he fell into step with her, determined to make conversation. "Do you know Reggie well?"

"As children, we played together before he went away to school. But seldom after that; never after he went into the army. Were you at school with him?"

Wes laughed and told her about his introduction to Reggie at Tattersall's.

"My grandmother is a friend of his mother. Gran got me to escort her to London with a view to Reggie's mother playing matchmaker for me."

She glanced at him. "And?"

"I'm, as you see, still a bachelor."

She looked over at him again. "Do you truly want to marry now? How old are you?"

"I've reached my majority, Miss Dunsford. How old are you?"

He saw the glint of a smile. "I'm four and twenty."

"Will it bother you that I'm a year younger?"

"What a widgeon you are," she said. "Why should I care?"

"Good," he said, and told her about his sojourn in York in the spring; about the beauty of the nearby Lake District; and more about his stepmother whom he'd just lost to a marriage he'd never expected.

"My gran lives at Twisden Manor, but she's often gone for weeks at a time to one spa or another taking the waters. She's in London now, but I don't doubt that she'll want to go north to the borders with Stepmama and Gus for a time."

And he would be alone, just him and the servants. He'd be comfortable, it was true, but he'd tried abiding at home last spring after his stepmother went down to York. Restless, after meeting his distant cousin Gus at a horse fair, he'd persuaded Gus to come along with him to York for the races there.

"Do you have brothers or sisters?" she asked.

"I had a half-sister. A sweet little thing. She died as a child."

She went quiet for a time and then raised the topic of his estate. He'd told her about it in the afternoon in her parlor, but she had more questions.

And he found he was able to answer them, telling her about the crops, the livestock, the tenants.

"How can you afford to remain away so long?" she asked.

"Our man is competent and trustworthy, and he sends me regular reports. When Reggie invited me down here, I thought, why not see

Brighton and wait for my stepmother when she returns from her honeymoon? She's with child, you know."

"With child? Ah. You mentioned that at the assembly."

"Shocking, isn't it? She's not so old—not yet forty. A bang-up great lady. She wrote to tell me they'd met one of Gus's friends in Palermo and will be sailing with him straight to Brighton, arriving any day now. I can't wait for you to meet her."

A stunned silence followed, and they entered a portion of the lane that had high hedges on each side and no verge. If a wagon came along, they'd be done for.

On the other hand, the hedges gave an even deeper feeling of privacy than the fog alone provided.

CHAPTER 6

W es reached for her hand and drew her to a halt, turning her towards him. "I'm surrounded by strong women, you see. That's one of the reasons I find *you* so attractive, Miss Dunsford. Sybil. Besides the fact you're a bang-up good-looking girl..."

She'd gone very still. Maybe he was talking too much. But he had more to say, and he might not be alone on a dark road with her again. He'd like to steal another kiss—a whole cartload of kisses.

She was quiet so long, he began to worry.

What did Sybil really want?

One thing he'd learned from his stepmother—not every lady craved jewels and finery.

What could he offer Sybil?

"My father," he said, "was wild for dogs. Prime hunters. While one doesn't really need more than a half dozen, he kept scores of them."

Braying and barking all night sometimes, and his father's favorites allowed into the house to climb all over the furniture. Being used to it, Wes hadn't really minded, but it was a wonder his stepmother had not poisoned the lot. "When he died, we sold all but a pair for breeding."

He took in a breath and squeezed her hand. "Those empty kennels might do for your little black and white pigs."

❦

Sybil felt heat rising into her cheeks. From the brandy surely, though she couldn't deny that the firm clasp of his long fingers was sending some of the warmth.

This wouldn't do. She had a farm to run. And she had the boys to look after. Lang had only just reached his majority. And the twins... She couldn't run off with Sir Westcott, no matter how well he kissed.

She glanced both ways on the road. They were completely alone, swathed in the damp fog. Neither of them had moved, but she felt herself being drawn to him, and him to her.

Mustering a breath, she said, "I can sell you some piglets to take home with you and breed."

His lips quirked and moved close to hers. "Will you come along too and show me how the breeding is done?"

She gasped, a giggle bubbling up within her. "I ought to slap..."

The touch of his lips silenced her. Her response came as naturally as the dawn would come in a few hours. Softly, he kissed her, and she went along willingly, warmth fizzing inside her, melting away the cold and the loneliness and the *fear*.

He angled his head and took the kiss deeper, and on a shocked murmur she felt the touch of his tongue to hers. The soft kiss soon became hotter, more intense, passion building as she pressed herself closer, a deeper awareness blooming within her.

"What's all this?"

A man on horseback blocked their way, looking down at them, and another, barely visible through the fog, had stopped behind him.

She would have sprung back, but Sir Westcott's arms held her tightly.

"Reggie?" Sir Westcott said. "Is that you?"

The second rider moved up closer. "Why, it's Sir Westcott. Why are you kissing that fellow, sirrah? Didn't take you for—"

"Hello, Quinton," Sir Westcott said. "I was, uh, merely... That is, this is not..."

"I'm not a fellow," Sybil said.

She might as well spare them both further embarrassments. Quinton was a gossip, but perhaps Reggie could persuade him to keep his mouth shut for the sake of his friend avoiding the parson's trap.

A knot of worry formed in her belly. "Why are you here?" She nudged Sir Westcott away. "What's happened?"

Were her brothers all right? What if Crofton had been set free and gone straight to the Grange?

"We're hunting, Wes," Reggie said. "One moment we were talking, the next we noticed he'd scampered. Dozed off, we did." He laughed. "Shall I do the pretty, Syb, and plant him a facer, since Lang's not here?"

"Is that Sybil Dunsford?"

The speaker, a third rider, nudged his way between the other two horses, and her heart pounded. She recognized Eddy Simpson, the ne'er-do-well brother of her neighbors. Eddy held a regular bench at the Duck and Spoon and staggered from there at closing to wherever else he could continue drinking.

He was a worse gossip than Reggie's uncle and with a far broader audience. She was done for.

Eddie leaned in, wobbling in his saddle. "And dressed as a boy?"

"A lost pig," Sir Westcott said. "She couldn't very well go searching in long skirts. I came across her while I was, er, taking a walk."

"That so?" She could hear the amusement in Reggie's voice. "Did you find this little oinker?"

"Miss Dunsford twisted her ankle. I was, er, helping her to her feet."

Reggie hopped down. "Come on, Syb. I'll put you up. The lane to the Keep is right here. We'll let our housekeeper have a look at your ankle."

Blasted Sir Westcott. He'd chosen the wrong lie, and Reggie *would* choose this moment to play the gentleman.

"No." She made a shooing motion. "I'm fine. Reggie, you're foxed. Go home and take Sir Westcott with you. I'll make my own way home before my brothers start worrying."

Reggie laughed. "As if they would."

"What of your missing swine?" Quinton asked.

And that was another problem with lying. One was always forced to dig in deeper.

"I'll send Emmet to look tomorrow."

"Loan me your mount, Reggie," Sir Westcott said. "I'll take Miss Dunsford home."

Reggie and Sir Westcott exchanged a look like the ones her brothers' often shared—a whole wordless conversation.

"We'll both go," Reggie said. "Too many goings-on in the Dyke tonight. Brought my pistols, just in case. Uncle Quinton, off you go. Past your bedtime."

Quinton lifted his chin and sent Reggie a haughty gaze. "Of course, I'm coming along with you, ready to offer my sword, Miss Dunsford. It's been many years since I've assisted a damsel in distress, and never a damsel as becoming as you are even in trousers. One might say, especially in trousers."

She rolled her eyes. "Foxed," she muttered.

"Cut the flirting, uncle. Eddy, you can go on home to your bed. All's well, that ends well."

Eddy swayed in his saddle, tipped his hat to them and rode past.

"He'll blab," Reggie said, watching the other man disappear into the fog. "Good thing he was too far back to see you, er, helping our Syb with the cut on her lips."

"Stow it, Reggie," Sybil said.

"With luck," Quinton said, "he's so bosky he won't remember a scene of romance on a dark country road."

Sybil had had enough for one night. "There's no romance. Nor will anyone care."

Except possibly Crofton. That thought sent a shiver of fear through her. What would he do after his minions came along and released him?

She must get to the safety of home.

She stepped out briskly, but Sir Westcott took her arm, scooped a hand under her bottom, and plopped her onto Reggie's mount.

"You're not walking home alone. What are the odds you'll have someone waiting for you there? We might need Reggie's fists and his pistols."

"A mill?" Reggie said. "Capital."

⚜

"What really happened?" Reggie asked, riding next to Wes.

They'd seen Sybil safely home and turned her over to Cass, who'd greeted them with an old-fashioned blunderbuss in hand. Lang was still out with the revenuers. Wes had promised to call the next day and waited while she locked all the doors before retrieving his horse where he'd left it.

For all that Reggie acted the dunderhead, he sensed he could trust his friend's discretion. He wasn't sure about Quinton, so he kept his voice low and told him about the night's events.

"Knew that pig story was a bouncer," Reggie said. "Going to marry her?"

Wes grinned. "If she'll say yes."

Reggie grunted. "Could do much worse than our Syb. Have to deal with Crofton. I can tell him it was me came along and let you out."

"I won't pull you in any deeper," Wes said, thinking. "Didn't Captain Moonlight rob Crofton last night? Who's to say he wasn't following him again and wanted to put another spoke in his wheel?"

"He might think you're Captain Moonlight."

"How could I be?" Wes said. "I just arrived here. Plus, no one thinks I'm clever enough to be a highwayman."

"Shhh." Reggie reined up and signaled to them to do the same and then drew the pistol from under his coat.

A group of riders appeared out of the fog.

"Who's there?" one called.

The lead rider, in uniform, saw the pistol. "Put that away, Dalrymple."

"Ah, Miles. Caught anyone tonight?"

"It was a wild goose chase."

Wes brought his mount closer. "Is Lang Picard still with you?"

"I'm here, Twisden." Lang made introductions.

"Why are you out tonight?" Lieutenant Miles asked.

"Wes here wants to run into Captain Moonlight," Reggie said. "Any luck?"

"No," Wes said. "But here's something: I heard a couple of fellows in an old granary not far from here talking about a load of casks coming up tonight from Beachy Head."

Miles and Lang Picard exchanged a look.

"I know that place," Lang said.

"We stopped by Devil's Dyke Grange to tell you," Wes said. "Your brother met me with a blunderbuss, and your sister wasn't happy about being woken up."

Lang gave him a long look, nodded, and rode off with the others.

"You didn't tell me about a load from Beachy Head," Reggie said. "Is that true?"

"It's what we heard."

"Good thinking," Reggie said. "Didn't know you had it in you. If it wasn't for Uncle Quinton here, I'd offer to go with them."

He'd been thinking about what Sybil had said about Crofton's new home. "Quinton," Wes called. "What sort of document do you suppose Crofton has that makes these swindling mortgages legal?"

The old man had claimed he once worked with a solicitor for a time and was happy to impart more knowledge than Wes cared to know.

When they reached the gate where they'd set the horses loose, he reined up.

"That's the Lewis farm," Reggie said. "Crofton's moved in here."

"I'm going to pay the farmhouse a visit," Wes said. "Care to loan me your pistol?"

"Nah." Reggie laughed. "I'm comin' with you. Wait here, Uncle Quinton, and you can raise the alarm."

"Housebreaking," Quinton said. "I can deduce what you're looking for. I'm coming, too."

A few days later

Only a few locals sat drinking in the tap room of the Duck and Spoon when Wes entered and found a table. He ordered a pint for himself and drinks all around, and was surprised by the friendly greetings of the men gathered there.

Crofton had been arrested, along with Butley and some men from Hastings, and no one seemed to mind. The free trade was important here, but Crofton's swindling had been widespread.

Wes had received the news in Brighton, where he'd gone the day after Sybil's adventure. He'd only just settled Gus and his stepmother at Highcross Keep and arranged this meeting.

A tall dark-haired fellow in uniform entered and looked around. The presence of Lang Picard brought a pause, and then the conversations resumed.

Wes called him over and shook hands. "Thank you for meeting me," Wes said.

The younger man's eyes twinkled, despite the obvious fatigue shadowing them. "Your tip the other night has kept us busy," he said in a low voice. "But I found time to stop by the farm and get what you asked for."

He pulled a paper from his coat.

Wes unfolded the document, Sybil's copy of the promissory note signed by her father.

"It's a fake," Wes said. "The original that Crofton bought out showed a debt less by a factor of ten."

Picard frowned. "And you know this how?"

"I saw it."

"Will you take it to Sir Peter?"

Wes tugged at his neckcloth. "He'll want to know how I came by it."

"Well then," Picard raised his glass, "here's to putting his swindle to an end."

"Sybil has paid that debt in full and then some."

"Sybil, is it?" He lowered his voice again. "Cass told me she went out that night and that you escorted her home. What else happened?"

Wes pressed his lips together. Picard wasn't asking about shifting casks or escaping the granary. Like any good brother, he wanted to know about the kissing. "Nothing. That is... I'd like to... to court her. And she told me quite firmly I'm not to ask your permission."

"That sounds like Syb. She's been bossing us around since the first day I met her."

"She's spirited."

"She won't give you any peace."

Wes laughed. "Wouldn't want a boring girl."

"You won't have that. The truth is, we'd like to see her married to someone deserving. I have plans that will take me away from Brighton, as does Cass. He wants to go to sea, and he can go as a cabin boy now, if we can find him a spot. Paul's the studious one. He'd like to go on to Oxford, or failing that, to clerk for a solicitor or banker."

Picard called for another round. "So, tell me the whole story. What happened that night?"

Before Wes could answer, the door slapped open and Sybil stomped in.

"You," she said, wagging a finger at her brother, and then she spotted the mortgage document. She looked from the paper to Wes, her eyes spitting blue fire.

"Sir Westcott wanted to see it."

"You had no right to go through my things, Lang. And you, Sir Westcott... I am perfectly competent to handle my own business. You can take yourself away and go back north and stop meddling."

"Look here," a man cried, his voice foggy with drink, "Ish a loversh' tiff."

⚜

Sybil froze. The taproom had gone still as death, the eager eyes of Normanton's worst idlers and gossips trained on her. And Eddy Simpson was here.

Her cheeks heated with embarrassment and fury.

"Haven't shaid a word 'bout her shpending the night with thish foreigner."

"I did not..." She spluttered, too mortified to go on.

"Sorry, Sybil," another man said. "Been running his mouth about catching you and Twisden kissing."

"Well," Eddy staggered to his feet, "What'd ye expect? After she'd been making free with Crof—"

"Enough." Sir Westcott shoved chairs aside and slammed his fist into Eddy's jaw. Another customer took umbrage and punched Sir Westcott.

"No one talks about my sister like that," Lang said, jumping into the fray.

Sybil froze, horrified, while the tavern maid ran to fetch help.

Remembering the promissory note, she grabbed it and, holding her head high, walked past the curious bystanders and left.

CHAPTER 7

T*wo days later*

Sybil closed her account book and wiped her pen, wondering whether the documents Lang had slipped to her late the night before truly meant she was free of Crofton's demands. The dastard had been taken to Horsham to face the next assize court; not many people in Normanton and surrounds were mourning his absence.

Lang had assured her she wouldn't be called to give evidence. She prayed that was true.

The clacking of wheels outside drew her to the window. A coach was wobbling down the lane, followed by a rider on a dappled gray horse.

A very tall rider.

She watched as two gentlemen stepped out of the coach, the second one offering his hand to the round little lady who followed him.

Their housekeeper and cook, Mrs. Hayward, was in the midst of baking, the maid was outside hanging washing, and Lang had gone to fetch the boys home from their studies, which had resumed once Paul began to feel better.

Sybil glanced in the mirror and sighed. The gown she'd donned in the morning was three years old and looked it.

Still, it wouldn't do to keep a pregnant lady standing outside while she changed. Tucking a hair in place with a trembling hand, she went to answer the knock on the door.

This visit might be one more step in Sir Westcott's attempt to woo her. Or it might be him saying goodbye.

To which she would add good riddance. His presence, his kisses, his fisticuffs, none of that would restore her good reputation in Normanton. That would take months, perhaps years, of her good behavior.

She opened the door and at the sight of Sir Westcott's face, her breath caught. His jaw bore a dark bruise. One swollen eye sat in a circle of purple worse than the bruise below.

His grin, though, never faltered, as he brushed away comments about his injuries and made introductions.

Mrs. Honoria Kellborn was a pleasant-looking lady with hair that was either light brown or dark blond, and eyes that radiated good humor and kindness. Major August Kellborn was a handsome man of middling years, dark-haired and shorter than Sybil. The man with them was Gus's friend, Lord Edward Greely, a wealthy baron who owned the yacht that carried the Kellborns home. He'd come along to join the party at Highcross Keep for a few days while his yacht went on to Southampton for repairs.

The scent of baking cakes and bread filling the air, Sybil assembled a tea tray. Sir Westcott's stepmother had insisted on following Sybil into the kitchen. She'd settled happily at the plain deal table where Mrs. Hayward had only recently been rolling out dough.

Far from being put out by the invasion, the servant had, after the initial shock, happily compared recipes for apple tarts.

When the water had heated and Sybil had piled a tray high with cakes and biscuits, they moved back to the parlor to await the men, who'd gone to look over Sybil's Essex pigs. She wondered if Sir Westcott's stepmother had arranged this chance to interview Sybil alone.

While they made small talk about the Kellborns' travels, Sybil couldn't avoid a spark of envy, wondering whether that was how her brothers felt when they watched the ships sailing past Brighton.

"You have a fine kitchen here," Mrs. Kellborn said. "I fear my new home, Whitlaw Grange, might not be quite as modern."

"You haven't seen it yet?"

"Not as yet. Major Kellborn whisked me off to the Continent a few weeks after our marriage." She reached for a portfolio that Sybil hadn't noticed. "Come and sit next to me. I'll show you some of the drawings that Wes always teases me about."

Sybil moved next to her, conscious of the lady's mild floral scent and the swell of her abdomen under her modest carriage gown. There were sketches of the cathedral in Palermo, others of Paris and York, and some of a large Tudor-style manor house of gray stone.

"Twisden Manor," she said proudly. "It's a fine old house. Larger than this one, but not so grand and stately that one can't find a warm room in the winter. After Wes's father's death, we gave it a most thorough cleaning from attic to cellar. He was excessively fond of dogs. We also installed a marvelous bathing chamber, which Gus has promised to replicate for me at Whitlaw Grange."

Sybil's stomach churned with a rising discomfort. Sir Westcott had brought this kind lady to tempt her.

I'm not going to marry him. She wanted to shout the words.

But had he actually asked her to marry him? He talked about courting. He talked about moving her pigs there. He kissed her.

"I fear..." Sybil cleared her throat and began again. "Your son has told me he'd like to court me. I don't know if he still holds that wish, but please know that I have no intentions of marrying. I have great responsibilities here with the farm and my brothers, especially the younger ones."

"And boys can be such a challenge," Mrs. Kellborn said. She went on to tell stories of Sir Westcott's childhood, his peccadilloes, and his attention to Twisden Manor and to her, both before and after his father's death.

The lady's description of Sir Westcott's appearance on her doorstep in York with Major Kellborn and the Major's dog in tow made Sybil laugh.

"Yes, he can be impetuous," Mrs. Kellborn said. "What young man isn't at times? Like when a young man is defending a lady's honor." She tilted her head, studying Sybil and finally smiling. "At his core, he is steady. And good. Like my Gus."

The steady and good men entered then, escorted by her three brothers whom they'd met near the stable. While Sir Westcott and the boys attacked the cakes, Sybil poured tea and answered the major's questions about her pigs.

Without looking, she could feel Sir Westcott's attention upon her, so much so that instead of calling for Mrs. Hayward to bring more tea and cakes, or sending the boys, she went off to the kitchen herself.

Sir Westcott caught up with her there.

"I'm to help you carry things," he said, standing too close.

The servant cast a curious glance their way, her mouth dropping open at the sight of him.

"Ignore the, er, bruise," he said, and complimented her baking, and while Sybil busied herself with filling the tray, Mrs. Hayward chatted away with him.

"Your mother's a dear lady," the servant said.

"She is indeed."

"Here now, Miss Sybil, you and your young man leave that. I'll finish and I'll carry it in."

"He's not..." Sybil bit down on the rest of the sentence and allowed herself to be shooed out of the kitchen.

Once in the outside passage, Sir Westcott pulled her aside.

"I've been worried about you," he said. "I ought to have come sooner, but this is the first day I can see out of this eye."

She scoffed. "A brawl, Sir Westcott. I fear you've made matters worse."

"Then let me fix them."

Before she could find words, he'd tucked her hand over his arm and towed her along to the parlor.

All heads turned their way. Wes's mother beamed her a smile. The men's eyes twinkled, and her brothers smiled slyly.

"Well?" Lang asked.

Her breath fled her on a sudden attack of panic. Sir Westcott clamped a hand over hers.

He turned to face her. "My dear Miss Dunsford—"

"*Sir Westcott*," she hissed quietly, "let me go."

He went on, ignoring her. "I dare not kneel lest you try to scarper in the midst of..."

With a deep breath, he smiled a nervous smile. Perspiration sheened his high forehead, illuminating another bruise that she hadn't noticed.

Heart pounding, she looked up at him.

Up. That was certainly a consideration.

"Miss Dunsford," he said in a strong voice, "marry me. Make me the happiest of men."

Warmth rushed into her cheeks, draining all the blood from her brain, rendering her speechless. She looked straight ahead at his lips —spotting another healing battle wound there—fearful of what she might see in his eyes. Triumph? Oh, that would make her spit nails.

One of the twins giggled.

The chill of his hands made her look up again and her breath caught on what she saw there. Not triumph, but vulnerability in Wes's eyes, the eyes of a steady and good man who was offering his heart and tempting her beyond her wildest imaginings.

Quickly glancing away, she saw that the major had taken a seat next to his wife and was holding her hand.

Affection between a man and wife. Might she have such a marriage with Wes?

Wes. She was thinking of him as *Wes*. What was wrong with her?

Ducking her head, she cleared her throat, finding some moisture.

The big booby watched her with his black eye, bruises and that open-faced look of expectation and worry.

Moisture threatened, and she blinked it away, mustering some dignity.

"You do me a great honor, sir."

That was true, she realized. He could do better than a farm girl on the lowest rung of the gentry.

Instinct and her own common sense told her he wasn't a fortune hunter. Not that she was in possession of a fortune.

They shared a passion for farming. He was amiable, slow to anger, and loved his stepmother. He was quite handsome. And so very tall. And he kissed so very well.

Was that enough to pledge the rest of her life?

In all their interactions, he'd been kind, to her as well as to her brothers.

Her brothers. The boys whom she'd raised and promised a home forever. Her only family. She must think of them.

She shook her head. "You do me a great honor sir, but... Devil's Dyke Grange... the farm... this is our home. Mine and my brothers'."

"Sybie," Lang said, reminding her that they had an audience and sending another rush of heat to her cheeks. "Cass, and Paul, and I, we're not farmers. It's not in our blood like it is in yours. Our da was a merchant trader. You'd never have found him chasing pigs or over-seeing a harvest."

"We don't begrudge you getting the farm instead of us," Paul said.

"Yes." Cass picked up the thread. "Why not marry Wes? He's a trump fellow. Besides, you'll never meet anyone as tall as him."

Before she could answer, Mrs. Hayward bustled in from the kitchen with a tray.

"How delightful," Sir Westcott's mother said, "won't you stay a moment Mrs. Hayward and tell me your recipe for these delicious lemon cakes?"

⚜

Wes watched the color that had drenched Sybil's cheeks drain away, and her hands were trembling. Or maybe he was the one trembling.

She was going to say no, if for no other reason than out of pure embarrassment.

Taking advantage of the cook's distraction, he led Sybil out into the hall, and all the way to the warm kitchen.

"You don't have to decide now," he said, turning her to face him.

Eyes shining, she shook her head. "That night, Sir Westcott, I... The rumors will die down. It was only a kiss. Or two. There's no reason to think you must marry me, and I won't be forced into it."

"No. I wouldn't want that either. I'd want you to marry me because we share things. A love for the land. And our families."

He eased in a breath, watching a new blush tint her cheeks and her eyes grow shiny. He wasn't the most persuasive of fellows, but he must find a way.

"I... I would hope that you might, someday, see how much I admire you. And care for you. If you don't care for me now, I'd hope that I might someday win your love as you have won mine."

The astonishment on her face made him huff out a laugh and nod. "Yes. It's true. I love you."

He'd rendered her speechless, and he gave into temptation, touching his lips to hers—tenderly, given his injuries—and then he pulled her closer. His hand trailed down to her waist, and then instinctively moved lower.

She pulled away quickly and ducked her head, resting her forehead against his cheek. "Crofton. Is it truly over with him?"

"It will be soon. Butley's turned on him. Besides that, there's a magistrate in Brighton looking into the loans Crofton bought. Lewis might even get his farm back."

"How?"

"Seems someone got hold of all of Crofton's records, not just yours."

"How... what did you do?"

"I'll tell you later. After... well, you know a wife can't give evidence against her husband."

Sybil laughed and shook her head. "The farm—"

"I have an idea about that. If you say yes."

She eyed him speculatively. "And then you'll tell me? Well, I won't have a husband who brawls. You mustn't go to blows on my account."

"If I'm not your husband, I needs must defend my own reputation as well as yours, at least until I leave Sussex. But if I *am* your husband, as the luckiest man in the world, I'll be above all of that."

He swept a thumb along the smooth skin of her cheek. "Say yes, Sybil. Put me out of my misery."

Eyes shining, she nodded, and with a whoop, he picked her up, swung her around, and then kissed her.

Ever so gently.

EPILOGUE

W es tossed the lines to a grinning Hayward, jumped down from the gig he'd hired a few days ago, then reached for the bundle that was a shivering Sybil.

Shivering from the late October chill or were her nerves thrumming like his?

He lifted her down and set her on her feet and dropped a quick kiss. A longer one was in order except that the Haywards were present, Ruth looking on expectantly from the front step of Devil's Dyke Grange.

"How was the ball, dear ones?" Mrs. Hayward asked, opening the door for them.

They'd left the ball at Normanton House early, abandoning the Picard boys to find beds for the night elsewhere.

"Eventful," Sybil said. "A duke attended wearing a footman's livery, Foreign Office men arrested a spy, a Bow Street runner accused a guest of being Captain Moonlight, and more than one betrothal was announced."

"And did anyone mention *your* marriage?" the housekeeper asked.

Wes grinned and handed the housekeeper Sybil's blanket. "We didn't stay long enough for an announcement."

They'd discussed calling banns, but when the Kellborns changed their plans about staying longer, Wes fetched a common license from Chichester. He and Sybil had been married that very morning in the village church by the local curate, Mr. Pendleton.

At the threshold, Wes hoisted his new bride, evoking a protest. "You did this part already."

"With so many blasted people around, we didn't get to proceed to—"

She set a finger to his lips, while the housekeeper turned away chuckling.

"Left some of those meat pies you liked so well, Sir Westcott," she said. "'Spect you'll be hungry in a bit."

"Best let these young people get on with it, Ruth," Hayward called. "They'll be wanting to get to bed."

The chuckling servants led the gig around to the back of the house.

"Finally," Wes said. "We're alone."

He eased her to her feet in the small hall and pushed back her heavy mantle. The pale blue ballgown was the same color as her bridal gown, but this one, with its low neckline and shimmering trim, showed off her creamy skin and the diamond-framed sapphire nestling above her breasts, his wedding gift to her.

"You were, truly, the most beautiful lady there tonight." He blinked, suddenly overcome that a girl so fine should throw in her lot with a fellow like him.

"It's the gown. How kind of your mother to help me decide on the color."

"It's not the gown making you beautiful. In fact..." A hot rush of desire had him easing in a breath. They hadn't had more than a moment's privacy since they'd said their vows. "In fact, let me get you out of it and check whether I'm right."

⚜

Sybil heard rustling at the grate and her eyes flew open to bright daylight. For one startled moment, her gaze filled with the backside of a man bent over the hearth.

A very tall, very naked man with a very well-muscled backside.

She closed her eyes tightly as the big body sank onto the mattress making the bed ropes creak and her insides heat with anticipation.

Her wedding night had been a revelation.

A shivery cold finger traced a line down her cheek, and she bit back a smile.

"You're not asleep," Wes said. "Thought I'd feed the fire before we get up. It's well past dawn." He pressed a kiss to her cheek. "*Should* we get up?"

A chuckle escaped her, and she turned toward him. "We're to call at Highcross Keep this afternoon." Gus and Honoria had decided to set out the next day for home, traveling by easy stages. Lord Greely would leave as well for Southampton, bringing along Cass to join his crew, and Lang, whom he promised to introduce to a friend with a shipping company. Paul would return to school.

He nuzzled her neck. "That's hours away."

"And we need to settle a few things with Reggie."

Reggie's mother, brother, and his brother's surprise new bride had unexpectedly arrived in time for the Somerville ball. The new mistress of Highcross Keep was a starchy earl's daughter. When Wes and Sybil suggested he lease Devil's Dyke Grange, Reggie jumped at the chance. And of course, Quinton was joining him.

"Reggie's not really a rattlepate," Wes said. "Devil's Dyke Grange will be fine in his care." He trailed kisses along her jaw and murmured, "I adore you, you know."

"Oh." A surge of moisture made her sniff.

It had taken some convincing, and a well-written marriage settlement leaving the farm in her ownership, but she'd finally seen that Wes genuinely understood her.

In her experience that was a rare and very dear quality. She wiped away a tear and smiled. "I rather like you, as well."

He lifted his head. "Like?"

"Very well, love. I love you, Sir Westcott Twisden. You've stolen my heart."

A sly grin curved his lips. "My darling girl. We'd best stay in bed longer. We have plenty of time until the afternoon," he said, and then set about proving it.

THE END

If you enjoyed Wes and Sybil's story, check out the sweet romance of Wes's stepmother, Honoria:

After years of tolerating her late husband, Honoria Twisden has escaped to York to enjoy her new freedom. Then her stepson unexpectedly appears with a long-lost relation in tow. Find **Lady Twisden's Picture Perfect Match** here https://books2read.com/LadyTwisdensPicturePerfectMatch.

SOCIAL MEDIA FOR ALINA K. FIELD

You can learn more about Alina K. Field at these social media links:

Facebook: https://www.facebook.com/alinakfield
X: https://X.com/AlinaKField
BookBub: https://www.bookbub.com/authors/alina-k-field
Instagram: https://www.instagram.com/alinak.field/
Goodreads: https://www.goodreads.com/author/show/7173518.
Alina_K_Field
Pinterest: https://www.pinterest.com/alinakf/
Newsletter signup: https://landing.mailerlite.com/webforms/landing/
z6q6e3

ABOUT ALINA K. FIELD

USA Today bestselling author Alina K. Field earned a Bachelor of Arts Degree in English and German literature but prefers the happier world of historical romance fiction. Her roots are in the Midwestern U.S., but after six very, very, very cold years in Chicago, she moved to Southern California where she shares a midcentury home with a golden-eyed terrier and a feisty chihuahua and only occasionally misses snow.

Learn more about Alina at
Website: https://alinakfield.com/
Newsletter signup: https://landing.mailerlite.com/webforms/landing/
z6q6e3

THE CASEBOOK OF
PRINCIPAL OFFICER ROBERT
PIERCE

Brighton and surrounding districts

Lieutenant Miles has his man, or a man, anyway. A fellow named Crofton was caught imprisoned in a shed full of contraband. His accomplice claims that the ghost shut the door on them. Whoever locked them in, there's no doubt that Crofton is a villain. Not only was he smuggling, but he was forging documents to blackmail people out of their properties.

On my own cases, I've had nothing but frustration. I keep trying, and sooner or later, the clue that is the key to the whole puzzle will come to my attention.

A DUKE IN PERIL

MEARA PLATT

A Duke in Peril
By Meara Platt

Lady Florence Swann's quiet life is upended when she finds a handsome soldier wounded on the side of the road near Swann Hall, the country estate where she and her grandfather reside. Captain James Ryder claims to be the Duke of Wellbourne's emissary and carries a letter concerning a Foreign Office matter. Is he more than he appears, and perhaps the duke himself? Can Florence trust her heart to him?

CHAPTER 1

Swann Hall
Sussex, England
October 1817

"Samuel, stop the carriage!" Lady Florence Swann called to her driver when she noticed a massive black stallion standing by the side of the road and nibbling on sweet gorse. The beast was saddled, but it was the rider sprawled motionless on the grass beside the animal who commanded her attention.

Was this another robbery attempt gone bad?

Were those men galloping off in the distance the ones who had attacked him?

Lately, these robberies had been happening with concerning regularity along this quiet stretch of road between Brighton and her grandfather's country estate, Swann Hall.

"Whoa," the faithful family retainer cried and immediately drew the team to a halt. He reached for the hunting rifle kept close at hand. "Be careful, m'lady. It could be a trap."

"Aye, m'lady," said Ethan, the young footman who had been assigned to accompany her on her errands upon her grandfather's insistence because of the lurking dangers. "Stay inside the carriage while I see what's what."

She waited with impatience, worried about the injured man and knowing she had to get to him fast.

"All clear, m'lady."

She hopped down and ran to the fellow, kneeling beside him to carefully check the damage. "Ethan, did you notice those men riding off as we approached? They must have been the ones who set upon him, for his wounds look fresh. Oh, dear. Why would they hurt him?"

"Good thing they left his beast alone," Ethan muttered. "Magnificent bit of horseflesh."

"Which suggests his rider is a gentleman of means. Only the elite could ever afford a horse as fine as that Friesian."

"Why did they not steal it?" he asked.

"Too distinctive an animal for them to dare take. A fine specimen, isn't he?"

The footman nodded as he cautiously approached the skittish horse and patted him gently to soothe him. "Look at the muscles on the fellow."

The same could be said of his rider, Florence noted as she carefully ran her hands along the man's broad shoulders and back while he lay face down on the grass. "A thief could never sell such an exquisite beast without immediately arousing suspicion. I'm glad those brigands did not harm the horse. Unfortunately, his rider did not fare so well. But I think we might have saved his life by coming along when we did."

"Aye, true," said Samuel, stepping down from his driver's perch to assist her as she struggled to turn the man over without causing him more harm. "I was about to blow my horn to scare off his attackers, but they must have seen us first, for they rode off right quick the moment our carriage came over the rise. Still, be careful, m'lady. The bloke looks to be a big fellow and strong."

"I wonder who he is?" Her heart fluttered as she perused his face and muscled form. "But look, he must be army. He's wearing an officer's uniform. Keep alert, Sam. You too, Ethan. Those brigands might become emboldened and decide to return to finish the job they started."

"Unlikely, m'lady. But we'll be ready if they do," Samuel assured, raising his hunting rifle to show her that he had it in hand.

Ethan also had his weapon drawn, holding it in one hand while keeping hold of the Friesian's reins with the other.

This recent spate of highway robberies had everyone on edge. Florence had taken to carrying a lady's pistol in her reticule for this very reason, although she hoped never to have to use it.

Were it not for her need of new clothes, particularly a suitably elegant gown for the ball to be held at Normanton House next week, Florence would not be making these constant visits to her Brighton modiste. But Aria Rocatti was a wonder, and Florence refused to consider going elsewhere for her new gowns.

The horse snorted several times and skittered backwards, but Florence's gaze was fixed on the handsome fellow on the ground. His hair was as black as the coat on his stallion. His face was manly but still held a youthful vigor, so she estimated his age to be in his late twenties or early thirties.

There was an ugly gash on the man's forehead that was dripping blood down the side of his face. His knuckles were bruised and swollen, and so was his face. "He must have fought fiercely."

She quickly checked the rest of his body and inhaled sharply upon noting the pool of blood on the wool of his uniform jacket. "Oh, dear. He's been shot. There's a tear in the fabric just below his ribs."

She unbuttoned his jacket to get a closer look at his wound, then withdrew her handkerchief and carefully dabbed at the blood that had soaked his shirt bright crimson at the spot. "I think the ball went clean through, but hard to tell for certain. There's a lot of blood. Poor fellow. However, I see no other serious wounds."

She put a hand over his chest in the hope of feeling a heartbeat. "Ethan, he's alive, but barely. We must get him to Swann Hall right away."

"M'lady, is it wise?" His eyes rounded in surprise at the suggestion. "We have no idea who he is. He might have been one of those brigands and had a falling out with his companions."

"Highly unlikely, the fellow is obviously rich," she said, taking the shawl off her shoulders and wrapping it around his torso to fashion a tourniquet of a sort. She hoped it would hold sufficiently until they got him back home. "His horse alone gives him away. But also look at the fine leather of his boots." She groped around the inside of his jacket for some document or other item that might give hint of his identity.

Goodness, his body was quite solid.

"I feel something," she muttered, withdrawing an official looking document. "The seal is broken. It is a letter addressed to the Duke of Wellbourne. Oh, a meeting of some sort to take place between someone by the name of Lord Meade and the duke's emissary. This man must be the emissary."

"Seems someone meant to stop him from ever reaching their meeting spot," Samuel remarked.

She perused the letter that gave a vague reference to a dangerous plot, details to be given when he and Lord Meade met at the Somerville ball to be held next week at Normanton House.

The very one she was attending.

She did not see how this man would heal in time. Only someone with the constitution of a bull could ever recover so rapidly.

Should she get involved? Offer her assistance?

After all, she and her grandfather would be there. It would take but a few minutes to seek out Lord Meade and tell him what had transpired.

"M'lady, we ought not linger," Ethan advised.

"Right." The letter caught in the stiff breeze and fluttered in her hand. She tucked it into the bodice of her gown for safekeeping, and then glanced up at the row of soft, white clouds dotting the deep blue sky. It was a cold afternoon, particularly cold for October, and not even the brightness of the sun could provide significant warmth. "Help me get this man into the carriage."

The footman sighed and shook his head. "It'll take more than the two of us, m'lady." He called Samuel over, and the three of them finally managed to haul him onto one of the leather seat benches.

Florence scampered in and decided to squeeze in beside him rather than sit across from him, carefully maneuvering so that his head rested upon her lap. This way, she could keep better hold of him during the ride home. It would also be easier for her to apply pressure to his ribs in order to stem the bleeding.

Ethan mounted the big Friesian who proved to be a gentle creature and offered no resistance when he climbed onto the saddle.

"Well trained beast," he told Florence, giving her a nod of approval when she peered out the carriage window.

She eased back against the squabs and studied the man quietly resting in her arms. "Let's hope you are as tame as your beast, sir."

Samuel snapped the reins and the carriage jerked forward at a lively pace, unfortunately seeming to hit every bump in the road as they traveled fast. "Hold on, sir. We'll soon have you home and properly tended."

But she was worried.

Both her shawl and handkerchief were completely soaked in blood, and she could not tell if her ministrations were slowing the flow.

The gash on his forehead also oozed blood, but it was now a mere trickle.

"How much longer, Samuel?" The injured man was restless, and Florence's arms were beginning to ache from the effort of holding him in place.

"Swann Hall coming into view, m'lady."

"Thank goodness," she muttered, afraid he would knock them both off the seat bench if he persisted in trying to sit up. "Please, sir. You mustn't. I have you, but you must lie quietly. We're almost home."

She kept her voice soft and lilting since this seemed to soothe him.

"Turnin' up the drive, m'lady," Samuel called out as the horses sped toward the manor house, a lovely brick structure with ivy climbing up the walls.

Ethan rode ahead to summon their staff for help.

A small army of footmen scurried out of the house along with her grandfather as the carriage drew up in front of the house.

"We're here, sir," she whispered, leaning closer.

The man's eyes flickered open to stare at her.

Her breath hitched, for his eyes were extraordinarily beautiful, a magnificent, dark gray. Quite splendid...and dangerous. "You're awake."

He drew her even closer, as though to whisper something in her ear.

But instead of talking, he captured her mouth in a scorching kiss that lasted no more than the count of three.

Dear heaven.

It was enough to mark her soul.

He released her with a groan and sank back onto her lap. "Who are you, lass?"

Lass?

She was a lady and almost the age of three and twenty.

"Lady Florence Swann," she said stiffly. "Something you might have bothered to find out before you kissed me."

His chuckle was deep and resonant. "Do not berate me, Florence."

Ugh.

Why was he being so familiar with her?

It was bad enough he'd kissed her, but to now address her as though they had been lifelong friends?

Sighing, she decided not to chastise him since he was not well and the damage had already been done. "Why did you kiss me, sir?"

"It was most improper, I know. But should I not be permitted to kiss my angel?"

She laughed. "Oh, I hardly think I am that."

"You are an angel, Florence. *Mine,*" he insisted, taking hold of her hand as it rested on his chest.

Honestly, if he knew her better, he would not be calling her anyone's angel.

Much less *his.*

Nor should he be holding onto her hand.

In truth, it felt awfully nice even though his palm was rough and his knuckles were bruised and swollen.

She meant to protest but never got the chance, for the man had gone limp in her arms again.

Her grandfather threw open the carriage door and stared at the big fellow lying motionless in her embrace.

"Hello, Grandfather."

"Oh, Florence. What mischief have you got into this time?"

CHAPTER 2

"Bloody blazes." James Ryder, Duke of Wellbourne, awoke to bursts of pain as he tried to sit up. Apparently, being a duke did not magically exempt him from the aches and pains of lesser beings.

Not that he ever believed in such nonsense about the privileged peerage.

"Sir, lie still."

He blinked against the glare of sunlight as a woman with an achingly sweet voice he recognized from earlier put a moistened handkerchief over his eyes, no doubt to calm his restlessness.

He fell back against a soft pile of pillows, relieved to be in the care of his gentle angel. "Florence?"

"Yes," she said with a merry lilt that warmed the corners of his heart. "I'm surprised you remembered my name."

He recalled everything about this young woman, even though he had known her for the length of a carriage ride and been out cold for most of it.

"Please lie still. I'm right here and can fetch you whatever you need."

"And where is 'right here'?" The last he recalled before the lovely

Florence had saved him, he was sprawled on the hard ground along a roadway north of Brighton, oozing his lifeblood.

Having spent much of his adulthood in the military, he had resigned himself to dying on a battlefield or in some other valiant manner and found it galling he had almost died at the hands of some inept brigands while on his way to meet Lord Meade.

Indeed, how galling to have almost lost his life when he was about to bring his Foreign Office assignment to a successful end.

Florence cleared her throat. "Right *here* happens to be Swann Hall, the home of Lord Rupert Swann. I am his granddaughter."

"That's right," he said with a slight nod, "you mentioned it when you rescued me."

"More important, do you remember *your* name, sir?"

Fortunately, he did.

But he also knew it was safest not to disclose he was the Duke of Wellbourne. Apparently, not everyone was pleased with the work he had been doing on the Continent alongside Lord Castlereagh to secure a lasting peace.

Just who was undermining his mission was a mystery about to be revealed when he met with his stepbrother, Lord Meade, the one who had written him the letter.

"Sir, can you tell me your name?"

Gad, her voice was a glorious mix of sweet and sultry, as deliciously smooth as a fine, aged scotch sliding down one's throat.

"I certainly hope so." He removed the moistened handkerchief she had earlier placed over his eyes, for he wanted a good look at her. "Captain James Ryder, at your service."

She cast him an indulgent smile, obviously waiting for him to say more.

Did she know he also happened to be a duke?

He thought perhaps not.

She was not fluttering or cooing around him as she would be if aware of his elevated status.

Perhaps he was making too much of his title.

He studied the angelic face he remembered looking down on him as he lay bleeding and certain he would die, quite entranced by those green eyes the color of dark emeralds staring back at him.

Florence was beautiful in a warm, and adorable way, what with the wild mass of ginger-gold curls that would look lovely tumbled upon a man's bed sheets, and a sweet, heart-shaped face that spoke of her lively intelligence.

Her ears were soft and small, and her nose was also small but had an impudent point at the end.

Her mouth also had an impudent look to it because the ends had a slight droop that made her look as though she were pouting.

It was a sensual pout.

Not that of a spoiled child.

Her lips themselves were shaped like an archer's elegant longbow. He had noticed their graceful curve while Florence fussed over him in the carriage.

How could he be faulted for wanting to kiss her, to taste the sweet honey of her mouth?

"I have not forgotten my name," he said, "nor shall I ever forget yours, or that you are the angel who rescued me."

She laughed once more as she sank onto the chair beside his bed. "I cannot take all the credit, Captain Ryder. I had plenty of help in saving you. It was a group effort to haul you into my carriage and then get you upstairs into one of our guest bedchambers. My grand-father is the one who stitched you up."

"He did?"

"Yes, he is not a surgeon by profession but was medically trained while in the army in his younger days. He is the one who really deserves the credit for saving your life."

"Then I look forward to thanking him, too." He went to touch his forehead, but she stopped him by taking hold of his hand.

Hers was soft and little, but purposeful as she set his own back at his side. "No, sir. You mustn't touch the stitches, they're still too fresh."

Which meant he hadn't been unconscious all that long.

Good.

By the position of the sun shining through the windows of his elegantly appointed bedchamber, he thought it might be late afternoon. The blue silk drapes had been drawn aside to allow light to flood into the room, something he appreciated because it allowed him to make a clear assessment of his surroundings.

He had been shot sometime in the early afternoon, which meant he could not have been unconscious more than an hour or two.

Not that it mattered, for he was receiving excellent care and felt he was now on the road to recovery.

Still, he did not like losing control of a situation or ever being at anyone's mercy, not even at the tender mercy of this beautiful young lady. When she leaned forward slightly, he caught the captivating scent of her, or perhaps he was merely hungry, for breathing her in was like breathing in a deliciously warm hot cross bun with a hint of cinnamon.

Lips of honey.

Cinnamon scent to her skin.

Yes, he was definitely hungry for food as well as for her.

"I recall one of those bounders struck me with the butt of his rifle," he said, returning to the matter of the scoundrels who had set upon him.

She nodded. "Gave you a solid crack to your skull that required six stitches."

"Only six?" He cast her a sloppy grin. "Could have been worse, I suppose. Fortunately, I have a hard head."

"My grandfather thinks I am quite hardheaded, too." She returned his smile, but it was all too brief as she moved on to recount the rest of what had happened to him. "But another one of those villains came dreadfully close to doing you in. Fortunately, his aim was wide of the mark, and he missed your vital organs. You are also fortunate the shot went clean through, ripping through your skin just below your ribs. That wound required twenty stitches to repair."

He grunted, for he was feeling a sharp pain there, too.

"We gave you laudanum earlier and can give you more now, should you need it."

"No, Florence. I won't be needing it ever."

She frowned at him. "How do you know? You will certainly feel more soreness now that you are awake."

"I probably will, but I'm still not taking anything that might dull my senses. I need to keep my wits about me."

"Sir, you are safe here. No one is going to hurt you while you recover at Swann Hall. And do not think to get out of bed," she chided when he attempted to do just that.

A blinding pain immediately tore through him, and he fell back with a groan. "Botheration, that hurt."

"You stubborn man, did I not just tell you to lie still? You were badly injured and lost a lot of blood. Not even a prime specimen such as yourself can hop out of bed like a grasshopper on a jaunt through a spring meadow."

He grinned. "You think I am a prime specimen?"

She rolled her eyes. "I am sure every woman in England feels the same, Captain Ryder. But I am certain you know it. You do not strike me as particularly bashful."

"What makes you think I am not bashful?"

She emitted a trill of laughter. "Because you are obviously comfortable wearing not a stitch of clothing. Do you not realize you are *naked?*" She whispered the word as though she were speaking of something sinful. "Why do you think I stopped you from pulling your covers aside?"

He looked down at himself, noting his bare arms and chest.

He peeked under the covers, as well.

"Oh, good grief," she muttered, turning away with a light blush to her cheeks.

He smiled, liking that she was modest and not suggestively gawking at him as most women would do. He understood the fairer sex found him attractive. "What did you do with my clothes, Florence?"

"Sent to the laundress in the hope of removing the bloodstains. She is a wonder and seems able to get stains out of everything. I'll do my best to mend the damage to your shirt and jacket once she has them cleaned. And just to be clear, I did not undress you. In fact, I was banished from the room while my grandfather and the footmen attended to you."

"But you are here now, and I am still without clothes."

"You are fully covered," she insisted.

"That begs the point. Why has your grandfather allowed you to remain by my side without a chaperone?" He understood the impropriety of a genteel, young lady in his bedchamber and wondered if he was being purposely placed in a compromising situation.

Had she seen the letter addressed to the Duke of Wellbourne?

Did she realize he was the duke and not merely his emissary?

Florence did not appear to have a conniving nature, but perhaps her grandfather was not so genial. Was this not something he needed to be more watchful of while in their care?

Ladies often flirted with him and welcomed him into their beds. However, he was always careful to choose his conquests for their lack of innocence, their shoddy morals, and their already married status.

Yes, married ladies were safest, and he liked it just fine that way.

No complications.

Florence regarded him oddly, and pointed in the direction of several large, cushioned chairs beside the hearth. "But I am not alone with you, Captain Ryder. I have never been left alone with you. My grandfather is here with us, although he seems to have fallen asleep in the chair. The poor dear stayed up all night by your bedside to watch for signs of infection."

"All night? Wait... how long have I been unconscious?"

"A full day, and I will not deny you had us quite worried. But I think it was a good thing you were not awake while we cleaned the blood off you and attended to the most serious injuries. Our ministrations would have given you agonizing pain otherwise."

He was still in significant pain but had no intention of complaining about it.

Florence frowned and then continued. "My grandfather managed to get a little laudanum in you while he stitched the gash to your forehead and the wound just under your ribs, but it wasn't nearly enough and has long since worn off. The other cuts and bruises were minor and easily treated, so we gave you nothing for those."

She nibbled her sweet lips for a moment before reaching out to lightly run the back of her hand along his neck.

He liked her gentle touch.

"You haven't developed a fever yet. That is very good, and your eyes look clear."

"Another good sign?"

She nodded. "Do you know who attacked you?"

"No, my angel."

She rolled her eyes. "I am not your angel."

Yes, she was.

He continued to study Florence because he seemed unable to tear his gaze away.

She had dimples when she smiled, and her eyes had a lovely sparkle to them.

Well, seems he had a weakness for dimples and sparkles.

He cleared his throat. "I had a letter with me..."

She smiled again just as the sun burst forth from behind a soft cloud and shone through the window to encircle her in a golden light. "Oh, yes. I have it in my bedchamber for safekeeping. Give me a moment and I'll fetch it for you. Shall I also have some broth brought up? Are you hungry?"

"No food yet, I'm not certain I can hold anything down. But I would like that letter. Did you read it?"

She gave a curt nod.

"Then you know who I am?"

"Yes, Captain James Ryder, the Duke of Wellbourne's emissary. Obviously, this correspondence is quite sensitive. I only read it because I was looking for something to identify you in the event... well, in the event you did not survive. You were in a very bad way yesterday."

"Who else knows of my connection to the duke?"

"Besides me, only my grandfather, our carriage driver, Samuel, and our footman, Ethan. Samuel and Ethan escorted me to my Brighton modiste."

"And were with you when you found me?"

"Yes, but you needn't worry about them gossiping. And I've only shown my grandfather the contents of your letter. I've warned them all to tell no one of your relation to the duke. They can be trusted to keep a confidence. Lord Meade was not wrong in his concern for you, apparently. I assure you, we shall all remain tight-lipped for now."

"I hope you are right. Servants have a tendency to gossip."

"Samuel and Ethan are more like family than servants. They are completely honorable and know how to be discreet. Same for me and my grandfather. No one has to know anything until you are ready to reveal yourself."

He chuckled. "I fear I have already revealed too much of myself."

After all, he was stark naked beneath the covers.

She may not have seen all of him, but those covers were only drawn up to his waist. Was this not scandalous enough?

The girl was innocent, he realized when the jest brought a soft blush to her cheeks.

He liked this about her, too.

"Captain Ryder, if anyone asks about you, what shall we tell them?"

He gave it a moment's thought, not liking to hide his true identity from Florence, but it was necessary for now. "Just tell them I am an acquaintance of your grandfather's who was set upon by brigands while on his way to Swann Hall."

"All right, but I might have to embellish a little. Those men who attacked you were not our usual crop of highwaymen." She edged her chair closer to his bed. "Do you know who they were?"

"Not a clue." He studied her when she leaned her elbows on the mattress and tried to stifle a yawn. He realized she must have been up much of the night along with her grandfather and was now exhausted, although she had managed to hide it well until now.

Her eyes still had a pretty sparkle to them.

"I only saw your assailants from a distance, but there appeared to be six of them, by my count," she said, nipping her lower lip as she gave the incident some thought, "I did find it odd there were so many. I have never known our local brigands to operate other than alone or in pairs, such as our Captain Moonlight, since it means more profit for them if they do not have a gang to share the spoils."

He arched an eyebrow. "My, that was quite detailed. Does this mean you are friendly with your local thieves?"

"Well, no," she said with another blush to indicate she was not being completely truthful with him. "But one does have one's suspicions, doesn't one? Especially when one has lived here all of one's life and has come to know most people around here."

"Is that so? Are you *one* of those local brigands? Is this how you and your grandfather maintain your elegant home?" he teased, suspecting Florence had not an ounce of larceny in her soul. In truth, she seemed good in every sense of the word. Good-hearted. Good-natured. Good morals – *too bad about that one.*

Since she was not the sort to give away her favors, he had to keep his hands off her even though he would have liked to have them all over her. "Or perhaps you are Captain Moonlight? How intriguing, a female highwayman."

"I have never stolen so much as a button in my life," she retorted, unaware of his straying thoughts. "It is simply that *our* thieves do not attempt to kill their quarry."

"Are you saying they are kind and gentle thieves?"

She sighed. "You are mocking me, but it is true. No one around here would do you such harm. Perhaps we ought to send word to the local magistrate. Would it not help to have him and his constables on alert? The more hands, the better, you know. This crime was egregious and really ought to be reported."

"No," he insisted. "Those men were after me and have no interest in harming anyone else. Nor will your magistrate ever find out who they are because I am certain these culprits are not local."

"Then it has to do with London and the Foreign Office?"

"Florence, I cannot talk about my business."

Florence pursed her lips. "Should you not get a missive off to Lord Meade? Will he not be worried, or perhaps might not attend the Somerville ball if he thinks you are dead?"

"Those villains cannot possibly be certain they killed me because they rode off before confirming I had drawn my last breath."

"But what if they lie about this in order to collect their fee?"

He cast her an indulgent smile. "You like this sort of thing, don't you?"

"What? Intrigue? Not really. I am more of a homebody. But you are in a dangerous situation, and does it not make sense to talk through all the possibilities?"

"That is good of you, Florence. But I am experienced at this sort of thing. Lord Meade will attend the Somerville party. He will not believe I am dead until he sees an actual body."

"Oh, I see. Of course. Captain Ryder——"

"Call me James when we are in private. Captain Ryder when among company. Frankly, in time I hope you will call me something far dearer."

"Dearer?" She shook her head, apparently confused.

Her eyes were already big, but they widened to the size of saucers when she finally caught his meaning. "Are you suggesting you have intentions toward me?"

"Suggesting it? No, I am stating it as fact."

"What sort of intentions?"

"Honorable ones, I assure you," he said, noting the blush on her cheeks and her sudden wariness. "Did you think I was delirious when I kissed you and called you my angel?"

Florence hastily glanced at her sleeping grandfather to make certain he was not listening in. Only then did she release a soft breath. "Yes, I did."

Since she sat close to him, it was no hardship to reach over and give her hand a light squeeze. "I was in full possession of my faculties. It was you I kissed and wanted to kiss."

She opened her mouth to speak, then closed it again, only to open it again a moment later. "You cannot be serious."

"Why not? You are beautiful, intelligent, caring, and obviously of good character without being insufferably priggish."

"Good grief."

More in her favor, she was not a practiced flirt.

Not once did she bat her eyelashes at him or pretend he was

witty, smart, or otherwise magnificent, as any other young lady would have done.

Then again, she had no idea he was actually the duke.

The *unmarried* duke.

She suddenly leaped to her feet. "Stay right there. Do not get out of bed. I'll be back in a moment."

"Wait!" He tried to reach for her hand again but she had already taken a step back, so all he managed to do was hurt himself. "Where are you going?"

She cast him an uncertain look and then hurried out.

"Blast."

Had he revealed too much of his feelings? Moved too fast?

She was a modest girl, after all.

Perhaps this was something he needed to work on.

He had never wooed a young lady before.

His encounters with the female persuasion were best described as assignations. Seductions. Eye contact. A quick nod. A meaningless amusement in a boudoir or secluded niche.

Gad, he needed reforming, and Florence was just the woman to do it.

Would she give him the chance?

CHAPTER 3

J ames grew impatient while waiting for Florence to return.

He considered getting out of bed to find her, but he had no clothes on and had to rule out that option.

Besides, he would probably collapse before getting to the door.

A snore emanated from the plump chair beside the hearth, reminding him that her grandfather was in the room.

Was the old man really asleep or had he been pretending in order to listen in on their conversations?

No matter.

He was serious about courting the man's granddaughter, although he was going to wait until he caught the villain who wanted him dead before making any public declarations.

The room seemed to brighten when she walked back in.

"Where did you go?"

"To fetch your letter. Here it is... James," she said, her face flushed from rushing to her bedchamber and back.

He smiled at her. "Thank you, Florence."

She appeared shy and flustered. "I had better see about getting you clothes to wear. If yours cannot be repaired, I'll look for some-thing among our servants' livery to hold you over. I know it is hardly a proper replacement for your army uniform, but it is a uniform of a sort."

Now that was an interesting idea.

"No, stay another moment. *Hmmm*."

"What is that *hmmm* about?" She settled in the seat beside his bed and eyed him curiously.

"You read all of Lord Meade's letter, did you not?"

She cleared her throat. "Um, yes. I told you that I had. But only because–"

"I am not admonishing you, Florence. I would have done the same had our situations been reversed. What matters is that you know I am to provide Lord Meade with some vital information at Sir Peter Somerville's ball."

She nodded. "I am sure my grandfather would have no objection to your riding with us, assuming you are fit enough to attend. However, it is less than a week away and I do not think you will be in any condition to travel."

"I will be."

"Oh, is that so? Because you have decreed it?" She laughed as she rolled her eyes. "I think you are just stubborn enough to manage it. We'll have to find you formal attire. I can go to Brighton first thing tomorrow and–"

"To find me a tailor? It isn't necessary, nor would I ever allow you to make this dangerous trip on my behalf."

She shook her head. "It is only dangerous to you. I've told you, our brigands do not make a habit of murdering their victims."

He frowned. "Do not be lulled into a false sense of safety. It is not such a far step from stealing one's valuables to committing murder."

"Which is why Ethan always accompanies me on my trips to Brighton. I have to return there anyway to pick up my gown for the ball."

"Don't go, Florence. Can you not send a servant for that task?"

"Yes, but the gown might need a minor fix or two, and it is most convenient to have it done there on the spot." She sighed when he continued to frown at her. "Well, I suppose I can easily tuck in a stitch or two myself, if needed."

He nodded. "That eases my mind greatly. If those scoundrels who shot me are still in the area, I—"

"But you seemed certain they were headed back to London."

He shrugged. "I could be wrong. What concerns me is that if you saw them, then they probably saw your carriage and might have seen *you* hopping down from it to come to my rescue. So, I would rather you stayed close to home until I have met with Lord Meade and addressed the matter. That's all I am saying."

"What do you plan to do?"

"Not sure yet, but it is to my advantage if the parties involved continue to wonder whether I am dead or alive."

She shifted even closer so that her body was pressed to the mattress as their discussion drew her in. "How are you to hide your identity if you appear at the ball?"

"Who says I must come as myself? I could attend as your grandfather's valet or perhaps as one of your footmen."

Her lovely emerald eyes widened again. "That is ridiculous."

"Why? Lord Meade will recognize me and find a discreet way to approach me. Meanwhile, few others will notice me, for the high and mighty rarely deign to look closely at their inferiors. Who among them will pay attention to a Swann footman?"

She laughed. "Oh, I think the women will immediately notice you. But why bother with the subterfuge?"

"It will allow me to prowl around the Somerville estate using the servants' stairs and back hallways so that no one is going to know I am there until I am ready to reveal my identity. It will also allow me to overhear gossip about the guests because those who serve the Upper Crust often see and hear things that we might not. I would not be surprised if the servants already know who is trying to interfere with my mission."

"Your nemesis would be awfully stupid to talk about it openly and risk a dozen people pointing fingers at him."

James shrugged. "I'm not saying he will be reckless, just

remarking on the fact that servants often know things we do not. I think my plan is an excellent one."

"If you do say so yourself," she muttered.

"Just get me something suitable for a footman to wear. Do you have anything that might fit me?"

She sighed. "I'm not sure. You are bigger than anyone currently on our staff, even bigger than Ethan and he's a bull of a fellow. We would not have been able to lift you into our carriage if not for his brawn."

"Ethan's father was in service before he passed on and was about the same size as you," her grandfather said, now rising from his chair and ambling toward the bed. The elderly man was of average height and slender, obviously more of a scholar than an old warrior. He had the same color eyes as Florence, but his hair was white and thinning.

"Lord Swann, you're awake," James remarked, noting the obvious. "Your granddaughter tells me you are the one who stitched me up. Probably saved my life with your fine handiwork. Please allow me to express my gratitude."

"None required, my good fellow." He waved a hand in dismissal and gave a wheezing laugh. "Glad I could be of help, and quite relieved Florence wasn't the one who shot you."

"Grandfather!"

Lord Swann laughed. "Just teasing you, love. You'd never be so foolish as to shoot a duke, especially an unmarried one."

"I would never shoot anyone," she grumbled, her cheeks turning crimson at the suggestion James was marriageable. "Besides, Captain Ryder is not the duke but his emissary."

"Ah, my mistake. I must have slept through that part," her grandfather said, eyeing him intently. "Forgive the error, Captain Ryder."

James realized he had not fooled her grandfather who had been awake the entire time and must have overheard their conversations.

What gave him away?

"I despise having to carry that lady's pistol in my reticule," Florence continued to grumble, unaware of the silent exchange between the two men.

"But it is necessary," James warned, for he had been trained to be prepared for the worst and always remain on his guard, a teaching that had served him well for survival in battle. "The world is not a kind place, Florence."

"I know," she admitted. "But I go nowhere without an armed footman close by, and our carriage driver also keeps a weapon or two at the ready."

"Still," he cautioned, "that pistol ought to remain with you at all times when you are on the road, even if you never have cause to use it. I hope you never do. But this makes me like my idea all the more."

"About coming with us to the ball as our servant?" she asked.

He nodded. "The disguise is doubly useful. If there is no need to protect myself, then I can better protect *you*."

The remark had Florence laughing again. "Who on earth would wish to harm me?"

"Seriously, Florence? Have I not made the danger to you clear?"

She snorted.

"The villain who wants me dead will not hesitate to use you against me if he senses I like you."

"There is a simple solution to this," she said with marked irritation. "Do not like me."

"All right. Done. I shall forget the angel who nursed me back to health. I shall ignore any feelings I have for you."

"Good."

He sighed. "Florence, I could no more stop liking you than the sun could stop shining or the moon could stop glowing."

Next, he turned to her grandfather. "I would like permission to court your granddaughter."

Florence made a strangled sound. "Ignore him, Grandfather. He is delirious."

The old man patted her arm before turning back to James and addressing him. "I shall be available whenever you are ready to speak to me."

Florence shot to her feet. "Grandfather! Do not indulge him. How can he possibly feel anything toward me when he has been lying in this bed like a dead fish since I brought him here?"

James laughed. "You certainly know how to flatter a man."

She winced. "Sorry, but is it not the truth? We know nothing about each other."

"We know he has fine boots and an even finer horse," her grandfather interjected. "We also know he is a man of importance."

"Why? Because he is acquainted with the Duke of Wellbourne?" she retorted.

Her grandfather chuckled. "I would say Captain Ryder is very well acquainted with him."

She stared at James. "Obviously, important people trust you. But I fear their trust in your judgment might be misplaced. After all, what do you know about me? *Nothing*," she said, responding to her own question that was meant to be rhetorical. "If you did know me, then you would realize I am rather inept around men. Having to make small talk is very hard for me."

James cast her an affectionate look. "You seem to have no trouble talking to me."

"That is different."

"How so?"

She sighed. "It just is. But in social situations, I am lost. I cannot pretend to find superficial *ton* conversations scintillating, nor can I pretend to be fascinated by the gentlemen who initiate them. I shall never be sought after or declared the belle of the ball. Not that I care, since I have yet to meet any man at these elegant affairs who makes my heart flutter."

"And what of the men you meet outside of those affairs?" James asked.

"Such as you?"

He nodded. "Florence, do I make your heart flutter?"

CHAPTER 4

"Do not be absurd," Florence muttered, tossing James a frown and another at her grandfather when he chuckled at the man's remark.

She would never admit being attracted to this ridiculously handsome army captain even though she was strongly attracted and this scared her.

Why was he persisting in this nonsense?

How could it end other than badly when they inevitably parted ways?

Flutters, indeed.

So what if her heart beat like a butterfly's wings whenever he was near?

He cast her a steamy glance. "Why won't you believe I am sincere?"

"Stop it. Just stop it, James. You will be gone after the Somerville ball and I will never see you again."

"Not true. Admittedly, I may have to go to London to discuss my attack with the Foreign Office, and I may have Wellbourne affairs to handle…"

"On behalf of the duke," she said with a nod.

"But I will come back for you. I give you my word of honor. If I do not return, it will mean I am dead."

She gasped. "Do not even suggest such a thing. I would never wish to see you hurt."

"That is very good of you, Florence."

His gaze was still steamy and he was now grinning at her affectionately.

She looked away. "Do you have any idea who would want to interfere with your assignment? I mean, there ought to be some obvious suspects."

"Oh, I'm sure there are."

"Who?"

"That is confidential information. Nor will I make any accusations until I am certain I have the right man. Of course, I could make a list of those most likely to want me dead, but that could run the length of an entire book. I have been offending people since I was a toddler in nappies."

He was making a jest of it now and she found it irritating.

If he wanted to play, then let him play. She was not going to stop him when he raced headlong into danger.

"You are frowning at me, Florence. All right, I'll be serious." He arched an eyebrow. "I will be on my guard, and you are to keep away from me once we arrive at the Somerville ball. Understood?"

She nodded. "And you will be in your disguise as our footman?"

"That is correct."

"Why did Lord Meade plan to meet you there? Why not just have you ride to London? Is it not odd?"

"I do not know why he was so secretive about it," he admitted. "And yes, I do find it troubling."

"Then you suspect him, too?"

"Florence, everyone is a suspect for now. But there are innocent reasons for this meeting to be set outside of London. Lord Meade may be worried about a traitor of high rank within the Foreign Office and wants to alert me beforehand."

"Hence the reason for your disguise. I understand now. Since my grandfather seems to have no objection to our turning you into one of our servants, let me scavenge some of Henry's old uniforms."

"She's referring to Ethan's father who was a big hulking Viking of a man," her grandfather explained. "Built like a warrior, much like you. I am certain his clothes will fit you."

"Warrior indeed," Florence sniffed. "Hopefully, the moths will not have eaten through the old fabric and left too many holes to mend."

She hurried out of the room and left the men to themselves, cringing as they both began to laugh.

Her grandfather, usually quite sensible and wary, seemed awfully quick to accept James and trust him.

Who was James exactly?

Obviously, a man of some importance and wealth.

Perhaps the duke himself?

She dismissed the possibility since a handsome duke would have his pick of the loveliest, wealthiest, and best-connected young ladies were he ever to enter the marriage mart, so why would he bother with her?

If he were the duke, then his fawning attention had to be a pretense, a game to amuse himself while he recovered.

Yet, he did not come across as the sort of man who would behave so trivially.

Nor would her grandfather ever allow anyone to treat her badly.

He was usually such a wise, old bird. As wise as an owl, she had always thought. He even looked like an owl when he donned his spectacles. Perhaps this manor house should have been called Owl Hall instead of Swann Hall, and their family name should have been Owl instead of Swann.

She coughed as she entered the storage room where their old belongings were stowed. "So, you want to be a footman, do you?"

Layers of dust had collected atop the trunks strewn about the musty place, for no one had been in here for months. There were dozens of trunks, and finding the one in which Henry's old uniforms had been packed would not be easy.

The first one she opened contained her mother's clothing.

"Mama," she whispered, running her hand lovingly over several of her elegant gowns.

An ache tore through her, so she slammed the lid shut.

However, the ache would not go away and she soon felt the urge to cry. "It's the dust," she told herself, wiping away a stray tear or two, and then more tears, with the sleeve of her gown.

When that became soaked, she took out her handkerchief and held it at the ready while moving on to the second trunk. Another mistake, she quickly realized, now staring at mementos belonging to her father.

She slammed the lid shut on those memories, too.

And then cried some more.

The third trunk she tried contained her own clothes from when she was a child. Atop those infant outfits was a tiny gold bracelet with a heart at the center that was marked with the letter 'F' for Florence.

She gave up and went running back to her grandfather who was seated beside James, the two men conversing quietly.

"Florence? What happened, dearest?" her grandfather asked, turning toward her and rising when he noticed her distress.

He opened his arms to her and she flung herself in them.

"I couldn't find the clothes," she said, and burst into tears again.

"Oh, my sweetheart." Her grandfather sighed. "I think it is not so much what you did not find as what you encountered while searching for them. I should have realized what else was stored in there. All right, child. Take my seat while I go speak to Mrs. Lynch. She'll send someone to search for the footman's clothing later."

She nodded against the lapel of his jacket, soaking it because she had turned into a watering pot and could not seem to stop.

"I'll also ask Mrs. Lynch to bring us up some tea and cakes. How does that sound?"

She nodded again. "Fine, Grandfather."

"Sit down, Florence. You stayed up all night while we tended to our patient and this has left you exhausted. All your defenses are down, dearest. Get off your feet and close your eyes for a moment. I'll be right back."

She said nothing as she watched him leave.

Nor did James speak, either.

He kept his gaze on her all the while.

She felt the power of his presence, especially now that they were alone. "Forgive me. I never fall apart like this."

In truth, she had not cried this hard since losing her parents all those years ago. James would not know about her loss or her upbringing, of course.

What did he think of her now?

"There is nothing to forgive, Florence," he said, his voice exquisitely gentle. "You are a sentimental thing, aren't you?"

"Yes, far too sentimental. I'm sure it is a trait you will find most irritating about me." She did not wish him to think of her as his angel any longer.

He sighed. "I find it endearing. Do you think any man wants a cold and unfeeling wife?"

"Oh." This was not the response she had hoped for.

She sank into the chair her grandfather had just vacated and let out a heavy breath. "I'm sorry for that completely...utterly ridiculous display, James."

"As I said, nothing to apologize for." He studied her a moment longer. "What happened to make you cry, love?"

She ought to have chided him for using the endearment. It was entirely too forward and he needed to be scolded for his impertinence.

But it sounded wonderful, and she did not have the heart to be angry with him.

Besides, her grandfather would return shortly, and James would not dare be so familiar with her in his presence.

"Nothing."

"It wasn't nothing, Florence."

She cast him a stubborn look. "I'm fine. Truly, I'm perfect."

"Oh, yes. You are perfect, but you are also heartbroken. Not to mention, you are a terrible liar." There was warmth in his voice, and she sensed the concern in his tone. "Must I get out of this sickbed and coax the truth from you?"

She laughed despite her sorrow. "No, the naked sight of you is more than I can handle just now."

"I would have wrapped a sheet around me, I'm not that big of an arse. Tell me what upset you so badly."

Unable to resist his gentle manner, she relented. "Oh, where to start." She released a ragged breath. "And do not blame me if I bore you. You asked for this."

"I will not be bored," he assured. "I have nowhere to go and plenty of time on my hands."

Odd, but she somehow knew he would be a good listener.

She stared at her hands as she spoke because she was not quite ready to meet his gaze. "My parents died when I was six years old."

"I'm sorry, love. It must have broken your little heart."

She shrugged. "It was so long ago, over sixteen years now. When I went to look for those old footman uniforms, I happened upon the trunks where my family's belongings were stored."

"And the memory of their loss rushed back and overwhelmed you? I'm so sorry, Florence."

She glanced at him and nodded. "It suddenly felt as though I had lost them only yesterday. Look, this is the bracelet I wore when I was but an infant."

He took it from her hands and studied it lovingly.

His smile as he handed it back to her was devastatingly gentle.

"Time is supposed to heal these raw wounds." She took the bracelet and tucked it into a pocket of her serviceable gown. It wasn't even a pretty gown, yet James was looking at her with that hint of heat in his gaze that made her feel beautiful. "But I was caught by surprise. James, losing someone you love is such an awful feeling."

"I know, but it is also a part of life. We do not live forever."

"I wish I had been given a little longer with them. They were the sun and the moon to me. Losing them left such a hole in my heart."

He took her hand but said nothing more.

After all, what could he say?

He did not know her and had never known her parents. Not even she had truly known them since her view of them had only been through six-year-old eyes. The only reason she remembered their faces was because of the family portrait painted of them shortly before they died and now hanging prominently over the mantel in the parlor.

The artist had depicted them with serious expressions, but she remembered them as always smiling and with a glint of love in their eyes.

This is how they remained fresh in her memory. Young. In love. Happy.

Her grandfather returned, followed by their housekeeper, Mrs. Lynch, who wheeled in a cart containing a soup tureen, bowls, a pot of tea, and an assortment of fresh breads and cakes. Florence rose to assist Mrs. Lynch in setting out the bowls.

"Captain Ryder," her grandfather said, "I hope you do not mind this lighter fare. It is not wise to give you anything heavier than this onion soup just yet. We shall improve the menu and offer you something more substantial tomorrow."

"Is this all you are having, too?" James asked, noting Florence had set out three bowls on a small, side table.

Her grandfather nodded. "I am a frail, old man with little appetite, and Florence," he said, giving her cheek a gentle caress, "does not have the heart for anything more tonight."

She nodded. "It has been an eventful few days."

James frowned. "I've disrupted your household."

"Not at all," she assured him, returning to his side to assist with his bowl since she wasn't certain he could hold it steady yet. "Your arrival, albeit under unusual circumstances, is a welcome change. We were growing too complacent in our dull routine until you came along."

"And shook things up?"

Her grandfather laughed. "Being jolted out of complacency is not a bad thing. I may be an old man now, but I was quite a hell-raiser in my youth. Ah, those were the days. Battles. Adventure." He waggled his eyebrows. "Romantic entanglements. Of course, I reformed my ways once I met and married my wife. My point is, I've lived my life to the fullest and now enjoy this quieter existence. But this is not right for Florence. She is young and vibrant, and it is selfish of me to keep her shut away with an old man like me."

"Grandfather, that is not so."

"No, child. It is the truth. You are good and devoted, but I have taken too much advantage."

"How? I've had my London seasons, several of them." She turned to James and ladled some broth into his mouth. "I had my come-out at the age of nineteen and endured another two seasons after that. Believe me when I say that I do not miss that horse market at all."

She ladled another spoonful into his mouth, surprised he was allowing her to coddle him in this manner.

He struck her as a man who liked to do things for himself. "My grandfather has not deprived me in the least. I was the one who asked to come home after a couple of months of endless and quite meaningless balls, routs, and musicales."

James frowned. "Because you were hounded by unwanted suitors?"

"I did have several," she admitted, "but they were mostly spoiled wastrels and only interested in whatever they could get for themselves. How could I fall for any of them when it was obvious they did not care for me?"

"Florence, I think you are being hard on those gentlemen. I'm sure many of them sincerely liked you."

"And I assure you, they did not. The marriage mart is little more than a horse auction where that year's crop of hopeful young ladies is trotted out before a host of eligible bachelors. They ogle us, check our teeth and backsides, and ask about our bloodlines as we stand there dressed in expensive silks and our hair done up stylishly in the hope of attracting these clots."

"Ouch," James said with a chuckle. "You do not hold back, do you, Florence?"

"Sorry," she said with a grimace, all the while certain to be gentle while ladling another spoonful of the onion soup into his mouth.

He swallowed and cast her a grin. "No apology required. I expect to feel no different once I am back in London. That horse auction goes both ways. The ladies and their families are also inspecting the men. My family is quite prominent and that alone is going to attract a lot of interest. And by 'interest' I mean they are going to descend on me like a plague of locusts."

Her grandfather laughed. "Gad, the two of you are a pair. The marriage mart is a venerable institution. Many good matches have been made there."

James did not appear persuaded. "The only reason I may go to London after the Somerville ball is to find out who within the halls of power wanted to stop me in my mission."

"About that," Florence said, spooning more soup into his mouth. "How can you be sure Lord Meade is not the one?"

"Florence, do not interfere in matters you know nothing about."

"Or what if the attack had nothing to do with your government business? What if it was a jealous husband. A woman scorned. A partner in a failed business venture? A political rival?"

He shook his head. "I've spent my life in the army and most of those years outside of England. There are no bad business ventures, and certainly no political rivals. As for women or jealous husbands..." He paused and cleared his throat. "That is an inappropriate topic of conversation to be had with you. However, there cannot be any women who feel scorned or would wish me ill. I have never seriously involved myself with any ladies, and certainly never courted any unmarried ones, nor to lead anyone to think I wished for something more permanent."

"So, you sought out only married ladies? What did their husbands think about your actions?"

"The women I chose to...er, entertain had bad marriages and husbands who did not care what they did or with whom they did it. Most did not even care if we were discreet or not. However, there will be no more of those sorts of engagements for me."

"Has your near-death experience made you see the error of your ways?" she asked.

"Not at all. I am changing my ways because I have found something more important and valuable, and that is you."

She set the spoon in the bowl with a clatter and frowned at him. "You must not speak to me that way. I do not need your flattery, so pray stop. We both know you will forget me once you reach London."

"I am aware of no such thing. Do you think I care a whit for this year's elegant crop of diamonds? Why are you pushing me away?" He frowned back at her. "I do not flatter. I speak what's on my mind and tell the truth."

"And I am supposed to believe you?"

"Yes, even though you think of me as a dead fish."

She smiled even though she did not mean to. "I only described you as that because you were unconscious for so long. It had me very worried. But you are not dead at all, thank goodness."

"And this frightens you?" He arched an eyebrow when she attempted to protest.

"I am not afraid of you."

"Good, because you will face some hard choices if you decide to marry me."

She set his bowl aside with a *thunk* and rose from his side with her hands curled into fists. "Why are you persisting in this fable? I forbid you to mention that word to me."

"What? Choices?"

"No, *marry*. That is not a word to be spoken to anyone upon a day's acquaintance."

"You are absolutely right, but you are not just anyone. Do not ask me to make sense of my feelings. Perhaps having a brush with death gives a man clarity."

She snorted. "I doubt it. You are obviously not thinking clearly."

He cast her a melting smile. "Stop being sensible, Florence. Sometimes a thing is so obvious, it defies reason or logic. I know you are feeling it, too."

She tipped her chin in the air. "What if I am not?"

"Then I'll wait for you to catch up to me. Is that a workable plan for you?"

CHAPTER 5

J ames was feeling much better by the fifth day of his recovery. His wounds were still tender but manageable so long as he did not lift any heavy objects, which was not a problem since Florence would not permit him to lift anything heavier than a teacup.

He liked the way she quietly fussed over him.

The Swann housekeeper had found the footman's livery that he was presently wearing, and Florence now had him standing up straight while she pinned the sleeve cuffs that were too long for him. "Do not move, James."

"Not twitching a muscle," he assured, but wished she would hurry up because he found standing in one place, even for a short while, harder on his body than simply walking around.

Ethan's father must have had the arms of a baboon.

The sleeves dangled past his fingers, but Florence appeared to have no difficulty in making the alterations. She took a step back to admire the result when she finished placing the final stitches on the cuffs. The entire outfit perfectly molded to his frame as though it were made to order. "How do I look?"

She smiled at him. "Like a footman."

He chuckled.

"You ought to change out of these clothes and don your captain's uniform," she said, tucking her needle and thread back in her sewing basket. "I'll leave the room while you do. Shall I summon my grandfather's valet to assist you?"

"No, it won't be necessary. I can manage on my own."

The housekeeper had returned his uniform several days ago cleaned, pressed, and the holes in the jacket imperceptible because Florence had done such a fine job of mending that, too. He was relieved to have his own clothes back and be able to walk around.

He had felt trapped while being forced to remain languishing like a lump in bed, a *naked* lump for those first few days.

"Let me make this quick change and then I should like a tour of your home. Is that acceptable to you, Florence?"

She nodded. "Yes, it is time you stretched your legs a bit. The Somerville ball is only two days away and we ought to know whether you are recovered enough to make the trip."

"There is no question I am making this trip," he said with finality. "Your grandfather assured me that my head wound is healing nicely."

"But you were also shot, and that injury will take longer to properly heal."

"I do not care. Neither Sir Peter nor Lady Somerville is going to change the date of their ball to accommodate me. I just need to be able to move around their residence without attracting notice. You'll have to draw me a rough outline of the place so that I know where best to meet Lord Meade. It is imperative he and I speak."

"Understood. This is all quite clandestine."

He arched an eyebrow. "Do you want to beg out of my plan, Florence? I would not hold it against you. Same for your grandfather. In truth, if there was any way not to involve either of you, I would gladly pursue it."

"But there isn't, so you mustn't fret about us. My grandfather and I have little to do other than pass a message on to Lord Meade mentioning where to meet you."

He eyed her thoughtfully. "Your grandfather must be the one to relay the message. You are to keep away from Lord Meade."

She regarded him with some surprise. "Why? Is he not your prime suspect?"

In fact, Meade was his stepbrother, slighter in build and several years younger, so that James had always felt protective of him. "My point is, he will be closely watched. If so, I want you to keep your distance. My enemy will not think twice about an old man such as your grandfather approaching Lord Meade to relate a made-up story about Meade's grandfather being an old schoolmate of his."

"While whispering instructions where to meet you?"

He nodded. "However, were a pretty thing like you to approach Meade? All eyes would suddenly be on you, and no one is going to forget you."

She sighed. "Fine."

He tucked a finger under her chin and tipped it upward so that her gaze met his. "Do not play the hero, Florence. Someone is trying to sabotage the efforts of Lord Castlereagh and the Foreign Office to keep peace on the Continent. There is a dangerous game afoot and the players are in the highest echelons of government. I cannot be worrying for your safety, too. And do not dare say that you can take care of yourself, because you cannot do it under these circumstances."

"Are you not exaggerating the danger to me?"

"Perhaps, but that is not a mistake I wish to make. You cannot match a man's strength, and if anyone were to attempt to harm you..."

"What would you do?"

He sighed. "Move heaven and earth to save you."

Her eyes widened. "Even if you stood to lose your own life in rescuing me?"

"Without a moment's hesitation. How could you think I would ever do otherwise? It is my duty to keep you safe."

She cast him a surprisingly sweet smile. "That is the nicest way of telling me to keep my snoopy nose out of your business."

He laughed and gave her a chaste kiss on the forehead. "Let me change out of this livery, and then I'll join you downstairs for that tour of your home."

Once Florence had walked out and closed the door behind her, James made quick work of donning his uniform. However, the stitches tugged painfully against his ribs when taking off his shirt and putting on another. It did not help that he took less care than he ought to have done because he was eager to be in Florence's company again.

How could he not marry this girl when he enjoyed being around her so much?

She thought she had made a fool of herself the other day by bursting into tears over those old memories of her parents. But it had only drawn him closer to her, for he loved that she was sentimental and compassionate.

Was this not better than involving himself with someone adept at lies and manipulation?

He looked forward to getting to know her better, although any courtship undertaken now would be interrupted by this Foreign Office business which had to come first. Still, he wanted to learn as much as he could about Florence and her life at Swann Hall while he had the chance.

It was partly selfish of him.

He knew he had competition for her heart, but it was not from any other suitor. His greatest rival was the loving grandfather who had raised her since childhood.

How was he to convince Florence to marry him and become his duchess when it meant leaving this old man and forging a new life without his daily presence? This was the true hurdle to be overcome, something he was not certain would happen even if she fell in love with him.

Well, nothing to be done about it now.

She did not even know he was a duke.

He strode into the parlor and found her waiting for him. This seemed a good place to start their tour because the portrait of her parents had been placed here. Seeing their portrait, listening to Florence as she told him about her past, added an intimacy to their tour. "How did your parents meet?"

She smiled at the portrait. "At one of those horrid *ton* affairs during my mother's debut season."

"Ah, the marriage mart you so detest."

"They were fortunate to find each other, and I'm sure there was a good crop of men that year."

"Unlike your years on the marriage mart? There are good and bad in every year, Florence. But the bad ones always seem to pounce first, don't they?"

She nodded. "Why is that?"

"Because they have little to lose and everything to gain. The good ones are more deliberate and know they must take their time in finding the right wife. Deciding whether or not to take the next step is important because they cannot risk making a mistake. The bad ones? They have no scruples and could not care less."

"I see."

"Had you waited out the full season, I expect you would have found several good men to your liking."

"Perhaps." She nodded. "But does this mean you are bad? You waited no more than a day before asking to court me."

He laughed. "No, it only means I know my mind. I'm a soldier and trained to act decisively. But it was your behavior that swayed me."

"How did I behave?"

"With grace under pressure," he said as they moved on to the next room which turned out to be the dining room. It was elegant, but not grand. The rosewood table was large enough to accommodate twenty and there was a massive silver epergne sitting atop it. The drapes were a dark green damask silk that seemed to bring out the red tones of the wood. "You were calm, efficient, and compassionate while treating my wounds."

"I could not leave you to die."

"Others might have." He shrugged. "So, what would any sensible man do when looking upon a young lady with those strengths who is also beautiful enough to have been declared a diamond, which you would have been had you bothered to remain in London. But it is the quieter life in the countryside that calls to you."

"We have an active social life here, even if it not quite the London whirl. Brighton is not far away, and particularly popular in the summer. This is where we go if we are of a mind to seek more elegant company."

"Are you ever of a mind to do so?"

She laughed. "Rarely, although it is fun to spend a day or two by the sea in summer. Brighton has excellent shops near the beach promenade including one to rival the ices to be had at Gunter's."

They moved on to the library, perhaps the most impressive room yet. "This is my grandfather's favorite room in the house."

It came as little surprise to James. Florence's grandfather was a scholarly man and had amassed an excellent selection of books. "I can see why. It would be mine, as well."

"Yours, James? That is surprising. You strike me as a man of action."

"Can I not be both?"

She nodded. "I suppose."

When they completed the tour of the main floors, James suggested they walk outdoors. "I haven't seen Pegasus in several days," he said, referring to his trusted steed.

"He is being well cared for. Ethan takes him out for a run every day. But I'm sure Pegasus is missing his master." She donned a pelisse and led him to the stable. "Do not overdo it. Honestly, I'm not certain we should be taking any hikes outdoors yet, even if it is only to the stable."

"I am not doddering, Florence. We won't stay long. I just want to see my horse."

"Where did you get him?" she asked when they reached his stall.

"On the Continent during the war. He was too fine an animal to leave behind." He shook his head and chuckled. "His passage to England cost more than mine."

She smiled at him. "I can see why. He's a handsome fellow."

"And I am not?"

She nudged him playfully. "You know you are, so do not pretend to be coy about your looks. I can see you riding into London on that magnificent beast and catching the eye of everyone you pass."

"That is not necessarily a good thing. In fact, the last thing I need is attention, especially if I am required to hunt down this nemesis of mine."

Pegasus munched on his hay, ignoring both of them as they stood beside his stall and stroked his coat.

Florence looked up at James again. "You know...."

"What, Florence?"

"If you wish to remain incognito, my grandfather and I could open up our London town house and bring you along as our footman."

James arched an eyebrow. "I would very much enjoy touring the sights of London with you as your devoted servant, but I dare not involve the two of you any more than I already have."

"Think about it," she said in earnest. "I'm sure my grandfather will be all in favor of the idea. There is nothing to hold us here after the ball."

"Nothing at all?" He took a moment to ponder the notion. "Although I have seen little beyond your manor house and this stable, I know Swann Hall operates as a working farm."

"Our estate manager will take care of whatever crops are left to be harvested, and Mrs. Lynch runs an immaculate home without need of our guidance. It won't take me or my grandfather long to pack since we each keep a full wardrobe at our London residence. As for Pegasus, he can either remain here or Ethan can ride him to London any time you like."

"No, Florence."

She stared at him while she digested his refusal. "Oh, I see. You do not want me around."

"I do want you with me, just not yet. I'll send for you once it is safe to do so, but not before."

She cast him a vulnerable smile. "You won't send for me. Let's not pretend that you will."

He took her hand when she turned to leave. "I could admit that you are right, that I am no better than a schoolboy whose head will be turned by all the tempting bosoms on display in a glittering ballroom, but that would be a lie. Why are you so reluctant to admit there is something between us?"

"Why are you so stubbornly insistent that there is?" she tossed back.

"Shall I kiss you to convince you, Florence?"

She let out a soft breath. "I am sure I will like it because I expect you are quite expert at making a woman melt in your arms. They all melt, don't they?"

"It so happens they do. But that is not the question you should be asking me."

She frowned. "What should I be asking?"

"Whether kissing *you* makes *me* melt...and do you wish to know the answer to that?"

CHAPTER 6

F lorence put her hands over her ears to keep from hearing his
response.

He took gentle hold of her wrists and drew them off her ears.
"You do, Florence. You make me melt and yearn and hope for a
bright future with you. How is that for an answer?"

"Completely absurd."

He laughed. "Care to explain why you find it impossible?"

"First of all, I had never kissed anyone before you pasted your
mouth to mine when we first met. Something you probably guessed
because how could our kiss be anything but clumsy and unmemo-
rable to you? I do not know how to kiss. Was it not obvious?"

"Yes, a little obvious. But that made it all the sweeter for me."

"How?"

He took her hand as he led her from the stable back to the
house. "You said it yourself just now. You had never been kissed
before. I was your first and only. Do you have any idea how special
that is to a man?"

"No." She tried to slip her hand out of his, but he stubbornly
kept hold of it. Fortunately, there was no one out here to notice

other than a few geese waddling by. "Perhaps it was special for me, but it was just one among many for you."

"Completely wrong, Florence."

She paused just outside of Swann Hall's front door. "How am I wrong?"

"I have never been anyone's *first* kiss before. So, it could be said this was a first for me, too."

She snorted. "Be serious."

"I am. I could tell you were innocent. Don't ask me how I knew... a man can just tell."

"Oh, really? You could tell? Even with your head cracked open and a nasty shot ripping through your ribs? Not to mention you lost enough blood to fill a bathtub."

"Now that is an exaggeration."

"But you could still tell our kiss was wonderful and melted your heart?"

He nodded. "As I hope it melted yours. In fact, I know it did."

She sniffed in dismissal.

"Sniff and snort all you like, but it won't change anything. A man can always tell how his kiss is received. You liked it. So did I. My point is, I have never kissed an innocent before, so that kiss was a first for both of us."

"Dear heaven, this is ridiculous."

"Protest all you like, but you cannot hide the truth." He took her arm as they continued inside, he leading the way even though he was injured and should not have been walking around with this apparent ease.

Obviously, the man was strong as a bull.

His strength continued to improve.

To Florence's amazement, he seemed to have recovered most of his vigor by the day of the Somerville ball. There were a few telltale signs of his lingering discomfort, for he winced when having to stand up or sit down, and he still allowed Ethan to exercise Pegasus, a sign he did not trust himself to ride the beast yet.

But these were minor irritations, and she was glad he was well on the mend.

However, stepping into the carriage was a bittersweet moment for her. She watched James take his place at the rear, resplendent in his footman's livery. They had spent an entire week together, neither of them seeming to run out of conversation, and it would now come to an end.

Day by day, little by little, she had lost her heart to this man she still knew almost nothing about. Yes, he was the Duke of Wellbourne's emissary and carried himself with confidence and authority.

He was educated and well spoken, and obviously came from wealth. Even his saddlebags were of the finest quality leather.

Yet, he had not spoken a word about his family.

Was he related to the Duke of Wellbourne? A brother or some other close relation?

Even her grandfather had at first mistaken him for the duke.

Could he be Wellbourne himself? Most telling was the way he simply assumed she would marry him if he asked.

Would a mere army captain ever presume such a thing?

CHAPTER 7

J ames smiled as he assisted Florence into the carriage for the ride to the Somerville residence on the night of the ball. "You look beautiful," he said, quite taken by her appearance, for she was stunning in a forest green gown of finest Italian velvet that matched the color of her eyes. The garment had little adornment other than a bit of silk trim in a slightly darker shade in a belt that circled just below her shapely bosom.

But this was Florence, knock-out of a figure and at the same time practical.

Most of the female guests would be wearing delicate silks and freezing in the chill of an October evening, all for the sake of attracting a man.

Not Florence.

She had fashioned a perfect life for herself at Swann Hall and had no wish for any man to disrupt it.

James hoped she would make an exception for him.

"You are in the role of footman now," she reminded, slipping her hand out of his when he held it for too long. "And I am to be addressed as Lady Florence. You look wonderful in your livery, by the way."

"Thank you, m'lady." He grinned. "May I say, you will be the envy of every lady at the ball. You look delicious enough to eat."

She laughed. "A proper servant carries out his task without need for comment."

Her grandfather hurried out of the house and came scrambling down the steps. James helped him to climb in as well. "Thank you, lad. By the way, what shall we call you?"

He shrugged. "Just James will do. It is a common enough name and should arouse no suspicion."

He climbed onto his post at the rear of the carriage, wishing he could sit beside Florence, but that pleasure would have to wait for another day. They did need to talk seriously and would after he completed his business at Normanton House.

The Somerville home was another of those charming country estates nestled amid rolling hills and gentle valleys. The ball would be a crush, drawing families from Brighton to Chichester, if the carriages lined up in queue along the drive were any indication.

James noticed lit torches at measured intervals around the front of the manor and more ablaze throughout the surrounding grounds. He had studied the map Florence made for him of this estate, so he knew exactly where to meet his stepbrother.

Ah, Meade. Let me be wrong about you.

He only needed Florence's grandfather to relay the meeting location, and then proceed to enjoy the ball with Florence. He'd warned the old man not to allow her to wander off to a quiet corner.

She was safest amid a crowd.

Several Somerville footmen stood by to assist the guests as their carriages drew up. However, James took charge of the Swanns because he wanted to give Florence a final word of caution. As she climbed down, he took her hand and leaned close. "Stay with friends at all times. Keep to the center of the room. Do not stand near doorways or curtained niches."

"Are you going to instruct me on how to powder my nose, too?" She sighed and moved on.

Was she going to defy him?

Her grandfather overheard the exchange and quickly reassured

James. "She's worried about you, and does not want *you* distracted by worrying about *her*. She will do as you ask. Take care of your business, and I'll watch over my granddaughter, as I always have."

"Very well, m'lord," he said, turning his head away as a Somerville footman approached. It would not do to be recognized too soon.

James waited for them to enter the manor house before he strode to the servants' entrance. Samuel had driven the carriage to an area near the stables where the drivers had been instructed to park their conveyances.

He had no idea when his stepbrother would arrive, but did not think it would be until later. This was Meade's fashion, to show up late, make a grand entrance, soak in the admiration, and then depart for a gaming hell or *demi-monde* party.

He had behaved similarly at Meade's age, for was this not commonplace among the privileged elite?

However, James had always worked harder than most because he had also been raised in duty. First looking after the Wellbourne interests and then answering the call of duty while war raged on the Continent. These last two years had been spent beside Castlereagh, striving to ensure a lasting peace.

And now, he was ready to make a life for himself with Florence.

After making a quick reconnaissance of the house and grounds, he joined a group of footmen having a smoke outside the kitchen door. "Who are you?" one of them asked brusquely, not recognizing him as one of their own.

"Lord Swann's man. James is the name." He offered the man one of his neatly rolled smokes.

"Where's Ethan?" another asked, also eyeing him warily. "You're a big brute like him. You haven't replaced him, have ye?"

"No, he's my cousin. I happened to be visiting, and he asked me to help out when he sprained his ankle while assisting Lady Florence."

"I heard she found an injured man on the side of the road several days ago," the first man said. "Some no-accounts tried to kill a man working for the Duke of Wellbourne. Carrying secrets for the Crown is what they say. But you ought to know. Who is he really? Did they do him in?"

"He's back at Swann Hall recovering." James held out the last of these smokes he had purposely prepared in order to ingratiate himself with these fellows. "He's an army captain on his way to London to report to Lord Castlereagh. But he doesn't know who tried to kill him. Have you heard anything about those no-accounts?"

Apparently, revealing he was Ethan's cousin immediately made him one of them. No one hesitated before repeating the gossip they'd heard. Much of it was nonsense, but one reference drew his attention. "Sally at the Boar & Bull tavern overheard those men talking the night before, and she said one of them mentioned Dolby Grange."

James arched an eyebrow. "The Earl of Westling's home?"

They all eyed him curiously.

"How do ye know that?" a third man asked.

"Being in service runs in the family. I worked for Viscount Evesham until he passed away a few months ago. I was a footman in his home near Dolby Grange," he said, improvising. "But Evesham's son closed up the house upon his death and discharged us all. That's how I came to visit Ethan."

"He discharged ye with references, I hope," the first man remarked with a disdainful snort.

"Yes, and I might return to the area to ask if Lord Westling is hiring staff."

"No, James," another of them said. "Do not mess with Westling's lot. He's into some very shady dealings, and I think something's going to take place here at this very party."

"Seriously?"

Dear heaven.

How did these servants know this?

"Yes, Westling's here. And Tom," he said, pointing to one of the smokers, "says several lords from the Foreign Office are here, too. I think they are onto Westling and watching him."

"Makes sense," James said with a nod, his heart thumping because this night was going to be more than a quick meeting between him and his stepbrother. "Perhaps I ought to warn Lord Swann. The captain is still recovering at his home. I wouldn't want any harm to come to him or Lady Florence."

They all murmured in agreement.

"Aye," said the first man, "she's a sweet lady."

"She's got true class," another said. "Better make sure you protect her, James. Westling's just the sort of vindictive rat to do her harm if he thinks it will gain him some advantage."

"I'll speak to the Somerville butler right now and tell him the situation. Ethan is counting on me to protect the Swanns and I mean to do just that."

He strode off toward the rear of the house and the ballroom that opened onto a terrace. He saw Florence and her grandfather speaking with several of their friends near the terrace steps. He recognized some of them from London parties and one or two from Vienna such as Lady Aitken whose trill of laughter proved her to be as jovial as ever. Lord Fontus Leigh mostly frowned, for he was a serious man.

Also looking serious was the Marquis of Corey who strode by James so quickly, they almost bumped into each other. James fell deeper into the shadows, knowing he could not afford to be recognized.

Sir Peter Somerville joined Florence's circle of friends briefly, whispered something to his wife, Lady Somerville, who was among those chatting with Florence, then stepped away. Sir Peter's brother was supposedly in attendance, but James did not see Robin Somerville among this crowd. Well, it did not matter since he was here on Foreign Office business and had no intention of catching up with friends.

Then he saw Lord Meade.

Florence's grandfather also noticed him and excused himself from the circle to approach him and convey the requested message. James watched the exchange, and then disappeared into the garden knowing Meade would not be far behind.

"James, blessed saints! Thank goodness you're alive," his stepbrother said a few minutes later as they met by the fountain. "I thought they had left you for dead on the side of the road."

James let out a heavy breath, for how could Meade, who was newly arrived to the area, possibly know how seriously he was hurt or *where* he had been accosted? "Was it Westling who sent those men to stop me?"

"Westling?" Meade repeated, sounding hesitant. "Yes, we were onto him early in our investigation, but dared not stop his activities until we found out who was providing him sensitive government information. That traitor within the Foreign Office is the one we are hoping to draw out tonight."

"And now he is drawn out," James said, his heart in a twist as he stared at his stepbrother. "Why, Meade? Why did you do it? I was praying you would prove me wrong."

"Me?" He laughed and shook his head. "What makes you think I had anything to do with the traitor?"

"Because you are the traitor. No one in the Foreign Office could have known I was injured on my way here, much less left for dead. Did you order it or did Westling decide to act on his own?"

"Westling's idea." Meade emitted a deflated breath. "How long have you known about me?"

"It was mere suspicion until you wrote that letter asking to meet 'the duke's emissary' here tonight. You knew I would never send an underling to meet you, and would come here myself. Who else is here with you?"

"Allenwood and Grimshaw. We are all three here on orders of the Foreign Office. Do they know I'm the one they're after?"

He nodded. "Possibly. I don't know how much Castlereagh has told them."

"Lord Castlereagh's not one to make accusations without solid proof. I'll wager it is only you who truly suspects me." Meade sighed. "The other two, Allenwood and Grimshaw, are busy watching Westling. They'll be very disappointed when they find you dead, and those secret documents planted on *you*. Sorry to besmirch your sterling reputation, but you've left me no choice."

"Stop dreaming, Meade. It is over. Castlereagh will never believe

I was the inside man. Plant whatever you like on me, plant a bloody garden on me, but it will do you no good. Castlereagh will never let you or Westling get away." James felt a deep sorrow wash over him. "If you needed funds, you could have come to me. I would have given you whatever you asked."

"And have me be forever indebted to you? Knowing I could never pay you back?" He raised his pistol and aimed it at James's chest. "My mother always adored you. How do you think that made me feel when I was her blood son?"

"She was a good woman and loved us both. She opened her heart to me, just as my father opened his heart to you. They were good and decent people."

Meade shrugged. "I grew to hate them."

"And me, too, apparently."

"Actually, I like and admire you very much. I'm sorry it has come to this, James. Brother against brother. Desperate times call for desperate measures. If anyone is to take the fall, it will be you. All I need is a minute or two to plant the evidence and make it point to you. I'll take my chances with Castlereagh. I can be convincing when I put my mind to it."

"You'll never get away with this, Meade. Put down your pistol and we'll work it out."

"No, too late for that. Westling's usefulness is also at an end. I've told him to join us out here. He should be along shortly."

"I see. You're going to kill him, too."

Meade nodded. "He's going to take the blame for shooting you. And then I will conveniently shoot him before he can confess anything to Allenwood or Grimshaw."

"I would rethink that plan," a sweet, feminine voice called out from the shadows behind Meade. "I have a pistol trained at your head, sir."

Florence.

James growled in frustration.

Why choose now to use that blasted pistol when she never even wanted to carry it in her reticule? What did she plan to do next? Fire the pistol? And then what was she going to do when she missed

Meade, as James knew she would because this girl did not have the killer instinct? "Florence, get out of here."

"No. And by the way, two very formidable-looking men have just joined me. I believe they must be the gentlemen, Allenwood and Grimshaw, you mentioned. They are pointing pistols at you, Lord Meade. They've heard most of your admission. So, please put your weapon down and let your brother do whatever he can to save you from the gallows."

"Westling has also been taken into custody, Your Grace," Allenwood said, stepping forward to address James. "Lord Castlereagh appreciated your cooperation and apologizes for taking so long to set up this plan. We'll next be rounding up the Westling underlings who attacked you."

Grimshaw stepped forward to disarm Meade, who offered no resistance. "Will you be returning to London with us now, Your Grace?"

"Yes, *Your Grace*," Florence said, her ache evident. "Do let us know your intentions."

He sighed. "Florence, I can explain."

"Do not bother. I'd rather hear no more lies from you. In fact, I would rather never hear from you again. Lord Allenwood can give my grandfather and me a report once the matter is concluded."

"Ignore her, Allenwood," James said. "I shall deal with Lady Florence and her grandfather."

"But I do not wish to deal with you, *Your Grace*," she retorted. "Or should I still refer to you as Captain Ryder? Why give me any of your time when there must be hundreds of elegant bosoms awaiting you in London?" She huffed, obviously still overset, and stormed back toward the house.

Allenwood and Grimshaw chuckled.

Even Meade was amused. "Worth being caught just to see you taken down a peg, James."

He frowned. "Whose bright idea was it to involve Lady Florence?"

Allenwood cleared his throat. "She took it upon herself, hoping to stall your brother while one of Somerville's footmen brought us her urgent message. Do not be angry with her, Your Grace. It was our fault for losing sight of Lord Meade. She saved your life with her quick thinking."

"Assuming my brother would have shot me," he said, still hurting over Meade's downfall.

"Sorry, James. I would have done it," Meade replied with a careless shrug.

James was not certain he believed him, for Meade had plenty of chances to do so before Florence arrived to save him, and even afterward because she was obviously not a trained agent and had no idea about defensive protocols. "Do you have further need of me, Allenwood?"

"No, Your Grace. Grimshaw and I are here with a team of agents. We'll get your brother and Westling back to London."

"Good, then I'll return to Swann Hall and see you in London next week." He strode off in search of Florence and caught up to her as she was about to enter the ballroom from the terrace.

He took her by the hand and dragged her back into the garden. "Do not struggle. My ribs are killing me."

"Too bad, *Your Grace*. Did you not think it important to tell me who you really were?" she asked, sounding obviously overset. "But then, you were only amusing yourself. How convenient to court me as Captain James Ryder, only to disappear forever once you were healed and the game no longer held any interest for you."

"Florence, you were never a game for me." He drew her into his arms, wanting to soothe her because perhaps he should not have waited so long to reveal his identity to her. But the Foreign Office matter was sensitive and delicate. Surely, she had to understand that discretion was necessary. He breathed a little easier when he felt her soften against him. "I will admit to being at fault for keeping the truth from you, but I only did it to keep you out of this intrigue."

"I was involved from the moment I rescued you," she countered. "That's twice I've saved your life, if you count last week and tonight."

Now, it was his turn to frown at her. "Why in hell were you hiding in the bushes tonight? Have you ever shot a pistol? Do not bother to answer, I know you haven't. For future reference, if you are going to shoot someone, aim for the body, not the head. The body's a bigger target and easier to hit."

"I only meant to distract him, not actually fire a weapon."

"Even worse, for he could have turned and shot you. Can you not see that you placed yourself in greatest danger? This is the last thing I ever wished you to do."

"Why should you care? You were only playing with my affections."

"You know it is not true. The only reason I withheld my identity is that I did not want word getting around and placing you in danger, something you managed to do tonight anyway despite my best efforts. I'm the one responsible to protect you, not the other way around."

"That is ridiculous. You are my *James*, even if you lied about being a duke. I had to save you. Why did you tell my grandfather and not me?"

"I did not tell him. He guessed the truth, so I swore him to secrecy. Glad to know he is a man of honor and never let on to you."

"We are both honorable and trustworthy. You could have revealed yourself to me, as well."

He laughed. "I did reveal too much of myself by spending three days naked in your bed before I finally got back my clothes."

"It was a guest bed. Not mine."

"Then I hope to soon be in your bed, sharing quarters and sharing a lifetime with you as my wife and duchess. Florence, I am in love with you. I knew it the moment I set eyes on you——and do not make a face at me," he said with a chuckle, for he loved her big eyes and dimples, too. "I am not a fool. I know what I have been missing in my life and in my heart. *You*. Do not make me beg for your forgiveness when I never meant to hurt you, only keep you safe. And I am willing to honor and protect you until death do us part."

Her eyes widened as she stared at him.

"Marry me, my angel. Say you will."

"What about my grandfather? How can I abandon him?"

"You would break his heart if you gave up your happiness for his own. Nor do I wish to see either of you hurt. Have him come live with us."

She swallowed hard, still staring at him. "James, he will never leave Swann Hall."

"Then visit him as often as you like. I am not trying to take you away from him, just asking for a space in your heart for me. I cannot move down here when I must spend so much time between London and my estates up north. Florence, we will work it out because I do not want to be without you. I *cannot* be without you. What do you say, love?"

"I don't know. I am still on the fence about you." But her lips twitched, so he knew she was struggling to suppress a smile. "Will you kiss me, James?"

"Here and now?" At her nod, he crushed his mouth down on hers and kissed her with all the depth of promise in his heart. "I'll kiss you every blessed day of our lives, Florence. I'll kiss you and love you, and I'll always be true. I'm so sorry I did not tell you I was Wellbourne. Perhaps I was too cynical, and perhaps I liked the way you saw *me* and not my title. I wanted us to get to know each other better without any trappings to blind us. If it is any consolation, I quickly saw that I could trust you."

"Yet, you still did not tell me."

"Because I enjoyed being James to you and watching you fall in love with me, as I was falling in love with you. But I also needed to concentrate on bringing this matter of the Foreign Office traitor to a close, and did not want to be distracted any more than I already was. The traitor is now discovered, and my greatest fear has come to pass. I wanted so much to be wrong about Meade."

"I'm so sorry," she said with sincerity.

"In worrying about him, I've hurt you. For that, I am the one who owes you the apology. My duties with the Foreign Office are now at an end and I am all yours."

She said nothing for a long moment, and then smiled. "Your kiss was nice."

He let out a breath. "Will that sway your decision about marrying me?"

She shrugged. "It might."

"Close your eyes, Florence."

She laughed. "Why?"

"Because I think you need a little more convincing. I love you, Florence." He kissed her again and again. "Be my wife."

She cast him a dimpled smile when he ended the kiss. "Yes, James. I'll marry you. I love you, too."

"Hallelujah," he muttered and kissed her breathless.

THE END

A Duke In Peril is a stand-alone novella written for the Bluestocking Belles' latest anthology, *Love's Perilous Road*. If you enjoy Meara's humorous historical romances, then read her *Silver Dukes* series, *Farthingales* series, or *Book of Love* series. For a more heartwarming read, there's her *Moonstone Landing* series, and if you love dragons and epic battles between Fae warriors and Dragon Lords who rule the underworld, then try her *Dark Gardens* series.

SOCIAL MEDIA FOR MEARA PLATT

You can learn more about Meara Platt at these social media links:

Facebook: https://www.facebook.com/AuthorMearaPlatt/
Bookbub: https://www.bookbub.com/authors/meara-platt
Website: www.mearaplatt.com
Newsletter: http://bit.ly/meara-platts-newsletter

ABOUT MEARA PLATT

Meara Platt is an award winning, USA TODAY bestselling author and an Amazon UK All-Star. Her favorite place in all the world is England's Lake District, which may not come as a surprise since many of her stories are set in that idyllic landscape, including her paranormal romance Dark Gardens series. Learn more about the Dark Gardens and Meara's lighthearted and humorous Regency romances in her Farthingale series, Silver Dukes series, and Book of Love series, or her warmhearted Regency romances in her Moonstone Landing series and Braydens series by visiting her website at www.mearaplatt.com

Sign up for Meara newsletter at http://bit.ly/meara-platts-newsletter

THE CASEBOOK OF
PRINCIPAL OFFICER ROBERT
PIERCE

Brighton and surrounding districts

As if matters were not complicated enough, with smugglers and ghosts to confuse the trail of my sneak thief and at least two highwaymen! Today, I received a letter from my superiors instructing me to stay out of the way of the Home Office, unless they specifically ask for my help.

Given that the Home Office has not deigned to tell Bow Street who their agents are or what they are doing, I cannot understand how they expect me to stay out of their way. I have enough trouble with my own cases, without interfering in anyone else's.

STOLEN KISSES

CERISE DELAND

Stolen Kisses
By Cerise DeLand

When Lance Winters kissed Emma Tomkins pretending to be a highwayman years ago, she was ruined. Now she has a fortune—and vows to remain a spinster. But Lance, newly retired from the army, wants Emma to laugh again...and love again. So he'll dress up like a highwayman again. But can he kiss some sense into her?

CHAPTER 1

"Stiff upper, Em." Kaitlin Manning threw a fake smile toward Emma Tomkins. "Here comes another."

Emma fought the pain she knew wreathed her face. Her friend Kaitlin had agreed two weeks ago to act as Emma's second in her duel to fight off the men with marriage on their minds. This garden party was the latest soiree where Emma tolerated the hordes of fellows who were intrigued by her eight-thousand-a-year inheritance.

"Do I know him?" Emma hoped not. Aside from making a mash of long, funny names, she was discouraging fellows who thought they had a shot at getting her to marry them. Her resolution was to grow old and remain a grumpy spinster—with money to burn.

"Merton," Emma's young cousin, Diana, patted her mahogany hair and coughed out the name.

Emma searched her memory. "Where did we meet? Tell me quickly."

"Day before yesterday."

"Not the one with garlic on his breath!" Emma winced and pushed back tendrils of long fire-red hair that escaped her coiffure.

Diana chuckled.

Kaitlin, a married viscountess who'd been at this society business for eight years now, sent Diana a telling glance. "No. From Devon. Likes to swim? Your remem...Well, good day, Lord Merton." Kaitlin was always at the ready to save Emma with smiles and all the correct names of the one hundred.

"Lovely to see all you ladies." He gave a little bow. "You are all looking well."

"Thank you, my lord." Emma did her bit for the conversation. Heaven knew Lord Mutton, or whatever his name was, had little to contribute.

"I say, do you still go to Brighton next week?" he asked Emma.

"We do. Why do you ask?" *Want a newsy tidbit to offer up at tea time?*

"I just heard this morning from a friend that his sister's carriage was attacked on the Brighton road by a highwayman."

Emma froze. Kaitlin had told her about the incident this morning as they came to Lady Trilling's garden party. Highwaymen were not a subject Emma encouraged. One such friend—in a moment of impulsive desire—had masqueraded as a highwayman and kissed her. One lady had witnessed this and spread rumors which told of Emma's ruin. She'd suffered from the ton's disdain for more than ten years. She wished never to meet another highwayman, real or imposter, ever again.

"That is terrible," Emma commiserated. "I hope your friend's sister is well and that the fellow did not rob her or her fellow passengers."

"No, for some odd reason, he seemed to be in it only for the show."

"Very odd," Kaitlin said. "But it is so wonderful no one was robbed or hurt."

"You won't go to Brighton, will you, Miss Tomkins, until this man is caught?"

"Oh, I dare say, Lord Mut—" Kaitlin shook her head at her—"my lord, I am not put off by such shenanigans."

"Many robberies of shops here in town." He knit his brows. "A few in Brighton, too, in the Lanes. Not good, you know. Not proper."

"No, well, I—"

He dithered on. "I would worry about you, Miss Tomkins. Your young cousin here, too." He flashed a smile at Diana. "Little Dorothy, is it?"

Di would have corrected him, but Emma sent Di a pointed look. *Not the only one who botches names, am I?*

"I beg you to be careful," Mutton rambled on. "Wait a few days before you leave London. Do come to my reception next Wednesday for the ambassador to Berlin. Smart fellow. Hates schnitzel though."

"That is bad," Diana offered. "Hope he likes beer."

"Hmmm. Yes, good thought." Mutton focused once more on Emma. "But...but really, my dear Miss Tomkins, do remain in town. Come to my party. I have no hostess, but I would love it if you would consent to act as such for this occasion."

"Oh, Lord...my lord. I am honored at your invitation and your trust in me, but you must understand I have been in society only these two weeks and I recall few rules. My education in social arts began eleven years ago, sir, and one forgets all the tiny ins and outs." *One also remembers those who shut me out after my own highwayman pulled me from that horse and kissed me.*

"Phooey, Miss Tomkins. Put your worries of that in a boat and send them out to sea. I care not for the past."

She had to smile at his solution. He might be a jolly fellow after all. "I thank you for your concern, sir." She'd avoid using his name altogether. She'd murdered so many. "But I have appointments in Brighton I must keep."

"Do you go by private coach?"

"I hoped to take the public one from London, yes."

"Ah, but my dear Miss Tomkins." He drew himself up into his protective mode. "Do you think that wise?"

Men who had better ideas than she and who offered them up like rules to follow, set her teeth on edge.

"I do. For years, sir, I have travelled up and down the roads of England without incident."

He cocked his head. "Except for that one...."

He'd just ruined all the good will he'd stored with her in the last few minutes. She bristled.

"Have you a small pistol for your reticule?" He went on, impervious to her glower and her clenched fists.

"I do." She didn't, of course. She would never own a weapon. Life was too precious to threaten another with harm. She'd had enough of that from her father's fists. "My cousin and I will be safe, sir."

At her clipped retort, he saw the error of his ways. Smart to retreat, he offered the tip of his head and his excuses.

"Mutton-head," she seethed.

"Now, now." Kaitlin shot Emma a frightened look. "Gather yourself. Here comes Lady Shackleford."

Disaster. Emma had managed to avoid the notorious tattletale at the previous events she'd attended in London. But today was the end of her reprieve. She'd do her duty and pretend she remembered not one thing the woman had spread about her.

"Good afternoon, Lady Shackleford," Kaitlin did the honors. "I am certain you remember my dear friend, Miss Emma Tomkins, and this is her young cousin, Miss Diana Tomkins."

The lady was taller than Emma, towering over most in the room, even the men. She was thin, too, so much so that a strong wind might not only destroy her wiry grey coif, but pick up her bony body and blow her out the garden wall.

Oh, what mercies joyful to behold. Emma grumbled to herself as the woman and Diana exchanged pleasantries.

Then the woman turned her spectral face on Emma. "I am happy to see you back in society, Miss Tomkins."

What a lie. You are the one most responsible for me being excluded from society ten years ago. But this was her mother's best friend's garden party and Emma could not strangle this woman in the midst of her friends and the last whiffs of the fragrance of roses.

"Thank you for the welcome, my lady. My cousin and I are delighted to share in the good society."

"I understand," she said with a lift of her monocle and a survey of Diana's hair and demure décolleté. "You come to renew old acquaintances. How lovely."

Emma would give this busybody nothing to carry from her presence. "We are."

"And next you close your uncle's house in Queen Square and go to Brighton."

That bit was public knowledge. "It is so."

"It is also rumored you wish to sell your uncle's house. Why? It could serve as your residence when in town for the Season?"

"It could," Emma said with a nod. "But it won't." She intended to bring out her young cousin, Diana Tomkins, in Brighton. A smaller community that swelled when the Prince Regent came to visit, Brighton's pleasures were more manageable for Emma and for Diana. Her seventeen-year-old cousin was a new heiress, a rich merchant's cousin, and a smart young thing who deserved to take her time selecting a husband. If indeed, Di wanted one at all.

"I understand," the lady said as she leaned close and tried to pry news from them, "you wish to formally come out while in Brighton."

Emma shot Di a warning glance. Her cousin was well aware of Lady Shackleford's behavior and Emma's dislike of the woman.

"I take my cousin's recommendations, my lady. She knows so much more than I."

The lady pursed her tiny lips together. "Yes, well."

"Forgive me, my lady," Emma had had enough of her snooping. "I must go sit in the shade."

"Ah, yes, your freckles will multiply, won't they?"

Along with my anger. "Good afternoon, madam." Then Emma, her cousin and her friend strode away.

The three women found an empty garden table and four chairs.

"Wine is in order," Kaitlin said as she tried to catch a footman's eye.

"Make that two for me," Emma groused. "Sorry," she said to Di, who knew she drank only in moderation, but to whom alcohol was an anathema.

Di shook it all away. "I know who you are, Cuz. Have two if you wish. We'll just say you're having one for me."

"You are a dear." Her young cousin was not yet out in formal society, but Emma took her along to less formal gatherings like this one to allow her to become comfortable with the goings on in town.

Kaitlin murmured her appreciation as a footman appeared and set before them four glasses of white wine. "If you could bring us a lemonade for our young friend, I would be most happy."

As Emma watched him leave, her gaze fell across the French doors to the main salon of their hostess's home. And she gulped.

What is he doing here?

Why? Why now?

Obvious, old girl. Building his new reputation as an earl. Or was it as viscount? With some never-ending title, too.

Emma could not recall. She'd stopped reading the bits in the newspapers about Lancelot Winters, the young cousin of some funny-named earl or baron or whatever who'd inherited his relative's worldly goods. *Good for you, Lance. You deserve some rewards for what you have endured.*

She wanted to go to him, stand near, inhale his devotion to lemon-scented soap and remember his endearing friendship—and dashing courtship. She should go and express her delight at his appearance, if only in form...if that were even acceptable. Which it was not. Still, quite a formidable figure he cut, too. And luscious to look at for a man who was....

Let's see. I am now twenty-nine, so Lance, you are thirty-one.

"Cuz!" Diana sat wide-eyed and nigh unto panting at the vision of handsome Lance at the door. "Who is that?"

"The new earl or...um...something." Honestly, she never remembered names. They were like recipes, long and too involved. "I don't remember."

"But you looked at him for ever so long, so you do know him, though?"

"She did," Kaitlin rolled her eyes at Emma. "Very well."

Diana shivered. "Oh, you must be thrilled. I mean. Will he come introduce himself?"

"If he presents himself, Di, he does because it is the correct thing to do." And if he does venture this way, he'd better make it all brief. *The Shackleford Woman took no prisoners. Ever. And with his appearance and hers, the biddy would make a fuss to compare only to Waterloo.*

Emma's sketchy understanding of formal rules of the *ton* left her bereft of the rule for who greeted whom. Man to woman? Old friend to renewed? Emma hated the *ton's rules.* None had ever helped her. Until now when society curried her favor because she had money.

She did her best not to sneer at the very idea. Money. Quite a bit. More than many a lord or lady could strangle from their impoverished estates. For her new-found wealth—they honored her for its acquisition, inherited though it was. Let her back into their graces, as if she'd forgotten all ridicule—and forgiven it, too.

And she did. She did it for Diana's sake.

"Don't worry, Diana," Kaitlin said with a wicked smile on her face. "If he does not appear—which I sincerely doubt— you and I can stroll his way and renew my acquaintance with him."

"Thank you, Lady Lawton. But why not you, Cuz?" The girl knew nothing about the disaster of years ago, only that the gossiping likes of Lady Shackleford had done her worst.

"Why? Because, Di, we are no longer friends. We were once, but now Lord... Oh, drat it, Kaitlin. It begins with a 'w'. What is his new title?"

"Weatherby-Soames of Pickford and Fife." Kaitlin winked at Emma, her whimsy to fill in such silly gobs of information for her scatter-brained friend.

"My, my," said the girl, dreamy-eyed, "all that and such dashing good looks, too."

Emma hummed. She refused to feast on the mature looks of the man her childhood best friend had become. Refused to turn or acknowledge the powerful picture of his sun-streaked cinnamon hair, broad shoulders, bronzed cheeks and of course, his lips. His unforgettable sensuous lips.

"He's not married," supplied Kaitlin for Diana, though she kept her merry gaze on Emma. "But the *on dit* constantly heard is that the man is looking for a spouse."

Emma set her teeth at that. She'd told Kaitlin she would not discuss Lance Winters. Not his new title and wealth. Not his soldier's past in the Army Engineers. Nor his love of horses and mules. And definitely not what he'd done one fine afternoon in Derby as Emma passed through a small village in a hired coach with six other passengers on board.

"How old is he?" Diana asked, now besotted. Beneath those mischievous sea green eyes, the girl clicked the locks on leg-shackles to poor Lance Winters.

"What is he, Em? Thirty-four? Five?"

"One," she let out through pursed lips. "One and thirty."

"So just the right age to marry," said Diana with a satisfied giggle. "And set up his nursery."

That Emma would not discuss, so she sprang to her feet. "I do believe the sun has doubled every freckle I own. Come, Di, we'll say our thanks to our hostess and find our way home."

"No!" The girl pouted. "We just got here."

"Not really." For effect, Emma lifted the tiny face of her watch pinned to her the shoulder of her jade sarcenet gown. "One hour and eleven minutes."

Diana frowned. "Cuz, please. Let us stay long enough for Lady Lawton to approach Lord Weatherby-Sizzle and Fizzle or whatever his name is. You know I long to do well in society, now that we have..." she leaned over the table to whisper "...you know, filthy lucre." Di thought the *ton*'s need of wealthy women a joke on their short-sightedness.

Emma sat quite still, her blood gone cold over the idea of money. Her cousin knew nothing about how their wealth had resurrected Emma from the low rungs of the social ladder. It was best she not know. Neither would Emma ever tell her. What had happened ten years ago on that Derbyshire road would stay there. Her cousin would benefit from not knowing...just as Emma would from never looking back.

"We are leaving. Come, Di." She leaned toward Kaitlin to buss her cheek in goodbye.

Her friend allowed the kiss then cocked a brow at her. "You do not wish to do the gracious act of congratulating the new viscount of Weather and Storm personally?"

"No." Emma ignored how her dear friend tormented her by calling Lance by an obviously wrong title. Instead, she yanked on her gloves. "And you know why."

"Why?" asked Diana, her sea foam gaze full of innocent inquiry.

❧

Lance Winters stood in the entrance to the garden and searched for his hostess. The one whom he'd spotted the minute he'd entered was the one he purposely sought. But he needed entry, didn't he?

He did not court society. This garden party, like the two balls he'd attended a few nights ago, was a maze to him. Rather like looking at the horizon of strange uncharted Spanish territory he had to conquer.

"At least, with my horses, I knew I had friends to help me out." Here? The best he could hope for would be a sympathetic hostess who'd take pity on him and introduce him to a few.

Especially to the only one who mattered to him.

The best he could hope for would be that his hostess, Lady Trilling, would take pity on him at once and lead him over to Emma. He had hopes that Em had not spied him and that he had time to play at a being a good guest, then somehow get Lady Trilling to help him over to Em and her friend Kaitlin Manning, whatever-her-married name was, and allow him a few moments of success.

Yes, he was here for Emma. Who the hell else would he want in this crowd of giggling ladies, and self-impressed peacocks, eager for the right chance?

But he would be a good boy in these circles. So, he followed the footman to the gazebo with an eager smile. He sought to ingratiate himself with these people. If only to get Emma to smile at him. *Or more than.*

"Lord Weatherby!" His hostess trilled out his name in her glass-breaking soprano. How fitting to be named 'Trilling'. "We are delighted to welcome you to our little gathering. I understand you are ever so busy moving into your homes in the north and in London."

"Just so, my lady." He gave her his most charming smile. It was the best he could do with his valet having tied his cravat to a murderous inch. He bowed, too, as he took the woman's hand. "But I am keen to meet so many and I am grateful for your kind invitation."

"We are thrilled to have you, my lord. Many in London are affable and good hearted. And we are especially thrilled to welcome into our fold former soldiers who did so well in Spain and France."

He wanted to scoff at that. London had not been kind to Emma after he so brashly ruined her ten years ago. He disliked whoever had demeaned her by implying she had done something wrong when he had been the 'bandit' who kissed her. Indeed, he cared not for accolades for his military service. War was a dirty, nasty business. He'd much preferred his assignment to the wilds of Canada last year. Yet now, his sole objective was making his life round and plentiful—and doing the same for Emma Tomkins too. "I look forward to the acquaintance of those who will be so kind as to smooth my way into my duties. I am green at this business and I am not averse to admitting it."

The lady extended a hand. "Allow me to introduce you to a few of those."

He offered her his arm, and as they strolled by little groups of her guests, he did the pretty and won them to his purpose.

"All the ladies will be fluttering like butterflies to learn more about you, sir."

From the corner of his eye, he saw Emma shoot to her feet. *Leaving are you? But then you don't flutter, you fly.*

"Well, my lady, I will tell you now that not much is intriguing about the life of an Army Engineer."

"In that corps, you do not fight other soldiers but the very earth, sir. That, in itself, is a Herculean effort."

"Often one more fit to be ascribed to Sisyphus."

She tipped her head, her eyes locked on his, truly interested in her response. "How so?"

He inhaled, his vision filled with the sight of a pontoon across a slow-flowing Catalan river. He'd calculated every angle, depth, speed of water, height of obstructing rocks. But he'd been wrong. His team of four horses stuck in the silt of the bed and his flat blocks over which all would travel—men, mules, cannon—had stuck. Pulling the mess from the river took three days and nights. Thus, the British missed their advantage over the French exposure.

He credited Lady Trilling for her interest, and softened the blow of his bitter memory of the disaster. "One's miscalculations are as misfortunate as those of one's enemy. War is a constant battle to gain sight of tomorrow. One day's labor is often a duplicate of the last."

"Oh," she said with a frown and a pat of his arm. "I fear too many of our returned soldiers tell tales of tedium and delay."

"I'm sure many do. We mustn't criticize them, but know they do that to repress the nightmares of bullets, bombs and men screaming for their mothers."

"My dear Lord Weatherby, should you need anything—and I do mean anything—to aid you now that you are home, you must tell me."

He met her with frankness in his gaze. "You were once my mother's best friend and in that spirit of good heartedness I ask you if you have you heard of my behavior ten years ago to a certain lady who is your guest?"

Her myriad wrinkles melted into each other as she beamed at him. They had stopped, away from others to have this conversation. "I have. A sad, unnecessary wagging of tongues. But only murmurs of it remain, thank goodness. Why, I do believe I hope you are interested in redeeming yourself for that peccadillo?"

"I am. Very much so."

"Do enlist me in your campaign, my lord."

"Then please. Lead on. I need all the help I can get."

Just in time, too, as from his right, Lance saw a swish of jade skirts. So, his Emma came, not to greet him. No, no. She was here to bid *adieu* and escape him.

Lady Trilling had another idea. With a pat to his arm, she stepped toward Emma...and his darling was suddenly in front of him with nowhere to run. "My dearest Miss Tomkins!"

Emma stood frozen.

"Forgive me, Lady Trilling," Emma said to her hostess while she herself remained standing face- to-face with the very man she had tried to avoid.

"Not leaving so soon, my dear! Why, you have not greeted our newest guest. I understand you are childhood friends. Miss Emma Tomkins, allow me to reacquaint you with Lord Weatherby."

"Miss Tomkins." Lance did the necessary, smiling broader, wishing harder than any time in his life that Emma would show some friendliness toward him.

"How wonderful to see you again, sir. You look fit." What in hell was she going on about? "Congratulations are in order, too, for your new title and responsibilities."

"The title is one I know so little about. Since I've been home, I've done nothing but walk the land and read the estate records of the past decade. It's a mountain of information."

"So, you have visited your estate? Forgive me, I cannot recall if you had ever been to your cousins' home."

Her voice quivered. She sounded like a schoolgirl. But then she remembered some manners and said to her cousin, "Allow me, my dear, to present Lord Weatherby. Miss Diana Tomkins, Lord Weatherby of ...of Sloan and ...and..."

"Firth." The girl stepped into the breach of Emma's lapse, the smile on her face aglow with a thousand lights and expectations. "My lord." She curtsied. "Delighted to make your acquaintance, sir."

"As am I, Miss Tomkins."

"I hope you will be out and about at future parties," the girl put in.

He looked startled at her forwardness. "I receive invitations by the dozens. Society has been welcoming."

"Miss Tomkins," Lady Trilling put in with a helpful tone, "is not yet out but her cuz brings her to less formal gatherings."

"How kind of your cousin." Lance took in the beauty of Emma, so full of trepidation at his nearness that he wanted to sweep her up and carry her away. But then, that was his usual reaction to Emma... and it only caused scandal. "I know her to be the most generous soul. You are fortunate, Miss Tomkins."

His compliment pinked Emma's cheeks and she shook herself to answer. "Lady Trilling, thank you for the lovely afternoon. My cousin and I have enjoyed it tremendously."

"You must return then. Next Friday? I have begun these little affairs on a weekly basis."

"Thank you so much, but I must decline. My cousin and I go to Brighton next week."

That was news. What was attracting her to Brighton?

Well, wherever she was, there he would be also. "How long do you stay?"

She met his gaze with sharp lift of her chin. "Forever. I will buy a house. It has always been my fondest wish to live close to the sea. Now...with my new circumstances, I can do this."

"I see. I am happy for you," he said with a sincerity motivated more by his desire to uplift her. God knew he did not wish to see her leave London. Not when he had so nearly arrived and tried to settle himself into the social scene, only to lose her to Brighton.

"When do you leave?" Lady Trilling did his work for him.

"Friday, we go. My cousin is very excited. I am, too."

Lance could not hide his gloom. "I am sorry to hear you leave town. I would like to resurrect our friendship."

"Thank you, sir. That is kind. Perhaps if you ever visit Brighton?" She was too enthusiastic, pretending she wished to see him. He could see her warning to him to stay away, But, she offered her hand in parting.

Bad as he could be, he bowed and took it. Her long warm fingers tugged, like bands around his heart. "I will make a point of it now."

He could see how she wanted to reprimand him, but she held her tongue.

With that, she and her cousin trailed off toward the main salon and Emma's escape from him.

Wily woman. Ever was she the prankster, the escape artist, the one who brought mystery and laughter into his life.

Well, Emma Tomkins. I do not care how you wish to escape me. I have waited too long to see you again. Avoided your presence for years because I had nothing to offer. But I need you. Your humor. Your valor.

I will follow you.

CHAPTER 2

E mma dropped her shears in her apron pocket and admired her trimming of the rose bush.

This was her garden, her refuge in her Uncle George's house. It was lush, only a hint of its regular fragrance now in mid-October. But she had tended it so carefully, that it sported one enormous red rose. If she sold the house, she would miss this and more of what she'd created here in this plot in the midst of the city. There was not much she adored that still existed. Her first pony, gone to an arthritic old age. Her kind and loving governess, banished by her father. Her oldest friend, gone to war, home now to...to...torment her with his bright green gaze and earnest behavior.

None of that had she any control over. But now at Uncle George's passing, she had the freedom to live as she chose, to ignore what had come before. Her uncle had ensured that for her...and for Diana.

Freedom that took her out into the world of which she knew so little. Freedom that took her to garden parties where Lady Shackleford spoke about her behind her long skinny fingers. Freedom where she had stared at the woman with knowledge of what she did...and what she had done years ago to sully Emma's name.

But then the image of the new, the vital, the dashing Lance Winters rose up before her like a genie from a lamp. He'd seemed to grow taller, broader, more imposing, and impossible to ignore with his sunny good looks and disposition. What was she doing, silently yearning for a moment alone with the Lance of her youth and the entrancing Lance who'd appeared yesterday?

Oh, yes, she shivered as she closed her eyes to chase him away. But he remained, stubborn fellow. And why not? He deserved more than a moment's regard. After all, she was proud of him.

He had endured. Survived the worst that life can give a man. War had built him, broadened him, rewarded him with vigor and health. He'd served faithfully in the hellish war against Napoleon. Then, so said her uncle, he'd been sent immediately to Canada. New colonists there needed protection from raging waterways and flaming forests. Army engineers built roads and bridges, tunnels and dams. Then suddenly on the death of Lance's cousin, fate had granted him wealth and status he'd never sought to claim.

His health and prosperity was another sign that some elements of her youth lived and flourished. She could celebrate his success as she should now celebrate her own change of circumstances.

She smiled to herself and touched her fingertip to the velvet petal of her last red rose of the year. *Perhaps I shall keep this house. Why not? It pleases me. If and when it doesn't, I can decide to sell.*

"P-p-pardon me, m-miss," her butler Jeffries came to the salon door.

Emma swung around to face him. Sans hair on his head and eyebrows, he had piercing blue eyes—and a palsy. Despite that, he would not allow her to pension him off. He'd served her Uncle George for more than thirty years and deserved a restful retirement. Poor fellow was right as rain in his head, but he had a terrible time talking. "You you you have a a c-caller."

"This early?" She did not know many rules of proper society but she did know no one called on another before two or three in the afternoon. When she'd come out here to prune her roses, the hall clock was just striking eleven. "Who is it?"

Jeffries winced. "Lord Weatherby, miss."

"Lance?" She let slip his given name.

"Yes, Miss. What shall I say? Do you re-receive?"

She whirled about, facing her roses and the white pagoda where she spent so many hours in silent joy. *Why did he come here and attack her serenity?*

"Miss?" Jeffries urged, his tone wobbly with worry. The old fellow had been in service to her Uncle George when she'd been disgraced years ago. He knew what receiving Lance could cost her.

"Let me in, Emma."

At the sound of his voice, her mind was flooded with old memories of how assertive he'd always been. Defying rules of his uncle not to ride the prize thoroughbreds in the family stables. Crawling up the drain spouts on her family's house to her bedroom and crawling along the branches of the old yew to scramble inside her room.

Years ago, she had thrilled to his escapades. She did now at this, too. Some things never changed. But the stakes were higher now, and just as treacherous.

She took him in, his power and might. Her hands perspired in her anxiety. She patted the palms of her hands on her yellow gardening smock. She'd have done with this matter now and for good. "Do, yes, come join me."

His magnificent physique was nothing to his grin of delight at her acceptance.

"Jeffries, please bring us tea and whatever Cook has available. Please ask Miss Diana to attend us here."

Lance strolled toward her, handing over his hat and gloves to Jeffries as he passed. "We don't need your cousin to chaperone, Emma. We are such old friends, how could we endanger each other's reputation?"

She dropped open her mouth. "You cannot be serious!"

"I am," he said as he stood right before her. So close, too close, she could inhale the scent of his morning bath. Lemon-scented soap. "It's been years. Ten of them. Too long."

She scoffed. A good thing, too. Looking up at his perfection burned her eyes. She would not fall prey to his charms. "Clearly, you must work the receiving lines more frequently. Did you meet Lady Shackleford at Lady Trilling's?"

He laughed and availed himself of a garden chair. No invitation to sit necessary for *such old friends* who have ruined each other, eh? "The woman with the silver hair?"

"And silver tongue."

"Yes." He crossed one long leg over the other, looking like a rogue in command of all before him. "I must say I expected her to slither along the floor."

Emma snorted. "She would want to show you her most sterling characteristics. She has two daughters in the marriage mart."

"And two bricks tied to each ankle," he crooned as he pressed a hand down his thigh, "wishing you to come drown in her cesspool with her. I've nearly drowned in clearer eddies."

She smiled at his joke.

He pointed a finger at her. "I see that."

"It's gone now." She grimaced at him, and he had the audacity to chuckle. "What do you want? Why are you here?"

His expression tightened. "Well, I did not come here to argue."

"I want to." Oh, she was being irrational and he always caught her out at that.

He winced. "Did your cook put sand in your tea this morning?"

"Oh! Get on with it!"

"I cannot rub along with you if you insist on being a harpy!"

"Did you just come here to tease and torment me?"

He lost all pretense of humor and locked his verdant green gaze on hers. "You know I've come to make you laugh."

"That day is done. I do not smile."

"You just did. Perhaps I can help you do it again?"

"How can you say that?" She swept out an arm, flabbergasted. "You honestly don't know why I cannot be gay?"

"Know what? What's happened to you? I know your father is gone and your uncle, too. Your cousin is with you. But what else can I know, Em? How can I? I am only down from the wilds of Northumbria since last week. There ever since February to take over for my dearly departed cousin. Before that I was in Canada, Em. For nearly two long years." He cursed beneath his breath and ran a hand over his hair. "Do you have any idea where Canada is?"

"Don't be ridiculous." She rolled her shoulder and sniffed. She'd worried and wondered about him for years off in the wilderness with wild animals and native peoples. "Of course, I have a globe."

"The mail gets to our encampment once a month. Little though that matters because you never answered my letters."

"You wrote?" She was crushed, appalled that someone—her father?—had kept Lance's letters from her.

"Of course I did." He looked stricken, as if she had wounded him. "You did not write to me. Neither would your father send me word of your health and—"

"You wrote my father?" She was stunned. The man had never told her.

"When I had no word, I knew not what else to do. He told me to forget you. No kind word of his regard. Not that I expected that of him. He was not one to offer solicitations in peace or war."

"I'll say!"

"Finally, I wrote to your Uncle George and he told me you had retired to his country house in Derbyshire. He reported you were well and wished to remain there. I speculated as to your reasoning, but then I knew you preferred your uncle's company to your father's." Lance stepped near again and urged both her hands from her pockets. "I promised I'd write. I keep my promises."

"That day when you kissed me you also promised to return for me. But you never did. I lost hope."

"I nearly did myself, Em. I was sent to Canada immediately after we occupied Paris. I never came home until February, then I went north immediately. My cousin Thomas, my predecessor, was dying and I was to replace him immediately. I had no say in any of my destiny. None."

He learned forward, his attitude one of a supplicant. "Please come sit and talk to me, Em."

His tender plea touched her heart. She sat, chastising herself for acting like a twit, sorrowing for what they had lost. Peaches came to purr around her legs and then his.

He put out a hand and circled one of her wrists with firm fingers. "I came to renew our friendship."

She took back her arm and shoved her hands in her apron pockets. "That is not possible."

"Why not?" He cast about the garden as if looking for others. "Is there some man for whom you have an *entendre*? I asked about, but no one mentioned any attachment."

His admission swelled her heart. He had inquired about her affections before he came here. She bit her lower lip. Well, he might have done but that still did not change what had happened between them ten years ago. Within days of that fiasco, he had left for war and Spain. She had suffered the nightmare of the *ton*'s scourge. Courtesy, of course, of one of the witnesses of their madness, Lady Shackleford.

"I have no attachment, no tender feelings for any man." *Only you. Ever you have I valued. Near, far, here, not.* "But you do not know how cruelly society cut me from their regard."

"I did not know that." He paused, somber as if ingesting its meanness. "Does it go on? After ten years? What folly is that?"

"The *ton* does not care for pranks. Not for jokes between friends. Especially not between male and female."

"What I did that day was in jest, and I regret that it hurt you so badly. But that is over, done. Ten years ago. How many highwaymen are there in England? The antics of Dick Turpin and his ilk are gone. It was I who had taken you from that coach and kissed you in the glen."

Tears burned her eyes. Her anger cooled to heartbreak, she saw him as she had that day. Awash in black, his body lithe and agile. His blond curls hanging from the bandana too loosely tied to his head. "I had to leave London. My come out was no more. I could not bear the whispers."

"Oh, Em, if only I'd been here." He went to his knees before her and circled his hands around her waist. "I would have helped—"

The sound of someone clearing their throat froze them both.

"Excuse me," murmured Diana, eyeing the way Lance's hands were still on Emma. "Jeffries asked me to come." She pointed her thumb over her shoulder and gave them a forced smile. "I—I can leave though."

Emma pulled from Lance's arms. "Stay. Do."

The girl licked her lips and looked back into the dark of the house. "I left my embroidery in the morning room and I can get it if—"

"Don't bother, Di. I'm certain you remember Lord Weatherby from Lady Trilling's party. He is just leaving."

"You'll throw me out?" He arched a brow, partly shocked and partly humored as he rose to his feet.

Emma swallowed. "You've overstayed your welcome."

"Have I?"

"Has he?"

"How?" He stared at Emma.

"I cannot see you, sir. Not anywhere. Not here. Not in public. People remember and they talk."

"To hell with them!"

Diana clucked in agreement.

Emma shook her head at the girl and then at him. "I cannot allow it, Lance. You must leave off."

"Why?" he asked.

"Yes, why?" Di persisted.

Her young cousin had too much pluck—but Em went on, "Diana and I have new opportunities. With Uncle George's generosity, both of us can now see bright futures. But it means I'll have no resurrection of the past. What you and I did on that road ten years ago ruined me."

"What did you both—?" Di began.

Emma quashed the girl's question with a scalding look. "I want a clean slate for Diana. I want her to be able to choose a good man who loves her. I want her to stand tall and proud among her peers. I will not do more than nod and pass a few words with you, Lance. I will not risk it."

"Then allow me to tell you why I am here, my dear Emma. I regret the past and how you suffered for my actions. But I will make amends to you. I swear it.

"I do not care how you wish to escape me. I have come to see you again because for the first time in my life, I have something to offer. As of February, heaven help me, I am the proud possessor of hundreds of acres of prime farmland. I have twenty-five tenants. Forty head of prime cattle. Nine goats. Four mules, two elegant Arabians I find of no practical use to me, but four strong Percheron horses I ordered from a friend in Brittany and shipped home."

He bent and snatched up Peaches from between his legs.

"I have no cats, but I welcome this one to join us. I have need of a good mouser."

"Peaches is not a mouser." Em reached to take the cat from his arms, but the animal batted her hands away.

He chuckled. "I dare say, she'll give me a go, won't you, Peaches?"

The cat snuggled up under his chin and gave him a good rub, purring loud as a beating drum.

Em could only marvel at how he'd commanded her garden, her cat, and destroyed so much of the past that had plagued her.

"I am rich, Em. In land, title, money and hope. I have spent my life, even after that disastrous comedy on that Derbyshire road, wanting only you. Needing only you.

"But you have changed. I see it. You've lost your funny bone. Become a grump—and a bit of a witch, too."

"Oh, you dare...!" *Where was her dignity?* Gone with his charm, by Jove.

He grinned. "I do dare. I want you. And I will show you I am to be relied upon. I am a gentleman in very fine fettle. You'd do well to allow me to court you. But if you don't, well...I will anyway. Do be prepared.

"The *ton* was cruel to cast you out. I could care less for any one of them. It's you I want. So do stand at the ready, my darling. You cannot get rid of me."

Then he turned on his heels.

As he dropped the affectionate Peaches into Diana's arms and picked up his hat and gloves from an open-mouthed Jeffries, Di curtsied and wished him a very good day. "It took weeks for Peaches to like me. Do you think it is his lemon bath soap she likes?"

CHAPTER 3

"Cuz!" Diana burst through the morning room door, aflutter and brandishing a green box in her hand. "Look what just arrived!"

Emma happily closed the ledger of household expenses and pushed aside Peaches who'd inspected the pages more than Emma had. She'd meant to tally the month's current household expenditures, but she'd allowed Peaches her way. Nor did she blame the cat for her failure because in truth for over an hour, she had fiddled and fantasized that she was a different person from the one who had been such a nitwit toward Lance yesterday. She really was in need of a change of scenery—and heart.

"What do you have there?" Smiling, she beckoned Di. "Who doesn't like surprises, eh?"

The box, a sage green satin affair, had clearly been hand-wrapped. The huge white satin bow intrigued her, too.

"Oh, I am certain you'll like this one, Cuz." She pounced it down on the desktop and put her hands behind her back. Di's usual expression of joy was rising repeatedly on her toes. Her father, Emma's father's younger brother, had been an exuberant fellow, even when in his cups which was daily. Unlike Emma's father who drank to indulge his rage, Diana's had brought up his child with a sense of impetuosity. Emma delighted in the girl's tendency to find joy in life's little pleasures.

Em had found a similar joy at the advanced old age of twenty-five after her father's death when she'd gone to live in London with his oldest brother, her Uncle George. Those four years had brought back some of her positive outlook on life. The fortune her uncle had granted her upon his demise went a long way to making that more of a reality. Di's presence did, too. And now, only days ago, the return of Lance Winters to her life injected an air of frivolity. Would that she could apply that happiness to all her days. That nothing the *ton* did or dictated would threaten to hurt her.

Best to begin with this box! She wiggled her fingers over the lovely thing like a magician eliciting treasures.

"Hurry, hurry!" Di grasped her hands before her in prayer. "Gifts are meant to be opened wide with great abandon."

Emma took the girl's words with a jolt to her heart. She hadn't known a moment's abandon since one special man had swept her off her feet and kissed her madly ten years ago.

She cleared her throat. "Let's do it!" She tugged at the luscious white satin bow and it melted to the desk like new butter. "Hmmm. Whoever wrapped this knew how to do a good job."

"Yes, yes." Di was in raptures. "What do you think it is?"

Peaches jumped up on a nearby table, curious too.

"Well! I have no idea. Did Jeffries say there was a card?"

"No. It must be inside. To keep you guessing, eh?"

Emma rolled a shoulder. She liked surprises. Savored them. She'd received so many bouquets from suitors in the past week that the main parlor looked and smelled like a hothouse. She'd appreciated them all and written effusive thank-you notes, even though she knew she encouraged the men beyond necessity.

But a box of green satin was an appealing new gift. Like the wild-flower bouquets Lance used to pick for her. The gaily wrapped rose bush cutting he'd given her years ago when she'd admired his father's garden in the cold northern plains. Now, now there was this lovely thing.

She licked her lips, lifted the box and found the main closure of the green satin. She grinned as she burrowed her fingers between the tightly wrapped fabric. Only one who knew how to build bridges or connect old roads would know how to enclose a box as deftly.

Inside were a jumble of items from Fortnum & Mason. A tall tin of tea leaves. Biscuits. A smaller round tin filled with sugar drops, pale peach, and to Emma's mind, most likely that same flavor. Finally, an embroidered tea towel. Emma shook it out and Lance's card drifted to her desk.

"Charming," Di enthused as she sat and Peaches jumped toward her to settle on her lap. "And the card says...?"

Emma held it, the paper fragrant with tea and candied peach. "'The sweets I missed yesterday I hope for tomorrow.'"

"Oh, I am sighing, Cuz. I like him even more than yesterday. But wait, he can't have tea tomorrow with us," Di frowned, disappointed. "We'll be gone to Brighton."

Emma was certain he knew they left then. They'd discussed it at Lady Trilling's.

"What will you say?" Di leaned over the desk and the gift box, eager for a sweet.

Emma offered her the tin to choose as she wished. "To Lord Weatherby?"

"Yes, won't you pen a note of thanks?"

"I will."

"Do add that we go to Brighton tomorrow."

"He knows that from discussion, Di. But wherever we are, I should not receive him. That would be unfair to him and I don't want to encourage him."

"But do tell me, Cuz, why not?"

Emma rose from her desk and walked to the window overlooking the rose garden. Browning to the colors of autumn, all nature anticipated winter. She awaited a new beginning for herself. "I know I've been secretive about why I remained out of society. I can tell you. I can. I find it useful only as a cautionary tale for you."

"Lord Weatherby and I have had a special friendship, borne in our youth. We understand each other. Complete each other's sentences. Know intuitively what the other wants, thinks, hopes for. Except for one thing. Weatherby has a funny bone. A silly streak. I lack such a thing.

"One day ten years ago, he dressed in black, climbed his horse and waylaid the coach I rode in. He did it as a lark. I laughed at first as I climbed down. I recognized him immediately, of course. He took me to one side and kissed me. Quite..." She recalled the moment his firm hot lips met hers. "Quite madly. There was another passenger in the coach who took delight in telling one and all about it, including news to a paper that printed the story. I was ostracized. Ruined. Unfit for good society. I retired to a secluded life. Soon after that day, Lance...Lord Weatherby who was an army engineer in the Royal Corps went off to fight in the Peninsula. I did not hear from him. I thought he did not write. I was bereft. I had to label the incident over and done...and disastrous. Only when he visited here the other day did he tell me he had written, even to my father and my uncle. My father did not reply to him. Uncle George did and it seems he miscommunicated the reasons for my retirement to his house in the country. It all seems such a tragedy over what was intended to be a bit of fun."

Diana grew angry, pointing at Emma. "But you did not ride out dressed like a bandit and kiss someone! Cuz, Lord Weatherby did!"

"But I paid the price for it, Di. Women do. Even though—"

"Even though what, Cuz?"

"I loved his dash, his abandon. We had been friends for years, his family's estate close by my uncles in the north. I had encouraged Lance, loving his pranks...and he liked mine. We were quite a pair." In her reverie, Emma felt the joy of that day as he leapt off his horse. The thrill of his hot embrace. And the rapture of his kiss. "He played a joke that day. He thought no one would care. Not as much as they did."

"So, it was others who spoiled that for you," Di said with bitterness. "Who are they to speak ill of you?"

"One of those in the coach that day was Lady Shackleford."

"Oh, no!" Di froze, her sea green eyes sad. "And she used it to carve a space for herself among those with small minds and small intentions."

"She did." Emma stroked the white satin ribbon. "But over time, I did learn one thing from her. Never hold your breath for anyone. Do what you know is right and ignore any criticism for it. You will sleep better at night and perhaps even live longer!"

CHAPTER 4

Emma could not leave London fast enough. In her haste and delight to be gone, she grinned at her maid, then recounted the two trunks and two valises—one each for Diana and herself—that stood before her in the hall. She patted the one tucked under her arm that contained all her financial documents.

"As soon as I find a house I like," she told her maid and Jeffries, "I will send for the rest of my clothes and Diana's too."

"Miss," the young woman bobbed. "I'll be happy to do that and join you as well."

"Just take good care of Peaches while we're gone." The cat wound round the maid's ankles. "I'd love to take her with us, but I fear the hotel may not accept animals."

"We will. Never worry, Miss," said Jeffries who stood to one side, his craggy face a mix of his worries and his joys. He and Emma had had a long discussion about him remaining to run the house here after she and Diana left. He wished to come and attend them in Brighton. He was right—and Emma understood his affections—when he declared that he'd served only the Tomkins family all his adult life. He did not wish to stop now. Emma had honored his wishes and told him she would summon him to Brighton, if he wished. He did.

He also worried about their travels being disrupted by attacks of a highwayman. "The South Downs," he had said at least three times these past few days, "have been plagued with the fellow since summer. They cannot seem to catch him!"

But Emma had been adamant. They were leaving. Highwayman or not.

"Jeffries," she addressed him now, her hands out and a smile on her face, "be good to yourself while we are away. Rest. We have given you quite a charge here the last month. I am grateful for your service, sir."

"Anything to m-make you happy, Miss. You deserve the best and I wish to see you receive it. Always."

"Thank you, sir. Now, Diana?" She called up the stairs.

The girl floated down to the foyer. Her wavy mahogany-colored hair she'd caught up in a loose coil and her sea green eyes, the singular Tomkins trait, sparkled with excitement.

"Are you ready for our new adventure?" Emma teased, for Diana wore her delight like a new gown.

'Our new adventure' was what Diana called each new experience she and Emma had since they heard the reading of their Uncle George's will four weeks ago. That gentleman's dictates to give the running of his merchant business to his chief clerk, and to grace his only two heirs—his cousins Emma and Diana—with eight thousand pounds a year each had changed the two women's lives for the better.

Emma returned to society from obscurity, but now an heiress of note with the family characteristics of flaming copper hair and sea blue eyes, still a beauty at twenty-nine. Emma's young cousin and daughter of the third Tomkins brother, Diana, was a young woman of good education thanks to Uncle George, and a bright future as anything she wished, married or not.

Emma thrilled to their prospects. *Bless you, Uncle George, for offering us hope and joy.*

"Let's be on our way, Di. We do not want to miss the coach stop." She turned, left the house she'd come to love and climbed into her uncle's twin coach, then sank to the squabs. Diana followed and sat opposite. Jeffries climbed in beside Diana, having argued to sit up in the box with the family coachman, but Emma would have none of that. He was too frail for such acrobatics, though she dared not voice that. So, he came with them to the public coach stop at the corner of Piccadilly. He'd insisted it was his duty to supervise their departure and ensure their comfort.

The transfer was quick. Lucky for her and Di, only one other person traveled with them. They were to travel the turnpike and if they had no accidents or challenges with the horses, they'd stop only at Crawley at a carriage inn. From there, Brighton was only two hours way.

Emma sank into her seat beside Di with a sigh. She was tired of the round of London parties, receptions and callers. Brighton would be less hectic. More discreet. Initially, she and Diana would take rooms in the Old Ship Hotel. There they would remain until Emma found a house she liked that she wished to purchase. She might even like one close to the shore. The sea breezes and the sight of waves had always soothed her. Again, the one to thank for that fond memory was Uncle George. He'd been the leader of the family, the responsible one of three brothers, the businessman par excellence. But he'd also been the kindly, watchful father-figure who had cared for his brothers' only children through the men's gambling fiascos, wild business ventures and poor health.

But all that was done. She would carve a new life for herself and for Diana, too. Seeing Lance had revived her dedication to it. Nothing was so bracing as hearing someone speak of your youth and help you to remember that life, despite its setbacks, once upon a time had been a treasure. That what one thought and what one wished for was a viable and peaceful existence. That laughter was essential to survival and that one should not stop striving for the joy of it, even unto one's last breath.

She welcomed that revival of laughter and joy. After all, she headed toward a tiny perky town, refreshing all who strolled there with the smells of salty air, the sight of endless sea and sky, and glorious sunshine.

After so many years shivering and lonely, Emma most of all valued sunshine and the warmth of others.

Lance had had enough of the rules and those who implemented them without regard to kindness.

In truth, he always had.

As he led his horse walked along the hedgerows near the highway, he frowned at what society had done to Emma after his attempt to lift her spirits.

So few had ever honored her with the good things of life. She'd grown up, a little girl with only a father—and an abusive drunkard at that. Yet she had found laughter in the tidbits of daily life. A pianoforte she played well, though badly out of tune. A stray kitten she'd nursed to health and tamed. Her constant hope that when she grew up, she'd have a better life, happier, free of her father's power... and in a home of her own where she was unafraid, comfortable and loved.

When he and she met, they were so young. He was ten and she eight. She'd come north to her Uncle George's country home that marched along the border with his uncle's. Both were visiting for the summer. Their friendship was that of shared moments of pleasure and the youthful acceptance of one for the other.

More than eight years later, after Emma's father died and Lance had come north during recess from his Oxford studies in physics, they had renewed their friendship and he had fallen in love with her.

He'd never voiced it. He'd had no future of any substance to offer her. He was a second son of a second son, with no inheritance. His future life in the military could be one of hardship and he would be paid poorly for it, too. But he'd rejoiced each time she came running toward him over the hill, her heart in her eyes, her desire on her lips. God, he had savored her.

But at the end of his first year at Oxford, his cousin who had paid for his studies recommended he join the Royal Corps of Engineers. Off Lance went to Woolrich to study. He excelled at his work.

Lance's skills with calculations of geometry were the perfect ones necessary to the expanded war effort beginning in Portugal. The corps of Engineers was a small, highly trained segment of the British military. Every man knew how to make something out of nothing. A wall from earth. A bridge from rocks. A road from dust. No engineer was without purpose—and all rallied when a new commander arrived to take charge of the heretofore failing effort. Arthur Wellesley was no laggard. His reputation marched before him and those who implemented his vision were the engineers who cleared the way and built new ones for the thousands of soldiers who came after.

Lance cocked an ear. A coachman's crack of whip and the grinding of wheels signaled his darling came near in her coach to Brighton.

"I saw you climb in this morning," he murmured to himself. "I doubt you've stayed in Crowley."

He had seen her and her cousin Diana climb down for a respite at the carriage inn when the coach stopped. But he had not waited for Emma or Diana to get back inside. He'd spurred his horse on to the bend in the road. Here he had waited patiently to demonstrate to his beloved that time had not destroyed his love of her. And that the *ton* could go hang by their own silly rules.

He was here, standing and delivering like a true highwayman that love and laughter went hand in hand—and he'd give it to her from this day forward.

From his vantage point, he saw the dust cloud billow above the hedgerow—and at once, there was the coach, fast on approach.

He put up his half mask and brandished his wooden pistol. Then he charged forward.

Headed straight for the carriage, he halted a hundred yards or so from view and encouraged his horse to paw the air. He'd even asked the groom where he'd rented the horse if the animal could and would do that on command. He did now....and Lance grinned at the image he must make. A black horse, large and rearing, upon which sat a large man in black, his face half concealed by his black scarf.

"Halt! Halt, I say!" He shouted as the coachman slowed his horses and came to an idle, then stopped.

The fellow stood in the box. "What ho, sir? Ye don't want to hurt us, nay!"

"Order your passengers out."

The man sank to his seat. "No!"

"I say..." Lance waved his replica of a fine pistol. "Tell them to come out."

The man turned and yelled towards the cab.

In the window, Lance saw Emma's face. At first she was bewildered, then frightened. But now, as the coachman left his perch and jumped down to open the door, she met Lance's gaze and her fear went to shock, then to recognition.

She took the coachman's hand, climbed down and approached Lance. "Why do this?"

He met her and let his horse dance around her. "You know why."

"No. I am at a loss."

"How many in the carriage?" He knew she'd be concerned about gossip of this, but in Crawley he'd seen the other passenger. The woman was young, pretty—and already tipsy when she joined Emma and Diana in the coach.

"Only three," shouted Diana from the window. "My cousin, me and Miss Frobisher, Mister Highwayman, sir. And ...um...sir? Miss Frobisher is very frightened." But by the grin spreading across Diana's glowing features, Lance could tell the girl enjoying this tremendously.

"Tell Miss Frobisher, she need fear no one." He walked his horse nearer Emma. "Certainly not me," he crooned as he slid to his feet, removed his mask and took Emma in his arms to put his lips to hers.

Willing, pliant in his embrace, she allowed him his kiss. Long and soft, intrusive at the end, but quickly satisfying, his capture of her mouth was just as he had hoped.

"Why?" she asked him, dazed, as he pulled away.

"Because you need surprise and laughter."

Her arms, tight around his neck, she sank her fingers into the wealth of his silky hair at his nape. "Why could you not wait and do this properly?"

"In a ballroom? Or church?"

He took her lips once more, a leisurely claim of reassurance. "I'll do that too. And soon. But I wanted you to remember and value what had happened that day."

"Oh, I do recall every moment."

"That I kissed you?"

"Thoroughly."

"That I told you I loved you?"

"Unforgettably."

"And that if I ever had the means, I would return for you and carry you away to happiness....and marriage."

"Oh, yes, such a declaration a woman never forgets."

"I renew it all now, my darling."

It was then Lance felt the barrel of a rifle in the small of his back.

"Ye'll take yer hands off the lady." The coachman was at the ready to do Lance in.

Emma nodded at Lance that he should obey. "Best to do it."

"Aye." He put up both hands in surrender and faced his captor. "Sir, I know you think I—"

"Yer Captain Moonlight. Aye! Fer certain. But no more. Ye cannot have her money or the other ladies'. And ye'll not be abusing them with kisses."

"Sir, I am not ab—"

"Well, it looks like it to me. Give me your pistol."

Lance handed over the imitation weapon he'd crafted the day before just for this occasion. "Take it. Note its craftsmanship, sir. It's fine grain."

The coachman, who'd taken Lance's wooden toy with one hand, stared at it as if it were a crawling creature. "What is that?" He cried and fingered it round and round in his hand.

"It's—"

The man scrunched up his nose. "It's wood? Ye...ye attacked us with this?"

"Yes, it worked. You thought—"

Emma came around to stand between them. "Lower your rifle, sir. This gentleman is no Captain Moonlight. He's...he's a friend who came to make a point with me."

"And frighten us out of our trousers?!" Word was that one high-wayman had robbed a fellow only of his breeches.

"Yes, well, there is that," she admitted with a snicker.

"But as the lady says," Lance began.

But the coachman cut him off. "I should tie ye up and take ye to the nearest magistrate."

"I know, but I really meant no—"

"There's Bow Street Runners after ye, too. Did ye know?"

"No." Lance went still. "That is news."

"Right you are! Got to catch ye. Stop ye."

"But, sir," Emma said, thoughtfully pointing a finger at the coach-man, "this man is harmless. He carries a dud and wanted no money or valuables. On the contrary, this so-called Captain Moonlight high-wayman rides with one other man."

"That's correct," Lance added. "I am alone."

"Ba! And you?" The coachman inched closer to Lance. "What's yer purpose? Kissing all the ladies in the land?"

"Only one," Lance said with a smile at Em. "Only this one."

"Oh, pull-eese!" Came a lady's cry from inside the carriage.

Lance and Em glanced over. The coachman took a step to look toward the carriage.

Miss Frobisher, red in the face, and brandishing a shiny silver flask, stood before the carriage, weaving. "Talk, talk, talk. Enough, I say. Can we get on? Eh? He didn't shoot us. Thank you, sir." She gave a graceless little bow. "He didn't shoot her. Ha! But he did take your breath away, didn't he, duckie? Takes mine, I tell you. Captain Whateveryourname is, you can come kiss me any time. Now!" She burped. "You, sir, you tuck your rifle away. You, Mister Dashing, take back your big wooden thing. Kiss your lady once more good-bye. I heard your proposal, so you'll find her later. And I wish to get to Brighton before my bladder bursts. Never did like a *bourdaloue*."

And at that, she hoisted herself up—rather gingerly—into the cab.

In the window, Diana stared at the three on the ground and chuckled.

The coachman cursed roundly, threw up his hands and strode away, muttering he was going to the Runners, he was!

Emma stared at Lance for a shocked minute.

He gave a laugh, then bussed her on the cheek. "I say *adieu*."

"And to you, Captain Weatherman or whatever you call yourself—"

"Weather of Cork and Pork."

"Oh, stop! You incorrigible man! At least this time there is no Lady Shackleford, but we don't know about Miss Frobisher."

"She'd be no tattletale," Lance reassured her. "She won't remember a thing!" He tipped his hat and escorted her to the carriage. "To Brighton, miss. Where I have plans for us."

"No more of this, I do hope." She flicked the edge of his black scarf.

"None. All above board, quick and neat."

"You are very determined."

"I have had ten years to do nothing but hope one day our challenges might drift away. Then, suddenly, they disappeared, and I had a few months to plan to make you mine."

The mellow adoration in her eyes nearly sent him to his knees. "I am so glad you're back."

"And this time I'm not going anywhere without you." He took up her gloved hand and kissed the back.

"Brighton, sir." She had to tease him. "Before our coachman changes his mind and arrests you for attempted robbery and indecently assaulting a lady."

"Get inside now. You focus too much on the negative."

"I've had practice."

"A bad habit I will rid you of."

She cupped his cheek and murmured. "I await the correction with anticipation."

He indicated she must get in and sit down, then he closed the door. "Watch me."

CHAPTER 5

Emma left the reception foyer of the Old Ship Hotel and strolled out onto the promenade of Brighton. With a satisfied sigh, she took the wooden stairs down to the beach.

Upon the stony shore, she paused to breathe in the briny air and close her eyes. The sun was just peeping to the east over the rolling seas of the Channel. She'd risen early, leaving Diana asleep in her room, and shocking the servants in the foyer at the sight of a lady out so early.

She'd bid them good morning and a quick goodbye. One had scurried behind her to ask if she might wish his protection, but she smiled at him and refused. "I don't think many are out so early. I will be safe. Thank you."

She curled her heavy shawl around her and began to pick her way along the shore. A few fishermen were out to sea, their multi-colored boats bobbing in the water like a kaleidoscope of children's toys. One sleek sloop was anchored about a mile out. The weather was sunny and gay.

Just like Lord Weatherby.

Just like my heart which he has so consistently touched these past few days. If she did not know him so very well, she might question his pursuit of her hand. But she'd known him as a youth and as a young man, when one's ability to conceal one's true nature is nigh too impossible. Yes, she knew Lancelot Winters, through and through.

So much so, that his dedication to courting her had turned her mind from solitude and grumpy spinsterhood to the delights of a union that could bring joy to both their lives.

"And we deserve to have it," she said to the sea and the sky. "He has done his duty to King and Crown and I...I am finished with being captive to convention. Now I have a future that has set me free and given me even another chance to have that one person who would make my life sublime."

Smiling to herself, she strolled west along the shore. The maid who had helped Diana and her unpack their luggage last night had told her about a new set of townhouses soon to be built west of the Steine and the Pavilion.

"Facing the water, it is to be, miss."

To be able to wake up each morning, see that view and be able to walk the beach was a thrilling thought. *I wonder if Lance would welcome that possibility, too.*

Just then someone hailed her from the promenade above.

The strings of her heart played a happy tune at the familiar voice. A hand to her brow, she squinted at the sight of the magnificent fellow with red-gold hair and bright white smile upon his handsome face.

What is he doing out so early in the morning?

Lance took the nearest set of stairs down at a clip. In what seemed like a heartbeat, he was beside her. "Good morning, my darling." He bowed formally for all who might observe. "I thought you might be out with the sun."

"You remember all my foibles."

"I remember all your habits." He offered his arm and the two fell in together.

"Hmmm. Even those that got me sent to my room without dinner?"

He stopped and lifted her chin. "You will be coming to our room after our dinner and the delights there will cancel out all the past."

She swayed toward him. "How I have needed you."

He took her in his arms and put his lips to her cheek for the bliss of a moment. "And I, you."

Tears marred her view of his grin.

"Don't cry, sweetheart. All is good going forward."

"I trust you have done away with your highwayman's attire?"

"In my trunk at the Old Ship. Under lock and key."

"Say you will not do that again. If a Runner is on the trail of this...this Captain Moon-whatever then you must not chance appearing again."

"I won't. I promise that the only appearances I shall make will be by your side."

"Thank heavens."

"Because I do need to kiss you again. Today and tomorrow and all our tomorrows."

She threw her head back to laugh. "No more scandals!"

"None!" He held both her forearms, looked above to the promenade and crushed her close. "I am kissing my fiancée." And then he did that with a lingering ecstasy that stole her breath.

Her eyes still closed, she said, "You make my day heaven."

"I have a license from Doctor's Commons to make it so."

She gasped but could not resist grinning at him. "When did you get that?"

"Last week. Wed me, my darling, here, tomorrow."

"Oh, but I—"

He feigned a frown. "Have appointments, do you?"

"Well, I...yes. I mean no. This is sudden. You jumble my thinking. I...I came here to buy a house. Do you like Brighton? Shall I buy one? Would you live here with me...or come for a week or so in the summer when—"

He swept her up against his strong body and said, "Yes. Let's buy a house."

"And I promised to bring Diana out here. I cannot renege on that. She is a dear and deserves—"

"Everything. She does." He brushed tendrils of her hair behind her ear. "You wore no hat this morning. One of my duties as husband will be to ensure you dress well...and undress even better."

She guffawed and tore away to cuff him. "You are quite risqué."

"Do I thrill you?"

"Yes, by god!"

He looked enormously pleased with himself. "Good. I mean to tempt you because I will press for you to marry me soon. I can, as your husband, you must realize, also help bring out Diana."

"There is that." She tipped her head. "I do love you."

He went quite still. "I know. I've always known."

A movement down the beach caught Emma's eye. She'd noticed it earlier. A man out early. She thought him a fisherman or a shop keeper. But now. He was tall, thin, dressed in black with a red waist-coat. Alarm swam through her. A Bow Street Runner?

"Casually as you can, look behind you," she said to Lance as she clutched the lapel of his frock coat.

"Yes, but why?"

"I think he follows me...or you."

"Why would—? Oh, I see. You question if he is a Runner?"

"I do. Did you notice him earlier? Before you found me?"

"I did. But thought little of it. Now his continued appearance gives me pause."

She noticed the man in question stood still, looking out to sea and mimicking their own actions. "He stops when we do."

"When I return to the hotel, I will ask if a Runner has registered as a guest."

"And if he is," she said shivering in fear, "we should seek other accommodations."

"No. If he follows me, that would only add suspicion. He'd seek me out. We will stay where we are." He ran his thumb across the edge of her lower lip. "We will go about our lives as if he is not there."

"Difficult to do. I want us to be happy."

"We will be."

"That's right. You are not Captain Mmmm..." She winced.

He laughed. "No, I'm not. And a Bow Street Runner can follow me forever, but he cannot prove me Captain Moonlight."

She cast off her fears. "What would you say to a few days here? To tell Diana about us. To allow me to catch my breath that I am so fortunate to be the one you love."

"That's the spirit." He patted her hand and turned them back toward the center of town. "Now, first thing we need to fetch Diana to come down to breakfast and there, you will tell me where we go today."

⚜

Emma and Diana gasped at the huge size of the modiste shop which the hotel reception clerk had recommended. Their walk from the Old Ship Hotel up to the Lanes had been brief and beautiful in the late afternoon sunshine. When the winds off the Channel stirred high now and then, they lifted the collars of their pelisses to keep them warm.

Mademoiselle Vernet, the owner of the shop, sailed from her workroom at the rear toward Emma. She was a petite brunette with a quick step and an air of efficiency that assured Em the lady was adept at serving her customers. "I am happy to welcome all of you here."

Diana had presented both their calling cards to the dressmaker's assistant as they had entered so Emma had no need to introduce herself. She'd never indulged in fashion, having little need for it. But now, she rejoiced in the opportunity to have a more complete wardrobe. She turned to the modiste, full of expectation.

"I am impressed by your array of fabrics, Mademoiselle Vernet. My cousin and I have need for a few items. We did not bring all our wardrobes with us although we expected to spend the winter months here." That plan would change now that Emma had accepted Lance's marriage proposal.

"I understand, Miss Tomkins. The winter soon approaches and what seems pleasant today can change tomorrow." Vernet spoke English with little accent.

"My cousin wishes to have a new wool cape and a walking dress to keep her warm as she enjoys the promenade." Diana had envied Emma's early morning stroll and at breakfast had said she would love to join Emma in the mornings.

Emma added, "Diana in addition has need of a ball gown." Emma had received an invitation to a grand event five days' hence at Normanton House, where one of Emma's childhood friends was now wife of the owner, Sir Peter Somerville. The house was less than an hour's ride from Brighton, and Emma was excited to see her old friend, Penelope. "I also need a ball gown and one other."

The modiste was happy to oblige. "Of course, Miss Tomkins. I can do this for you. When would you like these? And do tell me about your color preferences."

The bell over the front door jingled and Emma, Diana and the modiste turned to watch Lance enter the shop. He glanced about the tables where fabrics spilled across the expanses. He took his time surveying the walls where dozens of bolts of fabric stood for the customers to view. But then he headed for a glass case where ribbons were displayed.

Emma felt the warmth of his presence, and put her mind to business. "I would like not only a ball gown of deep green, I think, but a day gown of some presence. You see I am getting married in a few days' time."

"Congratulations, Miss Tomkins! That is wonderful news. I have a few new silks here from Lyon and from Lucca. Come to the far table and I will bring them from the workroom to show you."

The modiste showed them to a broad display table, then fluttered away to disappear behind the door.

Standing by the far wall, Emma and Diana had a clear, direct view of Lance.

He left his examination of ribbons and came to take Emma's hands in his own. "Hello, my darling. See anything you like? What about you, Diana?"

"What are you doing here?" Emma silently praised his selection of chocolate brown frock coat and fawn trousers, with cream wool waistcoat.

He winked. "I buy gifts for my fiancée."

Another tinkle of the doorbells caught their attention. Miss Frobisher swept inside with a look of alarm on her face. But when she spied Emma and Diana, she rushed over.

"I am so delighted to see you both." She glanced at Lance, her examination of him one of a person trying to recall his name.

Diana introduced her to him.

The lady took his name with no sign she remembered him from the road. "Pleasure to meet you, Lord Weatherby. I say, are you enjoying the town?" She kept glancing at the shop entrance. "I am. I am."

Emma nodded. "We take a morning walk along the promenade each morning. Perhaps you would like to join us?"

"I would. I would. Thank you."

Then the shop bell ting-a-linged again. A tall thin man in informal top hat, black frockcoat, trousers and bright red waistcoat filled the doorway.

Emma did not move a muscle.

Nor did Lance.

Miss Frobisher waved a hand in front of her face in a tizzy. "I'm here for a fitting. You? What do you do here?" She focused on Emma.

"We need a few items and Mademoiselle Vernet has been recommended."

One of the clerks appeared before the four. "I am ready to assist you, Miss Frobisher. If you will come this way."

"Yes, yes. Of course. But, you see, I realize, I am not ready. Not really. I must return."

"Oh, but when?" The young clerk was confused. "You wanted this gown by tomorrow."

"I know. I know. But I will return, say, in the morning?" Without waiting for an answer from the girl, off Miss Frobisher sailed.

Once she had disappeared, Emma returned her interest to the tall, thin fellow in the shop.

"Lance," Emma said with lowered voice, "I think that is the same man we saw this morning on the beach."

"The one who concerned you?" He positioned himself so as not to gaze at the man in question.

"Just so." She nodded.

Diana leaned in and quietly asked, "Is something wrong with him?"

"No, no. Not really," Emma replied.

"We had the odd sensation he followed us," Lance told her.

"Hmmm." Di thought a minute. "Tell you what we will do. He seems to be interested in muslins, though heavens knows why. One of the clerks has gone to welcome him so we shall see what he wishes to buy."

"What if—?" A horrible thought crossed Emma's mind. "Do you think he might be the Runner who searches for that highwayman?"

"No." But Lance's face fell. "Just because he seems out of place is no reason to suspect that."

"But he could have followed us," Emma added.

"You mean me," Lance said with concern lining his brow.

Diana folded her hands before her, and pursed her lips, looking very much like a stewed prune. "Let's continue with Mademoiselle Vernet and order our clothes. We shall see how long he remains."

"I can leave now," Lance offered.

"Do that," said Diana. "If he departs soon afterward, I will suddenly need the air. Stay within sight of the shop, my lord, and I will watch his moves."

⚶

The three of them met for dinner that night in the dining room of the hotel. The ladies had spent the rest of the afternoon at Vernet's shop as three seamstresses took measurements and both ladies selected fabrics and trim for their gowns. They had not seen Lance since he left the dressmakers.

As the waiter left their table with their orders, the three finally had privacy.

"We must know about the Runner," Emma prompted him.

"He left two minutes after you did, sir, and stood on the curb for quite a while watching you walk away," Diana said. "Then he hurried down a small alley. But I know not what he did after that."

"What happened?" Emma felt the old familiar vise squeeze her heart. Society would once more ruin her life, her plans...and now, her love. A Runner, of all people, would take Lance from her and send him to gaol.

Lance sighed and dropped his voice. "The news is not good. He followed me at a distance as I visited a book shop and a tailor's. I lingered so long in the book shop, he finally came inside. I could see him walking all the aisles."

"And at the tailor's?" Emma asked.

"He did not enter the tailor's but took a seat outside on a bench. He'd bought an ice and sat eating it. I could see him from the window. I could not tell if he focused on the patrons of the sweet shop or of me. In any case, he must have tired of his watch because when I came out, he was gone."

"You didn't see him after that?" Emma had to know.

"No."

"I suppose," Emma said, "he's read the daily newspaper with word of our arrival here." She'd read the latest edition of the town paper upon her return to the hotel from the Lanes. Her heart in her throat, she'd cursed the reporter who written it. The article, brief but brutal, resurrected all the old scandal for which she had paid such a dear price for so many years.

The Sussex Express posted news daily of those of note had arrived in Brighton and who had left. Often, the reporter added personal information about the arrivals. Emma and Diana were described as '*The London heiresses who intend to remain in our fair city. Sadly, their journey here was marred by the attack of a black-cloaked highwayman. Oddly, the man took no money or property from the Misses Tomkins nor from their fellow traveler, Miss Rebecca Frobisher. He took only kisses from one lady, who has had previous experience with rapscallions such as this.*'

Lance shook his head. "I bought a copy of the newspaper on my way here from the tailor's. I could not believe they had the nerve to write all that."

Diana agreed. "Miss Frobisher acted oddly with us in the shop. I wonder if she met with a newspaper reporter."

Emma clutched her hands together. *Disaster. It was happening again.* "Or a Runner."

"Now, now, my dears," Lance said, brushing off their fears, "we speculate. Not good to do so."

Diana frowned. "If the coachman told the tale at a pub or two around town, then there is another source. The reporter should have come ask us to reveal details."

"Oh, no." Lance was adamant. "That would be too intrusive. Plus, they know we would discourage any mention of that past."

Diana groused. "Better to be nasty. That gains more readers. But ohhh... look who comes to dine."

Emma recognized the tall thin fellow immediately. "No. Don't look."

Attired in the same clothes as those he wore earlier, their supposed Runner loped into the dining room behind the *maitre d'hotel.* He took a seat at a table for one, which he had probably asked for, because it provided a straight view of the three of them.

Emma gritted her teeth. *At least, he has the courtesy not to stare at us.*

"We will ignore him." Lance bit off his words.

"I have lost my appetite." Emma felt the pinch of that old vise.

Lance covered her hand with his. "You will not look at him. None of us will. Instead, you will tell me about your purchases at the dressmaker's."

Lance's determination filled Emma with confidence and she launched into a discussion of style and fabric. "I can see by the way your eyes glaze over," she said with a chuckle as three waiters came with covered trays, "that you have learned enough about silks."

He sat back, allowing the servers to place their dinners before them. "Tell me about Sir Peter Somerville and his wife Penelope. I wish to be a knowledgeable guest."

CHAPTER 6

Emma, Lance, and a maid hired to accompany them to the Somerville ball sat in the traveling coach Lance had engaged for the evening.

He sat across from Emma and the sleeping maid, as the coachman took them over smooth roads.

Lance pulled Emma over to sit beside him. "Even though Diana is ill, I'm relieved you decided to come to the ball, my dear. The excitement will be good for us both."

Lance and she had explained to the maid earlier that day that they were affianced, and that Em had hired her to be their chaperone, so to speak, for the evening. The girl, who worked at the Old Ship, had thrilled to the opportunity. Her immediate concern had been what she herself should wear and she'd hurried off to her friends to consult them. She'd worked herself into a frazzle, it seemed, because she slept—snored, really—all through the journey to Normanton House.

"I wish Diana had felt well enough to come," Em said.

"She'll rest and be the better for it in the morning," he whispered as he put his arm around Emma and drew her near.

"Di caught that cough walking in early morning along the beach without a proper wool coat."

"Thanks to Mademoiselle Vernet," he said, "she has one now."

"I won't let her go so early in the morning though. She must wait for the afternoon and full sunshine."

"Her reason for going so early was honorable." Lance commended Em's cousin for her attempt to comb the coast for sight of the Bow Street Runner.

"But none of us," Em said with a small smile, "has seen him again."

"He's on the trail of a true suspect."

Emma grinned at him and cupped his cheek. "That would be smart of him."

Lance took her hand and dropped a kiss to her palm. "We are embarking on the new phase of our lives together. Tonight, I plan to dance with you until your slippers fall off."

Giggling, she pecked him on the cheek.

⁂

Sir Peter Somerville and his wife of eleven years, Penelope, stood near the orchestra dais, looking well-pleased with themselves and each other.

"Your friend from school is a charming lady," Lance offered.

"She is." Emma recalled how Penelope had remained steadfast, writing often, offering stories about her debut and wedding, encouraging her to attend and accepting her refusal, yet making Emma feel as though she was a part of the social whirl. "Always was. We've kept up a correspondence for more than sixteen years. A true friend, she certainly is."

"There are a few good-looking gentlemen here. Bachelors, at that. Diana would have enjoyed herself."

"She'll have her day. I'll see to it."

Lance glanced out over those dancing to the latest country round. "Do you resent not having had your debut and a chance to—"

She put a hand to his chest to stop him. "No. It was so long ago and in many ways, I did dread the constant round of receptions and balls. I find so many rules of society to be restrictive and others silly. Those things I fear, not only for me but for others. Besides, as I heard of others like Penelope who found good lives within the restrictions and sometimes despite them, I had already found a man I loved—"

"And by his silliness," he said looking repentant, "he took from you the chance to find a better man."

"Oh, Lance," she said, wanting to rid him once and for all of his remorse, "you are the best man I have ever known. I love you. Never—"

He clamped one of his hands atop hers. "Em, look who is here."

"What? Who?" She looked around to pause at the sight of the Somerville butler introducing Sir Peter and Penelope to the man whom she and Lance had assumed was a Bow Street Runner.

"No," she breathed. "No."

"Don't panic."

"But," she gulped, "why is he here?"

Lance narrowed his gaze on their host and hostess. "They have a long conversation."

Two of the other guests whom Lance and she had met appeared in front of them. The Marquess of Corey and his wife were newly-weds and looked every bit enchanted with each other.

The Marquess knit his brows. "I heard Sir Peter tell others earlier that they'd had a visit from a Runner. He searched for a highwayman. Been a nuisance here in the South Downs from what I hear. Calls himself Captain Moonlight."

Emma leaned back against Lance, who braced her, hands to her waist. "When was he here to speak with Sir Peter?"

"Yesterday morning," said the marquess. "I saw the fellow arrive. In a rush, he was. My wife and I were out walking in the garden."

"Do you know if he has found his man?" Lance asked.

"I have no idea," said the marquess. "Let's see what he does."

What the man did was come straight for Lance and Emma. Accompanied by their host and hostess, the fellow stood politely and waited as Sir Peter introduced them all around.

Lance suppressed his anger that the man would single them out in front of other guests. Emma had gone white as a ghost when the man arrived at their sides. Lance would not have her suffer any more insults. She was his to protect.

Officer Robert Pierce was his name, and almost in contradiction of Lance's supposition, he was a polite and articulate chap. "I am pleased to meet you both. I wonder, Miss Tomkins and Lord Weatherby, if you would join me in a private conversation?"

Sir Peter and his wife took a step back and engaged the marquess and his wife as Emma and Lance followed Pierce out of the crowded ballroom. At the doorway, Normanton's butler spoke with Pierce and the servant led them onward to the morning room. Then he shut the double doors to afford them seclusion.

"What is this about, Sergeant?" Lance stood, in no mood for more niceties. "We've seen you out and about in Brighton."

"I knew you were aware of my presence, my lord." He took up a spot by the sculpted marble fireplace and, hands behind his back, shot up and down on his toes.

Nervous, was he?

Odd. Runners tended to be overconfident in their demeanor.

"I was in Brighton on assignment. I searched for three criminals. We are short of staff, you see."

Lance cocked a brow, impatience making him boil. "And?"

Emma, who had taken a seat on the yellow chintz settee, stirred. "Who are they? What have they done?"

Pierce smacked his lips. "I searched for a highwayman. One with and another without an accomplice. This Captain Moonlight, as some call one, is a jokester and has caused all kinds of problems and consternation."

"He is the one who steals men's trousers?" Lance asked.

"As far as I have learned, yes. But he has a streak of retribution in him too."

"How so?" asked Emma.

"One of his victims was a corrupt revenuer who was blackmailing a pub owner."

"And you know this because," Lance said as he dared to breathe more easily, "you have caught him?"

"Last night."

Emma's mouth dropped open.

Lance had stopped breathing.

"I also have assurances..." Pierce paused to roll his eyes about the room, indicating Sir Peter was his source of information, "that he will not ride again."

"You believe that?" Lance asked.

"One takes the word of a gentleman, doesn't one, Lord Weatherby?" Pierce held Lance's gaze like a magnet.

"Indeed."

"As I now will take yours." Pierce stopped rising up and down on his toes.

Lance stared at the man—and knew what he had to do. "I am no highwayman, Sergeant Pierce."

Emma stared up at Lance, her relief coming with a gasp.

"I know you are not, my lord. I have spoken with the coachman who brought you, Miss Tomkins her cousin, and Miss Frobisher to Brighton."

"He told you," Emma said, brightening, "that what Lord Weatherby did was in jest?"

"To kiss you, Miss Tomkins?" Pierce chuckled. "Indeed!"

"He's done that before," she said.

"That I learned, too, from the person who wrote a story for a newspaper. While I could ask why you did this once more, Lord Weatherby, I do understand that a man who wishes to gain favor with a lady does...shall we say, odd things."

"Very odd," Lance said. "Sometimes rather rash, as well."

"So true." Pierce smiled broadly.

"Clarify for us, Sergeant Pierce," Lance went on, "who the third criminal was whom you sought."

The man smiled. "A thief of great skills. Robbing travelers in and out of London for more than two years. Always kept us at Bow Street on our toes, changing routes, tactics, feeding folks food tidbits with laudanum in them, sometimes sharing a special tea with unhealthy doses of the poppy. We were run wild trying to find her."

"*Her?*" Both Lance and Emma asked as one.

"Shocking to think her so skilled, eh? She'd change her hair color often. A wig of course. She'd change her accent. East End, one time. Scots, the next. Irish, too. A real charmer. This time, she was careless and told her escapades to a publican in the Lanes, yesterday. She likes her whisky, poor thing."

"Miss Frobisher!" Emma clapped her hands together. Her laughter rivaled her shock. "Oh, my!"

"I put her in gaol this afternoon, ready for the Sussex assizes. Funny lady. I wish she were an honest one." Pierce inclined his head in a bit of homage. "I was following you both on the beach that first morning. But later, to the dressmaker's shop, it was she I trailed. I collected information as I could. Your coachman was helpful as well as the newspaper reporter. But now, I came tonight to relieve you both of any worry."

Emma shot to her feet, offering her hands to the Runner. "Thank you for this, Mr. Pierce."

Lance shook hands with the man. "This means a lot to us that you took time to do this."

"It is my duty and my pleasure. I assume you, sir, will not play at the highwayman again?"

"Never."

"Good man. I take my leave. Enjoy the evening." He stepped away but stopped to turn at the door. "I understand congratulations are in order. You are to marry soon."

"We are." Lance beamed, his arm around Emma.

"Long overdue, it is." Emma grinned.

"Better late than never, eh?" Pierce said. "Some things are meant to be, regardless of what society dictates."

"So true," Lance told Emma after the Runner left them. "Some people are meant to love each other, no matter what society rules." His kiss affirmed that all was at peace. "We are to marry in two days and whom God hath joined together decades ago, no one will ever again put asunder."

EPILOGUE

Lance and Emma put his marriage license to good use two days later in a small church not far from the Regent's Pavilion. Diana was in attendance, beaming at the pair. Sir Peter and his wife Penelope came south from Normanton. Plus Kaitlin Manning, Lady Lawton, traveled south from London to celebrate with her friend, Emma.

At the Old Ship, Emma had ordered a wedding breakfast celebration for the guests. Lance had argued that the party should last an hour at least, while Emma simply could not wait to leave everyone behind and go away on her honeymoon with her new husband.

Well past noon, however, it was Lance who took his bride's arm and urged her upstairs, away from everyone. In their suite, the door closing behind them, Lance took his wife in his arms and gave her the kiss that equaled the first one in Derbyshire and the second in Sussex.

"My," she crooned as he drew away to press kisses down her throat, "you do that so well, sir. Are you certain you do not steal kisses from lady travelers everywhere?"

"Only you." He led her past their sitting room into their bedroom. There, he drew her to sit beside him on the bed. "We must be about this, wife. You made that appointment to look at houses for sale tomorrow afternoon. We have little time to make this union legal."

She chuckled as she pulled the ends of his cravat and kissed his jaw. "Twenty-seven hours are not enough, eh?"

"We have ten years to make up for, my darling. I have not a minute's patience."

But his restraint showed him to be such a man of rare tendernesses that Emma marveled at his fortitude. She rewarded him for his skills with an eagerness to repeat all the charming intimacies he'd shown her.

Dusk sent shiny rays of sunlight through their windows as he rose to pour them each glasses of white wine. "To you, my dear lady!"

She drank and met his mellow gaze. "You are perfection, my dear lord."

"Hardly, madam. Were it not for Officer Pierce's quick thinking and sound skills of investigation, I might be cooling my heels in Brighton City gaol."

"I long to match you, sir, in perfection."

"You do." He pulled back, alarm on his face. "What worries you?"

Emma hated she had failings. "I don't dance."

He cocked a brow. "Then I won't either."

"I don't embroider."

He hooted. "I don't need fripperies."

She swallowed hard. "I do not remember names. I do not get your title correct. Lance, people will think me stupid or rude."

"Darling," he bent and gave her a smacker of a kiss. "Do call me whatever you like."

She rolled her eyes. "How about Whether-Be of Pickle and Fork?"

Lance cringed and swept her up into his arms. "That is a tad unruly, darling. Just stick to Weatherby. And stick to me. That's the finest I've ever asked in life...and now I intend to keep you for years to come, happy and my very own Lady Pickle."

THE END

❦

I hope you have had a good chuckle with the doings of our highwayman who stole kisses from his lady love. My latest new series, *Scarlett Affairs*, will give you a tingle of intoxicating romance suspense—and a dash of the real danger so many faced during the Napoleonic wars.

Learn more about about my work on my website at http:// cerisedeland.com

SOCIAL MEDIA FOR CERISE DELAND

You can learn more about Cerise DeLand on these social medial links:

Blog: https://cerisedeland.blogspot.com/
Facebook: facebook.com/CeriseDeLandAuthor
Instagram: https://www.instagram.com/cerisedeland/
X: twitter.com/@cerisedeland
BookBub: bookbub.com/authors/cerise-deland
Goodreads: goodreads.com/author/show/2940404.Cerise_DeLand
Pinterest: pinterest.com/frenchcherryred
YouTube: https://www.youtube.com/channel/UCba82P_Q1kUr JUVVWoCwJmw/

ABOUT CERISE DELAND

I'm Cerise DeLand and tickled to be a part of this wonderful collection of stories.
I am also a USA TODAY Bestselling Author who believes love brings rich rewards from a life lived with honesty, valor—and a functioning funny bone.
Known for my poetic elegance and accuracy of detail, I've won awards for many of the more than 90 novels she's written.

Learn more about Cerise on her website at http://cerisedeland.com

THE CASEBOOK OF PRINCIPAL OFFICER ROBERT PIERCE

Brighton and surrounding districts

For a short time, I thought I had a third highwayman to chase after. However, it quickly became clear that the man in question was merely a suitor with a flair for the dramatic. Suffice it to say that the only thing he intended to steal was a kiss from his beloved, and I gather she was happy to bestow it, so no larceny was involved.

At first annoyed at the distraction, I became glad of it when it led me to become aware of another passenger on the robbed coach. As I tell my young constables, you never know when a clue will lead to the needed result.

As a result of my investigations following this robbery-that-wasn't, I now have a name and a face for the thief previously known as Larcenous Lucy, and she is in custody.

CHARRED HOPE

CAROLINE WARFIELD

Charred Hope
By Caroline Warfield

A fool threw her and her miniature away. A wiser man treasures them both.

Major Titus Brannock believes the charred painting that fell into his hands must be valuable to its owner. When he finds her, he finds a true treasure. Tessa Fleming's first instinct was to burn the miniature her late husband scorned, but the admiration she sees in Titus's eyes gives her different ideas. Perhaps the little gem will give them both a pearl beyond price.

CHAPTER 1

Robert and Tessa Fleming were nothing to him. It was only by chance that a precious relic of them, a trifle really, fell into Titus Brannock's hands. The smoke-damaged miniature left behind when Lieutenant Fleming departed on the patrol that would be his last must have meant little. What provoked Titus to go to such effort to return it?

He couldn't answer that. Riding a rutted road through the South Downs, his impulsive quest felt like a fool's errand: find the widow; return the miniature; leave.

He was tempted to turn around, but it had taken him three months to dig up her whereabouts. The obscure corner of the war office that dealt with widows' pensions was harder to find than he expected. It seemed a pity to stop now. Besides, he needed a distraction from his pointless life.

As the road meandered, so did his mind, while Hannibal, reliable though weary steed that he was, trudged on dutifully. Titus entertained himself by pulling up his few pleasant memories of his time in Portugal and Spain. Women bent along river banks, laundering their belongings and those of men who paid them. Women cooking over open fires. Women carrying their children on their backs and their goods in a sack on long marches. Women singing by campfires. Somehow Tessa Fleming's image appeared in all of them, her hair shining golden in the sun like a beacon leading him on. He shook his head to dispel that bit of nonsense. He hardly knew the woman.

He came at last into the village of Normanton, pulled up at a weathered inn whose sign proclaimed it to be the Duck and Spoon and left Hannibal with the ostler for a bit of feed and water. The keeper bustled over with an ale to greet him jovially when he carried his saddlebags into the tap room.

The man introduced himself as Tobias Hooper and sat down for a chat without waiting for an invitation. It being the slow time betwixt lunch and evening revelry, he showed no signs of rising, happy to regale a stranger with bits about Normanton. When Titus could get a word in, he asked directions to Tessa Fleming's place.

"Easy enough. Turn ye down the second lane on yer right after ye ride out to the west. Look sharp so y' don't miss it," he said. "But ye'll not be back before dark," he added glancing at the window. "Unless it is your intent to stay over w'the widow, o'course," he added with a leer.

What must this man think of the woman?

Titus didn't like the implication. Worse, he wondered whether perhaps he had reason. Was she a widow with easy morals?

"I'll have a room for the night," Titus said, biting out the words. "And another ale." Hooper stayed where he was, gesturing to a boy cleaning the tap to bring two more. Titus suspected they'd both be on his tab.

"Have business with the widow, do ye?" The rotund innkeeper's eyes glittered.

None that is any of your business. Titus held his tongue and sipped his ale. Unless he was mistaken, a woman watched from the kitchen door.

When Hooper gave up with a sigh and changed topic to the state of the roads, the woman came out of the kitchen with a rag in her hand and basin of soapy water on her hip and began to wash the filthy tables. Lunchtime had passed, and the evening had not yet begun. Again, those hard-working women in Spain came to mind. He recalled Tessa Fleming as a tiny bit of a thing, but, like all women who followed the drum, she was a tough piece of work. She could carry her load and then some.

Titus rose to escape the incessant chatter, asked for a bath, and followed the innkeeper, now vociferously describing the inn's ancient history, to a room.

Titus opened the door and paused. As the keeper thudded down the steps, he heard the woman say: "Don't talk much, do he?"

He heaved his saddlebags on one of the two chairs pulled up to a table and hung his greatcoat on a hook by the door. Rolling his shoulders to relax them, he glanced around. The room at least was quiet and clean.

A traveler could only hope the promised bath would come soon and the water be hot. He removed his boots, undid his cravat, and rooted through the saddlebags for a clean shirt. He missed the spaciousness of his battered army trunk that had followed him on campaign.

He thought again of Robert Fleming's trunk. It and the man's worldly goods had been shipped home with the widow and, if Titus recalled correctly, little boy. When the officer who inherited the dead man's quarters brought him the damaged miniature, he said only that it had fallen behind a cot.

A knock at the door interrupted Titus's wandering thoughts. A burly sort in rough clothes dropped a tin tub by the hearth. "Best make yer own fire. Will be a bit to haul up all that water Bess's heating." He hesitated, hoping for a vail then shuffled out.

Bess, Titus assumed, must be the innkeeper's wife. He did as the man bid and made a fire from the wood in the box next to the hearth using his own flint.

He stood coatless with his shirtsleeves rolled up staring into the fire. So far, the place seemed decent enough. He'd visit the widow in the morning, return for a night, and then set off home.

He shuddered. Home meant Astlough Hall, where he'd grown up and where his brother now presided as earl. His welcome there, well-intentioned but lukewarm, wasn't enough to satisfy. He needed purpose, and they all knew it. He haunted the halls and walked along the Norfolk cliffs and crannies, avoiding London and the lure of drink and dissipation that swallowed so many returning soldiers.

The constant melancholy that followed him threatened to take hold. He reached in the bag and pulled out the miniature. Titus brushed off what dirt he could and tried to make out the face of the woman. Tessa Fleming. Damaged as the picture was, he had tossed it in his own trunk three years ago and forgotten about it. He told himself he didn't remember Fleming's wife, but when he stared at the miniature a clear memory of her crossing a mountain torrent, baby on her back, skirt pulled above shapely calves, hair glowing in the sun, came uninvited.

Stuff and nonsense. He didn't know the woman. He wrapped the blasted thing back up and lay it on the table, relieved when a knock signaled his bathwater had arrived.

The following morning, Titus reserved a second night and called for Hannibal early.

"Good y' didn't try to go last night," Tobias Hooper said, pausing for the obvious question. When it didn't come, he went on. "Roads are dangerous at night in these parts. Never know where Captain Moonlight himself will appear."

Titus rewarded the little display of drama with merely a raised eyebrow.

Stuff and nonsense. Gentlemen of the road are always a danger. That is why I never travel unarmed.

The innkeeper's wife stood at the roadside in front of the inn in earnest conversation with two well-dressed ladies so much alike they must be sisters. When Titus trotted out of the yard, they followed him with avid eyes. Riding away he made out a few words of their whispered conversation... widow Fleming... handsome rogue... great beast... highwayman...

Great gods of Egypt, what do those gossips think I am?

He rode a little faster. The road arched over a hill and the village disappeared behind it before he spied the second lane on the right.

Robby burst into the little cottage calling for his mother. "Mam! There's a rider coming down the road."

Tessa gave him a swift hug. "He's likely on his way and will pass by." She didn't like how cautious Robby had become. She had explained that no matter what the boys at the new school said, no night rider would attack them in their own home. Besides, it was still morning.

He nodded and turned toward the door.

Still, there were other fears. Ones she preferred not to tell a child. Fears specific to a widow living alone. More than one man came knocking, looking for things she had no intention of giving. She'd learned to be cautious.

"Robby," she called. "Stop right there. Don't you have reading to do for Mr. Weatherall?"

The boy's chin dropped. "Yes Mam."

She heard the sound of a rider coming closer. "Take a biscuit and get you up to your loft," she instructed him, making shooing gestures. He did as he was told.

The moment he disappeared, she barred the door and stood by it, listening. It wasn't long before a firm knock, a man's knock, echoed in the cottage. She held her breath, hoping Robby's obedient nature won over his curiosity. She couldn't think of any reason a man would approach her house. At least, no good one.

He knocked again. She ignored him again. The third knock was louder.

When she didn't respond, a deep voice rumbled through the door, "Mrs. Fleming, I don't know if you are in there or not, but I mean you no harm."

So you say... "What do you want?" she demanded through the door.

"I— That is, I knew Lieutenant Fleming in Spain. I brought you something."

After a moment she lifted the bar, unable to imagine who it could be. She'd heard from none of Rob's colleagues in the years since she came here.

"Who are you?" she asked through a narrow crack.

"Titus Brannock," he replied.

The name meant nothing to her, but something in the gentle voice that vibrated through her reassured her. She opened the door a bit wider. "I don't know you. Again, what do you want?"

The tall stranger, hat in hand, gazed down at her with eyes the rusty brown color of oak leaves in winter. A shaft of sunlight splashed his brown hair with chestnut highlights. She held her breath.

"It is something of yours that came into my possession when you shipped home. It may be a trifle, but I think you might want it." His voice wrapped around her like a warm quilt, a treasure she hadn't had since her grandmother's passing.

Don't be a ninny Tessa, you know better than to go soft over a man. She held her ground.

"I've come a long way to bring it, and I have a long way home," he went on. She thought he sounded hopeful.

She opened the door to face him, but if he thought she would invite him in, he was mistaken. She stepped out and pulled the door behind her. "I'm not in the habit of entertaining strangers, but you may leave this 'trifle' with me and be on your way," she said.

He studied her long and hard as if she were a mystery to solve. It took strength but she met that piercing gaze. She peered back up at him experiencing a flicker of recognition, one that wouldn't come into focus.

This one is a soldier for certain. It is in his bearing. In his confident determination. He wasn't dressed like one; he wasn't dressed like a poor man either.

At last, he nodded and tapped his hat back on his head. He reached into his fashionably tailored coat and pulled out an object wrapped in dark cloth and held it out to her.

When she took it, their hands touched briefly, and a jolt of feeling went up her arm to lodge somewhere in her center. She yanked her hand away.

At her gesture his lips quirked and he touched his hat. "I'll leave you in peace. If you have questions for me, I'll be at the inn in

Normanton the rest of today. I'm leaving tomorrow." He turned and left her murmuring belated thanks.

Tessa took the object to her kitchen table and unwrapped it. What she saw made her throat thicken. Tears, unanticipated and unwelcome, overtook her.

The miniature. The one I had made for Rob. The one he tossed aside so carelessly. As he did me.

She swallowed hard and pulled herself together, still staring at her own image, young and hopeful and yet covered in smoke and plunged in grey disappointment. She glanced at the door.

"Who was that man, and how on earth did he find it?" She ran to the door and looked down the road, but he was gone.

CHAPTER 2

Bess Hooper brought Titus an extra-large slice of warm apple pie when he returned to the Duck and Spoon. Her sharp eyes studied him, as avid as they had been in the morning. "How did you find Widow Fleming?" she asked.

That little widow is no light skirt, if that's what Bess wants to know. What the devil is wrong with people?

"I found her to be courteous and careful," he replied warily.

The innkeeper's wife chuckled. "Sent you away with a flea in your ear, did she? Coulda warned y'."

It wasn't at all what he expected. His brows shot up. "Why didn't you?"

Bess shrugged. "Starched up and virtuous is the widow. Doesn't stop men from trying their luck. I always wonder how long she'll hold out, a woman alone like that. Poor as she is." She wandered off shaking her head.

Titus's peace didn't last. When the last table cleared, Tobias plopped down across from him. "Can't blame the women y'know. They're just curious. A widow alone like that is always going to draw men to try their luck."

"She struck me as proper. Prim even."

Tobias nodded. "She is that. As good as a widow can be. Could loosen up some. Always serious. I expect any woman would be, though—on her own without two farthings to do for her boy. Tis all she can do t'feed him, a growing lad like that. Works hard with that lace business."

"Lace?" *A widow's pension, thirty pounds a year, might stretch to rent and little else.*

"Sells it to Burgess. Damned hard on the eyes, lacemaking. Pity in a pretty young thing." He glanced sharply at Titus. "Is that what you were doing? Buying lace?"

"Not even close. I knew her husband."

"Soldier, were you? Officer I'll warrant."

Titus nodded. "Dragoons. Major, not that it matters now."

"Shoulda told me. I took the king's shilling and marched for twenty years," Tobias said. "Next ale is on the house."

Tobias fetched a flagon of ale. "So, was th' woman happy with the what-not?"

"She sent me on my way sharpish before she opened it," Titus said rubbing his chin. "She'd have made a good sergeant."

Tobias found that to be hilarious. "I bet she would. Lot o' those army women learned how to give orders."

A disturbance at the door drew Tobias away. Customers came first, and these two were a cut above if Titus could judge by their Hoby boots and the quality of their coats. They approached a table near his, but one of them spied Titus before they could sit.

"Don't I know you?" the stranger asked studying him carefully.

His friend joined him. "Captain Brannock is it? Didn't we meet in that little scuffle off the coast of Santoña?"

"Santoña" brought a memory, one Titus was unlikely to forget. He stood. "Major now if half-pay, and I remember it well, Lieutenant Weatherall."

"First Lieutenant or would be if I was still navy," Weatherall said. "Do you recall Captain Somerville here?"

Titus studied their companion. "Yes, of course. The action was brief but memorable. I didn't often get an opportunity to deal with the navy," Titus chuckled.

"How could any of us forget those Frenchies running like scared rabbits when your squadron came out of the woods from two sides. Scared damn rabbits," Somerville laughed. "I presume you got the, erm, delivery to Wellington's headquarters safely."

"It may have been short a bottle or so more than the two we drank on the shore that night, but yes indeed. It was delivered." Titus gestured for them to sit. Tobias Hooper smiled contentedly as he took their orders.

"I certainly didn't expect to see you in the South Downs," Titus said.

Somerville laughed. "I grew up here. My brother, Sir Peter Somerville is the local magistrate," he said and clapped Weatherall on the back. "Justin here is now our schoolmaster."

"What are you doing in this part of England, Brannock?" Weatherall asked.

"Duty among soldiers," he replied. He told them his story.

"Odd they'd leave something like that behind," Somerville said.

"Aye. There's probably a story behind it, but I'm not privy. The painting came to me via a junior officer. I didn't know Fleming well. I didn't much like what I did know, truth be told." Titus studied his ale for a long moment.

Neither of his acquaintances spoke, thinking no doubt of the many ways a man could part from what he loved at war. Titus took a deep drink and broke the tension. "In any case it has been delivered, and I'll be on my way tomorrow."

"What then?" Somerville asked.

Titus opened his mouth to answer but the man went on, "How are you occupying your time now that you're back?"

"Not doing a damn thing worthwhile."

"Moping around your family's pile searching for your lost purpose?" Somerville asked. "I felt the same."

"Something like that. My brother is Earl Astlough now and preoccupied with the estate. He gives me projects, but they feel like charity. He urges me to take control of my own property, some nice acres in Lincolnshire left by a great uncle."

"At least you have property! Why don't you?"

"The land is fine. The manor is sound enough, too, but dreary, shabby, and in need of repair. Worse. It is empty. Just empty. I have no heart to do it." He swallowed and told them the rest, "Estabelle, my brother's wife, told me I need a wife, and says I'll never find one in Norfolk."

"A woman's answer to everything," Weatherall said. They shared a companionable laugh.

"I tried London for a bit. An earl for a brother opens doors. But society didn't suit, not with the poverty I saw on the streets. Damaged, starving soldiers were the worst of it. At least in Norfolk we're trying to care for our own."

Somerville studied him closely. "Do stay a bit, Brannock. You might like the South Downs." Weatherall cast Somerville a puzzled look but didn't speak.

"I could use company for certain," Titus replied rubbing his chin. "Tobias will be happy to give me a room for a few days at least."

"My sister-in-law is hosting a house party just starting at the manor, I could use an escape now and then," Somerville said.

House party? No thanks. Before Titus could think of a polite response, Weatherall added, "Besides, the South Downs is as pleasant a piece of earth as you'll find on our fair island. You should stay a while."

The innkeeper who had been hovering near strode to the door, drawing their attention. "Mrs. Fleming, may I help you? Tea in the private dining room perhaps?"

At the sound of the widow's name, Titus rose to see the woman with a small boy holding her hand. His eyes met hers, deep blue and alive with intelligence and anxiety. He couldn't look away.

What on earth must he think of me? Tessa shrank under the man's intense gaze. She took a deep breath for courage.

"Mr. Hooper, would you please ask the gentleman if I could have a word with him?" Tessa blushed. Approaching a strange man was not ladylike—not that she had any remaining pretense of being a lady.

"Which gent?" Tobias asked. She noticed belatedly that he had been sitting with Sir Peter Sommerville's brother and Mr. Weatherall.

"The, erm, stranger," she replied.

The gentleman—she didn't recall his name though he surely gave her one—pulled himself together and approached.

"May I be of assistance, Mrs. Fleming?" he asked.

He looked vaguely familiar, but she still couldn't place him. Her cheeks flamed hotter. "I'm sorry, we've not been properly introduced."

He gave a slight bow. She feared mockery but saw nothing but concern in his expression. "I apologize. Our circumstances prevented proper introduction. Titus Flavius Brannock, lately major in the 11th Dragoons. Now simply Titus Brannock. At your service, ma'am."

I prevented proper anything. I all but chased him away.

His words fell into place, and she lifted her chin to look at him again. *Of course, Major Brannock.* "You were in Colonel Foster's battalion. Our paths didn't cross often," she said.

"No ma'am, but I recall seeing you pass by a few times in winter quarters."

The silence that followed became uncomfortable, but Tessa couldn't think what to say standing as she was at the door to the tap room with two of Normanton's influential citizens looking on.

"You have questions. I can see that. Perhaps we should take Hooper up on that private room," he said.

Tessa gazed around. The room might be too private. "If you wouldn't mind, there is a small tea room close by. It might be more..."

"Appropriate?" the major suggested with a twinkle in his eye.

She glanced at Mr. Hooper. "No offense, but—"

"None taken. You ladies like yer cozy comfort." The innkeeper patted her hand as a grandfather might.

She led the way in awkward silence. Irene's Tea Salon would be fairly private this time of day but still proper. Besides, Irene Foster would take Robby so she could speak freely.

"May I have a Chelsea bun, Mam?" Robby asked when they neared the door.

Her heart sank. Even a few pennies were dear, but she brought this expedition on them. She stepped inside and had a few whispered words with Irene, the proprietor. Irene shot a curious glance at the major but she led Robby to the back with no questions. Tessa and Brannock took a seat at a small table by a sunny window with pretty curtains and a jar of wildflowers on the table.

"Major, I—" she began, clasping her hands to keep them from fluttering.

"Please no 'Major.' I'm plain Mr. Brannock, now." He smiled up at the young girl, Irene's niece Carrey, who came to ask what she could bring them. He ordered China tea and a plate of pastries before she could object. "And don't forget a Chelsea bun or two for Master Robby," he added.

"But I can't—" Tessa sputtered.

"Surely a treat from a gentleman is innocent enough, particularly as an apology for disturbing your peace yesterday."

He upset it more than he knows.

She was at least relieved not to worry about paying for their tea.

"Now, what is it you wished to discuss. Earlier you couldn't get rid of me fast enough," he said.

No point in beating around the bush. She removed the little bundle from her reticule and unwrapped it on the table. "Where— that is how did you acquire my miniature?"

He paused, staring at it, obviously choosing his words. "Someone brought it to me after you shipped out."

"But—who?" she stuttered.

"The officer who took your quarters after—after you left. Honestly, I don't recall his name," Brannock answered.

"But where was it? How did he come to have it? It was lost. I don't understand," she said staring down at her own image.

When he didn't answer right away, she peered up at him. "Do you not know? Is the answer terrible?" She couldn't imagine how it could be worse than she already knew.

Kind eyes met hers. Brannock swallowed deeply. "Not so terrible. He told me he found it against the wall under a cot."

She stared down at the table again, eyes blurring. After a few moments he spoke softly. "Do you have any idea how it got there?"

She shrugged, hesitant to speak. *You're made of sterner stuff, Tessa. What difference will it make? Tell the man. He was kind enough to bring it.*

"I wondered where it fell after Rob threw it at me," she said at last. "I couldn't find it." Brannock looked ready to ask more questions. She rushed ahead. "It was damaged. 'Useless,' he said, and should have been discarded long ago."

"Burnt."

She nodded. "Rob knocked it into a campfire. By accident he said."

Brannock raised one eyebrow, skeptical, but had the good grace not to voice it.

She shrugged again. "It was worthless. He was right. It ought to have been discarded." After a sigh she added softly. "It should never have been made."

She wiped her fingers across the picture, and gazed back up at him. "It looks as if someone tried to clean it. Was that you?"

Color, faint but unmistakable, ran up his neck to his cheeks. She found that endearing. He nodded.

"I brushed it a bit. It seemed a pretty thing that deserved better."

Her throat tightened. "But I left Spain in 1813 when we were in winter quarters, almost four years ago. Why now?"

"To be honest, I meant to discard it when the officer handed it to me, damaged as it was. I don't know why I tossed it in my trunk, but I did. I forgot about it until a few months ago when I was finally cleaning my things out, discarding things I no longer need."

He chuckled. "I put more back in than I left out. There was your miniature. I thought that, if I found it hard to dispose of objects from back then and the memories, perhaps someone would care about a painting they had troubled to have created."

Do I? Do I want those memories? Her hands closed over the miniature; she wrapped it back up and put it away. "Thank you, Mr. Brannock. You are very kind."

She sipped her tea and found it cold. Her escort requested a fresh pot.

Searching for a topic she asked, "How did you find me?"

His answer was simple enough, and he gave no indication of the amount of trouble it must have taken. She murmured thanks again, and this time savored the luxury of warm, strong, China tea. Brannock had made short work of the sweets. He pushed the plate in her direction, offering her a lemon biscuit. She took one and nibbled it.

After a moment he spoke again. "Did you commission it?"

She choked on the biscuit and needed a deep gulp of tea. She was too disconcerted to lie or evade the question. "Yes," she rasped. "The first time I was left behind in Lisbon soon after we were married. It was a gift. Foolish waste of money." She prayed he would drop the subject. Rob had shouted at her over the expense.

Blessedly he did, sensing her discomfort. Even better, Robby bounced back just then, crumbs from his treat on his cheeks. She rose and hugged him, and Brannock rose as well.

"We best be going, Robby. Mama has a stop to make before we go home."

"To fetch the money Mr. Burgess owes us?" Robby asked.

She bent to whisper, "We don't speak of that in front of people," and then kissed his cheek.

She rose, thanked the man, and walked away with as much dignity as she could muster. She could feel his eyes on her back all the way down the street. The miniature in her reticule bumped against her side.

I'll burn it. Destroy it completely once and for all, along with the memories that do me no good at all.

CHAPTER 3

Titus stood at the window watching the woman and her son until they entered a building. What kind of husband disdains a gift like that? He had no answer. He'd done his duty. What happened to the tiny painting was no longer his concern. Neither was what happened to Widow Fleming.

By the time he paid their shot, studiously ignoring the curious glances of the woman who took his money, Somerville and Weatherall were gone.

Damn. I looked forward to sharing war stories. There are a few more hours of light. Maybe I should leave now.

He stood at the entrance to the tap room, rubbing the back of his neck, trying to decide what to do for the rest of the day.

"Major!" Hooper bustled over. "Somerville left ye a note." He handed Titus a folded piece of foolscap, and waited. Since it wasn't sealed, he had probably read it and was waiting to see Titus's reaction.

Titus tapped the paper to his forehead in a quasi-salute, and then turned to take the stairs two at a time. He dropped into a chair as soon as he reached his room and unfolded the message.

Brannock,

I hope you'll take me up on the invitation to stay around for a while. Come to Normanton House tomorrow afternoon. We'll have a good ride, and I'll show you around the Shire. Justin can join us when school is done.

Robin Somerville

He sat for a while with no sound except his own breathing for company. *Why not? What else do I have to do?*

He wrote to his brother, telling him about his visit to the widow and warning him that his plans had changed. Then he reviewed what little he had packed. Clean clothing appeared to be his most acute necessity.

Tobias Hooper happily set the letter aside for the post and supplied him with directions to a laundress. He rubbed his hands with delight at the thought of having Titus's custom for a few more nights.

By the time Titus found the laundress, stopped at the sundries store, and walked the length of Normanton, it was suppertime. Soon after, the taproom filled with farmers and locals. That suited Titus, who was tired of his own company. Of Somerville and Weatherall, he saw no sign.

Drinks flowed, and he happily told sanitized war stories, dodged mention of his brother the earl, and answered curious questions about the Fleming widow with the simple truth. He delivered a package. He didn't know her.

The place grew more raucous as the evening went on, and the gossip and teasing became more ribald. Stories and disputes about the local character, Captain Moonlight, became more and more outrageous. He was a murderer. He was a kissing bandit. He was a Robin Hood. He was a gentleman. He was a menace to women. He only attacked the town's merchants. He attacked lone riders. He only attacked carriages. He had a gang of twelve. He rode alone. By night's end Titus could write a novel. Maybe he should.

The crowd thinned eventually, though the diehards were still going at it when Titus sought his bed. He slept the sleep of the just, and awoke the worse for drink, feeling less virtuous, and stumbled down for some coffee.

Tobias and Bess, who were already up and nauseatingly cheerful, saw to the coffee. He refused anything else except toast.

"Y'held yer own last night, Major. They liked the funny ones— the real stuff not so much. Y'done well. The ladies of the night jumping into the river to save that keg had 'em in stitches," Hooper said.

In the light of day, that story wasn't so funny. One of the camp followers had drowned. He must have been drunk, more so than in a long while.

"What's with all the nonsense about this Captain Moonlight? He'd have to be here, there, and everywhere at once for all that to be true," Titus said, sipping the hot black coffee.

"Isn't nonsense for sure. He's out there all right. Hit Burgess's coach again last night. Took the man for all he had. Summ'un saw him later up the west road," Tobias replied.

"West?" That would be close to the Flemings. *Not your problem, Brannock.* He smiled anyway.

"I'm feeling better. I'll take Bess up on a plate of those pancakes, if she has jam to go with them."

She did and the food helped to settle him. Thirty minutes later, he was riding west out of town. He'd see Somerville in a while. It wouldn't hurt to drop by on his way and make sure the widow was safe.

⚜

Tessa hummed as she kneaded dough. Baking always calmed her nerves. The rent would take her last penny and she worried how they would manage until her quarterly widow's pension arrived. For now, she had bread to bake. Robby fed their little flock of chickens and weeded the vegetable patch. They would manage even if Burgess continued to pay her unfairly.

She had just given the dough a final hard thump, when a knock on her door sent her heart racing. *Now what?* She picked up a towel to wipe her hands and waited. Whoever it was knocked again.

"Mrs. Fleming, it is Titus Brannock. I won't trouble you long. I just stopped by to be sure you and the boy were well."

When was the last time someone cared if I was well? She shocked herself by opening the door wide and smiling at him. "As you see, sir. Why would you worry?"

He smiled back, and her toes curled.

What foolishness, Tessa. You are too old for that nonsense.

He removed his hat and inclined his head. "Captain Moonlight was on the road last night. I heard he was out this way, and I thought..."

"Captain Moonlight, whoever he is, doesn't bother poor widows," she replied, tightening her lips against a wide grin that threatened.

"Good to know," he said.

They stood there staring at each other for long moments before he glanced behind her into the house. She was tempted to invite him in, but that wouldn't do. Just then Robby bounced into the yard, home early from school, and gave her a hug, reminding her she lived without chaperone or companion. He smiled shyly at the major.

"It is a lovely day," she said instead. "Would you care to sit in the sun for a while? I have no lemons for lemonade, but I have cold spring water to offer you."

His smile widened. "That would suit me very well."

She sent Robby off for water and gestured to the bench she had placed at an angle so she could sit and enjoy the patches of flowers she planted under the windows and next to the door.

He waited for her to sit, and she realized belatedly how narrow the bench was, barely wide enough for two. She sat as far to one side as she could, but, when he joined her, it was difficult to keep her shoulder from leaning against his.

She could think of nothing to say. Even if she could, she wasn't sure she could get the words out.

He glanced at her hands. "You've been baking."

She blushed at the sight of her hands, ungloved and speckled with bits of dough. "Bread for a few days," she said.

That topic covered, she thought he might leave, but he did not move. He peered up at the cottage as if studying it.

"It looks solid." He cleared his throat and went on as if to explain the observation. "Your thatch is good and your foundation is firmly set."

Odd that he should know property. It confirmed her belief he wasn't poor. "It is warm, dry, and comfortable. Enough for Robby and I." As if his name conjured him, the boy appeared. He handed them cups of water. Their little dog Ginger followed him.

"May I run Ginj up the hills Mam?" he asked.

Should I keep him near? She didn't. She let him go on his way.

"Fine boy," Brannock murmured.

"Very," she replied, swelling with pride. *How awkward could this be?*

"Is this area home to you? I mean, are your parents nearby?" he asked.

She shook her head. "They live in Lincolnshire."

His eyes widened. "I have property in Lincolnshire. What is your family name?"

"Reynolds. My father is Harold Reynolds." She swallowed. If he knew Lincolnshire she may as well go on. "Baron Wolfecliff. Does that surprise you?"

He peered down at her gravely. "Not in the least. You are every inch a lady in manner and speech."

The kind words warmed her, but something in his expression alerted her that he knew her father or at least his reputation.

"He, erm, he's a stern man," she said. "Stern" was a mild way to put it.

"How is it you are here?" Brannock asked, the concern in his tone stopping short of pity.

She frowned at her clasped hands.

"Sorry if I'm intruding."

She gazed back up. "You will have guessed I wasn't welcome home after defying them by running off with a junior officer with naught to his name. I hadn't left Lisbon when I got a letter telling me so. As to Normanton..." She shrugged. "We disembarked in Plymouth. I enquired of an estate agent. Houses there or in Brighton were too dear. I can manage this one—warm and solid as you said—on my widow's pension. So here we are in South Downs."

His smile warmed her deep in her center. "You handled Spain. Coming here must have been easier. I admire your enterprise and courage."

Their eyes held for a long while, and she knew it couldn't go on. She cleared the tightness in her throat. "I best see to my baking."

He nodded. "And I'm expected at Normanton House."

He rose, but before he could leave, Robby came running, the dog on his heels. He handed Tessa a small bag. "It was in the top of the chickens' nesting box," he said.

Her jaw fell open when she peered inside it. "Coins? What on earth?" A half crown, and a handful of smaller coins. It was enough to augment her pension for the next quarter and more.

She stared down at the coins. "Three shillings are exactly how much Burgess shorted me," she murmured. It was as if someone knew. "But I only told Rachel Pendleton about it."

She glanced back up at the major, and shook her head.

"You have a benefactor." He grinned. "Perhaps Captain Moonlight paid you a call after all."

She gave his arm a playful swat. "Captain Moonlight indeed."

"It is Mam; it must be!" Robby said rocking on his heels.

"It is not and don't you go telling tales, Robby," she chided.

The major smiled at the boy. "Tuck it away," he said. "I won't tell. The neighbors don't need to know."

"As long as whoever left it doesn't come back or want something in return," she said. *I'll have to spend it sparingly to avoid notice.*

"Don't look your gift horse in the month, Mrs. Fleming." The major donned his hat and went on his way, leaving her perplexed.

Titus had meant every word he said about courage and enterprise, especially when he learned her origins.

Wolfecliffe's daughter. That man's unyielding self-importance would make any young girl's life a misery, push her into defiance.

It was obvious to him that the little woman overcame it all. *She is something remarkable. Something...* He couldn't put what into words. One thing was certain. The coins had been a shock. She'd had no idea they were there.

Titus sent a swift prayer that whoever left the little hoard meant it kindly and that Tessa would have the good sense to hang on to it. It appeared he'd be staying around for a while, just to be sure.

CHAPTER 4

Somerville, as good as his word, led Titus through river valleys, along wetlands, and across green fields. The South Downs was a glorious mix of all that and more. Weatherall had just appeared as they left the Somerville stables, and the two friends took turns regaling him with information about the Downs, its natural beauty, and its history.

They rode in a wide arc around Normanton up and down hills. Houses, farms, and even whole villages appeared and disappeared around curves. Twice he glimpsed the sea from a high ridge. Once Brighton in the distance.

They galloped at a racing pace across an emerald field and up into a deep stand of wood, dismounting in the shade of ancient trees. Somerville uncorked a flagon of rum and passed it around.

"Incredible. Beauty—mystery—it's all here. No wonder your Captain Moonlight finds it a fruitful arena." Titus stared around himself.

"Why do you say that?" Weatherall asked, peering over the flagon.

"A spiderweb of roads, winding curves, and hills to hide behind. He can strike one moment and be out of sight the next." Titus waved his arms at the tree cover. "And places like this into which he can disappear."

"So, you believe in our phantom?" Somerville asked glancing at Weatherall.

"I don't believe all the fantastical stories, but he's real alright." Titus took a turn with the flagon and wiped his mouth with his sleeve before asking the question that had bothered him all afternoon. "Have you ever heard of Moonlight leaving coins to someone needy?"

The other two men eyed each other, but Somerville spoke. "Why do you ask?"

Titus cleared his throat. "I heard Robin Hood stories at the pub." He wasn't about to reveal what he saw at Tessa Fleming's cottage.

Weatherall spun a story about the family of one of his students whose father was injured finding mysterious coins the morning after a reported Moonlight raid.

"Then there was the vicar's claim about the charity box filling up after the church roof sprung a leak," Somerville said with a mischievous glance at Weatherall.

"Not to mention the Sailors' Rest in Brighton has been flush with cash since Moonlight began his rides. Not that anyone there will explain where the sudden money came from," Weatherall added, clearly amused.

"How is the Widow Fleming, Brannock? Have you seen her again?" Somerville asked with a knowing smirk for Weatherall.

"Well." Titus regretted answering so quickly. "That is, I saw her once in town as you know."

A raised eyebrow greeted that.

Titus went on as smoothly as he could. "I stopped in this morning on my way to your place. Since Moonlight had been on the road out that way last night. She appeared perfectly fine." He shrugged casually.

They walked their horses to the edge of the wood. "Looks like the weather may take a turn," Somerville said peering up at the western sky. "Head for home?"

They cantered along companionably until they came to the

Normanton Road and Titus waved good-bye. Somerville pulled up and put out a staying hand. "I almost forgot. If you're staying on, my brother plans a ball a week from Monday. I was assigned to extend an invitation."

"Kind, but I fear I have no evening clothes with me," Titus replied.

"You could wear my navy dress uniform," Weatherall teased with a grin.

Titus shuddered dramatically. "Spare me. The army would disown me."

"Most of the shire is invited. We'll find you something," Somerville said. "Come. I insist."

With that they departed, leaving Titus to wonder if Tessa Fleming would attend that ball.

❧

The next morning, at loose ends, he left the Duck and Spoon to stretch his legs. Something in the air felt different. He hadn't walked far before he saw what it was. A raucous crowd had gathered in the market square.

Shock struck him when he walked closer. A man was fastened head and arms in the ancient pillory that had been sitting unused since Titus arrived in Normanton. The miserable individual was the object of taunting and laughter. While Titus watched, Samuels the grocer trotted to the square with a large basket over his arm. It didn't take long to realize the basket was full of rotten vegetables and fruit.

"Thank 'e Samuels," a man said grabbing a rotten onion and throwing it at the man in the pillory. It was a dead hit and a cheer went up. More hands reached for ammunition, and the folks in the crowd began amusing themselves lobbing disgusting vegetable matter at the helpless victim.

Titus wondered if he should intervene, uncertain what to do. It seemed unlikely that legal authorities had ordered such a barbaric punishment. He glanced around the square and found Robin

Somerville leaning against a building watching the proceedings. He clearly felt no need to intervene.

Somerville struck Titus as upright and likeable but something about him puzzled Titus as well. He sauntered over.

"What on earth is going on here?" Titus asked.

Somerville didn't take his eyes off the man in the pillory. "A little rough justice," he replied. He glanced at Titus briefly and returned to his study of the action. "If you pity him, don't. He's a lying cheat who has caused much misery. Besides, my brother will be here soon enough to rescue him. If he can find the key."

"Key?"

"To the pillory. Hasn't been used in decades. He may need a hacksaw." Somerville still kept his eyes on the victim.

"Is this another of Captain Moonlight's escapades, like the drawers hanging from the church tower?" Titus asked.

"Likely," Somerville drawled.

"You approve of this?" Titus asked.

"Don't you? Sometimes it is the only way," Somerville responded. "Do you see the paper pinned to him? It is proof of his crime. When Peter gets him, he'll be locked up."

The crowd ran out of vegetable waste and began to disperse, only a few lagged behind to shout insults. Somerville pushed himself upright. "Join me for a drink?"

It was early for that, and Somerville looked a little the worse for wear. *As if he has been up all night.*

"Coffee maybe," Titus said. He had more questions.

Moments later, seated at the Duck and Spoon with a mug of blistering hot coffee, strong enough, he thought, to wake the dead, Titus asked the first question nagging him.

"This Moonlight. He takes it on himself to dispense justice?" Titus asked.

"In this case, to make sure the authorities do. Sometimes he needs to bring something to their attention. You said you've been doing what you can up in Norfolk—for the way our returning soldiers are treated at least. What would you do if nothing else worked?" Somerville's eyes bore into Titus.

"Nothing so drastic. But I can understand it."

"With the coast nearby and the ports, we have more than our share." Somerville peered down at his coffee.

"So, Moonlight targets criminals?"

"Criminals, cheats—anyone taking advantage of others. Burgess of course would disagree. Our miserly local merchant thinks of himself as practical, not greedy." Somerville's bitterness was palpable.

A conclusion that had been lurking in Titus's consciousness off and on resurfaced. *Could Somerville...* He didn't voice it. Instead, he revealed something he'd promised Tessa he would not.

"Mrs. Fleming was a beneficiary of Moonlight's bounty," Titus said eyeing his friend.

"Oh?" Somerville cocked one eyebrow, amused at Titus's prodding.

"She said it was a half crown plus coins that totaled exactly how much Burgess had shorted her. Something she'd told only to Rachel Pendleton."

"Miss Pendleton is a compassionate person," Somerville said. Something about his expression made Titus wonder if she wasn't much more than that to this newfound friend of his.

Curious. All of it. One more reason to stay around. Titus wanted to see how the Moonlight mystery played out, and what the consequences might be. It couldn't go on forever.

CHAPTER 5

After Saturday's rain, Tessa considered staying home Sunday morning, though attending church was the bright spot on her week. The choir was of the joyful kind and Mr. Pendleton, the vicar, was inclined to preach mercy and not drone on. What she mostly looked forward to was the socializing after, a time to chat with other women, the one thing she missed from her former life.

"We're going, Mam?" Robby gazed up hopefully. He enjoyed seeing school mates as much as she enjoyed chatting.

The sun shone and the lane outside her house appeared dry enough except in the worst ruts. She decided to make a go of it. "Yes. Your clean shirt is hanging in your room. Leave your boots by the door and I'll get them ready."

Tessa polished her half boots as well as can be, arranged her hair in a crown of plaits, and put on her Sunday dress—the same one she wore every week. She wrapped herself in her woolen shawl. It was one of her few nice things from home, and it still made her feel like a lady, though it had endured camp, survived marches, and held Robby as an infant. As had she.

Service proved to be as joyful as she hoped and fortifying for the week ahead. Robby pulled on her hand as they exited the church. He didn't have to ask.

"Go visit with your friends, but don't leave the church yard without telling me."

Peering around the church yard, an unanticipated thought struck her. Captain Moonlight could very well be one of these people she knew. She blinked. Not one of them looked the part. *Still, no highwayman in it for greed or desperation takes time to give money to his neighbors. Moonlight has another agenda.*

"Tessa!" Rachel Pendleton called. Rachel had become a friend, her kindness a boon to Tessa's loneliness. "You look far away. Come and join us."

Tessa approached the group that included Irene Foster.

"We're discussing your absence from last night's assembly. Tell me you don't plan to miss the Somerville's ball. It isn't just for their fashionable guests. They've invited the local gentry. You did get an invitation, didn't you?" Rachel demanded while Irene looked on sympathetically, thinking no doubt what Tessa was.

"I did but I sent regrets. I have nothing to wear, and I can't leave Robby. It is impossible. Besides, I'm not sure how I qualify as 'gentry.'" Tessa said.

"That, my dear, is, the most ridiculous thing I've ever heard you say." Rachel exclaimed. "If you aren't gentry, I'll—I'll eat my best bonnet."

Tessa had told Rachel about her parents in a moment of weakness. She held her breath, glaring at Rachel and praying she didn't babble about the "Honorable" nonsense. Tessa was Mrs. Fleming. Period.

"Of course, she is. Anyone who listens to her speak knows that," Irene said. "The rest is nonsense too. Robby can stay with me."

"I still have no dress and it is in eight days," Tessa replied.

"You can sew, can't you? I could help," Irene said, sounding hopeful.

The sight of Titus Brannock speaking with Sir Peter and Lady Somerville distracted her. He laughed at something Lady Penelope said, his eyes crinkling in the corners. A wave of longing came over her. If he was staying nearby, they would no doubt invite him.

"Tessa?" Rachel prodded.

"I'm sorry, I was woolgathering," Tessa said.

"I can see that," Irene responded with a sly smirk. "I said that you have time to sew."

"Do you have some suitable fabric?" Rachel asked.

Tessa thought of the coins locked in a box in her kitchen. She couldn't afford to use it all, and certainly not for silk, but a decent muslin was possible. "Yes," she said with a note of defiance. "I can manage it." She could. She even had scraps of lace put away that would trim it, and a ribbon she had salvaged when her wedding dress had been irrevocably damaged in the mountains in Spain. She resolved to go.

The Danvers sisters wandered their way, all determination and avid curiosity. Visitors at the Hall, they already had a reputation for spreading gossip and were rumored to be reporters for *The Teatime Tattler*, a notorious gossip rag. Tessa couldn't be certain whether they were bringing gossip or hoping to gather some. Either way, she bowed to her friends and left, feeling more cheerful than she had in weeks.

She scanned the lingering crowd, telling herself she looked for Robby, but deep down she knew she hoped to see Titus Brannock, and wasn't disappointed. He leaned against one of the yew trees that lined the church, deep in conversation with Justin Weatherall. She took a few steps in his direction.

I should speak with Justin about Robby's schooling, shouldn't I? He's the schoolmaster.

She hadn't gone far when a tall man stepped in front, blocking her path. Oswald Neale, intrusive man of business, unctuous would-be gentleman, and persistent rake, blocked her vision and revolted her senses. He smelled of an excess of bergamot and rum.

"Ah the delicious widow has left her cave," he drawled.

She frowned. "I'm here every Sunday."

"Perhaps I shall find religion again, in that case," he said leaning toward her.

She took a step back. "I need to fetch my son and go home."

"Really?" He glanced over his shoulder at Brannock and the schoolmaster. "I thought perhaps one of those two gentlemen had caught your fancy and made it through that impenetrable wooden door of yours," he said, studying her from neck to knees with unseemly attention.

Tessa shivered. Neale was one of the reasons she kept her door barred. He had trapped her against it once, and she'd avoided him ever since. She had met him in Portsmouth when she needed a place to stay, and he arranged the rental of her cabin. Thankfully he wasn't the owner, and she had hoped he would stay away. Unfortunately, he did business throughout the county and was occasionally in Normanton.

"Good day, Mr. Neale," she said turning to walk away.

"Farewell for now, but we'll meet soon, I am sure. I am a guest at the Somerville's house party," he said smugly. "Society hereabouts is close knit, is it not? I don't mind, of course, but one is surprised they socialize with a woman who followed the drum."

She spun around, just out of his reach.

His smile, slow and smug with no amusement whatsoever, shook her. "After all, some people know such women existed for the ease of the troops."

His twisting of "ease" made his meaning clear. He didn't mean laundry. He meant—*It is a threat, Tessa. He means to ruin you.*

"My friends know better," she said. "I've made a life here."

"Rachel Pendleton? Naïve. She'd be shocked by what I could tell her. What would her father have to say? Or the very social Somervilles?"

Tessa tightened her spine. It took every bit of effort. "No one would believe you." She turned her back and departed.

Tessa walked Robby to school on Monday morning, eager to get what she needed for her new gown. Miss Margaret Martin kept an unpretentious establishment in Normanton, stocked with fabric and copies of *La Belle Assemblée* only slightly out of date. Those with more money and a taste for fashion took their business to the better shops in Brighton or London.

The seamstress greeted Tessa with a wide grin. "Mrs. Fleming! What a joy to see you here at last. How may I help you?

"I need fabric for a new gown," Tessa replied.

"For the Somerville Ball, I suspect," Miss Martin said, drawing her brows together in thought. Soon they were clucking over bolts of cloth of various kinds and price points.

Tessa settled on a pretty flocked muslin ornamented with long blue stripes. She would make it up with the stripes running vertically from hem to bodice. Her bits and pieces at home would finish it off nicely. She described her plans and asked for enough to accommodate a ruffle for the bottom and long sleeves as protection from the inclement weather.

"I wish I had enough coin to ask you to make it up," Tessa said.

Miss Martin patted her hand. "It is just as well. I have plenty of work between now and that ball." She bundled Tessa's purchase in brown paper.

Tessa was handing over her coins when a sound behind her made her skin crawl.

"The lovely Mrs. Fleming. How fortunate to find you in town."

Oswald Neale! He has no business in this shop. Tessa kept her back to the man and refused to answer.

Margaret Martin frowned, her eyes darting to Tessa. "May I help you, sir?" she asked. Butter wouldn't melt on the ice in her voice.

Tessa gripped her purchase, still facing the proprietress, visualizing the path to the door in her mind.

"You have nothing I would want," Neale said. The arrogance in his voice made the hair on Tessa's nape rise. "I am here to escort Mrs. Fleming home."

Tessa turned slowly. It took courage to meet his eyes. "I fear you are mistaken, Sir. My son Robby is awaiting me. We have plans."

Forgive me Robby for using you.

She swallowed hard and raised her chin. "I neither need nor want your escort." She attempted to step around him.

Neale blocked her way. "Tessa, don't play demure with me. We both know better, don't we?" He glanced slyly at Miss Martin. "Camp followers can't pretend to be shy." It was an insult, and also a sample of how he threatened to smear her name if she didn't accept his advances.

"You are very much mistaken in me, Mr. Neale. Kindly move aside," Tessa demanded, grateful her voice didn't shake. She sidestepped one way and then went the other.

She managed to slip past him and out the door. His footsteps followed, and she could feel his heat as she stepped out. Tessa swallowed panic, determined not to show fear. She would not run.

CHAPTER 6

Titus watched the tall gentleman from across the street. It was the same man he'd seen accost Mrs. Fleming—Tessa— at church on Sunday. Tall, arrogant, and confident, the man had deliberately stepped in front of her that day. At first, Titus had assumed he was a friend or acquaintance, but her unhappiness had quickly shown itself. Before Titus could intercede, Tessa appeared to manage the thing. It wasn't his place to interfere, yet he couldn't help thinking the little widow needed his help.

This day, the stranger glanced around before entering the modiste's shop. Titus was certain he'd seen Tessa enter that same place shortly before. He always knew her whereabouts. Awareness of Tessa Fleming had begun to seep into his soul. He sensed her presence whenever she was near, and his heart followed her moves even when his eyes didn't. He had not yet had time to unravel what that meant or could mean.

Something isn't right. What business could a man like that have with the modiste? Ordering for some provincial mistress?

Crossing the street Titus groped for an excuse to follow him in. Titus had no business in the establishment either. Perhaps he would casually walk past the window and—

Before he could cobble together a plan the door flew open and Tessa Fleming stepped out, her sweet lips in a hard straight line of determination, her posture stiff. The stranger followed her closely. Too closely.

Titus hastened his steps. "Thank goodness. I was afraid I was late," he said, offering his arm to the lady.

The relief in her eyes told him everything he needed to know. It took all his effort to keep his focus on the woman beside him, and not turn around and pummel the man following her.

"Yes. Right on time. As we planned." The tremor in her voice was slight but definite. "Robby is so thrilled you are coming with me to greet him at school." Her steady gaze urged him to go along.

Titus forced a chuckle. "Well, he might be, the rascal. I promised him we'd practice bowling.

"Why, Mrs. Fleming, who is your new friend?" The stranger oozed out his words with inuendo and malice.

"And what business is it of yours?" Titus demanded, glaring at the man. *Something is off about this one. A day ago, I suspected Somerville as the night rider, but this one reeks of villainy—as I might expect of a brigand.*

"Only someone with a concern for the lady's reputation. A widow. Alone. She can't be too careful." The vile man eyed Tessa as he spoke.

Titus didn't miss her intake of breath. The urge to knock the man down shook him, but that would only cause a scene. Tessa didn't need two men brawling over her on a public street. He forced his attention back to the lady.

"We should be on our way. We don't want Robby to worry if we are late." Turning his back on the stranger, Titus put every ounce of encouragement he could muster into his voice.

"Yes. We best hurry on," she replied. "Good day, Mr. Neale."

Neale. Titus needed to investigate the worm. Robin or Justin would know.

They walked the length of the market street without speaking, Titus's back to Neale but every sense focused on the man's whereabouts. Tessa's dainty hand gripped his arm. It might have delighted him if he weren't so conscious of her fear.

"Is he the reason you bar your door so firmly?" Titus asked when he was certain they were alone.

"One of them," she replied. She started to say more and stopped abruptly. He'd been wrong. They weren't alone. Someone had spied them from the window of the tea shop. She approached at full sail.

"Mrs. Fleming, well met. It is such a lovely day," the woman cooed. She gazed at Titus expectantly, obviously fishing for an introduction.

"Miss Prudence Danvers, may I present Major Titus Brannock? A friend of my husband's from the fighting in Spain." Tessa's throaty voice sounded strained.

"Delighted! Irene, Abigail, and I were just saying how lucky you are to have the attention of not one but two handsome gentlemen. That was Oswald Neale I saw you with earlier, wasn't it?"

Titus peered at the tea shop. Tessa's friend Irene stood in the window looking fretful and unhappy about the confrontation.

"Actually, it is young Robby who has my attention, Ma'am. We're on our way to fetch him for some promised cricket practice," Titus said.

"Oh." The woman's avid eyes darted from one to the other, groping for her next verbal dart.

"And we best be on our way," Tessa said, tugging his arm.

Titus happily obliged. When they were out of earshot he said, "Gossipers are everywhere."

"Gossip can be vicious. It does real harm," she replied bitterly.

He stopped abruptly to peer at her. "You've been threatened." He wasn't sure where that insight came from, perhaps her tone.

She stared at the ground.

"Tell me," he said softly.

"A widow alone is a target for men without scruples. And for talk," she said without looking up.

"And Oswald Neale?"

"He threatens to tell the good people of Normanton stories of camp followers, luridly enhanced and full of implication." She raised her eyes to his. "I won't let him bully me, but I can't stop him."

Titus held his rage in check. "Your behavior speaks for itself, and your friends aren't fools. Shall we fetch your son as we told people? I'll escort you home."

He didn't give her room to object. He would see them home, and he would examine that cottage for signs of vulnerability. Barring the front door was hardly enough.

❦

The major wouldn't take no for an answer, and, if Tessa were being truly honest, she was relieved. It took him two hours to examine the kitchen door, the roof, and every window and to craft stronger security bars. He spoke little to Tessa.

Robby followed him around but never seemed to try his patience. Brannock—Titus as he urged her to call him—explained what he was doing, gave the boy little tasks, and praised his efforts. Tessa's heart melted at their interactions.

Tessa made a stew while he worked, but he declined dinner. "It won't do to have that Danvers woman see me coming back to town after dark," he said. She finally convinced him to sit for a few minutes for tea and fresh baked biscuits.

Robby picked up his school material to clear space.

"What is this?" Titus spied the miniature at the corner of the table when he sat down. "It looks a bit better."

Tessa's face heated. She had meant to burn the thing completely, but something held her back. "It seemed a pity not to try," she said.

Try what? You tried with Rob, she had chided herself. *He never did value much of what you did. Much of anything about you after the heat of the first few months.*

"A bit of olive oil cut with a soft soap seems to be taking much of the soot. See the corner there? It seemed too precious to simply toss away," she added. And it was. It had been a loving gift even if it wasn't appreciated.

"That is what I thought when I found it in my things. I'm glad I brought it to you."

Their eyes held, and for a moment Tessa wondered if he was glad about more than just the little painting. It was she who broke away. "And I thank you for it," she murmured.

A few moments later he rose, bowed politely, and she walked him to the door.

"Dare I hope that bundle you carried out of the modiste's premises means you're preparing for the Somerville ball?" he asked from her front step.

"My friends wouldn't let me say no," she replied lightly.

"I'm glad. Will you save me a dance?" he asked.

"I would be pleased to," she replied. *I would save them all if it wouldn't cause a scandal.*

His smile warmed and almost melted her bones. "Excellent. I'll see you then if not before." He touched his hat, nodded, and left. For one insane moment she wanted to call him back.

Don't be a nodcock, Tessa. Just because the man is kind doesn't mean he has a serious interest. In a week he will be gone. Back to Lincolnshire.

CHAPTER 7

The Somerville butler showed Titus to a private sitting room. Still puzzled over the message he had received from Robin, he paced the room, and didn't have to wait long. Robin entered followed by a footman with a bottle of good Strathnaver Scots whisky and two glasses.

Robin gestured for him to sit and handed him a glass without asking if he wanted one. "Drink up. You may need it."

Titus, eyes studying Robin in search of sense, sipped cautiously.

"Justin was injured last night." Robin's words were bald and frank. One of them registered harder than the rest.

"Night?"

"You will have guessed Moonlight has more than one identity," Robin replied impatiently.

Of course, he does! "How bad is he? Is he—" Titus sputtered.

Robin waved the words away. "Well enough. He'll recover."

"And what is this to me?" Titus demanded.

His mysterious friend appeared momentarily sheepish. "I need help."

"With Justin?"

"God no. He's well cared for. With another ride."

Titus blinked, unable to parse that out for a moment. "Ride? You mean—"

"What it sounds like. Captain Moonlight doesn't ride alone. Too easy to get caught; too hard to confuse people." His determined gaze held Titus's.

A sigh came from deep in Titus's chest. "Who is the victim?"

"One of Brighton's gambling sharps. He fleeced Tobias Hooper's nephew out of twenty pounds."

Titus whistled. "What was the lad doing with that kind of money?"

"It wasn't his. His employer told him to take it to the bank. The nodcock thought he might use it as stake and make a few of his own before depositing it," Robin said with a wry smile. "The loss might be a lesson except his master is threatening deportation. The lad was cheated."

"Fair enough. I'm in, but you'll have to tell me what to do." From the gleam in Robin's eyes that would not be a problem.

Hours later Titus shivered in the shelter of a thicket on the coldest night so far along the Brighton-London Pike waiting for Robin to identify their quarry. He'd been dressed in black with a flowing cape. He and Robin were meant to look identical, or as close to, so that if they fled in opposite directions, it would confuse witnesses. Two others—Somerville grooms, unless he missed his guess—rode with them. His heart pounded in his chest.

He was almost at the end of his endurance when Robin shifted in his saddle and raised his arm. How he knew, Titus didn't ask. They all pulled their masks over the lower part of their faces, and Titus patted his horse's neck, preparing himself. In a flash they galloped onto the road, riding in circles around a cabriolet, shouting, and confusing its single horse, forcing it to stop. Their basic goal was to sow confusion and fear and be done before the victims could think.

There were two passengers, both men. Robin pulled up on one side, loudly demanding their purses. Titus, as instructed, kept to the other side. He knew the pistol Robin aimed at the driver was unloaded, as was the one Titus waved at the passenger. When the driver tried to demur, one of the grooms yanked him by his neckcloth and groped inside the hapless victim's coat, pulling out a heavy purse.

In a flash it was over, Robin and one groom riding off one way up and over a hill; Titus and the other in the opposite direction down a lane and around a curve.

It was an hour before dawn when Titus reached the Somerville stables to find Robin still dressed as Moonlight counting their take. Robin looked up and nodded. "Well done."

Titus stripped off his dark cape and put his own coat and hat on. "How much?"

"Twenty-three pounds sixpence, plenty to bail the young fool out," Robin said. "Do you want a pound or two?"

"I don't want any of it," Titus replied, "But I know someone who could use it."

Robin grinned.

Titus took a half crown and several pence. More would draw potentially unpleasant scrutiny to Tessa.

"I'll be on my way. I have another stop to make tonight," he said.

Robin waved him on. They didn't discuss doing it again, and Titus rather hoped they would not. Captain Moonlight was riding closer and closer to discovery.

❦

The night had turned from deep black to grey when a sound outside awoke Tessa. Wrapping a blanket around her, she stepped warily to the window facing the rear of the cottage. In the gloom she saw a shadow moving around the chicken enclosure.

A thief? We can't afford to lose our birds. As near as she could make out the enclosure was intact. She clutched the blanket closer and sharpened her gaze when the figure moved around the side. It was a man, definitely a grown man—tall and well-built who moved with the confidence of a soldier. *Captain Moonlight? Again?*

The mysterious figure walked toward the side of the house, close enough to make out his outline. She sucked in a breath. He resembled Titus! The tilt of his head, the graceful posture...

When he disappeared from view, she tamped down the urge to run out and confront him. She could very well be wrong and whoever was out there might be a brigand or at least a poacher. She held her breath, listening. Soon enough, she heard the sound of a horse being led away at a walk.

No poacher came by horse. But what would Titus Brannock want in her chicken house in the dark of night? Or Captain Moonlight for that matter. Another gift? She would leave it for the light of day.

She lay back on her bed. "I ought to be terrified," she said to the empty room. Oddly, she felt safe and protected. She smiled into the night and drifted off to sleep.

It wasn't many hours before the sound of Robby banging down the stairs woke her again. She dressed quickly and followed him to the kitchen.

"Breakfast, Love? Are you packed up for school?" she asked.

"No school, Mam. Mr. Weatherall is injured, remember?" Robby answered.

"Porridge?" she asked picking up a pot.

"Yes, and an egg please. I'll go see what the girls have for us," Robby chirped. He was out the door before she could stop him.

Tessa froze with indecision. If she ran out to fuss, and there was no sign of an intruder, she would frighten the boy needlessly. On the other hand, if anything odd appeared, Robby would—

The door slammed open. "Mam!" Robby stood in the doorway. Coins blinked in the sunlight on his open hand. He deposited the money on the table as carefully as if it was the treasure of the pharaohs.

A half crown, and eight pennies. A treasure indeed. Tessa stared at it her heart racing.

"Captain Moonlight was here again," Robby enthused.

"We don't know that," Tessa told him cautiously.

"Davy says Moonlight knows those as are in need. We have need, don't we?" Robby objected.

"Even if it is from Moonlight, it will be ill-gotten," she replied, guiltily remembering the previous bounty, most of which was still in her lock box.

"Davy says he only takes from them that can afford it, ones that take too much from good folk."

His prattling went in one ear and out the other. Tessa's mind was processing the windfall. *I can't take charity from Titus Brannock. But if it was Moonlight...*

"I can't wait to tell Davy that Moonlight was here," Robby exclaimed.

"Don't you dare! I told you last time to tell no one. Please assure me you didn't say anything."

"I dint, Mam. Truly I dint. But it was hard, and now it will be harder."

"Sometimes important things are hard, Robby. We don't need the neighbors knowing our business. Now you go fetch that egg you wanted and one for me too," Tessa said.

When the boy scurried off, she removed her lock box from its hiding place and put the coins in before locking and returning it.

She turned back to fixing porridge, her mind a confused maelstrom. Only one thing was certain. She would have words with Titus Brannock. At the ball, if not before.

CHAPTER 8

I rene Foster whisked Tessa's gown, carefully wrapped in sheeting, upstairs to her cozy apartment over the tea shop. She laid it across the bed in her room, and exclaimed over it. "Oh well done, Tessa! That sprigged muslin is lovely and the lace at the neckline precious. I know you make your own lace but that embroidered blue ribbon you used at the bodice to set off the vertical blue strips must have cost the moon."

"It cost me nothing. I salvaged it from my wedding dress after it was all but destroyed in a river crossing," Tessa murmured.

One of the few bits of my former life. Baron Wolfecliff's daughter may as well have died in that river.

"Well done, my girl. You will look a treat tonight," Irene enthused, oblivious to Tessa's emotional reaction.

Tessa shrugged. "It will do, but it won't hold a candle to the ones the London guests are wearing."

"Your lace is exquisite. Where ever did you learn to make it?" Irene asked.

"In Lisbon." Tessa smiled. "It was good to learn something useful."

"Come have tea, Tessa. We have an hour or so before you have to leave."

Robby was already happily into a game of cards with Carrey, Irene's niece. He would be content here for the night, and Tessa would return to sleep whatever was left of it on Irene's floor. Tobias Hooper had put together transport up to the manor for those who had none of their own, sparing Tessa the need to spoil her slippers walking. All was in order; she felt her anxiety ease. It was one night, and she would enjoy the music and the dancing.

Later, entering the candlelit ballroom behind Rachel and her father, tension rose again. This glittering world had not been hers for five years. She felt like an interloper, especially as a single woman, even though Sir Peter and Lady Penelope welcomed her warmly. Whatever were they thinking to invite her on her own?

She peered around the room, hoping, she was forced to admit, to see Titus. She didn't. Perhaps he was late.

"Oh, my dear Mrs. Fleming have you heard?" Prudence Danvers had swanned up to her.

I'm sure you will tell me. Tessa gritted her teeth.

"It is about that young major of yours."

Titus? Her attention sharpened. *He isn't my major.* "Is there a problem?"

"No, dear. Well hardly, unless you include deceiving the shire about his identity." Prudence gazed at Tessa's face as if she could dig out some nugget of truth. "Please don't claim you didn't know."

"Know what?" Tessa's shock had to show at this point.

Prudence leaned in confidentially. "Why, his brother is the Earl Astlough. And him staying at the Duck and Spoon! Lady Penelope must be mortified. That Robin Somerville knew, but never thought to mention it. She put Mr. Brannock in the guest wing as soon as she knew. Imagine!" The old gossip studied Tessa avidly.

Tessa's heart sank. *Astlough! Their family seat is on the coast in Norfolk, twenty miles from my father's. How could I have failed to recognize his family name?*

Hope she hardly realized she harbored shriveled inside her. An earl's son wouldn't look at a poor widow with anything but pity—or lust—and she knew him to be too kind to act on the latter.

"Did you?" Prudence prodded.

Tessa, confused, didn't respond.

"Did you know he was an earl's son?" Prudence repeated.

"I had no idea," Tessa murmured. *More fool me.*

Prudence bustled off, no doubt to describe Tessa's reaction in any listening ear. They would laugh at her expense. She stood rooted to the spot battling temptation to turn around and trudge back to Normanton.

The receiving line must have finished because Lady Penelope approached, smiling kindly. "It can be a bit daunting, I know," she said. "Let me introduce you to my guests." She swept Tessa along with her, introducing her as Mrs. Fleming and subtly let it be known that she was a "heroic war widow."

Tessa bowed to so many well-dressed folks, some curious, some skeptical, some kind, she feared she'd never remember one from another. A few gentlemen signed her dance card. Mr. Smallwood, the rotund, avuncular squire who lived near her asked for the opening set.

A burst of hushed conversation behind them caught her hostess's attention. "Ah. There he is at last," she said.

Tessa turned and her breath caught. As much attraction as she felt for Titus Brannock in travel clothes and dust paled when compared to the sight of him in formal dress. Though it must certainly be borrowed, his dinner coat fit him to perfection, and his trousers clung to muscular legs. Tessa's face heated.

He walked toward them, and her eyes fixated on a jeweled pin gleaming in the bright white folds of his cravat, made all the more noticeable by the severe black of the rest of his ensemble. He looked every inch an earl's son tonight.

"Mrs. Fleming, may I present the Honorable Mr. Titus Brannock, a friend of Robin's." Lady Penelope's delight in this new guest resonated in her voice.

His answering smile warmed Tessa to her toes. "Mrs. Fleming and I are acquainted. We met in Spain."

476

His deep voice reverberated through Tessa. She couldn't help but return the smile in kind, her eyes held by his.

Lady Penelope gazed from one to the other shrewdly. "I'm neglecting my duties; I must speak to the musicians. I'll leave you to get reacquainted."

"You are beautiful," he breathed, swallowing before adding in a clearer voice, "tonight. The dress is a treasure."

His words broke Tessa's spell. "Now you talk nonsense. It is well enough, but kindly look around you." She gestured at the sea of well-dressed guests.

"Now you talk nonsense. I know I am late, and you must have been inundated with invitations. Did you save a dance for me as you promised?" he asked.

She glanced at her dance card with its few scattered names. He took it and scribbled his name once, and then again, before handing it back. He had taken the supper dance. A waltz! His name had also been added to the final dance of the evening.

They smiled at each other in silence—like a pair of lunatics, she thought later. A commanding chord from the musicians' gallery broke the spell.

Titus bowed. "I'm meant to dance the opening set with Lady Beatrix Sandrow. We'll talk later."

Tessa stared after him. She would have his company, if only for tonight. She let Mr. Smallwood lead her out. Something magical about the ball filled her with hope.

◈❧◈

The gossip, the choreography of precedence, the preening feathers— Titus had never much enjoyed society. Tonight, however, the promise of a waltz with Tessa gave him every incentive to throw himself into the spirit of the thing.

No matter his partner, no matter his own whereabouts, however, he never lost sight of Tessa. She danced with Major Kellborn, with Lord Meade, and with Robin Somerville. The first were strangers to him, and a fierce protective urge overcame him. He had to remind the sharp clawed falcon in him to let the lady make her own decisions. He felt better when she sat out a dance with Rachel Pendleton, the two deep in some feminine sharing.

Sometime later that falcon took flight again, claws out. Oswald Neale had been slithering around the perimeter of the dance floor all evening. Once Titus saw Tessa change direction to avoid the worm. It put Titus on alert, but the Somervilles kept him busy with introductions and partners, and the ladies in their circle seemed all too happy to oblige. He lost sight of her.

He bowed over Mrs. Kellborn's hand and led her back to the major. "Thank you Major Brannock," she said, endearing him by the use of his rank rather than the honorific.

The man smiled at his wife. "Just in time for the supper dance!"

At last! Titus left them, eager to find Tessa, but his quick glance showed she was not nearby. A vague sense of alarm came to life

He circled the floor as people milled about locating partners; she had disappeared. His alarm grew, and he strode out to the terrace, afraid some miscreant had escorted her there with ill intentions. She wasn't there. Nor was she in the card room.

He encountered his hostess being led out as the first notes of the waltz began. "Have you seen Mrs. Fleming? We're to have the supper dance."

Lady Penelope smiled at him. "Patience, Mr. Brannock. I believe she stepped out to the ladies' withdrawing room. She'll be here momentarily." She floated off with her partner, and Titus circled back around the room.

He paced by the door to the interior hallway, but impatience soon got the better of him. He went out and collared a passing footman carrying a tray to ask the direction of the ladies' withdrawing room. He earned a disapproving scowl, but the man gave him the information, however reluctantly.

Titus climbed the stairs and located the closed door to the room the footman had indicated. A maid came out carrying towels.

"Is Mrs. Fleming well?" he asked, unable to keep worry from his voice.

"Why yes, Sir. She left a few minutes ago." The maid bobbed a curtsy and moved on.

Titus ran a hand through the hair Robin's valet had so carefully brushed hours ago. Where can she be? He couldn't shake a bad feeling. He decided to go down the second stairs at the other end of the hall.

He hadn't gone far when the sounds of a scuffle behind one of the doors caught his attention. A man's angry growl impelled him to act, flinging open the door.

The sight of Tessa, pinned against a wall by Neale's bulky torso made his blood run cold. Oswald Neale had one hand clamped over her mouth while his other groped her. "You'll learn soon enough not to defy me," the beast growled.

With a full-throated cry that had terrified French infantrymen, Titus attacked. He clasped the villain's face with the splayed fingers of one hand and yanked his head back, while his arm went around the man's throat. Titus pulled the snake off her and threw him to the ground, knocking him against a heavy table. Neale rolled to one side, dazed.

A wracking sob drew Titus's attention to Tessa, bent double, still leaning against the wall for support. He reached for her, every instinct telling him to grab her into his arms, but an inkling of wisdom slowed him. She'd just endured one beast mauling her; she didn't need another.

He touched her elbow with a shaking hand, and lifted her chin with two fingers of the other. "You're safe, you're safe, you're safe," he whispered.

"He..." her eyes, wide and agonized bore into him.

"Shh. I saw."

Panic gripped her, and she screamed when a scuffling sound rose behind him. He pushed her to his back and turned to face her attacker. There was no need. The coward scrambled to his feet and ran to the door.

When he turned back, Tessa melted into his arms and clung like a limpet, while sobs wracked her. He lifted her gently and carried her to a nearby sofa, cradling her in his lap while she wept against his shoulder. "Shh," he whispered. "You're safe. I'm here. I will always protect you." *Always.* He knew the truth of that to the depth of his very soul.

CHAPTER 9

Tessa sighed against Titus's shoulder, breathing in the scent of sandalwood. She had rested in his arms for several moments—or perhaps an hour. She couldn't bring herself to move as she knew she should. Their position was entirely improper. Still, she couldn't move. She felt safe. Protected. Cared for, as she had never been. Had she really heard him say "always?"

When he leaned down and kissed the top of her head, she couldn't stop herself. She tilted her head back and sought his mouth, saying with her kiss the things she had no words for. He accepted the tender kiss, pulled back a few inches, and searched her face. If he sought permission, he had it.

His kiss matched hers with gentleness at first, but when she responded, he deepened it, pouring out his passion, filling her with need, and leaving her breathless.

"Shocking. As I told you!"

Tessa jerked upright and gasped at the sight of Oswald Neale at the door. Titus held her firmly in his arms when she would have leapt up. "Easy," he whispered, rising without hurry, helping her up, and holding her arm on his.

Sir Peter and Lady Somerville stood at the doorway, Neale a step inside the room. As she rose, Tessa, saw Prudence and Abigail Danvers come up behind the pair, peering over their shoulders into the room. Tessa felt sick. Only Titus's support kept her upright.

Neale denounced Tessa in an irrational tirade. "I saw her entice him in here. I saw the maid come to tell him there was an emergency in the ladies' withdrawing room. I followed and watched her invite him. She—"

"He lies," Tessa shouted, as the Somervilles followed Neale into the room.

"She was a camp follower," Oswald Neale shouted back. "You know they are no better than whores and—"

Titus silenced the maggot with one blow to the jaw. Neale fell to the floor, unconscious and blessedly silent. Tessa felt a surge of triumph, all too brief.

For a moment, the only sound was a gasp from Abigail Danvers. Sir Peter finally cleared his throat. "I assume that is your way of disputing Oswald Neale's words, Brannock?"

"I found him assaulting the lady. He escaped before I could pummel him completely. I'm glad for the opportunity," Titus said. "He is a lying pig."

The Somervilles glanced at one another. "You and I will speak about this in the morning, Brannock," Sir Peter said. "For now, I'll send a groom to see Oswald Neale to his room and lock him in until I can deal with this." He shook his head in disgust.

"I mean to make this lady my wife," Titus declared, startling Tessa. When she started to object, he grasped her hand, squeezed it, and looked down at her, nodding in the direction of the watching Danvers sisters. "We will talk tomorrow, also," he said. "For now, I think I need to get you home."

Lady Penelope broke in. "Mrs. Fleming, we will have someone see you safely home. For now, I think it might be best if Major Brannock returns to the ball as if nothing has happened. I hear the last strains of the waltz. Supper will be starting." She glanced up at her husband who seemed to agree. "We best see to our guests—if the Misses Danvers will excuse us." She shooed the notorious gossips out.

Their host nodded, but as they all walked away Tessa heard Sir Peter grumble. "This house party has been entirely too eventful. I will think twice before we have another."

Tessa had no idea what Sir Peter meant; she had eyes only for Titus.

"You can't mean what you said," Tessa told him. His abrupt announcement of intentions bothered her. She cared too much to have him coerced by gossip. She'd been someone's burden of a wife before. She wouldn't do it again.

"We'll talk in the morning," he said. "As much as I hate to admit it, Lady Penelope had a point. It is better for your reputation if I stay and put on a brave face," he said.

They certainly had little opportunity to discuss it just then. Lady Penelope didn't waste time. Servants arrived swiftly to accompany Tessa to a waiting conveyance. One footman glanced down at Oswald Neale. "And I'm to keep this one in here until we can haul him to his room."

Tessa started to speak, but Titus put a gentle finger on her lips. "In the morning," he said. He kissed her swiftly and left.

CHAPTER 10

Dealing with Neale and the aftermath of their confrontation took longer than Titus expected. Normanton House had rung with both happy announcements and less joyful upheaval the night before and the morning wasn't much better. When Sir Peter finally turned to deal with Titus, he made short work of it. Titus rode out far later than expected but confident he had Sir Peter's support of his version of the incident. As it turned out, many others distrusted Neale. The worm would be held over in Brighton for the assizes.

Tessa's friends warned him she would be at Irene Foster's home, not her own, and so he set out for Normanton planning ways of getting her alone and private spots suited to a marriage proposal. What he found put period to his romantic notions.

A crowd of people filled Irene's tea shop, and Tessa stood in the center in a state of panic. She rushed to him and grabbed him by the lapels.

"Titus, Robby has gone missing. We've looked everywhere! Does Neale have him?" she demanded.

He removed her hands but kept one of them firmly in his. "Neale is under lock and key at Normanton House. He won't bother you again." He glanced around the room. "Back up. Explain what happened here."

Tessa heaved a breath. Irene's niece spoke before Tessa could. "It is my fault. He woke early and I fed him porridge down here in the Tea Room so as not to wake Mrs. Fleming, her being out so late. I left him for two minutes to fetch my pinafore from the kitchen. When I got back, he was gone. Vanished." She repeated "gone, vanished," three times, weeping as she did.

"Did anyone see him leave?" Blank stares were all the response Titus got from the townspeople.

"Where have you searched?" Everyone spoke at once, giving Titus the impression there had been a disorganized search of every building in the village. Tobias had been certain he'd gone to visit the horses, but the ostlers had seen no sign of him. Others tried the school and various stores, most of which weren't even open.

"And the church?" Titus asked, thinking the quiet might have drawn him.

"Yes," Tessa said, still clutching his hand. "And the cemetery, the vicarage, and the church hall."

Titus bit his lip. "Is there somewhere nearby he likes to play? A pond, a small thicket?"

"None of that matters if someone took him," Tessa exclaimed.

True but improbable. Titus thought it much more likely the boy had wandered off in pursuit of some boyish interest. All eyes watched him. Waiting.

"Here's the next step. Divide into groups of two or three, each head in a different direction searching within a half mile or so of the village in a wide circle. Can you do that?"

Heads nodded and the villagers eagerly began to do as he said. He gazed down at Tessa.

"In the meantime, you and I are going to ride out to your cottage," he said.

"You think he went home?" she gasped. "I didn't think of that."

"It is the one place you haven't searched." He raised his voice to the group. "Mrs. Fleming and I will search her cottage. If we don't find him, we'll be back."

He lifted Tessa onto Hannibal's back, and leapt up behind her, pulling her precious body against him and holding her with one arm. Tessa, rigid with fear, sat stiffly in front of him.

He leaned down and kissed the top of her head. "We'll find him," he murmured. When she sank back against him with a sigh, her trust made him feel as if he could conquer the world for her. He resolved to move heaven and earth, if he had to, to retrieve her son.

※

Tessa let Titus's heat wrap itself around her like a protective armor. Her fear for Robby didn't leave, but hope nudged it aside a bit.

He set the horse from a canter to a gallop when they cleared the village, which ought to have terrified her, but, anxious as she was to get home, the speed didn't penetrate.

They arrived to find the cottage shuttered and the door locked as she had left it. He dismounted and pulled her down against him for a swift hug before she began calling Robby's name.

They did not go far. When they reached the rear of the cottage, Robby came running with his dog trotting at his side. "Mam! You're home. Hello, Major Brannock. Look Mam, I finished all my chores. The eggs are in a basket by the door, and I—"

Whatever the boy meant to say next was smothered against his mother's breast when she engulfed him in a powerful embrace. He tried to wiggle loose, complaining it was too tight.

You frightened me, young man!" Tessa scolded. "You are not to wander off without permission or telling me where you're going. We looked all over the village for you."

Robby looked baffled. "Why would I wander around the village? The chickens needed to be fed, and you told me to sweep out the enclosure and put down clean straw. Carrey said you needed sleep, so I couldn't tell you."

Tessa glanced back at Titus who appeared to be struggling to hold back a grin.

"I did my chores, Major Brannock. Exactly as my Mam wanted.

Ginj and I just went for a quick run after," Robby said. The gangly dog sat next to him, his tongue lolling out.

"Well done, Master Fleming, but you know now you frightened your mother. She had the entire village looking for you. There was fear you were abducted."

"Ab— you mean like captured by Captain Moonlight? He would never," Robby replied.

Titus went down on his haunches to Robby's level. "You're right, Captain Moonlight would not abduct little boys, but your mother knows there are bad folks out there, and she worries." He glanced up at Tessa, "Even though you've been walking into the village on your own for months now."

Tessa refused to feel foolish for worrying, even though she ought to have known he might go home after a night at Irene's.

Robby peered up at his mother. "I've always been careful. I can take Ginj with me for protection, if you would feel better."

Titus's smile lit his face; he put a hand on Robby's shoulder. "Just remember, mothers worry. Always tell her where you are going, even if Carrey says she needs to sleep."

Robby nodded back seriously. He walked over and hugged his mother. "Sorry, Mam. I didn't mean to scare you."

Titus rose and gazed down at Tessa. "Do you think you trust him enough to go back into the village to tell them he is safe? He can take Ginger for protection," he added with a twinkle in his eye.

"But we can all go," Tessa said, unwilling to let her boy out of her sight. She caught the glint in Titus's serious expression. "Or we can follow him shortly."

Titus turned to Robby. "Your mother needs a rest, and she's correct. We will follow you shortly. And then I can have you up on Hannibal to come home," he said.

Robby shouted "I can do it," and was on his way, the dog trotting along his side. All Tessa could do was call after him to be safe.

She turned back to Titus, and felt that sense of safety down to her toes. *As long as he is near.*

CHAPTER 11

N othing had gone as Titus hoped, yet here he was. Alone with Tessa. "Now that our boy is safe, we need to talk."

"*Our* boy?" her eyes went wide.

"I'm getting ahead of myself, aren't I? I told you we would talk in the morning, and now it is well past noon."

"Please don't feel obliged by what you said to the Somervilles," she muttered.

"Somervilles? You forget Abigail and Prudence Danvers. They convinced everyone at Normanton House we're betrothed."

He meant to sound teasing, but it didn't help. She shook her head. "Gossip dies down. You mustn't be coerced." She didn't appear convinced.

"Before they came in, while we were on the sofa, with your sweet hands on me, did I seem 'coerced?'" he asked.

She blushed scarlet, and he had to raise her chin to meet his eyes. "You gave yourself to lovemaking sweetly, to my great joy. It was all I could have hoped. Surely you must believe my intentions were honorable."

"Rob's were. At least he married me when he couldn't bed me any other way. But he tired soon enough. He left me in Lisbon the first time, before I learned to follow the troops. He came to resent being tied to me. I won't be some man's burden again."

How could Fleming not know what a treasure he had? Titus's heart ached for her. He reached for her but she pulled back.

"Please, Titus. You are kindness itself. Please don't do that to me." Tears pooled in the blue eyes he loved.

"Tessa, I'm not Robert Fleming. I'm the man who loves you heart and soul. I had decided to pursue you properly before last night. I know you trust me. I can feel it. Don't punish me for what that man did."

Her eyes stared back, wide and searching. When he took both her hands she didn't resist.

"You are a precious treasure, Tessa Fleming. You deserve a husband who values you above all things. Let me be that man. Will you marry me?" When she hesitated, he rushed on. "Tell me you think you might come to love me as I love you. Please. Let me care for Robby as my own. Be my wife."

Her tears flowed then, and her words were soft but he heard them loud and clear. "I already love you."

He gathered her close and bent to kiss her but stopped inches away. "You didn't answer me. Will you?"

"Marry you? Oh yes, I—"

It was all he needed to hear. He kissed her with all the hope he had been clinging to, all the love that filled him, all the passion that overflowed and came echoing back in her response.

When they came up for air at last, he cradled her against him. "We should probably try to catch up with Robby," he said.

"You sound reluctant." She laughed.

"To let you go. Yes. But better we do before I forget my training as a gentleman and rush my fences."

They started to the front, hand in hand, but he paused at her kitchen door. "Tessa, would you entrust your miniature to me?" he asked.

Tessa didn't voice the puzzlement he could see in her face, but she unlocked the kitchen door, retrieved the little painting and brought it to him.

When he unwrapped it, her precious face shone clearly back at him. "You've cleaned it!" he said.

"As well as I can," she replied. He loved the pride in her voice. *Is there a note of defiance, too?*

Titus wrapped it up and put it in his inner pocket over his heart. "I will treasure it always, as it should be; I will treasure the miniature and you both, as you deserve to be."

Tessa sank against his chest and he held her close. "I love you, Titus," she murmured. Her love and trust were all he needed. Holding her close, he thought of that manor house in Lincolnshire. It didn't seem empty anymore.

THE END

ॐ

Charred Hope is a standalone novella. Caroline's two most recent interconnected series are *The Ashmead Heirs* and *The Entitled Gentlemen*, tales of the impact of a particularly devious will and a fraudulent succession. You can find those and other standalone books at www.carolinewarfield.com/bookshelf.

SOCIAL MEDIA FOR
CAROLINE WARFIELD

You can learn more about Caroline Warfield at these social media links:

Website: http://www.carolinewarfield.com/
Bluesky: https://bsky.app/profile/gma-roddy.bsky.social
Goodreads: http://bit.ly/1C5blTm
Facebook: https://www.facebook.com/groups/WarfieldFellowTravelers
X: https://twitter.com/CaroWarfield
Email: warfieldcaro@gmail.com
Newsletter: http://www.carolinewarfield.com/newsletter/
BookBub: https://www.bookbub.com/authors/caroline-warfield
You Tube: https://www.youtube.com/channel/UCycyfKdNnZlueqo8MlgWyWQ

ABOUT CAROLINE WARFIELD

Award winning author of family centered romance, Caroline Warfield has been many things (even a nun), but above all she is a romantic. Someone who begins life as an army brat develops a wide view of life, and a love for travel. Now settled in the urban wilds of eastern Pennsylvania, she reckons she is on at least her third act. When she isn't off seeking adventures with her grandson down the block, she works happily in an office surrounded by windows where she lets her characters lead her to even more adventures in England and the far-flung corners of the British Empire. She nudges them to explore the riskiest territory of all, the human heart, because love is worth the risk.

Learn more about Caroline at:
Website: http://www.carolinewarfield.com/
Email: warfieldcaro@gmail.com
Newsletter: http://www.carolinewarfield.com/newsletter/

THE CASEBOOK OF
PRINCIPAL OFFICER ROBERT
PIERCE

Brighton and surrounding districts

The life of a solo highwayman is usually extremely short—a thought I am pondering today after viewing the body of the villain I believe to have been the man plaguing the London to Brighton road.

He has been robbing isolated coaches with some success, picking on those where the coachman was not armed, and where there were no outriders or grooms. His luck ran out yesterday, when the passenger in a carriage he attempted to rob shot him point blank as he opened the door.

I thought I had Captain Moonlight, caught under the same circumstances. But there proved to be innocent reasons for the wounds on the man I arrested, so I had to let him go. Still, I will be keeping an eye on him and his friend. There is more to the story. I am certain of it.

LOVE BY MOONLIGHT

ELIZABETH ELLEN CARTER

Love by Moonlight
By Elizabeth Ellen Carter

By daylight, he's a gentleman. By moonlight, justice is served.

In the quiet village of Normanton in the autumn of 1817, Captain Robin Somerville returns from naval service to find peace elusive. By day, he's a charming second son living at his brother's estate. By night, he becomes the enigmatic Captain Moonlight—a highwayman with a code of honor, redressing wrongs in secret. When Rachel Pendleton, the curate's daughter, begins to suspect his dual identity, her heart must weigh law against love. As romance blossoms amid secrets and schemes, a shared pursuit of justice could cost them everything.

DEDICATION

Dedicated to the always patient and kind Bluestocking Belles. And also dedicated to you, dear reader. This will be my last story for a little while. I hope you enjoy it.

CHAPTER 1

Early September 1817
Normanton House

The junior footman eyed the stack of mismatched plates in his arms and rounded the corner into the hallway at pace, nearly barreling straight into Captain Robin Somerville, who averted disaster with a well-timed sidestep.

"Forgive me, sir! I didn't see you."

"A miss is as good as a mile, Scottie," the handsome young naval officer replied.

The youth nodded his gratitude and continued his errand—at a much slower pace this time—through the morning room and out the French doors onto the lawn, making a beeline for a marquee that had been set up for today's gathering.

Through the doors, Robin took a moment to observe the cook and kitchen staff setting out dishes for the guests in attendance.

A well-run household was very much like a well-run ship, and his sister-in-law Penelope was a very able captain, he mused.

It was days like this—with all hands on-deck—that the sea called to him like a beckoning tide. He missed the surge of terror mixed with excitement that came with spotting a ship bearing French colors.

But alas, there were no wars to fight now that Bonaparte was safely incarcerated on Saint Helena, and with that fact came the inconvenient truth that there was no need for a large standing navy, let alone a surfeit of officers.

And many of those men had settled back into civil life with gusto —and a few with good fortunes, himself among them—however, Robin could not seem to quell his restlessness.

The expression 'all at sea' was obvious and hackneyed, but in truth, he couldn't think of another that suited him better.

Shaking off his introspection, Robin stepped out onto the lawn, taking in a moment to feel the warm early autumn sun on his face and to observe who was in attendance—which seemed like more than half the town of Normanton.

Firstly, he spotted his nieces and nephew, Victoria, aged ten, Christopher, aged eight and little Isabella, just turned five, playing with some of the village children. He regarded the three fondly— they were lovely children with the curiosity and energy from the Somerville side of the family and good-natured kindness that was clearly their mother's influence.

Not surprisingly, his brother, Sir Peter Somerville—tall, with sandy brown hair—was at the center of a gathering of villagers.

Robin dropped his head to hide a smile as he approached. After eleven years of marriage, the pair still held hands like newlyweds.

Yes, he might tease his older brother, but he had to own to a small bit of envy that Peter was so happily situated. As the youngest of the Somerville family and the second son, Robin was aware from a young age that expectations were different for him—especially as the baby of the family.

Enlisting as a naval officer had been a way to forge his own destiny, and he had attained the rank of Captain just as the war with Bonaparte was coming to an end. And in truth, Robin had enjoyed living like a gentleman of leisure for the first few months of his furlough but now, six months later, inaction chafed.

If it hadn't been for his friend and fellow officer Justin Weatherall, he might have gone stark raving mad but now...

Robin listened in on the conversation.

"Did you hear what happened to William Burgess?" said one of the villagers, who then paused for dramatic effect. "He was set upon last night by that highwayman and his brigands."

Anything to do with the highwayman who had been accosting travelers along the road from Brighton to London over the past few months always attracted interest, so Robin stepped closer, as did a few other people.

"Oh, how dreadful," said one woman.

"Frankly, Burgess got what was coming," muttered a man.

"Well, the law is the law, and one shouldn't go about trying to take it into one's own hands," another woman sniffed.

As far as Robin was concerned, William 'Bill' Burgess got *exactly* what he deserved—a tweak of his nose, a little public shaming, a touch of humiliation. Burgess prided himself on being a pillar of their small community. However, he was just a merchant who cleverly shortchanged his customers and was always late paying his suppliers.

Across from him, also listening to the conversation was Rachel Pendleton, the rather pretty daughter of Clive Pendleton, the town curate. Robin had learned from her that Burgess' latest victim was a widow who earned her living making piecework lace. The woman had been promised three pounds for her fine work but when she had counted out the coins, it had been three shillings short.

Not a fortune to be sure, but enough to make a difference to a young mother with two children who were only just getting by.

"Still, the man is quite a few pounds lighter today," someone else remarked.

A small chuckle went up from the audience, Robin included.

"According to his driver, a gang of them emerged out of the blackness and yelled, 'Stand and deliver!' Burgess was ordered out of the coach and to hand over his purse, then take off his trousers."

"His trousers? Whatever for?"

"Heaven knows why Captain Moonlight does what he does."

"Did Smith get a good look at the man?"

The storyteller shook his head slowly.

"One of the gang slapped the horse on the rump, which set it off in a gallop. By the time he managed to control the beast, he was close to home and thought it better to raise the alarm than go back."

That news was greeted by murmurs of approval, followed by a large tut-tut by another man.

"Robbery is a motive I understand, but was there any need to humiliate the fellow?"

Why, yes. Yes, there was, Robin silently mused.

The loss of half a crown was nothing to Burgess, the loss of his reputation on the other hand...

He peeled away from the group, lest they see the grin that threatened to spread across his face.

That *had been* a particularly satisfying adventure.

Tomorrow morning, Burgess would find his trousers flapping high on the flagpole atop the roof of the church and Mrs. Timmons, the widow, would find three shillings in the chicken coop when she went to collect the eggs.

Robin walked into the sunshine, letting the early autumn sunlight warm his face. It felt good to be outdoors, better still to be doing some good for others.

❧

Rachel listened to the tale of the infamous Captain Moonlight, conscious of the weight of an iron key in the pocket of her day dress.

She had thought it unusual when Robin asked her to bring the key to the church tower here today. Now she was beginning to have her suspicions that it might have something to do with the unfortunate incident with Mr. Burgess.

Livid had been the only word to describe her feelings when a tearful Mrs. Timmons told her about being done out of her proper wages, and Rachel had made no secret of that in recounting her visit over dinner that Captain Somerville had attended as her father's guest.

Surely, *he* had nothing to do with highwaymen. After all, Robin was an officer and a gentleman in His Majesty's Navy.

Still, there was something about his expression when Mr. Creighton was recounting the tale that made her think that Robin knew something more than he should. Why had he whispered in her ear after dinner that night to bring the key with her today?

She watched him leave their group and admired his form as he crossed the lawn toward the gardens in long unhurried strides.

How long had she held him in such affection? Too long. Forever, perhaps. Certainly, ever since she saw him in his crisp lieutenant's uniform that day he'd come back to their village to say his farewells before he taking up his commission.

How handsome he looked in his blue and white uniform and bicorn hat.

Now, after three years at sea, Captain Robin Somerville carried himself with the confidence of a man, rather than with the braggadocio of a youth. The sun had also tanned his skin, which only added to his handsomeness and now, hatless, his hair shone like a newly minted penny.

The group's conversation had left the subject of Captain Moonlight behind, so Rachel used the opportunity to withdraw from the group and head in the direction she had spotted Robin going.

She spied him wandering among the terraced gardens, where the last blush of summer lingered in the form of pale pink roses—fewer now, but no less fragrant—nestled between late-flowering marigolds. Rather than directly approach, she paused at one of the nearby bushes to admire the silkiness of the rose petals and take in the sweet scent.

"Pleasant day, Miss Pendleton."

The sound of Robin's voice never failed to warm her from head to toe. It was a well-modulated voice, very pleasant, and yet it was more than that. It was the knowing tone—one that sat just on the correct side of mockery.

She paused a beat before answering. Captain Robin Somerville might know a lot, but she would never reveal to him her tender feelings.

"Ah, Captain," she answered before taking a good few steps away. A moment later he was in step with her.

She felt the touch of his hand at her waist as he subtly directed her to one of the lower terraces, where a decorative iron garden bench offered a charming view down the valley and the sea beyond.

Rachel fished in the pocket of her dress for the key and pulled it out. But before she could present it to him, both of his hands covered hers.

He raised her hand to his lips and kissed it while his fingers tangled with hers to remove the key. Rachel gasped softly and moved half a step toward him, her eyes locked to his, a quicksilver grey-blue.

What would it be like to kiss him properly?

In her mind's eye, she could feel him touch her lips. She released a soft sigh.

Did he know what she was thinking? He appeared to. A faint smile passed briefly across his face and he released her hands.

"Thank you," he whispered.

"Why do you want the key?" she asked softly, despite the fact there was no one in earshot.

"It is to be a surprise."

"For Burgess?"

Robin briefly touched one of his fingers to her lips.

"Shhh, ask no questions."

Ah...

That was all the answer she needed. Rachel raised an eyebrow which was matched by Robin's boyish grin.

"Let's return to the party before people start to wonder where we are," he said.

Yes, it was wise to change the subject.

This was dangerous for any number of reasons.

CHAPTER 2

Normanton House
One week later

R obin set down his freshly drained teacup and had it immediately whisked away by an attentive maid clearing away the afternoon tea dishes.

If he closed his eyes for a moment, he could imagine himself back onboard ship where the senior officers issued commands and they would be carried out with well-timed efficiency. It had to be this way, the lives of hundreds of men were at stake, not to mention the success of their assignment to protect England and defeat Napoleon.

And yet he wasn't at sea, he was in his brother's stately home overlooking Normanton, and the one issuing orders was the home's beautiful and gracious mistress.

And the battle plans being made were for the Somervilles' annual autumn house party.

After so long at sea, Robin had forgotten what an important event it was and, as a youth, he had not realized how much work went into such an affair.

The servants at Normanton House had never been slack in their duties, thanks to the diligence of the butler and housekeeper, but now their efforts were redoubled.

The scent of beeswax and hearth smoke hung lightly in the air as the household prepared for cooler evenings. The days might still be warm, but the nights had already turned brisk.

Robin left the dining room, lest he be picked up and tidied away along with the dishes, and made his way to the lady's study.

Penelope was seated at her writing desk and Peter sat on a leather couch nearby, reading the newspaper that had come direct from London on the final post of the day.

"There," Penelope announced, setting aside an envelope freshly sealed with wax. "The last of the invitations."

Robin hid a smile as he watched Peter lower the paper to take in the high stack of invitations.

"How many are we inviting this year?"

Penelope shrugged daintily, a curl of dark brown hair bouncing with the movement.

"Only a dozen, the same as last year."

Peter picked up the list at Penelope's elbow and started reading aloud:

Sir Westcott Twisden, Lord Rupert Swan, Lady Florence Swan, Lady Josephine Cranfield, Viscount Weatherby...

Robin knew many of these people. Some were old family friends, others he only had a passing acquaintance with.

"...Felicity Belvoir..."

Robin pricked up his ears.

Well, someone was going to be very interested in that news.

He smiled to himself. Peter continued with the roll call of names, then another one caught his attention.

"... Victor Grant... do I know him?" Peter asked.

"Oh, we met him in London some months ago," she said with a dismissive wave of a hand. "He has quite a *tendre* for Lady Felicity Belvoir."

Now seeing Robin in the doorway, Penelope looked at him and smiled. "Thank goodness you're here this year; it would have been that much harder to get the numbers right."

Robin offered a small bow.

"Always a pleasure to be of service—after all it's the least I can do since you're giving me room and board."

Peter left his place and clapped a hand on Robin's shoulder.

"I know you can have a home of your own wherever you wish, but I'm glad you've chosen to stay with us."

The kindness of his brother's words struck a chord deep within him. He loved his family, and the time he had spent with them so far had caused him to think of a life beyond the relentless, unyielding discipline of the navy.

A home, a wife, family of his own...

The thought warmed him from within.

"My brother, there is no place I would rather be."

"And yet..." Peter knew him well. A desire for a home and hearth couldn't vanquish his restlessness.

Robin let the statement hang.

"And yet, I feel the need to be of assistance to my dear sister here," he said before nodding to Penelope. "If I leave now, I can be assured to have your invitations on the next mail coach to London."

He watched his sister-in-law spare a glance to her husband before turning back to him.

"There's no need to put yourself out, I can send someone from the house."

Robin shook his head and picked up the invitations and bowed.

"I am your servant, madam."

Penelope smiled at him with all the indulgence a woman could bestow on a beloved younger brother.

Robin opted for the mile-and-a-half walk into the village, cutting through the edge of the woods where the bracken had begun to brown and the leaves hinted at turning.

So far, his family remained utterly oblivious to his occasional nocturnal activities as Captain Moonlight—as well they should—for the cost to their reputation would be immeasurable should he be killed.

And should he be captured... the penalty would be the same— death, this time at the end of a hangman's noose.

That brought him back to Penelope's guest list.

Victor Grant.

Robin gritted his teeth.

Now there was a name that he hoped never to hear again.

They had butted heads in the past while in service. Although it had been years since Robin had seen the man, it still didn't make him any more kindly disposed to the cur.

Setting aside his own dislike, Robin knew of one other person who would like this news even less.

❦

Rachel stepped into the kitchen, slipped on an apron, sat on a stool by the window, and placed a large bowl of freshly harvested peas on her lap. Mrs. Rolf, the vicarage housekeeper, currently elbow-deep in flour, looked up at her.

"How are the Swenton family?" she asked.

"They're getting along," she said. "The eldest boy has been able to take on his father's carpentry work, although it will mean taking the youngest out of Mr. Justin's school to do his brother's chores."

Mrs. Rolf shook her head and clucked with sympathy.

"Such a shame Swenton broke his arm. School has been good for those children." she said. "I suppose we can thank God that the father didn't suffer worse than a broken arm, the way he fell off that roof."

Rachel started shelling peas, listening to Mrs. Rolf chatter away about other news in the parish.

Like Mr. Burgess' trousers hanging from the church flagpole in time for Sunday service last week...

"And no one can work out how Captain Moonlight actually did it," said the housekeeper. "The door to the church tower was locked, and the key never leaves your father's office unless he is carrying it."

Rachel held her breath waiting for a question. Did *she* know anything about it?

All in all, she would prefer not to lie, but neither could she possibly confess that she had taken it, because that would raise even more questions and that would lead to Robin Somerville.

"It's to remain a mystery, it would appear," she offered.

Fortunately, that was enough of a response for Mrs. Rolf to consider the subject closed and continue down another path, that being the arrival of Lady Penelope's house party guests.

Robin Somerville was Captain Moonlight.

Rachel released a breath. It was beginning to seem more like a statement than a question.

Really? Could it be?

If only she could remember all the times and places the highwayman had struck. Could Robin account for his whereabouts?

In truth, she didn't know. And it wasn't as though she could make inquiries of her own without impugning his character—or looking foolish if her suspicions were unfounded.

But what if she wasn't?

What she *did* know was that Robin chose to sit next to her at church on Sunday and sing from her hymn book rather than his own. And, at some point, she had no idea when, he managed to slip the key into her reticule, a fact she only discovered when she opened it to pull out coins for the offering box.

Rachel continued her task, listened to Mrs. Rolf's chatter while watching the view from the window, past the little kitchen garden and the little picket fence to the churchyard beyond.

A familiar figure came into view and her heart tumbled a few beats—it was as though she had conjured him up by thinking of him.

Robin.

"Ah, there's Captain Somerville," Mrs. Rolf announced, quite unnecessarily.

Rachel set her aside her bowl of shelled peas and glanced down at the apron filled with hulls. She stood, holding up the corners of her apron with one hand and announced her intention to feed those scraps to the chickens.

Robin waited for her there. On seeing her, he removed his hat. Curly sandy locks framed his face.

Rachel shook out her apron and the chickens hurried to peck at their treat.

"Have you time for a walk, Miss Pendleton?"

She paused a moment and regarded him intently.

"Have you come to ask me to purloin another key for you? If so, I shall have to decline. These things have a habit to of ending up in the wrong hands."

The corner of Robin's mouth lifted in a cockeyed smile. "The wrong hands, you say? Heavens, that will never do. What is this good borough coming to if a man cannot come to church without seeing his unmentionables flapping in the breeze."

Rachel found her tongue planted in her cheek to prevent a smile. "Indeed."

She searched his face, looking for the truth, and found herself taking in the shape of his jaw, the line of his lips, and then his soft blue eyes.

The look he offered her in return was no less intense.

Would he take her into his confidence?

Rachel held her breath a moment.

His eyes never left hers, and she felt the slight brush of his fingers run down her arm to her hand, caressing each finger before threading his fingers through hers.

Part of her mind clamored danger. She should not entertain thoughts about his good looks or risk her heart to someone whose social standing was far above her own. Yet she did not object as they walked hand in hand around the church grounds.

A neatly tended cemetery with weathered headstones attested to the age of the village—named for the very Normans that stepped on the shore not so far from here. Her father personally oversaw the gardens. Drifts of pretty little flowers in white, pink, and purple spread amongst soft greens of the grass and the tall yew trees that bounded the graveyard.

Lengthening shadows were a testament to the lateness of the day.

That still, small voice that had tried to warn her was soon quieted by the conversation which flowed effortlessly between them. She spoke of her visits to families in the parish and Robin shared Penelope's plans for the autumn house party.

"In truth, I was glad to get out from underfoot," he concluded.

Rachel squeezed his hand softly. Her heart went out to him. It mustn't be easy for a man of action to return to a life of genteel civility.

"You miss your time at sea, don't you?"

She received a shrug in reply.

"Would you go back into the navy?"

There was silence, and Rachel wondered whether it would be yet another question that would remain unanswered. They stopped at a tree at the corner of the churchyard. Some yards away was a two-story cottage, modest but well kept. But here they were not overlooked by it.

"No, I think not," Robin answered at length. "That part of my life is over."

"Then what is next? A man needs something productive to occupy his time; to have purpose. Or..." Rachel dropped her voice to a whisper and took a half step closer. "Have you already found it?"

There could be no mistaking the real question she asked; they knew each other too well for that. And she would know whether or not he told her the truth.

He let go of her hand and reached down to a patch of grass at their feet.

Robin plucked a four-leafed clover. A symbol of luck. He considered it for a moment then offered it to her, as a suitor might do with a bouquet of flowers.

"Perhaps," he replied mildly. "Who's to say?"

An answer, but not an answer.

Rachel accepted the offering, twirling the greenery around with her fingers.

"Would you stay here?" she asked.

Oh no, that sounded intensely personal.

"I mean, in the district."

And it was only because she was watching him so carefully that she saw his eyes soften, as though he'd read her thoughts.

At that moment, the door of the two-story cottage in the field burst open and out tumbled four rambunctious boys, having apparently reached the limit of their ability to sit still to learn.

Their enthusiasm made Rachel smile.

"School is out," she said.

Robin offered her a heart-stopping grin.

"And I'm here to see the teacher."

"And I will bid you a good evening."

As Rachel turned towards home, Robin snagged her hand and squeezed it briefly.

"Thank you," he said.

That could mean anything. But most of all Rachel suspected that it was for keeping her silence about the escape with the key.

If only she had the courage to ask directly, but as it was, Captain Robin Somerville was already striding across the lawn to where Lieutenant Justin Weatherall, their local schoolmaster, lived.

CHAPTER 3

R obin approached the cottage, accepting the greetings of
another six children as they departed.

It had been no easy task to persuade parents to allow their children to miss four hours of a perfectly good working day to learn the
essentials of reading, writing and arithmetic.

But Justin was a determined man and one with a gift of
persuasion.

And yet Robin couldn't help but think that, despite the worthi-
ness of this cause, Justin's talents might better be used in more
elevated society.

He paused at the threshold and took in the single room domi-
nated by two tables and a dozen or so mismatched chairs. Inside was
his friend, methodically putting away books on a small bookcase.

The scent of chalk and lamp oil lingered in the room, mingling
with the faint smoky smell of the hearth Justin had lit earlier against
the chill.

"If you're going to stand there, then you might as well as make
yourself useful by rearranging the furniture," Justin called out to him.

Robin walked in to move the chairs, along with the table, to return the room to its primary function of combined parlor and dining room.

"The invitations have gone out for Penelope and Peter's house party," said Robin conversationally.

"I'm sure you'll all have a wonderful time," Justin answered.

"Felicity has been invited, too."

Justin halted, then deliberately put down the chair and glowered at him.

Robin put up his hands.

"Nothing to do with me, it's all Penelope's doing, but I thought you might appreciate knowing in advance."

Justin shrugged before going over to a bookcase to retrieve a bottle from a high shelf—well out of the way of the children who came to receive their education.

"There's another guest on the list I thought you might want to know about... and this one I did try to dissuade Penny from inviting... Victor Grant."

Robin watched the look of displeasure cross his friend's face. He chuckled, because he was pretty sure he had worn the same expression when he saw the list.

"That man is trouble," said Justin.

"And you and I both know it. Sadly, no one else does."

"Will he come, do you think?" Justin's voice sounded hopeful, but both men knew the truth. Yes, Victor would be there—especially if Felicity was in attendance.

Justin sighed, knowing the answer to his own question.

Robin felt sympathy for his friend. He knew how much the man loved Felicity, and how much of a bright future they would have together if he wasn't so bloody prideful. While not exactly a pauper, Justin certainly didn't have the means to make an offer for someone of Felicity's station—even if her own heart was secure.

Robin examined the glass of spirits that had been placed before him and waited for Justin to finish pottering about and join him. The two of them had received their commissions on the same day and received the same commendations and promotions along the way.

And it was only because of the Somerville name that Robin was promoted to captain ahead of his friend.

The man was his equal in every way. If the war with Napoleon hadn't come to an end when it did, there was no doubt in Robin's mind that Justin would have been awarded command of his own ship and made his own fortune. But that wasn't to be.

Justin sat down heavily on a chair opposite.

"You didn't come all this way to tell me news I couldn't possibly care about."

"No, not entirely. It's a new moon three weeks from now. I think Captain Moonlight and his gang need to make another appearance."

Justin took a sip from his glass, and raised an eyebrow in mute enquiry.

"There is an Excise man by the name of Jimmy Hall who is over-charging on the taxes, but more than that, he is confiscating contra-band and selling it on himself," he said.

"And how has he been getting away with that?"

"He's blackmailing a publican with a small pub close to the coast."

Justin set down his glass. A smile slowly spread across his face.

"Well, we'll just have to make sure this chap receives his just desserts. A visit to the publican?"

"Indeed," Robin agreed. "Tonight?"

☙❧

The lamps had already been lit by the time Rachel returned to the kitchen and stepped back into the familiar, comforting routine of the evening meal.

The smell of pork resting on the bench was delicious, and Mrs. Rolf continued her work in the kitchen, removing a pan of roast vegetables from the oven.

Rachel walked through to the dining room and set the table, and heard sounds from the study across the hall that announced her father's presence.

"Hello, Father, dinner is ready to be served," she said. "How is Mr. Douglas?"

"Stubborn as always. No matter how much his daughter wishes that he would give up his cottage and live with her and her family, he has no intention of giving up his home."

Clive Pendleton offered an indulgent shake of his head. "Equally stubborn daughters, what should we do with them?"

Rachel grinned. "If that is a pointed dig at me, dear father, I shall not rise to the bait. I am as meek and biddable as they come."

Her father snorted with laughter and held out his hand to her. Rachel went to him and gave him a hug.

"I couldn't wish for a better daughter," he whispered.

Rachel closed her eyes and squeezed her father tight.

She loved her father so much that the thought of leaving him was almost unimaginable.

"Mrs. Rolf said Captain Somerville came calling his afternoon."

Rachel leaned back to look into her father's eyes.

"Captain Somerville came to *call* on Lieutenant Weatherall," she said firmly. "He happened to offer greetings as I was feeding the chickens."

"Ah, I see."

That merry twinkle in her father's eye was worrisome. It meant he had thoughts that he should not think about herself and Robin.

She stubbornly raised her chin and said nothing.

"No time for a stroll?" her father continued. "How disappointing."

Before she could think of a retort that would settle her father's unreasonable expectations, Mrs. Rolf announced dinner had been served.

The evening passed convivially as it always did in the Pendleton household—dinner followed by a lively game of cards, followed by an hour or so reading before the pull of lethargy drew its inhabitants to bed.

Rachel readied herself for bed in her upper-story room. The book she had started reading was fascinating, and she wanted to read just one more chapter tonight. She raised the wick on the lamp she placed on her dressing table, then opened the curtains and raised the window sash an inch.

She breathed deep and took in the landscape beyond just as the last of the twilight ebbed. From her vantage, she could see the corner of Lieutenant Weatherall's home through the trees. Was Robin still there? Probably not. Dinner most likely awaited him at Normanton House, perhaps one of those fine dinner parties that Sir Peter and Lady Penelope were famed for hosting.

Rachel sat down on the little bedroom chair with a sigh and picked up her book.

It really *was* thoughtless of her father to tease her about Robin. His restless spirit wouldn't let him settle in a little village like Normanton, and besides, his wealth and position would likely have him seek a wife from his own station.

Some hours later Rachel woke with a start. Her room was in semi-darkness. She'd fallen asleep in her chair while reading, and she could see the pages of her book gleam white in the moonlight that streamed through the window.

Indeed, the moon hung high, large but not quite round, lighting up the hill overlooking the town. A faint mist was rising across the churchyard, turning the yew trees into dark silhouettes.

She stood and stretched, then bent down to pick up her book and place it on the dressing table.

In the stillness, Rachel heard the sound of hoofbeats at a gallop.

It was late. Who could be out at such an hour and in such a hurry?

She stayed at the window, peering into the night. Was there an emergency? Was someone coming to them in need of help? Rachel waited at the window, but the sound didn't get closer.

There on the brow of a hill, she caught the glint—stirrups, perhaps, or sword hilts—as two figures galloped over the brow of the hill, their cloaks billowing out behind them, before disappearing on the other side of the rise.

Captain Moonlight?

Only time would tell.

CHAPTER 4

R obin gave his horse its head. The black gelding extended its stride and kept its footing sure on the moonlit road.

Even though the English Channel was three miles to their east, the briny tang of the sea air filled his lungs.

This. This was the cure for the restlessness that gnawed at him. Anticipation that thrummed through every nerve; his senses heightened, alert to danger—whether it be from the man, beast or nature herself.

It had been like this onboard ship, every time they sailed into a storm or faced an armada. It was there, the tension that made his hands and feet feel as though they were almost tingling, his jaw tightened until his teeth ached.

Damn it, he felt *alive*.

Captain Moonlight had started as a semi-drunken jest with Justin one evening after he'd listened to his brother recount his disquiet over the belittling treatment of Lady Georgina at the hands of her brute of a husband, Lord Farthingale.

Penelope had said that she tried to gently broach the subject with the lady herself, but the poor woman insisted nothing was amiss.

The man's lack of consideration towards his wife bothered them all, but what could they do about the domestic matters of another household? And if something should be done, then how could it be made to happen in a way that wouldn't leave Lady Georgina in a worse predicament with her husband?

The man needed to be humiliated in front of others and in front of his wife, Robin had decided. And thus, the idea of a highwayman was born and tonight saw him galloping along the road at midnight for the start of another escapade.

Robin glanced across at Justin who raced alongside him. His friend turned and also flashed him a grin.

Brothers-in-arms once more.

Farthingale had received his comeuppance a month after a dinner party at Normanton House. He and his wife were travelling down from London with two other couples when a highwayman ordered their carriage to stop.

Like the coward Robin knew the man to be, Farthingale's initial bluster turned to blubbering as he was liberated of his fancy gold hunter pocket watch and other valuables, and was made to strip off his own clothes and then rob his fellow passengers.

Robin had then ordered the other passengers back into the coach and sent it on its way, leaving Farthingale alone, vulnerable in the middle of a deserted highway, in the middle of the night. By morning, Farthingale had been found tied to a tree, his buttocks striped purple and black, caned by an expert hand.

As for the purloined jewels—they were delivered intact a fortnight later by the royal post to a solicitor in London, who received with it a full accounting of the evening penned by Captain Moonlight himself.

The next time the Farthingales dined at Normanton House there had been a marked shift for the better in the man's demeanor.

Yes, it had been a risky endeavor, and Robin freely acknowledged it. So much could have gone wrong but, by God, how satisfying it was to deliver a little extra-judicial punishment to those who deserved it.

And that's what tonight was going to be about.

Word had reached them via a former midshipman of their acquaintance who had newly joined the Preventative Waterguards, a division of His Majesty's Excise Service, that his superior, Jimmy Hall, was purposefully working in league with a gang of smugglers and enriching himself handsomely as a result.

And a large haul of tobacco, brandy, and silk was expected to be diverted to an isolated coastal inn on top of a headland. That's where they were heading now.

The building sat low and squat on the headland, its whitewashed stone glowing in the bright moonlight.

Robin and Justin brought their horses to a halt. The sea was below them, and the sound of waves crashing over rocks brought the smell of salt air even more acutely to their noses.

From their vantage point, they could see cuts in the rock that indicated steps down towards the water.

"No easy task to bring contraband back up to the top," Robin observed.

"There might well be caves below, and a second way down from the inn," Justin added.

"You mentioned innkeeper George Blunt is a reluctant participant in Hall's scheme?"

"Apparently so. Not without a sideline of his own, I'm given to understand, but he has serious reservations about this one."

"We'll take Midshipman Younger at his word," said Robin, pulling his tricorne hat lower over his eyes and pulling up the corners of his coat. "I see lights in the window. We'll see if Mr. Blunt will stand us a pint."

There were three men inside, one slumped in his chair by the fire and snoring loudly. Two others were hunched over a set of dominos, half-full tankards at the elbow.

He and Justin went straight to the empty bar. Blunt appeared almost immediately and eyed the two of them with suspicion, until Justin slid over a half a crown and a playing card—the ace of spades —a pre-arranged signal.

Blunt, a tall, solidly-built man with a head as bald as a new-born babe's, nodded grimly, poured two pints, then nodded to a curtained-off area behind him. Robin and Justin silently followed him into the kitchen.

"I want to get one thing straight," the man whispered harshly. "I ain't never been a turncoat in my life. My family have been running this area for more than a hundred years, and we've never betrayed one of our own.

"I took a big risk trusting Younger and a bigger risk letting you two in here, but there is one thing a man won't stand for, and that's when someone threatens his family."

"We understand, Blunt," said Robin.

"Do you?" The man's weathered face wrinkled into a sneer. "I have a daughter who's fifteen. She's a beauty, just like her mother were, and Hall said when he comes back next, he'll..."

Blunt's words failed him at that moment. He hung his head, shook it, and drew in a deep breath. Anger and fear were painted across his ruddy visage.

Robin's jaw tightened, and he squeezed his hands tight to manage his own anger.

"Have no fear for your daughter," he said. "We'll get her away from here. She'll stay with a very respectable young lady in Normanton until this is over."

Long silence ensued. Robin had the sense that the man was arguing with himself.

Then finally, a single nod.

"What do ye want me to do?" he said.

Justin immediately jumped in with questions, pressing him for more details of Hall's accomplices, their number, whether they were armed, and the manifest.

Blunt answered without reservation; they would be dealing with a core group of six. Hall, he knew carried a pistol—he'd seen it—and there was no doubt that all of them were carrying knives. He knew nothing more about the manifest, but he was to receive a barrel of brandy for his trouble.

An hour later, Blunt showed them out the back way to where their horses waited. It was obvious the man had questions of his own, and they had seen the effort it had taken to not ask them, lest he appear ungrateful.

Just as Robin mounted his horse, Blunt called out the one that was obviously the most pressing to him. "What do you want in return?"

"Nothing."

The man's brow furrowed.

Robin shook his head and flashed a grin.

"Believe it or not, Hall will pay for the pleasure of our company."

Given all the preparations required for the house party and associated social events that went with it, for Rachel to receive a note kindly requesting her presence at Normanton House was not entirely unexpected.

This major social event often required more staff in attendance than would be required day-to-day, and many of the villagers enjoyed the opportunity to earn extra money as gardeners, scullery maids, odd-jobs men, laundresses, and the like.

It often fell to Rachel to assist Lady Penelope in managing the additional personnel, and house party season was a time that she looked forward to. She'd only been to London twice in her life and never in elevated society, and it was intriguing to see the ladies' maids and valets behaving like lords and ladies below stairs, as their masters and mistresses did above it.

Moreover, it was exciting to catch a glimpse of ball-goers in their satins, silks, and glistening jewels.

As she made her way to the house, she was struck by an image of Captain Robin Somerville in his evening wear. He danced well—she knew it from the country dances he attended from time to time—and in her mind's eye she saw him smiling, dancing, and conversing with these sophisticated London ladies.

He would look handsome in black.

The sharp pang in her chest surprised her.

Somehow over the past year, she'd got herself into the habit of thinking of Robin Somerville as *hers*. While he was always polite and considerate to everyone he came across, she liked to think that he held her in some special regard.

There had been enough lingering glances and touches that suggested so. But was she truly deluding herself in harboring an affection greater than was wise?

Rachel hesitated at the fork in the path. The left would take her to the front door; the right to the servants' entrance. Where did she belong, *really*? She was only the daughter of a humble village curate, after all.

With her mind made up, Rachel turned to the right, going to the entrance she had always used.

Robin was never really hers. He belonged to the same society as his brother, and he ought to have a wife who elevated his status, and the sooner *he* acknowledged that fact, the better off she would be.

Any concerns Rachel had that her brooding thoughts lingered on her face was dispelled when she was ushered by a housemaid to Lady Penelope's study, where the lady of the house greeted her warmly.

The women settled down to business and had all the arrangements largely agreed upon when a maid arrived with tea and a small tray of delicacies.

"Cook has found herself in possession of a French cookbook that Robin brought with him when he returned from sea. She has discovered a new set of recipes for *petits fours*, and we are trying a few of her favorites," said Lady Penelope. "Will you stay for tea?"

"I'd be honored."

Before her was a selection of macarons and duchesses, as well as glazed little cakes, beautifully decorated, in addition to little eclairs and tartlets. To Rachel, they all looked and tasted delicious, but Lady Penelope made notes on each one.

"I have to confess something to you, and I know I can trust you to keep this in strictest confidence."

Lady Penelope's words surprised her.

Rachel took a sip from her teacup and set it down on the table.

"Of course, my lady."

"Sir Peter and I are concerned about Robin. He has been home for nearly a year."

"Surely that is a good thing? I know how much Sir Peter has enjoyed having his brother home."

Penelope inclined her head lightly in acknowledgement. "As we all have. The children adore him as do I, but we worry about his restless nature. It's not good for a man of his disposition to remain still for long. He needs a home and a family of his own."

"I think that would be good for him, too."

"I'm so glad you think so. The reason I raise this is that sometimes Robin will go missing for two to three days at a time, and no one knows where he goes off to. That's not to say that we keep him a prisoner in our home— he's free to come and go as he wishes —but he occasionally disappears in the dead of night."

Rachel breathed in slowly then exhaled, then breathed in once more.

Captain Moonlight.

She held her breath, waiting for Lady Penelope to draw the same conclusion as she had, but she did not.

"I know he is fond of you and your father. If by some opportunity, you could persuade your father to speak to him and find out if aught is amiss..."

"Certainly, my lady," said Rachel. "He holds the captain in high regard."

"I think it would do as well if you spoke to him as well."

Rachel frowned.

"Me? I could hardly persuade a man of his stature."

Lady Penelope raised her teacup and brought it to her lips, and if Rachel wasn't very much mistaken, it was done to hide a smile.

"I believe you underestimate Robin's regard for you," she said softly.

What could she say to that? Rachel dropped her head to hide the flush of color she felt rise on her cheeks.

"I want you to be our guest for the house party next month," Lady Penelope continued. "I would like for Sir Peter to get to know you better."

CHAPTER 5

Early October

R obin woke with a start.

For a moment he'd lost his bearings, thinking at first he was back on board his ship, then the next, his room at Normanton House. It wasn't until he heard the sound of a rooster and chickens clucking that he remembered where he was.

Justin's cottage.

He'd slept like the dead on a small cot by the fire in the kitchen. It wasn't the first time he'd done it. In fact, it was a useful cover. He could claim that he'd been drinking and dicing with Justin well into the night and decided it wiser to sleep there than stumble his way home.

Better being thought *louche* than trying to dodge servants who might find themselves wondering aloud why Captain Somerville was sneaking in and out of the house at all hours.

Over the past couple of weeks, he and Justin had spent long days studying their quarry, learning Hall's routine and identifying men who were members of his inner circle, and longer nights working out their plans.

The first priority was to keep Blunt's daughter, Mary, safe.

Upstairs, the sound of heavy feet landing on the floor told him that Justin was awake also. By his estimation, the two of them had only had about three hours' sleep.

There was a lot of planning needed if they were going to catch Hall and put an end to his scheme, and there was one person he needed to bring into his confidence if this was going to work.

Robin rose and put away the cot, then set about reviving the fire in the stove and setting a kettle over it. The soft grey light of dawn was getting brighter. It was about six o'clock by his estimation—too early to go home and far too early to pay calls.

What he really wanted was breakfast.

Eggs. At least two.

Perhaps three.

Mrs. Rolf should be up and about at the vicarage, and she might be persuaded to feel sorry for two bachelors and give them a half-a-dozen. Robin smiled at the thought.

Rachel would likely still be asleep. In his mind's eye, he saw her tousled brown hair spilling across the pillow, full pink lips slightly parted...

Robin shook his head briskly before the half-formed thought of kissing her awake became something more vivid in his mind.

He headed outside into the fresh, chilled morning air and took a lungful to clear his head, then followed the sound of clucking chickens. Robin let himself into their yard and strolled to their coop. Through the slats, freshly laid eggs waited.

"A fox in the henhouse, I see."

He started and turned, inwardly cursing at having been caught unawares. Rachel stood there with a basket in both hands, her expression amused. A lock of hair escaped from a ribbon that tied her hair away from her face.

She used one hand to sweep it back over her ear and Robin felt a sudden longing to have done that for her himself.

Rachel giggled. "Cat got your tongue?"

Robin offered a sheepish grin in return.

"You see, I was..." he began, glancing across to Justin's cottage.

Rachel's grin broadened. "Oh no, you don't have to explain yourself to me, Captain. How two bachelors choose to spend their evenings is not for the knowledge of a humble spinster."

She stepped around him and released the latch to the coop. Robin stepped back to avoid being stampeded as chickens spilled out, rushing around him to start pecking at the grass. One of the hens managed to find a sluggish worm, and soon a squabble erupted.

"I suppose you and Lieutenant Weatherall would like some eggs for breakfast."

Robin looked around for Rachel. She was already inside the coop, gathering the eggs.

"If you can spare some, two poor bachelors would be eternally grateful."

"I'm sure we can oblige. The girls have laid well overnight."

Rachel backed out of the coop and into Robin's chest. She gasped with surprise. Eggs rattled in the basket. Robin steadied it by placing his hand over hers. It was close to an embrace, but not quite, not as he found himself longing to do.

"Careful," he said softly, near her ear. "We wouldn't want to lose something precious."

Rachel slowly turned. Her soft brown eyes, opened wide, looked into his and then went deeper, as though she had touched his heart, his soul—certainly that primitive maleness that had now roused itself.

How much did he want to kiss her right now? Her own unguarded expression told him that she would have no objections if he did just that.

But.

But, but, but...

Robin pulled himself together and let out a long sigh. When he looked at Rachel again, her expression was composed.

"I need to speak to you on a matter of some gravity," he said urgently, "but I need to do so alone, without risk that we will be overheard."

Rachel seemed to catch his mood. Her expression revealed surprise, revelation, before settling on resolve.

She knew! She knew his secret.

Robin's heart tumbled a few beats. Delight and fear mingled. He ignored his feelings and pressed on.

"I can't explain here and now, as much I want to," he continued. "And I am committed to attend Penelope's at-home today. Can you meet me at four o'clock at Justin's cottage?"

It was clear to him that Rachel had questions. Of course she did. Any sensible person would. He waited for her to ask them. Instead, she nodded once.

Relief flooded his being. Before he could check himself, Robin leaned over the basket of eggs between them, cupped her face with his hands and kissed her. Thoroughly.

The soft lips that he'd once touched with his finger, he now touched with his lips, and they were as soft and pliant as he'd dreamed.

"Thank you," he whispered as he pulled away from her. Robin's eyes remained on hers as he pulled out four eggs from the basket.

He held them up to show her what he had taken. "You've stopped two grown men from starving."

Rachel's expression, which had regarded him gravely just moments before, now dissolved to laughter.

"Go on, you scamp, don't let it be said that hospitality has ever been denied here."

Robin grinned and bowed formally before heading back to Justin's cottage, his heart feeling a lot lighter than it had before. There were no other women in the whole world like Rachel Pendleton, and he was glad of it.

CHAPTER 6

I t was clear her father and Mrs. Rolf didn't notice her distracted state over breakfast, and for that she was grateful. While she was well-accustomed to keeping confidences when visiting parishioners on her rounds, never before had she felt compelled to keep a secret from her father.

He'd kissed her.

Rachel replayed the moment in her mind over and over again.

The kiss was arousing, but it was also colored by urgency, telling her without any doubt in her mind that Captain Robin Somerville was Captain Moonlight and further confirmed that Lieutenant Justin Weatherall too was involved.

But the costs of not keeping the secret were worse. The penalty for being a highwayman was death by hanging and harboring knowledge of such a criminal carried its own punishment. While the townsfolk of Normanton considered the antics of Captain Moonlight to be amusing escapades, many others did not.

Why did he need *her* help? He had the entire resources that the Somerville name could muster, not to mention the many former sailors who had returned to civilian life along the Sussex coast.

Her curiosity would have to remain unsated until four o'clock.

There was nothing for it but to get on with her day and try to forget the feel of his lips on hers.

As if she could forget.

Today, being Wednesday, saw Mrs. Rolf spend the night with her sisters while her father locked himself away in his study to pray and prepare for next Sunday's sermon, which meant Rachel could make her rendezvous without awkward explanations.

She brought with her a basket with more eggs, and a bouquet of freshly picked leeks from the garden—a thank you gift for the village teacher.

The front door was slightly ajar.

"Hello?"

There was no reply.

Rachel walked through the front room out to the kitchen and set the basket on the dresser. She cocked an ear and heard a booted foot on the stairs. She exhaled with relief to see it was Robin.

The broad smile she received from him was like basking in the warmth of the sun. She couldn't help giving him one in return.

"I hope you haven't been waiting long."

She shook her head.

"Not long."

He closed the door behind him.

Somehow, he seemed to exert a magnetic pull and she approached him, standing so close she had to look up at him.

"I know your secret," she blurted out. "You're Captain Moonlight."

He didn't answer, instead closing the distance between them until she found herself in his embrace.

"Do you trust me?" he asked softly. The desire for him she felt that morning returned full force.

"I trust you," she replied. "Just as you trust me."

He lowered his head. Rachel anticipated a kiss, but instead his forehead rested on hers. A look of relief flittered across his visage.

"Thank you," he whispered. "I need your help but it's not without risk. You need to know exactly what's going to happen, but you cannot breathe a word of this to another living soul."

"You have my promise."

"Have you heard of the Anglers' Arms inn just up the coast?"

Rachel nodded. "I know of it. I've never been there, but my father has. He hasn't said much about it, except that it attracts a rough sort of custom."

Robin kissed the top of her head and released her from his embrace. He lit a couple of lamps, placing one of them on the table. Rachel watched him set the kitchen fire.

"The owner needs our help," he continued. "We need somewhere for his daughter to be safe until we..."

Robin glanced at Rachel, then turned his attention to the fireplace. "...we do what needs to be done."

"There is no need to alter your words on my behalf," she said. "You're not talking to a missish ingenue."

"I know you're not," he said. "But I don't want you in any danger either. And anything to do with Captain Moonlight *is* dangerous. If something should happen to Justin or myself and the authorities discover you had anything to do with this, it would put you and your father in an invidious situation I want to avoid at any cost."

Rachel listened to Robin give a brief account—a customs man by the name of Jimmy Hall had turned smuggler himself and was not above using violence to suit his ends.

"What do you need me to do?"

"Mary is a fifteen-year-old girl, and Hall has made threats against her to ensure her father's cooperation. I need you to keep her here overnight while we deal with the matter, but no one must know she is here."

"She can stay with me in the vicarage—"

Robin shook his head.

"No one, particularly your father, must know. Too many people come and go. We have to get her here unseen."

Rachel nodded her understanding.

"Just tell me the part I need to play."

Robin closed his eyes and sighed with what to her looked like relief. Perhaps he thought she would be difficult about it and ask more questions than he felt comfortable giving answers to.

"Lady Penelope worries about you," she said. "Your absences from the house have been noted."

Robin grimaced.

"Do you think she knows?" he asked.

Rachel shook her head. "She and Sir Peter have determined it is restlessness after no longer being in command of a ship. It is her ladyship's sincere opinion that you ought to settle down on your own estate with a family of your own."

His expression changed—surprise, thoughtfulness and, if she wasn't very much mistaken, faint amusement crossed his face in quick succession.

"And what was your considered position on the matter, pray tell?"

Was he...? Rachel frowned. Why, he was teasing her!

"Is there a reason why I should be expected to have an opinion?" she asked.

"My sister-in-law thinks enough of your good opinion to confide in you."

"As do you, I should point out."

At that Robin burst out laughing.

Then she found herself hauled into his arms for an embrace.

"No wonder I love you," he said.

Then there was silence save for the crackling of the fire.

Robin's expression was of surprise, and Rachel suspected that her own expression revealed the same.

"I didn't mean to say it aloud," he said softly.

She wriggled to extricate herself from his embrace, but he was stronger.

"Did you mean to actually say it at all?" she griped.

"I did."

Rachel ceased her struggle.

"I didn't want to tell you like this, but now the truth of it is out, I'd be a fool to lie to you as well as to myself." Robin put a finger under her chin and silently urged her to look at him. "I've fallen in love with you, Rachel, and as soon as I'm free to retire Captain Moonlight, I will court you properly, but..."

Rachel studied his eyes, searching for the truth in them, since she wasn't sure she could trust her ears. Those soft blue eyes drew her in until she felt she could see into the very depths of his soul.

He had asked her to trust him and she'd given her word.

She pressed a finger to his lips.

"Then don't speak the words until you're free to do so," she said. "You asked for my help as a friend, and I freely give it. If you're asking for my heart, then know it has always been yours."

This time, Robin's kiss didn't take her by surprise. She anticipated the softening of his lips against her finger, the press of his arm to draw her closer to him. His lips on hers were soft, yet heavy, sweet but also seared into her soul.

She followed his lead, returning kiss for kiss until desire burned hot in both of them.

CHAPTER 7

The last of the dew was long gone from the rose leaves when Robin found Felicity Belvoir in the garden. She sat on a low stone bench beneath the arbor, sketchbook open on her lap, pencil moving in quiet concentration.

Most knew her as a guest of Lady Somerville, a lady of impeccable breeding and wit—but Robin knew her as something more: the woman Justin Weatherall had loved and left, and now couldn't seem to stop watching from afar.

The morning sun dappled the walk with shadows, and for a brief moment, Felicity looked like a figure caught between worlds—genteel society and something wilder, more uncertain.

"I hope I'm not interrupting the birth of a masterpiece," he said.

Felicity looked up with a smile that didn't quite reach her eyes. "Only capturing a fleeting moment before everything changes. Sit with me, Captain."

"You know I prefer Robin," he said, taking the seat beside her.

"And yet you persist in behaving like a man who enjoys having secrets," she replied mildly. "It rather suits the title."

Robin chuckled and leaned back on his hands, letting the quiet moment stretch between them. The garden was peaceful. The only sounds were the distant murmur of Penelope's voice through an open window and the rustle of leaves overhead.

"The house feels...tense," Felicity said after a moment. "Even the children are quieter today."

"Perhaps they sense the grown-ups have things on their minds."

She turned to him, her expression unreadable. "Is it something I should be concerned about?"

He glanced at her sidelong, appreciating—as he often did—how unflinching her gaze could be.

"Possibly," he said. "You really do care for him, don't you?"

She closed the sketchbook and drew a line down its edge with her finger, then said, almost casually, "Whatever you and Justin are planning... be careful."

Robin stilled.

"I haven't asked. I won't," she continued. "But if your silence is meant to protect me, it's unnecessary. I've lived through darker intrigues than anything Sussex can throw at me."

"This one's more... personal," he said finally.

She looked at him for a long time. "Then make sure it doesn't cost you more than it's worth."

"That's the trick, isn't it?" He offered a wry smile. "Knowing what it's worth, and who's counting the cost."

She returned the smile, but there was sadness in it. "Justin thinks he's the only man with something to lose. He isn't."

Robin didn't answer. The wind shifted slightly, carrying the sound of the clock inside the house striking eleven.

"You should go," she said. "I imagine your day is only beginning."

He rose, brushed his hands down the thighs of his trousers, and inclined his head. "You always did see more than you let on, Lady Felicity."

"That's what makes me dangerous," she said.

The cart, drawn by a single horse, waited patiently on the edge of the markets for Rachel to finish her errands, as outlined by Robin in a note she found yesterday afternoon left on her dressing table, along with a small purse of coins for the purchases.

She wasn't sure that she wanted to know when he had come into her room, or how, except she was reasonably certain that her bedroom window was open a couple inches more than it had been when she had left the vicarage that morning.

Waiting patiently by the cart was Justin, looking non-descript with a tricorne hat pulled low over his brow.

Rachel reached for a modest sack of apples the greengrocer had wrapped in oilcloth, but Justin stepped in, hand already halfway to it.

"Here, allow me—."

They said nothing more until they were well out of town, and the tense shoulders of her driver relaxed after they left the outskirts of the village.

"Do you think we're quite safe, Lieutenant Weatherall?" she asked.

"We're *playing* it safe, Miss Rachel."

Justin turned his head and offered a reassuring smile. "But we can't discount the fact that Hall will have people watching."

Rachel nodded and turned her attention to the landscape around her.

Surely to anyone observing them, they would appear to be on an errand—just the delivery of goods. But now she viewed the landscape as she imagined Robin would if he were beside her and had no doubt that was what Justin was doing right now.

Here, near the coast—so close that Rachel could smell the brine —torrential rain and ferocious storms frequently turned the area marshy, but Justin picked his path carefully until they started on the rise. Around them large rocks jutted out of the landscape; small shrubs huddled by them as if for shelter.

Perfect places from which to launch an ambush.

This was dangerous, but the fear was not for herself—it was for Robin.

Rachel braced herself against a gust of wind that hit the cart head on, then breathed deep to steady her nerves.

She squeezed her eyes tight, and at that moment she saw Robin in his highwayman's guise on this midnight road. A muzzle flash. A scream. A figure falling down dead.

Rachel clenched her fists and forced her eyes open.

That seemed real. Too real. She had allowed her imagination to run away from her, surely. But the vision seemed real enough.

A glance toward Justin revealed no change of demeanor on his part, so Rachel forced her fears down.

"What was life like at sea?" she asked.

Justin glanced her way and relaxed for a moment.

"For myself and Robin?" he asked.

Rachel nodded, and she received a soft smile.

"Monotonous routine with the occasional spike of terror," he answered.

"Then why would anyone do it?"

"The glory of king and country is not enough?"

Rachel wrinkled her nose at him.

Justin's smile became the flash of a grin that quickly faded.

"Men are not made for an easy life. They must strive to make their way in the world, and the navy is as good a place as any for a man to make his fortune."

"And that's what you and Robin have done?"

He shrugged.

"He had more success than I. He did very well—especially after being promoted to captain. My fortune was far more modest."

"And yet you don't resent him for it."

It was a statement, rather than a question. Robin, she had known for years. Justin was relatively new to their village, but it was obvious to anyone who looked that the two men were friends as well as brothers-in-arms.

Justin's shrug was the answer.

"The only thing a man needs after finding his purpose is to win the love of a good woman," he said.

"Well, you and the captain have no shortage of women to choose from," she replied.

"Ah, well that's where you're wrong. As it turns out, not any woman will do. The heart is a very fickle thing. And when the damned thing has decided what it wants, no amount of very excellent reason or logic can dissuade it."

Rachel silently absorbed the bitterly-spoken words. Clearly, he referred to himself and no other. Who was this woman? Did she know that Justin was desperately in love with her?

The conversation ceased, and the sound of the seabirds and the salt-tinged wind filled the void. Over Justin's shoulder, the waters of the English Channel glinted in the daylight.

"Well, it is not always easy for women, either, Lieutenant," she said, mostly to herself.

"Why did you agree to help us?" Justin asked suddenly.

Because Robin asked me.

"Because I am a curate's daughter and it's my duty to help a parishioner in need," she replied.

"Is that the only reason?"

Rachel refused to answer. Robin's declaration of love was made out of relief that she had been able to solve a problem for him, and even if he did feel anything more, there was also the expectation that he ought to marry someone more in keeping with his status.

"If you mean to winkle out of me a confession of love, you'll find that I'm a far too practical creature to set my sights higher than I ought, Lieutenant Weatherall."

At that, Justin laughed.

"Then we're more alike than I thought."

"Then heaven help the both of us!" said Rachel.

"Heaven help us indeed."

CHAPTER 8

Not being a frequenter of taverns, Rachel labored under no expectations of what she should expect of the Anglers' Arms. She was not left disappointed. The low ceilings and brine-stained windows made the room seem small and dingy. At least the thick walls stopped the howl of the wind outside.

But still, the crackle of the fire in the hearth added warmth as well as cheer, although there were no customers to take advantage of it.

Rachel set the heavy basket of goods on the table.

The innkeeper, a burly man with graying whiskers across grizzled cheeks, looked up from polishing tankards.

"You made good time from Normanton. And you've brought company," the man said gruffly.

Justin smiled faintly. "I'll do the introductions, I suppose. May I present Miss Rachel Pendleton? Miss Pendleton, this is George Blunt, proprietor of the Angler's Arms and a man who brews an ale strong enough to rouse the dead."

Rachel bobbed her head. "A pleasure, Mr. Blunt."

The man's demeanor softened.

"You do me an honor, Miss—especially since you're here to protect my daughter."

At that, the curtain that covered a doorway parted. Entering the taproom was a pretty-looking girl with light brown hair, aged about fifteen, drying her hands on her apron.

"This is my daughter, Mary. With her mother gone, she means the world to me."

The girl echoed her father. "Pleasure to meet you, Miss."

Rachel looked to Justin, unsure what to do next, but he was studying the view outside the window.

"We were followed."

Rachel started.

"Followed? By whom?"

Justin shook his head.

"Didn't get a clear look. Just the sense of a rider keeping to the trees. I didn't want to worry you—until I had reason."

Blunt frowned. "You're safe under my roof. No one causes trouble here uninvited. Mary, go make our guests some tea."

The girl nodded and disappeared into the backroom.

"Uninvited is just the problem, isn't it?" Justin muttered.

Rachel sensed the mood of the room change. She felt the prickles of unease in the air like the charge in the air of a looming thunderstorm.

Blunt dropped his head.

"Hall was in here last night. The shipment's coming in with tonight's high tide. I want Mary well away from here. Well away from *him*."

Justin's face hardened. "Then Captain Moonlight has to ride tonight."

Alarm clamored in Rachel's chest.

Robin was expected at a dinner party tonight at Normanton House. He couldn't be in two places at once.

She caught Justin's eye and whispered.

"He'll be missed."

The lieutenant offered a small smile of reassurance.

"There is another way," he said softly, then louder to Blunt.

"I need to see the cellar. And the way down to the caves below the headland."

Blunt's surprise was apparent on his lined face.

"You know about the caves?"

"We were naval officers, Blunt. We learned to read the land, and the smuggler's paths haven't changed much in fifty years."

After a beat, Blunt nodded.

"Come with me. Bring a lantern. I'll show you the way."

Rachel followed the two men into the room behind the bar. It was a kitchen with two doors leading off the room. One, painted black, she suspected went to a parlor and bedrooms beyond. The other door, unpainted but darkened by age, must lead to the cellar.

It was that one that Blunt unlocked.

Justin glanced back at her, and his silent message was clear.

Stay there with Mary.

Rachel nodded her understanding. When she turned to Mary, who was pouring the tea, the small pot was shaking in her hand.

"Mary... you're trembling. What is it?"

"It's Hall. He frightens me, Miss Pendleton. The way he looks at me... like I'm something he's already claimed. He's a bully, and worse when he's been drinking."

With more confidence than she felt, Rachel sought to reassure the girl.

"You're safe now. You have my word."

"He frightens my father, and that scares me most of all. Captain Moonlight has to stop Hall tonight. If he doesn't, Hall will have power over everyone from here to Brighton."

Rachel reached out and squeezed Mary's hand, her voice steady despite her racing heart.

"Then he won't get it. Not tonight. Not while we still have friends willing to ride under the moon."

Their conversation ended in silence save for the crackling of the fire. After fifteen minutes or so the large cellar door opened, hinges groaning. Justin and Blunt stepped back into the room, boots damp with salt air and lantern light flickering over their faces.

"We've got our route," said Justin briskly. "The caves are sound. But we need a distraction... and I have one in mind."

He addressed Rachel, his tone gentle but firm. "I need you to take the cart back to Normanton."

Rachel was startled. "Why? Where are you going?"

"I'm going out to sea to enlist some help. If Hall's men are watching, they'll expect to see a man and a woman returning to town. That's what we'll give them."

He looked to Mary, then back to her.

"Mary will wear your clothes, bonnet and all. At a distance, she'll pass for you. You," he said, nodding at her plain riding coat, "you're nearer to my size. If you wear my greatcoat and hat, with your hair tucked up, you'll pass for me."

Rachel nodded slowly. "And once we reach the village?"

"Take Mary straight to my cottage. Remember, not the vicarage —it's too exposed," he said. "You'll be safer there. Bar the door, let no one in. Then send word to Robin. Tell him the shipment is tonight, Hall's involved, and that Captain Moonlight is needed tonight—urgently."

Mary looked alarmed, gripping the hem of her apron.

"But what if Hall knows? I've never done anything like this..."

Rachel reached across and squeezed the girl's other hand. "You won't be alone. I'll be with you every step until we reach the village."

Blunt nodded sharply. The man looked worried. "It'll have to do. Some plan is better than none. Go with Miss Pendleton, Mary."

Rachel nodded.

"Take the basket that I brought in and put your things in there," she instructed. "We will start as we mean to go on."

Father and daughter left the kitchen. Justin turned to Rachel and spoke softly.

"I wouldn't ask this of you if there were another way. But if we can deceive Hall and buy ourselves some time, we'll have a chance to intercept him before the goods change hands. And before he thinks to take Mary."

Rachel straightened her shoulders, fully resolved.

"Then we'd best get changed. We've a moon to ride before he does."

Justin nodded once, a flicker of admiration in his expression.

"Godspeed, Rachel. I'll see you at dawn."

CHAPTER 9

T he old cart rattled over the rutted road as the horse plodded patiently along, the twilight deepening into full darkness.

Rachel held the reins, her hands steady despite the cold twist in her stomach. Mary sat beside her, swaddled in Rachel's cloak and bonnet, small hands clasped tightly in her lap. They spoke little on the journey—too much could go wrong. Silence was safer.

They reached the edge of the village without incident. No shadows in the hedgerows, no pounding hooves behind them. Rachel breathed a silent prayer of thanks.

Mrs. Rolf was still away visiting her sister, and Rachel's father was spending the evening playing chess with Dr. Standish and wouldn't return until late. She steered the cart toward Justin's cottage, helped Mary down, and led her quickly to the door.

Inside, the little house was dark and quiet. Rachel lit a single lamp and turned to Mary, her voice gentle but urgent.

"Stay here. Don't open the door unless it's me, Justin, or Captain Somerville. No one else."

Mary nodded, wide-eyed. "I'll keep the latch down tight."

"Good girl." Rachel gave her hand a squeeze, then slipped out into the night once more.

She left the cart tied up behind the vicarage and made her way on foot to Normanton House. The path wound uphill, moonlight gleaming faintly on dew-slick leaves. At the rear of the house, the kitchen door glowed warmly in the dark.

Rachel knocked twice, then once more for good measure. A moment later, the door opened to reveal Bessie, one of the maids she knew from parish work.

"Miss Pendleton!" Bessie blinked. "You've come all this way?"

"I need a message taken to Captain Somerville. At once. Quietly."

"Warm up here then, while you wait for the response."

Rachel shook her head. "No response."

Something in Rachel's tone silenced any questions. The maid nodded, disappearing into the bustle of the kitchen.

The laughter around the Somerville dining table swelled like the tide itself—warmed by good wine, a lavish meal, and the crackling hearth. Robin had played his part well, sharing a naval anecdote or two, letting the weight of his smile carry through the evening.

Across from him, Lady Felicity Belvoir and Sir Westcott Twisden traded barbed witticisms, while Emma Tomkins charmed with a droll observation that drew chuckles even from staid Lord Langley.

Then the kitchen door creaked, and a footman stepped in, quietly making his way to Robin's side, a folded note was discreetly placed at his hand. Robin's brow twitched—but only slightly—as he opened it beneath the table.

Change of plans from Justin. It's tonight's tide. Urgently meet at his home.—Rachel

He didn't blink. Didn't let the corners of his mouth shift. But inside, a cold finger ran the length of his spine.

Tonight.

He glanced up slowly, calculating. Two and a half hours until the turn of the tide. That was both a blessing and a curse—barely enough time to prepare, but just enough to slip away unnoticed.

"Something amiss?" Lady Felicity's voice was low but keen, her eyes narrowing just a hair. She'd seen it—the subtle shift, the way his shoulders had tensed for half a heartbeat.

Robin offered her a languid smile. "Merely a reminder I've left something undone. Nothing that cannot be mended."

She raised a brow but didn't press. That was Felicity's gift—sharp as a tack, but generous with her silence.

The dinner wound down near ten. Guests staying at the house lingered over a final glass of port, while others wrapped themselves in cloaks and stepped out into the cool night. Among those retiring upstairs was Felicity herself, and Robin caught her giving him a backward glance as she ascended, unreadable but knowing.

Once the house was quiet, Robin slipped out through the service corridor. The air had cooled sharply; dew already settled on the grass. He moved swiftly along the village path, cutting through a stand of oaks and down toward Justin's cottage, his thoughts turning to the work ahead.

Their disguises were stored in the shed. The horses—sure-footed, dark-coated geldings —were stabled just beyond in the small barn. Everything needed for Captain Moonlight's midnight theatre. Everything *should* be ready.

He arrived at the cottage and frowned. No lights. The front stoop was in shadow, the windows dark—but one curtain moved faintly.

He reached for the latch, paused.

The key—Justin's spare, always left beneath the third floorboard just inside the stable—was missing.

Robin's heart gave a cautious thud.

Someone was inside.

He stepped back, narrowed his eyes, and studied the front window. A silhouette moved behind the glass—slender, upright. Watching.

He whispered, "Rachel?"

A pause. Then a faint shuffle, and the door cracked open just wide enough to see her eyes in the dim light.

"Robin," she breathed.

He stepped through, swiftly closing the door behind him.

"Curtains," he said at once. "All of them. Now."

"I left them open so I could see if anyone came," Rachel said, already moving. She crossed the room quickly, drawing down the heavy fabric until the room was sealed from view.

Robin struck a flint and lit the oil lamp on the table, turning it low. The shadows grew steadier.

"No key in the stable," he said quietly. "You have it?"

She nodded and pulled it from the pocket of her borrowed coat, handing it over. "I thought it best to keep it close. I wasn't sure who else might come."

Robin gave her a sharp look of approval.

"Well done," he said. "We've got two hours before the tide turns. Get your breath while you can, Miss Pendleton."

He went back outside, already shifting into the man he needed to become.

The fire in Justin's hearth was low, casting soft golden light across the room. Mary sat curled in the armchair, her frame still tense, but no longer trembling. When Robin re-entered the front room from the shed—dressed now in the dark coat, scarf and tricorne hat—she looked up and gave a small gasp.

But then recognition dawned.

"It's you," she said softly. "Captain Moonlight."

She glanced at Rachel, half-smiling. "I heard the stories but never really believed them to be true. Mrs. Timmons! And that Burgess got what was coming."

Robin's mouth quirked into a wry smile. "And now it's your turn to be safe, Mary. You did well getting here."

The girl's relief faltered as she leaned forward. "But my father— Hall's turned vicious. He says if Da doesn't start keeping the ale flowing to *his* men and looking the other way, he'll have him arrested for harboring smugglers. Or worse."

Rachel stepped in, her face grave. "I've had no word from Justin. I expected him to meet us back here and ride with you but...."

She hesitated.

"He didn't tell me the details of his plan. He asked Mr. Blunt for a boat. Which can only mean he meant to sail back against the tide."

Robin exhaled slowly. He had no doubt of Justin's ability as a sailor, but it added a complication he hadn't counted on. If Justin was delayed, or worse—intercepted—it put them all in danger. Himself. Rachel. Mary. A house of cards that could come down with the lightest breeze.

He checked the time. Midnight approached.

Still no sign of Justin.

The original plan had been simple: intercept Hall *after* the contraband arrived. Catch him red-handed. But if Hall caught wind that his leverage—Mary—was missing, he might alter course. Or bolt. Or lash out.

Robin flexed his gloved hands. He couldn't wait any longer.

He crossed to the door, fastened his cloak, then turned back to Rachel. "Secure the house after I leave. Don't let anyone in until Justin returns. When he does—tell him everything."

She stepped closer, her eyes luminous in the lamplight. "Robin... be careful."

Their gazes locked.

Robin hesitated for the briefest of moments before cupping Rachel's face in his gloved hands, his thumb brushing her cheek as though memorizing her with touch alone. The tension between them, taut as a drawn bowstring all evening, finally gave way.

He leaned in, slowly, giving her a chance to stop him—she didn't.

Their lips met, soft at first, the world narrowing to just that moment, that breath. Rachel melted into the kiss, her hands gripping the front of his coat, holding him there as if by sheer will she could make time stand still.

When they finally parted, their foreheads rested together, breath mingling in the stillness.

"I was afraid," Rachel whispered, her voice barely more than a breath. "That you'd ride off and I'd never see you again."

Robin's smile was faint, but warm. "Not if I have any say in it."

She looked up at him, her brows drawing together. "You don't have to do this alone."

"I know." He brushed a lock of hair behind her ear, fingers lingering. "But I have to do it anyway."

Her lips parted, as if to say more, but she stopped herself. She understood. There wasn't time—not for confessions, not for promises.

Robin kissed her again, this time tenderly, lingering a heartbeat longer.

"When this is done," he murmured, his voice low and rough with emotion, "I'll tell you everything. If you'll still want to hear it."

Rachel reached up and gently tugged his collar straight. "Just... come back. That's all I want tonight."

"I will." He stepped back, his fingers slipping from hers like the last threads of something unspoken.

Then, in a swirl of cloak and purpose, he turned and vanished into the night.

Rachel stood in the quiet, her fingers still tingling from his touch.

CHAPTER 10

Robin's horse galloped beneath him with smooth, rhythmic power, the moonlight carving silver shadows along the path ahead.

The wind rushed past, tugging at his cloak, and the salty bite of the nearby sea filled his lungs with every breath. He kept his eyes forward, posture low and balanced, guiding the gelding with the ease of a man who knew every tree, every fencepost, every deceptive hollow of the Sussex countryside.

Rachel's face flickered across his thoughts—her hand trembling slightly in his, the taste of her kiss still warm on his lips. He forced himself to push the memory aside. There would be time for that later.

He *hoped* there would be time for that later.

As long as Justin's deception held, Mary's disappearance wouldn't be discovered—not yet. Rachel's part in it would remain unknown, her position safe. That was the only thought that steadied his heart now.

The girl was in good hands. But Justin... Robin gritted his teeth. His friend's absence gnawed at him. He should have returned by now.

Still, there was nothing to be done. He couldn't go back. Not now. The mission had to go forward, with or without his friend.

The crossroads north of the Angler's Arms loomed ahead—an unassuming fork where the old Roman track met the smuggler's lane that wound toward the sea. Here, the cart would pass, hauling contraband up from the coast and into Hall's domain. If Robin was right, they'd be using the quieter, inland route. Hall wouldn't risk the main roads, not with talk of customs men sniffing about.

Robin dismounted swiftly and led the horse into a copse of trees. He crouched low behind the brambles, pistol in hand, eyes trained on the road. His breath came slow and steady, and he counted each one as the minutes passed. The waning moon was no more than a sliver—but the stars looked down, bright, cold, and relentless in their watchfulness. Nearly one o'clock. The tide would have turned.

The only sounds were the wind in the trees and the crash of waves breaking against the rocky headland below. But then...*there!* Faint at first but growing clearer. The jangle of a bridle. The low creak of a cartwheel struggling against a rut.

Robin tensed.

He rose from cover, stepping out onto the road with confidence and a booming voice trained by years of command.

"Stand and deliver!"

The cart stopped abruptly. Two figures froze on the driver's bench, eyes wide, hands lifting as instructed. For a moment, Robin thought it would be simple.

Then one of the men—burly, thickset—narrowed his eyes and spat. "It's just the one. Take him!"

Robin had only a moment to react. He fired his pistol—not at them, but at the ground beside the cart. The shot sent a sharp crack through the air. The harnessed horse panicked, rearing and breaking the traces, throwing both men from the bench in a tangle of limbs and curses.

The first man hit the ground hard, rolling and groaning as his head struck a rock. The second recovered faster, drawing a dagger from beneath his coat and rushing at Robin with a growl.

Robin had no time to reload. He tossed the pistol aside and drew the blade from his belt. The two men clashed in a brief, furious dance, blades catching the moonlight. Robin took a shallow cut across his left arm but ducked low and slammed his shoulder into the man's gut, knocking the wind from him.

The man staggered. Robin pressed the advantage, pinning him to the ground with a knee to his chest. The man struggled, and Robin earned another slash—this one across his side—but he gritted his teeth, struck the knife from the man's hand, and wrested a length of rope from the cart.

With swift, practiced hands, he tied the man's wrists behind his back. Just as he rose, the other man—the one who had struck his head—began to groan, lifting his head groggily.

Robin didn't hesitate. He located his pistol, crossed the space in two strides and brought the butt of his weapon down sharply on the man's skull. The groan stopped.

Breathing hard, blood soaking through his shirt, Robin dragged both men to a nearby tree and bound them tightly. He gagged them for good measure and shoved their own cloaks over their faces for concealment. They'd live, but not comfortably.

He stepped back, surveying the scene, checking again for movement along the road. Nothing.

And yet... something was wrong.

He frowned.

Neither of the men was *Hall*.

He cursed under his breath.

The real mastermind hadn't been in the cart at all. Which meant...

"Damn," Robin muttered.

He vaulted back onto his horse with a wince. The slice on his side stung with every breath, but he had no time to tend it. If Hall wasn't part of the transport, then he must already be at the inn. Waiting for the shipment to arrive. Coordinating. Watching.

And now—possibly realizing his men weren't coming back.

Robin pushed the horse hard, galloping toward the Angler's Arms. The wind cut against his cheeks like ice, but his mind was racing faster than the hooves beneath him.

The whole operation was unraveling faster than he'd planned.

If Hall caught wind of what was happening—if he even suspected that Mary was gone—it wouldn't just be Robin and Justin in danger. Rachel, Mary, even the innkeeper himself—they were all exposed.

He urged the horse faster.

He would stop Hall. Whatever it took. He just prayed he wasn't already too late.

Robin's side ached as he slipped through the narrow path that led from the bluffs to the hidden cove beneath the headland. The pain was sharp, but he ignored it—tonight, they would put an end to Hall's games, and nothing short of a bullet would stop him now.

The moon cast a silver sheen on the waves below, and in the shallow water of the cove, the contraband boat had already arrived. Smugglers moved like shadows along the shore, unloading casks and crates with quiet urgency. No torches. No idle chatter. They were good—well-practiced.

Too good.

Robin crouched low behind a stunted gorse bush, hand already reaching for the small mirror in his coat pocket. The soft rustle of movement came from the path behind, steady and practiced. He didn't turn—he knew that gait.

"Late, as usual," came Justin's voice, dry as ever. "But I see you've started without me."

Robin grinned, despite the tension. "Had to warm things up."

He turned and saw not just Justin, but six more figures melting from the darkness—grizzled, watchful men. Old shipmates. Men who owed Robin and Justin, or simply couldn't resist a cause worth fighting.

As the group crouched behind the ridge, Robin angled toward Justin.

"Lady Felicity would tan your hide if she knew you were out here."

"She might," Justin agreed, the corner of his mouth lifting. "But I'd rather face her temper than sit this out. Besides..." He glanced toward the glow at the inn's windows. "We are nearing the end of Captain Moonlight, are we not? This might be our last ride."

Robin passed him a second mirror. "Then let's make it count."

He raised his voice just enough for the others to hear. "We ready?"

Justin nodded. "We keep it quiet. Rope in as many as we can before steel sings. But if it does, we end it quick."

"Right," Robin murmured, and gave the faintest flash with the mirror.

The men fanned out, splitting into pairs, navigating around the edge of the cove. Robin and Justin moved together, each step sure-footed, guns loaded and cocked ready. They waited until the next crate touched dry land before making their move.

Robin stepped into the open, pistol raised. "Hands where we can see them. Captain Moonlight requests your company."

A moment of shocked stillness. Then chaos.

Two smugglers lunged for their weapons. Robin fired—one shot to the sky, not to kill, but to scatter. Justin was already in motion, slamming one man to the ground while another sailor wrestled a second into submission.

More men joined the fray. A knife caught the moonlight, and a blow landed against Robin's ribs. He grunted and countered with a brutal elbow that sent the man staggering. Ropes flew, boots scuffed in the sand, and shouts were muffled by fists and force.

Within moments, it was over.

Ten smugglers lay bound in the shallows or slumped unconscious. The boat, loaded with tobacco, silk, and brandy, remained beached on a small stretch of sand.

Justin rolled his shoulder and offered Robin a half-smile. "I'd say that went well."

"Suspiciously well," Robin muttered.

Because something was off.

No sign of Hall.

Robin stalked through the subdued prisoners, scanning faces. None were familiar—none bore the smug sneer, the cruelty he had come to associate with Jimmy Hall.

"Where is he?" Justin asked, coming to the same conclusion. "He should be here. This was his shipment."

"I don't think he came."

Robin's voice was low, cold. "He sent them. But he stayed in the shadows."

Justin looked toward the bluff, eyes narrowing. "You think he knew?"

"I think he's cleverer than we gave him credit for."

Robin scanned the cliffside, heart thudding. Hall wasn't foolish—he'd never place himself in a fight he could watch from afar. And if he'd guessed something was amiss...

"We've cut the legs off his trade," Robin said, "but not the head."

Justin nodded grimly. "Then we find him. Before he starts growing new ones."

The wind shifted, bringing the scent of the sea and something else—smoke, faint and acrid, from the direction of the inn.

Robin's stomach turned.

"Come on," he barked. "Mount up. He's not here... because he's already made his move."

CHAPTER 11

Who'd have thought that sitting and waiting could be so nerve-wracking?

Rachel shifted in the straight-backed chair in Justin's bedroom, pressing a hand to her stomach to quiet the uneasy flutter there. The air was still, the kind of silence that made every creak of the floorboards sound like thunder.

Beside her, the lamp burned low, its wick turned down to conserve oil, casting long, slanted shadows across the walls.

She glanced at the bed. Mary lay curled beneath the blanket, one arm flung over her head in deep, untroubled sleep. Rachel envied her. The girl had been through so much—yet now, at least for a few hours, she was safe.

Rachel had tried to distract herself with one of Justin's books—something about the Napoleonic campaigns—but the words had blurred after the first chapter. She'd closed it nearly an hour ago. Since then, it had been only the tick of the mantel clock and the occasional pop of the fire downstairs to keep her company.

Then—movement.

Her heart leapt.

A faint light swayed outside the cottage, just beyond the shutters.

She rose and moved carefully to the window, lifting the edge of the curtain an inch. Her breath caught—then released.

It was her father. The lantern in his hand bobbed with his measured pace as he walked the narrow track from Dr Standish's house, as he did every time he stayed later than expected.

Her father.

Typically, she would have been the one waiting up for him. Had he assumed she was already asleep? Or would he check her room and find it empty?

She should have left a note. Something—anything. Staying with a sick parishioner would have done. Not quite the truth, but close enough not to burden her conscience.

But now… perhaps something closer to the truth was better.

Justin's cottage stood less than a hundred yards from the parsonage. If she hurried, she could reach the house before her father noticed she was gone, explain something believable and *mostly* true, and be back before Mary even stirred.

Resolved, Rachel snatched up her cloak and tiptoed down the stairs, careful not to disturb the girl's sleep. She unlatched the door and stepped out into the cold night. The wind nipped at her cheeks. She locked the door behind her, pocketing the key, and started toward the parsonage at a brisk but quiet pace.

She was only a dozen paces from the gate when a shape stepped out from the shadow of the hedgerow.

A man.

He grabbed her arm hard enough to make her gasp.

"Where is she?" he snarled.

Rachel's blood ran cold. Her pulse roared in her ears. She tried to pull away, but his grip only tightened.

"Don't think to lie to me, girl. I know she's not at the inn."

Rachel squared her shoulders despite the fear climbing her throat. "Let me go, Mr. Hall."

Hall started at the sound of his name on her lips. Rachel tugged her arm and almost had it free, but his grip firmed again.

"You're going to take me to her," he hissed, "or I swear, you'll both be sorry."

Rachel barely had time to scream.

Hall's hand clamped over her mouth, hard and unrelenting. His other arm snaked around her waist, dragging her back into the shadows. She kicked, twisted, tried to scream again—but the pressure of his grip, and the glint of a knife catching the moonlight, stopped her cold.

"Don't struggle," he hissed in her ear, voice controlled, sober, and all the more terrifying for it. "Tell me where she is."

"Rachel!" The call came from the direction of the vicarage.

Rachel's mind reeled. She clawed at Hall, her fingernails catching his face. A lucky strike—he grunted, and his grip loosened. Rachel wrenched free and stumbled back.

"*Father!*" she screamed, throat raw.

But Hall was quick. He lunged and caught her again, this time with the blade pressed against her throat.

"You've got one more chance, girl."

Rachel froze. The steel kissed her skin. Her eyes darted to the road, willing her father's lantern to appear sooner, faster—

A sudden *crack* split the air like thunder.

Hall jerked, stunned, the knife falling from his grip.

Rachel hit the ground hard, the breath driven from her lungs as she landed beside the unconscious Hall. For a heartbeat, she lay stunned, cheek pressed against the cold earth, her heart slamming against her ribs.

Her fingers brushed damp grass—and Hall's sleeve. She flinched, but the man was utterly still. Then a shadow fell over her, and a gloved hand reached down. Her gaze travelled upward—from the familiar scuffed boots to the tailored coat, to the scarf and hat silhouetted against the moonlight. The breath she'd lost caught again in her throat—not from fear, but recognition.

Robin!

He crouched beside her and, with the utmost care, helped her upright. Her hand lingered in his just a moment longer than necessary. She gave the faintest nod, and his grip softened.

"Rachel!" her father's voice called again, closer now.

Lantern light bobbed into view, then flared across the scene as the curate hurried into the lane, eyes wide with panic. He stopped short when he saw her.

Then his gaze lifted to the cloaked stranger at her side.

His expression shifted from fear to alarm, and then to something far harder to place. Protective fury, certainly, but layered with something else. A dawning suspicion.

"You," he said hoarsely, his hand tightening on the lantern. "You're Captain Moonlight!"

Rachel stepped between them, raising her hands.

"Please, Father. Wait."

The Reverend's voice was taut, firm. "A masked man standing over my daughter with a pistol. What in God's name is going on?"

Rachel looked from her father to the man beside her. "He's not the threat. *He saved me.*"

It took a moment for the Reverend to see what she meant. Then his eyes dropped to the figure crumpled on the ground.

"Is that—Jimmy Hall?"

"Yes," she said. "He was waiting for me. Demanding to know where the innkeeper's daughter was."

Her father's brows knitted tightly. "Hall? He's one of the newly-appointed Excisemen. I spoke with him just last week. He seemed... overzealous, perhaps, but not violent. Was he drunk?"

Rachel's mouth twisted. "He wasn't drunk. He was... prepared. He knew what he was doing."

The Reverend looked again at Hall—then slowly returned his gaze to the masked man.

Captain Moonlight hadn't moved. He stood slightly apart, silent, observing.

Then, in a voice Rachel knew was deliberately altered—low, gravelly, disguised—he spoke.

"Is everyone safe?"

Rachel understood. It wasn't a general question. It was *his* question, meant only for her. Meant to ask if Mary Blunt was still hidden, still protected.

"Yes," she said, holding his gaze through the shadows. "Everyone is safe."

The captain nodded—just once—and then began to step back, his eyes flicking to the dark hedgerows, the forest beyond.

"Wait," the Reverend said, voice still edged. "You—you can't just disappear. There's a matter of law—"

"Father," Rachel said firmly, stepping closer to him. "Please. Let him go."

He looked at her for a long time, eyes flicking over her face. She could see the questions in them—the rising suspicion, the deep unease, the growing awareness that his daughter had been somewhere, somehow, caught up in this for longer than he knew.

But he said only, "Is he... truly a friend?"

Rachel nodded. "Yes. He's kept more people safe than you'll ever know."

Her father's jaw worked for a moment. Then he lowered the lantern slightly and said, "I suppose... I should thank you, sir."

Captain Moonlight tipped his hat ever so slightly, then turned, disappearing into the mist without a word.

Rachel stood in the quiet that followed, only the crash of distant waves breaking the silence.

Her father exhaled. "There's much you haven't told me, Rachel."

"I know," she said softly.

"Then you'd better begin atthe beginning and let our friend here finish what he's started."

CHAPTER 12

Robin grunted as he hoisted Jimmy Hall's unconscious body over his shoulder. The man was heavier than he looked, all thick muscle and mean arrogance. Robin's side throbbed where he'd taken a dagger swipe earlier, but he set his jaw and pressed on, one step after another along the moonlit track.

The village green was quiet, bathed in silver light. A pair of owls called to each other from the trees beyond the chapel, and the cold night air burned in Robin's lungs.

In the center of the green stood the old stocks—weathered and long forgotten, half-swallowed by the grass. A relic from a more public sort of justice. Tonight, it would serve again.

Robin dropped Hall unceremoniously to the ground and pulled open the wooden device. With practiced hands, he arranged Hall's limbs—arms through the top, ankles through the bottom—and slammed it shut. The wood creaked but held. He secured the latches with metal pins that still, miraculously, moved.

Hall groaned once, but didn't wake.

Robin reached into his coat and pulled out the note—the one they'd intercepted earlier, bearing Hall's rough script. *"Keep your mouth shut and the goods safe, or your girl pays the price."*

He read it once more, jaw tight, then pinned it to the top of the stocks with his belt knife. Let the village see him for what he truly was.

A coward. A bully. And not above threatening a man's child to keep his schemes running.

Robin stepped back, surveyed the scene, and nodded. It was a fitting end.

The journey back to the Angler's Arms was agony. The adrenaline had faded, leaving only exhaustion and pain. His side throbbed with each step, and blood had dried stiff beneath his coat. His arm was little better, but still usable.

Just one more task tonight, he told himself. Then you can rest.

He reached the inn's rear courtyard just as the first hints of dawn began to stain the horizon.

Inside, the taproom glowed warmly, firelight flickering through the leaded panes.

Robin pushed open the door and stepped into a scene that was oddly festive.

Justin sat at a long table, flanked by the men they'd both once sailed with—their old shipmates, now scattered but still loyal. The air smelled of roast meats, aged cheese, and fine French brandy— smuggled delicacies, seized during the raid.

Someone cheered as Robin entered, raising a cup.

"Look what the wind blew back in!" one of the men laughed.

Justin stood, a half-grin tugging at his mouth. "I take it Hall's not going to be joining us?"

Robin sank into a chair and poured himself a small glass of brandy. "No. He's taking in the night air. In the stocks. I left one of his own notes pinned to his chest for company."

A ripple of laughter passed around the room.

"He'll be the talk of the village by morning," Justin said. "Good."

Robin took a long drink, then sighed. "This is the end of it, though. Captain Moonlight's had his last ride."

Justin nodded. "We've unmasked ourselves, whether we meant to or not."

One of the sailors raised his glass. "Moonlight or not, you two kept the right folk safe and gave the bad ones something to fear. That's all that matters."

The others murmured their agreement.

Robin looked around the room, weariness settling in his bones. "Thank you. All of you. But if anyone asks…"

"Never heard of him," one sailor said with a wink. "Must've been a ghost."

Robin smiled faintly.

"Aye," he said. "Just a ghost in the moonlight."

The taproom had quieted. Most of the men had either dozed off where they sat or stumbled up to the loft rooms offered by a grateful innkeeper. The fire had burned low, casting long shadows across the floorboards, and the clink of bottles had dwindled to silence.

Robin and Justin sat in the corner, nursing the last of the brandy. The weight of the night pressed down on them—not just the skirmish, but the knowledge that something had ended. Captain Moonlight was no more. What came next was something neither had dared to speak aloud until now.

Justin broke the silence first. "We've no masks left, Robin. No more pretense. Feels strange, doesn't it?"

Robin chuckled softly. "I thought you'd enjoy the quiet life."

"I *do*. More than I expected. But…"

Robin raised a brow, inviting the words Justin hadn't yet said.

"She'll leave again," Justin said at last. "Felicity. If I don't give her a reason to stay. And I don't mean throwing myself at her feet. I mean *truth*. A life built on something solid."

Robin leaned forward. "Then build it. Stop waiting for permission from the world—or from her brother. You love her?"

"I do."

"Then don't let your pride be the thing that drives her away."

Justin gave a lopsided smile. "Is that what you're planning to do? Follow your own sage advice?"

Robin glanced into his glass, then back at his friend. "I am."

"With Rachel?"

"Aye."

Justin studied him. "That girl's got steel in her bones."

Robin nodded. "She's braver than half the officers we ever sailed with."

There was a quiet moment between them, not heavy, but full.

"You're serious?" Justin asked.

"I am. I don't know what form it will take yet, but I mean to find out. No more hiding behind the mask, even if I liked the freedom it gave."

Justin raised his glass slightly. "Then to truth. And to the women who saw through us, even when we wore masks."

Robin clinked his glass against Justin's. "To the ones who never needed us to be legends—just honest men."

Robin slipped in through the servants' entrance at Normanton House just as the sun began to rise behind the downs. His limbs ached, his side throbbed, and his head was heavy with fatigue.

The night had stripped him down to bone and willpower, and now, with Captain Moonlight laid to rest, all he wanted was a bath, a bandage, and a bed he didn't have to spring out of at the drop of a pistol hammer.

He collapsed into it moments later, not even bothering to draw the curtains.

It was not yet noon when the knock came.

He groaned.

"Go away," he muttered into the pillow.

The door creaked open anyway.

Peter's voice, annoyingly bright, drifted in. "Thought you might want to hear that the notorious Captain Moonlight has outdone himself again. Seems poor Jimmy Hall was found locked in the village stocks this morning—gagged, bruised, and pinned with one of his own threats."

Robin moved, but not fast enough.

Peter stepped into the room—and stopped.

Robin had thrown the sheets off in the warmth of the morning sun, and the bruises across his ribs, the dried blood at his side, and the livid scratch across his collarbone told a story all their own.

Peter let out a slow breath.

"You idiot," he said, not unkindly.

Robin winced and cracked one eye open. "You're not going to ask?"

Peter just shook his head. "No need. I've known since the second week you were home. I chose not to know, but it seems now the choice is gone."

Robin sat up slowly, wincing. "You always did let me get away with too much."

"I always did," Peter agreed, then paused. "Are you finished now?"

"Yes," Robin said. Then he smiled. "But I've started something new."

"Oh?"

"I've signed a contract on a small estate—two valleys over. Not grand, but prosperous. Peaceful. I mean to make it home."

Peter's brow arched. "And this wouldn't have anything to do with a certain vicar's daughter?"

Robin said nothing.

Peter grinned. "Well, then. I hope she says yes."

"I hope so too."

Peter clapped him gently on the shoulder, mindful of the bruises. "Your secret is safe with me."

Robin looked at him, hearing the double meaning behind the words—the secret of Captain Moonlight, yes, but also the deeper one: of the man Robin truly was, behind the mask, behind the uniform, finally at peace.

"Thank you," he said quietly.

Peter smiled. "Get some sleep. You look like hell."

"I feel worse."

"Good. Means you're still breathing."

Robin chuckled, and as Peter left the room, he allowed himself—for the first time in years—to rest. Really rest.

And to dream of a future that felt, finally, within reach.

CHAPTER 13

The village of Normanton was abuzz. From the thatched rooftops to the green outside the church, not a soul had missed the morning's spectacle. Jimmy Hall, tied in the old stocks like a medieval criminal, a note pinned to the stocks in his own scrawled hand, was the talk of every baker's wife, cooper, and stable boy.

They called it justice.

They called it poetic.

They called it Captain Moonlight.

Robin walked through it all with a quiet smile and a tipped hat, nodding politely when someone greeted him. All they saw was Captain Robin Somerville, younger brother to the local squire—and that was as it should be.

If anyone of them entertained the thought that the two captains were one and the same, they never said anything to him.

A respectable gentleman, a highwayman? It was unthinkable.

Robin's stride never wavered. His heart was fixed on a single destination—the parsonage.

He saw them before they saw him: a small gathering beneath the ripening apple tree in the front garden. Rachel stood with her father, her hair braided simply, her cheeks touched pink by the wind.

George Blunt stood nearby; his broad frame squared with unusual stillness. Beside him, Mary, in a new shawl, clutched her father's arm and whispered something that made him chuckle.

Rachel looked up first. Her eyes met Robin's.

And then the innkeeper saw him.

"Captain!" George Blunt strode forward, grasping Robin's hand in both of his. "I owe you—no, we all owe you—a debt I'll never be able to repay. I've told the Reverend everything—how you helped keep Mary safe, what you and Justin did. My girl told me the rest."

Robin, slightly taken aback by the man's genuine fervor, returned the handshake. "You owe me nothing, Mr. Blunt. I'm just glad Mary's safe."

Blunt shook his head firmly. "You were the only one with the spine to take on Hall when the rest of us were too scared to even name him out loud."

"Speaking of names spoken out loud, all I ask is that you never mention myself or Captain Moonlight in the same sentence. It wouldn't do for people to get the two confused."

Blunt laughed and shook his hand once more with vigor, while he fought a wince of pain over the cuts and bruises he carried.

Robin's eyes slid to the Reverend Pendleton, expecting disapproval, or at least surprise.

But Rachel's father merely nodded once, slowly.

His beautiful Rachel, however, gave a slight, knowing smile.

Robin understood. She had told him everything.

But no one said a word more about it. It didn't need saying.

"I was hoping," Robin began, his voice warming as his eyes returned to Rachel, "that I might speak with your daughter alone, sir. Just for a moment."

"Of course," the Reverend said. "I believe Mrs. Rolf has prepared cinnamon cake for afternoon tea."

Rachel stepped forward as the others retreated into the house, and they were left alone in the garden, the air scented faintly with camellias in bloom.

"You came," she said, her voice quiet and sure.

"I could do nothing else."

She watched him, waiting.

"Captain Moonlight is no more," Robin said after a pause. "The cloak's been hung, the pistols stored away. No more midnight rides. No more masks."

"I'm glad," she said softly. "Though I'll miss him—just a little."

He chuckled, then sobered. "There's another role I want now. One I've never wanted more."

He took a step closer, then reached into his coat. From inside, he drew a small, deep-blue box. It wasn't ostentatious, but the ring inside, with a center stone of ruby, gleamed like morning dew in the sun.

"I don't need the disguise anymore," Robin said. "But I do need you. I love you, Rachel Pendleton. I want to build something real.

"I've bought a little estate nearby, not far from Normanton. It's modest, but it's mine. And I want it to be yours, too. If you'll have me."

Rachel's eyes shone. "You're serious."

"Entirely."

She didn't hesitate. "Yes."

The ring slipped onto her finger, and Robin kissed her hand, then her lips—soft, reverent, and full of promise.

When they parted, she smiled through the tears that had risen in her eyes. "You always knew how to make an entrance."

"And now I hope to master staying put."

Together, they walked back toward the house.

Inside, they found the Reverend in his study. He looked up as they entered.

Robin cleared his throat. "Sir, I've asked your daughter for her hand. And she's accepted."

Reverend Pendleton looked between the two of them, and for a long moment, said nothing. He rose and came to stand in front of Robin.

"I wasn't sure, in the beginning," the Reverend said. "You seemed... guarded. Restless."

"I was," Robin admitted. "But I'm not anymore."

Pendleton nodded once. "Then I give you my blessing. On two conditions."

Robin straightened. "Name them."

"First," the Reverend said, placing a hand on Robin's shoulder, "you keep her safe. Not from highwaymen or ruffians—I've seen what you can do—but from the slow creep of disappointment. Be the man you are, not the disguise you wore."

"I will."

"And second," the Reverend added, eyes twinkling faintly, "if you want the key to the church tower... you'll ask me directly."

Robin laughed aloud, the memory of the Burgess incident flashing in his mind.

"Understood."

With the air cleared and futures laid bare, the four of them sat together, sipping tea, sharing cake, and planning—tentatively, joyfully —for what came next.

Robin Somerville had finally found the one thing he'd never fought for before.

A home. A purpose. A future—with Rachel.

And this time, he meant to live it not under cover of darkness... but in the full light of love.

EPILOGUE

Late November, 1817—The Somerville Estate, near Normanton

The first frost had settled silver on the hedgerows that morning, and the orchard stood bare-limbed and quiet.

Inside the low stone house nestled at the foot of the rise, a fire crackled in the hearth, warm against the chill pressing at the windows. It smelled of pine and apples—Rachel's doing. She'd tucked slivers of dried fruit into the kindling when Robin wasn't looking.

He caught the scent now as he set down the last of the unpacked books onto a freshly dusted shelf.

"Smells like pudding in here," he said, not displeased.

Rachel looked up from the armchair, where she sat curled with her knees drawn close and a letter open in her lap. She wore a soft wool shawl and an expression that danced somewhere between amusement and affection.

"I'll take that as approval," she replied. "Better than sea salt and cannon smoke, wouldn't you say?"

"Debatable." Robin crossed the room to her, pausing to kiss the top of her head as he passed. "Who's the letter from?"

She lifted it with two fingers. "Felicity. She and her brother have arrived in London. Justin joins them next week."

Robin raised an eyebrow. "So soon?"

Rachel smiled. "He's giving up the schoolhouse. Sold his cottage to a vicar from Lewes. They're to marry at St. George's in two weeks."

He let that settle a moment, then exhaled quietly. "Good. He deserves her."

"And she, him," Rachel said. "She enclosed a note for you, too. Said to tell you not to make me climb any more bell towers."

Robin chuckled, then dropped into the chair opposite hers. The firelight cast soft shadows across his face—no longer guarded, no longer restless. He looked, at last, like a man at peace.

They sat in companionable silence for a time, listening to the crack and pop of the logs. Somewhere outside, children were calling to one another, chasing something down the slope toward the old fence line.

"Captain Moonlight's gang," Rachel said softly, tilting her head toward the sound.

Robin leaned his head back. "Already recruiting again, is he?"

"They've tied tea towels around their faces," she said with a grin. "One of them demanded a biscuit at lunch with the words 'stand and deliver.' My father was most impressed."

Robin closed his eyes briefly, a half-smile on his lips. "Well, at least someone's keeping the roads safe."

Rachel set Felicity's letter aside and stood, crossing to his chair. She slid into his lap with ease, tucking herself beneath his chin as if she'd always belonged there.

"Tell me," she murmured, "if I hadn't given you that key—would you have kissed me anyway?"

Robin tipped her chin up and met her gaze, the corners of his eyes crinkling. "Every version of this story ends the same way, Rachel. With you in my arms."

She laughed, quiet and sure, and kissed him soundly.

Outside, the children's shouts rose and fell like gulls on the wind, and the fire burned low, and the world—at least for now—was exactly as it should be.

THE END

"Great is the art of beginning, but greater is the art of ending."—
Henry Wadsworth Longfellow

SOCIAL MEDIA FOR
ELIZABETH ELLEN CARTER

You can learn more about Elizabeth Ellen Carter at these social media links:

Website: http://eecarter.com
Facebook: https://www.facebook.com/ElizabethEllenCarter
Pinterest: https://www.pinterest.com/eecarterauthor/
Instagram: https://www.instagram.com/elizabeth_ellen_carter/
BookBub: https://www.bookbub.com/authors/elizabeth-ellen-carter
YouTube: https://www.youtube.com/c/ElizabethEllenCarter

ABOUT ELIZABETH ELLEN CARTER

Elizabeth Ellen Carter is a USA Today bestselling author known for her evocative historical romances filled with intrigue, adventure, and heart. Her popular titles include Moonstone Conspiracy, Dark Heart, Captive of the Corsairs, and Live and Let Spy.

With a passion for history and storytelling, Elizabeth brings the past vividly to life.

Learn more about Elizabeth Ellen at:
Website: elizabethellencarter.com

THE CASEBOOK OF PRINCIPAL OFFICER ROBERT PIERCE

Brighton and surrounding districts

Miles and I met for another drink last night. Whether for commiserations or congratulations is uncertain, since the occasion was the arrest of a crooked revenue officer and his gang. A person in my position cannot admire a criminal. But the way that Captain Moonlight's men overcame the gang and Captain Moonlight rolled up the arch-villain himself...? I serve justice, as does Miles. In this instance, Captain Moonlight stood our friend.

I am still determined to uncover the man, however. And I think I know who he is.

FOREVER & ALWAYS
THE SECRETS OF FONTUS LEIGH

RUE ALLYN

Forever & Always
The Secrets of Fontus Leigh
By Rue Allyn

She loved him then left him. Now he's desperate to find her before secrets and deceptions can destroy them both. They must unite and defeat their enemies in order to share love forever and always.

CHAPTER 1

Rilbridge Cottage, Late September 1817

L ady Deoiridh Aitken entered the kitchen, setting her basket on a side table.

"Greta," she called.

Her maid of all work appeared from the scullery. "Yes, my lady?"

"Please put these lilies in the breakfast nook. Then deal with the herbs beneath the lilies."

"Immediately, Lady Deoiridh."

"Tea must be ready by two o'clock. Lady Somerville is bringing a guest she thinks I should meet," Dee smiled, heading for the stairs and her bedchamber.

"Certainly, my lady."

"Thank you, Greta."

The foyer clock struck one.

Dee hurried. An hour was sufficient to dress and arrange her hair. Much less time than needed to dress for the French court.

That life had been fun, even exciting. However, she enjoyed her present quiet life as well. If she needed social activity, she could visit Normanton House. She and the Somervilles were friends.

The couple, distant relatives of her mother, had been happy to shelter Dee when she'd sought refuge with them.

As she changed from her gardening frock, she recalled the argument she'd had with Major Lord Mars Leigh, her husband's brother, as he guarded her on her journey here in spring of 1815.

She had insisted he leave her.

"Tell me," she asked when he protested. "Am I safer with you knowing my location or not?"

Not until she revealed one of the two fancy pistols she used for protection did Major Leigh concede her point.

A knock on her chamber door, recalled her to the present.

"Yes?"

"Your guests have arrived, my lady," Greta called.

"Thank you. I'll be down shortly."

Dee checked her reflection. Satisfied, she reached the foyer at the same moment her guests entered.

"Allow me to take your outerwear, ladies," Greta said.

One foot on the last tread, the other poised in mid-air, Dee stared at the woman preceding Lady Somerville.

Busy with Greta, the woman did not notice Dee until she moved aside for Lady Somerville and raised her head.

"Deoiridh!" Lady Aitken threw her arms wide. "Come give your mother a hug."

Dee shot off the stairs and was wrapped in her mother's arms before that lady finished speaking.

"I am so glad to see you." She tightened her arms around her mother. "How come you to England? How did you find me? How did you get here? How is Louis? Are our court friends well? Are you certain it was safe for you to leave? Have you come to stay? With me?"

"I am delighted to see you, daughter." Mother placed hands on Dee's shoulders and gave a small shove. "However, if you squeeze much tighter, you shall deprive me of breath, and I won't be able to answer."

"Oh," she released her mother, stepping back. "I'm sorry, I just... that is...I wish.... You should have told me you were coming."

"Darling, that would risk the letter getting into the wrong hands."

Dee nodded. "Come to the parlor. Greta will bring tea, and we can talk."

"That will be very pleasant," Lady Somerville agreed.

Dee took her mother's arm and saw her installed on a settee. "Penelope, please take a seat. Thank you very much for bringing Mother to me. Greta will need some time to put the second bedchamber to rights."

"I didn't tell you Lady Aitken was coming because I wasn't certain she could," Lady Somerville informed her.

Dee blinked; her brow furrowed. "I don't understand."

"I know you wish to live retired," Lady Somerville continued. "However, I knew you would not mind if I wrote to my cousin and informed her you were safe here. In that same letter, I invited her to visit. Nearly three years is too long for mother and daughter to be separated."

A frisson of worry travelled up Dee's spine. Letters at Louis Bourbon's court were nearly always read by the men who kept Louis safe. Hence nothing was ever completely secret. One of the most notorious of those men, Monsieur Aristide Barbeau, had been an unwanted and all too persistent suitor. Given Lady Somerville's letter, Barbeau must know of Dee's whereabouts. He would certainly act on the information, but when and how?

"How thoughtful of you," she said to Lady Somerville. The lady intended a kindness. As happy as Dee was to see her mother, she wished Lady Somerville had not been quite so kind.

"I was too eager to see you to reply and would arrive before any letter. So, I just came," her mother confessed.

"Your mother's arrival last night was a surprise," Lady Somerville continued. "However, the hour was too late to visit. She spent the night with us, and this morning I sent the request to come to tea."

"I am quite comfortable at Normanton House and prefer to continue there. Lady Somerville assures me I may stay as long as I like."

"Are you certain, Mother?"

"Positively. You know I despise rusticating. Lady Somerville says she is very active in local society."

"Worry not, we shall keep Lady Aitken well entertained."

"Thank you. I'll not worry for my mother, though she may exhaust you and Sir Peter.

Lady Somerville smiled, sipping tea while Dee and her mother exchanged news of the French court.

"... Did Louis feel obliged to put on an entertainment that shamed the Belgians with its grandeur?" Dee asked.

"Of course."

"Speaking of entertainments," Lady Somerville interjected. "Peter and I are hosting a house party next week. We hope both of you will attend."

"I'll be delighted," said Lady Aitken.

"Send me the schedule of events, please. I'd prefer to remain here, but I will enjoy attending some of the entertainments."

"Splendid." Lady Somerville smiled.

"Are you worried that Captain Moonlight will accost some of your guests?" Dee asked.

"Captain Moonlight?" Dee's mother lifted a delicate brow.

"Oh, I've not had time to tell you about the highwayman haunting our country roads," said Lady Somerville.

"*Un Agent Routier*? How very exciting."

"You mean how very annoying." Lady Somerville set her teacup and saucer on a nearby table. "It is most vexing. A common thief bothering travelers just as we invite nearly the entire shire to our home, to say nothing of the friends traveling greater distances."

"From what I've heard Captain Moonlight is at pains to be courteous and courtly to his victims, save for a few whom he deems worthy of public embarrassment. He's never caused anyone injury while lightening their purses," Dee commented.

"So, when caught, he'll only be transported and not hung. Stealing is wrong despite any courtesy." Lady Somerville resumed her tea.

"*Chere ami*, please," Lady Aitken said. "Have *charité* for the poor fellow. Imagine the opportunity to charm him into giving back the jewels. Is he handsome? Perhaps I should ask for a kiss. *Un baiser* from a handsome thief is a memory to keep a woman warm at night."

Lady Somerville straightened. "Lady Aitken, you cannot be serious."

"*La*, my dear, of course not. Still, what a tale to tell my grandchildren." Her mother cast an arch glance at Dee. "You are not getting any younger dear, and cradling *un bebe* in my arms before I am too old is a devout wish."

Dee's cheeks heated. "Really mother. That is not a subject for polite discussion. Please forgive her, Lady Somerville."

"Certainly. Now, as lovely as this tea has been, I must get home. With less than one week before guests arrive, I have no spare time." Lady Somerville stood.

Lady Aitken followed suit. "I shall go with you and help."

"Thank you for your hospitality, Lady Deoiridh," Lady Somerville said.

"You are always welcome." Leading the way, Dee rang for Greta.

Amid a flurry of capes and bonnets, Dee managed to hug her mother.

"I'll see you soon, *mignon?*"

"Yes, Mother."

"Come to tea tomorrow. We'll be very casual. The house guests won't start to arrive for several more days." Lady Somerville invited.

"I will, thank you." Dee watched them leave. "You may find me in the book room when supper is ready, Greta."

"Of course, my lady."

By writing to her mother of Dee's location, Lady Somerville had created a worry. The time was long past for Dee to act in her own best interests.

She settled at the small desk in the snug little room. From the center drawer she withdrew a letter. She'd started writing it shortly after arriving here.

Why haven't I sent this?

She had no answer. The law required that she, personally, initiate the request for annulment. Once made, she'd hire a solicitor to guide her through the process, which could take years.

Why did I waste so much time?

Reviewing the letter's words prompted memories of Fontus Leigh. His smile, his laugh, the strength of his arms as he'd held her while hiding beneath that hay from Barbeau and his men. The quiet conversations during their escape to Dieppe. The kiss they shared before she'd left him on the ship in Brighton harbor.

Had she imagined the affection growing between them? Imagined his pleasure in that kiss? A kiss she had, for days, wished him to take. Her heart had melted when he respectfully asked for a farewell kiss. Pleasure had swelled that same heart when the kiss became more than the polite peck she expected.

She forced her attention back to her request for the annulment she'd said she wanted on the first day of their marriage. The marriage kept her safe, should Barbeau learn where she hid.

Now, because of Lady Somerville, Dee must decide to send the letter or not. At present she could not bring herself to do so. However, she would ask help from another quarter.

She put the letter back into the drawer. Then drew clean paper from a second drawer. Quill and ink from a third followed. She trimmed the quill and wrote.

To His Grace Lovis Leigh, Duke of Leigh...

Would the duke believe what she wrote? Or would he ride post haste to deal with an assumed pretender?

She stared at the letter until Greta summoned her to the evening meal.

If only she could speak with Fontus. They'd become friends, sharing histories and opinions. Not always in agreement, she felt more comfortable with him than any other man. Their one kiss had left her longing to stay with him and perhaps enjoy more intimate pleasures. She shook her head. Best to not think of Fontus Leigh. Dreaming of him caused her entirely too many restless nights.

CHAPTER 2

Normanton House, October 1817

F ontus stared at Normanton House. A month gone, and he'd not
found his wife. His brother Mars had left a note, suggesting
Dee might remain in Sussex, not too far from Brighton. Were that
the case, she may have already received the annulment, and he'd be
free. What an irony if Dee were living near Normanton House.

His brother Lovis, the Duke of Leigh, had ordered him here to
court Lady Beatrix Sandrow. The proposed marriage was a peace
offering to the Earl of Sandrow.

Fontus much preferred marriage to Dee over the misery of
wedded life with a woman who hated him. Of course, without the
annulment, having Dee and Lord Sandrow in close proximity could
be disastrous. Perhaps not finding her was best.

Time to dance to whatever tune fate played for him. He cantered
down the drive and dismounted before the impressive portico.

Fontus took his bags in hand, while a groom led his horse off to
the stables.

A footman opened the front door before Fontus could knock.

"Welcome, sir?"

"Lord Fontus Leigh," he informed the man as he entered.

"May I take your..."

"No, thank you. I prefer to keep my things." Keeping his belongings close was a habit learned for survival.

"As you wish. I'll see you to your room, my lord."

On the second story, the footman stopped and opened the door at the far end of a corridor. "I'll direct your valet here, when he arrives."

"I did not bring a valet. I shall ring for assistance should I need any."

"Then I shall return in an hour to escort you to the grand salon."

Fontus put his hand on the door's inner latch. "Thank you. However, that too is unnecessary, Captain Somerville and I are friends. I visited Normanton House frequently as a lad. Please inform the captain I am here."

"Certainly, my lord.

Fontus closed and locked the door then wandered to the window to look out at the gardens behind the house. Two female figures ambled along the pathways admiring the fall foliage. One of them removed her bonnet, fanning her face with it. Sun glinted off hair the color of freshly minted pence.

Surely not. It could not be Dee. I'm imagining things.

She looked up as she returned her bonnet to her head.

He stepped aside, wishing to avoid being observed himself.

His time with the French resistance taught him caution. Before leaving England, he'd been open and carefree. The duke called it careless and irresponsible. Years of war and diplomacy changed a man. For the better he hoped. Marriage came with responsibilities alien to a youth exiled from school and family. The young man Fontus once was would not understand.

What might wedded life be like? He imagined easy days of sharing work and confidences with Dee. Nights, mornings, perhaps an occasional afternoon of making love. Maybe a copper-haired child or two with expressive lapis eyes. However, Dee might not be the woman to bear his children.

An enduring marriage with Dee was an unlikely pipe dream. He would never hold her to an arrangement made solely for her safety. She undoubtedly had a number of suitors and wished herself shed of her once convenient spouse. He'd see it done, surprised to find himself more interested in her happiness than his own. Of course, he must find her first.

A knock sounded.

He unlocked and opened the door. On the other side stood Robin Somerville, wash water and towels in hand. "By all that's holy, has your brother lost his fortune and pressed you into service?"

"I encountered the maid on my way here and decided to save her a few steps."

"Come in. Just like you to consider the needs of a servant, or anyone else for that matter. How you managed to exert any discipline over ordinary sailors is a mystery to me." Fontus closed the door.

Robin set the towels, wash bowl, and pitcher of water on a table beneath a mirror opposite the bed.

"Ship's discipline is essential for the survival of all aboard. I am nothing if not a creature of necessity."

"True, you've been more than a good friend to me when I was in need," Fontus remarked. "Your occasional help kept me alive during the war. You must tell me if there is ever an opportunity when I can return the favor."

"We both survived some excessively dangerous situations," Robin said. "What brings you to Normanton House?"

"I am here on Lovis's orders and an errand of my own."

Robin's brow rose. "Care to share?"

"It's complicated. Let's sit, and I'll explain." Fontus gestured to a pair of cushioned chairs near the windows.

"Certainly. I'll ring for whisky. Peter has some very good Strathnaver."

Eventually, settled with drinks in hand, Fontus began. "I'm searching for a woman."

Robin laughed. "There will be respectable women aplenty at the house party. If another sort of woman is your preference, I can introduce you to the local madams."

"Thank you, but I've no need of a prostitute. I'm looking for one very respectable woman in particular."

Both of Robin's brows lifted. "Do tell."

"If you are acquainted with her, you'll recognize her as Lady Deoiridh Aitken."

Robin laughed so hard he was forced to set his tumbler on a nearby table.

Fontus waited. "What is it you find so funny?" he asked, once the laughter became chuckles.

"She's here."

"She's living with you and your brother? Please tell me you haven't married her?"

Robin's chuckles ceased. He stared at Fontus. "Certainly not."

Fontus sighed.

"Why should Lady Aitken's married state concern you?" Robin asked.

A few more words assured Fontus he had no serious competition for Dee's affections.

"Are you in search of a wife?" Robin queried.

"Not precisely."

"Well, if you've marriage to Lady Deoiridh on your mind, you've your work cut out for you."

"How so?" Fontus queried.

"My sister-in-law has been playing matchmaker for more than two years with no success. Lady Deoiridh has refused every suitor thrown at her."

Has it been so long? I recall our kiss as if it just happened.

"Including you?" he asked of Robin.

"Heaven forbid. The lady and I are friends. Indeed, we help each other avoid Penelope's machinations." Robin's gaze narrowed. "Not that I'd object to a little dalliance were Lady Dee interested."

Despite Robin's teasing, Fontus wanted no doubt that Dee was his.

Until the annulment, that is.

"Is she interested?" He studied Robin.

"Not in the slightest."

"And you've tried?"

"No, and I've no intention of trying."

"Good." Fontus sipped his whisky.

"You've obviously set your sights on her yourself. How did you come to meet her?"

"I was in Paris, drowning my sorrows at the news of Boney's escape from Elba. I over-indulged and slept in the tavern. The next morning a young lady woke me, seeking help."

"She obviously didn't know you," Robin said. "Or she would have run the other way."

"She was fleeing the attentions of an unwanted suitor, name of Barbeau. We managed to escape his search. Then she asked me to marry her."

Robin straitened abruptly. "You're joking."

"Not at all. She insisted the marriage would be one of convenience, and when she knew she was safe from the dastard chasing her, she would seek an annulment."

"You agreed to this?" Robin's jaw dropped.

"My affections were not tied elsewhere. She was attractive, intelligent, and intriguing. Yes, I agreed."

"Then what?"

"We were married by a traveling vicar who witnessed the marriage lines. Since my wife wished to be able to annul the marriage and it was never recorded in any church register, I left the document with her. Immediately afterward, her friends in the resistance spirited us away. We rode non-stop then took ship from Dieppe to Brighton harbor where we parted. I've not seen her since. Now the need to find her is urgent."

"Amazing."

"Please, Robin, do not reveal our marriage to anyone."

"Obviously, since she will obtain an annulment."

"Now that she's found, I can speak with her about it. For all I know I'm a free man."

"Do you want that?"

"I only spent a few weeks with her," he hedged. Weeks that lingered in his dreams and every waking thought.

"In close association. It is enough, I believe."

"Perhaps, but my wishes cannot matter, and there is a complication."

"What can be more complicated than not being able to find your wife?"

"You remember Lovis?"

"Indeed. Once one encounters the Duke of Leigh, one does not forget the experience."

"My brother made possible my return to England. He achieved a rapprochement with Sandrow."

"Truly? Did the earl forgive you for the death of his son in that duel?"

"Not that I am aware." Fontus stared into his whisky. "I aimed to miss. Vincent moved in the same moment I fired."

"I know," Robin soothed. "The incident was reported accurately in that rag *The Teatime Tattler*. Too bad, Lord Sandrow cannot believe it. He has wanted you hanged for years. What changed his mind?"

"Lovis persuaded him I would be an excellent husband for his daughter."

Robin barked a laugh. "And you already wed. That's rich. Will you commit bigamy with bird-witted Beatrix, or will you be forced to leave England again?"

"Lady Beatrix is a bluestocking and far from bird-witted. I intend to find out if I am still wed. If I am not, I shall bow to Lovis's commands."

"And if you are wed?"

"Then I must beg Lovis's assistance to resolve the situation. I lack enough influence to obtain an annulment, or appease Sandrow."

Robin shook his head and drained his tumbler. "I don't envy you."

"Also, I must keep my wife safe from that French worm, Barbeau. With Napoleon at St. Helena, the Bourbon monarchy is assured. I understand Barbeau managed to hang onto the fringes of Louis' favor, and continues to seek a fortune. If he learns where Deoiridh is, he may renew his efforts to force her into marriage."

"I've heard the name. Describe him, and I will spread the word among the servants and local residents to be alert."

"Barbeau is about your height and coloring. Dark hair, brown eyes. He is loyal only to the highest bidder. During the war, he spied for both sides."

"A truly despicable character."

Fontus drained his glass and set it aside. "Does your sister-in-law still keep country hours?"

"Indeed, so I'd best be on my way."

"It is good to see you, Robin."

"You as well, Fontus."

"Lady Deoiridh has been invited to dinner." Robin spoke with his hand on the doorknob.

"She doesn't reside here?"

"No, she occupies a small cottage, Rilbridge, a short walk from the rear gardens. The lady claims she'd rather live retired. So, my brother gave her the cottage for as long as she needed."

"Yet, she intends to be present at some of the house party events?"

"As her mother is one of the guests, I believe that is so."

"Her mother is here?" Horror chased relief around Fontus's stomach. Lady Aitken complicated matters.

"You've not met your mother-in-law?"

"If Deoiridh's mother could find her, Barbeau will too. I doubt she knows I exist. How long has she been here?"

"About a week. I understand she intends to return to the French court. Evidently she's some sort of confidant to King Louis."

"Deoiridh told me of the relationship. That court is rife with rumors about an affair between the two, but Dee says they've never been more than good friends."

"I admire Lady Aitken then. Friendship with a royal is never an easy burden."

"The reason, I suspect, King Louis values Lady Aitken over other women."

"It is none of my business. I'll see you in the Grand Salon. We still gather there before dining."

"Until then."

Robin left, and Fontus locked the door.

He must plan for Deoiridh's safety. He also must decide how to approach the topic of their marriage. Before having that discussion, he should probably decide if remaining married to the most fascinating woman he'd ever met was what he wanted. Lust, pleasant as it was, could not serve as foundation for marriage. Nor could memories, no matter how delightful. Years passed, and people changed.

Had lust ever driven me where Dee is concerned? If so, why did I not take advantage of the opportunity marriage provided.

He knew why. He respected the lady. He admired her courage, her inventiveness, her determination. She spent most of her life as part of the Bourbon court, yet remained more unassuming and candid than any courtier he'd yet encountered. At the same time, she kept a high standard of courtesy, decorum and discretion. Lovis would love her, another motive for remaining wed.

Furthermore, he now had prospects to offer a wife that he had not had previously. Given his work with Castlereagh, he could present himself as employed and possessed of an excellent future. She would make a splendid diplomat's wife. Would she want that role? Did he want to ask her? He simply did not know. He'd give it more thought.

Meanwhile, he settled at the desk, and started his message to the Foreign Secretary regarding information learned over the past month. He followed that with a note to Lovis, requesting help finding Barbeau, but gave no explanation. Last, he rattled off a missive to Castlereagh informing him of the delay in his return to the ambassador's service. For how long, he could not say.

CHAPTER 3

Normanton House, that evening

"I look forward to meeting the other guests. Lady Somerville plans several enticing entertainments."

Dee nodded as they entered the Grand Salon. Mother headed straight for their hostess where she stood talking with two gentlemen. One, Captain Robin Somerville, blocked Dee's view of the second man.

What little she could see of him felt familiar.

She followed her mother. Then as the second man came into view, she froze.

Fontus. Impossible. Given the history he had confided in her, he could never set foot in England.

His gaze met hers, and she gave the slightest nod.

Lady Somerville made the introductions.

"I am pleased to meet you, Lord Fontus," Lady Aitken purred. She shifted to bring Deoiridh into the group. "Dearest daughter, I present to you this charming young man, Lord Fontus Leigh.

"Lord Fontus, my daughter Lady Deoiridh Aitken."

Deoiridh recovered sufficiently to smile and offer her hand.

He bowed over her hand before returning her smile.

Her face heated.

"Delighted to meet you, Lord Fontus."

At that moment supper was announced. Sir Robin did his duty as escort to Lady Aitken. Dee accepted Fontus's arm.

"We must talk," she said sotto voce.

"Indeed," he agreed.

"Ask me to walk in the gallery after dinner."

"I will." No time remained before he pulled out a chair for her and helped her to sit then found his own seat at the far end of the table.

That meal was the longest of his life. He endured enquiries into his past, present and future from Dee's mother. Every attempt to re-direct the conversation met with polite resistance and a return to discussion of him and his circumstances.

What, he wondered, did Lady Aitken know, or guess?

"I heard murmurs that you may take up a diplomatic post?" asked Lady Somerville.

"Nothing has been decided for certain."

Before his hostess could make further inquiries, Lady Aitken joined the conversation. Fontus let the gossip and talk of female frip-peries flow around him, adding an occasional nod or murmur. Fortu-nately, the rest of the meal passed with very little of interest save the laughter and smiles shared between Dee and Robin.

He glared at them.

She's my wife, and you know it. Keep your smiles and jokes to yourself.

"Oh dear," Lady Somerville said. "Is something wrong with the trifle, Lord Fontus?"

He blinked. He'd lost track of the conversation at his end of the table. "I beg pardon. The trifle is delicious. Strawberries are my favorite." He hated strawberries but nonetheless popped a large spoonful into his mouth.

His hostess smiled. "I'm delighted. For a moment, you looked decidedly, ah, put out."

He chewed.

Lady Aitken joined in. "Indeed, Lord Fontus. Had I received such an expression from my late husband, I would have quaked in my dancing slippers."

He swallowed as his face warmed.

"Ah, forgive my lapse in manners. It was the trifle, so to say."

"What is wrong with it. I must tell cook."

"Nothing is wrong. I did say it was delicious."

"But you also said...?"

"The berries are especially sweet and remind me of a not-so-pleasant encounter with a few of Napoleon's Imperial Guard. The matter is not one for polite conversation. You will forgive me if I do not share any details save that the encounter occurred in a strawberry field." He lied.

Lady Somerville, placed her napkin on the table and stood. "Lady Aitken, Lady Deoiridh, let us retire to the music room, while the gentlemen drink their port. Husband, do not linger. I told Lady Aitken of your splendid voice. I very much want you to entertain us with a song or two."

"Of course, my dear. We shall be along shortly."

Fontus watched the ladies leave before rising at nearly the same moment as Robin to move closer to Sir Peter at the head of the table.

The port was served.

"You may leave us," Somerville directed the footman.

They conversed about general topics of interest, including the local smugglers and highwayman, Captain Moonlight.

"Something must be done," Sir Peter insisted.

"Have you specific plans?" asked Robin. "I am happy to assist."

"I as well," Fontus offered.

"No, not at this time. However, if either of you has a suggestion, I'm willing to listen."

"Should anything occur to me, I will inform you," Fontus said.

Robbin nodded in accord.

"Thank you, both," Sir Peter replied. "Are you ready to rejoin the ladies."

Fontus was more than ready,

The men trooped from the room.

Ask me to walk in the gallery after dinner.

The challenge was seeing their conversation remained private. He wanted no chaperones within hearing distance of what he must say to his wife.

CHAPTER 4

Normanton House, that same evening

Five songs later, Robin excused himself. Dee watched Fontus walk over to where her mother sat with their hostess.

"Lady Somerville, I recall the gallery here at Normanton House has some spectacular pieces. Might we take a tour?" He queried.

She smiled. "Why yes, that is a lovely suggestion. Peter, will you come with us?"

"You know much more of the art than I my dear. I've papers to attend to in the library. I will decline, if you do not mind."

"Not at all, my love. I'll come to you in the library when we finish. Lady Aitken, Lady Deoiridh, Lord Fontus, follow me please."

The gallery was a cavernous room, with portraits of Somerville ancestors three columns high lining all four walls.

Dee, her mother, and Fontus dutifully followed their hostess around the room as she gestured to each portrait and related the family history.

"Did Somerville's ancestor truly fight a duel with Cromwell during the Long Parliament?" Lady Aitken asked.

"That is what our ancestor's papers claim. Although no other evidence exists, and no one can recall the cause. The supposed duel was fought with swords and daggers." Lady Somerville unlocked a black lacquered chinoiserie piece, opening one of several drawers hidden behind the cabinet doors. "We own both daggers."

Lady Somerville lifted an ivory handled dirk and handed it over to Lady Aitken.

"Quick," Dee whispered to Fontus. "While they are occupied, take me to see the first Lady Somerville's portrait."

He took Dee's arm, strolling with her to the far side of the room.

"How did you find me?" she asked.

"Pure luck and a bit of speculation. I hadn't expected you to be living here, but Mars left a note suggesting it might be a good place to start."

"Your brother is entirely too clever. My mother is here because our hostess thought to do a kindness and invited her. The letter reached Mother at court, where keeping secrets is impossible. Barbeau still has connections there, so I fear he may know where I am."

"We must get you away."

"If I leave before the end of the house party, I risk raising questions that are better unasked."

"Robin Somerville is a friend. I've confided in him."

"You told him we are wed?"

"Yes. He promised his silence and will help keep you safe."

"I suppose having help is wise. Please do not confide in anyone else."

"I'm afraid I must."

"Why?"

"Because Lovis has arranged..."

"Daughter, our hostess insists we should continue here as long as we like. However, she must attend on her husband. I said goodnight for all of us."

"Thank you." Dee saw Lady Somerville leaving the room.

"Now, what were you and Lord Fontus whispering about?" Lady Aiken asked.

"I was asking Lady Deoiridh about something Lady Somerville

said." Fontus blamed that lady for gossiping without a blink. "That a gentleman of Louis' court was paying unwelcome addresses to Lady Deoiridh."

"The monsieur is *un canaille*," Lady Aitken informed Fontus. "He serves only himself. He has been absent from court for some time. I had hoped he found another quarry, and my Deoiridh could at last come home."

"I could set about some inquiries. Both my brother, the Duke of Leigh, and Castlereagh can learn nearly anything to be learned of Louis' court and its members."

"That is appreciated, Lord Fontus. Nonetheless, we must double our efforts here to keep Deoiridh safe."

"I agree. I will share the problem with Captain and Sir Peter Somerville at my first opportunity."

"Thank you."

"Meanwhile, ladies, I am at your service. Lady Deoiridh, I hope I may call on you tomorrow?"

"I would enjoy seeing you again, Lord Fontus."

"Perhaps we could ride together?"

"After breakfast perhaps. I rise fairly early."

"Perfect, thank you. Most of Somerville's stable comes from Leigh Chase breeding. You will be well mounted, if you permit me to select a horse for you?"

She inclined her head. "I trust your judgment."

"Then I will bid you both goodnight." He bowed over their hands and left.

Dee watched him go. She soothed her tiny disappointment at his departure with her delight that she would see him again soon.

"Mother, much as I enjoyed seeing the gallery and our conversations tonight, I must retire if I am to attend breakfast here tomorrow."

"Oh, I had hoped you and I might share that meal at your oh so *joli petit chalet*. Lady Somerville will not mind?"

"It is a charming cottage," Dee agreed while taking her mother's arm. "However, I no longer stand on ceremony with Sir Peter and Lady Somerville. In the morning, tell her I invited you."

"Perfect."

"Let us walk to the central stairs together," Dee said. "I should be able to find a footman there who will see me safely home."

She wished that Fontus were her escort, despite the impropriety. They had much to discuss.

How best to achieve the annulment? Where she should remove to prevent Barbeau finding her? Then there was that strange comment of his suggesting that he must confide their secret to his brother who had arranged something. Mother, bless her, had interrupted before he could explain.

Ever since her mother arrived, Dee had felt a looming sense of disaster. A long discussion with Fontus could do much to ease her worries. That was the only reason she was so eager for tomorrow morning's ride. Really.

CHAPTER 5

Normanton House, the next morning.

Fontus sent a note to Dee delaying their ride. He claimed an urgent matter required his attention. Best not to put any explanation on paper. He would tell Dee all as soon as they could take that ride.

He'd been surprised at breakfast to find Lady Beatrix and her father had arrived the previous night.

Lady Somerville performed the introductions.

"I heard a great deal about you, young man, from your older brother. He seems to believe you have matured." Sandrow's stern expression indicated that he was not confident of Lovis's assessment.

"It is a pleasure to meet you, finally, Lord Leigh." Lady Beatrix's frozen smile was even less welcoming than her father's dubious greeting.

The idea of making peace with Sandrow while avoiding an engagement with the lady was daunting. Fontus prayed his diplomatic skills were sufficient. He owed Lovis that much. However, he believed telling the truth would embarrass Lady Beatrix and anger Sandrow.

The Earl slapped his daughter's upper arm with the back of his hand.

She turned a furrowed brow on him.

"Your hand, daughter. Offer Lord Fontus your hand."

She blushed and extended her gloved fingers.

Such an insensitive reminder shamed the father more than the daughter.

"I am, of course, delighted to meet you both," Fontus lied and bowed over her hand. His lips grazed the material of her glove.

When he straightened her face was red.

"Perhaps I could escort you on a tour of the Somerville gardens after breakfast, Lady Beatrix?"

Mute, she looked to her father.

"Take your maid with you," was the man's terse approval. The earl turned and left, heading to the dining room without another word.

The lady's head swiveled between her father and Fontus. Clearly, she did not know what was expected of her.

Fontus offered his arm. "May I escort you to breakfast?"

"I... uh... I suppose." Gingerly she laid her palm on his forearm.

No cozy clasp around his elbow for her. Was her distaste for her brother's killer so strong, or was she afraid? Angry or fearful, she must be feeling vulnerable, perhaps powerless. On their walk he would empathize and establish common ground. Then he would see where the conversation led.

Seating at breakfast was less formal than at other meals. Fontus led Beatrix to a chair beside her father. Then he chose a seat at the table's opposite end.

He watched Lady Beatrix. She smiled and spoke easily to all. She felt comfortable enough to converse with other guests. Nonetheless, when she glanced at her father, she stiffened and immediately focused her gaze on the table before her. The earl had not even noticed her attention. He was deep in conversation with a gentleman on his other side.

Another late-night arrival? The man was unremarkable, brown hair, brown eyes, brown attire, a very simple cravat, and not a single gem or jewel in evidence.

Too much distance lay between them for any conversation, so Fontus turned to his hostess. "Who is the gentleman in brown?"

"Mr. George Froppin, a member of the Society of Friends. He champions causes of interest to Sir Peter. My husband is hoping to enlist Mr. Froppin's aid with the wording of some legislation Peter wishes to present to Parliament."

"Fascinating, I shall enjoy meeting him." Cultivating varied people was a cornerstone of how Fontus believed diplomacy should be conducted. One never knew when a contact with someone, whose beliefs or culture differed from one's own, might prove useful.

"Lady Aitken says you asked her daughter to ride with you later today."

"I did," he nodded. "However, something has arisen, and I let her know that unfortunately I had to postpone the ride."

Lady Somerville's gaze narrowed, and her smile turned sly. "Might that something be the arrival of Lord Sandrow and his daughter?"

"I see the duke has enlisted your aid in furthering my betrothal with Lady Beatrix."

"It would foster peace between your families."

Peace was good, but Fontus preferred Sandrow's complete indifference. He could not propose marriage to Lady Beatrix when he already had a wife.

He suspected Lady Beatrix had as little wish to marry him as he did her.

Lady Somerville looked at him expectantly.

"Yes, a connection with Sandrow could create an environment to nurture peace."

"You sound doubtful."

"Any man on the cusp of proposing must have doubts, Lady Somerville."

"Indeed. When your brother asked us to invite Sandrow and help you pursue a resolution to problems between your families, we were quite happy to assist. You must let me know, if I can do aught to aid with your courting."

Fontus quailed at the thought but pasted on a smile. "I will certainly keep that in mind. For the present, Lady Beatrix has accepted my invitation to walk out among your roses after breakfast."

"A splendid beginning. "Lady Somerville turned to the guest on her other side.

Fontus finished his meal at about the same time as Lady Beatrix rose to excuse herself. He managed to leave the room beside her.

"I will go up for my cloak," she said as they lingered in the foyer.

"Nonsense." He ordered over a footman. "Please go up and obtain Lady Beatrix's bonnet and cloak. Tell her maid to join us."

"Thank you." Her lips formed the words, but her gaze was glacial. When the maid, cloak, and bonnet finally arrived, the lady sighed and allowed Fontus to help her.

"Come." He held out his arm to her. "I know the shortest route to the rose gardens."

Lady Beatrix ignored his arm in favor of clasping her maid's hand.

He still intended to establish common ground with her, but her patent disapproval complicated the task.

As they entered the garden, the maid dropped back some, allowing them space to speak privately.

"You know why I am here?" Lady Beatrix stopped walking.

Fontus nodded but did not show his surprise that Lady Beatrix had taken the initiative.

"Indeed, Lady Beatrix. My brother informed me of his arrangement with your father."

"That's just it, the arrangement is with my father. No one asked me if I wanted to marry a murderer." She punctuated the statement with the stamp of a foot. "No one consulted me as to whether or not I wished to marry." A stronger stamp of that foot followed.

His head snapped backward. "I gather you find no favor in the idea."

"I am not in favor of marriage. I saw what it did to my mother, and I will not permit that to happen to me." She began to walk away.

He suppressed a sigh of relief and followed. The difficulty Lovis's meddling had put him in might resolve itself.

"Why did you come to Normanton House then?"

"You've met my father."

Fontus saw resignation in her eyes.

"Is your first impression of him as a gentle man?" she continued. "A man who considers the wishes of others?" Her tone was flat.

"To say otherwise would be rude." He'd yet to find his footing with this enigmatic woman. Shy to the point of awkwardness in her father's presence, she was much different without him.

"Even if it is the truth?" she asked.

Fontus decided to be as forthright with Lady Beatrix as she was with him. "My first impression of your father is that he is a forceful man who demands conformity from everyone he knows."

"That is fair—kind even." She stared off to the low stone wall separating the garden from the surrounding pastures and woodlands. "He only relents with people who are above him in station."

"I see." Her father made no attempt to hide his social ambitions. He shared directness with his daughter. However, Fontus believed she would not be pleased by the comparison. "So, my brother made an impression on Lord Sandrow."

"Father was most eager to meet with the Duke of Leigh. When he realized what His Grace had in mind, he cagily thanked him, but said he must take time to consider what is best for my future."

"Lovis would think that quite reasonable," Fontus stated. He had some small hope now that his present marriage might not be a problem.

"Father sent word within the week, that he wished for you and I to meet before any announcement was made. Your brother suggested this event. No doubt he knew the invitation would please Father."

"My brother is nothing if not observant. Your father might imagine himself canny. However, Lovis certainly expected just such a reaction and put the wheels in motion for the invitation to be sent before he received your father's reply."

"His Grace sounds like a very interesting man." Her lips gave an upward twist before resuming their usual straight line.

"Many people find him so." Now was not the time to explain that Lovis could be more demanding than Sandrow.

"What of yourself?" She queried

"Have you any other siblings?" He avoided her question, thinking to establish the common ground of difficult family. The moment he saw the color leave her cheeks; he regretted the question. Idiot, he cursed himself.

"No, you took care of that."

Her tone chilled him.

"It is not enough, but I deeply regret the events that led to Vincent's demise."

"No," she replied. "It is not enough."

"However, I think I may be able to make a small gesture that could ease your sorrow, somewhat." He tried for some humor.

"How?" Her nose twitched. She all but sniffed.

"I will happily accept your rejection of my proposal," Fontus offered.

She smiled, quickly covering her mouth before revealing a face colder than before.

"I find that acceptable. However, my father will call you out if we do not wed. My refusal might be your death sentence."

"Or his."

Her jaw dropped. "Oh, I hadn't thought of that. Father is a much more skilled marksman than Vincent."

"I could attempt to refuse his challenge," Fontus offered.

"And be branded a coward? I hear you embark on a promising diplomatic career. What will happen to that? A coward can hardly be an effective negotiator."

He'd known she was much smarter than the ton branded her.

"I see your point. Lovis is the one who created this conundrum. We must enlist him to resolve it." Fontus was not at all sure the duke would want to help.

You will never learn responsibility as long as I continue to support you. Henceforth you are on your own... Lovis's words to him after the debacle of the duel echoed in Fontus's memory.

"Would he do that?" she asked.

"If he understands you are being forced into a match you do not want. He's not a cruel man, and while he might think I deserve marriage to a woman who hates me, he would not see you in the same light."

"I don't hate you, precisely."

She gave a good imitation; despite the small indications of thaw he'd seen in the ice.

"My brother was a fool," she confessed. "While I loved him dearly, I had no doubt that the accounts of your duel were correct, when they reported he moved into your line of fire."

"I wish your father could believe that."

"He doted on Vincent, spoiled him shamefully, and was constantly disappointed by him. Though Father will never admit such. The manner of Vincent's death gave Father an opportunity to re-direct his anger and frustration from Vincent to you."

"You are a very perceptive young woman."

"Now you are having me on." Her lips curved upward. "I am at least five years older than you."

"Age and wisdom are not the same. Your age suits you, as does your insight into others' behaviors."

She rolled her eyes, "You will be a very successful diplomat, if you can gammon foreign dignitaries as you are trying to gammon me."

He mimed sorrow with an exaggerated frown. "You wound me for speaking a truth I sincerely believe."

"Such was not my intent. I apologize."

He saw sympathy reflected in her gaze before resuming his smile.

"Then let us plot how to resolve the problem of the proposed betrothal neither of us wishes."

"I think writing to your brother is the best start. I will simply tell him how I feel. Although you must ensure that Father does not see my letter."

"I can do that. I will suggest to Lovis that he invite you and your parent to Leigh Chase for a visit. I will also warn him that he must find a different way to mollify your father."

"Speaking of my father, he plans to announce our betrothal at the ball at the close of the house party."

"You must tell him you need more time."

"I doubt he will listen to me." Her brow furrowed.

"Perhaps if he believes I am actively courting you, he may be willing to delay."

She turned to look at Fontus. "He must believe that matters will turn out as he wishes."

"Do you think you could pretend to like me enough to bill and coo like a betrothed couple?"

"Must you kiss me?" Worry strained her face.

He placed a hand on his chest and widened his eyes. "Of course not. I would never go beyond the pale with the woman I love."

She laughed. "You don't love me."

"No, but I'm coming to like you very much."

He took her hand and kissed it.

"Ahem."

He dropped her hand, and saw Lady Beatrix blush as he turned around. "Lady Aitken." He grinned at her hopefully. "Good morning. May I introduce Lady Beatrix Sandrow?"

"Enchanté," Lady Beatrix." She moved between them, grasping that lady's arm. "You must tell me about yourself, Lady Beatrix. I'm certain Lord Fontus will not mind if I interrupt your *tête-à-tête. Non?*

Lady Aitken stepped out, forcing Lady Beatrix to come with her or create a scene.

Fontus, motioned to the maid she should go with her mistress.

"We will speak again later, Lord Fontus," Lady Beatrix called as she dragged her feet to slow her progress.

"I am at your service, Lady Beatrix. You as well, Lady Aitken."

Lady Aitken shifted to look back at him.

Fontus did not care for her toothy smile.

"Certainly, Lord Fontus. You and I must find an opportunity to converse."

As he escorted the ladies back to the house, he wondered, exactly what Lady Aitken had seen? Had she overheard his conversation with Lady Beatrix? Would she tell Dee? Of course, she would tell her daughter. But what? He must speak with Deoiridh as soon as possible and explain the plot he and Lady Beatrix hatched. Pray heaven he could explain before his wife saw or heard anything she could misunderstand.

CHAPTER 6

Rilbridge Cottage, the following afternoon

"I don't believe it, Mother."

Lady Aitken shrugged. "Choose, if you wish, Deoiridh to turn a blind eye. However, I know lovers when I see them. While Lord Fontus's kiss of Lady Beatrix's hand was quite proper, I know I heard him call her 'the woman I love.'"

Sick to her stomach, Dee longed to rush up to her bed and bury her face in her pillow so no one might hear her cry. She and Fontus were wed on paper only. She had no right to weep. She still planned for an annulment. Did she not? No, she should be glad he had found someone to love, to share his life with.

"How he could prefer her over you, I cannot imagine," Mother continued. "She is comely, but she has no presence. When her father is near, she cowers. Behind the earl's manners, probably lies a fearsome temper. No doubt his daughter learned to keep her mouth shut." Mother paused to take a sip of tea then set down her cup and saucer. "Did you hear me, Deoiridh?"

Dee forced a smile. "Certainly Mother. I'll remind you that Lord Fontus's affaires are none of my concern. As for Lady Beatrix, I will keep your comments in mind but decide what I think of her when I finally meet her."

"So, you say." Mother sipped again. "However, I did not think you unhappy to receive his invitation to ride out. How unfortunate that an urgent matter forced him to postpone your riding engagement... indefinitely."

Mother is fishing for details. However, Fontus's note provided no explanations.

At the time the lack made sense. Should anyone else see the note, details must arouse suspicion. Her mother's information forced Dee to consider Fontus may possess more than one reason to omit explanation for the delay.

"My dear, you are quite distracted. Is something bothering you?"

A dozen things, none of which she wished to confide in her mother. The last thing she needed was Mother interfering.

"Nothing of any import. Tell me, what will you wear tonight? I gather most of the guests arrived, and Lady Somerville plans an evening of music after dinner."

"She does, indeed," Mother confirmed. "I shall probably don my midnight blue evening gown. It will give me opportunity to show off the sapphires your father gave me."

"That is a lovely gown, and those gems are stunning. You'll be the belle of the evening."

"Lady Somerville will clear the music room floor for impromptu dancing. I intend to share a waltz with that scamp, Robin Somerville."

Dee lifted a brow. "Please tell me you do not possess a *tendre* for him."

Her mother waved a hand in the air. "Of course not. Recall, please, how much I enjoy dancing and rascals. Now tell me, what will you wear?"

"I am uncertain." Part of her wanted to sparkle so much Fontus could not look away. He must know what he is missing. *I'll show him. I'll flirt with every other man and leave him to suffer with his new beloved.*

Not that he and she had been in love. Theirs was strictly a

marriage of convenience. Once Barbeau was no longer a problem, she'd wish Fontus well of Lady Beatrix Sandrow.

"Let us go up and examine your gowns. By now, all your clothing must be new. Perhaps, I can help you decide."

"That is a good idea, Mother." Normally, Dee would politely decline the offer. Mother's tastes were a bit more flamboyant than her own yet still very proper. However, if anyone could suggest an ensemble to draw a man's attention, it was Mother.

⚜

At dinner, Dee flirted shamelessly with the gentlemen partnering her. From her peripheral vision, she saw Fontus staring. He and every other man had paid serious attention when she entered the grand salon before dinner.

The ice-blue velvet gown showed her figure to perfection, and contrasted nicely with her lapis eyes. The pale blue topaz parure, borrowed from her mother drew all attention to her face.

"You are very lovely tonight Lady Deoiridh," murmured Sir Peter Somerville.

Penelope Somerville surveyed the room to see who was looking. "Indeed, my friend, you captivate every man present. I know some husbands who will receive scolds from their wives later." She smiled.

"Thank you. It is always gratifying to hear one appears her best."

"Come with me," Lady Somerville said." I will introduce you to everyone. All our guests are here, save for Mr. George Froppin. He arrived yesterday. Shortly after breakfast, his valet informed me Froppin felt ill and would spend the day resting. He expects that his master will be fine tomorrow."

"I shall look forward to meeting him then."

Lady Somerville introduced a number of guests, among them a viscount and his wife, a couple of lords, colleagues of Sir Peter Somerville's in parliament. They crossed the room to the only people Dee had yet to meet.

"This next introduction is to Lord Sandrow and his daughter Lady Beatrix Sandrow. Sandrow is a life peer, and not normally someone we would include. However, we invited them at the request of His Grace of Leigh. Evidently, he and Lord Sandrow arranged a match between Lord Fontus and Lady Beatrix. I don't know if you are familiar with the difficulty between the two families. You see..."

"I am aware of the history between Lord Fontus and Sandrow's son." Dee kept her tone casual. Inside she was shaking. Angry, frightened, confused, sad.

How could Fontus propose to someone else and not tell me?

"Oh good, then you will understand when I ask you to make a friend of Lady Beatrix. She is painfully shy, especially with her father nearby, and a bit awkward. I'm sure Lord Fontus would appreciate any kindness shown his prospective bride. Although the betrothal has not yet been announced. That should happen before the end of our house party."

Less than two weeks. Hopefully the engagement would last a year or more. That had to be enough time to obtain the annulment.

Lady Somerville halted before the Sandrows and performed the introductions.

In conversation with Robin, Fontus stood watching a few feet away.

"We met your mother, Lady Deoiridh. She is French but wed a Scot." Lord Sandrow sniffed. He used 'French' and 'Scot' as condemnations.

Color left Lady Beatrix's face.

"Her friendship with King Louis is long-standing," Dee informed.

Sandrow's brows rose. "Really." He drew the word out as if there might be some question. "Do you approve of such an arrangement?"

Beside him his daughter paled even more, and swayed.

Dee stepped closer to the woman, leaning her shoulder into the lady's side for support.

"Lady Aitken does not need her daughter's approval or anyone's." Lady Somerville answered.

"Harrumph," Lord Sandrow snorted. "I also note she is well acquainted with Lord Fontus." In Sandrow's mouth, 'well acquainted' indicated inappropriate intimacies.

Dee usually tried to be patient with idiots like Sandrow, but she found her temper slipping from her grasp. Beside her, Lady Beatrix trembled.

"Lady Beatrix, are you quite well?" Dee asked loudly enough to draw the attention of anyone able to hear.

"Oh dear," Lady Somerville uttered. "I'll send for your maid."

"N...n...no, pl...ease." Lady Beatrix whispered.

"Don't be mawkish, daughter, you need..."

Dee interrupted, "Lord Sandrow. I believe your daughter is in need of some wine. Please get her some," she ordered. "You will find us on that settee near the fire."

She guided Lady Beatrix slowly around to the designated settee.

The lady's father frowned and signaled to a footman.

Fontus spun on his heel, intercepted Sandrow and the footman. Sandrow left to speak with another guest. Fontus took the wine from the footman then approached Lady Beatrix.

As the two took places on the settee, Fontus appeared at Lady Beatrix's side, and offered the glass of wine he held. He smiled at both Dee and the other woman.

Dee gave a nod of thanks but did not answer his smile.

"Thank you." Her voice raspy, Lady Beatrix drank deeply.

"Better now?" Dee asked.

"Yes, thank you for your help. My father is not always the most tactful of men. He had no business implying anything about your mother."

"He said nothing I haven't heard before. Too many people prefer to think badly of someone rather than learn the true circumstances."

"I'm glad you understand, Lady Deoiridh," Fontus said.

"Do I?" She referred not to the incident with Lord Sandrow but her husband's relationship with the man's daughter.

He gave a slight nod of comprehension. "Perhaps we could clear up matters by taking that ride I requested tomorrow?"

So, he wanted to explain. She wanted to refuse, but in light of her own comments about pursuing the truth, she accepted. "After breakfast?"

"Yes."

Aware of their audience, Dee turned to Lady Beatrix. "Do you ride Lady Beatrix?"

"I know how," she stated. "However, it is not my favorite activity. You need not invite me to join you. I shall enjoy a little solitude in Sir Peter's library. He has a collection of works by Pliny the Elder that I have not yet obtained for my own library."

"I am certain you will enjoy them. I prefer the younger Pliny's work. However, reading one in light of the other, enriches the knowledge of both."

Fontus blinked.

Dee smiled. No doubt her husband's very English education included some of each Pliny. He must be surprised she knew of the Roman authors let alone admitted reading their works. It was obvious that Lady Beatrix's mention of her reading preference astonished him.

Lady Beatrix perked up. "Perhaps we could share tea in Somerville's library later and discuss both Plinys."

"I would love to." Dee said. "Shall we say tomorrow? I can ask Lady Somerville to serve us tea separately in the library, if that suits you."

"Please. I'd rather not ask in front of my father. He's sure to scold me for spending time on musty books when I could be..." She trailed off into silence. Her shoulders slumped, and she lifted a stricken face to Fontus.

"Shall I tell him that Lady Deoiridh is a friend, and I asked her to spend some time with you?" Fontus suggested.

"That is kind of you."

Dinner was announced.

"Ladies may I escort you?" He offered both elbows.

However, Lord Sandrow hurried over and asked to escort Deoiridh. Courtesy forced her to accept. She prayed for a seat quite distant from him.

In between bites and conversation with her dinner partners, she pondered about the ride with Fontus in the morning. Did she really hope he had a reasonable explanation for courting Lady Beatrix?

He'd proven himself trustworthy to this point. Would he lie to her now? Would she be able to tell if he did?

She recalled a conversation on shipboard while crossing the channel.

"I do not think you lied to me. When you do play someone false, I'm certain you believe it necessary," she had said.

"You are determined to think well of me." he had replied.

"You give me no reason to think otherwise." Nor had he now. She must be patient and not jump to unwarranted conclusions.

Tomorrow, she would learn whether her trust had been misplaced.

CHAPTER 7

South Downs, the following day

Side by side, Fontus and Dee galloped away from her cottage, until they arrived at the top of a broad ridge. A groom trailed behind, remaining within sight for propriety's sake. They dismounted, gave their horses over to the care of the groom and walked along a slight path worn into the ground.

"Captain Somerville was right," Dee remarked." The view from this ridge is spectacular, and not just the expanse toward the estate. The other side of the rise is a picture of forested mystery. See how the late morning fog lingers between the trees."

"Indeed," Fontus agreed from beside her. However, he was not admiring the rolling vista of the South Downs. She was as beautiful in an elegant riding habit as she had been in borrowed peasant's clothing, or last night's gown. He expected she would be just as entrancing on the dance floor. Or perhaps tousled and rosy from love making.

She shifted to look at him.

He shook his head to clear the inappropriate fantasy. He'd kissed her only once. A delightful, if unsatisfyingly short, embrace. Never before had he fantasized about one woman with such persistence. Women came to him with relative ease. If one left, another eventually appeared.

Deoiridh's endurance in his imagination was unique. He'd never tried to cajole or lure her into a compromising position. She was a lady. Of course, he had treated her with every respect.

She trusted me, needed my help. She did not need to be seduced. Nor would she have welcomed it.

His inventive mind did not care. There, the intimacies shared with Dee were legion. All previous encounters with women paled.

"I was thinking last night of all the items we must discuss."

Despite her stern tone, his heart warmed. She thought of him when she was alone.

"I suppose you want to know why I appear to be courting Lady Beatrix," Fontus stated.

"Appear? Lady Somerville informed me that Sandrow and daughter were invited so you could learn to know your future bride. She said your brother had arranged the match. Does he know you are already married?"

"Not yet. I had hoped to discover that the annulment was final and no obstacle existed to my marriage with Beatrix."

Dee paled a bit, and she stiffened. "How disappointed were you when you learned otherwise?"

Fontus peered closely at her." Do you think I want this marriage?"

Dee straightened and lifted her chin. "Which marriage? Your current one, or the one you wish for."

He snorted. "I do not wish to marry Lady Beatrix Sandrow."

"Your actions suggest otherwise." Her gaze narrowed.

"That is for her father's benefit," Fontus said. "You saw how he browbeats her with degrading remarks. She has no more interest in our betrothal than I."

"How do you know?"

Was that hope he saw beneath her slitted lids?

"Because she told me."

"Hah," Dee scoffed. "She's too afraid of her father to say that."

"You are right. She would not tell me had her father been present," Fontus remarked.

"You spoke with her alone?" Her scorn turned glacial.

"We walked in the rose garden. Her maid was with us, and we could be seen from the house."

Dee's expression softened a bit. "That's when my mother came upon you."

"Yes."

"She heard you call Lady Beatrix the woman you love."

"Had Lady Aitken seen our faces, she would have known we were joking. The remark was taken completely out of context."

Did Dee just sigh? All stiffness left her.

"Tell me what the two of you said."

He summarized the conversation. "I agreed to behave like a suitor, until Sandrow receives my brother's invitation to visit Leigh Chase. That should happen soon, as I sent my letter and one from Lady Beatrix to His Grace yesterday."

Something like dismay crossed Dee's face so quickly he was uncertain he'd seen it.

"He will agree?"

"If not for my sake, for Lady Beatrix. Lovis is not cruel. He would not wish her to suffer simply to make my life easier," Fontus explained.

Dee laughed. "I doubt life would be easy for anyone with Sandrow as a father-in-law."

"Agreed. Whomever I am married to, I will travel widely. Lovis, when I spoke with him last, implied that my permanent employment with the diplomatic service was all but assured."

"Do tell?" Her brows rose.

"He attempted to soften the news of my arranged marriage with the comment that a wife is an asset to a career diplomat."

Dee nodded. "That much is true. Do you believe Lady Beatrix is the best choice?"

"When out of her father's orbit, she is delightful," Fontus mused. "Away from parental browbeating, Lady Beatrix's wit and intelligence will shine."

"That may be," Dee admitted. "Even on short acquaintance, I am certain she could learn quickly. However, a woman of more worldly experience is a better choice."

Does Dee mean herself?

"Have you someone in mind?" he asked.

"Ah," she paused. "Not at the moment. Nonetheless, I am happy to assist you in making a selection."

"Marriage for career advancement is fine, but what if I wish to marry for love?"

Fontus needed to know if Dee shared that wish?

"I had not taken you for a romantic. Is that what you want?" she asked.

A light shone in her lapis eyes. He might imagine she wanted him to marry her for love.

"I am not opposed to the idea of being in love with my wife."

She walked in silence.

"What of you, wife? When we are no longer wed will you follow your heart into your next marriage?"

"I'd not given it much thought." She spoke slowly.

But you gave it some thought. Who did you imagine as the man you might love?

The conversation was becoming fraught. Better to change the subject.

"We must consider our futures carefully. My primary concern is your safety," he said. "I propose that you move to Leigh Chase in Leicestershire. There is no safer place I can think of than the ducal seat. If we take Lovis into our confidence, he'll not only see you safe, but he can speed along the process of annulment."

She blushed.

The color in her face was becoming, but he'd no desire to embarrass her. "You do still wish for an annulment?"

"I...I believe so. However, I must confess, that while I started the letter necessary for requesting one, I've not yet sent it."

His brow wrinkled. "You've had close to three years. The process could be complete by now. Why the delay?"

"Please don't be angry with me."

Fontus softened his expression and placed a hand over hers at her side. "I apologize if you thought I was upset. I could never be angry with you Dee."

"Truly? You don't know me well enough. You cannot be certain."

"I take your point. Nonetheless, I can think of only one thing that might cause me a moment's irritation with you."

She tilted her head. "What would that be?"

"If you took an unwarranted risk with your life. I would never forgive myself if anything should happen to you." He kept his tone and expression level. He wanted her to know she mattered to him.

"But you said, 'if I took the risk' not you?"

Fontus grinned. "Strange is it not, for me to feel responsible for your actions."

Now Dee's brow furrowed. "Indeed, I'm not certain I like that."

"It doesn't make me happy, precisely. But there it is. Since the day I left you with Mars at Brighton Harbor, I've been unable to shake the feeling that I need to be the one to protect you."

"Hmmm. Perhaps not so strange. Not, if you loved me."

"Indeed." He looked away.

Now was not the time for confessions of imaginary love. They needed time to examine their feelings. Logical, yes. Reasonable, yes. Satisfying, far from it.

"You don't love me, do you?" she asked.

He turned back to find her peering at him as if he were some strange creature she'd seen for the first time.

"I don't know. Never, for any other woman, have I had the feelings I have for you. I think about you and what life would be like if our marriage was real—if we spent our lives together. Am I in love? I don't know." He could think he was in love, but that wasn't enough to declare himself. "I've never been in love before, so I don't know what it feels like. What about you?"

"What about me?"

"Have you ever been in love? Do you know what it feels like?"

She shook her head. "I know what my mother told me about loving my father."

Fontus waited.

"Mother said, the feeling crept up on her when she wasn't looking. Father had courted her in the standard manner. He was eligible. He proposed, and she accepted. She liked him, she said, as well as any other suitor. She had not realized how much she loved him until he was gone.

"I recall how deep her grief was after he passed. I could say nothing, do nothing to lift her spirits. It was King Louis, actually, who insisted on meeting with her to talk. Initially they spoke of my father, for he too had loved Father in the way kings love their few friends. They helped each other mourn, and eventually both of them became happier. Their conversations continued, though on other subjects. I believe they love each other, but in the way of friends rather than the passion of lovers…"

She and Fontus ambled to a halt to sit beneath a tree. He removed his coat, spreading it on the ground to protect Dee's dress from stains and damp.

"So, your mother was surprised by love?"

"Evidently."

"If what I feel for you is love then I hope I realize it before I lose it," he confessed.

"My hope for myself is the same."

"You asked if I love you," Fontus reminded. "I cannot say for certain. I can say that I believe I could love you."

She gave a small smile. "I, too, think that might be possible. For me to love you, that is. However, marriage involves many other matters than love."

"Indeed, but I hear that love makes it easier."

"Since neither of us is certain, let us put the topic aside."

"Yes, will you come to Leigh Chase after the events here at Normanton House?"

"I find myself reluctant. I will agree, since your arguments are sound. However, I comply on the condition that it is temporary, and other arrangements are made for my continued safety."

He nodded." We will make more definite plans after we speak with Lovis and get his help with the annulment."

Her smile faded.

Did the thought of an annulment sadden her? She'd not said she wished to remain wed.

In the distance, one of the horses snorted. Fontus heard the groom murmur to it.

He became aware that the sun stood high in the sky.

"We've been gone longer than I expected. We should head back now, or we'll be late for luncheon."

"I will need to change," Dee said. "We should go to my cottage first."

"Of course. However, I've a few small items to do before we sit down to eat, so I will leave you there.

He signaled to the groom.

They turned their mounts toward her cottage.

CHAPTER 8

Normanton House, later that same day

Footsteps sounded on the stairs as Dee entered the Normanton House foyer.

"Ah, it is Lady Deoiridh Aitken." Lady Somerville said. "Permit me to introduce you."

To avoid a collision, Dee halted and looked up.

"No." She breathed the word. One hand went protectively to her chest. Looking at her was an all too familiar face. However, instead of formal court attire he wore a light brown wig and excessively simple brown clothing. Wide with feigned curiosity, his brown eyes, sparkled.

What is Barbeau up to?

Lady Somerville performed the introductions, adding that, "Lady Deoiridh's mother is visiting us also, I will introduce you after luncheon.

"I gather she is a French woman and has spent time in the Bourbon court." His English was perfect, bearing no sign of years in France. "I look forward to meeting her."

Luncheon was announced.

"Ladies," Barbeau said. "May I escort you in?"

Dee must think of him as Froppin until she could tell Fontus and the Somervilles the truth.

Common courtesy forced her to accept the unwanted escort. Unlike Lady Somerville, who had grasped the offered elbow, Dee placed her hand very lightly on his arm.

He had the audacity to move her hand himself from his arm to the crook of his elbow compelling a more intimate contact.

She wanted to toss his arm back at him, rush to her rooms, and scrub clean the skin beneath the sleeve of her dress. She might even burn the dress.

As soon as they entered the Grand Salon, Lady Somerville aimed for her husband, pulling Froppin with her. "Sir Peter asked me to seat you at his left, so you might discuss political matters easily."

"Of course, Lady Somerville. I am delighted to assist him."

Dee excused herself and joined her mother speaking with several other guests.

Mother and daughter exchanged warm greetings.

"We were discussing the local highwayman..." Robin said.

"The man who just entered the room with you and Lady Somerville, is he the Quaker gentleman?" her mother asked. A puzzled frown crossed her face. "He seems vaguely familiar."

"You've met him."

"Really, I do not recall knowing any members of the Society of Friends."

Dee looked at Robin, uncertain how to proceed.

"If you will excuse me..." he said.

"No, please. It is important that you know who Mr. Froppin really is. We must also inform Sir Peter and Lady Somerville."

Robin tilted his head. "Froppin is not who he claims?"

"No," Dee replied. "He is Monsieur Aristide Barbeau. He trades in lies and deception."

"I believe Fontus mentioned him to me, though I cannot recall the details. Why do you think he has come here?"

"He is here because he wishes to marry my fortune," Dee stated.

"But..." Robin halted. "I will certainly warn my brother and his wife that the man is a threat and not to be trusted."

"Thank you," Lady Aitken said.

"I am safe enough when I am not alone." Dee explained. "He has always done his dirty work in the shadows, far from prying eyes and listening ears."

"No doubt you are correct, Lady Deoiridh," Robin said. "However, I prefer to take precautions rather than regret not doing so."

"I agree and established my own safeguards at the cottage."

"That may not be good enough, daughter. I shall feel more comfortable if you moved to Normanton House while Barbeau is here."

"I don't think that is..."

"A capital idea," Robin enthused.

"I'd rather not inconvenience Lady Somerville," Dee said. She had no wish to live so close to her mother, not until the marriage to Fontus was resolved.

"No inconvenience. In fact, it may solve a problem," Robin admitted.

"How so?" Dee inquired.

"With Froppin's arrival, some of the guests may be forced to share quarters. If Lord Fontus and I remove to the cottage, that will free up two bed chambers."

Dee bit her lower lip but remained silent.

"What of my daughter's safety? Your absence will give Barbeau greater opportunity to accost her."

Dee agreed.

"Not if she is always in company," Robin stated. "You did suggest he acts in secret. In addition, we will alert the staff and keep a footman on watch near your rooms."

"Very well," Dee nodded. "Let us speak with Sir Peter Somerville together. Can you arrange that?"

"Certainly. We value friends highly. I am certain my brother will wish to ensure your safety."

Dee spent the afternoon discussing Pliny with Lady Beatrix. The meeting with the Somervilles followed. She was pleased to see Fontus there. Silence reigned for a few moments after she finished explaining, and Robin proposed his plans.

"I think my brother's ideas are good," Sir Peter said.

"We should waste no time removing Lady Deoiridh to another location," Fontus insisted.

"No. The man will simply believe he is found out. He will go to ground, and we may not be able to prevent an attack." Robin pointed out.

"Could you not arrest him now and put him in jail?" Lady Somerville asked.

"On what grounds, my dear," her husband replied. "This is England. People are not imprisoned without cause."

"Lady Deoiridh's safety is sufficient cause, as I see it."

"An excellent point, Sister," Robin soothed. "However, the need for caution is not evidence of a crime. The law prevents imprisonment simply on the basis of threat or suspicion."

"I agree with Sir Peter and Robin," Deoiridh said. "Barbeau's arrest and imprisonment must be accomplished with legal means, to be permanent. However, until we achieve that, I shall never go anywhere alone."

"Not sufficient," Fontus muttered.

"It must do," Somerville said. "For now."

As they left Sir Peter's study to dress for dinner, Fontus pulled Dee aside. "We can leave immediately if you like?"

"No, not only would it be discourteous, but I want Barbeau to be removed from my life before I go anywhere. Staying here is my best chance of that."

"Very well, all shall be as you wish," Fontus agreed.

She could tell he wasn't happy, but this was her life and her problem. She needed to be the one to resolve it. To do that she required some idea of what Barbeau might do. She could speak with him directly, though she doubted he would tell her much. Perhaps Greta could question his servants under a guise of friendship.

The house party continued for the next week or so, with no response from Lovis. It wasn't like the duke to remain silent, especially where his plans were involved.

"Looking forward to making a special announcement at the ball," Sandrow had said, one afternoon when he and Fontus happened to be observing the activities. "M'daughter's not said a word about your proposal. You asked her?" His stare stabbed Fontus in his conscience.

"We are still becoming comfortable with one another."

"Comfort can come after the bedding," the man snapped. "I won't wait much longer. Get to it." Sandrow walked away.

Fontus wished Lovis would act. However, his concern over Barbeau's intentions toward Dee bothered him more. When would the man make his move?

One unusually warm day, Lady Somerville informed her guests they would be having a picnic on the ridge where he and Dee had taken their ride.

Most of the men rode, along with Dee and her mother. Froppin had chosen to drive his own curricle. Rather pretentious for a member of the Society of Friends. Barbeau must not know as much as he imagined about that group.

What other mistakes might he make?

Once they arrived at the picnic site, luncheon was served immediately.

In between bites of chicken and glasses of wine, Sandrow made pronouncements disagreeing loudly with current political and economic policies. Few of the diners replied. Those to either side of him made polite murmurs, but no one would give the man the argument he appeared to wish for.

As to Froppin, Barbeau paid court to the Danvers ladies, letting them rattle on about the latest *on dits* while he surveyed the rest of the party.

What is he looking for?

After the meal, they dispersed, some to sit on blankets under shady trees, others to wander, admiring the various views. Still others simply stood about talking.

Fontus settled his ladies on a blanket.

"Are you certain you do not wish to marry?" His wife was asking Lady Beatrix.

"Most definitely. I've no need of a husband, who will do little but forbid me my small pleasures, and most likely take on a mistress while he gambles away my fortune. My father will leave me in very comfortable circumstances when he passes. He is not a person to leave money to charities or distant relatives."

"Meanwhile, you are forced to live with him, cater to his preferences, and submit to his restrictions," Fontus commented.

"I know little different. My mother died before I had my come out. For the most part Father ignored me until after...." The lady looked stricken.

Fontus had been glad when she forgave his part in her brother's death. Now, she was blaming him, inadvertently, for the misery of her life since then.

"You and Lord Sandrow must join Fontus and myself at Leigh Chase," Dee said. "However, my stay there will be short. Why don't you come with me when I leave? You can tell your father you are visiting a friend to help her settle into a new home. You may stay as long as you like. Indefinitely, in fact. I shall live quietly, but if you want to travel, you may do so and always return to me rather than your father."

She assumed Fontus's claim that Lovis would help was the truth. He could not know for sure. However, Lovis did not tolerate cruelty, and any marriage between Fontus and Lady Beatrix promised multiple miseries.

"That's a splendid idea," Fontus said. If he and Dee dissolved their marriage—and he prayed that would never happen—having someone stay with her would ease his mind considerably.

"I don't know." Lady Beatrix dithered.

"You need not decide right now. We've several days before the party ends," Dee said. "I will ask your father for your company while we travel to Leigh Chase, so we can come to know each other better."

Lady Beatrix smiled. "I should be able to decide by the time we arrive there."

"Wonderful. I want to go for a walk. Would you care to join me, Lady Beatrix?" Dee invited.

"Yes, indeed."

Fontus leapt to his feet and helped the ladies stand.

"Lord Fontus," Dee's eyes sparkled. "You need not accompany us."

"What if I wish to?"

"I... ah..."

A ruckus on the far side of the picnic area interrupted her reply.

"I tell you, that woman should be burnt at the stake." Sandrow shouted at the top of his lungs.

Red-faced with fury, he pointed at Lady Aitken.

"She's worse than that Wollstonecraft woman. Flaunting her affair with the French King and saying that the Bourbon court is better than Prinny's. Worse, she's French and married a cursed Scot."

About two feet away, Dee's mother stood between their hosts and laughed.

Most of the other guests simply stared.

"Excuse me," their host intervened.

Fontus ran to help Sir Peter Somerville.

"Monsieur Sandrow," Lady Aitken drawled. "You act the fool, speaking of things you know nothing about."

"Fool! Fool! You dare to call me a fool." He rushed at Lady Aitken, arms outstretched, hands curved like talons ready to choke the life from her.

Sir Peter stepped between the two.

Lady Somerville pulled Lady Aitken away.

Somerville seized one of Sandrow's arms, slowing him.

The earl snarled and swung at his host.

Fontus arrived in time to grab the earl's arm before the fist could land.

Still struggling to gain control of his limbs, Sandrow turned on

Fontus. "You! You are just like all the rest of them. Taking your plea-sure wherever, how, and when you wish without a thought to the grief you cause."

"Calm yourself, your lordship," Somerville soothed. "You are overwrought. Let us help you to one of the carriages. You will be far more comfortable out of the heat."

Sandrow stared at his host as if surprised to see him. Then he looked across to where Beatrix stood beside Dee.

His daughter's head hung in shame for her father's behavior.

His brow furrowed, and doubt filled his eyes.

"Overwrought? I'm not...ah...yes. Yes. Thank you, Somerville, I believe the sun has been too much for me."

Together, Fontus and Somerville walked with Sandrow to a coach.

Robin appeared at Somerville's side. "Peter, your wife said you needed me."

"Yes, go find one of the coachmen. Lord Sandrow is ill and needs to return to the house."

"Certainly."

The coachman was fetched.

"Perhaps I should go with the earl," Robin suggested after Sandrow had been loaded into the coach. That man sat slumped on the forward-facing seat. His cheek pressed against the coach wall, he snored. "I can see to his comfort in your stead, brother. You are needed here."

Somerville hesitated only a moment. "Thank you, Robin."

"I'll see you later then, my friend," Fontus said to the younger Somerville.

Back in the picnic area, Fontus found Ladies Deoiridh and Beatrix returning from their stroll.

"Did you enjoy your walk?" he asked.

"Very much so," Lady Beatrix enthused.

When everyone was ready to return to the house, the sun was low in the sky.

"Have you seen my mother?" Dee asked of Lady Somerville as

coaches were being brought round along with mounts for those who rode.

"No, although I received a note from her saying she wished to return to the house early. Her horse and one of the grooms are gone."

"She's probably soaking in a hot bath. The out of doors is not her favorite venue."

CHAPTER 9

Normanton House, that evening

Parting from Fontus, Dee made her way to the suite she shared with her mother. Removing her bonnet and cloak, she rang for her maid then knocked on her mother's bed chamber door.

Receiving no response, she cracked the door open and peered into the room. The sheet covered lumps in the bed implied Mother had one of her rare sick headaches and had decided to sleep it off. Dee closed the door quietly just as Greta entered the room.

"How may I ..."

"Shh." Dee placed a forefinger before her pursed lips. "My mother is sleeping. She never naps during the day, so she must have a sick headache."

"I'll be happy to prepare a tisane," Greta offered.

"No, she should be fine by the time we dress for dinner."

"Very well, my lady."

"I want a bath and will rest before dinner. Please wake me an hour before."

"I will arrange it."

"Thank you, Greta."

Night had fallen by the time the sound of her bedcurtains rattling woke Dee. She had Greta assist her with her ensemble and hair. Ready sooner than she expected, she decided to go down to the Grand Salon. Someone should be there. She was sure to find stimulating conversation. She tiptoed to her mother's door, and knocked softly.

Her mother had not moved.

She must feel very ill. If she is not better by the time dinner is finished, I shall ask Sir Peter to send for a physician.

"Mother is still sleeping," Dee informed Greta. "Please see that she is not disturbed."

"Yes, my lady. I will do your mending so as to be close at hand."

"Thank you, Greta. I shall relax knowing she is well cared for."

In the grand salon, she found her hosts conversing with Frobbin and the local vicar. Lady Beatrix sat on a settee near the far wall. Two young bucks, friends of Robin's, lay siege to that lady's attention. The lady blinked rapidly and moved her head slowly from side to side. Her gaze lifted to Dee's for a moment. Dee caught the unspoken plea for rescue.

She aimed in the direction of her new friend. Halfway there, Frobbin blocked her path.

"What do you want?" She wished she could give him the cut direct.

"I must speak with you privately."

"I do not care to converse with you, sir. Nothing you can say is of any interest to me." She used her iciest tone.

He arched a brow. "Not even if it concerns your mother?"

Dee lifted her chin and sniffed. "My mother is asleep with a sick headache and is no concern of yours."

Hands clasped behind his back, Frobbin rocked back and forth on his heels. "Really? Did you see her?"

"She is asleep, so of course I did not disturb her."

"Hmm. Perhaps you can explain a mystery for me."

"I tire of whatever game you play. Get to the point, so I may speak with someone else."

"I play no game. However, since you are so certain of your mother's location, maybe you can explain this note she wanted me to give you."

Without thinking, Dee took the offered slip of paper, unfolded it, and read.

Daughter, please do not do as this canaille asks. He dares not carry out his threats. Deny him, and I will be fine."

Beside her mother's signature, in very tiny script of an ancient style were the words *Neart agus Faireachadh*, war cry of the Aitken clan in her father's native tongue. *Strength and Vigilance.* Few people from other nations could translate the ancient Scots language, let alone the particular dialect used here. Hence, her father had established it as a way of verifying that any message was truly from family.

"I am surprised that you permitted my mother to write such a note."

Barbeau shrugged. "I care only that you understand she is my guest at a location I shall disclose later. You may of course do as she asks and ignore my warning."

"You made no threat."

"Immediately after the ladies leave the table, you must excuse yourself."

"On what grounds?"

"I don't care what lie you create." He snarled the words despite the smile he kept on his face.

"So, you wish to make a liar of me as well as a slave."

"Take care, Lady Deoiridh. I will soon be your husband. You will not wish to test my patience. Having excused yourself, get a cloak and bonnet. Steal one from the maids if you must, but do not return to your room. My associates among the footmen will tell me should you deviate from my instructions. Leave the house by a side door and make your way to the front gate. Stay within the shadow of the trees lining the drive. No one must know you left or suspect that anyone has gone from the house. I will meet you at the gate and take you to our destination. Bring nothing. I will provide everything you need once we are married."

Dee laughed. "You honestly believe you can coerce me into

marriage." She kept back information of her marriage to Fontus. She and Mother were safer if Barbeau believed her single, for now.

"I believe you would do anything to prevent your mother being sold into prostitution. Arabs with seraglios prize white women highly. While her age and experience make her less valuable than a young virgin, your mother is especially attractive and will fetch a high price. A small compensation for myself should you decide to sacrifice her and remain unmarried."

He would, do it. She must stop him.

But how?

She had an hour or so to plan.

"If you try to cross me, I warn you I will watch you carefully for the entire evening. Any appearance of conspiracy with another guest will result in very unpleasant consequences."

"You err if you imagine I cannot defeat you and your plot. Even if I go with you later, you may regret that you ever attempted to force me."

He issued another shrug. "Keep your delusions You need not tell me your intentions. Tonight, when you either appear at the Normanton House front gates or not, I will know how much you value your mother."

I will rescue Mother and visit vengeance on Barbeau so terrible, he will never recover.

Her smile showed her teeth. "You are incapable of understanding the depth of feeling Mother and I share."

"Perhaps. However, I know you would give your life to keep her safe. Ah, I see one of the Danvers ladies, beckoning me. I shall bid you good evening."

He walked away.

Dee stood staring into space.

Lady Beatrix rose and approached. The young bucks followed in her wake.

"Gentlemen, I wish a private word with Lady Deoiridh. You may leave us."

The bucks walked away, unable or unwilling to disturb a private conversation.

"My friend, are you well?"

Dee nodded, dropped her arms to her sides, crumpled the note, and stuffed it into a hidden pocket of her gown.

"I saw that horrible Quaker person speaking with you," Lady Beatrix continued. "Did he lecture you on the sins of self-indulgence and warn you to take up the first marriage proposal you received lest you come to a bad end."

Dee laughed at the irony. "Yes, we did speak of marriage. For a person of short acquaintance, I found him quite forward."

Lady Beatrix leaned close. "You are too kind."

She took Lady Beatrix's arm and aimed for the now empty settee. "He is not worth our attention. Tell me did you enjoy speaking with those two young men? I believe they are friends of Robin."

"Not very much. They spoke of little but horses, hunting, and racing carriages."

Dee and her friend sat.

"A shame that young men do not value intelligent women. Next time, start a conversation about Pliny. Their sort will disappear faster than you can blink at the mention of any topic that might require them to think."

Lady Beatrix giggled. "I had not thought of employing my knowledge as a shield."

"It is a trick I learned early from my mother to deal with presumptuous or unpleasant courtiers."

"Speaking of your mother," Fontus's voice came from over her shoulder. "Where is the lovely Lady Aitken?"

Dee fixed her smile in place before she shifted to include him in her view. Should she confide Barbeau's demands to him? Uncertainty kept her silent.

"I left her asleep in her bed," Dee lied. "She never sleeps during the day, unless she feels poorly."

"I am sorry to learn she is unwell."

"Can I do anything to help?" Lady Beatrix asked.

"Thank you both. Mother will be fine. Sleep is the best restorative. If you'll excuse me." She stood. "I must give Sir Peter and Lady Somerville her excuses."

"Of course," Lady Beatrix murmured.

"We will come with you," Fontus announced, assisting the ladies to stand.

Moments after speaking with their hosts, dinner was announced.

Throughout the meal, Dee felt his gaze on her. Could he sense something disturbed her peace? Would he think it simple concern for her mother? Did she dare confide Frobbin's threats to her husband?

CHAPTER 10

Normanton House, later that evening

The ladies left the men to their port for tea in the music room. While there, Dee accepted well wishes for her mother's quick recovery. As soon as she could, she took Lady Beatrix aside to a far corner.

"I need your help." Dee wished with all her heart she could confide in Fontus, but Barbeau would suspect. She had no idea which of the footmen might report any encounter with Fontus.

"Of course."

"First, you must act as if I am sharing an amusing story."

Lady Beatrix gave a sly glance and waved a hand. "Oh, la, Lady Deoiridh, I've never heard such a thing."

Dee smiled. "Perfect. What I tell you must remain in strictest confidence, until you can inform Lord Fontus."

"My lips are sealed." The lady added a giggle to emphasize the part she played.

"I must leave."

"Oh no, really?" The question was perfectly pitched to indicate amazement at someone's outrageous behavior.

"Indeed." Dee lowered her voice for Lady Beatrix's ears alone.

The Danvers sisters approached as Dee finished her explanation and stood.

"Good night, Lady Deoiridh," said Lady Beatrix, smiling.

"You cannot be leaving us this early," Abigail Danvers protested.

"We were hoping you would share with us the amusing tale you told to Lady Beatrix," Prudence said.

"I regret, I cannot," Dee replied. "I must attend my mother."

"I will happily share the story with you," Beatrix volunteered.

"Well then." Abigail nodded. "We will wish you a good evening."

"God speed your mother's recovery," Prudence added.

Dee left, giving her excuses to Lady Somerville. As instructed, she stole a cloak, the rattiest most worn-out garment she could find. Then leaving by a side door, she dashed to the cottage where she kept the pistols received from her father. Barbeau did not know she had lived in the cottage, and even if someone informed him where she'd gone, she doubted he would suspect anything, since the cottage was unoccupied for the evening. All too soon, she was seated beside him in his curricle, bowling along at a rate far too great for a dark country road.

He'd not said a word when handing her up and had remained silent, focused on guiding the horses with as much speed as possible.

Clouds scudded over the moon, gathering in clumps. The surrounding woods thickened to a dense forest, plunging the dark night into pitch black. The wind picked up. The air smelled of rain to come.

Would a storm help or hinder Barbeau? She supposed all was a matter of timing. Could he get her and her mother away before any storm kept them landbound, before Fontus could arrive with help, before she could bring one of her pistols into play?

Had Lady Beatrix delivered her message? Was Fontus even now searching for her? Would he find the bits of fabric she managed to tear from the cloak she'd stolen? Barbeau's concentration on driving made it easy for her to leave the trail. He never saw what she did.

CHAPTER 11

Normanton House, a short time later

"Calm yourself Lady Beatrix. Tell me once more what Dee said." Fontus used a soothing tone and handed the lady a cup of tea. Outwardly in control, inwardly he seethed. Barbeau is a dead man. His fists clenched and unclenched.

Beside him in the master's study, Sir Peter and Robin, listened to Beatrix's tale in silence.

"Steady man," Robin placed a hand on Fontus's shoulder. "We'll find her."

"Barbeau will be punished," Sir Peter insisted. "As magistrate, I will see to it."

"One more time, Beatrix," Fontus encouraged. He would find Dee. He must. He could not live without her.

Lady Beatrix repeated everything that Dee told her. More slowly this time, in between sips of tea.

"How long ago was this?" Somerville asked.

"I don't know. A quarter hour perhaps. She left the music room no more than five minutes before you gentlemen joined the ladies."

"Excellent." Fontus turned to his host. "I require five of your best men who can ride and shoot." His blood raced. They could not act quickly enough.

"I can help with that," Robin offered. "I know the men well. I also know the terrain. Barbeau will aim for the coast. A number of likely inlets and coves could be used to land a small vessel unseen. One of the reasons so many smugglers operate in this area."

"We must send men in other directions just to be certain," Somerville said. "I will give the orders and come with you."

"Ah..." Fontus hesitated. "I think it best if you remain here."

"Why?"

"Your guests will wonder and gossip should you disappear for hours at this time of night. Also, if you leave, the chances increase that Lady Deoiridh's absence and Barbeau's will be noticed. Even speculation about such a coincidence could harm her reputation. In addition, your wife might worry enough to try to follow."

"I don't like it, but you are right," Somerville acknowledged. "We must swear to secrecy the men Robin gathers to assist you. All of them with military experience."

"Good." Fontus turned to Robin. "Have horses saddled, and tell your men to meet me at the stable yard in five minutes. If we act quickly, we may yet be able to stop Barbeau." Could they? They must. The alternative was unthinkable.

"I will alert the men, then catch up with you. I have something vital I need to retrieve."

A considerable while later, Fontus despaired of ever finding Dee or Barbeau. The flambeaux and lanterns each man carried scarcely pierced the gloom, and a mist rose in the hollows. He would welcome a storm with its flashes of lightning. Fog would limit vision and deaden sound.

They had already passed three potential locations at Robin's insistence Barbeau would not use them.

Fontus feared they were running out of time. The only sources of hope he'd discovered were the ragged pieces of material found every few miles. He would not have that, had not Robin been so eagle-eyed as to notice the small patches of deeper darkness lying where no such patch belonged.

They paused at a fork in the track they followed while Robin and one of the other men searched each pathway for signs.

"He definitely took the right fork," Robin announced as he resumed his saddle.

Then they set off again. The pace was agonizingly slow. However, Robin assured Fontus care was necessary not to miss any sign of Barbeau's passing.

"What about the smuggler's croft?" One of the men said to Robin.

"A good point," Robin said. "Undoubtedly, Barbeau has hidden them away close to the river for easy access to any craft he's hired to take him from England. The best place for that is not widely known."

"Hence the reason smugglers use it," the fellow commented.

"Precisely." Robin described the hovel near the river where he believed Barbeau hid his captives. "If he expects the smugglers to help him, he'll be sorely disappointed. They had a run-in with Captain Moonlight recently, and are lying low."

All the men checked their weapons. Torches and lanterns were doused. Then they proceeded into the woods following Robin in single file.

"Look." Fontus whispered. "There's a curricle badly hidden in those trees." He pointed to his left. The carriage appearing in such an odd place gave him hope that they were close to finding Dee and her mother.

A few yards more, and they arrived at a structure, more hovel that croft.

"I suggest we surround the building then wait in the trees for one or more of the men with Barbeau to leave," said Robin.

"The problem is that we do not know how many underlings the villain hired or how loyal they are to the gold he promised them," Fontus replied. "Were I him, I'd not trust more than two or three men at most."

"I agree," Robin said. "Patience is our ally. We can seize them one at a time."

"That could take all night," Fontus warned.

"Not so. Once the first man fails to return, the second will emerge sooner to check on him. The same with the third, if there is one."

"Very well. Your logic is sound enough, if the men behave as you expect."

Robin chuckled again. "I know criminals and their behavior quite well. If we are lucky, Barbeau will also leave the women to learn what happened to his men. If not, we will rush the building and try to take him down before he can harm anyone."

Positioning themselves behind thick brush and trees surrounding the hut they waited.

Beside Robin, Fontus fidgeted.

"Be still," his friend whispered. "It won't be long now."

Whisps of fog drifted across the small clearing.

Eventually, the door opened with a loud creak. Two men left the structure together. They paused a moment before the closed door. Fontus could not hear what they said. Moments later they left, each man in the opposite direction.

"How odd," murmured Robin.

The thin man walked in their direction. The massive fellow marched off toward the nearby river.

Once the thin man stepped within the tree line, Fontus attacked, striking him with the butt-end of his pistol. The man dropped, unconscious.

"Here," Robin handed Fontus two long leather straps. "Use these to secure his hands and feet."

Fontus peered at the leather. "You always carry spare belts with you?"

Robin shrugged.

One of their men eased in close to them. "We had some trouble with the other fellow. However, he is now trussed like a chicken and sleeping. He'll wake with a severe headache."

"As will this fellow." Robin pointed out their captive. "Have some of the men to remove our prisoners. Leave them in that curricle we passed on the way in. We'll take care of them when we finish our business."

"How many more do you think wait in the hut?" Fontus asked.

"I suspect it is only our villain and his captives," Robin replied.

"Then send the rest of Somerville's men with our prisoners. The three of us should be able to subdue one man, even more than one."

The other man left and returned quickly.

"I insist on going in first," Fontus said.

"We will be right behind you," Robin confirmed

Fontus took one step toward the hovel when shouting came from that direction followed by the crack of a pistol shot.

"Dee!" Fontus dashed forward. He flung the door open and ran inside.

CHAPTER 12

The forest, while Fontus searches for Dee

How long they traveled from Normanton House Dee could not tell with so little light.

"I'm surprised you made no attempt to hide your destination. Now if I get a message out, I can tell my rescuers where to come."

"Shut up." Barbeau gathered the reins in one hand and struck her with the back of the other before resuming full control of the horses. "Time is too short to send messages, so what you know doesn't matter," he snarled.

Her cheek smarted, and her jaw ached. Nonetheless, Dee hid her smile. He was on edge. She set her mind to figuring out more ways to get him to lose control. If he lost control, he would be careless, and might present her an opportunity to attack.

The curricle turned into a lane nearly obscured by surrounding brush.

The dirt track was so narrow tree branches scraped the sides of the open carriage, forcing Dee to move closer to Barbeau.

The horses slowed.

Barbeau cursed the pair and whipped them. Instead of moving faster the steeds halted completely.

Muttering more curses, he leapt to the ground, came around the carriage, and offered his hand. "We'll walk from here."

Should I fight? A struggle here will delay him.

"Don't," Barbeau warned.

"Don't what?" She blinked all wide-eyed innocence.

"Don't resist." He reached up, dragging her from her perch.

He left her for a moment to force the horses and curricle into too small a space between the trees.

Should I run? No. Mother needs me.

He made no attempt to hide the vehicle more and returned to her side before she could change her mind.

"I instructed my compatriots to do what they will with your mother if I do not arrive when expected."

She swiveled her head but saw nothing other than darkness and even darker tree trunks.

"Where is our destination?"

"You'll know soon enough." He grabbed her arm and shoved her forward along the track." Get moving."

She was forced to lift her skirts and run to avoid falling on her face. Once she steadied, she kept the rapid pace, eager to put others, even his own men, between her and Barbeau.

How many henchmen did he have? Surely not more than one or two. The more people he involved, the less secure his plans. One of his so-called compatriots might already have betrayed him.

She heard the sound of running water, and Barbeau dragged her to a stop.

He studied the forest to the south.

"Ah, there."

She was pushed into motion once more. Unable to see where she stepped, she entered the trees with caution. Barbeau followed.

Eventually the trees thinned to reveal a very small clearing and hovel.

She could see no windows or openings, just the wooden door.

Beyond the hut she heard the rush of a river. Darkness prevented her from seeing the water. She peered in the direction of the sound.

"Yes, there is a river, as deep as this night is dark and very fast," her captor uttered. "I don't recommend it as a means of escape. Of course, you could choose to drown instead of marrying me and saving your mother. I will still make a profit."

She let him think she was desperate enough to consider suicide. She'd actually been contemplating murder. She was a strong swimmer and willing to take her chances. But was Barbeau?

Arriving at the door, he knocked in a complicated pattern.

The door opened. "'Bout time ye came back. We was startin' t' worry."

"Your job is to follow orders. Leave the worry to me." Barbeau chastised. Then he bowed to Dee and extended his arm.

"Ladies first," He mocked.

Dee crossed the dirt lintel.

Remaining outside, Barbeau closed the door behind her.

Inside, Dee discovered an iron stove in the center of the structure. Walking further within and finally able to see by the glow of the fire in the stove's grate, she noted two men. The one who opened the door was thin and possessed of dirty red whiskers. The other was massive. His head was bald, and his nose was crooked. He stood guard over her mother. Mother sat on the dirt floor, bound and gagged in a back corner farthest from the heat.

"Mmph." Lady Aitken made to rise.

"Sit down, yer Ladyship." Baldy ordered, shoving Mother's shoulder to add emphasis.

"Unhand her," Dee ordered and rushed to hug her mother. "Mother! Are you well? Are you hurt?"

Lady Aitken cast an accusatory glare at her daughter.

"Oh, I'm sorry." Dee removed the gag and released the knots that bound Mother. "Water," she ordered to the air.

Whiskers leapt to comply and left the hut. He hadn't questioned if he should take orders from her. Nor had Baldy done more than sneer at his partner's eagerness to please.

He returned in a trice with a tin cup, which he offered to Mother

As Mother took her first sip, Barbeau entered the hut.

"Go get the preacher," he ordered Whiskers. To Baldy he said, "Go down to the dock and signal our friends. Their passengers are ready to leave."

The henchmen left.

Dee didn't like having the men in different places. Of course, they might be easier to take down, one at a time. Not knowing how much time she had, she bent low and whispered to her mother. Under cover of their skirts, she slipped Mother one of her two pistols.

"Stop that whispering," Barbeau shouted. "Sit over there." He pointed Dee to a large rock on the opposite side of the stove.

Dee complied.

From her seat, she watched Barbeau pace. He occasionally thrust his hands through his hair and muttered unintelligibly to himself.

Long, silent moments passed with Barbeau pacing from one end of the small building to the other.

He paused once and stamped his foot. "Where are they? Those fools should be back by now."

Dee had no idea what the problem might be, but now was the time to act. She nodded at her mother.

Mother gave a nod of her own and rose.

Barbeau turned to pace back in their direction at the same moment. "What are you doing? Sit down." He grabbed Dee by the hair.

Dee could not restrain a wince and a small whimper.

"How dare you hurt my daughter." Lady Aitken lifted her pistol and fired.

The shot caught Barbeau high on his left shoulder. The force of the impact compelled him to release Dee, stumble backward, and fall.

Dee leapt on him. She bashed his skull with the butt end of the pistol she'd kept.

Barbeau went limp.

Lady Aitken ran to hug her daughter

"Oh Mother, did I kill him?"

"I don't think so," a wry voice said from the doorway.

"Fontus!" She rushed to him. He folded her in his arms and kissed her.

Robin and their compatriot squeezed past the couple.

"I am glad to see you, Robin Somerville," Lady Aitken said.

On the floor, Barbeau groaned.

Neither Dee nor Fontus noticed, too wrapped in each other and their kisses.

"Lady Aitken, please hand me those lines." He indicated the bonds that had once held her captive.

"Of course." She handed the ropes over with a grin.

"Thank you. While I take care of our injured friend, perhaps you could recall your daughter and her husband to our present circumstances."

"Husband?"

"Ah, forget I mentioned that. I am sworn to secrecy and spoke carelessly."

She laughed. "Not wise for a highwayman."

"How did you know?"

"It isn't difficult to learn the truth if one watches when you are gone and when the Captain rides."

"I have retired." He knelt beside the fallen man.

"Bien. Nonetheless, I regret I shall not have an encounter with Captain Moonlight to tell to my grandchildren." Lady Aitken crossed the room, leaving Robin to deal with Barbeau.

Robin rolled the villain onto his belly.

"Owww."

"It is your own fault for attempting to abduct women more than capable of defeating you on their own." He secured Barbeau's wrists behind his back. Then performed a similar action at the man's feet.

On the other side of the room, Lady Aitken tapped Fontus's shoulder.

"Ahem, *Monsieur*, unhand my daughter."

Fontus lifted his head, gifting his mother-in-law with a beatific smile. "It's all right. We are married."

Lady Aitken attempted to repress a smile. "So, you say. However,

I've not seen the marriage lines nor heard my daughter say she is wed to you."

Dee looked at her mother then rested her head on her husband's chest. "We are wed, Mother. Truly, Fontus has every right..."

"Perhaps," the lady replied. "However, for a husband, he neglects you shamefully. Are you certain you wish to be married to him? Louis could probably persuade the pope...."

Dee gazed up at Fontus.

His heart in his throat, he stared back.

"Do you wish to remain my husband?" Her expression and tone gave no clue as to her own desires.

"With all my heart, forever and always."

"There, Mother. You see he wants to be my husband."

"And what of you, daughter? What of your wishes?"

"Yes, my love, do you wish to remain my wife?" Fontus asked.

She saw fear in his eyes and could not bear to tease him.

"With all my heart, my love. I will be your wife forever and always."

He kissed her.

Her mother shook her head and turned back to Robin.

"These two will be of no help," she muttered.

"Then you must assist me, Madame, please." He gestured to a sack at his side.

"How?"

"Hold Barbeau upright while I dress him in my Captain Moonlight's garb."

Lady Aitken smiled. "You are very clever, Sir Robin. If everyone believes him to be Captain Moonlight, no one will believe a word he says about abducting me or my daughter."

"I have retired my pistols for more law-abiding activities."

"*C'est dommage.* I would so enjoy a kiss from the mysterious Moonlight."

He grinned at her. "Alas, my kisses are promised elsewhere."

"Ah, it was not meant to be. Let us get this canaille on his feet, and arrange for the homeward journey."

They dressed Barbeau in Captain Moonlight's cloak, gloves, mask and hat.

"It is good that you and our prisoner are of similar builds," Lady Aitken remarked.

"Indeed," Robin agreed. "Now he is properly attired, I can take care of Barbeau, if you will recall your daughter and her husband to reality."

"Certainment."

"Then I bid you adieu, madame."

"You will not return to Normanton House with us?"

"I think it best if everyone believes I was otherwise occupied all night. I shall see you in the morning."

EPILOGUE

Normanton House, the evening of the ball that ends the house party

Dee waltzed for the third time with her husband. A short conversation with the Duke of Leigh, who had arrived the day before, assured them that Lord Sandrow had accepted, with very little protest, an alternative arrangement for Lady Beatrix's future.

Indeed, the life peer had spent much of the evening whispering to the Danvers sisters. Whatever Sandrow and Lovis had agreed to would be widely known by morning.

Dee did not care. She had what she wished most.

The music ceased. Fontus escorted her to the refreshment table, taking beverages for each of them.

"Will you mind greatly the life of a diplomatic wife?"

"No, I always envied my father the traveling he did on diplomatic missions for Louis. He and Mother decided that taking a child along on such journeys was not wise. So, she remained at court—the court in exile—with me."

"Do you want children, my love?"

"Eventually. However, I refuse to be left behind in England when you are assigned elsewhere."

He nodded. "Then our children must come with us."

She smiled. "I agree. Do you know where your first posting will be?"

"I spoke with Lovis this evening. He talked with the foreign secretary who said he was considering India or the former colonies. Either way, he confirmed that I would be undersecretary to an experienced diplomat for long enough to cut my teeth. What is your preference? I shall request it."

"Hmm. I think I would enjoy either posting. As long as we are together."

"Ah. Being together brings me to another topic. We need a home in England to return to from time to time. Do you prefer London or the country?"

"Both. However, I think it wisest to first find a small residence in London while we await your new assignment. You will want to be close to the Foreign Office, and I have not seen London in an age. Some school friends still live there."

"We could visit Lady Beatrix. I am not certain what Lovis suggested to Lord Sandrow, but both he and Lady Beatrix seem content enough."

"I am certain the Danvers sisters will ferret out all the details. We will learn of them tomorrow."

"Lovis informed me he must depart in the morning. Evidently there is some crisis for which Prinny wishes advice from him and the Earl of Hythe. I will ask Lovis to have his man of business search out a home for us in London."

"It won't take me long to pack up my belongings at the cottage. Most of what is there, belongs to Sir Somerville."

"If you like some of the things, I could offer to buy them from Somerville."

"There are a few items, but I only want them if you approve."

"I suggest we give our goodnights and go to the cottage now."

"To examine the furnishings?"

"Hmm, among other things." He set their drinks on a nearby tray.

"Oh," She accepted his hand as he guided them through the crowd to their hosts. "Such as?"

"Well...in a manner of speaking, one activity I want to share with you is testing the beds."

Her cheeks heated. "I like the way you think, Lord Fontus."

Watching his brother and his sister-in-law depart, Lovis smiled. He'd not expected Fontus to ever settle. Lady Dee was perfect for him. Now if only he could solve the difficulties of his other brothers. Fontus may believe that all was well with his older siblings, but Lovis, as head of the family, knew better. They were all troubled in one manner or another. The problem was they refused to share their difficulties with him. Why they insisted on keeping secrets from the one man with the power to arrange their lives was beyond him.

THE END

If you enjoyed Deoiridh and Fontus's story, and would like more about the Leigh siblings, try *A Waltz for the Wallflower*, the tale of Fontus's sister Blythe.

Since her first stumble during her first season, she hasn't been able to live down her reputation as an accident waiting to happen.

Years after that unfortunate waltz, he still wishes he could change disaster into delight. However, she won't give him a chance. Can polar opposites find love together?

SOCIAL MEDIA FOR RUE ALLYN

You can learn more about Rue Allyn on these social media links:

Bluesky: https://bsky.app/profile/rueallyn.bsky.social
BookBub: https://www.bookbub.com/authors/rue-allyn
Facebook: https://www.facebook.com/RueAllynAuthor
Goodreads: https://www.goodreads.com/author/show/5031290.
Rue_Allyn
Pinterest: https://www.pinterest.com/rueallyn/

ABOUT RUE ALLYN

Award winning romance author, Rue Allyn has a life-long passion for happy ever after. She lives south of the border with her husband of more than forty years and their cat, Tanto. She has two sons and is a proud veteran of the US Navy. She writes heart melting romance in all sub-genres, but her favorite is historical romance, especially medieval.

Follow Rue Allyn on FaceBook, BookBub or BlueSky @rueallyn.bsky.social. Or keep up with her activities and **Subscribe to Rue's News where you may learn more about Rue and receive a FREE download https://www.rueallyn.com/subscriber-entered-from-online-profile/**

Learn more about Rue at:
Website: https://RueAllyn.com

THE CASEBOOK OF
PRINCIPAL OFFICER ROBERT
PIERCE

Brighton and surrounding districts

Captain Moonlight is in custody. Or, at least, that is what his cloak and mask suggest, and that is the evidence of those who captured him. The man himself denies it, but he would, wouldn't he?

The prisoner is certainly a villain. I have heard the evidence of his crimes, some of which cannot be prosecuted without damage to a lady's reputation. I am pleased to have him in custody, and if he hangs as a highwayman, it will be just recompense for his sins against the lady.

Captain Moonlight's career is over. I know this to be true, and that, in the end, is what matters.

A BEND IN THE ROAD

JUDE KNIGHT

A Bend in the Road
By Jude Knight

Justin is not worthy of Lady Felicity Belvoir. He hadn't needed her brother to point it out. Felicity is determined to marry Justin Weatherall, her brother be damned. Now that she has found where he is living, she needs only to convince him.

CHAPTER 1

Early October

"I suppose there is no point in me begging you not to chase away all your potential suitors while you are at the house party, Felicity," said the Earl of Hythe to his sister, as the carriage turned in through the gates to Normanton Hall and began the approach to the house.

Lady Felicity Belvoir grinned at him. "I suppose there is no point in me pleading with you to choose a bride while you are in Brighton, Hythe," she retorted.

Hythe shuddered. "At Prinny's Pavilion? Hardly. And you would not thank me if I did, Felicity, as you well know."

She chuckled, but she did know. Indeed, it was because of the Prince Regent and the company he gathered around him that Hythe didn't want her coming to Brighton with him.

She had been Hythe's companion and hostess in Vienna for the peace talks, in Brussels when the nations gathered there to counter Napoleon, in Paris after Waterloo, and then in London when his diplomatic duties called for his presence there. His reluctance to subject her to probable insult in the household of the ruler he served spoke volumes about his personal opinion of the man.

Had Felicity wanted to go to Brighton, she would have argued. Felicity was confident of her ability to discourage unwanted attention, even from royalty. However, she had her own reasons for accepting an invitation from Sir Peter and Lady Somerville to a house party at Normanton Hall. Indeed, unbeknownst to Hythe, she had written to Penelope, Lady Somerville, who was of an age with Felicity's sister Sophia, and therefore something of a friend.

"Hythe needs to be in Brighton for a few weeks and won't need me," she had written. "May I visit you? The children will be growing apace, and I would love to see them."

The invitation had arrived by return post. Penelope was having a house party and would be delighted to welcome her friend's sister. Felicity had not told Penelope her true motives, nor Sophia, either. A secret was best kept when it was only known to one person.

They would be at the house at any moment. "I will marry one day, Hythe," she told her brother. "And when I do, you will be in the suds! No hostess. No ear on the distaff side of the company. No chatelaine for your houses. Then, you will have to choose a wife."

The carriage drew to a halt, and Hythe used that as an excuse not to answer. Indeed, the point was unanswerable, as was the unfortunate truth that the pressure on a man to marry was less urgent than the pressure on a lady. As a wealthy and well-respected earl, Hythe would be an attractive marriage prospect well into old age. At twenty-three, Felicity would be on the shelf already, if she did not have an impeccable family name, the highest of social connections, a large dowry, and a personal fortune left to her by her maternal grandparents.

The footman opened the door and let down the steps, and Hythe bounded to the ground and offered his hand to Felicity.

Penelope was waiting at the foot of the steps leading up to the front door, and the next few minutes were devoted to the courtesies, Penelope inviting Hythe to stop for refreshments, and Hythe politely refusing for the sake of his horses, and so he could complete his journey to Brighton before nightfall.

By the time he had asked after Somerville and the Somerville offspring, and given Felicity a brotherly peck on the cheek, her luggage had been offloaded from the second carriage under the supervision of Felicity's maid, and footmen were already carrying it inside.

"I shall be on my way, then," Hythe said, with a polite bow. "Send me a message if you have need of the carriage, or anything else, my dear. Your servant, Lady Somerville."

"Let me show you to your room, Felicity," Penelope said, as the carriages retreated down the driveway. "I will leave you to freshen up, and you may join the company whenever you are ready. We are gathered in the large parlor this afternoon. I daresay you will know some of the guests. Lord Fontus Leigh? Lord and Lady Corey? Mr. Brannock? Lord Rupert Swan and his granddaughter, Lady Florence? Lord Langley?

She prattled on, with Felicity having to do little but make interested noises, but her ears pricked up when Penelope said, "We have a suitor of yours in residence, too."

Could it be that Justin had let Penelope know of his interest? But no, for her hostess continued, "Captain Vincent Grant was particularly pleased to know that you were coming, Felicity. He tells me he met you in Vienna. You have made quite a conquest there, my dear."

Grant. Bother. She supposed there was no harm in him, but she could not warm to the man. How would having him chasing after her affect her real errand? She could not think it beneficial. Justin and Grant had been at loggerheads in Brussels. Justin and Robin had both disliked the man, in fact, which did not speak well of Grant.

Was Robin here, too? "How is your brother-in-law?" she asked Penelope.

"My goodness," said Penelope. "You are not interested in *Robin*, are you?"

Felicity was not certain whether to be amused or irritated by Penelope's amazement. Robin's brother and his wife seemed to think the decorated naval hero had not changed since he was a mischievous child. "Not romantically, Penelope. But we are friends."

Penelope waved a dismissive hand. "He is living here, of course, as I am sure I've mentioned in my letters. What he gets up to I have no idea, and I am sure I do not want to know. Robin never changes. Still the same rogue as ever."

"He is a fine officer," Felicity commented, but Penelope waved a dismissive hand again.

"No doubt, but we are not at war now, and he needs to find something useful to do, Somerville says."

When Penelope quoted Sir Peter Somerville, there was no arguing with her. "I'll let you get back to your other guests, dear," Felicity said, "and I shall be down shortly."

Today's mission. Find out the program for the rest of the day and tomorrow, and what direction to walk to the schoolhouse, where Justin Weatherall had taken up the unlikely role of schoolmaster. It would have to be carefully managed, for she did not want to be missed, and she did not want company on the walk.

The road ahead of her had seemed clear before she met Justin. She was making a career out of being a diplomat's sister and expected to eventually be a diplomat's wife. But then along came Justin, and suddenly, the straight road, the safe road, was no longer enough.

She did not know what was around the bend, but she wanted to walk it with Justin.

Then... nothing. She assumed Justin had intended to send a message when he left Brussels without a word to her and disappeared from her life so completely. But what message?

I was merely an amusement. If so, her instincts had abandoned her entirely when her feelings became involved. She could have sworn his attentions were sincere. *He is afraid of commitment.* A possibility, but hopeful, for it would mean his thoughts were of marriage, and perhaps they could work through his fears. *He feels he is not worthy of me.* If he tried that one, she just might throw something at his head. Something heavy enough to knock some sense into his skull.

CHAPTER 2

Justin Weatherall dismissed the children for the day and set about straightening the schoolroom. Putting everything away where it belonged was the last task he assigned every day, but it never ceased to surprise him how much even the older children missed. A lid off an ink pot. A crumpled piece of paper tucked out of sight under the boys' table. Smoothed out, it proved to be the dart Gareth and Billy had been tossing back and forth until he caught them at it. He had wondered where that had gone.

Since there was no school tomorrow, he'd also move the chairs and tables to return the room to being a parlor. Not that he expected visitors, but he liked things to be ship-shape.

Several items went into his desk drawer for the next school day, when he would hold each one up and ask the owner to collect it. He hoped a moment of shame might make the perpetrators more careful in the future, but so far, it had not had the desired effect.

Was he expecting too much? The smallest of powder monkeys soon learned to keep his kit and his duty station immaculately tidy. Mind you, the navy used a heavy hand to enforce discipline, even on those most junior crew members. Justin had never liked the practice. Whipping or birching might enforce obedience, but it created fear and resentment, too. Justin had seen crews turn sour under the rule of a bully, and a surly crew was ripe for mutiny.

Justin would not have used birching in his schoolroom in any case, since he taught both boys and girls. No man worth his salt would raise his hand against a female, and Justin couldn't consider it fair to birch boys and not girls when they were being educated together.

"They are not a bad lot," he reminded himself. Their untidiness might offend his navy-trained sensibilities, but they were mostly good students. With a few notable exceptions.

"Milly Stone is heading for a sharp set down." Milly Stone was the daughter of the butcher, and reveled in her reputation as the prettiest girl in the village. She was fifteen, and her ambition in life was to better her mother's achievement of marrying when she was just turned sixteen and having her first child before her seventeenth birthday. Milly had set her sights on becoming the schoolmaster's bride, and was doomed to disappointment.

"Silly chit. She is half my age and has considerably less than half my wits."

As if his thoughts had conjured her up, Milly sashayed through the door, all ready for conquest. "Mr. Weatherall?" She'd either been stung by a bee or she'd been pinching her cheeks and biting her lips. Given that she had also unbuttoned the top of her dress and folded the pieces back to give herself a decolletage that would not have disgraced the seamier streets of Paris, Justin was placing his bets against the bees.

"Did you leave something behind again, Miss Stone?" He attempted to infuse his voice with both ice and long-suffering boredom. It worked about as well as he expected. Milly was impervious to hints.

"I thought I might be able to help you, Mr. Weatherall," the girl simpered, batting her eyelids so vigorously that Justin imagined he could feel the wind.

"No, thank you. It is time for you to go home."

Instead, she continued to advance across the room. "You are so diligent, Mr. Weatherall," she cooed. "So much better than our last teacher."

Justin had replaced an elderly lady who used to set the work for her pupils each morning and spend the rest of the day asleep. She had been thrilled to accept when Sir Peter Somerville, the school's patron, offered her a pension and a little cottage of her own. And Justin had been delighted to take her place—still was, Miss Stone notwithstanding.

"Mrs. Caldecott was an excellent teacher in her day, so I am told," he said. "Do run along, Miss Stone. It is not appropriate for you to be here with me when the other pupils are absent."

"I don't mind." There went the eyelashes again, stirring up a hurricane. "Da won't mind, either. He likes you better than my other suitors."

Good Lord. "Miss Stone, I am not your suitor."

Milly leaned forward to give Justin a better view of her mammary assets. "You could be, though, Mr. Weatherall. That's what I'm trying to tell you. It doesn't matter if you are poor. Da is rich, and he likes the idea of having a gentleman as a son."

Time for that set down, Justin. Pity you haven't composed one. He'd just have to improvise. "Miss Stone, even if I was in the market for a wife, I would not consider a child of half my age." *Or a chit with feathers for brains and no more idea about what marriage entailed beyond a pretty gown for her wedding and the chance to lord it over the other girls in the village.*

Another simper warned Justin that the palatable excuse had not been enough. "Da says a man is better to marry a young wife, so he can teach her how to go on."

Mrs. Stone was a timid woman completely in the shadow of her formidable husband and demanding daughter. Justin could not imagine Milly ever becoming a counterpart of her mother, no matter whom she married.

"You have my answer, Miss Stone. I will not change my mind, and if you continue to attempt to flirt with me, I shall tell your father you are learning nothing at school, which is no more than the truth, and that you should stay at home and help your mother."

For a moment, Milly looked her age, as she pouted and stamped one foot. "You are so mean," she declared.

An unexpected third voice joined the conversation. "Am I interrupting?" Every cell in Justin's body came to attention and his heart leapt, even before his eyes had confirmed what his ears had told him. Lady Felicity Belvoir!

It couldn't be, but it was. The woman his heart yearned for, despite the gulf between them.

"Miss Stone was just leaving," he told her, even while his mind was trying to babble all the reasons why it was even worse to be alone with Felicity than with Milly.

But Milly accepted her dismissal—even if with poor grace. She flounced out, Felicity moving out of the doorway to allow her passage, and if the girl had been a feline rather than the human version of the same animal, she would have hissed as she passed.

"A little young for you," Felicity observed. Did he sense a touch of possessiveness in that tone? Well. If anyone had the right, she did.

"A lot too young. Also too ignorant, too self-absorbed, too inclined to flirt with everything in trousers, too devoted to her personal appearance in lieu of any other redeeming features."

Felicity chuckled, as she walked past him. "Poor Miss Stone."

Justin inhaled the fragrance that said "Felicity" to him. Floral notes, with cedar undertones and a touch of musk, plus something indefinable that was all her own. It took him a moment to gather his wits., "Say, rather, poor Mr. Weatherall. Convincing Miss Stone of my complete lack of interest is proving to be a labor of Sisyphus. Every time I think I've routed her, she rolls right back to the bottom of the hill, and it is all to do again."

"Hmmm." Felicity seated herself at his desk, placed her reticule on it, leaned her parasol nearby, and folded her hands in her lap. He waited, but she said nothing. Just observed him from her clear blue eyes. He devoured her with his own. She shouldn't be here, said his mind, but the rest of him rejoiced in her presence.

To say he had missed her was like saying that an elephant was sizeable or that ice was cool. A totally inadequate statement to convey the full extent of the phenomenon. She was here, and the hollow place within that only she could fill was both appeased and desperate. Eased by her presence. Desperate for the closeness they had shared—was it for only a few weeks? It had seemed a lifetime. In the two years since, he had been only half alive.

Perhaps it was good she was here. For surely, he would find she did not live up to his memories of her. *She is not for you, Weatherall.*

As always where Felicity was concerned, his customary charm deserted him. "What are you doing here?" he demanded.

Her eyebrow formed an interrogatory curve. "We are to skip greetings then, and go straight to the point? I am a guest of Lady Somerville's. She and her husband are holding a house party."

She continued to gaze straight at him, her face calm, but he had been born, or so it seemed, understanding the words she didn't say.

"Did you come because you knew I was here?"

Her face changed at his question, and for a moment he saw such anguish in her eyes that his own heart clenched with pain. "You left. You gave me no reason, not even a goodbye. Not even a note. You said you would come the next day, and you did not. Then I found you were gone." She screwed her eyes shut as if to hold back tears, took a deep breath and composed herself. "I need to know what changed."

What changed was that he'd come to his senses. And yes, it had been a coward's part to creep away without speaking to her, or at least writing. The Earl of Hythe, her brother, had assured him he would soon be forgotten, especially if he simply left and said nothing. But Hythe did not know what had transpired between them. He should have ignored Hythe, insisted on staying to see her one last time.

"I owe you an apology," he conceded.

The lady gave no quarter. "You owe me an explanation."

"Come then." He would show her. He unlocked the door between the school room and his own quarters—he had kept it locked on schooldays since the day Milly Stone had been waiting for him in his bedchamber, sitting at his desk and leafing through his personal correspondence.

"Come this way. This is how I live. It is what I can afford, Lady

Felicity." During most of their acquaintance in Brussels, they had been on first-name terms, but he needed the reminder of her social status, far, far above his. "It comes with the position—one bedchamber upstairs, a small parlor that doubles as the schoolroom, a kitchen. I have enough for my needs, but any wife and family are far outside of my reach, let alone a wife like you."

He expected another sardonic comment, or perhaps an explosion of temper. She had one, as he had cause to know. Her question was asked in a contemplative tone, however. "An expensive wife, you mean?"

"Any wife, but particularly a well-born lady used to every elegance and comfort." And what was wrong with that? He lived in three rooms and was paid very little. Not enough to feed a wife as well as himself. And certainly not enough to pay a servant to cook and clean, even if he had room enough to house one. And yes, he had savings. But they would soon diminish if he tried to live beyond his means.

Just in case she had missed the point, he repeated it. "I cannot afford a wife."

There went the eyebrow again. "And this is the reason you abandoned the field? And me? Justin, whether I might agree to live in a three-room cottage with you is not a question we need to entertain. Or, at least, I had not thought you one of those arrogant fools who refuses to allow his wife to spend her own money on her own comfort and his."

So, Hythe had not told her. "Hythe will not pay your dowry if he does not approve of your husband," he explained. "And he made it very clear that he does not approve of me."

Both eyebrows shot up, signaling her surprise. "Hythe told you that?" She narrowed her eyes and her right hand drifted up to the desk, where she set one finger drumming, a single slow beat, as if setting the time for a funeral march. Hythe's funeral? Or Justin's?

"I cannot decide whether I am more cross at you, Justin, for discussing marriage with Hythe but not with me, or with Hythe, for telling you fairy tales."

Both of us, then.

She sighed. "If you had told me this in Brussels, two years ago, I could have explained that yes, Hythe could be silly about my dowry, though he would catch cold at that soon enough, but he does not control the bulk of my fortune. Or, at least, he is one trustee of three. And even if all three agreed to withhold my principal, the income has been mine absolutely since I turned twenty-one, and both dowry and principal come under my complete control when I am twenty-five."

With a casual wave of the hand, she dismissed his living conditions as an argument. "Your poverty is not an adequate argument for ignoring the promise of what we had together. You said you loved me, Justin, and that you wanted to be with me forever. I believed you meant it. At the time."

And to this day. Only the most iron of control kept him from falling on his knees at her feet and repeating his promises from two years ago. But his eyes must have spoken for him, for her expression softened. "You still have feelings for me," she said.

It was not a question, but he answered it anyway. "I cannot be your kept man."

"Good. Because I do not need a pet." She stood with a rustle of skirts, and picked up her parasol and reticule. "I have an opening, however, for a partner, a friend, a lover, a spouse."

"Justin! Just!" It was Robin Somerville's voice, and a moment later, Justin's dearest friend and former captain poked his head around the door from the schoolroom. "I beg your pardon. Oh, it is you, Lady Felicity. Good day."

"Good afternoon, Captain Somerville." Felicity had retreated behind her company manners. "You wanted Lieutenant Weatherall. I shall leave the two of you to your business. Lieutenant, we shall resume this conversation."

Justin bowed. "Lady Felicity."

She inclined her head to each of them in turn, and then left the room. Justin followed her out, and watched her exit the cottage and shut the door behind her. Robin prowled after him. "I thought you said she was no longer interested in you," he commented.

"That is what her brother said. Apparently, he was mistaken."

"Be careful," his friend warned. "I remember what you were like after Brussels. I'd hate to see her take you up and drop you again like last time."

"It wasn't like that," Justin protested. "I left her. Her brother said... But I was wrong not to tell her I was going. The fact is, Hythe was right. She is not for me, Robin. A lovely lady like that? An earl's daughter, and independently wealthy?" He shrugged. "She doesn't understand."

"I cannot say that I do. If she wants to marry you and you want to marry her, why not?" Robin waited for Justin's response, but he didn't have one. After a moment, Robin continued. "I just found out she had arrived, so I came to tell you. And I'll tell you something else that will interest you."

Justin didn't think he was likely to be interested, but Robin clearly wanted him to ask, so he did. "What?"

"I told you that Victor Grant was invited. My sister-in-law tells me that he is here as a suitor for Lady Felicity."

"Bloody hell." Not Victor Grant. Of all the people on the planet, Grant was the last man Justin ever wanted to see again, and he certainly didn't want the man anywhere near Felicity.

"My thoughts exactly," Robin said.

CHAPTER 3

Apparently, Captain Grant could not bring himself to believe that Felicity meant the firm 'no' with which she had greeted his proposals in Paris in 1815 and again in 1816, and the proposal that followed in London. He showed every sign that he was going to try a fourth during this house party. What a nuisance the man was!

He must have shared his intentions with Penelope Somerville, for he was assigned to take Felicity in to dinner two nights in a row, and when they travelled into the village to patronize the local shops, Penelope sent Felicity to ride in a curricle driven by Captain Grant.

He also followed her around, partnering her in every two-person activity if she had not been quick enough to find another partner, joining any group she was in, sitting next to her at tea, and constantly speaking to and about her as if they were an established couple.

She managed to deflect any attempts on his part to turn the conversation in a personal direction, and truly, if it came to the point, she would simply refuse him again. But it was exhausting.

Also annoying, for she had had no opportunity to make another visit to the schoolhouse, and Justin had not tried to see her. Robin, too, was playing least in sight, so she could not even recruit him to either carry a message to Justin or run interference with Captain Grant so she could be her own messenger.

"Penelope," Felicity said to her hostess after breakfast on the third morning of the house party, "Please stop pairing me with Captain Grant. I do not wish him to think I might be amenable to his courtship."

"But darling," Penelope replied, "Captain Grant has done me the courtesy of discussing his intentions towards you, and they are everything honorable. He is a gentleman of means, and while his father's family is nothing to speak of, his mother's people are mostly highly connected. Most highly indeed."

"Captain Grant has already proposed several times, Penelope. I have refused and will continue to do so."

Penelope could not understand it. "But Felicity, you cannot have thought. He is most eligible, I assure you, and so elegant in his manner. I cannot see any objection. Indeed, I am certain the Earl of Hythe and your sister Sophia would be most distressed if I failed to urge you to reconsider."

Penelope was quite out, there. Hythe disliked Grant, though he had declined to discuss why, which left Felicity with the impression it was to do with the secret work Hythe sometimes did under cover of his diplomatic positions. And Grant was not popular with Sophia, either.

"I have nothing personal against the man, Felicity," Sophia had said. "But I cannot warm to him. And His Grace has warned both me and James against becoming too familiar with Captain Grant, so I daresay he knows something to the man's discredit." His Grace was the Duke of Winshire, father to Sophia's husband James, the Earl of Sutton.

Even if Felicity had been partial to Captain Grant, she must have questioned her inclination once she discovered he had come to the attention, and not in a good way, of her brother and her sister's father-in-law, both of whom were active in His Majesty's service.

She could not tell Penelope any of that. It was probably some sort of top secret, and she did not have details, in any case.

"Neither my brother nor my sister would want me to marry

where I felt no affection, Penelope. Indeed, and I know I can rely upon your discretion—I cannot like the man. No doubt a fault in me, but there it is. I am certain you would not wish me to pursue an acquaintance with a person I dislike, for you are so very fond of Sir Peter, and he of you."

Penelope frowned, wrinkling her nose as if she might be about to cry. "Oh dear. Are you certain? Only, he seemed so certain you were merely showing maidenly reserve, and that his persistence would win you." She sighed. "I did think it romantic he would try and try again."

I find it disturbing. "I am certain. And truly, Penelope? Maidenly reserve? You have known me since I was eleven!"

Penelope giggled like the girl she had been when she first became friends with Sophia. "I suppose you are right, darling. You have always been very confident."

Not when she was eleven, and Sophia, Penelope and a cluster of other girls had been eighteen. Felicity had felt jealous, because Sophia, who had been both sister and mother to her since their own mother died, was part of a giggling group that Felicity was too young to join. Then, when she was eighteen herself, she found that giggling over ribbons and beaux did not appeal to her after all.

Penelope sighed again. "Oh dear, I did hope you had finally found a husband, Felicity."

So did Felicity. And it was not Captain Grant.

⬥

This stretch of the Brighton to Chichester Road had two advantages for a pair of highwaymen. It was isolated, with no dwellings for several miles in either direction. It was bordered on both sides by mixed stands of oak, elm and beech, with hazel, gorse, hawthorn and holly forming an understory.

As they waited for their quarry, Justin wondered what on earth he was doing here. It was not as if he hadn't tried to convince Robin this was a very bad idea. For one thing, they had agreed to stop just a few days ago, after a run-in with a revenuer and a group of smugglers threatened to disclose their identity. For another, rumor had it that there was a thief-taker out, determined to capture Captain Moonlight and win himself a fine reward and a place in history.

But Robin was determined, and Justin hadn't let Robin go into danger alone since they were midshipmen together. The cause was just. Robin was right about that. Their target was the steward of an absentee landlord.

He had been using his position to try to force one of his employer's tenants into an affair with him, telling the poor widow that he'd forgive the rent in return for her compliance. Each time she refused, he put the rent up.

Justin had found out and told Robin, and together they had found a new place for the widow and her two children—a position as housekeeper for another more prosperous widow, which came with accommodation. To Robin, it wasn't enough. He had discovered that the steward would be travelling back from Brighton this evening, and he wanted to teach the man how it felt to be powerless and threatened with disgrace.

What would Felicity think if she knew all? She had a wild streak, Justin knew that. She'd probably cheer Robin on. She hadn't been back since that day at the schoolhouse. Had she given up on him? It would be for the best, whatever his heart said.

And here came another carriage—only the third since they had been waiting. The threat of rain was keeping most people at home.

"It's him," Robin reported. He nudged his horse out of the trees and onto the road verge. Justin, watching from the gloom under the trees, saw the driver realize Robin was there. He moved, reaching for something, but Robin spoke before he could complete the movement. "Don't try it. I would prefer not to shoot you. Put your hands in the air and keep them there. My companion back there..." he indicated Justin with a wave of his head... "is an even better shot than I am."

The coachman cast a frantic glance at the shadows where Justin sat on his horse, and raised his hands. Justin rode forward to the head of the carriage horses, so they could not take off and spoil the fun.

Robin headed his horse along the verge and around the back of the carriage, to come up beside the door. He turned the handle and backed his steed before the door could swing open. They'd learned that trick on their second hold up, when the lady inside the carriage had hurled the contents of a *bordeleau* into Justin's face as soon as he opened the door.

"Come out with your hands up," he growled.

It all went smoothly after that, until it didn't. The steward was the only passenger in the coach. He handed over his purse with only a small bit of bluster. Under Robin's stern gaze and unwavering pistols, he stripped to his shirt, though he blustered a great deal more, threatening all kinds of retribution. When Robin instructed him to begin walking to the next village, he decided to make a stand.

"I will not," he said.

Uh oh. Robin had been a ship's captain for too many years to ignore such mutiny. He fired one of his guns, hitting the ground near the steward's feet, so that the man's bare shins were peppered with flying dirt.

The man set off at a run, but while Robin and Justin had been distracted by the steward, the coachman had found his courage and his weapon. He fired, and might have killed Robin if Robin's horse had not taken exception to his sudden movement. Its nervous side-step meant the shot missed.

Good. No one was meant to get hurt, especially not Robin. Still, Justin couldn't let the man hurt his friend, for the coachman was aiming again. The weapon must be double-barreled. Justin pulled his own trigger, aiming to crease the man's arm, and an oath proved he'd hit his mark, but it wasn't enough for the man, for he swung toward Justin and fired again.

Justin felt half a dozen sharp stings and flinched. *Damn*, he thought. *I've been shot.* Just then his horse shied sideways and tossed him. As he fell, he was vaguely conscious of the coach thundering past. The blast past their ears must have spooked the carriage horses.

He landed badly, his head thudding onto something hard. Hurt tumbled down on him—a thunderous pain exploded across his head, sharp stabs of agony lancing inward. He could hear Robin saying something. His voice seemed to come from very far away. Justin couldn't make out any of the words. He tried to tell Robin that, but darkness reared up and swallowed him.

⚜

Felicity went up to bed tired after another purposeless and dull day. She had avoided Grant as well as she could. She supported Penelope by pretending enthusiasm for the series of games the poor hostess had substituted for the outdoor games that had been cancelled by the rain. She did her best not to groan or fall asleep in the face of endless conversations about nothing at all.

The tiredness she claimed as her excuse to leave the drawing room was real. But it seemed to have faded into nothing by the time her maid had unlaced her and taken down her hair.

"Thank you, Carson. I shall read for a while," she said. "Have an early night yourself. You've certainly earned it."

She had brought books with her, but she had finished two of them and couldn't settle to either of the others. The attempt had eaten up perhaps half an hour. She sat and wrote a description of her day in the letter she was writing to her sister Sophia, making it much funnier in writing than it had been in reality. Another half hour.

Outside of her room, she could hear the murmur of voices and other sounds of people passing her room. The company must have broken up for the night. Felicity walked to the window. The rain had stopped at long last, but the night was still overcast, and she could see nothing but a sprinkling of lights off to the left. The stable block was there, with its loft accommodation for grooms. Otherwise, the world might be empty.

Felicity tried one of the rejected books, but it still failed to catch her attention. She blamed Grant. And Justin. Too many unresolved problems turning somersaults in her head. She could do with a cup of tea. "I wonder if someone is up in the kitchen." Probably not. But there was port in the library. She'd seen it there. If she went down to the library, she could get herself a book to read.

The noises of people seeking their bedchambers had ceased, though there was always a risk of meeting someone who was seeking someone else's bed.

What if she ran into Grant? Or some other amorous idiot with a yen for her dowry? But was she going to let fear rule her actions?

"No," she said, decisively. She exchanged the light robe she was wearing for a warm gown that she could do up without assistance from her maid. There. At least she would not be roaming the halls in night attire. Into the pocket she'd had sewn into the gown, she put her small muff pistol. Fully loaded, so Grant had better stay in his own room, and leave her alone!

She encountered no one as she walked through the hall and down the stairs. In the library, she lit a few candles from the one she'd brought to light her way. The port was right where she expected, and she poured herself a glass. Now for something to read.

She browsed along the shelves, with her glass in one hand and the candle in the other, stopping from time to time to put both down so she could examine a particular book. Finally, she settled on *The Abbess*, by W.H. Ireland, which she'd heard about. The library had all four volumes of the gothic romance. *I'll read a chapter, and if I like it, I'll take volumes 1 and 2 up to my room.* Felicity settled into a chair with her port, her candle and the first volume.

She was absorbed in the narrative when a sound attracted her attention and she looked up to see Robin Somerville just inside the door.

"Captain Somerville," she said in greeting. "I have not seen much of you today."

"Good evening, Lady Felicity. I saw the candle and wondered who was up," he said, approaching closer. "Trouble sleeping?"

Felicity gave a sound of assent. "I thought I'd read for a while."

"The port might help, too," he teased, even as he walked to the decanters on the nearby table. "I was looking for brandy, though. Ah, this will do." He lifted the decanter. "Yes, I'll take this."

Felicity put the book and her glass to one side and lifted her candle. Those marks on his arm were surely just shadows? She moved closer, then bent to examine them more closely. "That looks like blood. Are you hurt? Do you need help?"

Robin waved a dismissive hand. "A few scratches. Most of the blood isn't mine."

With her candle closer, she could see holes in his coat on the other shoulder from the bloodied arm. "You've been shot at. A poacher, Robin?"

"It is nothing, truly. Felicity, do you know where Penelope might keep dressings?"

"The housekeeper keeps them in a basket in the still room." An errant thought had her asking, "Who needs a dressing?" It couldn't be Justin. He must be safely tucked up in bed in his cottage, but the thought wouldn't go away.

Robin turned his head. "I must get back to my patient," he told her, ignoring the question.

It *was* Justin! Something about the way Robin avoided her eyes, made her certain. Or perhaps it was the way the restlessness that had affected her all evening suddenly coalesced into a pain in her heart. "What exactly are his injuries? I shall get what you need, and I am coming with you."

"Nothing too serious. A bang on the head that knocked him out for a few minutes, but he was conscious when I left him. Several shallow bullet wounds, some with projectiles still in them. The co— the villain was using a blunderbuss, so one shot, many projectiles. He has had worse, Felicity. We both have. I can handle it."

Hardly the point. Even a scratch could kill if the sufferer contracted wound fever, and bangs that knocked people out could also have dire consequences.

"So can I," she said. "Remember Waterloo?"

She and Justin had volunteered to assist the wounded, and had spent nearly three days in the houses that had been turned into field hospitals for those streaming back into Brussels after the battle. Hythe and Robin had been co-opted as messengers and spent the same days riding flat out across the landscape.

Robin narrowed his eyes at Felicity and must have seen how determined she was. "As you will."

Felicity ran upstairs for shoes and a cloak, then searched the still room for the supplies she needed, which she put into a basket. What had they been doing that got them shot?

She met Robin in the kitchen, where he had put together another basket, with the brandy and some food for Justin's larder.

"Ready?"

"Ready," she said.

He opened the door that led to the stable-yard. "This way. Are you willing to ride pillion? I don't want to wake any of the grooms."

"I can." Felicity had assumed they would walk, but a horse would be faster, at least one that was already saddled and bridled.

Robin had a horse hitched to a post just beyond the kitchen courtyard. He put the baskets on top of a wall. He then linked his hands for her foot, tossed her up, mounted and settled into the saddle behind her.

It was easy to collect the baskets from the top of the wall. The horse set off at a fast, smooth walk, and a few minutes later, she was dismounting outside the schoolhouse.

Justin was sitting on a chair in his bedchamber, dressed for riding, still in boots. He had his head tilted up and his eyes shut, but he lowered his chin and opened his eyes as they entered. She noted his wince. The movement had clearly hurt.

"I've brought reinforcements," Robin said. "Lady Felicity, I'll get you some hot water. Is there anything else you need?"

"More light," Felicity ordered. "Justin, how many fingers am I holding up?"

"Two," Justin said, correctly.

Good. "Show me all the places that hurt," she told him, "and we'll decide what needs attention first."

Robin lit a lamp and all the candles on a five-branch candelabra. "Better?" he asked.

It was, and it wasn't. Felicity could see much more clearly, it was true. What she could see was that Justin looked terrible.

"Should you be here?" Justin demanded.

"Should you be wounded?" she snapped back. "If you would prefer Robin to ride off and find a physician, say so. Otherwise, be quiet and bend your head so I can see where you banged it. We'll deal with that first."

He made no further protest, but bent his head. She'd thought that would silence him, for she had put two and two together and was reasonably certain she'd arrived at four. If they'd been attacked by someone up to something nefarious—a poacher, a smuggler, or a highwayman, for example—Robin would have taken his friend straight to a doctor.

That he didn't, suggested he and Justin were the ones up to mischief. Her mind had leapt to the highwayman who had become the hero of the countryside. Justin and Robin were Captain Midnight!

Felicity found the bump, which was covered with blood and still seeping. He must have fallen on the sharp edge of a rock, for when she washed away the blood, she found a gash an inch and a half long.

Robin splashed brandy onto the gash, causing Justin to suppress an oath.

"I'm going to put in some stitches, because it is still bleeding," Felicity said. She had come provided with a suitable needle and linen thread.

Justin gritted his teeth and neither moved nor complained while she set the stitches. It got worse, though. Next, he removed his coat, waistcoat and shirt, his shoulder and arm were peppered with wounds. Her mouth dried at the sight of his naked torso, but her physical reaction subsided as she examined and cleaned the wounds. She needed to dig projectiles from nine of them. Two of those also required stitches. All of them received the brandy treatment from Robin.

Felicity had no idea how much time had passed before every hurt had been treated and bandaged, but finally she looked up from Justin and fixed Robin with a stern glare. "Your turn," she said.

Robin had been right. He had fewer wounds, and only one needed a piece of metal dug out of it. Justin declared himself happy to administer the brandy, but he was in no fit state to do it. He could barely keep his eyes open, and his hand was by no means steady. Perhaps it was the headwound, or the impact of treating his other wounds. Most likely, it was the full glass of brandy that Robin had handed him— "For internal application."

Felicity splashed each of Robin's wounds in his stead. "There," she said at last. "Nothing serious, Robin."

"Thank you, Felicity. I'll see you home," Robin offered.

Felicity studied Justin for a moment. He had succumbed to his weariness, but he did seem to be asleep rather than unconscious, for as she watched, he muttered something and shifted restlessly.

"I am staying here," Felicity told him. "Justin has had a hit on the head. He should not be left alone tonight."

"Are you certain?" Robin examined her face, as if trying to read it for doubt.

She had none. "I'll give you a note for my maid, telling her to announce that I have a headache and will not be leaving my room. That should prevent scandal. As to the proprieties, even if Justin were not sound asleep, I have no concerns about my safety in his company."

"No more you should have. He is a gentleman to the core. But I gather you realize that. There'd be no impropriety if you married him."

"He would need to be willing," Felicity pointed out.

No one had ever called Robin stupid. "Meaning that you are willing. He's proud, Felicity, and he doesn't feel good enough for you. But when the pair of you parted after Waterloo, it almost broke him. He was a sad man for a long time—perhaps ever since."

"I did not want to part," Felicity said. "But…" This was not right. She didn't need to have this conversation with Robin, but with his stubborn, prideful friend. "I hope we can work things out, Robin. That is all I am willing to say to you, when it is Justin I need to talk with."

Robin waved a hand toward the bed. "You will have him as a captive audience for a short time. I'm certain you shall make the most of it." He flashed one of his mischievous grins. "Tie him to the bed if you have to."

Felicity was just desperate enough to try it.

CHAPTER 4

Justin did not sleep for long, and he was not at all pleased when he woke and found her still there. "Felicity, if you are discovered here there will be a scandal," he pointed out. He could not bear for Felicity to suffer in the least, and certainly not for her kindness toward him.

"I shall leave early tomorrow—or today, I suppose, since it is after midnight. No reason why I should be discovered. And my maid will tell anyone who asks that I am in bed with a headache."

"Felicity." He made a scold of her name, and she copied his tone in reply.

"Justin." She put her hands on her hips and glared at him. "I am not leaving until I am sure you are not going to have ill effects from that bump on the head. You might as well resign yourself to the fact. I shall be most displeased if you make your headache worse by fretting. Now..." she pulled *The Abbess* from the bag she'd brought with her. "We can talk, or you can rest while I'll read."

With a sigh, he gave up his objections. "Tell me about your book," he said.

"It is what they call a horrid novel," Felicity told him. "The hero and heroine are trying to escape the schemes of—well, everyone else, really. Parents, secret enemies, hidden burial chambers full of torture devices. Very gothic. Rather shocking. Most unlikely." Her eyes twinkled as she added, "I am enjoying it enormously."

"Read me some," he asked. He needed some distraction from the inappropriate idea that his body was having, despite how battered it was at the moment. Having Felicity alone with him in his bedchamber was a dream come true, but not to be acted on. He was a gentleman, dammit.

"The castle of Albano," Felicity read, "situated at the north-western extremity of the Venetian Gulf..."

As distraction, it was not working. Justin was seduced anew by the magic of her melodic voice, with the laughing glances Felicity cast at him, inviting him to share her amusement at the florid text. Seduced by dreams he should not have. She had always enchanted him, from the moment he had first seen her on the deck of the yacht *Sea Mist* off the coast of some remote English village. The sling that had lifted her aboard had been caught by a rogue wave before it lifted beyond the sea's reach. He was there to welcome aboard some earl's sister, undoubtedly indignant at the wave's *lèse-majesté* and ready to blame the nearest officer—him.

Then Felicity emerged from the sling, a laughing if somewhat drenched fairy, her golden hair sparkling in the sun, but not as much as her blue eyes, and he was her slave from that moment.

They had landed their passengers in Brest, but he and Robin had travelled on to Brussels with her brother's party, for Robin had a package of documents to deliver to the Duke of Wellington on behalf of the yacht's owner and his and Robin's temporary employer, the Marquess of Glenaire.

And each day in Felicity's company had enraptured him more. On the sea voyage, he had tried hard to convince himself that she was a social butterfly, all glitter and glamour. But watching her smoothly take charge on the canal boat and the midpoint accommodation house dispelled that impression, and a few days in Brussels taught him she was a consummate hostess, a skilled politician, a stateswoman and—as he worked beside her in the make-shift hospital that received Waterloo casualties, a strong and compassionate woman.

He loved her, and living without her was living with a gaping hole where his heart should be. It was hopeless, though. He'd known that even before her brother, the austere Earl of Hythe, had pointed out they were from two different worlds. The second son of a country schoolteacher and the earl's sister? The offspring of an obscure rural family and the descendant of one of the great families of England? The unemployed naval lieutenant and the diplomat's hostess? Ridiculous. It would never work.

The cadence of Felicity's voice changed, and when he heard his name, he realized she was asking him a question. "Are you feeling worse, Justin? Do you need a compress for your head?"

He had not heard a word for several minutes, lost as he was in his own thoughts. "I beg your pardon, Felicity. I was not concentrating. My mind drifted."

"To something sad, I gather," she said.

He was certainly not going to tell Felicity that he was thinking about her. He repeated his apology. "I'm sorry. That was rude of me."

"You are excused," she replied, her eyes twinkling. "First, you have a nasty bump on the head, and second this story is by no means gripping. I suppose it is just too unlikely and the characters too unlikeable. I keep wanting to tell the heroine to stop being so agreeable! As for the hero...! I do wish people in books would simply talk to one another like rational beings."

"You should write your own gothic novel," Justin joked.

Felicity blushed and looked down at her hands.

The woman never failed to surprise. "Lady Felicity Belvoir! You have written a novel!"

She lifted her chin, her eyes steady, and said, "I am writing a novel." She raised one eyebrow as she waited for his reaction, but he caught a hint of uncertainty in her expression.

"I am impressed," Justin said. "Have you always wanted to be an author?"

The starch went out of her spine and she smiled. "That was the correct question," she said. "Yes, Justin. I have wanted to write novels since I first realized that stories were created by actual people and did not simply appear in print. My father said that I would grow out of it. I never did."

"And why should you? Other women write novels. I think you must be good at it."

Her smile widened. "I have told very few people, Justin. Sophia said how nice that I had a hobby to fill my time. Hythe commented I could pay to have it printed if I liked, but I should not use my own name, because any future husband would not like it. You are the only one who thinks I might be good at it."

Justin shrugged. Her brother and sister looked at her and saw their little sister, he supposed. "I heard some of the stories you told to amuse the children who travelled on the barge with us to Brussels. And I remember you telling me you wrote for the *Teatime Tattler.* The reports they ran about Brussels during and after Waterloo, the ones by 'a lady'—those were yours, were they not?"

"They were," she acknowledged.

"Then yes, you must be a good novelist."

Felicity, whom he'd never seen at a loss, blushed and looked down at her hands. "You are too kind," she said. But he was being honest, not kind. She was a good writer, with a gift for vivid descriptions and a deft way of eliciting the reader's sympathy.

"I would love to read it," he said, meaning every word, forgetting that he was meant to be maintaining a distance between them. "If your dream is to write novels, then you should do it."

"Part of my dream," she admitted. "I dream of a home in the country. Not a large estate, but one that is large enough to be self-supporting, and not an enormous house, either. One that is large enough for a husband who doesn't mind if I disappear for a couple of hours each day to write. Children, and sufficient servants to keep us all comfortable."

"That doesn't sound anything like the life you have been living, Felicity," he said. *Who knew that her dreams marched so closely with his?*

Felicity got to her feet, to pace from one side of the bedroom to another. "I am tired of always moving about, Justin. I love Hythe, but he needs a wife of his own. One who enjoys being a hostess to political and diplomatic guests, always on show, always having to be polite while people talk about the same boring topics over and over. Oh, it was fun and exciting to start with, and what Hythe does is worthwhile. But it is his job, not mine."

"I thought it was what you wanted." Justin's head hurt like blazes, but even through the pain, he was seeing new possibilities.

"No. It was what I could do instead of dwindling into spinster-hood when I could not imagine marrying any of the men who asked. I have been good at it, I believe, and I've enjoyed parts of it. I love dancing, and parties are fun when with friends and family. But I danced and had parties back when I was a girl and lived year-round on Hythe's estate. I've had more fun at a country assembly where I danced with shopkeepers and farmers than I have ever had at a London ball, or a Paris one, for that matter."

"Have you not met anyone you wished to marry?" Justin asked. It was incautious of him, and he knew it when she turned to face him with her eyes blazing. She let out a huff of exasperation.

"One man, but he left me without a word, and did not speak to me for two years. It was only by chance that I discovered where he was, the dastard. And so, I invited myself to Penelope's party to find out whether I had imagined what we found together, and if not, whether there was something I could do to convince him to marry me. Is there, Justin?"

Ah. He had always known she was braver than him. "You humble me," he said. "Am I a dastard, then, Felicity? I thought I was doing what was best for you. Hythe said..." Perhaps not the most felicitous of comments. Her eyes were steely, and she grimaced.

"You and Hythe decided my future without consulting me. Is that the sum of it?"

It was, pretty much.

"I don't know what to say," he confessed, feeling at a complete loss.

"Tell me your dream," she demanded. "What life do you want, Justin? To be a country schoolteacher?"

"Would you want to marry a country schoolteacher?" he asked.

"If he was you. Is that your dream?"

Justin shook his head, cautiously, because it ached like the blazes. "No, actually. I needed a way to keep body and soul together while I tried to figure out how to have my dream. I have prize money, Felicity. Not a fortune. Not enough to buy a grand estate. But maybe enough for a small struggling estate. That's my dream. A home and a position all in one. I want the life of a country gentleman, looking after my acres, working alongside my tenants, socializing with my neighbors, raising a family with my wife."

He could see it in his mind's eye, and for the past two years, the once shadowy figure of his wife in that dream had been Felicity. For two years, he had been telling himself that she would not want such a quiet life, far from the political and diplomatic power that had been her life at Hythe's side.

"I don't mind if you disappear for several hours each day in order to write," he added.

"Why, Mr. Weatherall, is this a proposal?" Felicity joked.

"Felicity," Justin's groan was a plea for mercy, and she must have realized that, for she changed the subject.

"How long have you and Robin been Captain Moonlight?"

CHAPTER 5

V ictor Grant stood in the shadow of the trees watching the schoolteacher's house. Lady Felicity Belvoir had been inside for well over an hour. Furthermore, the lights that still showed were upstairs, in what must be the bedchamber. He had just returned from a meeting with the smuggler's leader when he saw her and Lord Somerville's care-for-nothing brother emerge from the manor house. *Just as well she has not developed a* tendre *for that scoundrel. Her brother might have approved the match.*

A second son, but from a good family, Captain Somerville might have been a rival. But Lady Felicity would not throw herself away on a country schoolmaster. She knew what was owed to her bloodlines.

Victor had seen her let Captain Somerville out of the cottage— had heard her insist she could nurse Weatherall on her own, and he need not send anyone from the manor. So, she was playing lady bountiful again, as she had in Brussels. She had been praised for her dedicated nursing, and no doubt it had gone to her beautiful head, and now she thought she could do as well as a doctor.

Women were so predictable.

He thought of waiting for her to emerge, and confronting her immediately, but she might be there all night. Indeed, she probably would be! Victor Grant did not wait on the whims of a woman! He would go back to Normanton Hall, and to bed. He would have a busy day, tomorrow, with a proposal to make and a visit to Brighton to tell those fools the Fenians that he needed them in two nights' time. And then he must be up late again that night, possibly for most of the night, to pay the second half of the smugglers' fee and to watch the Fenians take delivery.

Yes, a few hours' sleep, and his valet warned to wake him early.

His valet! That was an idea. Victor would wake the man and tell him to watch for Lady Felicity's return and then wake Victor. He would speak to Felicity before he went to Brighton. It would be good to have the question of his marriage settled.

There was no scandal in Felicity nursing a sick man, but perhaps the threat of scandal might be useful. He could tell her he'd keep her presence here secret, but in return, she must marry him. Or better! He could tell the Earl of Hythe. He would have time to visit the man during his day in Brighton.

He growled at the memory of his recent interview with the Earl of Hythe. *Pay your addresses, Grant. Felicity will accept or refuse you, as pleases her.* It would serve the dastard right to be among the casualties when that ornate monstrosity the Prince Regent was building near the Brighton foreshore blew to smithereens. If the Fenians managed to pull it off, which would be a miracle.

Whoever heard of a woman being able to make up her own mind about an advantageous match? A proper lady would be guided by her family, of course, as it should be. Not what pleased her. Not her own feelings. Ridiculous.

Hythe would have to change his tune when he realized that Lady Felicity had been alone with Lieutenant Weatherall. In his bedchamber, furthermore. And once Hythe ordered Felicity to marry Victor, Victor would have it all. Her wealth, her social connections, and her delightful body in his bed.

The Fenians needed a week to set in place the explosives he was supplying. It would be as well to marry the chit before the explosion, for he did not know who was likely to take over as her male guardian, and that might cause delays he could not afford. He needed to get his hands on her dowry as soon as possible.

And if she wanted to marry Weatherall instead? Unlikely, but Victor liked to cover all possibilities. He smiled at the memory of what he had found in the schoolhouse sheds, which he had examined closely after Somerville rode away. Yes, Victor had the evidence he needed to make certain that Weatherall was locked away, and—all going well—hanged by the neck until dead.

And Robin Somerville, too. The impertinent dolt. Vincent had never liked Somerville, and the scoundrel had the nerve to dislike Vincent, and to show it. He was polite to his brother's guest, exquisitely so, treating Vincent with the kind of punctilious courtesy that shaded into mockery, and all with a twist of amused contempt.

How dare he!

It wouldn't do to be too hasty, however. Perhaps Weatherall could keep his miserable life—a threat to tell what he knew might be just what Victor needed to force Lady Felicity's compliance. He chuckled to himself. The same applied to the captain. Sir Peter Somerville, unless he missed his guess, would pay handsomely to keep his brother's impudent neck out of a noose.

◈

By the time the sun rose, Felicity was content that Justin's injuries were as minor as he had claimed. "Uncomfortable, but not dangerous or even disabling," as he himself said.

He had told her a few of his adventures with Robin as Captain Moonlight, had slept a little, and they had kissed a little.

At Felicity's request, admittedly, but Justin had agreed that, since they had kissed in Brussels, a few more kisses would not go amiss. In fact, they had done more than they had in Brussels, when he had drawn back from their first gentle and relatively innocent kiss, declared himself unworthy, and left for Brest and his ship.

The discipline of a naval officer could be annoying, Felicity decided.

The thought made her smile, for he had drawn the line firmly again last night, but she had persuaded him to move it, not once, but several times. She was walking back to Normanton Hall a virgin because she chose not to push him further—she was confident of that. It would not have been fair to use his own desire for her to force him into actions he would later regret.

It was, in any case, wise, although wisdom had been the last thing on her mind while he showed her how much pleasure her body was capable of, and how much she could give him. They had not, to her understanding, gone very far at all toward the point of no return— but how glorious it had been!

Had he taken her fully, she might not have had the willpower to stop him. She had no reservations about anticipating her marriage vows, but he had not proposed, and if he had changed his mind about how unworthy he was, he had not told her. She supposed if he had fully bedded her, he would have married her despite his reservations, but it would be wrong to trap him like that.

In any case, they should avoid doing anything that would result in her conceiving a child without a wedding ring, for there was many a slip between cup and lip, as her old nanny used to say. Felicity had known several ladies left with child and alone after a much-loved would-be husband had unexpectedly died.

She wanted Justin's children, and would delight in having them. After they were wed. If they were wed. His kisses and caresses had given her hope, but she was by no means certain that he would not elude her yet.

"One more kiss," Justin said. He had insisted on coming downstairs with her, and escorting her at least as far as the kitchen door. "I am still not happy about letting you walk home without me."

"I shall go straight back to Normanton Hall," she said. "I have my muff pistol and the sun is up. And you shall go back to bed, Justin."

"Even so," he protested.

"Go back to bed, Justin. I'll escort Lady Felicity back to Normanton Hall." It was Robin, leaning nonchalantly against the side of the shed that ran along one side of the schoolhouse's small kitchen courtyard. He straightened. "But first, I need to catch… a… *rat!*" During the last sentence, he had prowled along the barrels, old furniture, and other items littered along the base of the shed's outside wall. With the last word, he pounced, and then stood tall again, a struggling figure dangling from his hand by its neck.

No, by the back of her dress, which he held at the neck.

"What do we have here?" he asked. "Is it a rat? It seems to be a girl. But not a well-behaved girl, or she would not be creeping around the schoolyard in the early morning light." He shook the girl, who threw back her head to shriek.

Felicity, catching sight of her face, said, "Put her down, Robin. Miss Stone, you are early for school, but you might as well go home. Let the village know that Mr. Weatherall has suffered a blow to his head in a fall, and will not be teaching today."

Miss Stone, dropped on her behind, scrambled to her feet and glared at Felicity. "So what are you doing here, then? In the middle of the night with two men. Some lady you are!"

"Miss Stone, you will apologize to Lady Felicity," Justin thundered a moment before Robin snapped something similar. Miss Stone cringed. Felicity almost felt sorry for the poor girl.

"Go home, Miss Stone," Felicity commanded.

"Mr. Weatherall would have married me if you never came," Miss Stone insisted. Really? The girl was utterly deluded.

"No," Justin said. "As I have told you before, Miss Stone. I will not marry you under any circumstances. I shall, I think, need to have a conversation with your father."

"And so shall I," Robin said. "My brother will not be pleased to know about your behavior, Miss Stone."

Oh dear. They meant well, but the two men were just making things worse. The chance of her keeping quiet about Felicity's presence here this morning had already been slender, but they had just narrowed it to nothing.

Miss Stone stamped her foot, expelled an angry shout, and stalked away.

Robin raised his eyebrows. "It is good to know that Normanton village has all the usual amenities," he commented, "for there went the village idiot."

"Poor girl," said Felicity, with a surge of fellow feeling. After all, like the village beauty, she had reached out for the man she wanted. Unlike Miss Stone, he wanted her, too. And Felicity intended he should have her.

CHAPTER 6

A ll Felicity wanted was a couple of hours sleep, which was surely not too much to ask. But apparently it was. She had talked to Robin for a few minutes and then gone upstairs to find Victor Grant waiting in the hall outside of her bedchamber.

"I trust your patient has not died in the night," he said, in a tone that implied the opposite.

The best form of defense was attack. "Were you spying on me, Mr. Grant?"

"Let us say, rather, I was looking out for the lady I mean to make my bride."

"I have already refused your proposal, Mr. Grant. I will not marry you."

Grant smiled. "I think you will. I hold your reputation in the palm of my hand, Lady Felicity. One word from me, and the whole of England will know you spent the night in the schoolhouse with Weatherall. And what is he, after all? A penniless schoolmaster. Distantly related to an earl, it is true. But by no means a match for a Belvoir, one of the great families of England."

"Of the United Kingdom, Mr. Grant," Felicity informed him, lifting her chin proudly. And yes, she was proud. The Belvoirs had served king and country since there was a country, and all without scandal staining their name. Grant was mistaken if he thought his threat would work on her, however. That very pristine reputation would protect her, and if it did not? Then better retirement to the country alone than marriage to a yellow-bellied cur.

"The answer is still no," she said.

The man had not expected that. His smile slipped, and he snarled. "Then I will have no choice but to tell that Bow Street Runner who is here looking for our highwayman that Weatherall is Captain Moonlight," he said.

Felicity absorbed the blow, schooling her face to show no expression. He could not know for certain, and even if he had witnessed something incriminating, it would be his word against Justin's. And her word. She would give Justin an alibi even if she had to perjure herself. "What utter nonsense," she said.

"I am going to Brighton today, Lady Felicity. I shall call on your brother and tell him what you have been up to. He, at least, will have a care to your reputation."

Felicity managed to say, quietly, "I am of age, Mr. Grant. I will make my own choices."

"Be sure that you make the right one," Grant insisted and swaggered off, leaving Felicity far more disturbed than she would allow him to see.

Justin dragged himself out of bed to answer a thunderous cascade of knocks on his door. It was Victor Grant, who raised his brow at Justin's appearance and said, "What does the schoolmaster get when he is late for school? Six of the best? Would you like me to administer them for you?"

"Get lost, Grant," Justin said. "I have nothing to say to you." He tried to shut the door, but Grant put his boot in the way.

"I have something to say to you, however," Grant said. "You have been annoying Lady Felicity Belvoir, and I won't have it. Stay away from my betrothed."

As had often happened in battle, Justin suddenly felt very calm, very much in control, all his emotions set to one side to be picked up again on the other side of the conflict. "No, Grant. It is I who say those words to you. Stop annoying Lady Felicity. We are to be married."

The reward for sins often arrived before the payment, and so it was in this case. Grant's jaw dropped, and his attempt to speak caught on a stutter. The payment would come when Felicity discovered what he'd said. No matter. Justin would pay whatever penance she demanded, and it would be worth it for the expression in Grant's eyes.

"Nonsense," said the man, gathering his usual cloak of supercilious dignity around himself. "Marry you? You are nothing and no one. She is a Belvoir, and one of the great beauties of our age. You are penniless, and she brings a fortune with her. You were a mediocre naval officer and are now a village schoolteacher. She is used to the highest of Society and is welcome in all the courts of Europe. A marriage between you? Ridiculous."

How odd. These were the same arguments that Justin had been using, but hearing them from Grant he could see how petty they were. If Felicity loved him as he loved her, and if she wanted the life he could give her, then what else mattered?

"It is you who are ridiculous, Grant. Chasing after a woman who has already refused you several times."

"A woman has a right to be pursued," Grant said, loftily. "A sensible man does not regard it as discouragement."

"A wise man assumes a woman like Lady Felicity knows her own mind. She has chosen me, Grant. Now go away." As he said that, he gave Grant a shove to move him from the doorstep, and slammed the door in the man's face. He latched it, locked it, and—for good measure—put the bar in place.

After a few minutes, he heard Grant's horse leaving.

But before he could go back upstairs to his bed, another knock sounded, more gentle but equally insistent. By pressing his face to the window, he could just see a skirt. Not Milly again, please God, no. But the figure stepped back to glance from side to side, and when he realized it was Felicity, he could not get the door open fast enough.

"Was that Grant I saw leaving?" she demanded, as he drew her inside and shut the door to protect her from the eyes of scandalmongers. "What did he want?"

"To tell me I wasn't good enough for you," he blurted.

She raised her eyebrows and gave an unamused chuckle. "At least there is something the two of you agree about."

I hurt her. Justin supposed he must have known it before, but seeing her use humor to deflect possible hurt brought it home to him.

"I told him we are betrothed," he blurted. "I shouldn't have. Not when I haven't even asked you. I love you, Lady Felicity Belvoir. I have loved you since I first met you. For the past two years, even while I kept telling myself that it was hopeless, and that I was an arrogant bumptious fool for ever thinking I was fit to touch the toe of your shoe, I have loved you. Will you forgive this poor fool for running away without talking to you?"

Somewhere in that impassioned speech, he had caught up her two hands. He lifted them to his lips, and then said, "Will you marry me, and join me in a partnership to make our dreams come true? Will you, Felicity?"

Felicity lifted her lovely face and touched her sweet lips to his. "Yes, Justin. Yes, I will."

During the kiss, Justin lost his wits for a while, allowing Felicity to instead fill his senses, sinking into the web of desire even as he wove it. He was not ready when she drew back after several glorious minutes, but he immediately loosened his grip so that she did not feel confined.

She had an urgent matter on her mind. "Justin, if there is anything in the school's outbuildings that can be traced back to Captain Moonlight, we must hide it. Robin and I led Grant here when I came to care for you last night, and he hinted that he searched the sheds and plans to have you arrested."

"Our cloaks, hats and masks," Justin said. "Also, plain tack for

Robin's horse. His own is too distinctive to use. And if they search the schoolhouse, too, my pistol."

"Quick," said Felicity. "Let us move them. The cloaks, hats and masks first, I think. The rest can be explained away if required. I'll do it. You're still recovering."

"We'll do it together," Justin insisted.

They wrapped the cloaks, hats, and masks in oiled cloth and hid them in a hollow Felicity excavated in the wood pile, putting back enough of the cut logs to seal them away out of sight. "Your pistol next," Felicity said. "I'll take it back up to the house with me and hide it in my room."

"That you will not," said Justin. "I shall wrap it well and bury it in the flour bin. As for the tack, I think we can forget about that. It is plain enough, and I can hang it up next to my own."

He didn't want Felicity to go, but surely she must have been missed by now? "Does Lady Somerville have nothing on today?"

Judging by her startled look, she had not given the house party a thought. "I shall be missed! We are meant to be painting watercolors on the other side of the lake. Justin, I must go, but I don't want to." She moved back into his arms for another kiss.

"I shall walk you back," he said.

"You shall go back to bed," she responded. "The wounds were trivial, Justin, but the blow to the head was hard enough to knock you out! It is full daylight, and I shall go by the road, so you need not fret."

Justin reluctantly let her go, but stood on the doorstep and watched her until she was out of sight.

He stopped in the kitchen to make himself a cup of tea before returning to bed, and it was there that he was found by Principal Officer Pierce, the Bow Street Runner who had been hanging around the district like a bad smell.

"Weatherall, is it not?" said the runner.

"I am Justin Weatherall," Justin admitted.

"Due to information received, I have to ask you how you were wounded, Weatherall," said the runner.

Information received from whom? Was this Grant's mischief? "An accident with a gun," Justin replied.

"Causing a head wound," the runner stated, which was not a great stretch, given Justin's bandaged head.

"And several wounds in the shoulder and arm, none deep or serious," Justin said. The bandage that held his dressings in place was clearly visible at the open neck of his shirt. Inspired, he added, "I suspect it was an *espingole*—a bit like a blunderbuss, but in pistol form."

It was unlikely the runner would accept the diversion, and he didn't. "And who shot you, Weatherall?"

Ah. That was a trickier question. Justin couldn't think of a safe answer. "I regret, sir, that I cannot say."

"Then I regret, sir, that I must take you into custody, on suspicion of being a highwayman," said the runner.

CHAPTER 7

F elicity still had a sense of dread, like a hovering cloud—far in the distance but sure to rain at just the wrong moment.

She hurried along the path through the woods, taking the turn toward Normanton Hall at such speed that she almost bumped into someone coming the other way.

"Lady Felicity." It was a woman she had met a few days ago—a widow of about Felicity's own age. "Mrs. Fleming."

"Is it true," Mrs. Fleming blurted, "that you spent last night in the schoolhouse with Mr. Weatherall?"

Felicity must have glared, for she quickly said, "It is none of my business, I am sure, though you should know that word has spread around the village."

As well to know, Felicity supposed. "Thank you."

"If it is true, if you know Mr. Weatherall well, can you give him a message? You probably know there are smugglers on this coast. I'm not going to name them, but if you can, tell Mr. Weatherall that I heard two of them talking about the shipment they are meant to be bringing in. They are worried about it. It is for a man called Grant, and they think he is up to no good. I thought Mr. Weatherall and Captain Somerville might know what to do with the information."

"I will tell them," Felicity promised, her mind racing. What was Grant up to? How delightful it would be to have a threat to hang over his head!

She continued through the woods, her mind returning to her betrothed, so that she smiled as she hurried.

When she came out of the trees, she could see two large open carriages drawn up at the steps, and people were already emerging to take their places. *Oh dear.* Felicity fairly ran across the grass, giggling at the thought of what Sophia might say if she saw her running like a hoyden. Her happiness was like the fine sparkling wine from the Champagne region that was often served in England on special occasions, and that the French affected to despise. It fizzed in her veins, sending up bubbles of delight to explode into smiles, giggles, and other exuberances.

She would join the painting party, since Penelope had been such a dear sweet hostess, and did not deserve to have her plans upended. And then she would write to Hythe and let him know that he might expect a visit from Justin. "And you must answer that I shall please myself, dear Hythe," she composed in her mind, "but I hope I shall have your blessing. I shall marry Justin with or without it, for I love him and he loves me. But I would like my brother to be happy for me."

She arrived in time to join the last carriage, but over the next hour, as they set up on the water's edge and attempted to put paint on canvas, her mind kept drifting to Justin. Was he truly recovering? What if one of the wounds became infected? Fear for him kept trying to infest her mind, but she fought it back. There was no reason behind her anxiety.

What she should be feeling was joy, and she did! She and Justin were betrothed. At last. Hythe might grumble, but once he came to know Justin, he would see what she loved in the man. Hythe wanted what was best for her, and she knew that was Justin.

Then Robin arrived. She saw him stop to greet Penelope then saunter along the line of painters, having a word with one and then with another. He stood beside her and said, in a voice just above a whisper, "Lady Felicity, the Bow Street Runner has arrested Justin on suspicion of being Captain Midnight or his associate." Her vague disquiet suddenly had a focus.

"The man says his wounds are proof enough," Robin said. "I'll have to hand myself in, Felicity."

"Take me to Justin," she demanded. "I have an idea." Without waiting for an answer, she hurried along the lakeside to Penelope. "Penelope, something has come up. Captain Somerville is going to take me into the village. May I borrow one of the carriages to return to the house? I will send it back."

"Yes, of course," Penelope replied. "I hope there is nothing wrong."

Felicity was going to have to tell her something. "Walk to the carriage with me," she said. When they were out of earshot of everyone except Robin, who had followed along, she told Penelope, "Mr. Weatherall and I became betrothed last night, Penelope, but we are not telling anyone until Hythe knows. Mr. Grant guessed, and has accused Justin of being the highwayman. Robin and I are going to talk to the Bow Street Runner and find out what Grant said so we can prove it is untrue."

"You must go, of course," Penelope agreed. "Oh dear. I had rather hoped you would marry Mr. Grant. He is distantly connected to royalty, though mostly Italian royalty, it is true."

"Mr. Grant's suggestions to me have been villainous, Penelope. Even if I were not most sincerely attached to Mr. Weatherall, I would never marry a man who threatens to blacken my reputation if I do not accept him. As for having Justin arrested! Words fail me."

"I could not agree more, my dear. I shall wish you very happy, then, Felicity, and when Mr. Grant returns from his trip to Brighton, Peter shall tell him he must leave the house party." She nodded decisively for emphasis. What a dear Penelope was.

"I have something to fetch from the house," Felicity said to Robin when she descended from the carriage. "I won't be a moment."

Robin nodded. "I'll have them harness my team to my curricle."

He was as good as his word, and a few minutes later, they were on their way to the village. Robin occasionally eyed the long pistol case on Felicity's knee, but he asked no questions. Just as well, for Felicity had no intention of answering any. She had taken her carriage pistol from her luggage, and fired it into the log basket. Despite her efforts to smother it with a blanket first, it had made an almighty noise, but no one came to investigate. The blanket was in no good state. She would need to buy Penelope another one.

The runner was staying with the village constable, Robin said. Justin was in the cottage's little lockup, waiting to be seen by Robin's brother Peter. Somerville was the local magistrate.

"I hope they have not made Justin's injuries worse," Felicity said. If he was sick again, someone would answer for it, or she was not a Belvoir. She led the way to the cottage's front door, and rapped on it without waiting for Robin.

"Lady Felicity Belvoir to see the gentleman from Bow Street," she told the maid who answered the door. "You may tell the gentleman that I am Mr. Weatherall's betrothed."

The maid let them into the hall and hurried off to announce them to the runner, who came out into the hall himself a few minutes later. "Lady Felicity, is it? I regret, my lady, that I am unable to allow you to see the prisoner. Nor you, Captain Somerville."

"I hope to see Mr. Weatherall, of course," said Felicity, "to be sure that he has not been put in danger by your rash action in arresting him."

The runner tossed his head back, jutting his chin belligerently. "I have it on the best authority, that the prisoner Weatherall was injured in the commission of the crime of highway robbery," he said. He might have said more, but Felicity interrupted.

"Your authority is, I believe, Mr. Victor Grant, a retired naval officer who asked me to marry him yesterday evening. When I refused, he threatened to harm Mr. Weatherall and also to damage my reputation. I have since been informed he is in league with smugglers. Hardly the best of authorities, and clearly no gentleman."

That bothered the runner, but he rallied. "We also have information laid by a young female, as to what she observed, plus there is the fact of Weatherall's injuries. One of the highwaymen in question was shot last night by a coachman, using a blunderbuss, and

Weatherall has wounds consistent with those made by a blunderbuss."

Milly Stone. Silly girl. Felicity was going to find her and give her a piece of her mind. Or better still, talk to her father. She was easily dismissed, and Felicity had an explanation for the wounds that the runner would find hard to disprove.

"The wounds were made by an *espignole*," said Felicity, holding out the pistol case until the runner took it. "You will find my *espignole* in that case." She blushed. It was a talent she had developed as a child, requiring only that she thought of something deeply embarrassing. "I shot my *fiancé*."

She fluttered her hands by her hot cheeks. "Oh, this is so mortifying. After I was threatened by Mr. Grant, I wanted to tell Justin. Mr. Weatherall. It is not a long walk to the schoolhouse, so I decided to go and see him, even though it was late at night. To protect myself, for there are desperate characters abroad, as you know—and besides, Mr. Grant had gone out again, though heaven knows why. Oh! Perhaps he had gone to meet the smugglers! I took my carriage pistol, which is an *espignole*."

She had him. The runner was hanging on her every word, and rather than give her away, Robin was merely staring at her with his mouth slightly open. Surprise had been the reaction she was looking for.

"I must have been more nervous than I thought, for when I heard a sound in the undergrowth, I inadvertently pulled the trigger, and the pistol went off." Felicity had no trouble calling tears to her eyes. She had only to think about how pale Justin had been last night while she was digging bullets out of his shoulder and arm. "I shot my own betrothed," she wailed.

Robin coughed. If the man betrayed her by laughing, he might be the one she shot. However, he got himself under control to say, "How frightening for you, Lady Felicity."

The runner either wasn't falling for her act, or he was too set on his arrest to accept her story. "I don't suppose Mr. Weatherall mentioned what he was doing out in the woods at night," he said, his voice heavy with doubt.

Felicity was ready for him. "He was on his way up to the house to make sure I was unharmed. Mr. Grant had called on Jus—Mr. Weatherall—to repeat his threats, and my betrothed was concerned he might have attacked me."

The village constable had been listening, and now he spoke up. "Sounds like her ladyship has the right of it," he said. "This Mr. Grant could be worth another look, Mr. Pierce. A right villain to go around frightening ladies and wasting the time of good men such as yourself by accusing our village schoolmaster for his own selfish purposes. And if it is true that he is in league with the smugglers..."

Oh, excellently well played. The constable's arguments swayed the runner, but he was not quite ready to give up.

"There is the evidence of Miss St... the village female," he said.

"Miss Stone is a silly child," Felicity said. "She has been attempting to seduce Mr. Weatherall in the hopes he would marry her. She took the news of our betrothal very badly. I really must make time to speak with the butcher. He needs to know what a scandal she will make of herself if she keeps up this behavior."

Once again, the constable supported her, saying, "Milly Stone has feathers for brains, right enough, and she is the apple of her Pa's eye." He clinched the matter by adding, "I'd not like to take the case before Sir Peter Somerville on the unsupported word of young Milly, and that's a fact."

And within fifteen minutes, Robin and Felicity were taking Justin home in the curricle. "Do not leave the village, Mr. Weatherall," the runner had warned. "I have my eye on you."

"I am in awe," said Robin, once they were comfortably ensconced in the schoolhouse, sitting around the kitchen table with a cup of tea each. "Felicity, you were magnificent. I know the truth, and I believed you!"

Felicity fixed him with a stern glare. "I lied, Robin. I do not like to lie. If you and Justin had not been playing at highwayman, I would not have had to do so."

Justin winced at her tone. She was not wrong. "It's over, Felicity. Robin, I won't ride out with you again, no matter how deserving the cause."

"It is time," Robin acknowledged. "This was too close a shave, and they'll be watching, now. We never intended to do so many, but after we fixed things for the Widow Bryant, we kept hearing about new offenses, and I suppose it made me feel useful. The people we've robbed have all deserved it, Felicity."

"Except for Lady Corey," Justin pointed out, "and that was a mistake. We thought it was someone else's coach. Anyway, we gave her rubies back to Lord Corey."

Perhaps he should not have mentioned that. Felicity cast her eyes upward as if sending a prayer for patience. "Lady Corey's rubies," she muttered, but it was not a question and Justin was not stupid enough to take it as one. Robin, too, kept silent.

"No more *highwaymanning*, then," Felicity said, her eyes on Justin.

"Never again," he vowed.

"It's a pity we can't find someone else to be Captain Moonlight," Robin mused. "The good work could carry on, but also, if he robbed someone on a night when we were both out in public and highly visible, it would eliminate the last of the suspicion."

Felicity looked as if she was going to eviscerate Robin as soon as she summoned enough calm to maintain her dignity. Justin spoke to save them both. "Robin, no more plots," he said. "Let's just allow Captain Moonlight to fade back into legend."

Justin got up to answer a knock on the door. If it was Milly Stone, he was going to blister her ears.

It wasn't Milly Stone. Standing on the doorstep with his hand raised to knock again was the consummately elegant Earl of Hythe. Felicity's brother.

"Ah. Mr. Weatherall," said Hythe. "I am pleased to see you on your feet after my sister shot you. Is my sister here?"

"Hythe?" said Felicity from behind Justin. He stepped out of her way and she greeted her brother with a decorous kiss to the cheek. "Come in, dear," she said. "The tea is still hot."

Hythe followed her into the kitchen. "Somerville. Are you

playing chaperone? Rather a change of roles for you. Yes, please Felicity. And congratulations on your betrothal. I heard about your dash to save your betrothed from the constable. Of course, firing off your espignole in a panic is just what I would have expected from you."

That was Hythe. Every word carrying half a dozen meanings. The man's thoughts twisted and turned, and zipped from place to place like dragonflies. Justin had played chess with him once. He'd felt good about his chess playing until that game.

Felicity showed she followed the man's mental gymnastics by saying, "You looked for me at the house and then at the village. Penelope told you that Justin and I were betrothed, and the constable told you I had accidentally shot Justin."

"Yes," Hythe commented, his tone dry, "you being such a nervous creature. How fortunate that your mistake inadvertently provided Weatherall with an alibi."

Felicity ignored the provocation, saying, "Grant visited you in Brighton, I suppose. He said he was going to do so."

"Grant!" Hythe's mouth screwed up in distaste. "He will not bother you again, my dear. I regret to inform you, Felicity, that you were not the primary reason for his visit. He has been meeting Fenian conspirators and is currently explaining his interest in their plots to a couple of friends of mine."

"Well!" Felicity said. "I knew he was a villain. Hythe, I have just found out that he has been meeting with the leader of a smuggling gang. What do you suppose he was having smuggled? Something in? Or something out?"

"Interesting!" Hythe stood. "The name of this leader?"

"I was not told," Felicity said.

Justin was able to supply a few more details. "Bert Gladwish. Ostensibly a fisherman. Lives in Lancing-by-Sea. He runs the gang that uses this part of the coast."

"Excuse me," said Hythe, with an abbreviated bow. He strode from the room, and they heard him in urgent conversation with someone outside. After a moment, he returned and resumed his seat. "Thompson will see to it that the smuggler is taken up for questioning," he said. "Well done, Fliss. We think the Fenians were planning to blow up the Pavilion next week when the prince has his brothers visiting. We suspect Grant was to provide the explosives. The smuggler's leader should be able to help us tie the whole problem up and put a bow on it."

"We," the man said. Justin's respect for Hythe shot up several steps.

"Oh. So that is why you had to go to Brighton," Felicity said. "And why you jumped at the chance to leave me here. Really, Nat. When are you going to stop trying to protect me out of all the fun?"

Justin rolled his eyes at Felicity's idea of fun, and noted with amusement that her brother was doing the same thing. Hythe gave him a quick conspiratorial smile before saying, "I gather I am expected to pass the duty of protecting you to Weatherall here. All my previous reservations still apply, Weatherall."

"About that, Nathan Anthony Charles Belvoir," said Felicity, sternly. "I am a grown woman, and I did not appoint you to act on my behalf. I am very cross about you scaring Justin off."

"He didn't scare me," Justin protested, outraged at the thought that this land-lubbing aristocrat could scare a war-hardened sea dog like himself. Although apparently there was more to Hythe than he had realized. "He just pointed out that I don't deserve you and I am not worthy of you. Both of which are true. But since you know that, and you want me anyway..." He shrugged.

Felicity gave him both her hands and leaned across the corner of the table to kiss him, then tossed her brother a saucy smirk. "*That* for your reservations, Hythe," she said.

"Hmm," Hythe said. "I take it you have given up being a highwayman's accomplice, Weatherall? With all due respect, Somerville, I can't have my sister perjuring herself to the law. Reputation of the Belvoirs, you know." A faint smile played about his lips. The sly dog! He'd taken a dig each at Robin, Justin and Felicity with a few carefully chosen sentences.

"We have your blessing, then, Hythe?" Felicity asked, amusement bubbling in her voice. She and Hythe were more alike than Justin had realized.

Even Hythe's shrug was elegant. "You will marry with or without it. It had better be with it, or I shall miss my last chance to give one of my sisters away at the altar. I don't want you running off like Sophia."

As Justin understood it, Felicity's sister had gone to London to be with her viscount when he was called to his dying grandfather's bedside. She had done so with her brother's full knowledge and agreement—hardly running off. "Thank you, Hythe," he said.

A wintery smile. "You are stealing my hostess and travel companion," Hythe complained. "But I suppose love will demand its toll."

"You should try it, Hythe," Felicity said. "A wife would be a much better hostess and travel companion than a sister."

Hythe sighed. "Why is it that all people in love wish to inflict the state on those in happy ignorance of its effects? What of you, Somerville? Are you, too, considering the married estate?"

Robin blushed, which was a sight Justin had not seen before, and answer enough.

Hythe chuckled. "I can see I am outnumbered. Are you ready to go back up to the Somervilles' house, Felicity? If so, I shall do myself the honor of escorting you."

Felicity's brother Hythe announced her betrothal at the ball several days later. Sir Peter proposed a toast to them both, and Penelope glowed with the satisfaction of a job well done, for Justin's and Felicity's betrothal was not the only one to come out of the house party.

The Fenians had been rounded up, the smuggling gang had given up the guns and explosives, and the Prince Regent was safe from everything but his own excesses. And the Bow Street Runner was happy, for he had an arrest. Froppin—his real name was Barbeau— kept protesting his innocence, but any witnesses in his favor were keeping quiet. Everyone clearly agreed that he was guilty—not, of course, of being Captain Moonlight, but of being a bully, a thief, and a cheat.

Felicity said her farewell to Justin the following morning, before leaving with Hythe for London. Her official farewell, that was. Her unofficial farewell had begun after the ball and lasted a fair part of the night. But Hythe did not need to know about that.

"I will see you soon," she said.

"Four weeks," Justin agreed. "It will seem forever, but I suppose it will pass, as time does." Justin had given Sir Peter four weeks' notice of his intention to quit, and would come to London after that. And in six weeks, they would be wed, in St George's with her family in attendance.

And perhaps some of Justin's, for he had written to invite his father and brothers.

"You do not have to hire somewhere to live while you look for an estate," Hythe said, and not for the first time. "I have plenty of room at Belvoir Court, and if you do not want to live under my roof, the dower house is kept clean and in good repair. It can easily be readied for you."

"We love you, Hythe," Felicity assured him, "but we want to live under our own roof." She was speaking for Justin on the second part of the statement. As for the love, Hythe and Justin were still circling one another like cats who had only recently met and who were forced to share accommodation.

"We do appreciate it, Hythe," said Justin. The two men shook hands, but when Felicity gave hers to Justin, he lifted it for a kiss.

As she and her brother drove away in the carriage, she cradled that hand in the other. Four weeks until she saw him again. Six weeks until they were married. They could not pass fast enough!

"I suppose you are going to beggar me buying paper and ink for your letters," Hythe commented. He was attempting to distract her, dear man.

"Probably," Felicity replied. A letter a day, they had promised one another. She smiled at the thought. His words would have to do for a few weeks, and then she and he would be joined for their lifetimes.

She had glimpsed the future that lay ahead around the bend in the road, and the vista was wonderful.

THE END

If you enjoyed Felicity's story, and want to know more about the Belvoir siblings, I've already told Hythe's and Sophia's stories. You can get *To Wed a Proper Lady*, in which James Winderfield crashes a house party to woo Sophia, here: https://books2read.com/CMK-Prop erLady

Another house party matches the very proper Earl of Hythe with the scandalous Amaryllis Fernhill, in *The Husband Gamble*. Buy links are here: https://books2read.com/HusbandGamble

SOCIAL MEDIA FOR JUDE KNIGHT

You can learn more about Jude Knight at these social media links:

Website and blog: http://judeknightauthor.com/
Subscribe to newsletter: http://judeknightauthor.com/newsletter/
Bookshop: https://shop.judeknightauthor.com/
Facebook: https://www.facebook.com/JudeKnightAuthor/
X: https://X.com/JudeKnightBooks
Pinterest: https://nz.pinterest.com/jknight1033/
BookBub: https://www.bookbub.com/profile/jude-knight
Goodreads: https://www.goodreads.com/author/show/8603586.
Jude_Knight

ABOUT JUDE KNIGHT

Jude always wanted to be a novelist. She started in her teens, but life kept getting in the way. Years passed, and with them dozens of unfinished manuscripts. She had a successful career in commercial writing, but the fear grew. What if she tried, failed, and lost the dream forever? The years since 2014 have seen more than a score of novels, twice as many novellas, 5 volumes of short stories, 3 awards, and thousands of positive reviews. The dream is alive.

Learn more about Jude at:
Website and blog: http://judeknightauthor.com/
Subscribe to newsletter: https://judeknightauthor.com/newsletter/

THE CASEBOOK OF
PRINCIPAL OFFICER ROBERT
PIERCE

Brighton and surrounding districts

With all three of my cases closed, I am returning to London. It has been an interesting interlude. Miles and I have drunk a final jug of ale in salute to our successes, and I have invited him to join me for another if ever he is in London.

The Home Office has also closed its case, apparently. I have not been told all the details, but I have had the honor of meeting two highly-ranked gentlemen who were involved in the investigation.

Smugglers, Fenians, explosives and more! Frankly, I would rather stick to highwaymen and sneak thieves.

THE BELLES WOULD LIKE YOUR HELP!

Book reviews help readers to find books, and authors to find readers. Please consider writing a review for **Love's Perilous Road**, even a couple of sentences telling people what you liked (or didn't like) about the stories. Reviews can be posted on Goodreads and on most eRetailers websites. For links to this book on those sites, see the *Storm & Shelter* page on the Belles' website: https://bluestockingbelles.net/belles-joint-projects/loves-perilous-road/

Malala Fund

The Bluestocking Belles have chosen the Malala Fund as the charity they support, and to which they donate some of their royalties. Periodically, they take on projects intended to directly support this cause, which exemplifies their personal values and intentions: the right of girls and women to do whatever they choose with their lives.

How can you help?

Make a donation at https://malala.org/donate

When a storm blows off the North Sea and slams into the village of Fenwick on Sea, the villagers prepare for the inevitable: shipwreck, flood, land slips, and stranded travelers. The Queen's Barque Inn quickly fills with the injured, the devious, and the lonely—lords, ladies, and simple folk; spies, pirates, and smugglers all trapped together. Intrigue crackles through the village, and passion lights up the hotel.

One storm, eight authors, eight heartwarming novellas.

Holiday Escapes (2020)

Holidays, relatives, pressure to marry—sometimes it is all too much. Is it any wonder a woman may need to escape? The heroines in this collection of stories aren't afraid to take matters into their own hands when they've had enough.

These stories are republished here at 20% of the cost of collecting them all from each individual author.

Two bonus short stories round out the collection.

Fire & Frost (2020)

In a winter so cold the Thames freezes over, five couples venture onto the ice in pursuit of love to warm their hearts.

Love unexpected, rekindled, or brand new—even one that's a whack on the side of the head—heats up the frigid winter. After weeks of fog and cold, all five stories converge on the ice at the 1814 Frost Fair when the ladies' campaign to help the wounded and unemployed veterans of the Napoleonic wars culminates in a charity auction that shocks the high sticklers of the ton.

In their 2020 collection, join the Bluestocking Belles and their heroes and heroines as The Ladies' Society For The Care of the Widows and Orphans of Fallen Heroes and the Children of Wounded Veterans pursues justice, charity, and soul-searing romance.

Valentine's From Bath (2019)

The Master of Ceremonies announces a great ball to be held on Valentine's Day in the Upper Assembly Rooms of Bath.

Ladies of the highest rank—and some who wish they were—scheme, prepare, and compete to make best use of the opportunity.

Dukes, earls, tradesmen, and the occasional charlatan are alert to the possibilities as the event draws nigh.

But anything can happen in the magic of music and candlelight as couples dance, flirt, and open themselves to romantic possibilities. Problems and conflict may just fade away at a Valentine's Day Ball.

Follow Your Star Home (2018)

Forged for lovers, the Viking star ring is said to bring lovers together, no matter how far, no matter how hard.

In eight stories, covering more than half the world and a thousand years, our heroes and heroines put the legend to the test. Watch the star work its magic, as prodigals return home in the season of good will, uncertain of their welcome.

Never Too Late (2017)

Eight authors and eight different takes on four dramatic elements selected by our readers—an older heroine, a wise man, a Bible, and a compromising situation that isn't.

Set in a variety of locations around the world over eight centuries, welcome to the romance of the Bluestocking Belles' 2017 Holiday and More Anthology.

It's Never Too Late to find love.

Holly and Hopeful Hearts (2016)

When the Duchess of Haverford sends out invitations to a Yuletide house party and a New Year's Eve ball at her country estate, Hollystone Hall, those who respond know that Her Grace intends to raise money for her favorite cause and promote whatever love-matches she can. Seven assorted heroes and heroines set out with their pocketbooks firmly clutched and hearts in protective custody. Or are they?

Eight assorted heroes and heroines find more than they've bargained for when they set out for Hollystone Hall for a charity ball.

MEET THE BLUESTOCKING BELLES

The Bluestocking Belles (the "BellesInBlue") are a group of very different writers united by a love of history and a history of writing about love. From sweet to steamy, from light-hearted fun to dark tortured tales full of angst, from London ballrooms to country cottages to the sultan's seraglio, one or more of us will have a tale to suit your tastes and mood.

Learn more about the Bluestocking Belles at:
Website: www.BluestockingBelles.net/
Newsletter: http://eepurl.com/dAJU_9
Teatime Tattler twice-weekly gossip magazine: https://bluestockingbelles.net/category/teatime-tattler/
Free books: https://bluestockingbelles.net/teatime-tattler-free-books/

 facebook.com/BellesinBlue
 x.com/BellesInBlue
 pinterest.com/bellesinblue
 instagram.com/bellesinblue